Beverley Harper was b[...]
twenty years in Africa. [...]
she draws inspiration [...]
She lives now on the [...]
New South Wales but regularly returns to Africa
for research purposes. Beverley is married to
Robert and they have three grown sons. When not
writing, which is hardly ever, Beverley enjoys
'being'.

Also by Beverley Harper

Storms Over Africa
Edge of the Rain
Echo of an Angry God
People of Heaven
The Forgotten Sea
Jackal's Dance
Shadows in the Grass
Footprints of Lion

SHADOWS
IN THE
GRASS

BEVERLEY
HARPER

PAN
Pan Macmillan Australia

First published 2002 in Macmillan by Pan Macmillan Australia Pty Limited
This Pan edition published 2003 by Pan Macmillan Australia Pty Limited
1 Market Street, Sydney

Reprinted 2003, 2004 (twice), 2005 (twice), 2006

Copyright © Beverley Harper 2002

All rights reserved. No part of this book may be reproduced or
transmitted in any form or by any means, electronic or mechanical,
including photocopying, recording or by any information storage
and retrieval system, without prior permission in writing from
the publisher.

National Library of Australia
cataloguing-in-publication data:

Harper, Beverley.
Shadows in the grass.

ISBN 0 330 36414 6.

1. Malicious accusation – Fiction. 2. Man–woman relationships – Fiction.
3. Scots – South Africa – Fiction. 4. Hunting – South Africa – Fiction.
5. Zulu War, 1879 – Fiction. I. Title.

A823.3

Map by Mike Gorman
Typeset in 11.5/13pt Bembo by Post Pre-press Group
Printed in Australia by McPherson's Printing Group

This novel is a work of fiction. Names and characters are the product of the
author's imagination or are used fictitiously and any resemblance to actual
persons, living or dead, is entirely coincidental.

This book is for
Robert, Piers, Miles and Adam,
solid as rocks in the sand dunes of my life,
and for Yvette, who came into my son's life like a
cyclone, so much so I named one after her in The
Forgotten Sea, *and for Jo and my granddaughter,*
Kayla, who entered this world as innocent as the
animals of Africa and just as beautiful.

It is customary for authors to thank those who have contributed, in any way, towards the writing of a book. In *Shadows in the Grass*, however, my research has relied completely on those departed souls who adventured in Africa in the nineteenth century. For various reasons many of them felt compelled to write of their experiences, and for this, I am extremely grateful. Their memoirs have provided the backbone for this story. They are, nonetheless, no longer on this earth and, inspirational as their written words may be, the acknowledgments page lacks a sense of here and now.

Modestly, therefore, in the absence of persons living to whom I can express appreciation for research assistance, I wish to acknowledge my own sheer hard work.

And to Cate Paterson and Sarina Rowell, structural editors of phenomenal skill, I acknowledge their valuable input. They tightened, tweaked and changed bits. Much muttering was heard coming from the author's study. 'You can't cut that,' she was heard to yell on more than one occasion. Angst and gnashing of teeth aside, their suggestions made sense and I thank them both.

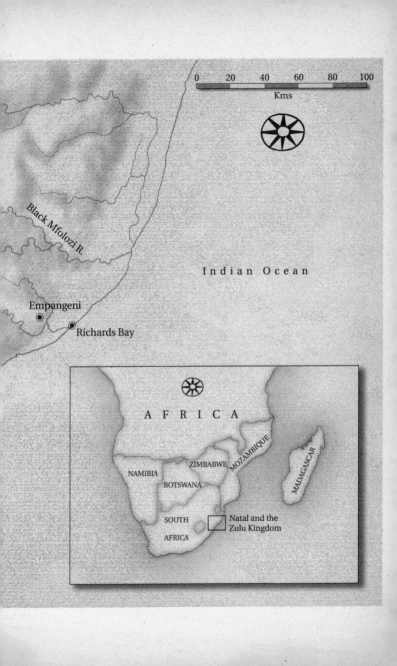

ONE

Late November in Scotland, cold and inevitably dank, promises the bitterness of winter, a depressing monotony of grey, wet days, weeks and endless months.

But as though unmindful of the forces nature massed against it, a determined early afternoon sun shines gamely on. Closed windows in the solid sandstone residence reflect its light with a deceptive brilliance. It ventures past the cream and brown damask patterned wool curtains of an upstairs room and lays a sheen of pale gold over deep blue and silver brocade covering the walls. Tentative fingers of yellow touch dark carved furniture. Gossamer fine, it inches forward over the richly woven carpet, one tiny patch finding a discarded slipper of black velvet. A delicate ray illuminates the rhinestones encrusting its toe. For a brief moment the sun's efforts combine with imitation diamonds to produce a spectacular and dazzling display in the large and ornately furnished bed chamber. But it has no real place in winter's bleak countenance and soon, too soon, the chilly gloom returns.

Nature's defiance went unnoticed by the two occupants. A coal fire, lit that morning by one of the housemaids, glowed in the hearth but did little to throw out any heat. Bed linen, once immaculately smoothed and tucked in, plumped pillows, starched frilly lace on the counterpane, carefully arranged so that the material fluffed and swirled where it touched the floor – all were crumpled and in disarray.

A naked pair on the bed had been absorbed in each other for several hours. The lady of the house was supposedly indisposed and strict instructions had been issued that she was not to be disturbed under any circumstances. The large household of servants – from butler to page, housekeeper to scullery maids – were not fooled but they knew that nothing short of fire, or an unexpected return by their master, would be reason enough to so much as knock timidly on the door.

Lord Dallas Acheson was as fine a specimen as could be found, with or without his clothes. Dressed, he was often referred to as dashing. Naked, the lady currently occupying his attention thought him magnificent. Youth kept his six-foot frame firm and well-muscled. He had a lean face and smouldering eyes. Unlike many he was clean-shaven, which emphasised his square jaw and long, strong nose. Very dark curly hair, heavy brows and thick, long eyelashes contrasted well with pale skin, another sign of approaching winter. A wide smiling mouth and the humour that glinted regularly in the depths of his eyes showed a touch of daredevil.

Young girls found his face handsome. Older women looked deeper and saw sensuality.

At twenty-one, Dallas Acheson was at the peak of physical fitness – a fact not lost on his ladyfriend. Also, to her intense delight, ardour and the pursuit of physical satisfaction were two activities to which he was prepared to devote much attention and energy.

Lady Alison de Iongh was not the only mistress Dallas had enjoyed but she was the first to take upon herself the agreeable task of educating him in matters pertaining to delights of the flesh. The affair, therefore, had continued for longer than either of them might have expected. Despite exceedingly good grounds to end it, the absence of resolve was stronger than a willing spirit. Lord de Iongh spent most of the year in London; his absences made it easy to dismiss discovery as a real threat. Had he stopped to think about the law of averages, Dallas might have concluded that he was using up an extraordinary amount of good fortune.

Alison was a woman most young men could only dream of knowing. At thirty-nine, having borne four children, two of whom had died at birth, Alison's figure was still slim, though a little stretch-marked around her abdomen, breasts and thighs. Her face no longer held the soft dewiness of youth. It was angular with fine lines around the eyes and mouth. She'd lost several teeth, the most noticeable of which was her upper left canine, which gaped whenever she spoke or smiled. Alison's hair was her best feature – golden, thick and glossy with no hint of grey. She was justifiably vain about it, especially as now when it tumbled over the pillows and spread around her face in a shimmering waterfall of vibrant colour. Cool grey eyes could smoulder with desire and her body responded to Dallas's lightest touch. Aroused, she could use the language of street urchins – a far cry from the composed and elegant figure who graciously received social callers in the drawing rooms of her many houses. Heady stuff for a young man usually denied that which he most desired.

Her fingers were lost in his hair. His tongue drew lazy circles around each nipple. They had made love twice but both were ready for more. Dallas pressed his erection against her leg and, as he had anticipated, she reached for him, long nails gently scratching the length of him. He rolled onto his back, enjoying her touch.

'Tell me what you want.' Her voice, husky and throbbing with desire, sent shivers through him.

'Take me in your mouth.'

She slid down his body, lips circling his engorged penis, small tongue darting, seeking out the most sensitive parts, teasing and playing his arousal until he was squirming with pleasure. Abruptly, she left him, rising and straddling his face. 'No,' she panted. 'Not yet. I am not ready.'

Dallas sought and found the bud of pleasure and, as she had taught him, gently brought her to the point of orgasm. Alison, head flung back in ecstasy, rode him until she teetered on the very brink of release.

'Now,' she breathed, rolling from him.

Dallas rolled with her, hands sliding under her knees, bringing them up.

Alison raised her legs over his shoulders. 'I want your cock inside me. Hard.'

He rammed into her and she gave a moan as her orgasm could no longer be denied.

Braced by his arms, Dallas looked down and watched himself thrusting at her raised body. Alison was whispering words of encouragement, basic gutter language which had long since ceased to shock him. She pushed her pelvis up to meet his, matching him stroke for stroke. Each time he drew back, his penis glistened with the wetness of her desire. She would come to him again soon, shuddering and whispering his name. Dallas lost himself in sensation. The need for quiet was forgotten.

Beyond the heavy oak door, a passing housemaid, arms laden with freshly laundered linen, cocked her head as lustful cries rang out. With a knowing smile, she bent an eye to the keyhole and was rewarded by the sight of nothing more than a solitary slipper on the floor. Straightening, she leaned closer to the door, listening. Feminine gasps and masculine groans, hoarse whispers, and finally, drawn-out moans of satisfaction. Intent on the activity inside Lady de Iongh's boudoir, she didn't hear the telltale jangle made by the housekeeper's symbol of status – keys of all description carried on a large iron ring.

Mrs Kelly – so-called though the woman had

never married, nor, as far as anyone knew, even had a suitor – invariably bore the sour expression of one who shouldered the burden of life's disappointments. Disapproval of others was second nature to her. The one exception was Lord de Iongh, whom she had known since he was ten. She became more of a mother to him than his own and the lonely spinster lavished the boy with love. As he grew older and relied less on her for company, Mrs Kelly drew comfort from the fact that her charge appeared to be shaping up splendidly for a life as one of Britain's elite aristocracy.

Then, at thirty-eight, he had become engaged to Alison when she was only seventeen. Lord de Iongh was bewitched by his beautiful young fiancée. Mrs Kelly took one look at the girl and knew she was trouble. Within a year of the wedding her worst fears had been realised. Lady de Iongh didn't have a loyal, or come to that, ladylike, bone in her body. As time passed, the aging housekeeper came to loathe her mistress. Although often tempted to drop hints in his lordship's ear about Lady de Iongh's indiscretions, Mrs Kelly knew she would come off second best. Lord de Iongh saw only his wife's demure side and fondly believed her incapable of anything even remotely unladylike. Besides, he was a member of the peerage. His full title was the Fifth Earl of Dalkeith but Lord de Iongh was one of the few who preferred to use his family name rather than that of a geographic location. A nobleman through and through, he would never stoop to hearing gossip from a servant, even if she had been with his family for nearly forty years. Mrs Kelly lived in the fond hope that one day Lord de Iongh would find out for himself.

On discovering the young housemaid with one ear glued to the door, the housekeeper did what was expected of her and dragged the girl away, scolding her as soon as they were far enough from the room not to be overheard. 'Whatever are you thinking, Mabel? How dare you eavesdrop on her ladyship?'

At thirteen, though innocent enough, young Mabel had grown up in an overcrowded cottage with a curtain separating her sleeping mattress from that of her parents. However, she widened her eyes and feigned virtuous incomprehension. 'Beggin' your pardon, Mrs Kelly, but I couldn'a mind the like of it.'

As Mabel had hoped, the housekeeper believed her. 'Of course you don't understand, you silly girl. It's not your business to know. Don't let me catch you at it again. Her ladyship was probably having a nightmare.'

A sly smile crept across Mabel's face. 'Beggin' your pardon again, Mrs Kelly, but it's half-ein in the afternoon.'

Housekeeper Kelly rounded on the impudent child. 'Go about your business, girl. It's not up to the likes of you to question her ladyship. Any more eavesdropping and you'll be back to peddling fish at the market. Go on, away with you. Make haste. Put away that linen and get yourself down to the dining room. The epergne is tarnished. Her ladyship will have a fit if she sees it like that. And don't get polish on the table. I'll be down later to check your work. Off with you now, you're not here to stand around.'

'Yes, Mrs Kelly.' Mabel scurried away. She'd caught a glimpse of Lord Acheson on his arrival and thought him the most handsome man she'd ever seen. With luck, if she took her time polishing the large candlestick cum flower bowl with its intricate carvings, figurines and clawed feet, all of which required painstaking care, she might just see him leave.

In Alison's boudoir, quite oblivious of matters domestic, Lord Dallas Acheson and Lady Alison de Iongh lay entwined in the languid, rosy after-hum of love-making. He would have to take his leave no later than two-thirty. As fate would have it, and much against his better judgment, he was madly, passionately, and unwisely in love. He was in a hopeless situation and knew no way out of it. Under normal circumstances, he'd have ended the affair with Alison, declared his feelings for the true love of his life and the two of them would have lived happily ever after. The circumstances, however, were far from normal. Lady Lorna de Iongh, Alison's seventeen-year-old daughter, would be waiting for him in the coach-house.

The year was 1871. The place Canongate, stately Edinburgh home of Lord and Lady de Iongh. Events of that afternoon were not at all unusual.

Dallas and Alison had been lovers for four months. With the earl away in London so much, they enjoyed each other's company several days a week. Alison's husband sat with the House of Lords, and parliamentary sessions normally ran from the beginning of the year until August. As a rule, Lord de Iongh would have returned to Edinburgh as soon as the annual session was over. This year, however, with the House of Commons gaining more power, not to mention public support, and facing a proposal that members of the House of Lords should be elected by secret ballot rather than remain the automatic right of social influence and affluence, Lord de Iongh, along with a handful of others who were genuinely concerned that the running of Britain was being taken over by the gentry as opposed to the peerage, stayed in London to lobby Queen Victoria to retain the status quo. Surprisingly, the queen was proving stubbornly resistant to the idea of keeping power in the hands of the House of Lords. Some whispered that ill health was the reason. Elections relieved the Regent of the responsibility of selecting her parliament. Others, more bold, suggested she was too enamoured with John Brown – the queen's Highland servant – to be bothered with anything else. Whatever the reason, Lord de Iongh's continued absence from Scotland left Dallas and Alison free to indulge their passion for each other.

Two months ago, what had been a perfect situation became complicated by Lady Lorna de Iongh. She had no idea Dallas was her mother's lover. Alison, likewise, did not suspect that Dallas had not only deflowered her young daughter but had fallen in love with her.

The folly of bedding mother and daughter simultaneously was exacerbated by several complicated issues. Lorna was betrothed to another. Even if she hadn't been, Dallas knew that Alison would never allow him to marry her daughter. Jealousy aside, the intricate and rigid rules that governed their highly class-conscious society meant that Dallas would be considered unsuitable as a marriage partner for Lorna.

Realising he was damned whichever way he turned, and cursing himself for being a weak fool, Dallas developed a head-in-the-sand approach to the problem, telling himself everything would work out for the best. Just how, he had no idea.

Dallas was the fourth son of the Earl and Countess of Dalrymple. As such, his future prospects were not exactly assured.

Custom decreed that the first-born son, Thomas, or Viscount Gilmerton since he was entitled to use his father's secondary title, would inherit everything – estates, country houses, town houses and social standing. Married with two children, Thomas stoically plodded his way towards old age and continuance of the Dalrymple family tradition.

A royal commission in the Scots Guards had been bought for Boyd, the second-born. To augment a meagre pay, his parents bestowed a generous stipend which kept him comfortable. While Boyd would not be considered eligible to marry daughters of the peerage, not socially desirable ones anyway, his lineage and army rank ensured that any future wife would at least be the daughter of a baronet or knight.

The third son had turned out to be a gentle, dreamy young man who had gone willingly into the church. Glendon had no ambitions other than to serve God. He was perfectly happy as a vicar, conducting services, tending the sick, performing his duties at christenings, weddings and funerals. He lived well enough on local tithes – one-tenth of the money earned by parishioners – and had access to the glebe, the parish farmlands on which he could grow his own crops or raise livestock.

To Dallas, Glendon was something of an enigma. That he genuinely cared for the well-being of those less fortunate than himself was in no doubt. Right from the time he was old enough to realise that social injustice and gender went hand in hand, he held genuine and deeply religious beliefs that it would only be a matter of time before inequality of this nature was eradicated. Yet he appeared actually to dislike women and often made uncharitable comments about them. Despite this, he was engaged to the impoverished and straitlaced niece of the bishop in his diocese. She was seven years Glendon's senior, looked, Dallas once confided to Boyd, rather like a starving sheep, and had no personality at all as far as Dallas could see. But her family connections were impeccable.

Of his three brothers, Dallas remained closest to Boyd. Thomas was stuffy and pompous and hardly ever ventured away from the family estates in Tayside and Strathclyde. Glendon, with his love of poetry and close relationship with one of the family retainers, left Dallas filled with an urge to frogmarch him off to a brothel.

There was one sister, Charlotte, for whom Dallas had always felt a protective affection, but being four years younger, and having only just come out, he still saw her as a child.

Of the five Acheson offspring, it was usually Dallas who incurred their father's disapproval. When Nanny's shrieking and dishevelled form burst from her room gibbering about a toad in the bed, all family eyes turned to Dallas. It came as no real surprise to Lord Dalrymple when his youngest son was nearly sent down from Eton for an innovative prank involving a chamber-pot, a disgusting and foul-smelling object collected from the Head's golden retriever, and a visiting dignitary. It wasn't the joke that infuriated Lord Dalrymple – indeed, when told of it he shut himself in his study for several minutes to control an hysterical urge to giggle – it was his son's apparent lack of concern that the school's very important visitor had been so unimpressed by the mischief that he'd withdrawn his considerable financial support to the institution. Dallas was suspended for the rest of that term.

Far from being contrite, Dallas was delighted. As punishment went, he couldn't think of anything more splendid. Three weeks' extra holiday was not to be sneezed at. But Lord Dalrymple punished his wayward son by annexing his services to the head gardener. This was not only for the three weeks of suspension either. Dallas toiled in the great outdoors for his entire summer holidays.

He seemed to skitter from one diabolical disaster to another. What Dallas perceived as a lark usually backfired with calamitous results. Who else, on building a small fire to toast marshmallows, could burn down an entire barn? Who else, on burrowing below the retaining wall of an ornamental pond to build a secret cave, could hit a weak spot and drain all the water, killing his mother's precious goldfish? Dallas sometimes wondered why these things only ever happened to him.

The sole member of his immediate family to whom he was really close remained his mother. While she sometimes despaired of her youngest son's escapades, she at least seemed to understand that he never meant harm. As Dallas grew older the confidences he shared with her invariably became more guarded; nonetheless, he knew that a special bond still existed between them. Personal matters were not discussed any more but it was with his mother that he often addressed the problem of what to do with his life. A military career or the clergy held no appeal whatsoever.

'Marry an estate,' Lady Pamela Dalrymple advised succinctly and seriously on more than one occasion.

It was common enough practice. Younger sons of the peerage, set to inherit little but the courtesy title 'Lord', married wealthy, titled, often widowed ladies in order to gain control of everything they owned. The only trouble with that was, as a general rule, eligible women of rank and wealth only became available for the very good reason that they were possessed of a difficult personality, plain appearance, bad reputation, or were over-the-hill. Some even enjoyed a combination thereof. Dallas simply wasn't interested.

'Banking,' he said gloomily when all other possibilities seemed unlikely.

'Go into trade? Heavens no!' his mother would exclaim. 'How frightfully vulgar.'

So Dallas did nothing and lived, as did many a young man or woman from the privileged class, spending his days indulging in one social activity after another.

During the 1871 London season fate finally took a hand. It was then that Dallas was diverted by Lady Alison de Iongh and bewitched by her daughter, Lorna.

Lady de Iongh seduced the good-looking young man on a train heading north from London.

Lorna de Iongh willingly gave up her virginity to him two months later, just after her seventeenth birthday.

TWO

The London season brought together anyone who was anyone and a few with enough new money and ambitions to become someone. Each year around fifteen hundred families headed from country estates for their residences in the West End. Some arrived as early as Christmas, especially the families of Members of Parliament, but the season proper only began after Easter.

Dallas and his sister, Charlotte, who was coming out that year, journeyed with the Earl and Countess of Dalrymple by rail early in April. It was a raw day: the sky promised late snow, or at least rain squalls, as persistent easterly winds funnelled cold air off the North Sea up the Firth of Forth. The sole method of heating their first-class carriage was metal foot warmers filled with hot water by a porter. Dressed for the cold in furs and snuggled under heavy woollen blankets, the family was tolerably comfortable.

This was the third time Dallas had made the trip from Edinburgh to London by train. He did not particularly enjoy the method of travel. There was no passageway connecting the carriages. Once in, one stayed in. No illumination – candles had to be brought from home, as did food since there were no facilities providing sustenance.

Worst of all, no toilets. Some women, especially if travelling in the exclusive company of others of their sex, carried a chamber-pot for emergencies, hidden discreetly in a basket. Men could purchase a long tube which they strapped down one leg and concealed under their trousers. Like most, Lord Dalrymple and his family found these solutions highly unsatisfactory and preferred to wait until the train stopped at a station, then, along with everyone else, make an undignified rush for the public toilets.

To amuse themselves, the family alternated between reading and playing cards. Charlotte chattered incessantly about coming out. It was an exciting time for a girl who grew up restrained by the shelter of class and convention. This season she could enter society, enjoy the attentions of young gentlemen, dress like a lady and be treated as a grown-up. Her best friend, the Lady Lorna de Iongh, was also coming out and Dallas idly wondered what society would make of the two of them.

Charlotte was excitable and easily led by Lorna who, it sometimes seemed to Dallas and everyone else who knew her, went out of her way to shock. When Lorna was six she kept a collection of live snails in her bedchamber and would hold regular race meetings on the outcome of which her friends were coerced into betting pocket money. When this practice came to the attention of her mother, it was stopped. The reason given was that it was unbecoming behaviour for a young lady.

Lorna, who regularly complained to Dallas about inequality between boys and girls – 'Why can't I climb trees if boys can?' or 'Why must I sit with my knees pressed together if boys don't?' – gave vent in her usual forthright manner. 'Why is it unladylike? I'm allowed to sit on the floor to play cards. My knees were covered.'

At ten, Dallas didn't know the answer, but he took a wild guess. 'You were holding a purse on the races.'

Lorna tossed her head. 'So what? You still couldn't see my knees,' and she hauled up her skirts to show him two bony little lumps which she firmly believed were responsible for the ban.

Staring at them, Dallas could see no good reason why they might be considered unladylike. At that moment Lorna's nanny came into the room. The resultant fuss was mainly caused by a highly embellished account of the event from Nanny Beth. Lorna was dragged off home, rolling her eyes in defiance. Dallas didn't understand what he'd done that was supposed to be so awful, and neither he nor Lorna could appreciate the reason given as to why they were chaperoned for months afterwards – 'It's for your own good.'

As they grew older, they often gravitated together to complain when they felt punishment for a supposed breach of good behaviour was too strict. They were bound in friendship by their inability to conform.

When Dallas reached puberty, and for no reason he could think of, his mother informed him that, 'for his own good' he and Lorna would, once again, be chaperoned. He put it down to one of the many confusing rules and regulations of life, never once suspecting that the day he was caught looking at Lorna's knees was the reason. The ever-present Nanny Beth was a challenge. Dallas and Lorna often amused themselves devising and executing ways to escape her attention. Eventually, their parents came to accept that the two were firm friends, nothing more, and allowed them reasonable freedom together.

And now, along with his sister, the little tomboy friend of his childhood would be coming out. God help the young suitors, Dallas thought. Particularly Lorna's.

The journey took twelve hours. When the train eventually reached London they were stiff and cold, though in very good condition compared with the frozen, sneezing and sodden third-class passengers who had made the journey in open trucks. It was a relief to return to the familiar, to have their coachman meet the train and turn the matter of their considerable luggage over to two grooms and a like number of footmen. The luggage travelled in one brougham, the family boarded a second.

'Nearly there, dears.' Lady Dalrymple yawned delicately, as the carriage set off. 'I can't wait to stretch my legs.'

Their town house was on Park Lane, the most fashionable part of London's West End. Years earlier, the earl's father had purchased another residence next door and, instead of keeping it a high, narrow building like most, combined the two houses making the Dalrymple address quite exclusive. The kitchen, scullery and laundry, as well as the cook's, housekeeper's and butler's quarters, lay below ground, in the basement. At street level were an imposing wood-panelled entrance hall, dining and drawing rooms and a glassed conservatory that spanned the back of both original houses. Above them, a billiard room, library and gallery. The second floor comprised three large bedrooms, with four more on the third. Other servants and storage took up the fourth floor and attics.

Despite their late arrival – it was nearly midnight when they drew up outside the house – the full complement of servants lined the entrance hall waiting to greet the family. Cook had a late supper prepared and hot water was ready to take upstairs so that any who wished to bathe could do so. Lady Pamela's personal maid – a young French girl of good breeding, exceptional prettiness and lively personality – waited to attend to her ladyship's luggage. The earl's valet was at the ready for his lordship. A housemaid would do likewise for Dallas, and his sister's governess waited for Charlotte.

Having not seen the London staff for seven months, proper greetings for the privileged, more senior, servants and gracious acknowledgment of the others had to be undertaken. Lady Pamela was particularly adept at praise, appreciation and gentle reprimand, managing to bolster egos as she instilled a desire to do better in future, without unbalancing the precarious pecking order so important in keeping the household running smoothly and trouble free.

It was gone two in the morning before any of the family could retire.

So began the season. Dallas would spend most mornings riding in Hyde Park, then home for a late breakfast. Afternoons and evenings would consist of one social engagement after another. Lunch at his club, calling on friends, dinners, soirees, the opera, concerts, art exhibitions, dances and various balls, the Derby and Ascot, Henley Regatta, cricket matches between Oxford and Cambridge or Eton and Harrow, even visits to Regent Street to meet unmarried ladies of a more sexually forthcoming persuasion than those young chaperoned girls whose mothers had entered into the marriage market.

His path crossed with that of the de Ionghs many times. Lady de Iongh and his mother knew each other well, although Lady Dalrymple sometimes intimated that Alison was, on occasions, 'a trifle too gay', meaning, as far as Dallas could establish, flirtatious. Dallas himself was friends with Charles, Lorna's brother. And the two earls were acquaintances.

After Charlotte and Lorna had been formally presented to Queen Victoria at St James's Palace, they were officially admitted into society.

Overnight, both girls became young ladies and, as such, could welcome the attentions of potential suitors.

The first time Dallas saw Lorna after her coming out he could scarcely believe how she had changed. The occasion was a ball, hosted by his parents – or more specifically, his mother. Her main objective was to introduce Charlotte to eligible young men. Invitations had gone out a month earlier and the Park Lane house turned inside out and upside down for the event. The concertina doors between the first-floor billiard room and gallery had been pushed back, making two areas into one large ballroom. Lord Dalrymple's library on that floor was transformed into a refreshment room. An orchestra – cornet, piano, violin and cello – were in one corner of the ballroom, discreetly screened behind a veritable forest of indoor plants.

At street level, the dining room was ready to feed more than two hundred while one drawing room had been turned into a card-playing area for those older guests who preferred whist, loo, vingt-et-un or speculation to the hurly-burly of dancing. Two bedrooms on the second floor served as cloakrooms.

Lady Pamela and Charlotte had spent weeks planning the menu, decorations, music and their own costumes. Dallas and his father were pleased to make themselves scarce. 'Don't know why all the fuss,' the earl grumbled. 'Anyone with half an eye can see that young de Iongh is besotted.'

Dallas was well aware of Charles de Iongh's interest in his sister. It had been there for years, way before etiquette allowed. Now that she had come out, Charles was free to declare his feelings. In fact, he envied his friend. As an only son Charles's inheritance was assured, making him highly acceptable to ambitious mothers not shy in pushing their daughters his way. Charles could have his pick. Not that he wanted it. Charlotte was the one. His only anxiety was whether she would accept him.

At eight o'clock on the night of the ball, Dallas, resplendent in formal evening wear, and Charlotte, dazzling in white and diamonds, were standing at the entrance with their parents to welcome guests. The de Iongh family, like most, were fashionably late.

Lady Alison pressed a cool cheek to Dallas's and murmured, 'How handsome you look.'

Dallas, who had known the countess for years, read no innuendo into her words. She was not much younger than his own mother and part of a different generation.

As was the custom, most women in the room wore white. Lorna looked bewitching. Her wild blonde curls had been tamed, swept up and caught with an intricate weaving into some kind of headpiece. A band of deep green velvet encircled her neck, a sprinkling of seed pearls sewn onto it not detracting in any way from pale, soft skin. Small emeralds and diamonds dangled from her ears.

Good Lord! Dallas thought, almost staring. What's happened to her?

Then she was in front of him, haughty and composed. 'Good evening, Lord Acheson.'

Etiquette decreed that he return the greeting, bow over her hand and turn to the next guest. Instead, he leaned forward and whispered, 'Is that really you?'

The old Lorna – the child of a few weeks ago – would have responded with a grin and perhaps a few cheeky words. The new Lorna – the young lady who had been instructed in the ways of decorum required from the instant she came out – lowered long blonde lashes over cool grey eyes, fluttered her fan and offered languid fingertips. Dallas was confused as he bowed over her hand. Why was his heart suddenly hammering? Surely a short ceremony and a few words from the queen couldn't have brought about such a change. This was the little grub who had pelted him with horse manure only last year. There was no sign of that child now. Where had she gone?

He had lingered for too long over her hand, aware suddenly that she was trying to withdraw it. Straightening, he looked into her eyes, noticing for the first time how the grey irises were ringed with a darker shade. 'Charmed,' he managed, feeling foolish.

Lorna inclined her head, expression polite, before turning away.

The de Ionghs went upstairs, Charlotte's eyes following, her brother's doing the same. 'Damn me, she's beautiful,' Dallas whispered.

'What?' Charlotte was still watching Charles.

'Nothing.' He shook himself mentally. This will not do. Pull yourself together, man.

Dallas nudged his sister. 'Mama is watching you.'

She threw him a grateful look before turning to greet the next guests. In a lull she whispered, 'He is so fine a gentleman.'

'Hush, Charlotte. Charles thinks the world of you. Don't be forward and you will get your wish.'

Shining eyes confirmed what Dallas already knew – that Charlotte's admiration for Charles was a reflection of his for her. A match. What's more, a love match. How lucky they were. If only . . . But no. Lorna could do far better than a fourth son with a courtesy title and few prospects. She was not for him. With an effort he forced himself to pay attention and greet the steady stream of guests.

At eight-thirty, reception duty was handed over to the butler, who would deal with the tardy few yet to arrive. Lady Pamela Dalrymple and Lady Charlotte moved upstairs to the ballroom to perform their next chore, the introductions. Despite the fact that nearly everyone knew each other, gentlemen wishing to dance with this year's crop of debutantes needed to be formally introduced.

Following his mother and sister up the sweeping staircase, Dallas wondered how long Charles and Charlotte would have to hold back before they could acceptably dance together. Not the opening quadrille. His sister would be required to dance with the second-highest ranking guest – probably that odious nephew of Her Majesty. No, they'd have to wait for the second or third waltz or galop.

Lorna? He could at least dance with her, it would be expected. Once only, however. Twice and tongues would wag.

The earl's job was to make himself available to guests, mainly the older men. To some extent Dallas was required to do likewise while, at the same time, keeping an eye out for any young woman sitting out a dance and going to her rescue.

When he saw Lady Bloomsdale bearing down on him his heart sank. She was a large woman who resembled a ship with all sails set. She was also the mother of perhaps the most unattractive daughter in the whole of London. Lady Bloomsdale, despite vast estates and wealth, all of which would go to her daughter, Bernice, and in spite of continuous and persistent efforts, had so far failed to find a match for the poor girl. Men, even those in dire financial straits, ran a mile from Lady Bloomsdale's non-too-subtle approaches. Bernice was now in her mid-twenties and, unless a blind fortune hunter materialised, unlikely to marry. This didn't stop her mother from trying.

'Lord Acheson,' she boomed in a foghorn voice. 'Be a dear and dance with Bernice. I fear her aloofness intimidates young men.'

There was nothing he could do but comply. Bracing himself against the torture of trying to make conversation with Bernice for perhaps ten minutes – an arduous task indeed since the girl was practically dumb with nerves and inclined to bray at the slightest thing – Dallas did his duty. It was agony. She trod on his foot several times, blushed continuously, answered his questions with barely more than a nod or shake of her head. To make matters worse, nervousness caused her to perspire freely and by the time the waltz was over, both gloves were wet through and disgusting rivulets ran down her face and neck, disappearing inside the scooped décolletage and wetting the bodice of her gown. It felt a bit like holding a damp sponge.

The music stopping did not put an end to the ordeal. Dallas had to promenade the floor with Bernice on his arm and then inquire if she would care for any refreshment. Thankfully, she said no.

On returning to the other side of the room – as far from Lady Bloomsdale and her daughter as possible – Dallas joined Lord de Iongh, Charles and Lorna.

'Young Acheson,' boomed de Iongh. 'Where's your damned father, boy?'

'He's here somewhere, my lord. I glimpsed him in conversation no more than a few minutes ago.'

'Good, good.'

Conversation with Lord de Iongh inevitably left Dallas feeling he'd missed something vital. 'Would my lord like me to find him?'

'Eh! No need. Damned fine show.'

'Thank you, my lord.'

'What's the occasion? The countess did mention it on the way here but I'm damned if I can remember.'

'My sister, my lord.'

'Good God! Is she old enough?' Lord de Iongh had obviously forgotten greeting Charlotte at the entrance and that she was exactly the same age as his own daughter.

Dallas answered patiently. 'Seventeen, my lord.' Out of the corner of his eye, he saw Lorna lean forward to peek at him. When he turned, she dropped her eyes, blushed, and moved back behind her father's formidable figure.

'Seventeen, eh!' mused Lord de Iongh. 'I swear, these young gels grow up too fast these days.'

'I'm sure they do,' Dallas said, keeping his eyes on where Lorna had disappeared. Sure enough, she couldn't resist another look, this time accompanied by a tiny smile and slight inclination of the head before leaning back. Dallas returned his full attention to her father.

'. . . the next thing one knows, one is attending their nuptials.'

Dallas assumed they were still speaking of Charlotte. 'No doubt she'll soon find herself betrothed.'

'Yes, of course.' Lord de Iongh's capacity for social chitchat had been exhausted. He had lost interest and moved swiftly to his favourite topic. 'Have you heard? That damned Ponsonby has had the temerity to question the queen's workload. The man is mad. He completely disregards medical advice. Her Majesty has been in delicate health since Albert passed away.'

'Well, Sir William should know best,' Dallas said cautiously, although privately he was inclined to think that the queen's personal physician tended to say whatever was demanded of him.

'Damned right, Acheson. Well said.'

Dallas relaxed. He'd taken a calculated gamble that Lord de Iongh was a royalist and it had worked.

The older man was staring reflectively into space, hands clasped behind his back, rocking on his heels. Each time he swayed backwards, Dallas caught a tantalising glimpse of Lorna. Next to her portly, florid-faced father, she had the appearance of a delicate flower.

Lord de Iongh cleared his throat and Dallas wondered if the man would ramble on in defence of the palace and its occupants. He tended to disagree with de Iongh's beliefs but was too polite to say so. The fact remained, however, that the popularity of Queen Victoria, in fact of the entire royal family, had been waning for several years and public opinion was divided over the cost to the nation of keeping the royals in such grand and opulent style. With the monarch's reluctance to be seen publicly, and her son, the Prince of Wales, preferring the pursuit of leisure and pleasure, the public believed they were not getting their money's worth. Republicans, becoming more outspoken, demanded to know exactly how a Civil List costing £385,000 a year could possibly be justified for a queen who was well known for her miserly ways. The Prince of Wales was proving irresponsible, indiscreet, and considered unsuitable as heir apparent to the throne. The Franco-Prussian War had fostered speculation that the monarch sympathised with Germany. William Gladstone, the Prime Minister, was increasingly preoccupied with what he called 'the royalty question' – how to convince Queen Victoria to be more available to her public. These days it was difficult to know who favoured the queen and who did not.

'Did you hear about that oaf Dilke's speech in Newcastle?' Lord de Iongh asked suddenly, his ruddy face taking on an expression of contempt.

Dallas, clearly at a disadvantage since he knew nothing about it, could only shake his head.

'Suggested that royalty cost the nation a million pounds a year. A million! What rubbish. Even went so far as to call it a mischief.'

'That's outrageous, sir.'

The older man leaned towards Dallas, a conspiratorial look on his face. 'The queen has asked for four hundred pounds a year for John Brown.' While his loyalty to the throne was not in doubt, Lord de Iongh, like most others in the land, had come to dislike the man who had started out as a stableboy at Balmoral, been promoted to gillie by the queen and Prince Consort, then, in 1864, elevated again to become the queen's Highland servant. Brown offended everyone with his brusqueness and the fact that, since her beloved husband's death, he and he alone enjoyed the queen's total attention. It was even rumoured that she had secretly married the man. No-one else dared speak to Her Majesty like Brown. He had been overheard on one occasion disapproving her attire. 'What's this ye've got on today, wumman?'

Derisive talk about John Brown was a favourite pastime for those privy to the comings and goings of the queen's household. The man's influence over the monarch was such that she used him to convey messages to those who had previously enjoyed access to her.

Dallas secretly approved of the rough-and-ready Brown. He rather hoped that the Scotsman had indeed found his way into Victoria's bed – it might relieve her sour countenance. Such feelings, however, could not be disclosed to Lord de Iongh. 'His responsibilities are great, my lord,' Dallas responded, adding quickly at Lord de Iongh's expression of disapproval, 'though not, I fear, as great as his affections for his influence over Her Majesty.'

He was rewarded with a bark of approving laughter. 'Damn me, Acheson, you'd make a fine politician.'

Dallas could at last move off the subject without appearing rude. 'With your permission, my lord, may I ask the Lady Lorna for a dance?'

'Certainly,' de Iongh said jovially. 'If indeed my daughter has room on her card.' He turned away to speak to someone else and Dallas found himself face-to-face with Lorna.

'If a dance is acceptable, my lady, it would be my honour.'

Her brother, oblivious of his friend's sudden interest in Lorna, laughed. 'She's been saving a space for someone, haven't you, sis?'

Lorna frowned at him. 'Not really. I don't see why I should accept every offer.'

Dallas raised an eyebrow. 'Who's the lucky man? I shall challenge him immediately.'

She giggled, remembered her manners, fluttered an ornate fan and consulted the dance card in an effort to hide her embarrassment. At seven, Lorna had told her governess that one day she would marry Lord Dallas Acheson, not understanding the response received as to why she couldn't. At twelve, though aware of the intricate do's and don't's of just who would make her a suitable husband, Lorna still had a secret crush on Lord Dalrymple's fourth son and she was flustered by the gleam of attraction she now saw in his eyes. There was one space left on her card. She showed it to Dallas. 'There.'

His eyebrows rose in mock surprise. 'Only one?'

'I think, sir, that one should be sufficient.'

He bowed over her hand hiding a smile. 'Then one will have to do. I shall count the minutes until then.'

Lorna only just managed not to smile with delight. Nodding gracefully, she moved a step closer to her father.

Charles, thinking Dallas was teasing his sister, said in an undertone, 'She still has the devil of a temper, old chap. She's taking this season so seriously. If you mock her too much you're liable to end up on the receiving end.'

Even though Charles was a close friend, Dallas could not tell him his true feelings. Instead he pulled a face and turned the conversation. 'Can you believe how grown up the two of them are?'

The other looked momentarily embarrassed, cleared his throat and ran a finger around the stiff dress-shirt collar. 'Your sister has become quite beautiful.'

'Indeed,' Dallas agreed.

'Ah . . . Then you know how I feel about her, don't you, old chap?'

'I have noticed your eyes develop bovine characteristics whenever she enters a room.'

Charles responded with a sickly smile. 'I'll speak to Lord Dalrymple, of course.'

'I'd advise you to speak to Charlotte first,' Dallas said with a grin.

'Indeed.' Charles gave a nervous cough. 'If I call on her, will she receive me do you think?'

'Last week I'd have said yes but she's a woman now.' Dallas shrugged. 'Far be it from me to speak for her.' Then, taking pity on his friend's desperate expression, added, 'At a guess, I'd still say the same.'

Charles, relieved, went off in search of Charlotte. Lorna turned back to him and Dallas gave her a dazzling smile. 'May I be permitted to say how fetching your gown is?'

'Thank you.' A flush rose to her cheeks.

'When are you returning to Edinburgh?'

'Mama wants to leave next week.'

'So soon!'

Lorna pouted slightly. 'Everyone I know will stay until the grouse season opens. It really is too bad of Mama to leave so early.' She fluttered her fan and inclined her head to someone nearby. 'Charlotte is staying on, I understand?'

Flashes of the child were still there, for which Dallas was grateful. With his interest aroused, it would be so easy to flirt. 'Why don't you see if you can stay with us? I'm sure your mama would allow it.'

Lorna's face brightened. 'What a wonderful idea. I shall speak to Charlotte at dinner.' She looked at him boldly. 'Will you be here?'

The fact that she returned the attraction he felt for her was not lost on Dallas. But what was the point? Both his family and hers would quickly forbid the development of a relationship destined to go nowhere. 'Alas, no. Papa wants me in Scotland to assist with preparations for this year's pheasants. Will you be accompanying your parents to Tayside this year?'

She hid her disappointment well. 'Of course.'

'Then I look forward to seeing you there.'

Music started for the galop and the next young man on Lorna's card appeared and bore her away.

A week later, only Dallas and Lady de Iongh travelled north by train. Lord de Iongh asked if Dallas would be so kind as to accompany his wife in their carriage. 'Her wretched maid is ill. God knows why she has to go now – says it's something to do with a church fete. Works too damned hard on charitable affairs if you ask me.' Lord de Iongh was clearly uninterested in his wife's reasons for cutting short the London season, merely vexed that he had to find a suitable travelling companion for her. Both Charles and Lorna would be spending several more weeks in London. The earl, having pressing political reasons for staying, was only making a brief return to Scotland for the start of pheasant shooting on the first day of October.

With Lady Dalrymple looking after Lorna as well as Charlotte and Lord Dalrymple's gout playing up, Dallas was the only one Lord de Iongh felt he could reasonably ask to travel with his wife.

Dallas, as was expected of him, courteously agreed. At least it would be company and he knew she played beggar-my-neighbour tolerably well, a welcome relief on the tediously long trip.

He was pleased to be leaving London. Dallas had been expected to escort Lorna to any function to which she had no-one to accompany her. It was a week of hell. At times he felt that his attraction to Lorna would burst from him. A chaste peck on the cheek in greeting or farewell had him burning to hold her.

In lucid moments, Dallas told himself his feelings were caused by wanting something he knew he couldn't have. By the time he boarded the train with Lady de Iongh, he'd managed to convince himself that Lorna was no more than the friend he'd always known. He was glad of that. To sit with her mother for twelve hours harbouring passionate emotions for Lorna would have been intolerable.

As they waved goodbye, Dallas actually felt quite proud of his restraint. It was the honourable thing to do. He was a gentleman. His conscience was clear.

He did not anticipate the bottle of wine and two glasses produced from a travelling basket as soon as the train gathered speed.

'The trip is so dreary,' Lady de Iongh explained. 'Join me.'

She kept Dallas off-balance and uncertain for several hours. She would lean forward to tap his knee with her fan, then sit back with a small frown. She introduced several topics not normally discussed in polite conversation, retreating modestly if he responded in kind but persisting when Dallas appeared unsure how to react. Playing cards, her fingers brushed his several times although she appeared not to notice. With darkness falling outside, Dallas was both aroused and scared. He had no idea what Lady de Iongh was up to or even if she intended anything at all.

In his limited experience, Dallas had met three kinds of women with two modes of behaviour. Either they did or they didn't. It was as simple as that. Those who didn't were to be treated with due regard for their virtuous natures. Those who did either worked in establishments operating specifically for that purpose or they openly accosted one in the street. The third kind was more difficult to read. Bored high-born wives looking for a diversion. Alison de Iongh was blurring the boundaries. He was uncertain what she wanted of him.

He was definitely not expecting a second bottle of wine.

'I do so hate to drink alone.' With one hand she opened her bodice slightly. 'I feel the heat terribly. Wine is so refreshing. Here.'

Unwisely, he held out his glass.

She steadied his hand with hers, laughing gaily. 'This wretched train shakes so.'

Dallas sipped sparingly but Lady de Iongh quaffed hers. 'I hope you don't mind, Dallas, I'm developing a headache. I must let my hair out.' With that, she stood, removed several silver combs, and tresses, gold and curly, tumbled free. 'That's better,' she breathed, tossing her head.

Dallas didn't know where to look. It was such an intimate act.

'Oh, come now, don't be so stuffy. It's only hair.'

At that moment the train gave one of its unexpected lurches and Lady de Iongh lost her balance and sat down heavily, right next to him.

Dallas fidgeted in his seat.

She made no attempt to move away. Her eyes locked on his. Dallas felt he might drown in the limpid pools. 'Do I shock you?'

'I . . . No, of course not.'

She smiled slightly. 'Of course I do. I shock most people. Have you heard of William Acton?'

Dallas tensed. The subject change was of no comfort. 'The doctor?'

Alison nodded and he watched fascinated as curls bobbed around her face. 'He's written a book.'

'Really?' What else was he supposed to say? Lady de Iongh watched him expectantly. 'What kind of book?' He knew what kind of book. Half the British Isles had a copy.

'About sex,' Alison said bluntly. 'The man claims ladies of quality have no sexual desires.'

'Oh.' Dallas ran a finger under his collar. It felt unusually tight.

'He's wrong.' She laid one hand on his leg, raising an eyebrow when he jumped. 'The earl is away in London a good deal. He is much older than me. Even when he is home . . .' She shrugged elegant shoulders. 'Do you understand?' An edge of exasperation had crept into her tone.

Dallas heard it. 'I . . . I think so.' *She's Lorna's mother, for God's sake!*

'Do you think I'm attractive?'

He'd never really thought about it. 'You are beautiful.'

Something glowed in her eyes. She reminded Dallas of a satisfied cat.

It was now or never. His heart was hammering wildly. There was a fifty-fifty chance of getting it wrong, whatever he did. Her face was close to his. The partially open bodice revealed a swell of milky breasts. Dallas felt desire stir. He tentatively leaned closer and she parted her lips. Dallas took the plunge. Her reaction exceeded his wildest dreams.

Alison de Iongh, Lady de Iongh, Countess de Iongh, wife to an earl of the peerage, a man who was a respected member of the House of Lords and one who had Queen Victoria's respect, gave a small cry, pressed herself closer, wrapped both arms around him and whispered against his lips, 'You can do whatever you like to me.'

It must be said in defence of Dallas that this particular temptation was damned near irresistible. He was like a small boy let loose in a confectionery establishment. When the train rumbled and hissed to a stop at their final destination, Dallas was in a daze. Alison had captivated . . . Well, it wasn't his heart. Reason and commonsense told him he was playing with fire. Prudence, however, had been overruled by a somewhat more basic desire. Justification seemed so flimsy – he was not being unfaithful to Lorna, she would always be out of his reach; it was once only, the earl would never find out; this was obviously not Alison's first extramarital encounter, nor likely to be her last; anyway, a man had to gain experience somewhere.

Expecting Alison would retreat into cool aloofness, the experience a never-to-be-mentioned or repeated thing of the past, Dallas was somewhat surprised, and more than a little alarmed, to learn she had other ideas.

'Friday,' she whispered before they alighted from the carriage. 'Come to Canongate at eleven.'

Friday! So far away. Only two days from now. What am I to do?

Dallas knew it was wrong. He was aware that the servants gossiped about them. They'd be found out eventually. Dallas didn't care. Alison was like a drug, likely to bring him down, yet intoxicating and habit forming. He'd leave her bed determined never to return but, by the time the next arranged assignation arrived, found himself eager and impatient, unable to deny the fires of longing that spread within him. 'Just one last time,' he told himself over and over again.

Guilt took up residence in his heart. Dallas was

betraying everyone. Still, he could no more end the relationship than fly.

One month into the affair with Lady de Iongh, Lorna's betrothal to the Marquis of Dumfries was announced. Lord Dumfries was a widower with no heirs. A dour and humourless man who had vast estates bordering with those belonging to the de Ionghs in the Dumfries and Galloway region, he was eight years older than Lorna's father. The marquis had not so much as glimpsed young Lady de Iongh when he decided to marry her. He had approached the earl and suggested that a marriage between their two families would strengthen both. The union, as far as he was concerned, was to produce heirs. In return, Lorna would enjoy the status of marchioness. A perfect business arrangement.

Without consulting his daughter, or even his wife, Lord de Iongh accepted Lord Dumfries's proposal. It made sense. Lorna would outlive the old man by many years. With luck, by the time he died, she would have produced a male successor to his lands and title. If the boy were young enough, Lord de Iongh, or his own heir, Charles, could exert considerable influence over the lad and control the administration of both estates.

Lorna was horrified. 'No, Papa, please. He's so old.'

She was even more disgusted on first meeting her intended. A plain, bony face with hooded eyes perched on stooped shoulders, giving him the appearance of having no neck. He was not tall, and skinny legs bowed outwards. There was something almost reptilian about the man's appearance, especially in his cold stare and bloodless lips. Lord Dumfries barely acknowledged Lorna other than to comment loudly and crudely that she appeared to have all the makings of an excellent brood mare.

Lorna's mother, equally aghast that her husband could be so uncaring about their daughter's happiness, and trying desperately to console the girl, unwittingly set in motion an event that would have far-reaching consequences. 'Calm yourself, dear child. You are no different from many women. Give the old wreck a son and look elsewhere for love and pleasure.'

Unfortunately, Lorna believed she had already found the man of her dreams – Dallas. Yet, like him, she accepted that a union between them would be impossible. Marriage to another was something that would be bearable if the man was young and possessed a modicum of good looks and humour. Lord Dumfries was more than she could bear. The mere thought of him made her flesh crawl. However, betrothed she was and married she would become, there was nothing Lorna could do about that. But with her mother's apparent blessing, she could make damned sure of tasting something infinitely more palatable before the old bastard got his hands on her.

Lorna had no idea that the subject of her intentions spent so much time at Canongate. Alison made sure her daughter was kept busy with social engagements and works of a charitable nature.

These, she attended to willingly. Indeed, it never once crossed Lorna's mind to pursue her plan while still in Edinburgh. The forthcoming pheasant shoot on Lord Dalrymple's estate in Tayside should provide an ideal opportunity.

The shooting party was expected to run for four full days. Dallas, as youngest son of the host, probably in the field with a gun for only two of them. For the rest of the time he would be expected to help entertain other guests. Lorna was sure a chance would present itself. Her father should be out on all four days. Her mother much in demand at the card table. Brother Charles, when not shooting, would be mooning around Charlotte.

The day finally dawned. Lorna and her parents travelled to Perth by train. A coach then took them on to Tayside. Charles would be coming over from the de Ionghs' Perthshire estate later in the day.

As they drew up outside the Dalrymples' imposing country residence, Lord de Iongh would have been astounded if he'd known that both his wife and daughter, unbeknown to each other, had plans for the good-looking young man who came down the wide stone steps, a welcoming smile on his lips.

For that matter, so would Dallas.

Lord and Lady de Iongh were shown to a sumptuous guest suite on the first floor, Lorna to the second floor where unmarried girls had their own rooms. Charles, when he arrived, would be at the other end of the house with the bachelors.

A housemaid took care of Lorna's unpacking and brought her hot water so she might bathe. Refreshments had been laid out. As with all guests, Lorna was expected to remain in her room until it was time to go downstairs for dinner.

Boredom was relieved by the arrival of Charlotte. She rushed into the room, kissed Lorna's cheek, then dropped all pretence and asked, 'Is Charles here yet?'

Lorna smiled at her friend's eagerness. 'He's coming over later this afternoon. Papa expects him around six.'

'I do hope he won't be late.'

'My dear brother is as keen to see you as you are him,' Lorna said, envying Charlotte's affection – both given and received. 'Wild horses could not keep him away.'

Charlotte blushed. 'Do not think me forward.'

Lorna caught Charlotte's hands and swung her around. 'You are a baggage but I forgive you.' Her face clouded. 'I daresay you know of my betrothal?'

Charlotte sobered immediately. 'Oh, my dear. How selfish of me. You poor darling.'

Tears formed in Lorna's eyes. 'He is quite hideous and does not try to hide the fact that an heir is the only reason for our union.' Lorna brushed her cheeks impatiently. 'But I will not think of him until I must. There. No more tears. Tell me about the other guests.'

The two girls gossiped until it was time to dress for dinner.

Lorna took great care with her toilette. As she descended the wide staircase, more than one pair of male eyes glanced up with admiration. But Lorna was seeking Dallas. He had already seen her and when she looked his way, both smiled in acknowledgment. To her delight Dallas excused himself from the group he was with and made his way to the foot of the stairs.

'How lovely you look,' he said softly, bending over her hand. All good intentions disappeared as the feelings evoked in London flooded back.

'Thank you.'

'Ah, there you are.' Lady Dalrymple linked her arm affectionately through her son's and smiled at Lorna. 'I swear, you young people cause such headaches. I was at a loss to know who to pair you with, my dear. An unattached male simply would not do with your fiancé so far away. Anyway, all's well now. Dallas has said he'd be delighted.' A small frown creased her brow. 'I do hope you don't mind. I'm sure it will be all right. After all, you're practically brother and sister.'

'I don't mind at all, Lady Dalrymple. It will give us a chance to catch up. We've hardly seen each other since London.'

'Good.' Duty done, the countess was anxious to circulate among other guests.

Left alone, Dallas had no choice but to offer his congratulations on the news of Lorna's engagement, though it was the last thing he felt like doing.

She glanced briefly at the diamond ring on her

finger and gave a small shudder, remembering Lord Dumfries's words when he put it there. 'Don't you dare lose it. It belonged to my grandmother. This ring is worth a fortune. You're a lucky girl.'

Dallas saw her shiver. He knew she couldn't possibly have feelings for Lord Dumfries but hadn't expected any outward show of revulsion. Ladies of quality had certain duties and went about them, irrespective of how onerous they might be, with the poise expected of them. 'Is my lady displeased with the arrangement?'

'You are my friend, are you not?' Lorna asked by way of response. Tears glinted in her eyes.

'You know I am.'

'Then do not speak to me as you would a stranger.'

Dallas leaned closer. 'Lorna, what is it? What ails you?'

'We must speak,' she whispered, head lowered. 'But not here.'

Dallas wanted to reach out and touch her. Lorna was clearly very unhappy. 'Perhaps a ride with Charles and Charlotte in the morning,' he suggested.

She fingered the locket around her neck and nodded. Her brother would welcome the opportunity to be with Charlotte away from prying eyes, which could very well give rise to a chance to be alone with Dallas. 'That would be most agreeable,' she murmured.

Parental permission to go riding the next day was happily granted by both mothers. What better way for youngsters to spend time than enjoying the company of friends? Being with Dallas and Charles, Alison and Pamela had no reason to worry about their daughters' well-being.

After breakfast the four set off. Charles and Charlotte rode on ahead, engrossed in each other. Lorna seemed subdued and silent. Dallas didn't push her, assuming she'd tell him why when she was ready.

They ate a picnic lunch beside a swiftly flowing stream that ran along the foothills of Glen Almond. 'Oh, my hat,' Charlotte exclaimed, packing away the last of the food. 'I couldn't eat another crumb.' She jumped up and stretched out a hand to Charles. 'Come on, lazybones. Let's walk off some of that food.'

Groaning, Charles allowed her to pull him up. 'Are you joining us?'

The question was rhetorical. Dallas and Lorna would not be welcome.

Lorna shaded her eyes. 'I'm far too comfortable here. You three go ahead. I'll be fine.'

Naturally, as Lorna had anticipated, she couldn't be left on her own and, as expected, Dallas said he'd stay too.

Charlotte and Charles set off, promising to be away no longer than a couple of hours. Watching his friend help his sister over the pebbly riverbed, Dallas said idly, 'Charlotte seems very fond of Charles these days.'

'Fond!' Lorna responded with a humourless laugh. 'She adores him.'

Dallas threw her a sharp look. 'You disapprove?'

Lorna's cheeks coloured slightly. 'Forgive me. My own unhappiness clouds sincere feelings of joy for Charles and Charlotte. Of course I am pleased for them. Charles could well declare his love this very afternoon and would do so with my blessing. He spent some minutes alone with Lord Dalrymple when he arrived last night. Charles has said nothing to me but from the way he's behaving, I'd say your father has no objections.' She sighed deeply. 'How lucky they are.'

'What troubles you then? Come, speak frankly. You are as close to me as my own sister.'

'Am I?' Pain crossed Lorna's face. 'You do not feel like my brother.' She plucked at her skirt before looking intently into his face. 'But I will be frank. There is no choice left to me.'

'So. It is your forthcoming marriage. It does not please you.'

'How could it?' Lorna cried out. 'He is an old man. He is nothing to me. I will hate him, I know I will. Why should I submit to this? It's not fair.'

Dallas watched a single tear slide down her cheek. Reaching over he gently brushed it away. To reveal his true feelings was impossible and his own pain was acute. 'I know it is hard but you will have children to love.'

'His children!' she said bitterly. 'What about the other kind of love? I will never know a lover's arms or the feel of his kiss. Not for me a wildly beating heart or the sparkle I see in Charlotte's eyes when she looks at Charles. The thought of marriage to

Lord Dumfries makes me want to die inside. And that is probably what I shall do. Become old and dried up before my time.' More tears fell and she shook her head helplessly. 'I am a woman yet I cannot choose my husband, I know that. If I could, I would choose you.'

'Me!' Dallas's heart skipped a beat. Her revelation had taken him by surprise. Lorna was well outside acceptable social boundaries. Eyes could say it. Words, however, should not be uttered. And yet he was glad she had spoken. Warning bells clanged. He was in dangerous territory in more ways than one.

'I cannot marry you, Dallas, I have always known that, even though it is what I desire most in this world. This sadness would be bearable if I married a kind and loving man. A young man.' Her eyes were still locked with his. 'But this old . . . disgusting creature with bony hands and watery eyes, his thin lips and yellow teeth, his stoop and pot-belly.' She shivered. 'He even smells old. How can I bear it?' Lorna bowed her head and sobbed.

Dallas moved quickly to her side and took her hands in his. 'Calm yourself, dear one. I am with you. Lord Dumfries is far from a pretty picture but, as you point out, he is old. Soon he must die. You will still be young. As a widow of means you will be free to marry whoever you wish.'

'You,' she whispered. 'I love you. Will you wait for the marquis to die?' She tried to read his look. 'Do my words shock your tongue to silence? Or do I hope for something you are unable to give?'

Oh, if only I could. 'Shush, Lorna. Do not torture

me, dearest, with what I can never have. You are betrothed to another, and even if this were not so, as we both know, more cannot be between us.'

'But it can, dear heart. And I mean it to be so.' She looked away, towards the distant hills of Glen Almond. 'Can you still see them?'

'Just.' Dallas pointed. 'There.' The indistinct figures of Charles and Charlotte moving further away. 'What are you saying, Lorna?' His heart beat a wild acceptance of what his head told him to refuse. Even if he promised to wait for her, even if Dumfries dropped dead on his wedding night, what about Alison? Would she stand by and allow her daughter to marry her own lover? Somehow he doubted it. All else aside, Alison's ego would not tolerate such a match.

Lorna took his silence as unhappy acceptance that they could never be together. She lay her head against his shoulder. 'I will marry Lord Dumfries and I will bear his children, but he shall not be the first man to touch me. You shall be that man. I give myself to you. I come to you freely and willing, asking only that you know I love you. Until the day I marry, I am yours. Will you take me, Dallas? Will you show me how love feels?' She turned her face to his. 'Can we not pretend, even for a little while, that we belong together?'

Her lips were close to his. Knowing full well what folly such weakness was, Dallas drew her towards him. It was a long kiss, full of yearning. 'Are you sure?' he asked breathlessly when their lips finally parted.

'Dallas, my darling!' It was a cry of despair. 'Give me a memory. Something I can take with me. I beg of you, don't let me go to his bed not knowing how it should be.'

She had made up her mind. To refuse her now would be cruel. Or so Dallas told himself. The irony never once crossed his mind that, had Lorna but known it, the man who introduced her to sensuality was merely passing on lessons taught to him by her own mother.

She was like a clean page, waiting for him to write his name on it. Dallas's lips found hers, again and again, feeling her quiver as passion swept all else aside. One hand found her breast, then his fingers slipped inside her bodice, caressing and stroking until Lorna was sobbing with desire. Very slowly, he removed her clothes, kissing each secret place with tenderness. When at last she lay naked and open beside him, Dallas ran his mouth and hands over her entire body before moving away and sitting up.

'No,' she moaned, reaching out for him. 'Come back.'

'Open your eyes,' he said softly.

Lorna watched while he removed all his clothes. Her lips parted in awed surprise when she saw the size of his erect and ready penis. 'Do not be afraid,' he whispered, leaning towards her. 'I want you to know me.'

He lay back and she propped herself over him on one elbow, running a finger slowly from his neck, around nipples and down again, her eyes following. 'You are beautiful,' she breathed. 'So different from what I imagined.'

'Touch me.'

A fingernail softly scratched the length of his erection before thumb and forefinger encircled it. 'What do I do?' she asked.

'What do you want to do?'

'You will think I'm shameless. Help me, Dallas, for I don't know what is right or wrong.'

'Nothing can be wrong between two people who seek the same thing.'

She lowered her head and explored him with lips and fingers until he gently eased her away. 'Your turn.' He moved down her body, his tongue finding and probing. Lorna gave herself up to the unknown pleasure and, when he had her trembling on the very brink of release, he rose and swiftly entered her.

Lorna tensed, then thrust back at him with a stifled cry as passion overrode all else. Moving together, time ceased to exist until he heard her call his name. Dallas gave himself up to his own sensations and his seed spilled into her body.

They lay together in silence, one of her hands gently stroking his hair. 'I had no idea,' Lorna whispered eventually.

He could feel her heart beating against his chest, wildly at first and then subsiding to calm. Her breath was on his cheek. Finally she stirred. 'Thank you, my dearest one.'

Dallas propped himself on an elbow. Lorna's eyes were shining with love, serene with satisfaction. 'No regrets?' He too felt relaxed and happy.

'How could I? When the old man dies we will be wed. He won't live long. It is right that you were the first.'

She had done no more than voice his own thoughts but a strange disquiet ran through Dallas. Lorna was headstrong, even a little spoilt. Could she be capable of hastening the demise of Lord Dumfries? As much as he abhorred the idea of her marriage, the thought of taking such steps to end it was even more unacceptable.

'Mmmm.' She snuggled against him.

He held her tightly, loving the closeness between them yet in despair. From whichever way he looked at things, obstacles seemed to rise up. Most had Alison's face. He had complicated his life beyond belief and could see no easy solution. In love with this girl, yet lusting after her mother. Dallas knew he'd have to find some way of ending his affair with Alison, it was the very least he could do. Reluctantly, he stirred. 'We'd better dress. Charles and Charlotte could return at any moment.'

By the time the other two did get back, Charlotte near bursting with happiness and Charles fairly glowing with excitement, Lorna and Dallas were sitting a discreet distance from each other discussing trivialities.

'You should have come with us. The view was well worth it,' Charlotte bubbled, glancing coyly at Charles.

By the look on his friend's face, Dallas suspected that he had found the courage to declare his feelings. And by his sister's behaviour, they were reciprocated. Lucky them, he thought, with no rancour.

That was nearly two months ago. Since that day, he and Lorna managed to snatch a few hours together each week. Her social commitments, and preparations for the forthcoming marriage, made manipulation of their combined engagements extremely difficult. Extricating himself from Alison's attention was even more so. In fact, he failed. If he raised the subject of servants' gossip or the possibility of Lord de Iongh catching them, Alison knew exactly how to take his mind off the subject. On more than one occasion, Dallas ruefully acknowledged to himself that most of his actions and reactions appeared to be ruled solely by one particular part of his anatomy. He was old enough to understand that the only real thing between himself and Alison was intense lust. He was too young, too full of juice, too fascinated by the forbidden to know how, or even wish to know how, to stop it.

Lying in Lorna's arms, a heart full of young love, his resolve remained strong. Easy. He'd simply tell Alison it was over. But the older woman held a strange power over him and, with her, he weakened time after time.

In one way or another, Dallas's complicated love-life occupied most of his waking thoughts. Lorna's wedding was set for a week hence and, as much as he dreaded the occasion, knew it would provide a partial solution to his problem. Then, as if life wasn't convoluted enough, came the final and inevitable catastrophe. Lorna told him she was with child.

'This is perfect,' she'd said happily. 'If it's a boy he will inherit the estates and title. The old fool will think it's his. When we wed, it will be your son, not his, who is heir.'

The winter sunshine had a watered-down appearance as it crept, triangular-shaped, over the tangled sheets. As usual, Dallas found himself cursing his weakness in allowing Alison, yet again, to waylay any more honourable intentions. The trouble was, even though his primary attraction lay at a most basic level, he liked her. As well as being gifted in matters carnal, Lady Alison de Iongh was intelligent and entertaining. Lying next to her, Dallas knew. *I've got to get out of this mess before it's too late.*

He stirred and sat up. 'I must go.'

Alison pouted. 'Stay a while, what's the hurry? My husband returns the day after tomorrow and remains until the new year. This might be our last chance.' Strong fingers gripped his arms. 'Oh, my dearest, I will count the days until he leaves for London again.'

Dallas had his mind set on the logistics of leaving the house undetected. He would have to reach the stables equally invisibly, and in a manner that made Lorna believe he'd only just arrived. Stopping in the act of pulling on linen under-breeches, Dallas glanced over his shoulder and smiled. 'You will appreciate me more after the enforced abstinence.'

Again she pouted, but her eyes teased him. 'I could not possibly appreciate you more than I already do.' She reached out and tweaked a buttock. 'You look so damned fetching in your underwear.'

He turned and fell on top of her, hands holding both arms above her head. 'You are utterly shameless. I could —'

Alison was never to know exactly what it was that Dallas could. They both heard the disturbance in the hall — a man's voice demanding to know what ailed his wife and the housekeeper imploring him not to disturb Lady de Iongh.

'Oh my God! It's the earl!' Alison gasped.

But it was too late to do anything about it. Dallas dived for his shirt. The door opened and a smile of greeting died on Lord de Iongh's lips. Behind him, Mrs Kelly smirked spitefully.

'You young puppy!' Lord de Iongh stepped into the room and slammed the door shut in the housekeeper's face. 'What is the meaning of this, sir?'

Dallas felt around for his buckskin breeches, his mind frozen.

Alison clutched the covers under her chin and began to weep. 'He forced himself on me.'

Dallas gaped at her.

Suspicion had replaced the initial shock on her husband's face. 'Have you no voice, madam, that you might have called a protest? Or do all our servants become deaf in my absence?'

'I swear, the intrusion so terrified me I could

54

utter not a sound.' Tears rolled down her cheeks in a thoroughly credible display of misery.

'Alison!' Dallas protested unwisely.

'Silence!' roared the earl. 'How dare you address my wife in such intimate terms? What say you, sir?'

Dallas eyed the earl's silver-topped cane. So far, it hadn't occurred to him to use it. There was nothing he could do but take the blame. Alison, in protecting herself, hadn't hesitated to place him in an impossible position. Unfair as it was, and the implications were only just beginning to sink in, Dallas had no option other than to behave like a gentleman. 'This was entirely my doing. The lady is innocent of any misdemeanour. My feelings for her overcame all reason. I implore you, Lord de Iongh, take whatever retribution you deem necessary.' He steeled himself for the stinging blows.

But Alison's husband was not convinced. He turned to her. 'In my opinion, madam, a man intent on ravishing a lady does not stop to remove every stitch of her clothing.'

Alison's performance did her credit. Her eyes filled with more tears. 'He said he would kill me. I was too afraid to resist.'

The earl looked back at Dallas for confirmation.

'It is as my lady says,' he confirmed stiffly.

Lord de Iongh nodded. 'Very well. I will wait for you in the library. As for you, madam, stay here. I will see you later.' With that, he turned and left. Dallas heard him bellowing at the housekeeper. 'What are you gawping at, woman? Go about your business.'

'Dallas,' Alison breathed.

'Do not trouble yourself with pretty excuses, Alison.' His voice was cold. 'I know my duty.'

'What else could I do?' she pleaded. 'Please, my dearest . . .'

'A seducer is one thing, Alison. A rapist quite another. You have condemned me to hell in order to save yourself.' He pulled on his boots. 'Good day to you, madam.'

'Wait,' she cried.

Dallas retrieved his waistcoat and coat. 'I will see the earl in private.'

'What will you tell him?' she asked fearfully.

'Trust me, Alison, the damage is already done. You can rely on me to behave impeccably. I only hope you sleep untroubled by your mischief. Since you accuse me of rape, my death at the gallows should relieve you of worry that the truth will out.' With that, and with Alison's now genuine sorrow filling the room, Dallas made his way down to the library.

Lord de Iongh stood facing the window, hands behind his back. He did not turn around. 'Your manners do you credit, Acheson, though I fear it is a little late in the day to remember them. My lady's accusation, and your own admission of guilt, leave me no course of action other than to inform the proper authorities. In deference to my friendship with your father, I will delay doing so for forty-eight hours.'

'Thank you, my lord.'

'If you know what's good for you, young man, you'll leave this country and never return.'

'Sir —'

'Silence!' roared the earl. 'I have no wish to hear more lies. Get out.'

Dallas waited but Lord de Iongh had finished. He gave a stiff bow to the ramrod-straight back and left the house. In the stables he had the groom saddle his horse and went through to the coach-house where Lorna waited.

'I cannot stay,' he said, holding her at arm's length.

'Whatever is wrong, my love?'

Dallas gave a twisted smile. 'No doubt the gossip will reach your ears soon enough. Try not to think too ill of me. I have been a fool but I am no criminal.'

'My darling, what are you saying?'

He bent and kissed her cheek. 'Forget me. It is best that you do.'

'Forget you!' Lorna stamped her foot. 'How? I carry your child. What has happened, Dallas? At least let me hear it from your lips.'

How could he tell her? He turned away. 'Goodbye, my love. We shall not see each other again.'

Lorna ran sobbing towards the house. Dallas strode to his horse and mounted, spurring it immediately to a gallop. He'd been caught out, as he well and truly deserved to be. Angry as he was at Alison's betrayal, furious with his own weakness and how it would cause Lorna pain, the overwhelming emotion of grief ran through him. He couldn't have the girl he loved but now he was unable even to remain in the same country. He had to get away. Fast. Turn his back on all he knew to save his own skin. *Forgive me, my darling.* How could she? Eyes streaming from the cold – or were they tears of terrible sorrow – Dallas did not look back, nor slow his pace until reaching the Grange.

Lady Dalrymple was in the drawing room, writing letters. Of his father, there was no sign. Dallas knew he had to tell his mother everything if she were to help him get away. And leaving was his only option. The disgrace when his supposed conduct became common knowledge would make his ongoing presence in Edinburgh, indeed, in the entire British Isles, impossible. Lord de Iongh had given him forty-eight hours. After that, he would be a wanted man.

Lady Pamela looked up and smiled when she heard his step. The smile froze as she sighted his expression. 'Something is amiss?'

Time was of the essence. She'd learn the details sooner rather than later. This was not the time to hesitate. Dallas told her everything. Well, everything to do with Lady de Iongh. There was no point in burdening his mother with Lorna and the baby as well.

She heard him out in silence as he paced up and down in front of her, eyes never leaving his face. Aside from turning very pale, Lady Dalrymple remained expressionless. 'There is no time to waste,' she said when, finished, he dropped to one knee at her side. 'You must leave here immediately.' Picking up a small silver bell she rang it urgently. A housemaid appeared.

'Ah, Abigail, have Mrs Potter and Victor report to me.' With the girl gone she went on. 'We'll need their help. Victor can go with you to Tynemouth.'

'Tynemouth!' Dallas said in surprise. 'Surely it would be better to head north.'

'It's winter,' his mother reminded him. 'Sailings are few and far between. North is exactly where the police will expect you to head. It will take some time for them to start looking over the border. I have a cousin in Newcastle and will provide you with a letter of introduction. He may be able to help.'

Panic rose within him. 'But where should I go?'

'The colonies,' his mother said calmly. 'Australia, Africa, Canada or India. Take whatever ship leaves first. I understand that life can be quite tolerable in the dominions.'

'Mama, I did not force myself on Alison.'

'Lady de Iongh,' his mother cut back coldly, 'is a strumpet with no thought for anything but herself. I am appalled by her betrayal. Come, Dallas, rid yourself of this woman. She is not worth the trouble. You are far from the first young man to fall for her charms.'

Dallas hung his head. The shame this scandal would heap on the shoulders of his family almost too much to bear. 'I am sorry, Mama. I have been a fool.'

'No more than many before you,' his mother continued in brisk tones.

She went to say more, but stopped as Mrs Potter and Victor knocked and entered. 'Come in.

Close the door behind you.' When the house-keeper and head groom stood before her, she spoke calmly, with no trace of panic. 'Lord Acheson will be leaving Britain immediately. Mrs Potter, pack his belongings for an extended sea journey. Victor, you will travel to Newcastle-Upon-Tyne and deliver him safely to my cousin. Neither of you are to discuss this matter with the other servants. Victor, prepare the wagon. I want you ready to leave within the hour.'

They left to carry out her bidding. 'Dallas, come with me.' Lady Pamela rose and moved swiftly towards the door.

He followed her upstairs and along the passage into her boudoir.

'Wait,' she ordered, stepping up to a painting and lifting it from the wall. Behind sat a small safe which Dallas had not known existed. Carefully, his mother withdrew two small pouches. She tipped the contents onto her vanity chest before crossing the room and sinking down on a chaise longue. 'They are rightfully yours. Take them and use their value as you see fit.'

Dallas stared at the jewels. Emeralds, diamonds, sapphires, rubies and pearls set in necklaces, rings, earrings and brooches of the finest gold. He'd never seen his mother wear any of them.

'Mama, this is too much. I cannot.'

'They're yours anyway,' she replied.

'I don't understand.'

'You will. Come and sit by me.' She patted a place next to her. 'I too have something to confess.'

Dallas hesitated then joined his mother.

'Those jewels belonged to your father's mother.'

'Then surely they now must go to Thomas.'

Lady Pamela shook her head. 'Under normal circumstances I would never have admitted to this but now you need to hear it.' She bit her lip, gave a little sigh, and went on. 'Lord Dalrymple is not your real father.'

Dallas couldn't believe what he was hearing. 'Not my –'

'Sshh, my darling. There's so much to tell and so little time. Hear me out.' She took a handkerchief and touched it to her eyes. 'It seems so long ago. I was young, foolish and desperately unhappy. The earl is a dear man and I'm very fond of him now but, back then, I dreamed of being swept off my feet. The chances of that happening were remote to say the least. Here was I, a respectably married woman with three sons. I had position, a title and wealth. Unlike some women, and I'm afraid, my dear, that includes Alison de Iongh, the taking of lovers was too vulgar to consider. Men sense when a woman might . . . indulge in such things.' She flushed with embarrassment but continued. 'I resigned myself to accepting that true love was the price to be paid for everything else in my life.'

Lady Pamela worried the handkerchief into a small ball in her hands. 'Then I met Jonathan.'

Jonathan! The name burned into Dallas. His father's name was Jonathan.

'Jonathan Fellowes,' his mother went on. 'Connected in some way to the Walshinghams of

Norfolk.' She smiled slightly. 'A bit of a black sheep, I fear, but so terribly charming. He came to Tayside for the shooting. The earl was . . . busy that year.'

Mistresses were not uncommon. Dallas knew what she meant.

'I was lonely. He came to see me, here, when the season finished. I . . . I became quite infatuated.' She shrugged slightly. 'It wasn't love but it felt so right at the time. I'm sure you don't wish to hear details.'

Dallas didn't. What with one thing and another, his entire world was suddenly in an uproar. Mothers didn't have feelings like that, only mistresses. He realised that this thought didn't make sense but couldn't reason his way around it. 'You bore him a child? Me? Are you certain he is my father?'

'Yes. Women have ways of calculating . . . Anyway, you look so much like him.'

'And my fath . . . the earl. Does he know?'

'I shouldn't think so. Oh, he was aware that Jonathan flirted outrageously with me but he had no reason to suspect that I reciprocated. We were very discreet and careful.'

Lorna flashed through his mind. They'd been discreet and careful too. But, as his mother had before them, Lorna was now carrying a child. 'Where is this man now?'

Lady Pamela rubbed at a small frown on her forehead. 'I don't know. He left England before you were born.'

'Because of your condition? What a cad!'

'No, no. Don't think that about him. He loved me, I'm sure of it. There was a scandal – something to do with the family fortunes. Jonathan lost everything. Even so, he gave me his mother's jewels. He said . . . he said I would know what to do with them when the time came. That time is now. They are yours.'

'Do you still think of him, Mama?'

She smiled. 'Every time I look into your face. I will be forever grateful to him for two reasons. He gave me you. And he brought me happiness, true happiness. At least I know how it feels. Don't look so sad, my darling, I am happy, happier than many. Memories fade. It was all so long ago. My affections for Jonathan transferred to you.' She looked sad, reflective for a moment, then brightened. 'Don't mistake me. I love all my children equally. You are just more special.' Lady Pamela smiled again and Dallas thought she'd never looked more beautiful. 'Have I shocked you?'

'No, Mama. You have explained something that has puzzled me for years. I know now why I'm so different from the others. Thank you for telling me.'

A knock at the door prevented further conversation. It was Mrs Potter. 'His lordship is in the library, my lady. He is inquiring about the wagon.'

'We'll be right down. Have you finished packing?'

'Yes, Lady Dalrymple. His lordship asks about that too.'

'Kindly inform Lord Dalrymple that we will

join him forthwith. And have footmen load the wagon.' When Mrs Potter had gone, Lady Pamela placed the jewels back in their pouches and handed them to Dallas. 'Go where you must, my son, do what you will, but always remember that the man who gave me these chose a hard road for himself so that I might never suffer in a similar fashion. It is easy enough that I pass them on. I trust you won't dispose of your inheritance so readily. Even though you did not meet your real father you hold in your hand proof of his love and very existence. Treat his possessions with the respect they, and he, deserve.'

Silenced by emotion, Dallas kissed her cheek.

'Come, my son. The next few minutes may be most unpleasant for his lordship will react as any father should. Do not forget that he too is worthy of your respect. Show him that courtesy before you leave.'

They entered the library side-by-side, an unconscious effort to present a united front. Lord Dalrymple poured three crystal goblets of red wine, handing Dallas and Lady Pamela theirs. 'Drink. Something tells me it is called for.'

His mother sipped, then slowly put her glass down and went to speak.

Dallas laid a hand on her shoulder. 'This is my doing, Mama, I will tell of it.' With that, he succinctly outlined the facts, neither taking full blame nor trying to excuse himself.

The earl heard him out. 'Well,' he said mildly when Dallas fell silent, 'at least you appear to have behaved correctly under the circumstances. It was decent of de Iongh to give two days' grace. He might not believe Alison's accusation of rape but the man still caught you in bed with her. Are you ready to leave?'

'Yes, Papa.' Dallas hid his astonishment.

Lady Pamela left the room saying, 'I'll have Cook prepare a basket, for the road is long.'

Alone, Lord Dalrymple crossed to his desk and opened a drawer. 'I keep some cash here for emergencies. Not much. A few hundred as a rule. You're in luck. I withdrew a large sum yesterday. Should be nearly two thousand.' He didn't bother to count it, simply thrust the wad of banknotes at Dallas.

'Thank you, Papa.' Dallas felt uncomfortable taking the money but knew he needed it.

'I should be angry with you.' Lord Dalrymple poured more wine. 'If de Iongh carries through and reports this, the scandal will be terrible. As it is, I rather suspect Charles and Charlotte's engagement will be terminated. Your sister will be heartbroken and you must carry the burden of that unhappiness. Glendon may be dismissed from the church and Boyd could well forfeit his commission. You have done nothing by half measure, Dallas. This family has nought to thank you for.'

Dallas was red with shame. All the earl said was true. And he only knew the half of it.

'A man takes his pleasure where he can,' his father went on reflectively. 'In my younger days I was no different.' He put his drink down carefully, and turned suddenly angry eyes on Dallas. 'But, by

God, sir, I was always mindful of the damned consequences. What on earth made you think you
could cuckold de Iongh and get away with it? He's
a family friend. You have behaved with the utmost
disrespect for one of Britain's most distinguished
gentlemen.' The anger passed quickly and Lord
Dalrymple gave a slight smile. 'Alison is still a fine-
looking woman. I daresay she made it difficult to
say no. Your audacity, though! I swear, I don't know
whether to despise or admire you.'

'Not for one second should it be the latter,
Papa, for I have most certainly ruined Charlotte's
life.'

'Aye,' the heavy response came. 'That will be
difficult for all of us.'

'I sincerely apologise, Papa, for I thought of no
others save myself.'

'No question of that,' the earl said gruffly. 'But a
man's inclinations make for a powerful persuader.'
He drained the decanter of red wine between
them then became briskly businesslike. 'Let us
know where you are. Send letters through your
aunt in Aberfeldy. I'll have her hold them for us.
You do realise, my boy, the gravity of this situation?
If you are accused of rape I have no option but to
disown and disinherit you. It's the only course of
action open to me. You will need to change your
name and never lay claim to this family again. I can
arrange to transfer a small stipend each year, but
that is all. You must learn to live on your wits and
this remittance.' Lord Dalrymple put out his hand
and Dallas gripped it. 'Godspeed, my boy.'

Dallas could have sworn that the voice of this man he had always called Father was husky with emotion. He realised suddenly that the man who represented authority and reprisal had only been discharging his parental duty. Now the time had come to say goodbye, Dallas knew how much he loved and respected this man. He might not carry the earl's genes but he bore his name and had learned by example all the decent principles and manners, family pride and self-respect held dear by him. A pity indeed that he hadn't paid closer attention. Lord Dalrymple turned and left the library. Dallas felt his throat suddenly choke with suppressed sorrow.

Lady Pamela returned and handed him an envelope. 'Victor is waiting. Here is the letter to my cousin. You must make haste.'

She walked with him to the courtyard. 'Change your name when you book passage to wherever. You must no longer use Acheson.'

'I know, Mama.' Dallas turned and hugged her tightly. 'I love you.'

'Go.' Her voice broke. 'Go now.'

He climbed into the seat beside Victor. As the wagon turned out of stone gates at the end of a long, tree-lined drive, Dallas could not resist one last look back at the Grange, a place he loved above all their other homes. 'Granger,' he thought. 'I'll change my name to Granger.'

And so it was that Dallas Granger set off into the unknown. He'd heard of remittance men. Their escapades and daring had always seemed wildly romantic. Well, he was about to find out first-hand if that admiration were justified. Would the life of a remittance man be one of adventure and opportunity? Or did something more sinister await him?

THREE

Dallas had never met his mother's cousin in Newcastle-Upon-Tyne. In fact, he knew virtually nothing about the man. Some years before there had been rumour of unscrupulous business dealings, leaving Dallas with the impression that Cousin Adrian was something of a black sheep. It emphasised the seriousness with which Lady Pamela viewed his current predicament that she was prepared to send him to the family rogue for help.

It was a journey that dragged on through six days and nights of unmitigated misery. Wet winter weather had turned the roads into a slippery quagmire of rutted wheel tracks and bottomless potholes. Their wagon lay open to the elements. Huddled on the unpadded wooden seat next to Victor, rain and sleet stinging slitted eyes, running down his neck to find its way inside an overworked oilskin cloak, Dallas soon lost his spirit of adventure. He was cold, wet and uncomfortable. By the time they eventually arrived, Dallas felt that every bone in his body had been shaken out of place.

They slept rough on the journey. Victor

inevitably managed to find shelter behind a hedgerow or in a secluded forest clearing. Suggestions by Dallas that they seek out a warm and comfortable inn at the end of each day's travel fell on deaf ears. 'Better not, my lord. There are any number of scoundrels who would sell you short for a shilling. Until you are well away from these shores it would be as well to exercise the utmost caution.'

On the second night they shared a shepherd's derelict stone hut with a herd of wild goats, the rank smell of droppings and urine being infinitely preferable to incessant rain.

The basket of food prepared by Cook soon emptied. Victor would leave Dallas shivering and hidden while he took the wagon into a village, returning with whatever supplies he'd been able to find. Dallas grew sick of bread sodden with rain, stale suet pudding and cured ham well past its prime. Cheese and onions were a favourite with Victor and so proudly did he return with these on two occasions that Dallas didn't have the heart to tell him he hated onions.

On their last night they stopped in a field just outside the small village of Higham Dykes. The rain miraculously cleared. Victor had managed to purchase a rabbit and some potatoes, and was now making a stew over a meagre fire. Wafting delicious aromas caused spontaneous waves of hunger in Dallas. 'There'll be a frost tonight,' Victor predicted pessimistically.

'Better that than what we've been living with.'

'Don't be too sure, my lord. Rain may be uncomfortable but the hoar bites deep.'

'Then we'd best fill our bellies with warm stew to keep out the cold.'

Victor shook his head. 'Aye, my lord. But Jack Frost will have us both afore daybreak.'

Dallas jumped to his feet. 'We reach Newcastle tomorrow. I smell like a beggar's armpit and cannot present myself to Lord Wedderburn in this state. A wash and shave in that stream is called for, though I swear the cold might damage my ardour for some time to come.'

Victor stopped him. 'We are not there yet. Stay your impatience, my lord, for many a man goes through a winter without seeing water. The police seek someone of means. You look and smell like a man of the road. It is better that you remain so.'

Dallas saw the sense but his whiskers and body itched terribly. And Victor was right about the cold as well. Curled hard into each other to stay warm, and despite taking cover under the wagon, by morning both men's hair was crisp with ice and their bones ached raw and deep from the frigid air. Even the horses seemed pleased to set off at a fast trot to get their circulation going again.

They found Cousin Adrian's address with ease – in one of the most elegant parts of town. It was a splendid house, almost vulgar in the excellence of quality of workmanship. No expense had been spared. Dallas could see a three-tiered, ornately carved fountain behind the imposing double wrought-iron gateway. On either side, set into niches, statues of angels with outstretched wings gazed reverently heavenward. A third struck a pious pose in the arch above.

Dallas would have opened the gate and gone in but for Victor's warning, 'Not through the front, my lord. You would never get past the butler.'

A side entrance brought them into a cobbled courtyard at the back of the house. Two of the finest carriages Dallas had ever seen stood there. Their arrival attracted the attention of a groom who spoke harshly to one of the scullery maids. 'Call a downstairs tweeny, you lazy girl, and tell her to inform Cook that strangers wish to see his lordship.'

They nearly didn't get past the cook. She took one look at the two of them and assumed they were tinkers. 'Be off with you. We need nowt of your trinkets and baubles today.'

Victor held his ground. 'Lord Dallas Acheson is calling on Lord Wedderburn.'

The cook placed chubby hands on ample hips and cocked her head to one side. 'Lord Acheson, is it? You cheeky beggars. Be off before I send for the peelers.' She gave a short laugh. 'Lord Acheson, indeed. What will you lot think of next?'

Dallas decided to intervene. 'Madam, my appearance is the result of six days' hard travel. I am indeed the son of Lord and Lady Dalrymple. Here is my introduction.'

The envelope, bearing the Dalrymple crest, was slightly worse for wear but the cook took it and sniffed derisively. 'His lordship has better things to do with his time than read begging letters.'

The woman was only doing her job. Dallas knew that beggars and tinkers were forever being turned away at home. He had to convince her he was telling the truth. 'My mother is Lady Pamela of the Grange, in Edinburgh. She and Lord Wedderburn are first cousins. Would you risk his lordship's anger at such discourtesy to his kin?'

She looked at him closely. Dallas stared back unwaveringly. His speech and manners were those of a gentleman but the man's appearance and smell were not. Dark eyes held steady though, and in them she saw desperation but no guile. The good lady made her decision. 'Very well, though a body is likely to get a scolding for her trouble.' She bore the envelope away.

The groom, who had listened avidly, chuckled. 'Always a soft touch despite her sharp tongue. You got away with it, lads, though I wouldn't want to be in your shoes if you're lying.'

Victor surveyed the stable hand with a stare cold enough to turn him to stone and the man, who knew seniority when he saw it, prudently left to go about his business. Ten minutes later, the cook reappeared looking slightly nonplussed. 'You may follow me.'

Victor turned to go too but was quickly stopped. 'It's Lord Acheson that his lordship wishes to see. You can wait in the butler's pantry. There's ale, bread and cheese, and I'll expect no trouble. If this gentleman is who you say, there'll be a good meal later. Until then, you mind your place.'

Victor, whose authority over grooms was

second nature, wilted under the cook's undisputed power in her own domain. 'Would there be an onion to go with the cheese?'

She tossed him a look withering enough to melt a gold ingot and waddled from the kitchen.

Dallas rolled his eyes at Victor's impudence, receiving a cheeky grin in response, and followed the cook through a series of opulent, high-ceilinged reception rooms to the main entrance where he was told to wait. 'Martin will be here presently.'

Martin was presumably the butler. While he did as instructed, Dallas studied family portraits on the walls. The butler's continued absence was bordering on impolite by the time he finally put in an appearance. And what an appearance it was. He was more unlike a major-domo than any Dallas had ever encountered – short and bow-legged, with the coarse, weather-beaten features of a man who worked out of doors. His hair was grey and curly, worn long and tied back so that it hung between his shoulderblades. Faded grey eyes, creased at the corners with a dozen or more laugh lines, were alive with humour, showing no sign of the glassy-eyed lack of interest of most who held his position. Martin's voice bore none of the affected disdain normally shown by the butler of a grand establishment. It was gravelly, strongly accented, holding no hint of deference. The man actually smiled as he spoke. 'His lordship waits for you in the Garden Parlour.' Martin turned, expecting Dallas to follow.

Observing the man's extraordinary rolling gait,

Dallas tried to remember what he'd been told of Lord Wedderburn. Most of his money came from owning ale houses, of which there were dozens. He also operated a brewery, a textile mill and a newspaper. Lady Pamela had hinted at a house of ill-repute but that remained a rumour. Dallas did know that his mother's cousin was partner in a small, privately owned shipping line which plied passengers and goods between England and France. It was through this that he hoped to leave England.

They stopped outside a closed door and Martin knocked.

'Come.'

Dallas was ushered in. The man in the room stared at him for a moment before dismissing Martin with a nod of his head.

Cousin Adrian, Lord Wedderburn, or, to be more precise, the second Marquis of Darras, was a tall, thin, humourless-looking individual with hooked nose, fleshy lips and cold blue eyes. He returned his gaze to Dallas with some measure of disapproval. 'So, you are my cousin's offspring. How nice of your mother to remember her kin when she needs help.'

There wasn't much Dallas could say to that, so he said nothing.

'How is Pamela?'

'She is well, sir.'

'And her whelp finds it prudent to leave England?'

'Yes, my lord.'

Cousin Adrian picked up the letter and flicked

his eyes over it. 'There's a berth on one of our ships leaving the day after tomorrow,' he said finally. 'Calais. Will that do you?'

'Thank you.'

'I don't suppose you can pay?'

Dallas flushed. 'Of course –'

Lord Wedderburn waved him to silence. 'No matter. I don't imagine that tightfisted father of yours sent you packing with much. Hang onto it. At least my dear cousin cannot accuse me of lacking in hospitality. 'Tis no pleasure but I'll do what obligation requires of me. I would prefer to think that you come to me out of fondness or respect, but since that is not so I refuse to tarnish my good name on your behalf. Should misfortune befall before you sail do not seek further assistance from this quarter. You will be smuggled aboard tomorrow night. That's the best I can promise. After that, you are on your own.'

Grateful as he was, Dallas could not help but feel resentment at such obvious animosity. 'My deepest thanks to you, Cousin Adrian. Were it not for the pressing circumstances in which I find myself, there would be no question of troubling you.'

Lord Wedderburn gave a sour smile and tapped the letter with a forefinger. 'Reading between the lines, I would say you have little choice in the matter.'

'Indeed, sir.'

'You do not shirk from the truth. That is in your favour. Of what are you guilty?'

'Gross stupidity, cousin. Nothing more.'

That seemed to amuse the marquis. 'How old are you, boy?'

'Twenty-one, sir.'

'Old enough to know better?'

'Yes, sir.'

'And young enough to think you'd get away with it, eh?'

Dallas looked embarrassed. 'Yes, sir.'

'Very well. If your mother is correct, it would seem that the constabulary may already have an interest in finding you. The ship's passenger manifest will list you as, let me see . . . hmmm . . . yes, Monsieur Debrett – a returning trader. That will do nicely. What name you use once in France is not my concern. In fact, I implore you not to divulge your intentions to me. The less I know of this unsavoury affair you flee from, the better. Martin will show you to your room. Dinner is at eight sharp. You will meet the rest of my family in the parlour, no later than five-and-twenty before the hour. Keep your true identity from them, it is best that way.' Lord Wedderburn rang a bell and Martin reappeared so quickly that Dallas thought he might have been listening at the keyhole. 'Take Monsieur Debrett to the Yellow Bedchamber. He's obviously in need of water to bathe. See to it.' With that, Cousin Adrian left the room.

Dallas followed Martin to the second-floor suite of rooms. It was very grand. In the main bedchamber, a simple but elegant stucco ceiling was enhanced on its four corners by a swirling fleur-de-lis frieze that had been picked out in vivid yellow. The cornice repeated a simplified version of this design. A gilt four-poster bed was finished with gold damask that matched the curtains, while other furniture, handmade from Spanish mahogany, was also upholstered in the same richly coloured silk. By contrast, the dark polished cedar floor set off a matching pair of Persian rugs, predominantly red in colour and of the finest, hand-knotted workmanship. Hanging tapestries were from Antwerp and well over a hundred years old. They both displayed intricate floral designs. Two magnificent gilt pier-glasses and console tables occupied space between the windows, and the white marble chimneypiece and mantel were Italian.

Off the main bedchamber was a dressing room in which the predominantly yellow and gold theme was continued. Adjoining this, the chamber boasted a hipbath and earth closet. Dallas had heard of, but never seen, these supposed innovative contraptions where fine earth, kept somewhere in the attic, periodically flooded the pipes helping carry waste to the cesspit. He was quite pleased to find a good old-fashioned commode as well.

Martin supervised the installation of his sea chest and valise before saying, 'I will light the fire, monsieur, then have hot water brought up.'

While Martin busied himself at the hearth, Dallas took in the view from a window. The weather had cleared. He could see High Bridge further up the road, a two-tiered structure with one level for road traffic and the other for trains. Cousin Adrian's house was on Grey Street, a tree-lined avenue fronted by many elegant facades. The street outside was busy with activity. Vendors pushed barrows, calling out the nature of their wares, carriages bore ladies of quality to and from social engagements, elegant gentlemen on horseback tipped their hats as they passed, ever-hopeful beggars sought hand-outs until moved on by the local constabulary, nannies returned from the park with their charges before the cold of evening set in. A lamp-lighter was already going about his business and a merry troop of thespians made their way towards the Theatre Royal in good time for the evening's performance. Dallas turned back into the room. 'Do not trouble yourself unpacking the chest, Martin. The small valise contains all that I need for now.'

'Very well, monsieur.'

Dallas wondered about Martin. The man had shown not a flicker of surprise when Lord Wedderburn announced that he would be staying. Given Dallas's rumpled and unsavoury appearance, most butlers would have managed to convey haughty disapproval. And an envelope bearing the crest of one of Britain's most prominent families would surely have caused curiosity, especially from the hands of such a dishevelled traveller, and particularly so seeing as that person went by the name of Debrett, not Acheson. Cousin Adrian had not considered it necessary to explain anything, unless of course he had done so before Martin fetched him from the entrance hall. Lord Wedderburn must place a good deal of confidence in his butler's discretion, since most servants would have been quick to gossip about such an unlikely guest.

Martin rose from the now crackling fire and collected up the shirt, breeches and jacket that he had unpacked. 'I will send hot water, monsieur. A maid will freshen these before dinner.' He looked Dallas up and down. 'If you wish, monsieur, I will arrange for the clothes you wear to be laundered.'

'That would be most welcome.'

Bucket after bucket of steaming water soon arrived. Dallas undressed and left his filthy clothes on the floor. Real soap, not the homemade tallow variety, was provided. Maids kept the water coming, one or two openly admiring the strong arms and shoulders of the young French trader who, surprisingly, was being shown the kind of courtesy usually reserved for visiting members of the peerage. Dallas seemed quite unconcerned by their shy giggles and the offer of one to scrub his back.

The relief of soaking in a tub and removing six days' grime and growth of whiskers was immense. By the time he emerged from the closet, Dallas felt more human than he had for days. His dinner clothes, freshly pressed, were laid out on the bed and his boots gleamed with polish. Coals glowed in the grate, sending out welcome warmth. His bed had been turned down and the curtains drawn. Of his discarded apparel there was no sign. This was life as he understood it. A copy of William Wordsworth's *The Prelude* lay on the mantelpiece and Dallas flicked idly through it to while away time until he dressed for dinner. He had to enlist the aid of a passing chambermaid to show him to the parlour where family members would be gathered.

'Ah, Monsieur Debrett, I trust you are refreshed?' Lord Wedderburn handed him a glass of wine.

'Thank you, my lord. I feel like a new man.'

'Excellent. Come, all are most anxious to meet you.' He led Dallas to the fire where a plain, slightly built woman toyed with a glass of cordial. 'May I present my wife, Lady Wedderburn. My dear, this is Monsieur Debrett who is to be our guest this evening and indeed, tomorrow.'

Lady Wedderburn inclined her head. 'Such a pity your visit is so short, Monsieur Debrett, for we would have been delighted to show you this fine city of ours.'

She spoke so softly that Dallas had to lean forward in order to hear. 'Alas, my lady, business demands that I return to France as soon as possible.'

'My son, Lord Rupert,' Cousin Adrian went on. 'He's home from Oxford.'

Dallas shook hands with a young man who appeared to be a couple of years younger than himself. Dallas had also been to Oxford but, of course, was unable to mention it.

Lord Rupert looked decidedly bored. 'In what do you trade, Monsieur?'

His father answered the question, which was just as well since Dallas couldn't think of a single thing. 'Monsieur Debrett is not a mere trader, Rupert. He is here on behalf of the French government and has held confidential discussions with the President of Council.'

Dallas was relieved to hear that. At least he could take refuge behind the secret nature of his negotiations and not have to fabricate a story.

'I see.' Lord Rupert didn't, but wasn't going to admit it. 'Is this your first trip to Newcastle?'

'Indeed. A very splendid city from what little I've seen.' Without being aware of it, Dallas had developed the slightest of accents.

'My younger son, Lord James.' Cousin Adrian indicated a gangly youth of around sixteen. 'He's still at Eton.'

Lord James shook Dallas by the hand, smiled toothily, and returned to contemplation of the fire.

'My dear, shall we go in?'

The dining room was every bit as opulent as the rest of the house. Family portraits adorned the walls, including one Dallas recognised as being of his own grandfather. Keeping up the pretence of being a French trader, he was unable to comment on it. What did strike him, however, was that the old man wore just as sour an expression in this portrait as he did in the one at home in Edinburgh.

Dinner was elaborate and, for Dallas, still suffering from Victor's culinary tastes, most satisfying. Thick artichoke soup, followed by red mullet on a bed of crisp cucumber. A marrow pâté preceded lamb cutlets with peas and asparagus. Roasted side of venison came next, duckling after that, with plovers' eggs in aspic before fruit, dessert, and a lemon ice finished off the feast. Wine, sherry, Madeira and champagne were served throughout the meal.

Conversation remained stilted but the younger son's enthusiasm for music became clear. He spoke incessantly of a Russian composer called Tchaikovsky who was set to take the world by storm. His observations revolved around such expressions as 'melodic vein', 'the brilliant colour of his orchestral power', and 'how he expresses himself with such strong emotion'. Interesting as it was, Dallas had the feeling the boy was quoting something he'd read in a book. The family had obviously heard it many times before and kept trying to change the subject.

Lord Rupert, by contrast, seemed determined to exclude Dallas. Having made it abundantly clear that whenever he wasn't at university he held a position of some responsibility and authority in one of his father's businesses, he kept returning the conversation to matters that were known only to himself and Lord Wedderburn. The lady of the house had very little to say on any subject and deferred most questions either to her husband or one of her sons. Midway through the meal, two little girls in nightdresses, their hair twisted into sausages by coloured ribbons, were shown in to say goodnight. They giggled shyly. One sucked her thumb.

After dinner, Cousin Adrian invited Dallas to take a stroll. It was then that his mother's veiled references to her cousin's unsavoury side were confirmed. Dallas never established whether Lord Wedderburn actually owned the house of ill-repute but noted that his host was greeted like a regular and favoured customer.

'Take your pick,' the marquis said magnanimously, disappearing upstairs with a flame-haired wench of generous proportions.

Dallas was only human.

They returned to Grey Street a little after midnight. Lord Wedderburn seemed in excellent spirits and said a jovial goodnight at the top of the stairs, whistling all the way to his bedchamber.

The fire in Dallas's room had recently been built up. He undressed and fell gladly into bed, wondering if Cousin Adrian regularly indulged in good food, wine, and other things. No comment had been made about their visit to the brothel, other than an inquiry as to whether Dallas enjoyed himself. He appeared amused by the younger man's enthusiastic response.

Other thoughts crowded for attention. This was only the beginning. From here, life would never be the same. Lying in bed watching the flickering firelight send dancing shadows around the room as he waited for sleep, Dallas allowed his thoughts to ramble. He was not yet safe and could never consider himself so until on board ship heading for one of the colonies. If he were apprehended, and a charge of rape were proved against him, irrespective of his social status and family connections he would be hanged. Whatever lay ahead had to be better than that.

And what of his new life? Dallas, for the first time, realised just how privileged the peerage actually was. Deference, respect, luxuries, everything he had taken for granted would suddenly have to be earned. As Lord Acheson, doors had opened. As Dallas Granger, there was no choice but to do the job himself. As Monsieur Debrett . . . but no, that was too temporary to even bother about. He was at least free of the somewhat restrictive rules of aristocracy. That was good. But the liberty which came with it was in itself a set of chains, tying him to the pursuit of life's necessities. Dallas realised he could face this in one of two ways. A challenge to be conquered or a threat waiting to bring him down.

Sleep eluded his restless mind. Where would he end up? There was not much point in speculating about a future until that at least became clear. Even then, what on earth could a man of his background actually do? He knew a bit about farming, could shoot and his manners were impeccable. Come on, Dallas thought, lying in the darkness. There must be more to my life than that.

There was. He'd had an excellent education, was young and healthy, and knew his way around a lady's body. Nothing there to reassure him much.

What did he want to do? Difficult question. Far easier to decide what he didn't want or couldn't do. A civil service position was out of the question. He would find the red tape, petty squabbling and repetition boring in the extreme. Dallas had always liked being out of doors. A desk-bound job would drive him mad. Besides, any civil or military employment meant he'd be working for the British government and that was a bit too close for comfort. Unlike brother Glendon, Dallas had no calling for the church and even less interest in doing good works. Which left what? He'd always been propped up and secured by the system. Dallas knew he could no longer rely on that. All he had was a bit of money and his wits.

His eyelids grew heavy. The last conscious thought before sleep overtook him was that everything that had made sense up until now no longer mattered. The future could become anything he damn-well pleased. If only he could work out what that was.

The next day passed at adagio speed. Lady Wedderburn, probably wondering why a French trader was staying in her home, didn't quite know what to do with the unexpected guest. She treated him to a tour of the gardens before excusing herself. Dallas found the library and read for a while. Cousin Adrian was nowhere to be seen. Rupert, if last night's conversation were any indication, was presumably off doing whatever he did in one of his father's enterprises. The younger son, James, and the two little girls whose names he had forgotten, came and went with nothing more than a surprised, 'Oh, good morning,' or, 'Good afternoon,' as though they expected him to have gone.

Bored, Dallas went in search of Victor, only to be told by Martin that he was already on his way back to Scotland. 'Left early this morning with a note for Lady Dalrymple from his lordship.'

'I would have appreciated the chance to bid him farewell,' Dallas said coolly.

'His lordship thought it best that he leave quickly. The servants talk, monsieur. Victor's accent marks him as a man from north of the border. Strangers excite attention and in order to gain access to Lord Wedderburn the two of you were not exactly discreet. It would be most unfortunate if your real identity became common knowledge, monsieur, so close to the time you leave. I have the utmost faith in Cook's discretion but cannot guarantee likewise for the groom. He has been allocated tasks that will keep him busy for a few days but may still gossip with the others. 'Tis impossible for me to keep them all under lock and key.'

Martin's expression remained unreadable but Dallas thought he detected sympathy in the man's voice. 'Quite so, I was not thinking. Thank you, Martin.' Dallas returned to the library.

At ten past six Cousin Adrian found him there. 'The police have been to see me,' he said with no preamble.

Dallas was dismayed. 'They know I am here?'

'No. But I must let them know should you seek passage on one of my vessels. They watch the port and have posted your likeness around town. So, dear cousin, I won't exactly be sorry to see you leave.' He moved to the sideboard and selected a decanter of claret, raising an eyebrow of inquiry and pouring two glasses when Dallas nodded. 'Naturally I have taken steps to cover myself against any question of aiding your escape. If it becomes known that you sailed to France under an assumed name, I'm afraid "liar" and "cowardly absconder" will be added to your reputation. I cannot be seen to have abetted you in any way. Regrettably that is the way it has to be. For myself it is of little consequence but no scandal can be allowed to touch my family. I do hope you appreciate the situation.'

'Most certainly. Rest assured, Cousin Adrian, that should I be so unfortunate as to fall into the hands of my pursuers your good name will remain unblemished.'

'I thank you for your undertaking, cousin. Your word as a gentleman is good enough for me. I'm pleased to be of assistance but it would help to know of what you stand accused. The police would give no details save to say that you are a desperate man who will stop at nothing to get away.'

'I am guilty of no serious crime, Cousin Adrian, though, to protect the honour of a lady, I find myself accused of the foulest deed. Bear with me and I will endeavour to put your mind at rest that you do not harbour a desperate criminal, merely a man who found himself in the wrong place at the wrong time. Should you then decide to wash your hands of me, do so knowing I bear no ill will.' Dallas outlined the events leading to his flight. 'So you see,' he concluded, 'there was little or nothing I could say in my own defence without tarnishing the reputation of Lady de Iongh.'

Unexpectedly, Lord Wedderburn chuckled. 'Rape, eh? Half the peerage know how impossible that would be. The lady in question has fewer morals than those good ladies you met last night. At least they conduct themselves with more restraint. Lord de Iongh is a besotted fool, though I daresay he's turned a blind eye more than once. It appears you have been grossly unlucky, though a man of your intelligence must have realised that the liaison could not carry on indefinitely. If you are guilty of anything it is lack of thought. We both know how it is when a man's blood is up. Dally once or twice, cousin, but always move on, irrespective of the lady's charms. Alison de Iongh was always a bewitching creature. You have good taste, young Acheson, I'll give you that. I have dallied there myself, many years ago, but she was too rich for my blood.' He chuckled again and shook his head at the memory. The smile was still there as he raised the glass to his lips.

Dallas drank too. Cousin Adrian's admission came as a complete surprise, making it even more evident just how big a fool he had been. Alison had relied on his gallantry and he'd obliged, ruining his reputation in the process. Not that he didn't feel guilt, but both of them were equally to blame. As for Lorna, Dallas shuddered. That was another matter. The consequences should have been foreseen and he should have known better.

'After dinner you will go with Martin.' Cousin Adrian became businesslike again. 'He will see you safely aboard ship. She sails on the tide tomorrow afternoon. Stay below and talk to no-one. Even in France you are not safe but there are any number of vessels leaving Calais. Take the first available. I need not tell you that until you are clear of the English Channel there is grave danger of discovery.'

'Thank you, Cousin Adrian. I am ill-prepared for a fugitive's life.'

'Life plays unexpected tricks on all of us. We must learn from our mistakes and go forth as wiser men. This has always been my advice to Rupert but I fear that he, like you, would trip over his own feet rather than benefit from the ramblings of an older man's memory. Ah well, 'tis the prerogative of the young, is it not?' He reached for the decanter. 'More wine, cousin?'

Dallas held out his glass.

Lord Wedderburn refilled it and his own. 'Nothing like a sip of wine in this weather, eh, Dallas? Warms you to your toes. Mind you,' he added with a twinkle in his eye, 'in summer I drink to cool down.'

Dallas laughed.

'My wife does not approve. Thank God for the sanctuary of this library. We will go to table like two innocent choirboys.' He chuckled, then turned serious. 'Thank you for your candour. Lady Pamela has good reason to be proud of you. To act with honour under such trying circumstances is admirable. I'm pleased to be of assistance.'

Dallas returned to a matter that was still worrying him. 'Why do the police search for me here? Was I seen on the road?'

'Lord de Iongh has a long arm, my boy. He is a very influential man, and highly regarded in circles that count. Alison has played him for a fool since they met but the old codger was so desperately in love with the wretched woman that, even in the early days of their marriage, he pretended not to know. But a man can take only so much. This time she's gone too far, carrying on right under his nose at home and in front of the servants. He had no option but to act. It's not you he seeks to punish, though God knows, catching you in bed with his wife can hardly have made your future well-being important to him. The scandal will be his revenge on Alison, with or without the rape fabrication. That's what de Iongh is after. Who knows, perhaps he thinks the shame will put an end to her indiscretions. Dammit, he's a decent man at heart. Why do you think he waited two days before reporting the matter?'

Wedderburn was hogging the fire, coat-tails raised to warm his bony posterior. He shrugged. 'In some ways you can count yourself lucky, though I will breathe more easily knowing you are well away from these shores. No, you were not seen on the road. But the police have no choice but to take the charge seriously. An early arrest will curry favour with the House of Lords. Even the Prime Minister urges a swift result. Unfortunately, you chose to cuckold one of Britain's most admired statesmen.'

Dallas turned and paced the room. 'If the police, as you say, are watching the docks, then how am I to avoid their scrutiny?'

'Fear not, cousin. Martin will get you safely on board. That much is easy.'

'You place much trust in the fellow. I pray it is not misplaced.'

'Martin is my man. I trust him implicitly. He has never let me down.' He went to say more but a tap on the door prevented further discussion.

A footman appeared. 'Dinner is served, my lord. Lady Wedderburn awaits in the dining room.'

'Thank you, George. Come, Monsieur Debrett, it would not do to keep the good lady waiting.'

After the meal, which was every bit as sumptuous as the previous night's, the family retired to the drawing room for tea and port. There was not much chance to talk frankly with Cousin Adrian but later in the evening he took Dallas to one side and said quietly, 'I will not see you again. Martin waits in your bedchamber. Do as he says and above all else trust him. Captain Ross of the *Newcastle Lady* is expecting you. Have faith in his allegiance to me but the less said to strangers, the better. Godspeed, cousin, and good fortune.'

Dallas wondered how Cousin Adrian would explain the sudden disappearance of their guest to the rest of the family.

Martin stood by the glowing fire, leafing through the same copy of Wordsworth's *The Prelude* as Dallas had the previous evening. He put it down hastily at Dallas's appearance, as if loath to be caught reading something so patently un-nautical. 'I have taken the liberty of laying out suitable attire, monsieur.'

Dark clothes and a long black cloak were draped across the four-poster bed. While Dallas changed, Martin disappeared with his discarded dinner clothes.

'Your sea chest is in the wagon, monsieur,' Martin said when he reappeared. 'I will take the valise.' He hefted it in strong arms. 'Follow me, please.'

They descended a set of back stairs out into the cobbled courtyard. Although it had not rained that day, everything dripped wetness. A dank mist, so thick the horses seemed headless, hung in the air.

'The weather works for us,' Martin observed, each word springing from his mouth in vaporised illustration. 'Peelers have no stomach for a night such as this. They will seek the cover of a roof at least. If we are unlucky and stopped, ask directions to an inn for the night.' Martin flicked the whip, softly clicked his tongue and the wagon pulled out into Grey Street, turning left. 'The *Newcastle Lady* is at anchor off North Shields. A dinghy will be put ashore at our signal.'

'Is she steam or sail?'

'The finest under canvas,' came Martin's proud response. 'Sailed with her myself.'

'You are a seafaring man?' Dallas was surprised. In his experience, sailors would rather die at sea than take a job on land.

'Aye. Until I broke my leg. Lord Wedderburn found me work ashore.'

'You are fortunate indeed.'

'Aye.' The butler's response held sadness.

'Though not fortunate enough to ever go back to sea. This leg troubles me greatly.'

Dallas sensed Martin's sadness. 'You would prefer the discomfort of a ship?'

'It was my life, the sea. There was freedom in full sails, a hiss of water under the hull, conversation aplenty in each groan and creak. A ship speaks and you learn her language, respond to her demands. She is like a woman. Even for that which a man desires most she obligingly lies at anchor waiting while you dally in foolishness and lose your hard-earned shillings. Then she forgives and forgets, once more bearing off with your very heart and soul.'

Dallas grinned. 'Like a truly good woman should? Is that what you're saying, Martin?'

'Aye. A ship knows a man's needs and makes no complaint unless he neglects hers.'

'So look on the bright side. Now you're a land-lubber find a real woman and settle down.'

Something like a grunt issued from Martin. 'In my view, sir, such a creature does not exist. If she did, the earth would have women with neither voice nor opinion. Instead, the good Lord chose to give them tongues and fill the world with their ceaseless prattle. Where am I to find a woman who neither nags nor complains? Where is the woman who, in return for a roof over her head, food in her belly and children by her knee, lives to cook and clean, keeping herself from my company until sent for? If I could find such a woman, sir, I would marry quick enough. All I ask is that, when I need her with me, she behaves in private as the finest waterfront whore.'

Dallas laughed softly as he thought what his mother's reaction might be to such an outrageous statement. 'Of course, Martin, such women are crying out for your attention, are they not?'

'I beat them off with a stick, sir,' Martin replied dryly.

'Mark my words, Martin. The day will come when a soft-eyed wench will tear your heart from within.'

'Beggin' your pardon, sir, but I have had many more years than you to find that the softest eye hides the hardest head. Women, I'm thinking, are far from the fairer sex. Their hearts are black as pitch. They are merciless, taking all that you have to give, and crying out for more. No, sir. Better the warmth of rum than that professed by a woman.'

'In truth, I do not share your jaded view, Martin.'

'You are young yet, sir.'

They fell silent after that. Dallas had enjoyed the exchange. Was this pragmatic honesty something to be found in whatever far-flung colony he would end up? Not only was it different but the prospect of unknown lands and customs with even less familiar people was suddenly quite exciting. He could make a good life. Provided, of course, that he made it safely on board the *Newcastle Lady*.

Through the misty night they travelled. Twin plumes of warm breath vaporised from the horses' nostrils, joining the river dampness that rose off the water and sat over it like a blanket of brume. This was made thicker by the inevitable swirling sea mist. All turned yellow in the gaslight from lamps along the street. Bearing left out of Grey Street, they faced nothing but darkness. The only illumination, lanterns hung from the wagon, their halos of dim light there more to be seen by oncoming travellers than to show the way.

'Nearly there, sir,' Martin announced when, after thirty minutes, they had not encountered man, wagon nor beast on the streets. He stopped the wagon and blew out both lanterns.

The clip-clop of hooves seemed muffled by the dampness all around as they set off again. Dallas could smell the river's salty tang and hear tidal wavelets slapping against the bank. Streetlamps on the far side were a mere suggestion, a hazy hint of brightness. After a few more minutes, Martin reined in the horses again.

'There's the *Lady.*'

Dallas could just make out a green light on the river.

'If the watch is awake they'll have seen our lanterns go out.' Martin jumped down and stood on the river's edge, staring out. There was no sound save for the ripple and lap of water. No dogs barked, no voices, no horses or wagons. Yet danger lurked. Out there in the night, eyes watched for him. Dallas was so close to taking the next step in his bid for freedom that anxiety rose and hammered in his throat. Fear of the unknown was nothing compared to his dread of being caught. *Where are they?* Just as he began to think that no-one was coming, a rhythmic sound of paddles broke the silence and a dark silhouette of a longboat slid towards them.

'That be you, Martin?' a voice hailed softly.

'Aye.'

'Jasus, it's colder than a witch's tit.' The boat turned effortlessly against the incoming tide and presented broadside to the riverbank.

Dallas eased down from the wagon and joined Martin. 'You'd be Monsieur Debrett?' A dark figure leapt from the longboat and approached. 'Fortune is with you. Police watch the docks but not the river. Only two patrols have we seen and neither showing much interest in being out. Not even cats venture far on a night like this. Come, men, load the luggage and let's be off. I've a warm berth awaiting and a dram of rum to help me sleep.'

Martin and two sailors loaded the sea chest and valise.

'Farewell, Martin. And thank you.' Dallas clapped his hand on the man's shoulder briefly before stepping into the boat.

The distinctive whistle of a lapwing reached them from further upriver. 'Patrol,' one man said. 'Wouldn't you know it. They'll be here in ten minutes. You'd best be off, Martin. Come, lads. Heave.' Four rowers bent their backs to the task and the longboat glided swiftly towards the *Newcastle Lady*.

Captain Ross waited in the chartroom to welcome Dallas on board. His greeting was perfunctory and the man got straight down to business. 'Jensen will show you to your cabin. It's small but the best we could manage. Stay there until the other passengers disembark at Calais. I've appraised Jensen of your circumstances and, aside from the longboat crew, trusted men and true, no-one else knows you are aboard. Jensen will attend to any needs and come for you when it is safe to leave your cabin. With fair winds you'll be in France in time to take passage on the *Marie Clare*. I'm assuming you intend to remove yourself from Europe as expediently as possible. To this end, the weather works for you.'

'The *Marie Clare*?'

'Steam, and brand new she is.' Captain Ross failed to hide the tinge of envy in his voice. 'She carries mainly cargo, though has berths for about twenty fare-paying passengers. Her captain is a tough man but one of the best you'll meet. He keeps his ship in the finest condition. I've not had the pleasure of boarding her but hear tell she is fit-ted with the best of everything. And fast. Sixteen knots in good conditions.'

'To where does she sail?'

'On this trip, to the best of my knowledge, Spain, Morocco, and down the west coast of Africa to Cape Town. She rounds the Cape of Good Hope and returns via the Red Sea and Suez, call-ing first on Mauritius. Will that suit you?'

Africa. Of the five destinations, it was probably the one he knew least about and would have chosen last. 'Perfectly.'

Captain Ross had not exaggerated the size of the accommodation allocated to Dallas. His sea chest had to stay on deck, there was no room for it. Jensen promised it would be safe but cautioned him. 'No offence, monsieur, but the family crest draws attention.'

Not only did it do that, it advertised who he was. Dallas realised that, as a fugitive, he had much to learn. How stupid of him to travel from Scotland with his family credentials there for all to see. 'You are right, Jensen. It must be removed.'

'I'll see to it, sir.' Jensen hovered hopefully.

'Thank you.' Dallas proffered a crown.

'Thank *you*, sir.'

With the sailor gone, Dallas winced at a generosity he could ill afford. The man would probably have been happy with a florin. Money, something he had always taken for granted, could no longer be splashed around.

With nothing to do, Dallas undressed and crawled into the narrow bunk, inside him an empty pain. This was his last night in Britain. Forever. To his horror, Dallas experienced the uncontrollable emotion of tears. To make matters worse, yesterday had been Lorna's wedding day. She was now married to a man she despised. Not that it made much difference. Despite carrying Dallas's child, Lorna would hate him too. Whether she believed him capable of rape, or merely thought him a callous seducer, the end result would be the same. He hadn't cried for years but gave in to grief as loneliness and fear engulfed him. Drained of emotion, Dallas lay with his eyes closed, unwilling to see the cramped cabin that would be his last contact with home.

While he was at first unable to sleep, the gentle rocking of the ship became hypnotic. Dallas woke at eight the next morning to the grinding scrape of anchor chains.

Jensen brought a tray of tea, bread and jam, and an apple. 'Captain's compliments, monsieur.'

'Thank you.'

'I'll fetch hot water once we clear harbour.'

'How long will that be?'

'Quite a while, monsieur. The ship is about to berth and board passengers. After that, we wait for the tide.'

'So when do we sail?'

'Four bells in the afternoon watch, monsieur.'

Two in the afternoon! That was six hours away. Resigned, Dallas dressed and ate the food provided. The cabin had no porthole, so he could only guess at what was happening outside. He felt the ship dock, heard shouted commands and sensed a bustle of activity beyond his small world. Passengers began to board just before ten. Dallas could hear voices in the passageway and envied those free to move around. He lay on the bunk, staring moodily upwards. Inactivity made him impatient to get going. The previous night's fear became boredom. His thoughts turned resentful. *Damn that minx Alison with her lust and lies. Damn her husband's idiotic devotion which left him no choice but to take her side. Damn his own weakness, without which the day's most pressing problem might be whether to play cards or go riding.* Feeling thoroughly out of sorts, Dallas made up his mind that no woman would ever use him again.

'Dallas Granger.' He tested the sound of his new name. *Mr Granger, I've heard so much about you. Welcome to Africa, Granger, we have several appointments that might suit you. Africa! God! What do I know of Africa?*

It made sense to board the first available ship out of Calais. The sooner he was away from Europe, the better. Looking on the bright side, Africa was at least being colonised by explorers, adventurers and missionaries. Not convicts, like Australia. So, if it was to be the dark continent, he would just have to make the best of it. Where exactly? Africa was vast and largely unknown. From what little he did know, each territory was flavoured by its colonial master. Dallas didn't fancy Arabic countries, nor ones occupied by the Spanish or Portuguese. He spoke French fluently and, when pressed, could manage German. Any areas they occupied might be possible. Having the choice, however, he'd prefer a British colony. The danger of detection would certainly be greater but at least he might find familiar customs. Britain dominated the south, so that was where he should head. He'd heard of Natal and liked the sound of it. *Dallas Granger from Natal.* Yes. It had a certain ring to it. Very British. Surely he could find something to do there.

But what? Yet again, it came back to the same depressing truth. He was qualified for nothing. Dallas daydreamed through the next few hours, considering his options. Deep in thought, he didn't hear footsteps hurrying down the passage and stop outside his door.

It burst open and Jensen rushed in. 'The peelers, monsieur. Quick! They are searching the ship.'

Dallas scrambled from his bunk and followed the sailor. They descended an aft companionway into what could only be the crew's quarters. Small, airless and slung with hammocks, the smell of unwashed bodies and damp was almost overpowering.

Jensen thrust some non-too-clean clothes at him. 'Put these slops on. Be quick. And take your boots off, they are too fine for a sailor.'

Dallas did as he was told, handing Jensen his discarded apparel which was quickly stuffed into a duffel bag.

'Wear this. Here, let me do it.' Jensen tied a bandana around his head, then messed his hair around it. 'That will have to suffice. Come.'

They set off again, Dallas following. He could hear voices coming towards them – one belonged to Captain Ross, who sounded irritated.

'This way, monsieur.' Beyond the crew's accommodation lay another companionway that brought them up into a sail storage area. 'Over here.' Jensen released the drawstring on a canvas bag and drew out a sail. 'Sit on the deck. Take this end. We're looking for tears. Check the reef point stitching and keep your head down. Pay attention to the clew, it rips first. Keep the sail over your feet, they're too white for a man who works on deck. Try to hide your hands as well. Look smart, here they come.'

Dallas bent his head over the sail, heart hammering, head spinning, not knowing what was a reef point and clew or how he was supposed to look as if he were checking them without using his hands. He risked a glance at Jensen. The man had both arms under the sail and was examining a short piece of line fastened through it on one of the corners. Dallas copied him.

'This is an outrage.' The indignant voice of Captain Ross. 'I tell you, sir, any who sail in my ship do so with port authority knowledge. If you delay us much longer we shall miss the tide. Time is money, my good man.'

Dallas heard footsteps climbing the companionway.

Captain Ross saw immediately what Jensen was trying to do. 'Is that jib seaworthy yet? Hurry it up, men, we sail in half an hour and the bobstay still needs tightening. Report to the officer of the watch when you're finished here. Jensen, have you seen to the mizzen crossjack?'

'All in order, captain.'

'Good man.' Captain Ross turned to the police sergeant. 'Are you satisfied?'

'Three of the cabins are clearly occupied and yet no-one was in them.'

The captain allowed impatience to creep into his voice. 'It is not my job, sir, to account for a passenger's whereabouts. Find them if you will. I have work to do.'

His obvious annoyance swayed the policeman's resolve and he backed down. 'That won't be necessary, captain. A look at the passenger list if you please. Then you are free to depart.'

Both men left the sail room and Jensen expelled air. 'Stay here, monsieur. I'll come for you when the coast is clear.'

Left alone, Dallas leaned back against a sail bag and closed his eyes. He hadn't dared glance up at the policeman but the man seemed to have little interest in the crew. Dallas remembered Victor's advice when he wanted to clean up before arriving at Cousin Adrian's. Victor had been right. Jensen too had known instinctively how best to escape detection. The police were searching for a gentleman. Right under their nose but disguised as a common Jack Tar, he became virtually invisible. It was worth remembering. Dallas recalled the generous tip he'd given. It hadn't been a waste of money after all.

Jensen only returned once they had cleared the river mouth. Dallas tried to thank him. 'There be toffs and toffs,' the man declared seriously. 'Wouldn't give the time of day to most. Drown 'em at birth, I say.' He spat on the deck. 'But once in a while, you meet one who is just like us common folk. Human like, know what I mean, sir? No airs and pardon-me-bloody-la-de-da. You be one of them, monsieur, and no mistake.'

Dallas managed not to smile. In his own rough way, Jensen had paid him the biggest compliment of his life and he felt absurdly pleased because of it. The sailor had simply stated a fact as he saw it and would probably not appreciate, or even understand, any kind of reaction.

Returning to his cabin, Dallas was in buoyed spirits. They were under way.

FOUR

Captain Ross sent for Dallas several hours after the *Newcastle Lady* had berthed. Up on deck, Dallas could see that Calais was in the grip of even more miserable weather than England. The prospect of warmer climes suddenly seemed very appealing.

The captain glanced up from a sloppily coiled mooring line, a look of displeasure on his face. He was preoccupied and abrupt. 'I have spoken with Captain Aujoulat. The *Marie Clare* sails tonight. For passage to South Africa he asks forty English guineas. Can you pay?'

It seemed a lot but Dallas had no option. 'For that much I expect a decent cabin.'

Ross laughed mirthlessly. 'Monsieur, I advise you to accept what is offered. Aujoulat suffers no airs and graces. He will treat you fairly but as an equal. Take it or leave it.'

Dallas had the impression that Captain Ross had done all he was prepared to do. 'Thank you, captain. I accept.'

'Good. You are free to board at your leisure.'

The man obviously couldn't wait to get rid of

him. Dallas realised that if Cousin Adrian hadn't been part owner of the shipping line, he would have seen little or no help from Captain Ross. 'Then I'll take my leave of you, sir.' He gave a formal bow.

The captain responded stiffly and turned away.

Jensen brought Dallas's valise on deck. 'I'll carry this, sir.' He nodded to two others who lifted the heavy sea chest. 'The captain requires that we see you safely aboard the *Marie Clare.*'

Although a welcome offer, Dallas wondered if Captain Ross was simply making sure his unexpected passenger remained a responsibility no longer than absolutely necessary.

Jensen led, pushing through the crowds and yelling, 'Make way, make way.' Dallas wished he would stop. People were eyeing him with curiosity. He tensed as two gendarmes appeared but the policemen obligingly stepped aside allowing Dallas to pass. Once again, he was struck by the English sailor's audacious cunning. A fugitive would hardly draw such attention to himself.

'You're a lucky devil and no mistake,' Jensen commented when they reached the steamship. 'I hear tell she's a beauty.'

They said goodbye on the wharf. Dallas thanking the man again.

Jensen shrugged it off. 'You're running from the law. The peelers never caused me nothing but grief. It's me moral duty, monsieur.' He stuck out a grimy hand and Dallas shook it. 'Would you take a piece of good advice, sir?'

'Indeed, I'd appreciate it.'

'Trust no-one.' With a cheery wave, Jensen was gone.

Dallas felt quite alone as he stood in line before a table where passengers' names were being entered in a large leather-bound ledger. His turn came quickly.

'You are the gentleman off the *Newcastle Lady*, I take it? Name?'

'Granger,' Dallas said self-consciously.

'Thank you, Mr Granger. Please present yourself to the purser of B Deck. He will have someone show you to your cabin.'

Dallas ascended the gangplank, awed by the steamship's sheer size. A smartly dressed officer greeted him at the top. 'First Officer Hardcastle at your service. Welcome aboard, sir. We trust you will have a pleasant trip with us. Should you have any complaints about our service, or any special requirements, do not hesitate to inform the deck steward. I'll see to your baggage, sir.'

Dallas registered that the officer appeared to be English, not French. There was no reason for him not to be, but a Frenchman would be less likely to have heard of the scandal.

He was pleasantly surprised by his accommodation. It had two portholes and the door opened straight out onto A Deck. Comfortably furnished, an arch led from a small sitting room to the bed-chamber. A plan of the ship on the back of the door showed him where to find the dining room, games room, library and bar. Other printed information on a small bureau told him that the journey from Calais to Cape Town, should no heavy weather be encountered, would take five weeks. On their passage south the ship stopped for several days at the ports of Bilbao, Oporto, Casablanca, Las Palmas and Freetown, before steaming on to Cape Town. Passengers intending to disembark in Durban had to allow another four days, including one stopover at Port Elizabeth.

Additional information explained how the valet and laundry service worked, gave mealtimes, library and bar hours, and outlined a rudimentary entertainment schedule. Apart from a dinner dance in the games room every Friday and multi-denominational church services held in the library three times on Sundays, passengers had to amuse themselves. The library contained a collection of short plays for those with amateur dramatic leanings. Those wishing to play cards should see the purser who, for some inexplicable reason, kept playing cards under lock and key.

Sporting activities – shuffleboard, quoits and deck tennis – could be played outside or in the games room, where all associated equipment was to be found. Gentlemen wishing to spar for recreational purposes should see the purser. The ship's doctor had his surgery on B Deck where there was also a small infirmary.

Queen Victoria's influence stretched even to a French steamship. The vessel's saltwater pool would be open to ladies on Monday, Wednesday and Friday. Gentlemen could swim on Tuesday, Thursday and Saturday. It was closed on the Sabbath. A gilt-edged card informed Dallas that he was invited to join the captain's table every Tuesday and Saturday. On other days he would take meals on table three.

Alcohol, according to company rules and regulations, was not allowed in passengers' cabins and, while the bar would be closed whenever the ship was in port, alcohol could be purchased in the dining room. Passengers were free to utilise A and B Decks but anywhere else was off limits unless accompanied by a ship's officer. Fraternisation with crew members was strictly forbidden. Dressing for dinner appeared to be obligatory but tea gowns for women and less formal men's attire remained acceptable for breakfast and luncheon. Sailing times would be strictly adhered to and any passenger failing to return to the ship would be left behind, irrespective of country, with no responsibility for any subsequent calamity accepted by either the captain or the steamship company.

The ship would sail from Calais at ten that night. It was now three in the afternoon. Unpacked, Dallas decided to explore. Promenading A Deck, he found fellow passengers doing the same. After several turns nodding and smiling politely, continued formality seemed a waste of time and groups of people gathered to introduce themselves. Very soon, Dallas had met everyone.

Captain Ross thought the *Marie Clare* had berths for about twenty passengers. Dallas counted sixteen on deck, including himself. They were a mixed crowd.

Reverend David Stone and his wife, Margaret, were bound for Freetown to save black souls from white-learned evil ways. They came from Bath. In their early thirties – as far as Dallas could guess – the missionary had an open, sandy look about him, his hair, eyebrows and lashes a kind of dusty white colour and eyes a peculiarly pale hazel. Margaret was a small, nervous woman with sensibly short dark curly hair. David Stone said little but Margaret seemed full of meaningless social chitchat which communicated even less.

A German couple, Herr and Frau Knappert from Munchen, were on their way to Oporto and the start of a new life. Herr Knappert was a man in his fifties, his wife a good twenty years younger. There seemed to be sadness in both of them, and a kind of barely controlled tension simmered between them.

The thin and sickly-looking Monsieur Arnaud from Paris was going to Las Palmas to, as he quickly informed everyone, recover his health. From what, he did not say and no-one was impolite enough to ask.

The rest were going to South Africa.

Lord and Lady Diamond from Chester were accompanied by their two daughters, the ladies Grace and Sylvia. Her husband, Lady Diamond monotonously told each newcomer, was to take up an administrative position in Cape Town. Dallas knew him by reputation – an astute and highly respected politician, well connected at court and known to put Britain's interests before those of the peerage. Extra care would be needed to hide his true identity from this man. Lord Diamond would surely know of the rape charge and may become suspicious of a man travelling alone with no tangible reason for doing so. The daughters were aged fourteen and twelve, impeccably behaved and the apple of their father's eye.

There were two soldiers. Lieutenant Dirk Elliot of the Grenadier Guards, a short, balding gentleman in his forties, was joining his regiment in Natal, and Ensign Nesbit Pool of the 17th Lancers, a young man of no more than eighteen, was to disembark at Cape Town but seemed uncertain as to where he would be posted after that. The soldiers had little in common but, because of their military connections and possibly because they were travelling alone, quickly formed an acquaintanceship and were soon discussing playing poker as a way of passing the time on board.

A large Dutch gentleman and his equally ample wife – 'I am Hanson Wentzell and my goot lady is Magda. We are from Cape Town,' he pronounced it *Kapstad*, 'where there is little need to stand on useless ceremony.'

'Oh, Mr Wentzell,' Margaret Stone was clearly dismayed at the big man's gruff lack of formality, 'it is so important to keep up standards, especially in front of the natives.'

'Madam,' Hanson Wentzell said heavily. 'After six months of where you are going I guarantee your precious standards will be of no account. Believe me, the Kaffirs will soon see to that.'

'Kaffirs?' Clearly Reverend Stone's wife had never heard the term.

'Natives, as you called them, madam. Every last one a heathen.'

Margaret Stone looked shocked.

'Come, Hanson,' his wife admonished. 'Do not frighten the poor woman with your rough words.' Magda Wentzell delivered Margaret a grimace that passed for a smile. 'Don't listen to him, my dear. It is true that the Boers are less formal but the British do at least try to keep up their traditions.'

Her clumsy attempt, meant to comfort the reverend's wife, had an opposite effect. Margaret took on the look of a frightened rabbit. 'Oh dear,' was all she could manage.

'And what do you do in the Cape?' Lady Diamond sought to change the subject.

'We're farmers,' the Dutch woman told her.

'Oh, how interesting,' was all Lady Diamond could think of to say.

'Interesting, is it?' Hanson Wentzell gave a bark of derision. 'Ja, I suppose, if you don't mind living a day's ride from another white face, lions eating your cattle, thieving Bushmen stealing them and disease killing off whatever's left. I tell you what's interesting, lady, it's you plurry British thinking you can tame Africa. Nobody does that. It will beat you every time. The sooner you learn that and go home, the sooner we Boers can get on with the job we started.'

An embarrassed silence followed, broken by a slow handclap. 'Well said, Wentzell. Still your old charming self, I see.'

The speaker was English. A tall, weather-beaten man of at least sixty. His smile did not match the cool disapproval held in his eyes.

'Burton!' Wentzell, obviously surprised, turned to face the newcomer.

The man gave an exaggerated bow and introduced himself. 'Logan Burton at your service, ladies and gentlemen. Pay no attention to my ill-mannered Boer friend. The man is outnumbered – a situation most of his kind try to avoid. Take it from me, Africa is very different from anything you've ever known. Attempt to bend her and, as Wentzell says, it will break you. On the other hand, it is not only the Boers who live in harmony with the dark continent. Learn to do that and you will be rewarded many times over.'

'What would you know, Burton? An adventurer who's never done a hard day's work in his life?'

Logan Burton raised a sardonic eyebrow. 'That's really what sticks in your gullet, isn't it, Wentzell?'

'Oh stop this.' Magda Wentzell moved her considerable bulk forward so that she stood between her husband and Logan Burton. 'You two are like squabbling children.'

'I couldn't agree more,' murmured a voice beside Dallas. He turned to see who had spoken and found himself looking at one of the most exquisitely beautiful women he'd ever seen. She looked straight at him. 'Why do men carry on so?'

Dallas smiled. 'Not all of us, madam.'

She held out a hand. 'Jette Petersen.'

Dallas took it and bowed low, brushing his lips

across the soft and faintly perfumed skin. 'Charmed.' Straightening, he added, 'Dallas Granger at your service.' He released her fingers reluctantly. It was unusual for a woman to go without gloves and the sensation was most pleasant. 'What takes you to Africa?'

Jette Petersen was Danish, travelling to Durban where she would live with a recently widowed aunt. Not long bereaved herself, the arrangement suited both of them. As she spoke, Dallas warmed to the sight and sound of her. Well-dressed and similarly spoken – her French and English both flawless – she was probably in her early thirties with lustrous blue-black hair, flashing dark eyes, alabaster skin and pearly white teeth. Her voice floated low and musical. He couldn't help but admire her manner. She spoke as an equal, showing no hint of shyness or feminine flirtation. Nor was she trying to make a point. Dallas had the impression that Jette Petersen would despise any man who attempted to treat her as an object of beauty alone. She regarded herself as being on the same social and intellectual level as men and it was obvious that she expected to be treated as such. The few Danes he'd met in the past demonstrated an indifference for protocol which tended to make them ostracised in English society. Here, with his circumstances so changed, and in the company of such a diverse group, Dallas found it easy to adopt a more informal outlook.

One by one, the unattached men gravitated to Jette and Dallas. Even sickly Monsieur Arnaud seemed captivated by the beautiful Danish woman. In a very short time Dallas found himself competing for her attention with four others. To all five, Jette spoke in the same straightforward way, responding to compliments with pleasure but displaying none of the coquettishness that could so easily have gone with it. One by one, the competition fell on their swords.

Ensign Pool of the 17th Lancers was first to go. 'I say, bit risky, don't you think? I mean, a woman travelling on her own – it's hardly the done thing. People might think . . . well . . .' He gave a self-conscious laugh. 'I'd be more than happy to be of service.'

Jette, perhaps taking pity on his tender years, merely smiled. But Dallas noticed that she excluded him from further conversation.

Monsieur Arnaud went next. Seeming to forget that he was supposed to be ailing, he made a classically French tactical move which Jette, and everyone else, saw as patronising. Enduring a string of transparent compliments about her eyes – Dallas couldn't believe that anyone could come up with so many similes in one breath – the Frenchman started on her hair.

Jette allowed eight words – 'You have such beautiful hair, madame, it's like –' before cutting in, 'You would too, if only you'd wash it.'

Oh ho, Dallas thought. There's a hard streak to this lady.

Lieutenant Elliot was physically out of his depth. Jette stood inches taller, which placed him at an immediate disadvantage. And he spoke French so badly no-one could understand him. To give Elliot credit, he withdrew any further expression of interest before it was done for him.

That left Dallas and Logan Burton. Although the older man had to be twice Jette's age, he was a fine physical specimen with a store of anecdotes that Dallas couldn't possibly hope to equal. Tales of wild animals, primitive people and daring deeds, coupled with a dashing air, infectious laugh and eyes that glowed with interest bordering on the indecent – given his age – had Jette highly entertained.

There was something about Logan Burton that Dallas didn't like. He couldn't have stated what it was, just a feeling that the man wasn't to be trusted. It was nothing he said – his stories were interesting and entertaining – and nothing he did – his manners were impeccable. Perhaps it was the fact that he effortlessly monopolised Jette's attention.

'What takes you to Africa?' Burton turned unexpectedly to Dallas.

'Adventure.' As the word came out, Dallas cringed.

Logan Burton pounced. He threw back his head and laughed. 'Adventure,' he repeated, looking at Jette. 'Oh well, the boy is young.'

'Indeed,' Jette agreed. 'Young and full of dreams. Better that than old and living on memory, not so, Mr Burton?' With a brief nod she left, walking with cat-like grace along the deck towards her cabin.

Burton gave a short laugh. 'I do believe the lady has slapped my wrist. And what a lady, eh?'

Despite his misgivings, Dallas liked the way the older man had accepted Jette's dismissal. Perhaps he'd been mistaken about him.

'How about a wager, young Granger? A guinea to the first in her bed. What do you say?'

No mistake. Burton was a crude and crass bore. 'No bet,' Dallas replied coolly. 'You said it yourself, she's a lady.'

'Come, Granger. We both know how it is with widows.'

'Not I, sir.'

Burton looked disappointed for a moment, then shrugged. 'So be it. The best man will win. I'll see you at dinner.' With that, he strolled away.

Dallas noticed the big Dutchman, Hanson Wentzell, watch him leave, a frown of dislike on the man's florid face.

'Surprising number of British on board.' Lord Diamond stood next to Dallas. 'Good to see so many heading for Africa. Damned Boers think they own the south.'

Dallas said nothing about being Scottish, and he knew little about South Africa. 'Is Wentzell typical of the Boers? He seems unusually aggressive.'

'All the damned same, if you ask me. There'll be trouble between them and us one day. Please God the man isn't going to make a nuisance of himself on this trip. There's bad blood between him and that Burton chap and our two military men certainly didn't like his comments about the British. Good job there are so many of us, eh?' Lord Diamond turned to watch Wentzell. 'If you get a chance to speak with our Dutch friend I'd welcome a quiet word about anything of interest he might say.'

'What sort of thing?' Dallas was astonished that Lord Diamond should ask such a favour.

'Oh, just general comments about the Boers – how they view the British, their vision for a future South Africa, that's all.'

'Certainly. Though I doubt Wentzell, given his obvious dislike for us, is likely to say anything much to me.'

'Good chap.' Lord Diamond sidled off towards Reverend Stone. Dallas wondered if he planned to ask all the British passengers a similar favour.

After a few more minutes watching the activity on the dockside, Dallas turned towards his cabin. Others were heading for their. Despite the shipboard feeling of informality, dressing for dinner was so deeply entrenched in everyone that all the passengers gave it their utmost attention.

Dallas, when he located his place at table three, found to his delight that Jette was to be seated on his right. She arrived just after him, her widow's black somewhat festive looking with a low décolletage, lacy and scalloped, revealing the milky swell of uplifted breasts. Nipped at the waist, the fine cloth fell in silky folds around her feet. Several of the women eyed her with open disapproval. The bustle was very much in favour, yet Jette's gown lacked one. She looked, Dallas thought, like God intended women to look. With black hair swept up leaving curly tendrils falling around her face and neck, a glitter of diamonds at her throat and ears, she outshone every other woman in the room.

Jette gave Dallas a brilliant smile as he rose to greet her. 'It is still raining. How I look forward to reaching a sunnier climate.'

Dallas helped her with the chair. 'Have you been to Africa before?'

'Oh yes. Many times. And you?'

He shook his head. 'Never.'

She clapped her hands softly, eyes twinkling. 'Then you are in for a treat. Forget all that nonsense Mijnheer Wentzell spoke earlier. The Boers are spectacularly pessimistic. Africa is harsh, I admit, but like most things rigid there is a soft centre. Treated properly it will deliver up its secrets and hidden depths to a lucky few. Have you not found this to be so?'

'Inevitably, Madam Petersen.' *Could he be mistaken?* The innuendo was so blatant that Dallas decided her words had to be innocent.

'Mind you,' she went on, 'I have found a great deal of comfort in things that are solid. They are real. One can rely on them. There are times when a woman needs such reassurance. In my experience, that which has no substance is inclined to let you down.' She clapped her hands again. 'But don't mind me. I prattle too much. Look, here is our dashing first officer.'

Dallas was relieved by the diversion. He'd had no idea what to make of Jette's astonishing words.

The officer who welcomed Dallas on board

introduced himself to everyone at table three. 'Good evening, ladies and gentlemen. My name is Jeremy Hardcastle. It will be my pleasure to join you at dinner each evening. I see everyone has met. Excellent.'

The greeting was repeated in fluent French and then German, the latter a pointless exercise except perhaps to demonstrate the Englishman's command of both languages. In addition to Dallas, Jette and Jeremy Hardcastle, their table seated Monsieur Arnaud, the Reverend and Mrs Stone and a late-arriving French couple – Robert Dupaine, a civil servant, and his wife, Comfort.

Table one was the captain's and set for six. This evening, his guests were Lord and Lady Diamond and their daughters, plus Logan Burton. At the next, number two, the purser played host to the German couple, Herr Knappert and his wife, Lieutenant Elliot and Ensign Pool, and the Wentzells – Hanson and Magda. A fourth table, set slightly apart, was reserved for the ship's doctor and several other officers.

The ring of a crystal bell captured everyone's attention. Captain Aujoulat rose to his feet, waiting with an indulgent smile while the babble of voices died down.

He looked every inch the sea captain, resplendent in immaculate white trimmed with gold braid. A short, slightly built man, fiftyish, face unlined and very tanned, not a hair on his head, he had about him a benign appearance contrasted only by the shrewdness in his eyes. He made a short speech of welcome, effortlessly switching between French, German and English. 'Normally my officers and I would be free to join you after dinner. This evening, however, we will all be fully occupied with preparations to get under way. You are most welcome to remain in the dining room and become better acquainted. A waiter will be on duty and I myself expect to join you for a short while. We sail, as you all know, at ten this evening. It should be a fine sight as we steam down the Channel. The bar will not be open but you are free to purchase your tipple here and take it to A Deck. I do hope you all have a pleasant cruise. If there is anything you need, anything at all, please do not hesitate to inform Mr Hardcastle, who is seated at table three. *Bon appétit.*'

Captain Aujoulat called upon Reverend Stone to say grace. The good man bowed his head and obliged with great enthusiasm, ending on a heart-felt plea that they all think of those who had no choice but to go hungry. Dallas didn't see much point in thinking of the starving – there wasn't a whole lot he could do for them, so why ruin a perfectly good meal. The missionary tucked into each course with a look of such pleasure on his face that Dallas wondered if he too had forgotten the less fortunate. Monsieur Arnaud hardly touched his food, citing 'stomach troubles' as the reason. This was too indelicate for Mrs Stone who approached her meal with apprehension, almost as if she expected the same complaint to visit herself. Robert Dupaine explained that he and his wife would disembark at Freetown and from there make their way to the Côte d'Ivoire on a smaller vessel. 'We're looking forward to our time in Africa, aren't we, *ma chère*? There is so much work to be done. France was granted permission to colonise the Ivory Coast thirty years ago but has done little so far except change the name. My wife and I are part of, what you British would call, the advance party. It is a challenge but one is always at one's best under such circumstances, are we not, *ma chère*?'

Comfort Dupaine smiled shyly and murmured, 'I do hope so.'

Dallas could not fault the meal, or the way it was presented. Set off by the finest Irish table linen, the crockery, cutlery and crystal were of the very best quality, each course delicious and the service superb.

Jeremy Hardcastle, seated on the other side of Jette, tried to do his duty and chat with everyone but it soon became clear that his heart wasn't in it. He kept turning back to the Danish woman and, finally, gave up, concentrating on her alone. Dallas attempted to keep up with them but they had discovered a mutual acquaintance in Durban. Feeling excluded, he turned his attention to Comfort Dupaine, who sat on his left. She, as it turned out, had grown up in Provence, a part of France Dallas knew well, yet, still being cautious, he did not reveal the fact. Monsieur Arnaud joined in from across the table and Dallas listened as they reminisced. Robert Dupaine tried to engage the Stones in conversation but the man of God was more interested in his meal and his wife held court with such a long and convoluted family history that the French civil servant had to draw on all his reserves simply to stay awake.

The time passed pleasantly and Dallas was in mellow mood at the end of it, especially when Jeremy Hardcastle excused himself saying he had things to attend to prior to their departure. He had Jette to himself again.

'My apologies, Mr Granger. I fear you have been ignored. Just imagine, Mr Hardcastle knows my aunt. What a small world.'

'Indeed it is. You are forgiven.'

Jette's eyes lingered on his face and a small smile touched her lips. 'For that I will reserve the first dance for you.'

'Alas, that is not to be until tomorrow evening.'

'Ah, Mr Granger, you did not allow me to finish. You may escort me around the room tonight.'

'That will be my pleasure, Mrs Petersen.'

Jette tapped his arm playfully. 'Mind you, Mrs Dupaine clearly found your company to her liking. I swear, you paid scant attention to me once in conversation with her. I should feel vexed with you for ignoring me.'

'I do apologise, madam. It was certainly not my intention to displease you.'

She pouted. 'Very well then, I forgive you. Do you think we might circulate? I have heard enough of Monsieur Arnaud's health problems to last me the entire journey.' Her voice dropped. 'I declare, he is the most tedious man I've ever met. Thank God he's only going as far as Las Palmas.'

Dallas smiled, rose and offered his arm. 'Who takes your fancy, madam?'

'Lord Diamond. He and his wife are most agreeable.'

'So be it.'

They made their way towards the captain's table, where Lord and Lady Diamond sat with their daughters. Logan Burton saw them approaching and rose smoothly to his feet. 'You join us. How delightful.'

A waiter brought extra chairs. Jette leaned closer to Captain Aujoulat and asked, 'How long before we reach Morocco?'

'Eight days out, usually.'

'So long?' She seemed surprised.

'The Bay of Biscay is unpredictable and always we have cargo to load in Bilbao and Oporto. After that it is a clear run to the north coast of Africa. Do you have pressing business in Morocco, madam?'

'No, no.' Jette sat back. 'I'm told it is such a fascinating place.'

'Fascinating!' Captain Aujoulat raised an eyebrow. 'That's not a word I would choose, particularly not where we are heading. Casablanca is little more than a fishing village. Rabat, if you can get there, is slightly more interesting. I've never ventured inland, though I'm told the cities of Fez and Marrakech are more worthy of a visit. Unfortunately there is not enough time on this trip, they are too far.'

'Then why do we stop in Casablanca?' Lord Diamond demanded. 'Surely Rabat makes more sense. It has a port, does it not?'

'Indeed, and we are regular visitors there. However, the supplies on board are bound for Marrakech. Casablanca is closer.'

Lord Diamond huffed disapproval but said no more.

'Well I think it's exciting.' Jette was not put off by the captain's assessment. 'We can still explore, surely? Perhaps a visit to Rabat will be possible. We remain at port two days, is that not so, captain? Would that give enough time?'

'I do not advise it,' Aujoulat said. 'The journey is rough and reliable guides near impossible to find. Remember too, we delay departure for no-one. Morocco is not a place to find yourself abandoned. If you will take my recommendation, madam, explore Casablanca by all means but do not venture further.'

Jette's face fell. Logan Burton laughed. 'I do believe our beautiful travelling companion will not be put off. If it pleases you, madam, I have undertaken the trip to Rabat several times. It would be my pleasure to accompany you.'

'Thank you, Mr Burton, but I feel it would be prudent to take the captain's advice. Regrettably, Rabat will have to wait.'

'As you wish, madam.' Logan Burton dismissed the refusal lightly but his eyes gleamed with disappointment.

Captain Aujoulat took his leave. Lady Diamond

and her daughters bade the others goodnight and retired. The Reverend and Mrs Stone, followed by Monsieur Arnaud were not far behind. Those left, mingled in the dining room until ten o'clock when the ship was due to depart. All opted to watch from A Deck.

Mixed feelings became apparent as mooring ropes were slipped from their bollards severing the ship's connection to land. It had stopped raining, though a swirling fog obscured all but the brightest of lights as Calais disappeared astern and the *Marie Clare* steamed down the English Channel. Jette, Logan Burton and the Wentzells were openly glad to be under way. Frau Knappert briefly gave in to nervous tears. The rest fell strangely silent as they wrestled with the differing emotions of leaving behind all that was familiar. For Dallas, teetering between relief and regret, it was a poignant moment, but he soon shook off any sadness as Jette's excitement transferred to him. Logan Burton ordered a bottle of champagne and all three of them toasted the continent of Africa.

By midnight, most of the passengers had retired. Dallas walked Jette to the door of her cabin and made sure she was safely inside before returning to his own.

He'd almost convinced himself that the comments she'd made during dinner were innocent of any double meaning. Certainly, he could not fault her manners since then. Deep in pleasant thoughts of Jette, he failed to notice a dark figure close to his cabin. 'Got a moment, Granger?'

Lord Diamond leaned against the railing, smoking a cigar.

'Certainly.'

'Damned cold night. At least the rain has stopped.'

'I'll not miss the winter.'

Lord Diamond drew with deep satisfaction on his Havana before releasing a pall of pungent smoke. 'Ah. But will you miss Scotland?'

Dallas turned suddenly cold. 'I beg your pardon?'

'Scotland, man. It's where you're from, isn't it?'

'How . . . What gives you that idea?'

'Your name. It's quite unusual. Gaelic, isn't it? Grampian region, if I'm not mistaken. Small place south of Elgin. Am I right?'

'You are much better informed than I, sir.'

'Hardly. The accent gives you away.'

Dallas remained silent.

'Lothians, Edinburgh, I would say. Did you hear about Lady de Iongh? Terrible business.'

'Lady . . .'

'Come, man, the whole country knows of it. Lord Dalrymple is scarcely able to show his face.'

Dallas felt his heart constrict.

'They're looking for his son. Young fellow, about your age. Same name. Bit of a coincidence, wouldn't you say?' He turned to Dallas, his face hard. 'Be aware that I'm watching you, Granger, if that is what you call yourself now. The scandal of your actions has rocked the whole of Britain. Lord de Iongh is a personal friend and your own father is known to me. I give you the benefit of any doubt because it is common gossip that Alison is, shall we say, free with her favours. A man should not be accused of such a crime if he is, in fact, innocent. My observations this evening lead me to the conclusion that you have quite an eye for the ladies. Believe me, I would not hesitate to have you arrested if, for one moment, I thought that the accusations against you were well-founded. It is only fair that you know that.'

Dallas leaned against the railing and stared at lights along the French coastline. 'My lord, there is no truth in the charges brought against me,' he said softly. 'I am guilty of nothing but stupidity.'

'You are responsible for a damned sight more than that, sir,' Lord Diamond snapped. 'You have bedded another man's wife.'

Dallas dropped his head momentarily, before looking back at the older man. 'What you say is true and I am not proud of myself. However, I am not the first to be guilty of that misdemeanour. Nor, in all likelihood, will I be the last.'

'That is no excuse, sir.'

'Indeed,' Dallas agreed. 'But she was damned hard to deny.'

Lord Diamond puffed for a moment, then flicked his cigar stub into the waters below. 'She's a vixen and you were out of your depth. I daresay few your age could have said no. I trust she was worth it.'

'Nothing, and no-one, is worth this much trouble,' Dallas said bitterly.

Lord Diamond's tone softened slightly. 'Put it

behind you, lad. You are paying a high price and it's no more than is fitting. However, unless I miss my guess, you do not deserve to be hanged.'

'No, sir. I do not,' Dallas agreed quietly. 'Nor do I deserve the future I must now face.'

'That's a matter of opinion. It is mine that the suffering you have brought to Lord de Iongh should not go unpunished.'

'My punishment goes further than you can imagine,' Dallas replied, thinking of Lorna in particular. 'However, what is done is done and now I must make the best of things. That is all I am trying to do.'

Lord Diamond nodded. 'We will say no more of this. Your secret is safe with me, for the moment. Goodnight, Granger.'

'Goodnight, my lord.'

Dallas stayed at the railing for some time, his thoughts swirling. He was still not safe. Would Lord Diamond keep his word? Despair settled on him like the cold night air. What bad luck that he was travelling to South Africa on the same ship as a man astute enough to have guessed his real identity. The Diamonds would disembark at Cape Town. All the more reason for Dallas to make for Durban. The further from British authority, the better.

The cold drove him into his cabin a little after one in the morning. By then he had come to the regrettable conclusion that, tempting as the idea might be, Jette was off-limits. Dallas could not risk anything that might cause Lord Diamond to think ill of him. Commonsense applauded the wisdom of that decision. The rest of him was profoundly depressed. Avoiding Jette Petersen was the last thing his healthy young body felt like doing.

It turned out to be easier than he expected during the next week. Jette was much in demand and, although she occasionally threw a questioning look in his direction, seemed perfectly happy with the attentions of others. Dallas remained polite and charming, but distant. He made no attempt to compete with Jeremy Hardcastle or Logan Burton, both of whom had made their interest abundantly clear. Although unintentional, the stance adopted by Dallas only served to intrigue Jette.

On their second Friday at sea they sighted the North African coast of Morocco. That same night there was to be a dance in the games room. Jeremy Hardcastle had virtually monopolised Jette's attention during dinner but before leaving the table she turned to Dallas and said, 'I did not have the pleasure of dancing with you last week, Mr Granger. I do hope you are planning to rectify that this evening.'

'Of course.' On the other side of her, Dallas saw the first officer's expression harden. He did not like the idea of sharing Jette with anybody else.

'Excellent.' Jette smiled. 'I will save the first waltz for you.'

There was nothing Dallas could do but accept. As he claimed her for the dance, he noticed Lord Diamond staring at him, an unreadable expression in his intelligent eyes.

· 'You are avoiding me,' Jette accused as soon as they swirled away. 'Have I offended you?'

'Not at all. Though you are hardly short of admirers.'

She gave a small smile of acknowledgment. 'Perhaps not. But I would add one more if that were possible.'

Dallas laughed. It was quite spontaneous. He liked the Danish widow immensely, finding her candour refreshing. 'Madam, were you not taught that greed is bad for one?'

'Oh yes,' she said gaily. 'Such a lesson was indeed drummed into my head. But in truth, Mr Granger, I was also taught that in order to get what is wanted, it is sometimes necessary to help oneself.'

'Tut!' he chided gently. 'You already have our dashing first officer eating out of your hand. The intrepid Mr Burton is smitten. Our two military men beg for crumbs. Even Monsieur Arnaud seems to be making a miraculous recovery. What more could you want?'

Jette glanced up through thick lashes. 'A woman's wants, Mr Granger, should remain her secret. Until she is ready to share them, that is.'

Dallas felt his heart skip a beat. Once again, Jette's words could be taken either of two ways. 'I am certain, madam, that any of those gentlemen would be more than willing to share a secret with you.'

Impatience crept into her voice. 'Most men are so obvious they bore me. But you? There is something rather . . . reserved in your manner that is both challenging and intriguing. I am a woman who hates mystery and warn you, sir, my intention is to ferret the reason from you. Will you walk with me on deck a little later?'

Alarm bells were ringing in Dallas's mind. He ignored them. 'It would be my pleasure.' He thought briefly of Lorna but pushed her memory aside. She was the past.

After their dance Jette announced cheerfully to Jeremy Hardcastle, 'Mr Granger has offered to see me safely to my cabin. Isn't that sweet of him, Jeremy? I know how busy you are. Now you need not bother yourself with my well-being.'

Hardcastle looked angry but gave a stiff bow and, a short while later, left the dance.

When Dallas walked with Jette towards her cabin, she took his arm and said, 'Let us stroll for a while.'

The weather had become progressively warmer as they steamed south, grey skies giving way to clear blue. At night twinkling stars and the cloudy slash of the Milky Way seemed to sit within reach overhead. A new moon perched on the horizon, a silvery sliver of light scything through the velvet black sky.

'Isn't it beautiful?' Jette murmured. 'I do so love Africa.'

The air had a softness Dallas had never felt before. 'Is Natal like this?'

'Oh, much better. At night you can smell flowers and the damp earth, listen to crickets and frogs. It's wonderful.'

'You can do all that in Europe,' he teased.

'Tch! Where's your sense of romance? Africa is different. Bird calls are unlike any other. You hear all manner of sounds, some quite frightening until you learn to identify them. That's part of the magic. There's a danger which heightens your appreciation of being alive.' She gave a small laugh. 'A lesson for all of us, Mr Granger. Where else can you go with the possibility that life could be snuffed out at any moment? It makes you want to live every second to the full. You'll fall in love with Africa, I promise.' Jette tossed her head, and hair, which she'd left loose and flowing giving her a gypsy appearance, rippled and settled softly around her face. 'There's a wildness, an unrestrained feeling which sets you free. Unless I'm mistaken that same wildness lurks behind your reserve, it just needs to be released.' Her fingers tightened ever so slightly on his arm. 'Or has someone already done that?'

No mistake this time. 'Perhaps,' he murmured, bending his head towards hers to create more intimacy. 'Although only a fool would lay claim to having nothing left to learn.'

Jette's laugh tinkled as she looked up at him. 'And you are not a fool, are you, Mr Granger?'

A reply did not make it past his lips. Jeremy Hardcastle blocked their way. Eyes blazing with jealousy, his words were harsh. 'So, you walk with this young puppy yet refuse my earlier offer. Tell me, madam, do you enjoy humiliating others in public?'

Jette did not resort to feminine flutters. She

stood her ground and spoke plainly. 'I'll walk with whom I please, Mr Hardcastle. And it pleases me to walk with Mr Granger. Now, if you'll excuse us.'

Hardcastle did not move. 'You led me to believe that the honour would be mine.'

'No, Mr Hardcastle, I most certainly did not. You came to that conclusion on your own.'

Jeremy Hardcastle was in a fit of jealous rage. Dallas eased Jette's hand from his arm, hoping the man could control himself. 'Let us pass, Hardcastle.'

'That I will not, sir.' He stepped towards Jette, a determined look on his face.

She appeared quite unmoved but her fingers once again found Dallas's arm.

'Your attention is unwelcome, Hardcastle. The lady has made that perfectly plain. Let us proceed, there's a good chap.'

The first officer rounded on Dallas. 'You dare to challenge me? Very well, I accept. The best man can take her.'

'Don't be stupid. You know the rules.' Dallas was standing directly in front of Hardcastle. 'Leave the lady alone.' He dodged a wickedly fast right jab and grabbed Hardcastle by the upper arms. 'I will fight if you insist but implore that you think again.'

The strength of his grip, steady eyes and calm voice broke through Hardcastle's anger. He shook Dallas off. 'Fortunately for you my position forbids me to take this matter further. Should I ever catch up with you ashore it will be a different story.' The officer turned back to Jette and bowed. 'Good-night, madam. Since you prefer a boy to a man, I wish you luck. You are likely to need it.' With that, he strode past them.

In the soft light outside her cabin, Jette's eyes glowed with excitement as she gazed into Dallas's face. She reminded him of Alison de Iongh and the thought made him angry. 'It might be wise, madam, if you place a barrier against your door. A duplicate key will be easy for Hardcastle to obtain and the man clearly cannot control his impulses.'

She noticed his annoyance but seemed unaffected by it. 'And you can?' Jette challenged.

'Indeed, madam. Goodnight to you.' Before bending over her hand he caught the look of surprise on her face. She'd been playing with him, of that he had no doubt, and the game had backfired. A fleeting feeling of disappointment ran through Dallas but he hardened his resolve. Once bitten. He had no intention of becoming Jette's plaything. She should know that he could not be trifled with. Turning away, Dallas thought of going back to the games room but decided against it. Instead, he went to his own cabin.

As the door closed behind him, a dark figure moved from the shadows. Lord Diamond had witnessed the entire incident. Young Dalrymple had acquitted himself well. That boy is no rapist, he decided. Making his way back to the dance, Lord Diamond was deep in thought. While he could never condone the cuckolding of de Iongh, neither could he fully blame Dallas. A lad sows wild oats where he can – Diamond had planted a few in his time – and a beautiful, willing woman was damned near impossible to refuse. Tonight Granger had proved that he could control both anger and desire. There was maturity and honour in the young nobleman, traits highly prized by Diamond. Given the chance, he would do what he could to clear Dallas of the charges standing against him. He'd never restore the boy's reputation – that damage would never completely go away – but he'd do his best. As for Jette Petersen? The Danish woman was trouble, no doubt about it. Lord Diamond was reasonably certain that she would find her way into young Granger's bed, if not tonight, then soon. He chuckled. 'Lucky devil!' A night with Jette could be a truly rewarding, if somewhat exhausting, experience.

The man was as good a judge of human nature as any. Thirty minutes after saying goodnight to Jette, Dallas heard a soft tap on his door.

She stood looking at him for a moment, as if gauging his mood, before speaking. 'I cannot sleep. Have I annoyed you in some way?' She brushed past into his cabin. 'Oh!' Jette exclaimed, looking around. 'This is much grander than mine.' She sank into a chair, her eyes large in the heart-shaped face that looked up at him. 'Please do not be angry with me. I'd like us to be friends.' Dallas was still clothed. 'I didn't wake you?'

'No. I was thinking of returning to the dance.'

'I too thought of doing so. But Jeremy may be there.'

'A word to the captain, madam, would see to it that he did not bother you again.'

'Oh, I have no wish to make trouble for him.'

'Why not? He was planning exactly that for you.'

She shook her head slightly. 'No, no. I don't believe that. Jeremy is a little . . . impulsive perhaps, but he is a gentleman.'

Dallas found Jette's nearness disconcerting.

She smiled up at him. 'I only came here to make peace between us.'

'There is no need. I was pleased to be of assistance.'

'But you are angry with me. I can see it on your face.'

'No, madam, you misunderstand. I was angry with Hardcastle and I am also annoyed at myself.'

'At yourself!' Her eyes widened in genuine puzzlement. 'Why?'

'You travel alone. Protection is needed.' Dallas was acting on instinct, wary of Jette yet sure that she would only ever please herself. At least she wasn't married, so where was the harm in taking what was offered? What could go wrong?

'Does the need to protect me displease you?' The coyness of her words could not mask the desire that throbbed in her low voice.

'Not at all. I am happy to be of service.' Dallas took a deep breath and plunged in. 'And yet, within myself I find the same base instinct that overcame Hardcastle. Madam, I am no better than he.'

Satisfaction gleamed in her huge dark eyes. 'Do not trouble yourself with such thoughts, for you have proved yourself many times more honourable. You flatter me, sir, with your admiration for I am much older than you.'

Dallas crossed the cabin and knelt by her side. 'Your age is of no consequence. It is the woman I much admire.'

'You are bold indeed, Mr Granger. Bold and direct. Allow me to be the same. I think we understand each other, do we not? Perhaps I shock you but it is not in my nature to be timid. We both want the same thing.'

Dallas rose to his feet and held out a hand. She took it in both of hers and he pulled her up. 'Since we are of like mind, madam, perhaps you should try calling me Dallas.'

'Indeed.' She stepped closer and wound her arms around his neck. 'And you should call me Jette.'

'An offer not to be refused, since I have no intention of knowing you from head to toe without being able to call your name in my pleasure.' Dallas bent his head and kissed her parted lips.

When they broke apart Jette gave a gurgle of delight. 'I see you are young in years only, Dallas, for your lips tell a different story.'

Dallas picked her up and carried her to his bed. 'It is my body, Jette, that is aching to speak to you.'

Lord Diamond was right in every respect. By the time Jette left for her own cabin shortly before dawn, Dallas was incapable of raising a smile, let alone any other part of his anatomy. They had made love more or less continuously throughout the rest of the night. She found ways to stimulate him that he wouldn't have believed possible. His entire body became her playground and he responded again and again to teasing fingers and lips. Her need of him had seemed insatiable and she displayed no coyness in providing Dallas with every pleasure imaginable, and then some. Leaving, she blew him a kiss, her eyes languid with satisfaction and pleasure.

Dallas knew she was trouble. A woman like Jette could never be content with one man, no matter how much he tried to please her. Physically, emotionally and intellectually, she would always seek out the stimulation of change. For now at least, her attention was on him and, as long as that lasted, Dallas was only too happy to enjoy it. The lessons learned with Alison and the alarm bells that warned him of Jette were ignored.

And Lorna? She was out of reach. He'd betrayed her trust and she was lost to him. Lorna would remain in his heart forever. It was all he had left of her.

They spent two days and one night in the seaport of Casablanca. Captain Aujoulat had been right in one respect, it wasn't much more than a fishing village. Still, the place had a distinct Arab flavour with a small mosque, narrow streets and sun-dappled courtyards. Its one and only souk displayed a disappointingly limited array of goods for sale. Yet the air vibrated with unfamiliar sounds – ironworkers and coppersmiths hammering, donkeys braying, roosters crowing, reedy music and raised voices shouting a strange foreign language. The *Marie Clare*'s arrival brought out the whole town. Tourism was a new concept to Casablancans but their natural inclination to barter had the Arab inhabitants offering everything from their sisters to lanterns made of silver. A scent of spices, fragrant and exotic, filled the air. Unwisely, Dallas sampled a bowl of food offered for sale by a doe-eyed boy. It was couscous with chunks of leather-tough meat, probably goat, and flavoured with mint leaves. Pungent and spicy, it burned his mouth, but with Jette's amused urging, he finished the lot.

They returned to the ship before dark. At dinner, Dallas had little appetite and felt unexpectedly tired. He put it down to the previous night's exertions with Jette but it didn't prevent him from suggesting she spend the night with him again. He was dismayed, therefore, when his body's response to her ministrations proved, at best, lackadaisical. She appeared not to mind and the two of them eventually drifted off to sleep.

In the early hours of morning, cramps woke him. He staggered from bed, trying not to waken Jette. Dallas had never felt so ill or known such excruciating pain. As first one end, and then the other, emptied, he was convinced death awaited. Jette waking and coming to his aid only increased the misery. He did not wish her to see him in such a state but she dismissed his feeble protests, pressing cold cloths on his forehead and wiping the sweat from his body.

Finally the desperate flux ran its course, leaving Dallas weak and pale. 'Go back to your cabin,' he pleaded with Jette, embarrassed by the foul stench in his.

But she stayed, bathing his body and dressing him in clean linen, even emptying his chamber pot over the ship's side. Then, kissing him gently on the brow, she left a fragrant handkerchief on his pillow and whispered a tender goodnight. Dallas barely heard her and within minutes had fallen into a deep and exhausted sleep.

A knock on his door woke him just after midday. It was the Reverend Stone and his wife, the latter bearing a bowl of broth. 'We understand you are unwell,' she said solicitously, bustling in. 'You poor dear man. The sooner we are away from this disgusting place, the better. I had no idea that Africa would be so filthy.' She threw a backwards glance at her husband as if to say, 'It's all your fault.' He seemed more fascinated by the sight of Jette's handkerchief, which was still on the pillow.

Dallas just groaned and covered his eyes.

'I asked the cook to prepare some chicken broth. Sit up now. Try and have a little.'

It was the last thing in the world Dallas wanted. The smell alone made his stomach heave. On a mission of mercy, the good Mrs Stone, who was convinced her destiny lay in helping others, bore down on him with a determination not to be thwarted. Dallas realised the sooner he swallowed at least some of the greyish watery-looking liquid, the sooner he could be rid of the domineering woman. He obediently allowed her to spoon-feed him. She prattled non-stop.

'Everyone was quite worried when Mrs Petersen said you were ill, weren't they, David?'

The reverend nodded, his eyes still on the scrap of perfumed linen.

'Just as well one of us knew. You might have died in here. Who knows what these heathens put in their food. Really, Mr Granger, I gave you credit for more sense. Fancy eating something off the street. I declare, you are lucky to be alive. Isn't he, David?'

Nod.

'Mind you, it hasn't deterred Mrs Petersen. Off she's gone today in a donkey cart. Quite alone she is too, aside from an Arab guide. She's a plucky little thing, though rather foolish, I fear. Even refused Mr Burton's offer to accompany her. Oh, I do hope she'll be all right. Do you think she will be, David?'

Nod. Grunt.

'And Mr Hardcastle seemed quite out of sorts at luncheon. He barely spoke to anyone. That nice Mrs Dupaine tried so hard to include him in conversation but he was barely civil. Quite unnecessary, wasn't it, David?'

Nod.

On and on she went. The reverend finally switched his attention from Jette's handkerchief to mournfully watching each spoonful of soup. Dallas had had enough. 'No more, please, Mrs Stone.'

'Just a teeny bit.'

Dallas warded off the spoon and shook his head. 'Thank you. I should sleep now.'

'I do hope you are well enough to join us for dinner. If not, we'll bring a little something to your cabin, won't we, David?'

Nod.

'Nice talking to you,' Dallas managed.

The comment went straight over Reverend Stone's head.

When Dallas awoke, it was to find that the ship had put to sea. The sun's angle suggested it was around four in the afternoon. He sent for hot water and washed. Still weak but feeling much better, Dallas vacated the cabin so a steward could clean up and make his bed. The fresh air on deck helped but a need for liquid had him go to the library for tea. He was finishing a second cup when Logan Burton found him.

'Have you seen Mrs Petersen?'

'No. Not today at least.'

'No-one has. She went ashore this morning and hasn't been seen again. I believe she's still there.'

'My God! Does the captain know?'

'I'm not sure.'

'Then we must find out at once.'

They left the library together and encountered Jeremy Hardcastle on B Deck. 'Captain Aujoulat made our departure time perfectly clear. He will not turn the ship back. Are you sure she's not in her cabin?'

'The door is locked and there is no response from within.'

'Maybe she's ill,' Dallas said, worried.

'Good God, Granger. Don't tell me she ate that local food too?' Burton looked as concerned as Dallas felt.

'Certainly not yesterday.'

'The purser has a key, I'll get it,' Hardcastle said. 'One of you wait at her cabin. The other might like to see if Mrs Stone would be kind enough to join us just in case.'

Dallas found the reverend's wife and swiftly explained.

'Oh dear. I do hope she's all right. Of course I'll come with you. You stay here, David?'

Nod.

Mrs Stone insisted on being the first to enter Jette's cabin, 'In case the lady is indisposed.'

She needn't have worried. Jette was not there. Nor, when they searched the cabin, were any of her belongings.

Captain Aujoulat refused point-blank to turn back. 'The fact that Mrs Petersen's luggage has gone would seem to indicate that she chose to leave the ship. I have no intention of falling behind schedule to rescue a damned headstrong woman who will not listen to advice and who probably has no wish to be rescued. That is an end to the matter, gentlemen.'

Even Jeremy Hardcastle appeared shaken by Jette's disappearance, although he could not resist a crude dig at Dallas. 'Perhaps the lady seeks a man, not a boy. She should have come to me.' Dallas ignored the comment. Hardcastle's jealousy was tedious to say the least. He hoped Jette would be all right. Her vanishing like that was a mystery but they all agreed with the captain: Jette had left the ship willingly.

Dressing for dinner, Dallas noticed a stain on his white shirt. He searched for the key to his sea chest to find another. It usually lay on the small bureau but there was no sign of it. Nor was it in any pocket of his clothing. He finally found it in the chest's lock. Frowning, for he did not remember leaving the key there, Dallas opened the lid. Then his brow cleared. Of course! Jette had insisted he put on fresh attire before going to sleep.

As Dallas removed a clean shirt he noticed that the chest's contents had been unusually disturbed. That was odd. His nightshirts were kept on top, Jette should have had no difficulty in finding one. A dreadful fear rose in him. Reluctantly, for he could hardly bring himself to suspect her, he lifted the layers of clothing.

Both pouches containing the jewellery his mother had given him were missing.

FIVE

The *Marie Clare* steamed southwards around the bulge of north-west Africa. Herr and Frau Knappert having left the ship in Oporto a week earlier, the unexplained defection of Jette – mysterious to all but Dallas, who had little doubt as to the reason why – reduced passenger numbers to fifteen.

On deck, the day after leaving Casablanca, Logan Burton approached Dallas offering a gold sovereign. 'You win.'

Dallas refused. 'If you recall, sir, I did not accept the wager.'

'No,' Burton agreed, still trying to press the money on Dallas. 'But unless my guess is much mistaken, you have recently experienced a not inconsiderable loss of funds.'

The gesture was brushed aside. 'Keep your money, Burton, for I am not so hard pressed as to accept that for which no claim exists.'

The older man shrugged and pocketed the coin. 'As you wish.' He turned to the railing and stared towards a distant horizon. 'I hope she was worth it.'

Dallas made no comment. Another woman had played him for a fool. Was he ever going to learn?

Perhaps reading his thoughts, Burton chuckled suddenly, shaking his head. 'You are a lucky devil, young lad, and no mistake. Youth is on your side. Take the loss on the chin, my boy. Africa awaits. Whatever that little minx absconded with, you can make up many times over. The rewards are there for those not afraid of a little danger. I see in you a Promethean spirit. You'll overcome this setback and move on to better things.'

Will I? Dallas wondered. Could he ever replace the one and only connection with his real father? Face expressionless, all he said was, 'I daresay you are right, Burton.' Inwardly, he puzzled at the older man's choice of words. Drawing on his scant knowledge of Greek mythology, Prometheus was a Titan who stole fire from the gods only to be chained to a rock as punishment. For all eternity, each day an eagle would eat his liver only to have it grow again during the dark hours and be eaten anew the next day. If that was Burton's idea of an analogy, Dallas wasn't sure he liked it.

Monsieur Arnaud left the ship in Las Palmas. No-one was sorry to lose his endless prattle about health.

A couple of nights later during dinner, Margaret Stone divulged that Herr and Frau Knappert had not been married. 'He left his wife and three children to run away with her,' she told the table in scandalised tones. 'No wonder they seemed so tense.'

Her husband raised pale amber eyes from his meal. 'Margaret! That is privileged information.'

'Don't be silly, David. What harm can it do? We'll never see them again.'

Dallas had been watching Reverend Stone. The man's mild expression didn't change but the knuckles of both hands turned white as he gripped his knife and fork. Nothing more was said.

For the rest of their trip to Sierra Leone, where the two missionaries as well as Robert and Comfort Dupaine were to disembark, Margaret Stone took meals in her cabin and was not seen on deck. The reverend excused her continued absence as 'A mild touch of the ague'. His explanation was accepted by the others with appropriate murmurings of understanding since everyone had been suffering to a greater or lesser degree from the water taken on board at Casablanca. But as they waited to go ashore in Freetown, a scarf did little to hide Margaret's bruised face. A man of God indiscreetly sharing confidences with his wife was one thing, her sharing them in public obviously another. Dallas, who didn't particularly like Margaret Stone, nonetheless felt that a good talking-to would have been sufficient to dissuade any repetition in the future. Looking at the Stones – she standing ramrod straight staring at the land, he with his arm protectively around her – a picture of married bliss, Dallas came to the conclusion that he wasn't the only one with secrets. He couldn't help but feel that, compared with Margaret Stone's, his problems were slight. Heaven help the heathens, he reflected, if David Stone needed such a heavy hand to get his way.

Down to ten passengers, since nobody new had joined the ship, they continued down the rugged and densely forested west coast towards Cape Town. Boredom set in. Life on board revolved around mealtimes. Most mornings, Dallas and Logan Burton joined Lieutenant Elliot and Ensign Pool at cards. The well-behaved daughters of Lord and Lady Diamond gave in to sulks, tantrums and petty squabbling. Hanson and Magda Wentzell kept pretty much to themselves, although the Boer farmer took every opportunity to snipe at Logan Burton.

'What's the man got against you?' Dallas eventually asked.

'I'm British. He needs no other reason.'

'He's not downright rude to the rest of us.'

'No,' Burton agreed with a chuckle. 'The rest of you haven't been involved with his sister.'

If an observation about Logan Burton were called for, it was that discretion rarely troubled him. Wishing to avoid a frank revelation, Dallas merely nodded, but the man was in expansive mood.

'Pretty little thing. Flirts like the devil. Called on her a couple of times. Wentzell found out and went off half-cocked. Said he didn't want a bloody Englesman anywhere near his family. Anyway, the whole thing was just a flash in the pan. She was a typical Boer.'

Despite his best intentions, Dallas had to ask what Burton meant.

'No sense of humour, my boy. Took everything literally. A word of warning, young Granger, steer clear of that lot. Boer fillies are as boring as a day in church. And, without fail, they run to fat.'

'Oh come, Burton.'

'It's true. Look around when we get to Cape Town. If you can find one that's married and slender I'll eat my hat. Wentzell's sister was no exception.'

'Many English women are the same. Anyway, you said she was pretty.'

'Was, my boy, was. A good twelve years ago.'

'And he still hates you after all that time?'

'Um . . .' Burton looked briefly conscience-smitten, before he laughed. 'A farmer's daughter, old chap. Grew up seeing animals doing what came naturally. We were in the barn, just larking about, you understand. Anyway, Wentzell caught us. Made a hell of a fuss. Before I knew it, his old man arrived with a sjambok. I was in for it, make no mistake. Those two were planning to flay the hide off me. I did the only thing possible under the circumstances. Told them I was in love and wanted to marry the girl.' He laughed again. 'Well, they weren't too happy about it but let me go.'

'So you jilted her?'

'Don't be silly. She didn't want to marry me any more than I her. She had an eye on some farm boy next door. As I said, we let it fizzle out. It's her brother who can't let it go.'

'What if she'd wanted to marry you? Would you have gone through with it?'

'Certainly. What do you take me for? I'd have settled down, fathered children, ploughed her father's fields and eaten her Ouma's terrible food. And one day, when she rolled over in bed, I'd have been squashed flat.'

Dallas shook his head, smiling.

'Don't believe me?' Burton chuckled. 'Ah, my young friend, your lack of regard for my honour cuts me. You must think me an awful cad.'

Dallas could never work out when Logan Burton was joking.

Apart from those whose turn it was to dine with the captain, the remaining passengers now sat together. Though Jeremy Hardcastle performed his duties without speaking directly to Dallas, the man's animosity was evident. Despite this, the night before they reached Cape Town, Dallas made a request for the address of Jette's aunt in Durban.

'And why should I pass that information to you?'

'I thought I'd pay her my respects.'

'Did you indeed? As it happens, Granger, I'll be calling there myself. I'm sure the good lady doesn't need to see you as well.' He smiled bitterly. 'Mrs Petersen made a complete fool of you. Forget her.'

Dallas contained a rush of anger towards the first officer. Damn the man and his petty jealousy. 'As you like. If you won't help, I'll find her aunt on my own.'

'I can't stop you trying.' Hardcastle's voice was tight. 'Go ahead. See how far you get.'

Logan Burton had been listening and interrupted

in a tone that was light enough yet had underlying impatience. 'It's hardly Granger's fault that you were smitten by the lady.'

Hardcastle glared at him. 'If memory serves, you too found her attractive.'

'To be sure,' Burton agreed affably. 'Very. But like Granger here, that's as far as it went. Wake up to yourself, man. None of us stands a chance with the likes of Jette Petersen. If you're lucky, bed them. If not, walk away.'

The first officer turned bright red. 'How dare you, sir. I demand a retraction.'

Lord Diamond, who had been following the exchange, intervened. 'If you don't mind, Burton, there are ladies present.'

'Quite,' the first officer snarled. 'What more can one expect from the likes of him?'

Lord Diamond's intelligent eyes showed irritation. 'I'd hold my tongue if I were you, Hardcastle. From an incident I observed on deck a few weeks ago you are hardly in a position to comment.'

'My lord, I have no idea to what you refer.'

'No?' Diamond stared him down. 'Think back. You, sir, wished to fight Granger for the lady's favours. Need I say more?'

Jeremy Hardcastle excused himself and left the table.

'Don't concern yourself about finding the aunt.' Burton turned to Dallas. 'As it happens, I know where she lives.'

'Of course you do,' Hanson Wentzell sneered suddenly. 'There's not a woman in Natal, or the

Cape Colony for that matter, whose address you don't have.'

'Thankfully,' Logan drawled, 'your sister's is not among them.'

Magda stopped her husband from rising. 'Let it be, Hanson,' she said quietly.

Logan remained outwardly relaxed but Dallas sensed him tense, ready to react if necessary.

'Dear me.' Lady Diamond fanned herself. 'I shall be glad of dry land. I think we're all a little unsettled after so long a journey. Mr Wentzell, you were telling me the other day of meeting that wonderful man Thomas Baines. Just think, an author, artist and explorer. How fascinating. Do tell, what is he like?'

The Dutchman laboured with his English, recounting a surprisingly favourable impression of the young British gentleman who was, in the main, a member of the Cape Colony's artistic fraternity – a far cry from his own world. Others around the table quickly lost interest but Lady Diamond appeared fascinated, even if she had only asked the question to divert a confrontation.

Looking decidedly bored, Lord Diamond turned to Dallas. 'A word on deck if you'd be so kind, Granger.'

Without waiting, he rose and left the table.

Dallas nodded an apology to the others and followed.

As soon as they were in the fresh air, Lord Diamond offered Dallas a cigar.

'Thank you, no.'

'Just wanted to put your mind at rest, Granger.

I'm a fair judge of character, have to be in my position. You've had a spot of bad luck rather than anything else and are obviously concerned that I could choose to expose you.' Diamond smiled without mirth, his expression grave yet uncritical. 'Well, your true identity and whereabouts are safe with me. I don't condone what you've done, de Iongh is a damned fine man, but you don't deserve to hang. As far as I'm concerned, officially anyway, you are who you say you are. If there's anything I can do for Dallas Granger I'd be happy to oblige.' He puffed on the cigar with enjoyment before continuing. 'None of my business, of course, but I'd suggest that Natal might be your best bet. Like you, it's just starting out. Ideal for somebody whose background would . . . ah, not stand up to scrutiny. There's a tendency up north, so I'm told, to judge a man by what he does today. Family connections matter only if they have relevance in Africa.' The nobleman smiled again and, this time, approval glinted in his eyes as his tone became almost conspiratorial. 'You could do worse than teaming up with Burton. The man's an honest rogue but that's desirable out here. You're a bit of an adventurer too. I think you'd do well together.' Lord Diamond extended his hand and Dallas grasped it. 'Good luck, Granger. I'll be listening out for news. I've a feeling you'll make your mark one way or another.'

With a brisk nod, Lord Diamond returned to the dining room, leaving Dallas wondering exactly what he'd done to so favourably impress the man.

Table Mountain, standing sentinel over the town and surrounds of Cape Town, came into view just after lunch the following day. It was a welcome sight and everybody stayed on deck as the *Marie Clare* drew nearer. The city, what could be seen of it, lay in a curve of the bay. Rising behind, richly wooded forests sloped towards a vertical wall of solid rock. White, wispy cloud billowed over the flat summit hanging, like a lace tablecloth, over the crags and crevices. It was windy, the blustery south-easter whipping the deep blue sea into choppy white horses. Dallas felt strangely elated as he counted a dozen or more ships riding at anchor.

Logan, one hand making sure his hat stayed with him, sniffed the air. 'Lunchtime. I can smell curry.'

'So can I. Does the wind always blow this hard?'

'In summer, yes. Locals call it the Cape Doctor. Always a south-easter. They say it carries germs away from the land. That may well be true. I've seen her blow hard enough to knock grown men backwards. When she stops, you can expect a day so serene, so gentle, you might as well be in heaven.' Logan broke off, looking surprised, as though he hadn't expected his words.

Hanson Wentzell stood nearby. 'Home. Thank God. No place like it.'

'Where will we live, Papa?' fourteen-year-old Sylvia asked Lord Diamond.

'I'm not sure,' her father responded doubtfully. He could see little to enthuse over. The architecture showed a distinctly Dutch influence and was not much to his liking.

'As far away as possible,' muttered Wentzell. 'That's the only place for you British. You think you are too fine to live in the city with the Dutch.'

'We'll live wherever the British government provides a house,' Lord Diamond rebuked mildly.

Wentzell turned away.

Ensign Pool was also dubious. 'That must be the fort,' he said, pointing. 'Not very big.'

'Where does soldier boy think he is?' Logan Burton commented in an undertone.

In such windy conditions the longboat trip ashore might have proved extremely difficult. However, as if on cue, the Cape Doctor abruptly ceased.

'Does that all the time,' Logan said. 'It could start up again in five minutes or stay away for days.'

Lord Diamond and his family said ceremonious goodbyes to both fellow passengers and crew. Hanson Wentzell and his wife barely waved.

Three single men and two married couples joined the ship in Cape Town. Of the couples, one was returning to England after being away for five years. The wife made no effort to conceal her delight at leaving. Her husband was less enthusiastic at the prospect. 'It's hard on the women out here,' he explained with no elaboration. 'But it's a grand life all the same.'

Dallas mentioned to Logan that no-one seemed ambivalent about Africa.

'Don't listen to any of them,' Logan advised. 'Keep your eyes and mind open. See for yourself.'

Dallas realised he had no choice anyway. He

might love Africa or hate it. Whichever way it went, he was here, and here he must stay.

The ship spent two days offloading and taking on fuel, fresh supplies and cargo. During that time, Logan decided to show Dallas around. Cape Town was a real melting pot. Its diversity of architecture may have been fascinating but what Dallas found even more so was the strange mixture of inhabitants. As well as the British – soldiers mainly, Hanson Wentzell had been correct that English settlers didn't seem to mingle – and the Dutch, there were Hottentots, Indians, Malays and mixed-race coloureds, each with their own distinct culture and language. They flavoured the streets with an exotic mix of colour, sound and an ever-present smell of food.

On their second day, with the Cape Doctor still mercifully quiet, they took the aerial railway car to the top of Table Mountain. From there, the full magnificence of Cape Town could be appreciated. It seemed to Dallas that he was standing on the rim of a gigantic basin. Away to the south-west, Cape Point thrust into the sea where two mighty oceans met, the Indian and Atlantic. Rugged mountains rose from the sea creating bays, beaches and cliffs. To the south-east lay more stunning scenery.

On the mountain slopes and between rocky nooks dotted here and there on the flat top, wind-stunted wildflowers grew in profusion, scarlet, gold-spangled, pure white, pinks, blues and yellows. The spectacle was further enhanced by brilliantly coloured nectar-seeking birds hovering over them.

Inland, the Cape Flats stretched towards another mountain range standing misty blue in the distance. Despite being summer, it was cold on the summit.

'What do you think?' Logan asked.

Dallas thought for a moment. 'Big,' he said finally, giving an apologetic shrug.

Logan smiled. 'You get used to the space. After a while it's difficult to live without it. Compared with this, England is a doll's house.'

'Well,' Dallas said reflectively, hugging himself against the cold, 'at least there you know where everything lives and how it all fits together.'

'To be sure,' Logan replied blithely. 'And just how boring is that?'

'It must be a comfort to some,' Dallas objected.

Logan snapped his fingers dismissively. 'Come, my friend. I know a splendid tavern where we can find a dram to warm us. Let us leave questions of comparison to another day. You cannot be expected to form an opinion in so short a time, though I confess some appreciation of the beauty around you would not have gone astray.'

'It is beautiful,' Dallas agreed. 'If, so far, only to my eyes.'

'A start, dear boy. We will continue this discussion some other day.'

On the way down, swinging precariously in the small carriage as it crawled along the cable above, Dallas fell silent. It was impossible not to be impressed. Everywhere he looked was nature at her finest. For admiration to become perception required, at the very least, familiarity. At best, acceptance. That took time. Luckily, that was a commodity he had in abundance. Dallas was content to take all that was needed. He had to admit, however, that as first impressions went, Africa was a pretty compelling sight.

Four days later, Dallas took in the sight of what promised to become his new home. It was completely different from Cape Town. Gone now the grandeur of rugged mountains, cosy inlets snugged between sheer cliffs, no more a wind-tossed deep blue sea. Where Cape Town had been crisp and sharp-featured, Durban was soft and gently contoured. The vegetation further south appeared almost European. Here, it was lush and tropical. The Indian Ocean was aquamarine in colour and indolent in its swell. Beaches lay long, drowsy sweeps with breakers almost reluctant to end their incessant journey. Cape Town displayed a sense of development and order. Durban looked untamed – a defiant spirit refusing to present something it was not. There was promise of a land wild and warm. Savage, to be sure, and unforgiving with it, but for all that it seemed to pledge welcome for those bearing love and respect.

Dallas shook his head at such fanciful thoughts. So much to learn. What lay beyond the tangled forests? What lurked beneath that wide blue sky? What manner of people would leave the comfort and security of a European background to live voluntarily in this hot and dangerous place? It was gut country. Take it and shake it land. Slip and it would go straight for his throat. It had thrown out its challenge and he felt the first stirrings of response.

'Beautiful.'

Dallas hadn't heard Logan Burton approach. The man moved like a cat. 'Beautiful,' he repeated. 'Yet much more than that, I suspect.'

'True. Every turn holds a surprise, each day a gift. Keep an open mind and, whatever you do, don't expect anything to be familiar. If it is within yourself to accept this place, no questions asked, then you will be happy. Try to bend Africa and not only will you fail, she'll break your spirit. This is a land of opportunity and excitement not offered to many. Love her for that and she'll give you everything in return.'

It was almost as if the man had been eavesdropping on Dallas's own thoughts. 'I admit it's better than I expected.'

Burton grinned approval. 'I came out here at about your age. It took me a month or so to work out that I could embrace Africa and be happy or hanker for England and get nowhere. There are no half measures here. It's all or nothing. Compromise doesn't work, though you'll find many a fool clinging to the old ways.' He squinted towards land. 'Jump in boots and all, laddie. I've a good feeling about you. You're going to make a life here, I can feel it.'

Lord Diamond had said something similar. Dallas wished he could see what seemed so clear to others. Was Logan Burton a success? He'd never mentioned what he actually did for a living. Tearing his gaze away from approaching land Dallas asked, 'What exactly do you do here?'

Burton's faded blue eyes twinkled. 'Anything that comes up. Hunt, act as a guide, trade with the natives, you name it. I'm a free man – no wife, no children, no home. It's the way I prefer it.'

'Don't you get lonely?'

'Rather that than face an infinity of dull company.'

'Well, you know what they say. The lone sheep –'

'Is in danger of the wolf.' Burton nodded with a smile. 'Yes, I've heard. Though that rather depends on the sheep, old chap.' Pain briefly clouded the older man's eyes. He clapped Dallas on the shoulder. 'Yes, a man does get lonely sometimes but there's many lonelier than I surrounded by a wife and children. And where's the happy man when driven only by a quest for position and possessions? I work so that I can live, Granger, not the other way around. What you haven't got, there is no fear of losing.'

'That's all very well,' Dallas objected. 'What happens when you are too old to fend for yourself?'

'With luck, my friend, the good Lord will have taken a swipe at me before then. When I no longer have enough energy to hope, then is the time to leave. I am a man who lives life. There is no point in losing my faculties and reaching a stage where I forget I once had any.'

'You paint a bleak picture, Burton.'

'Not one to concern yourself with. If I could

wish for anything it would to be to count youth on my side – have my time over.'

'Would you do things differently?'

Burton laughed. 'Probably not. I have a few regrets, of course I do, but given the option, not much would be different. There's not many can say that.' He changed the subject abruptly. 'Tell you what, a new bet. Ten shillings says we won't be ashore until morning.'

Dallas took the wager. After all, it was only midafternoon.

Lesson number one: If it takes half a day in Britain, the same thing can take up to a week in Africa.

The *Marie Clare* rode at anchor in the road-stead, on the seaward side of a submerged sandbar that prohibited large ships from entering the port itself. The entrance to Durban harbour was protected on its southern side by a spit of land called The Bluff. Its bush-covered bulk rose several hundred feet out of the sea with what appeared to be a recently erected lighthouse adding nearly half that height again. In front of this stood the signal station, built for the sole purpose of communication with arriving ships. Unfortunately, the signalman was not always on duty. When he was there, he was more often than not either drunk or asleep. Whichever was the case on this day, hours went by before the need for a tender could be communicated. Eventually a boat made its way out but only to inquire where the *Marie Clare* was from and were there any sick on board. By then, it was too late to bring passengers ashore and a frustrating overnight delay was experienced by those who wanted to feel dry land under their feet. Heat, humidity and a rolling swell added to their discomfort.

Paying over the ten shillings, Dallas asked Logan how he managed to accept such a delay with no sign of surprise or irritation.

'Remember what I told you. This is Africa. She moves to her own beat, at her own pace and in her own way. Lose your temper, demand action, insist on speaking to someone in authority and you will find yourself on the receiving end of what can best be described as African laissez-faire.' Logan paused briefly. 'It takes a bit of getting used to but the system won't be pushed. At best, you'll amuse the natives. At worst, alienate the authorities and make yourself look ridiculous. No, my friend, that's not the way.' He flung out an all-embracing hand. 'Take a lesson from what's around you. Nature is in no hurry, why should we be? It's a beautiful evening, the sun is still shining, you're alive. What more could a man wish for? Come, let's get a drink.'

'We're in port. The bar is closed,' Dallas reminded him.

'Ah, dear boy, where's your faith in this continent? Here the rules work for you, not against. Let's go. I'll buy the first.'

Not only was the bar open but Dallas and Logan were last to arrive. Passengers and officers alike ignored shipping line regulations about the sale of alcohol in port. Even Captain Aujoulat was there and, judging by his high colour, had been for some time. 'Welcome to your new home, Mr Granger. If you can't find what you seek here you'll find it nowhere. I would stay in a thrice, if I could.'

Logan overheard. 'What's stopping you?'

The captain shrugged, spread his hands and smiled. 'My wife.'

Everybody laughed. The gathering was reminiscent of a celebration. It had a finale feel, which, Dallas supposed, stood to reason. As the hour latened, so too did the bonhomie increase. Dallas lost track of time somewhere around midnight.

He did not appreciate the wake-up call at four in the morning. Others were already on deck in the pitch dark, all sourly wondering if someone was playing a practical joke. But no. At this time of year, announced an equally sleepy second officer, violent storms and sudden squalls were prevalent. The weather was more predictable, less volatile at this hour. Sure enough, as the horizon found its first hint of colour, a lighter could be seen making way towards the ship. Once alongside, luggage belonging to the departing passengers was lowered and stacked haphazardly on deck with little or no thought to the possibility of damaging any fragile items. Dallas, Logan Burton, Lieutenant Elliot, the three single men and one of the married couples who had joined the ship in Cape Town were then required to make the transfer. Nearly fainting with fear, the only woman was swung clear of the *Marie Clare* in a kind of makeshift chair and roughly lowered to the lighter below.

The men had to climb down a rope ladder and jump, an exercise hampered by a choppy swell that had both boats rolling together then parting, leaving a gap too wide to attempt. One misjudgment, one slip, and any of them could end up between the two hulls, to be crushed as they rolled together. By some miracle, tragedy was avoided. Not one of the men had enjoyed much sleep, their dexterity further hampered by limbs sluggish from hangovers. That everyone and everything made it on board the lighter without mishap was due largely to the competence of an all-African crew. Their deft footwork and steady hands guided and supported with unfailing accuracy.

Once on board, the passengers were asked to enter a kind of hold. Protests about the smelly, damp and dark area fell on deaf ears. Logan Burton reassured the others. 'It's only until we're across the bar, for your own safety.' Reluctantly, one after the other, all went below.

'They'll let us back on deck once we're in the lagoon,' Logan explained, though obviously ill at ease himself. Within a few minutes, Dallas understood why. The hatches were closed and the sandbar crossing made in total darkness. Tossed around by the swell, Dallas lost orientation and had no idea which way was up. The woman was seasick. Sour-smelling vomit mingled with already stale and fishy odours to set off a chain reaction. Already suffering headaches and queasiness, the men, in time-honoured tradition, joined the lady. The trip seemed interminable.

Blessed relief came immediately they reached the lagoon. The hatch was flung open and a smiling black face informed them they could now come up on deck. Emerging into sunshine and fresh air it was obvious why they had been subjected to the dreadful confines below. All their luggage, and the sailors, were drenched. Dallas breathed in deeply, willing his still-churning stomach to settle.

'Hell of a way to start a new life,' he muttered to Logan Burton.

The older man spat over the side, wiped his mouth and said grimly, 'Hell of a way to start anything, old boy.'

Dallas looked around with increasing interest.

A couple of small trading sloops were moored close in shore. Glancing down, he understood why larger ships could not enter the lagoon. The sandy bottom was no more than six feet beneath them in water so transparent he could see fish darting to and fro.

Once clear of the bar, depth returned quickly and Dallas turned his attention to sights above the water. Thick seaweed, like an ocean meadow, covered large parts of the bay. Small islands stood out, choked with mangrove jungle. Wild fowl, pink flamingos, pelicans and cranes in their thousands bobbed or strutted in search of a meal. The ears, eyes and foreheads of hippopotamus were visible as herds played a now-you-see-me-now-you-don't game, rising to the surface for air before disappearing again. To Dallas, who had only ever seen drawings of them, they looked like benign sea monsters.

The water abruptly lost its pale blue colour. It turned instead to a glaucous shade due, in no small part, to weed below and a deep blue sky above. Sunlight danced across the ripples of a turning tide. There was no wind. The temperature and humidity, already uncomfortably high, had them all sweating profusely.

Dallas looked towards land. The customs house occupied the Point, Durban harbour's northern extremity, a low spit of land fronted by powder-white beach. Next to it stood a small wooden cottage and warehouse. Several buildings were under construction but it was impossible to guess at their ultimate purpose. That was it. The town proper sprawled untidily beyond. A wattle-and-daub general store belonging to a man called Cato, who also owned the warehouse, appeared to be the commercial centre. Located nearby was a forge and blacksmith. Animals were being unceremoniously slaughtered outside a Wesleyan chapel and mission house, presumably for sale by the butcher next door. Grog shops and hotels, offices of the *Natal Mercury* newspaper, a music hall, a couple of other retailers and some houses straggled along the main streets. The 45th Regiment had their barracks and quarters behind the main part of town, a botanical garden was being developed, a racetrack wound its way through natural bush and a cottage served as the jail. It would have appeared as unplanned mayhem save for the fact that Logan Burton pointed out each feature as it came into sight.

Dallas felt a stab of disappointment. He hadn't known what to expect but this wasn't it.

Logan glanced at him and saw the dismay. 'Look through it. This isn't Africa. This is England trying to tame it. Get out of Durban as quickly as you can. Allow yourself to linger in this sorry place and before long, you'll become part of it. You are welcome to join me. After addressing a small matter of money owed to me I will be leaving for Zululand. Probably in about a week.'

Dallas didn't want to be reliant on anyone, tempting as the thought was. He had to stand on his own two feet. 'Thank you, but if I'm to make a life here I had best start as I intend to carry on and make my own way.'

'Well said. Just remember, we all need friends in a place like this. The offer is made. I'll say no more.'

Getting ashore was a process as unique as everything else. Passengers were carried the last few yards on the backs of black men. Dallas would have preferred to wade but seeing Burton accept a ride as if it were the most natural thing in the world, went along with it. The Africans who conveyed them to dry land were stripped to the waist and smelled strongly of perspiration, their grinning faces displaying square, brilliantly white teeth. The woman who had already come ashore in the same manner as the men was blushing furiously and avoided eye contact with any of the others.

It was eleven twenty-six precisely on a sticky

hot Saturday, 20 January 1872, when Dallas Granger first set foot on the shores of Natal – a place he would call home for the rest of his life. Tomorrow was his mother's birthday. It took a conscious effort to will his thoughts away from family in Scotland. Remembering the traditional champagne breakfasts, presents piled high for whomever was celebrating their special occasion, and for Dallas, even after he'd grown from boy to man, the warm glow that stayed with him all day irrespective of which family member was marking the passing of another year – all a thing of the past and best forgotten.

A short, clean-shaven man dressed in white, which included a wide-brimmed hat worn at a rakish angle, stepped forward to apologise for the length of time it took to disembark and for the unconventional manner in which it had been accomplished. He announced himself as G.C. Cato, owner of both the fine general store in town from which one could purchase everything, and the warehouse behind him. Anybody failing to find what they were looking for in the shop had only to ask and chances were it would be in the warehouse.

'Started as a simple trader,' Burton said in an undertone.

'Welcome to the fine borough of Durban, so named after Sir Benjamin D'Urban, Governor of the Cape, some thirty years ago. You are standing, ladies and gentlemen, six thousand eight hundred miles from England. Naturally, so far from home, you will find your surroundings a little strange at first . . .'

The speech went on for some twenty minutes, though at times it seemed more like a lecture.

'He does this every time a ship arrives,' Logan told Dallas with a grin. 'Regards himself as some kind of unofficial welcoming committee. The truth of it is slightly more pecuniary. He wants people on side so they shop at his store. If the speech doesn't work, he offers free refreshment.'

People were shuffling and looking bored. It was hot and they had no shade.

'Get on with it, George,' Burton called eventually. 'We're dying of thirst.'

Huffing with annoyance, G.C. Cato did just that. 'Please do not judge us by the unfortunate manner in which you were deposited on our shores. I do apologise, especially to you, madam.' He bowed deeply to the only female present. 'The journey ashore is never easy. Our problem, as you already know, is the sandbar. Large ships cannot pass over it, even at high tide. Many times we have tried to build a breakwater, even an outer harbour, but the sea always defeats us. Debris from the harbour mixes with sand drifting in the current and despite our best efforts, any progress made by dredging quickly fills and we are back to square one. One day the engineers may actually agree on a way to narrow and deepen the entrance in a manner that works. Until then, please accept my deepest apologies for your inconvenience.'

Logan yawned ostentatiously. Cato decided he'd

said enough and dramatically clicked his fingers. Servants appeared carrying trays of delicacies and pitchers of lemonade. 'Please feel free to partake,' he said expansively. 'It is a small gesture of welcome that I take upon myself.'

The speed with which the refreshments were surrounded put paid to any more verbosity on Mr Cato's part. He mingled with the group of new arrivals, dropping constant hints about the excellence of his general store.

'Clever,' Burton murmured. 'It costs little and earns their loyalty. Guess where most people go to shop?'

It was nearly time to part company with Logan Burton, yet Dallas found himself reluctant to do so. The big man had come to represent a kind of reassurance that life, irrespective of how different, was there for the living. Listening to his stories it was easy to accept the unfamiliar as a challenge, rather than a threat.

'I wonder if we'll meet again?'

'Bound to, old chap. Those of us who venture into the hinterland are forever stumbling over one another.'

'What are your plans?'

The older man smiled ruefully. 'There are a couple of traders who owe me money for ivory. Jette all but cleaned me out at cards, the little cheat.' He laughed. 'Oh well, I suppose it was worth it, though she failed to favour me with such close attention as you. Still, a man my age can't complain. After I sort out my financial difficulties,

I'll be heading north for elephant.' He gave Dallas a quizzical look. 'I trust our mutual Danish acquaintance didn't leave you completely without funds?'

Dallas shook his head. 'It could easily have been so. I was a fool.'

Burton shrugged. 'A man is at his weakest when a beautiful woman tells him how strong he is. I daresay the merry widow knew exactly what she was doing.'

'Then how is it you were not taken in by her?'

'Experience, old chap, though I would willingly have surrendered my meagre possessions for a night in her arms. Alas, it was not me on whom she set her sights. I've met women like Jette before. She's a professional thief, my dear fellow, and a very good one at that.'

Dallas winced. Would he ever learn? 'I fear you are right,' he admitted reluctantly.

'Do not judge Jette too harshly. If anything, admire her expertise.' He finished the glass of lemonade. 'I'll be off then.' His hand went out and Dallas took it. 'Good luck, Granger.'

'Where will you be staying?'

'At the Royal. Should be there about a week. It's not a bad place if you can't afford better. Five shillings a day. Snakes, rats and ants stay for nothing, but a man cannot be choosy. If you have the money, look for a room in a boarding house. There are a few just out of town that offer a clean bed and good food. Cheerio, old chap. Hope we run into each other again.' With a nod and quick grin, Logan Burton strode away.

Making inquiries, Dallas was directed to the Berea, an area where he might find decent accommodation. Mr Cato offered the use of a sulky to transport him and his luggage, 'For a nominal fee'. Dallas accepted. He could see no other way of getting around. A railway existed but the line only ran from the harbour to a quarry on the Mngeni River, a distance of six miles and not in the direction he wished to go.

Mr Cato had to be headed off from the subject of railways and future plans for extending Natal's before Dallas could thank him.

'My pleasure. The driver knows where to take you.'

They drove through the town centre. Up close, first impressions proved right. Durban was basic in the extreme. Its run-down appearance was further emphasised by evidence of heavy rain which had obviously fallen quite recently. Large puddles lay everywhere, some so deep that it was necessary to take a detour around them in order to avoid becoming bogged. Tracks of horses and carts churned the mud which on higher ground had already formed into hard sun-baked ridges and wicked wheel-trapping ruts.

The centre of town, which did indeed revolve around Cato's General Store, was alive with activity. Dallas saw gentlemen and ladies as finely dressed as he'd seen in London, yet they seemed so out of place in this pioneering land. More at home were tough-looking common folk – the men dressed in homemade clothing of varying materials, including animal skins, their women plainly clad in calico, cheap cotton or even sacking cloth. Weather-beaten, sun-darkened faces, unfashionable hairstyles and attire notwithstanding, there was pride, confidence and contentment in their bearing. These people would never grace the drawing rooms of aristocracy back home but something about them told Dallas that not one would swap places with those who could.

Children of the local gentry waited patiently in their parents' carriages while others, barefoot and plainly clothed, were less inhibited. Shrieking with laughter, they splashed through puddles, climbed trees or played hide-and-seek in a carefree display of health and happiness. The quieter, well-dressed children eyed them with envy but were bound by convention, afraid of being scolded by their parents if they joined in.

Africans seemed to be at work everywhere, bare torsos and arms shining with the sweat of their labours. Deep, melodious voices, the rhythm giving uniformity and cohesion to their mutual cooperation, combining effortlessly as they toiled in the hot sun. Skinny dogs and domestic pigs competed for scraps on the ground while vervet monkeys screeched and chattered in branches overhead as they foraged for fruit.

Beyond town, the ground rose steadily as they travelled inland. Looking right, an endless ocean sparkled clear to the horizon. Behind and below, back the way they'd come, the lagoon limited urban sprawl in that direction. On the other side of its deep, dark water rose The Bluff. From up here, Dallas could even make out the *Marie Clare* anchored in the roadstead. Turning from the view, he gazed ahead.

The Berea was favoured, Mr Cato had informed him, as a residential suburb. It enjoyed sea breezes which, each evening, brought a welcome fanning to relieve the day's stifling heat. And indeed, as they climbed, the air did become noticeably cooler.

The African driver reined in outside a neat, two-storeyed cottage. A steeply pitched roof and lacy curtains gave the place a homely, lived-in appearance. Flowerboxes overflowing with small, star-shaped petals from white to pink and deep red added further to its welcoming, friendly atmosphere. Brick walls had been recently whitewashed and the window shutters displayed a fresh coat of green paint. The cottage reminded Dallas of country Scotland and he felt immediately drawn to it. Set in a garden of lush lawn, flowering shrubs and large shady trees, the owner had much to be proud of. A sign on the picket fence read, 'A.M. Watson – boarding establishment'.

Dallas jumped down and opened the gate. A cobbled path ran through flowerbeds to the front door. He knocked and waited. It was opened by a black girl of around fourteen, dressed in stiffly starched white.

She couldn't possibly be the owner but Dallas was uncertain how to address her. He had yet to learn that asking to speak with the master or mistress of the house was the acceptable norm, rather as he might have done in Scotland. 'Madam, I believe you have a room to let.'

She stared at him in wide-eyed silence.

A voice called from inside, speaking a language he could not understand. The girl smiled shyly and beckoned, leading him to where a woman sat in a high-backed chair. She offered no greeting, looking him up and down with bright, intelligent eyes. Finally she said, 'You seek a room?'

'Yes, madam.' Dallas self-consciously tugged his jacket straight.

'How long do you wish to stay?' The question bordered on imperious but her tone conveyed nothing more than professional interest.

'I am not certain, madam, having only arrived this very day.'

'Oh? On which ship?'

'The *Marie Clare*.'

'French.' The woman sniffed. 'Damned frogs.'

Dallas didn't know what to make of her comment so remained silent.

'My name is Ann Maria Watson. I own and run this establishment. Do you have references?'

'No, madam. My travels bring me straight from home.'

'Hmm. You seem well educated.' She lowered her glasses and peered at him. 'Have you a position to take up?'

'No, madam.'

'What do you expect to do?'

'Start a business, madam. Trading perhaps.'

'For heaven's sake, young man, stop calling me madam. I've told you my name. What's yours?'

Disconcerted by her abruptness, and his own lack of manners, Dallas fumbled for a response. 'My apologies, mad . . . er, Mrs Watson. Dallas Granger, at your service.'

A glint had appeared in Mrs Watson's eyes as if she was enjoying his discomfort. 'Well now, Mr Granger, trading is it? Fancy yourself as a bit of an adventurer, do you?' She gave a sardonic smile. 'Many have tried. Some succeed. Most fall foul of the drink. Do you imbibe, Mr Granger?'

'No more than most men.'

'That's nothing to be proud of and no recommendation in this part of the world.'

'Not to excess, madam.'

'Mrs Watson,' she corrected absently. 'I assume you can pay?'

'Of course.'

There was silence while she seemed to come to a conclusion. Then a change of subject. 'My nephew is Thomas Baines.'

Dallas recalled Lady Diamond asking Hanson Wentzell about him the night before the *Marie Clare* docked in Cape Town, but for the life of him, could not remember a word of the Dutch farmer's reply. 'I'm afraid I —'

'No matter. He is an artist, an explorer and gold prospector.' She was obviously very fond of him.

'Did he paint that?' Dallas had noticed an exceptionally good watercolour on the wall and pointed to it. Not large, the predominant colour was an intriguing blue-green-grey tone that had been used to good effect to denote trees, cactus and foliage. There was a glimpse of open space beyond and in the foreground a line of men crossing a stream. The transient moods of weather and light were skilfully captured, a hazy wash in the far distance creating an impression of untamed infinity. At the same time there was a sense of order about the shapes in the foreground. The presence of people was almost an intrusion, though whether intentional or not had been left up to the observer.

The woman turned, rose and moved towards a fireplace over which the painting hung. Dallas was surprised at her agility. Out of the chair she seemed younger than he had first supposed. Mrs Watson examined the watercolour as though she'd never seen it in her life. 'Thomas did that eight years ago in the Zambezi Valley. He's travelled all over, you know.'

'It's very good.'

'Oh, do you think so?' She was pleased. It seemed to sway her in his favour. 'I can rent you a room but for how long I do not know. Thomas is up north working for the Gold Fields Exploration Company in Ndebele country. The company is rumoured to be having some financial difficulties so he could be back at any moment. Thomas worked with David Livingstone, you know.'

'Really!' Dallas was relieved to at least know something of the missionary.

'If he returns to Durban he'll need his room.'

'That's fine, Mrs Watson. I don't expect to be here for long.'

'A week in advance. All meals. The room is serviced and laundry done twice a week. That will be three pounds, ten shillings. I require seven days' notice, if you please. Otherwise money in lieu. Will that be acceptable?'

'Perfectly. Thank you.'

She called the maid and rattled off what were obviously instructions before turning back to Dallas. 'Mabel will show you the accommodation. If it's to your liking, you can move in immediately.'

He followed the African girl up a narrow, dimly lit set of stairs. A passage at the top was wide and pleasantly cool. The room faced east with views over Durban. More evidence of Thomas Baines's talent adorned the walls of the comfortably large bedchamber.

Going back downstairs, he paid Mrs Watson for a week's board and lodging.

She insisted on writing out a receipt, her neat copperplate handwriting obviously a source of great pride and taking an inordinate amount of time to complete. 'I have two other gentlemen staying here. You'll meet them this evening. Dinner is at six sharp. If you are late it will be kept for you to eat cold. The privy and washhouse are out back. Place any dirty linen in the bag provided behind your door. I expect my lodgers to keep respectable hours and show consideration for the sleep of others. Guests must not be entertained anywhere but the front parlour. Here is a front-door key. I hope you will be comfortable. Yours is the best room, the one Thomas uses when he is here. Mabel will assist the driver with your things. Breakfast is at eight.'

Several hours later, unpacked and bathed, Dallas met the other two lodgers. One was about to be married and owned a small trading company, somehow connected to Mr Cato. Dallas never found out exactly how but learned that the man exported meat, butter, maize and beans to the Mauritian sugar plantations and ivory to Britain. Imports came largely from England and the problem of chronic shortages dominated his conversation. The other guest worked for the *Natal Mercury* and advised Dallas to read the newspaper if he was looking for work. 'Everyone advertises,' he said. 'You'll find plenty of opportunities.'

The meal was plain fare but good. After dinner Dallas and the other two gentlemen went into the garden to smoke cigars. Listening to the conversation, Dallas learned a lot about this new land. Everyone, it seemed, needed a smattering of the native language, Zulu.

'Absolutely essential, old chap. You'll pick up the basics quite quickly. It's not difficult.'

Zulu kings and their tribal courts, British administrators and dirty dealings, scandals, skirmishes between African and European or Boer and British, petty in-fighting, rumours of gold, tales of hunters and explorers, wild animals – the stories kept coming. Although Dallas was well aware of embellishment for his benefit, the unfamiliar subject matter made the tales exotic and exciting.

At one stage, Dallas repeated their landlady's boast about her nephew, Thomas Baines. 'I understand he's an acquaintance of David Livingstone.'

The newspaperman laughed derisively. 'And probably wishes he'd never met the man.'

'Why not?' The name David Livingstone was revered throughout Britain. He'd had a private audience with Queen Victoria, the Royal Geographical Society presented him with a gold medal, and he was one of the very few to be granted freedom of the city of London. Funding for further expeditions was readily available from a variety of sources. His book, *Missionary Travels and Researches*, had been highly successful, making him a household name. The man was a hero, some even suggesting he was a saint. Now here was a hint that the missionary was not all he seemed. Intrigued, Dallas raised inquiring eyebrows and was rewarded with a frank response.

'I've spoken to a few who travelled with him.' The journalist seemed happy to elaborate. 'Men like Dr John Kirk, who was on Livingstone's Zambezi expedition with Baines. The great man falls out with everyone. He's arrogant, narrow-minded and not, it would seem, particularly Christian in his treatment of those around him. Thomas Baines was ill for a lot of that trip. Fever and sunstroke mainly. The poor chap was delirious. Livingstone accused him of malingering, fired the man for lack of attention to his duties. The claims are perfectly true.

Livingstone's behaviour has been confirmed by several who have been on previous expeditions with him. The Zambezi trip was especially bad and seems to have been doomed from the start. David Livingstone was difficult enough but his brother, Charles, caused most of the problems on that venture. Damned man was lazy as hell. He was the one who accused Baines of holding up the expedition, despite his own insistence on resting every half hour.'

Dallas found it difficult to accept such damning comments about a man as admired as David Livingstone. His expression must have reflected that doubt.

The newspaperman merely shrugged. 'Why are you surprised? Livingstone was human first, a national hero second. Like most daredevils, fame came as a consequence of his success. Had he failed, the man's character would have gone unrecorded. Irrespective of any weaknesses, he at least deserves our admiration for vision, perseverance and achievement.'

Dallas nodded. 'You may well be correct. However, telling such tales at home would need more than mere hearsay to avoid acquiring the reputation of a heretic.'

'Home,' the journalist scoffed. 'What do they know of this place? Let me give you some advice, sir. Forget England. Don't compare the two. You can't.'

Logan Burton had said the same thing, several times.

Turning in a little after ten, unique and strange as his new home may have been, Dallas felt the first stirrings of belonging. Whether it was having finally reached his destination, or a more basic empathy with the unconventional nature of things around him, he couldn't have said.

At breakfast, Mrs Watson produced a copy of the *Natal Mercury*. 'It's the latest issue. I'd like it back, please.'

One advertisement grabbed his attention. A trader by the name of William Green was looking for a partner to join him on a trek into Zululand. Dallas liked the idea of a partnership. He showed the advertisement to Mrs Watson. 'Do these opportunities come up often?'

She peered at the newspaper and sniffed. 'Never heard of William Green.' A stubby finger jabbed at an announcement about something called the Welbourne Scheme. 'That's a thing you should be looking at.'

'What is it?'

'Plans to extend the railway. This country will never move forward until we have an efficient railway system. A group of private financiers has been granted two and a half million acres of land by the Legislative Council to develop one. Get in on the ground floor of that, Mr Granger, and your future is assured. Not only do they have the land, the syndicate has negotiated an annual subsidy and secured a ten-year monopoly on the supply of iron and steel. There's some talk of government vetoing the idea but mark my words, if it's not the

Welbourne Scheme, then another will soon be up and running.'

Dallas didn't fancy the idea. The thought of an equal partnership had excited him. 'It sounds a bit too political for me, Mrs Watson. I think I'll reply to William Green's advertisement. At least find out what's on offer.'

She sniffed again. 'Be on your toes, Mr Granger. There is many a rogue in Africa ready to swindle a young man such as yourself.'

'Thank you for the advice, Mrs Watson. I'll be careful.'

Dallas received a reply to his expression of interest three days later. He had used the intervening time to set himself up with a few essentials. First, and most important, he needed a means of getting around. A horse seemed the best option and his landlady was able to assist. Mrs Watson knew a man who was returning to England and anxious to find a home for his favourite animal with someone who would take good care of her. The three-year-old chestnut filly's name was Tosca. Dallas was assured that she had a quiet and gentle nature yet was spirited enough to run when allowed. Tosca approached her new owner with suspicion but, once she'd sniffed the outstretched hand and felt his fingers gentle on her nose, she relaxed. The asking price paid, Dallas acquired one horse, the accompanying saddlery and several items he would find useful in the bush, including a bedroll. It was almost as though Tosca knew she had been sold. Man and beast left her old home, neither offering a backward glance.

A rifle was next. From a gunsmith recommended by the *Natal Mercury* newspaperman, Dallas purchased a .44 calibre, 1866 Winchester Yellow Boy. It was almost new with intricate engraving embellishing a brass receiver frame, buttplate and fore-end. He had no idea that it was far from ideal for African conditions.

He opened a bank account, depositing nearly one thousand pounds. The money his father had given him seemed like a lot at the time. When he realised how much he needed to outlay on basic requirements, Dallas knew he had to find a way of bringing in money, and quickly. What was left would not last forever.

He wrote a letter home. Dallas was anxious for news but knew it would be a long time before he received any. His mother would be equally eager to hear from him so he filled pages with details of his travels, leaving out any mention of the jewel theft, and ending with an assurance that he was well, in good spirits and asking forgiveness, especially from his sister.

Dallas would dearly have loved to write to Lorna but knew it was impossible. Not a day passed without a memory, however small, coming to taunt him. Knowing she was beyond his reach – geographically, emotionally and socially – should have helped put her out of his mind. It didn't. In Dallas's case, he had strayed too far over acceptable boundaries to forget her. His fault. The knowledge of that didn't help.

He found himself telling his mother of his

feelings for Lorna. The more he wrote, the greater his longing, but Dallas seemed unable to stop. Something, he knew not what, compelled him to share his pain with another. It was not a confession of indiscretion, he left all detail of their trysts out, rather a baring of his heart. Of all the people he knew, his mother would understand. The earl would read it with little sympathy, perhaps even anger, but Dallas needed to confide in someone.

Mrs Watson, once sure that Dallas was a gentleman to be trusted, allowed him to give her address so that correspondence could be sent to him there.

The response from William Green, handdelivered to the *Natal Mercury* and brought home by Mrs Watson's lodger, was badly written and brief: *I be down at Point Grog Shoppe Sunday. Me old partner died of the fever. If you be genuine come at midday. Will Green.*

Dallas was rather taken aback at the man's lack of education. He showed his fellow boarders the scrappy note. Both were understandably skeptical.

'Fellow is illiterate,' observed the about-to-bemarried trader. 'I know most of these travelling men. Never heard of Will Green.'

'I've met him,' the journalist said. 'Bit on the rough side.'

'Never mind that.' Dallas brushed their opinions aside. 'It will do no harm to at least meet the man.'

SIX

At eleven on Sunday morning, Dallas saddled Tosca and rode into town. Over the past few days he'd explored far and wide, becoming familiar with a number of the roads and identifying several landmarks. Quite by accident he'd found himself passing the address Logan had given him for Jette's aunt. He nearly paid her a visit but, in the end, decided against it. If the woman was aware of her niece's lucrative though felonious activities, she'd not be inclined to answer any of his questions. And if Jette's aunt had no idea what her relative got up to, there was no point distressing the good lady. Jette could wait.

Dallas found the Point Grog Shoppe down near the railway terminal. Like most buildings other than those housing government departments, it was roughly built of wattle and daub. The bar consisted of six wooden packing cases, stacked end to end, behind which a giant of a man with a bull neck and shiny bald head kept order, after a fashion. Off-duty military men joked, plied each other with alcohol and gambled. Sailors, equally rowdy, made up another group. The rest of the occupants were tough-looking men who sat in groups of two or three drinking steadily, most deep in conversation. Raucous laughter, shouted requests for more liquor and rough voices raised in good-natured bantering gave the place an atmosphere Dallas had never seen in Britain, probably for the simple reason that he'd never ventured into the less salubrious taverns back home.

Jeremy Hardcastle sat at one of the tables. Dallas barely recognised the first officer out of uniform. The *Marie Clare* had sailed three days ago. Why hadn't Hardcastle left with it? Had he been dismissed or jumped ship? From the man's appearance, he'd been drinking for quite a while. The company he was in was most definitely questionable. Sailors by the look of them, one sporting an eye patch, the other covered in tattoos. The three were hunched towards each other, as if discussing something they wished no others to overhear.

Dallas's gaze moved on, searching for anyone who might be William Green. In such a place his manner of dress was drawing attention. He noticed one man seated alone, staring at an empty glass in front of him. Dallas approached him. 'William Green?'

Faded blue eyes flicked up, almost in surprise. 'Who's asking?'

'Dallas Granger.'

Green's eyes raked him from head to toe, an expression of contempt clear in them. 'Didn't expect no gentleman,' he said finally. The voice was strongly accented. Yorkshire, Dallas thought.

'What difference does it make?'

'Young, too,' the man went on. 'Yer no more than a suckling babe.'

Dallas flushed. Open amusement showed on faces nearby and Green seemed to be enjoying the audience. 'Young I may be, sir, but dry behind the ears, you'll find.'

'Is that right?' The slumped form cackled suddenly, showing stained and decaying teeth. 'Well, that's as maybe.' He rose so swiftly that Dallas was taken by surprise. One of Green's hands shot out and grabbed a fistful of shirt front. 'Perhaps we should find out now. I've no inclination to do business with a nancy boy.'

Eyes never leaving Green's face, Dallas gripped the sinewy arm with one hand, fingers tightening.

William Green's eyes widened with surprise and he grimaced with pain as Dallas exerted pressure. He let go of Dallas's shirt. 'No need for that, youngster. It was just a bit of fun.'

Dallas treated him to several more seconds of his grip before relaxing it. Still holding Green's arm he said softly, 'Just so you know, Mr Green, I may be young but this gentleman is no milksop, nor am I a fool.' His fingers squeezed slightly. 'Now, do we have something to discuss or don't we?' The derision aimed at Dallas from those nearby transferred to William Green.

Aware of the shift, and glancing nervously around, Green nodded.

Dallas let his hand fall and sat down. After a few seconds' hesitation, William Green did the same.

Around them, men lost interest as the promising confrontation apparently fizzled out.

'Drink?' Green offered, his eyes now wary. 'Try the rum.'

Dallas accepted.

Green bellowed an order to the barman.

They waited in silence, each sizing up the other.

William Green, Dallas decided, was certainly a chancer. Happy to indulge in a little bullying but quick to back down when someone stood against him. Not promising traits for a potential business partner. However, having lost the first encounter, Green seemed happy enough to put it aside. Physically, he was an odd-looking individual. Short and slightly built, exposed face and arms burned brown, his body wiry with no excess fat. Dark-red frizzy hair looked as if it hadn't been washed for some time. It lay in limp, knotted strands down to his shoulders. Dark bushes sat atop faded blue eyes. A flowing beard, predominantly grey with patches of ginger around the mouth suggested maturity, but he could have been anywhere between thirty and fifty. Creases covered his forehead and deep crow's feet crevassed from eye to hairline. Yet the skin on his cheeks was as smooth as that of a much younger man's. He wore threadbare breeches tucked into homemade leather boots and held up by braces made from plaited hide. A grubby shirt with rolled sleeves, open at the collarless neck, had been patched many times and was in dire need of replacement.

Two none too clean glasses of rum were

plunked in front of them by a serving girl who Green treated to a slap on the rump. 'Cheers,' he said, downing his drink in one.

'Cheers,' Dallas responded, attempting to do the same. The spirit caught in his throat and he coughed for nearly a minute. 'God's teeth,' he managed eventually. 'This stuff would eat a hole in your guts.'

William Green's laugh was more of a giggle.

Dallas was starting to have serious reservations. However, he'd come here to discuss a partnership so he might as well get it over and done with. Leaning forward was not a good idea. It wasn't only the man's hair that needed washing. 'Your proposition, sir?' Dallas quickly sat back again.

Green's look turned smug. 'Not so fast, young'un. If I don't like you, there ain't one in the offing. Man's got to protect hisself, know what I mean? Just you hold on a bit and tell me of yourself.'

Dallas was prepared – he was the sixth son of an Edinburgh merchant and in search of adventure.

William Green listened intently, head cocked to one side. When Dallas fell silent, and with no change of expression, he said, 'There be more truth in a tart's tale of woe than that sorry story.' He lowered his voice, leaning forward. 'I don't want no details. Don't care if you knocked up the queen herself.' A grimy finger jabbed into Dallas's chest. 'You're one of them remittance men. Stands out a mile.' Green sat back, chewing the inside of his cheek, mouth screwed up, sucking air through the gaps in his front teeth. 'I've met good and bad of your kind,' he went on finally. 'Don't like toffs as a rule.' Dark-red eyebrows drew together. 'Don't take to criminals much, either. The way I see it, one lot wants to take everything I own and the others think they own everything already. I'm not saying you're neither, mind, but it's me that's taking a partner and I want to know what I'm letting myself into. Know what I mean?'

Green had some kind of strategy of his own invention, throwing his weight around a bit to impress and establish authority. It didn't call for an answer. Dallas remained silent.

His lack of response seemed to unnerve the trader. 'Some of you aren't that bad. Could be we'd get along fine. Man's got to make sure, though.' Green scowled again, aware he was on the back foot, talking too much, with only himself to blame.

Dallas sipped the remainder of his rum, holding down an overwhelming desire to cough.

Green tried another tack to regain the initiative. 'What did you do? With your kind, it's either thieving or murder.'

'Neither,' Dallas managed, though the liquor had his throat on fire. 'As I told you, I'm the sixth son –'

'Yeah? And I'm the bleedin' Pope.'

Dallas shrugged. He didn't care what this man thought of him, he'd already made up his mind not to become involved in discussion. 'Believe what you like.'

Green toyed with his empty glass, making meaningful glances towards the bar.

Dallas supposed the least he could do was buy the man a drink. 'Rum?' he asked.

By way of response, Green bellowed a new order to the barman. The prospect of more alcohol fuelled the man's desire to make his point. 'As I see it, the likes of you don't do business with the likes of me without a bloody good reason. So, you're either running from gambling debts or the law is after you. Makes no difference to me. I couldn't give a rat's arse what you've done, me fine fellow, but I don't need no bleedin' aristocrat pulling airs and graces. Your lot are trouble.' He changed tack suddenly. 'Can you ride and shoot?'

'Of course.'

'I mean ride, boy. Not your bloody "Tally-ho, there's the fox". I'm talking about twelve hours straight and still having the grit to dig out a bogged wagon.'

Now he'd got down to it, Green's demeanour had changed. He seemed very much in charge. 'I'm fit and strong enough, if that's what you mean.'

'It's exactly what I mean. There'll be no slacking. You'll have to pull your weight. No-one is going to run around and do your bidding. You might be somebody back home but out here you're no more important than the next man. Fair weather or foul, you work. Get injured, you still have to work. Get sick, that's hard luck. Dying is the only excuse I'll accept for laying about. As for whatever you're running from, if the law comes after you, I'll not lie to them. Don't expect no protection from me, you won't get it.'

'I –'

Green glared at him and Dallas fell silent.

'Ye puts up your share of the money, and keeps your mouth shut until you know half as much as me.' The little trader drummed dirty fingernails on the stained table. 'Right now, ye don't look tough enough.'

'Tough enough for what?'

'Tradin'.'

'I assure you, sir –'

Green spat on the hard-packed mud floor and wiped his mouth with the back of a hand. 'Drop the fancy talk,' he growled. 'Ain't no place for it in these parts. Me name's Will.'

'Dallas.' Despite misgivings, Dallas was sufficiently intrigued enough to find out more. 'Where and in what do you trade, Will?'

The Yorkshire man smiled humourlessly. 'Wherever and whatever.'

'That's no answer.'

Will scratched a mosquito bite on his forehead until it bled. 'It's the only one you'll get. Trading's not like a regular job. In this business the weather dictates where you *can* go, animal migration decides where you *should* go and fate usually plays a hand in where you end up. Natives warring with each other, the whereabouts of other traders, rivers too deep or bone bloody dry, there are a million and one things to consider.'

Dallas watched fascinated as a thin trickle of blood found a crease and ran horizontally along it. Will Green appeared oblivious to it. Tearing his gaze from the unpleasant sight, Dallas asked, 'Why animal migration?'

Green looked at Dallas as if he'd grown another head. 'What do you think we trade for? Bows and bloody arrows? We're after skins and tusks, boy. Skins and tusks. Those we can sell. That's where the money comes from. Anything else we pick up along the way we barter with the blacks.'

Dallas nodded to the serving girl who brought their drinks, noticing she kept well out of Will's reach. 'If what you say is all there is to it, what's to stop me going it alone?'

Will burst out laughing, treating Dallas to a full blast of fetid breath. 'By all means. Many a raw youngster has tried. Not many come back. Their bones feed the hyena. Africa is full of pitfalls. It's the ignorant who obligingly fall into them.'

'In that case, what exactly are you proposing?'

Will didn't hesitate.

'You put up fifty per cent of the goods we take with us.'

'Fair enough.'

'And fifty per cent of the wages, enough for six months. You give that to me for safekeeping.'

'Why you?'

'I'm the senior partner.'

A look of cunning had crept into Will's face. Dallas didn't like it. 'Fifty-fifty means no senior partner. My share buys equality. Take it or leave it.'

'Now look here,' Will reacted angrily.

'No. You look. You advertised for a partner. To me that means everything is split equally, costs and profit. I'll pay my share of wages, but not hand it over in advance.'

Will's eyes narrowed. 'Are you saying you don't trust me?'

'Exactly,' Dallas answered bluntly.

The brutal honesty took Will by surprise. 'What about goodwill?' was all he managed.

Dallas ignored the pun, which he was certain was unintentional. 'For what? Name three things.'

'Er . . . well, there's me contacts, they've taken years to build up. Knowledge of the country. I know it like the back of me hand. And . . . I speak Zulu,' he ended with a flourish.

'These things are indeed valuable, I'll grant you. Tell me, Will, why are you seeking a partner? With all that goodwill, you don't seem to need one. Unless of course you're broke. Would that be the case, Will? You weren't by any chance planning to take my money and run, were you? Let's be quite clear on one thing. If you ever tried that, Will, I would personally see to it that you regretted such an action until the day you died. And believe me, the burden of remorse would not be borne for very long. Still, it's trust that counts, isn't it, Will?'

Dallas deliberately kept his voice light but his dark eyes burned into Will's with such intensity that the man nervously licked his lips.

'I'll grant you, I'm inexperienced. However, I have something you seem to be short of. Money. With luck, I might just get away with ignorance. Without money, you go nowhere. We need each other. I could probably find another partner easily enough, but could you? I'm prepared to talk business. My trust is something you've yet to earn. The truth, if you please, Mr Green. You are without funds. Am I right?'

Will scratched his beard vigorously.

'I'm waiting.'

'The situation is temporary,' Will burst out.

'What situation would that be?' Dallas asked softly. 'Come, man, there should be no secrets between us.'

'There's been a mistake. I don't want a partner,' Will muttered, rising to his feet.

'Sit,' Dallas snapped.

'No, truly. I've changed me mind. I —'

'Sit.'

Will slumped back into his chair and stared miserably at Dallas.

The authority to which Will had so readily responded came as second nature to Dallas. He'd grown up with it dealing with servants and tenants. For all Green's bluster, he'd probably been at the receiving end of autocracy for most of his life. While Dallas didn't wish to play the master and he certainly had no desire to intimidate the man, adopting a position of strength could prove advantageous until he could trust him. Never slow to size up opportunity, Dallas felt his way around a plan that had been forming in his mind. The two of them needed each other. It wouldn't work with Will in charge, the man couldn't be trusted. Perhaps the other way round . . .

'You have a horse?' he asked suddenly.

Will nodded. 'A good one.'

'Rifle?'

'Yes.'

'Wagon and oxen?'

'Ah!' Will looked uncomfortable.

'What precisely do you mean by ah?'

'The wagon was old.'

'Was?'

'A temporary setback, I assure you.'

Risking the man's odour, Dallas leaned towards him. 'Empty your pockets,' he ordered quietly.

'Now, see here . . .'

'Just do it.' Dallas figured that Will Green would carry all the money he possessed rather than risk leaving it anywhere else.

Green turned his pockets out and the two men stared down at two crumpled notes and a handful of coins.

'Six pounds, four shillings and threepence half-penny,' Dallas said slowly.

Will shifted uncomfortably and said nothing.

'A fine start to our partnership. Did you really think I'd be fool enough to fall for a pack of lies? What was your plan? Take the money and disappear? Or did you have something more devious in mind? Murder, perhaps? How many others have fallen foul of your partnership offer?'

'No, no. You misunderstand me.' Despite being caught out, Green looked genuinely shocked at Dallas's words.

'Have you funds elsewhere?'

Will scratched and fidgeted.

'I see.' Dallas drained his rum and managed not to cough. 'What is the price of a wagon? The truth, man, not some cock and bull.'

Any bravado left in Will Green collapsed. 'One hundred pound,' he muttered. 'For a good one, anyways.'

'Oxen?'

'Depends where you get them. Another hundred should do it.'

'Trading goods and stores for us?'

'Another hundred.'

'Three hundred!'

'Six for two of us,' Will put in quickly.

Dallas was cautious. If he funded everything he'd be left with enough money for one more try at a venture. If this one failed, the next had to succeed. Prudence pulled him one way, excitement the other. Will Green was a gamble but Dallas knew of no other offers. Trading promised wide open spaces and adventure with only a possibility of profit. Was it worth the risk? He pulled his wandering thoughts back to what Green was saying.

'. . . there's no doubting that Cape wagons would be best. They're more expensive but designed for African conditions. We'll be in rough country.'

'What makes them different?'

'The sides, bottom and carriage are not joined together. Each is free to move on its own. More solid-built wagons tend to crack. And she's the right size, too – fifteen feet long. Nothing is better for heavy work.'

'I suppose speed depends on the conditions?'

'Fully loaded she'll do twenty miles a day over flat ground.'

Will obviously knew his wagons.

'How many oxen will we need?'

'Eighteen to pull each wagon and at least the same again to spell them. We'll lose a few. Lion take them, they break legs or get sick. Best to allow at least forty per wagon.'

'Forty!'

'Like I said, some die. Most people take more than that.'

'Can't we replace them as we go?'

Will shook his head. 'Won't get the good ones. Inland beasts are heavier and more fussy about what they'll eat. Coastal oxen are smaller, tougher and eat anything. They're used to the sour grass that grows here.'

Will knew his oxen too.

'What about supplies and goods to trade? Where do we buy them?'

'Cato's have a standard list. We can add or subtract as we wish.'

It was decision time. Dallas stared at Will. 'No partnership,' he said finally. 'If I'm putting up the money, it's my risk. You work for me.'

Will opened his mouth to protest, thought better of it and nodded unhappily. 'What do I get out of it?'

'Flat wage. Ten shillings a day. Since you're supplying the experience, or goodwill, if you can call it that, you'll get twenty-five per cent of my net profit.'

'Ten shillings?' Will protested. 'Labourers earn more than that.'

'Less actually. Between six and eight shillings a day.'

'Twelve at least,' Will wheedled.

'Ten.'

'Eleven?' Will asked timidly.

'Ten.'

Will whistled air and stared upwards.

Dallas took the gesture as acceptance. 'Give me an idea of what we can expect to be paid on our return.'

'Well, now, that rather depends on what we come back with.'

'Estimate only. You must have some idea.'

Will shrugged. 'I've made four hundred, I've made seven-fifty. Those who do the hunting themselves earn more. Tusks bring good profit. Couple of men I know say they clear near on a thousand each trip.' Will scratched his head. 'Dunno about that.'

'Do you hunt?'

'Some. Not elephants.'

'Any reason?'

Will sighed. It had the sound of a man who had just been asked to bare his soul. 'I'm a trader. What do I know about elephants?'

'You tell me.'

'They're big bastards. Some say easy to kill but I'm not so sure. Too many stories about near misses. I could name a few good men who met their maker trying to earn a quid from elephants.'

Dallas waited but Will had finished.

'In other words, you're frightened of them.'

'I didn't say that.'

'If you're scared, I'll do the hunting. I'd just like to know in advance about how much back-up I'll get from you. Out in the bush with a jammed rifle is not the time to find out.'

Will's eyes narrowed. 'I'm no coward.'

'And I never said you were.'

'Wait till you've seen one up close.' Defiance had crept into Will's voice.

Dallas left it. Will could be pushed into some things but he'd made it perfectly clear that elephant wasn't one of them. When it came to shooting, Dallas knew what he was doing. The Winchester Yellow Boy was not, he now realised, heavy enough for the larger animals. He'd buy another rifle and use the Yellow Boy as back-up. As long as he knew he'd get no help from Will, he could take other precautions against technical difficulties.

Talk turned back to more practical things. With the status quo reversed between them, it would not have surprised Dallas to find Will sullen and unco-operative. It was not so. The man seemed to shrug off any disappointment and was quickly getting down to details. As well as his experience with wagons and oxen, Dallas discovered that Will's knowledge of the tribes and their territories would take him years to match. If only the man could be trusted. If only he would wipe the blood from his forehead.

Dallas caught a sudden look of alarm on Will's face.

A voice behind him sounded slurred and angry.

Dallas looked around. Jeremy Hardcastle stood swaying.

'Granger. My, my, how the mighty have fallen. What are you doing here? Slumming?' The insult was clear. Resentment released by alcohol, Jeremy Hardcastle made no attempt to hide it.

A fight was probably inevitable. Dallas wasn't worried by the prospect. Hardcastle was so drunk he could hardly stand.

'You've no call to say that.' Will Green obviously resented the slumming reference and was indignant.

Hardcastle barely glanced at him. 'Shut up,' he snapped.

'Now, see here –'

Dallas intervened. 'What's your problem, Hardcastle?'

'You are. People like you think they rule this world. Well, I've got news for you. Not out here, you don't.' The first officer swayed back but managed to stay on his feet. 'I warned you. You're not a passenger now.'

'You're drunk.'

'And your chair is blocking the way. You don't own this bloody place. Let me pass.' The first officer placed a foot on one side of the chair and pushed. Dallas wasn't expecting it and reacted instinctively, both hands dropping to grip the sides of his seat. Legs splayed and braced, he avoided a spill but was still off-balance as he turned to face the sailor. A shocking pain exploded at the side of his head and everything went black.

'He's coming round.'

Dallas groaned and opened his eyes. A sea of strange faces peered down at him. He struggled, trying to get up.

'Take it easy, son. That was one hell of a knock.'

Willing hands helped Dallas to sit. His head pounded badly, vision blurred and the pain was acute. He raised a hand to the left side of his face and it came away sticky with blood. 'What happened?'

Will's face swam into focus. 'Some damned sailor took exception to you.'

Hardcastle. It was coming back slowly.

'Swung a chair at your head. You went down like a sack of shit.'

'Where is he?' It hurt to speak.

'You just missed him. Darn fool hit you right in front of an off-duty bobby. He's on his way to the lock-up. A few of us taught him some manners before he left.'

Dallas tried to stand and Will laid a restraining hand on his shoulder. 'Give yourself a minute.' Concerned eyes roved Dallas's face. 'Nothing serious unless your jaw's broke.'

Working it back and forth hurt like hell but at least it told Dallas that the bone wasn't fractured.

'The bloke was yelling blue murder when he hit you. Something about a yetta.'

Jette!

'Man must be mad. There's no such thing.'

Dallas cleared his throat and spoke around the pain of a rapidly swelling face. 'Not yetta. Jette. It's a woman's name.'

Will cackled. 'Aye, it usually is one of them that gets a man all vinegary. Well, chances are he's got more than that on his mind right now. Not only is sailor-boy under arrest for attacking you, seems like he also broke his contract and jumped ship. That means charges in France as well.' Will fumbled under his shirt and produced Dallas's money pouch. 'Here, took this off you for safekeeping. Lifted a couple of quid for me trouble but the rest's there.' Will held up a bleeding fist. 'Bastard had a jaw like an iron bar.'

'Thanks. Help me up.' His head swam and he felt sick as he sank onto a chair.

A stranger offered his pot of rum. 'Here you go. Swig that down, it'll help steady your legs.'

Dallas very much doubted it but drank anyway. 'I'll pay for any damage.'

'No need. Place gets done over every day. The furniture's cheap. Something more solid and you'd have been a goner.'

Dallas relished the thought of Mrs Watson's boarding house and his comfortable bed. 'We'd best start looking for wagons tomorrow. Any ideas?'

'Only one place to go. There's a man in New Germany –'

'Where?'

'New Germany. It's on the Mdloti River. A settlement of Germans. They grow vegetables there.' Seeing Dallas's blank expression Will added, 'Do you know where the main Pinetown road joins the Old Dutch?'

'North?'

'No. West.'

'I'll find it. How about ten o'clock?'

Will nodded vaguely, he had something else on his mind. 'Ah, Dallas . . . can ye pay for my drinks?'

'You've just helped yourself to a couple of pounds.'

'Aye, but I needed that for someone else.' He shrugged. 'Bit of bad luck with the cards last night.'

Grudgingly, Dallas obliged.

On his horse and heading back towards the Berea, Dallas was still pondering the wisdom of becoming involved with William Green. The man liked his drink and gambled to such an extent that he was prepared to sacrifice the tools of his trade. And yet, he had defended Dallas rather than run with his money. Dallas checked the money pouch. He'd gone to meet Will with no more than ten pounds on him. A thousand was safely in the bank and the rest was in his locked sea chest. A quick count revealed that Will's idea of a couple of quid was not the same as his. The man had taken five.

Mrs Watson was demonstrably unimpressed with Dallas. 'I run a respectable establishment, Mr Granger, and I do not expect my lodgers to behave like common ruffians.' She sniffed suspiciously. 'And you've been drinking.'

Dallas had a splitting headache and wanted to lie down. 'I apologise, Mrs Watson. It won't happen again.'

'Indeed it will not, Mr Granger. That is if you wish to continue staying here. Just look at you.'

'It's worse than it appears. I'll clean up and –'

'You have a visitor. He's in the parlour.' Mrs Watson sniffed again, turned on her heel and marched away, disapproval in the stamp of each foot.

Logan Burton looked mildly intrigued by the condition Dallas was in but confined comment to a couple of casual observations. 'Greetings, Granger. Heard you'd moved in here. Just passing. Thought I'd see how you're getting on. Wouldn't have picked you for a bar room brawler.'

'Very funny.'

'Indeed, from where I sit it's quite hilarious. You, of course, are free to disagree.' Burton grinned, curiosity getting the better of him. 'Did someone throw a train at you, old chap?'

'Look,' Dallas said impatiently, 'as you can see, I've had a bad day. If you'd be good enough to state your business I'd appreciate a chance to clean up and rest.' He crossed to a chair and sank into it, helpless to prevent a soft groan of relief.

The older man rose hastily. 'This is not a good time. I wanted to talk business. I'll come back tomorrow.'

'Spit it out, for God's sake, man.' Dallas closed his eyes briefly before looking up at Burton. 'I'm sorry. That was unforgivably rude. Please sit down and tell me why you're here.'

Logan paced instead. 'It's a bit . . . er . . . indelicate, old chap.'

Despite his condition, Dallas realised that the man was embarrassed. 'Please,' he said heavily. 'I'm in no mood for guessing games.'

Logan spread his hands in a helpless gesture before sitting down again. 'I find myself . . . Ah, well, the truth of the matter is, Granger, I'm looking for a partner.'

Dallas rubbed fingers across his mouth to try to hide the smile that involuntarily appeared. 'A partner,' he repeated eventually. 'I've been here six days and already learned that those seeking a joint venture are actually looking to part a fool from his money. How much do you need?'

Burton blinked in surprise at the blunt words. 'I'm not asking a lot. Just enough to —'

'How much?'

'Four hundred pounds.' The old hunter sounded defiant.

It was Dallas's turn to blink.

'I know it sounds like a lot, but —'

Fatigue and pain made Dallas impatient again. 'What's in it for me?'

Burton relaxed slightly. The question at least revealed that his request had not been rejected out of hand. 'The loan repaid twofold in no more than four months.'

An absolute gem of an idea popped into Dallas's head. Why not? He rubbed his jaw gingerly, making Logan wait. Finally, 'Tell you what, Burton, I'll provide the finance if you take me along. You'll work for me until you can buy out.'

Burton looked angry. 'Not a chance. I'm going

after elephant. It's dangerous work and hard enough keeping myself alive. There's no way I'm worrying about your skin as well. You'll get your money back. My word on it as a gentleman.'

'Sorry, Burton, but that's the only deal I'm prepared to discuss.' Dallas was getting the hang of this. He wasn't wealthy by any manner of means. But with a little juggling here and there the sums needed by Will Green and Logan Burton could be found, though it would leave him with less than he'd have liked. Tusks were profitable and Will was scared of elephant. Logan Burton wasn't. With the hunter along they'd need a third wagon. That meant extra trading goods with them and space for more ivory. Bringing Burton in would also reduce any temptation on Will's part to cut and run. It seemed like a pretty equitable arrangement for all concerned.

After a painfully long silence Burton nodded. 'Very well, I accept. On one condition, though.'

'And what is that?'

'I meant what I said. Hunting elephant is dangerous. You might be paying for this, which means I'm effectively working for you, but when we start hunting, do as I say, no questions asked. Is that understood?'

'Perfectly.'

'What are your terms?'

'You sign a promissory note guaranteeing repayment within a year. I'll pay you ten shillings a day and twenty-five per cent of the profit.'

'Gross?'

'Net.'

Burton shook his shaggy grey head. 'I'd be taking the risks.'

'I'm putting up the money.'

'The danger is considerable.'

'To me as well. You die, there goes my investment.'

'Charming!'

'Take it or –'

'Yes, I know.' Burton raised his hands in surrender. 'Or leave it. I'll take it but only because I have no option. With luck, I should be able to pay you back after the first trip. After that, I never want to see your cheeky young hide again.'

Dallas grinned then wished he hadn't. Lips, jaw and forehead objected strenuously. 'Suits me.' He hesitated, then went on. 'There's just one other thing.'

Burton looked suspicious.

'I've already got another partner. Well, a sort of partner. We're headed into Zululand in a few days. You'll have to join us.'

'For Christ's sake, Granger, this isn't a travelling sideshow.' In the face of an unwavering stare from Dallas, Logan relented. 'Is he a hunter?'

'Trader mainly. Shoots for meat and skins but not ivory.'

'Then let's keep it that way. Who is this man?'

'Will Green.'

Logan Burton tipped his head back and roared with laughter.

Dallas waited.

'Will Green,' Burton repeated, wiping his eyes

with the back of a hand. 'That little runt. I gave you credit for more taste.' He shook his head. 'I daresay you've struck the same deal with him?'

'Yes, I have actually.'

Admiration shone briefly in Burton's eyes. 'I'll say this for you, Granger, if you were thrown starving into a river you'd probably make it ashore with a fish in your mouth. Will Green knows more about Zululand than any other trader I've met. At least that's in his favour. He's not usually so broke that he accepts what you've offered.' Logan scowled. 'For that matter, neither am I. It would seem that your good fortune continues.'

'Is there bad blood between you and Will? The last thing I need is people problems.'

'Green's all right, provided you keep him on-side. I've never had much to do with him. He has a good reputation as a trader, which is more than can be said of his character. He'd take the flowers off your mother's grave if he thought he could sell them.' A thought hit Burton suddenly. 'He's not responsible for that face of yours, is he?'

Dallas shook his head. 'Jeremy Hardcastle.'

Burton whistled. 'I thought the *Marie Clare* had sailed.'

'It did. Three days ago.'

'Watch him,' Logan said quietly. 'Pushed too far he can be as dangerous as a cornered rat.'

'Hardcastle's behind bars.'

'Let's hope he stays there.' He stood. 'Right, I'm off. I'd suggest you get some rest.'

Dallas rose. 'Meet us tomorrow where the Old

Dutch Road joins the new one to Pinetown. Ten o'clock. We're going to New Germany for wagons.'

'Whose idea was that?'

'Will suggested it. He recommends something called a Cape wagon. Any problem?'

'No, they're the best. Besides, you can't beat those German craftsmen. You do realise the place is thirty miles from here?'

The information came as no surprise. 'Will omitted to mention it.'

They shook hands. 'I'll be there at ten,' Logan confirmed. 'You'll learn fast enough that Will Green needs to be squeezed pretty hard before he gives out all the information. Have you a bedroll?'

'Yes, among the bits and pieces that came with Tosca.'

'Who?'

'My horse, you haven't seen her yet.'

'I can hardly wait. Anyway, bring the bedroll with you tomorrow.'

With Logan gone, Dallas avoided Mrs Watson's accusing eyes, washing first then going upstairs to rest.

In the morning all three men arrived at the appointed spot within ten minutes of each other.

Will was the last to get there. 'What's Burton doing here?' were his opening words.

'He'll be joining us.' Dallas took in the appearance of his other partner – unshaven, bloodshot eyes, probably slept in his clothes, beard and hair unkempt, hands less than steady. Up close, the lack

212

of personal hygiene was even more unappetisingly apparent than yesterday. 'Let's get one thing clear, Will. In your own time you can do as you wish. In mine, please present yourself as well as prevailing conditions may allow. In short, you stink. I, for one, have no intention of suffering that awful odour for one minute more than is absolutely necessary. The first stream we come to you will remove those putrid garments to wash both them and your person.'

Will gaped, and turned to Logan for support.

None was forthcoming. 'Our young employer is right. I've smelled better in a fish market.'

'That be fine for you and your fancy digs,' Will complained. 'Ain't no such thing as a bath where I stay.'

'Then I'm sure you must be as anxious as we to rectify the matter,' Dallas went on smoothly. 'There's a good fellow. You'll feel so much better for it.'

Ignoring further complaint, Dallas remounted and turned Tosca westward. Behind him he heard Logan tell the Yorkshireman to shut up before, with his horse breaking into a fast canter, and the warm rush of air singing in his ears, Dallas gave himself over to the pleasure of the ride.

Reining in an hour or so later near a small tumbling stream, Dallas dismounted and ground-tethered Tosca. 'Off you go, Will.'

'What am I supposed to wear? I'll catch my death.'

'Go,' Dallas ordered. 'Unless you wish Burton and me to forcibly remove your clothes.'

Muttering about crocodiles, Will stepped into the cool water.

'There won't be any here, will there, Logan?' Dallas was suddenly concerned.

'There isn't a beast alive who would want him while he smells like that. Besides, crocs like still, muddy water with reeds.'

They watched in amusement as Will hopped on one leg to remove a boot, cast a beseeching look over his shoulder at Dallas, then wobbled some more till the other came off too.

'Poor devil has no stockings,' Dallas observed.

'Probably wouldn't know where to put them,' was Logan's only comment.

Breeches next, under which he wore nothing. His skinny white buttocks and legs looked pathetically undernourished. Will stepped further into the water. 'Shirt as well, if you please,' Dallas called.

The bottom was stony and slippery. Naked now, Will found a clear spot to sit and carefully lowered himself into the crystal water. Dallas moved closer and kicked the discarded clothes in as well. 'We've no soap but a good rub should help. Bend your elbow, Will, then toss them to me and I'll hang them over a bush.'

'Please, Mr Granger. I've got stones halfway up me arse.'

The formal use of his name told Dallas how miserable the man was but he showed no sympathy. 'Scrub, Will.' He would have to learn.

'It's cold,' Will whined.

'Then scrub harder,' Dallas advised. 'Wash your hair as well, you've got lice.'

Grumbling and swearing, Will washed his clothes and then himself. 'What am I supposed to do now?' he complained, when the job was done. 'Can't hardly walk around in me birthday suit.'

'Drip off. Your shirt's near dry already.'

'Nearly! I'd like to see you wear wet things. Likely as not I'll die of the consumption.' Dallas was aware of Will's continuing displeasure as he returned to the horses.

'Puny little bastard,' Logan grunted. 'Got a cod like a string bean.'

Dallas ignored the comment and opened his saddlebag. 'Fancy some bread and cheese, compliments of Mrs Watson?'

Logan licked his lips. 'Wouldn't say no, old chap. Haven't had a bite since yesterday.'

Will, looking ludicrous, his hair and beard straggled and dripping, the still-wet shirt clinging to his bony frame, skinny white legs sticking out beneath, joined them.

'Some food?' Dallas asked.

'Aye. Much obliged.'

Once again, Will's apparent lack of any grudge impressed Dallas. The man would whine and connive at every opportunity, yet, when faced with a fait accompli, good-naturedly accepted the inevitable and got on with things.

The three chewed in silence which, while not exactly companionable, at least was no great strain.

'How far to go?' Dallas asked, brushing crumbs from his shirt.

'Couple of hours,' Will told him.

'I hate to appear pedantic,' Logan said, 'but if wagons are available, just how do we get them back to Durban?'

'With extra horses,' Will explained, making it sound perfectly obvious. 'There's a man in New Germany who breeds trek ponies. They're all out of salted stock.'

'Excellent!' Logan sounded impressed.

Horses! Another little item Will had omitted to mention. 'Indeed. And what, pray, is a salted horse?'

Logan explained. 'It's one that's been north of the Limpopo River, suffered the tsetse sickness and survived. Not many do. If a horse recovers it seldom gets sick again. Foals born of two salted animals stand the best chance of surviving.'

Tsetse had to be explained too. 'It's a fly. Has a bite like a horse fly but carries something called sleeping sickness. If a man gets it he usually dies – just wastes away. Horses and cattle suffer in the same way. Ever heard of nagana?'

Dallas hadn't.

'Same disease, different name. Horses are particularly vulnerable. They develop what looks like a streaming cold. In the end, they choke on their own mucus.'

'Can't it be treated?'

Will smirked and Logan shook his head. 'There are all kinds of crackpot remedies. None has been proved to work. One fellow swore by brushing the inside of his horse's nostrils with tar. Others use sulphur, mustard poultices, quinine, even gin. More often than not, the poor bloody nag dies from its treatment. No, the best bet is to get your hands on a salted horse.'

'What about Tosca?' Dallas hadn't owned his mount for long but was already impressed by the animal and would have hated something to happen to her.

'Don't worry,' Will soothed. 'We won't be in tsetse country on this trip.'

'Who says?' Logan demanded. 'We'll go where the elephants are. If that takes us north of the Limpopo, then so be it.'

'I'm not going that far.'

'You will if it's necessary,' Logan told him flatly.

Dallas saw a clash of interests developing.

'This is a trading expedition,' Will protested. 'Not a bloody hunting party.'

'The best money's in tusks,' Logan pointed out.

Dallas cut in before the two were at each other's throats. 'We'll trade *and* hunt. Get used to the idea, both of you. And here's something else you might like to think about. I'm relying on the two of you for experience but this is my expedition.' He treated both to a silencing stare.

'I'm still not going north of the Limpopo,' Will muttered stubbornly.

Logan turned away, an exasperated look on his face, then spun back and shouted, 'Do you know what ivory fetches, you idiotic man? A pound a pound, sir. You would need to trade for bloody months to make that much.'

Will looked set to argue and again, Dallas intervened. 'For God's sake, just shut up, both of you.' He jabbed Will in the chest with a straight finger. 'We will go where I say or you are on your own. Which is it to be?' Without waiting for a reply, Dallas looked at Logan. 'The same applies to you.' He turned and took several paces away before spinning to face them both. 'We are three grown men. Any difference of opinion will be sensibly discussed. Is that clear?'

Logan, eyes brimming with anger, shrugged.

Will nodded reluctantly.

'Good. Now get dressed, Will, and let's be off.'

Logan couldn't resist. 'Yes. Best you cover that puny little excuse for a body.'

'Better lean than looking six months gone with child,' Will shot back.

The older man's hands dropped instinctively to his paunch. Despite the attack on his vanity he replied mildly, 'My dear man, much time and money has been lavished on this bay window. Do try to show a little respect.'

Will failed to notice that the cutting comment had hit home. Shaking his head he moved off to retrieve the rest of his now dry clothing.

Dallas swung into the saddle and waited. Logan did the same, muttering something about the lower classes always looking half starved.

Realising that it was only an attempt to salvage wounded pride, Dallas ignored the remark. He had already come to the conclusion that life on the road would be far from plain sailing. Logan and Will seemed to dislike each other on principle. Getting the best from both was going to be difficult, especially as his dependence on them would only undermine his authority. He could not be seen to take sides. Each could be sensitive. The two of them were down on their luck and had been forced to hitch up with an inexperienced younger man. It was something they resented. Both displayed a degree of vanity in the matter of their professional talents. Dallas fervently hoped that when the time came for Logan and Will to prove their individual worth, each would be good enough at what they did to elicit some respect from the other. That way, with luck, they might cease their pointless squabbling and get on with the job.

They found their wagons. Two brand-new, one a little work-scarred though structurally sound. It had been well repaired and the canvas was good. Dallas paid two hundred and seventy-five pounds for them, but only after Logan and Will had beaten the price down by fifty.

'Does Old Joe still sell salted horses?' Will asked the German wagon-builder.

'Ja. I tink.'

Dallas told him they'd be back later to pick up their purchases.

'He tinks,' Logan mimicked as the three men rode away.

'Shut up!' Will snarled.

Surprisingly, Logan did.

Old Joe, when they located him, was only too happy to sell them horses until he heard they would be pulling the wagons back to Durban. 'They're broken but not trained for that.'

'It'll be fine,' Will assured him.

Old Joe scratched himself thoroughly, stomach, head and crotch. 'They'll spook. Don't say you weren't warned.'

'That's all we need.' Logan looked disgusted.

'Believe me, it'll be fine,' Will repeated.

They had no option. 'How much?' Dallas asked.

Calculating eyes turned from one face to another, as Joe's expression went from doubt, through cunning to good old-fashioned greed. He named his price.

'Too much,' Will and Logan responded together. Will added, 'They might be salted but it's horses we're buying, not the bloody crown jewels.'

Dallas remained silent while the other three haggled. Against the combined skill of Will and Logan, Old Joe didn't really stand a chance, his initial confidence rapidly becoming a scowl of defeat.

'Eighty pounds and not a penny less. It's the best I can do.' They agreed, but the old man hadn't finished. 'Extra for halters.'

'Forget it,' Will said. 'We'll drive them to the wagons. It'll be easy.' Having beaten the price down by forty-five pounds there was no way he was prepared to let it go up again. Dallas saw his air of confidence and nodded acceptance.

Logan wasn't so sure, a fact obvious from his expression.

Of the nine horses they'd just purchased, two stood watching the men, one was drinking and the rest showed little interest in anything. They seemed docile enough. Dallas agreed with Will.

It was no more than a mile, along a road flanked by very European-looking dwellings. The horses, no doubt relieved by being released from the monotony of their small enclosure, celebrated in style. They made enemies of every establishment en route. Dallas retained a memory of that afternoon for the rest of his life. The animals ran amok and displayed total disregard for the property of others. Carefully cultivated flora disappeared into eager mouths, hooves trampled crops and gardens alike. Not even windowboxes escaped attention. A broom-wielding German frau in hot pursuit of a piece of female undergarment erroneously filched by a horse as a snack, brought an entire line of washing to the ground. The lady was determined to retrieve her corset, the horse just as anxious that she came nowhere near it. Two such diversely opposing, though equally urgent, requirements ensured disaster and the clean clothes were unfortunate victims. Dallas, with his sketchy though adequate knowledge of her language, had no idea German women were equipped with such an expansive vocabulary.

Dogs, barking hysterically, joined in the fun. Chickens ran squawking in all directions seconds before being trampled. Children shrieked, either from fright or excitement – Dallas didn't know which. Nor did he care. The end result was identical. Panic.

Total disaster was averted by the wagon-builder, who had heard the approaching pandemonium and blocked the way, forcing all nine horses into his fenced field where the wagons stood. Sweating, swearing and yelling, Dallas, Logan and Will followed close behind and swung the gate closed.

Once contained, the animals did a nervous circumnavigation, found no way out, and settled down to graze.

'I tink you haf to leave them tonight. Tomorrow they calmer. Den they like little kinders.'

Puce-faced with outrage and exertion, the broom-wielding frau waddled into sight. 'Mine, mine,' she screeched, pointing to her corset, which was still carried by one of the horses. As they watched, it shook its head vigorously and the garment flew, with unerring accuracy, to land on a fresh pile of dollops deposited by another. 'Nein, nein,' the woman yelled.

Dallas hastily retrieved the chewed and now yellow-stained undergarment and self-consciously returned it to its rightful owner.

Perhaps believing she was not understood, the woman delivered a stream of obscenities in her native language, describing in detail what she would do to his manhood if she could get her hands on a knife.

Dallas managed to keep a straight face.

They took the wagon-builder's advice and camped in the field. The man's wife brought them home-baked bread and a steaming pot of impala stew. Conversation around the fire was limited. Logan lay on his back gazing up at the night sky and smoking a cigar. Will stared into the fire.

It was Dallas who broke the silence with a question to which he was horribly certain of the answer. 'Do you two know the first thing about horses?'

'Don't be stupid.' Logan cleared his throat.

Will kept his gaze on the flickering flames.

'Do you?' Dallas persisted.

When they finally condescended to tell the truth, Dallas found he was not in the least surprised. His two associates knew how to ride, they could size up horseflesh and bark out orders. However, the actual working of animals was taken care of by their African employees. Knowing what should be done and actually doing it themselves were two totally different things.

'Somehow,' Dallas gritted, as the reality of their situation became evident, 'we must get this lot back to Durban tomorrow. It would seem that, of the three of us, I am actually the most experienced. Therefore, I'll take the lead.' In fact, Dallas didn't have much more practice than the other two but he certainly wasn't about to admit it. He had, at least, driven a pony cart in Scotland.

'I have experienced Zulu boys waiting in Durban,' Will offered helpfully.

'So do I,' Logan volunteered. 'They'll need to come with us for the oxen.'

'Damned right they will.' Dallas prodded moodily at the fire. 'A pity neither of you thought to bring them with us today. And I'll need staff myself. Any suggestions?'

'Behind Cato's store. You'll find any number looking for work.'

'If the cattle are anything like the horses,' Dallas said firmly, 'we'll need all the help we can get.'

In the morning, and not without assistance from the wagon-builder's Africans, they managed to hitch three horses to each wagon. Fortunately, most of their journey would be downhill. The animals were nervous and jumpy but, once rolling, with Will, Logan and Dallas riding in front and leading a wagon each, they managed to make the trip with only a few minor problems.

The journey, however, was slow and it was after five before they arrived back in town. By the time they'd unhitched the wagons and made arrangements to overnight the horses, it was too late to do anything more. Before returning to Mrs Watson's, Dallas said he'd meet Will and Logan outside Cato's at eight the next morning.

Under normal circumstances, it had not been a big day. A bash over the head with a flimsy chair and the acquisition of two partners the previous afternoon, Dallas could have taken in his stride. So, too, the collection and return of horses and wagons from New Germany to Durban today, through very unfamiliar territory with two strangers – one of whom held practical reality in contempt; the other, seemingly happy to sit back and criticise.

Added to everything else, however, by the time he reached Ann Watson's, Dallas was pleased the day was over. His head ached, as did his jaw. For that matter, so did the rest of him. As Will had said, riding in Africa was rather more than 'Tally-ho! There goes the fox!' Trying to absorb all manner of new information, whether it came from the mouths of his partners or was provided by sudden, and often very unwelcome, experience, had taken its toll. Dallas was more than ready to call it a day.

His landlady made a point of only offering cold food from the previous night's dinner but appeared to be genuinely sad to learn that her lodger intended leaving. A week's rent in lieu seemed to cheer up the good woman, who by the time Dallas bid farewell the next morning had reiterated her offer to hold any mail that might come for him. She also agreed to store his sea chest, valise, and any items of clothing or personal effects he wanted to leave behind. His belongings being reduced to the bare minimum seemed to increase Dallas's sense that his new life was about to begin.

It was already hot when, at six-thirty, he set off into town. That morning, Dallas experienced a heady mixture of anxiety and excitement. Ahead lay God knows what. Although ready to face the challenges, he could not help but wonder what they might be.

SEVEN

If Dallas thought he had a problem with Will and Logan not getting along, it was nothing compared to what he was about to see in town. Nobody had prepared him for the stark and uncompromising ferocity of tribal hatred. The first inkling of anything being amiss came as he rode up to Cato's store. Logan was already there, standing off to one side with three Africans. Dallas nodded in greeting but his attention was taken by a roughly dressed and noisy group of mainly white men intent on something taking place in a large clearing next to the store. 'What's going on?'

'Bit of a fight.'

At that moment, Dallas spotted Will, with a fist full of money, scuttling through the throng. 'What's he up to?'

'What's it look like?' Logan was clearly disgusted.

Dallas handed him the reins. 'Wait here. I'll fetch him.'

'I wouldn't if I were you.'

'Why not?'

The crowd parted briefly and Dallas saw two

Africans, one wielding a short whip, the other armed with a heavy stick, warily circling each other. Both men had skinning knives in their other hand.

Logan indicated the action with a jerk of his head. 'Fellow with the sjambok is Will's driver. He's a Zulu. The other is my skinner. A Sotho. Seems like we've got a slight problem. They hate each other.'

'Any particular reason?' Dallas winced as the whip whistled past the skinner's face. The crowd roared in approval.

'They don't need one. Tribal differences are usually enough to spark a fight. In this case it's not just that. Will's driver claims that my man got his sister pregnant.'

'Did he?'

'Christ! How the hell would I know? The bloody man dips his wick as often as he takes breath. He probably gets lots of them pregnant. Zulus call any girl from the same ancestor their sister. If you ask me –'

'No, you listen. We've got to stop them before they kill each other.'

Logan seemed to share none of his concern. 'Oh, one will kill the other, no doubt about that. The money's on my chap. Nice enough fellow, but as well as a propensity for the opposite sex he's a bit hot-headed. He's also devilishly accurate with that knife. Definitely not a good idea to get involved at this stage. Their blood is up and they'll fight to the death.'

'This is ridiculous,' Dallas snapped. 'We end up

with one man dead and the other charged with his murder. Why don't you do something?' He waved his arm towards a laughing, though tense, group of Africans who held back but were observing the action intently. 'Why don't *they*? They're Zulus, most of them. Why don't they step in and prevent their man from injury?'

Logan gave a bark of amusement. 'How? None of us is that stupid. Look, old chap, you'll just have to learn, you never, ever interfere in their arguments. Most of the time these boys simply pick up where they left off yesterday, the day before, last month – Christ, last year, who knows. One second everything is fine and dandy, the next they're ready to kill each other. It's too late by then. Try and stop it now and they'll more than likely turn on you. To the whites it's nothing more than entertainment, but to the Kaffirs it's a matter of honour. Will's driver is fighting for his entire clan. My man is equally committed to showing contempt on behalf of the Sothos.'

Dallas didn't want to hear the reasons. He was concerned with the delays such a depth of feeling and any subsequent confrontation might cause to the expedition's departure. Even more worrying was that one, or both, would be killed.

'We'll lose two good men.'

'One,' Logan contradicted. 'The other, unless his chief decides to take the matter further, will not be punished. Native law, old chap. A straight crime of grievance. It might cost the winner a beast of some kind but that is about all.'

Dallas pulled his rifle from its saddle scabbard. 'We'll see about this.'

'Make sure it's loaded, dear boy,' Logan advised mildly. 'Go in there, and chances are you'll have to use that fancy popgun.'

'Are you with me or not?'

Logan sighed and sent an African to fetch his own firearm.

They pushed their way through the rowdy crush. 'Stop!' Dallas shouted.

The two combatants were so intent on each other they gave no indication of having heard. Dallas now had a perfect view of the impending confrontation. Will's driver was slowly circling the Sotho, swinging the hippo leather sjambok, then striking out with deadly accuracy, forcing the other to keep his distance. Logan's skinner was contemptuously ignoring the near misses, seeming to know that his adversary was not yet ready to deliver a committed attack. The knife in his right hand looked loosely held. His left arm was extended, the stick constantly moving, fingers splayed for control as he weaved it in the air to divert attention and confuse concentration. Eyes locked, the two Africans moved around each other like wary leopards, each waiting for an opportunity or a wavering of confidence.

A hush fell as spectators sensed that the moment was near. Dallas could hear his heart beating. The early-morning drama seemed almost unreal, as though he would wake and find it had been a dream. Yet he knew it wasn't. Having interfered, he now had to follow through. Although Africans seemed to live by a code unknown to Dallas, one thing was perfectly clear. To win their respect his action would have to be quick and decisive. Anything less and the authority he needed to maintain would be doomed.

Dallas didn't doubt his skill as a better than average shot. On the grouse moor he had once equalled Lord Ripon's record of seven birds dead in the air at one time. Conscious thought left him as instinct took over.

How he sensed that the moment had come, that any more delay could prove fatal, he'd never be able to say. Perhaps a warning communicated from the contestants' hate-glazed eyes. It might have been a subtle straining of already taut muscle or a change of stance. Both men stood firm and rock steady. The whip arm of Will's driver may have come back a little further, or the knife point lifted slightly. Whatever it was, Dallas knew he had to act now.

The driver took a stamping step forward and swung. As the sjambok scythed towards Logan's man, the skinner's right arm pulled up and back. Simultaneously, the twirling, darting stick became a blur of motion. In that instant, before the knife was snapped towards its intended victim, Dallas worked the lever action of his rifle, shouldered and fired in one fluid and continuous movement. Without a moment's hesitation, he turned and fired again, this time at the Zulu.

Later, Logan admitted he'd never seen anything

like it. His skinner, braced and totally focused, bent back to avoid the murderously accurate whip. As he did so the knife and a finger were smashed from his right hand. An instant later, the Zulu dropped his own knife, clutching at his upper arm, blood streaming through his fingers. For a second, the crashing Winchester retorts seemed to suspend time. It penetrated the hate lust of both combatants as they turned unseeing eyes towards the sound, incomprehension evident on their faces. The Zulu then stared stupefied at the blood running down his arm. His Sotho adversary's blood-soaked hand worked spasmodically as if searching for that which was no longer there.

Dallas lowered his rifle but for a full few seconds stood frozen to the spot. The rim of spectators fell silent, momentarily stunned, waiting to see what would happen next. Some mouths were working but the scene appeared to be bound within a cone of silence.

'I've been shot.'

The bellowing, pain-filled howl broke through shocked paralysis, and a babble of voices suddenly erupted. Dallas turned dazedly towards the voice, his mind scrambling for purchase, ears still singing to the reverberating blasts. Impossible! The bullets would have gone too high.

'Help! I've been shot.'

A man stood with both hands pressed to his head, blood seeping through spread fingers.

'Shit!' Dallas heard Logan's loud expletive over the shouts of others. He watched, rooted to the spot as his partner moved to examine the wound. Logan blew a breath of relief from puffed cheeks and said in a voice clear for all to hear, 'You haven't been shot, man. Looks like you've been hit by the knife.'

Logan's words caused a fugitive mirth but it was short-lived. In pendulous mood the crowd swung. They had wanted blood, even been prepared to bet on it. What they'd seen hadn't been enough, there was no clear winner. The African observers turned away, an air of resignation, or even dissatisfaction, clear in their expressions. What was nothing more to them than a matter of honour had been thwarted by ignorance, something they were learning to live with as their contact with whites increased.

Those betting on the outcome had a different outlook. Instead of taking a cue from the Zulus, they turned on Dallas.

'Just who do you think you are?'

'I bet good money on this little scrap.'

'Interfering bastard!'

'Where's me shilling then?'

'This is a set-up.'

'What say we take it out of your hide?'

'Give us our money back.'

'Where's Will?'

The anger was growing. Dallas, an outsider who dared to interfere, had cost them hard-earned money. In the centre of an outraged phalanx he was the obvious medium for a quid pro quo. Rat-like cunning was essential. The mention of Will gave him an idea. Pointing in the first direction that came to mind, Dallas yelled, 'There he is. Will's got your money.'

Unfortunately, and purely by coincidence, Will was, at that very moment, sidling quietly towards his horse. Dallas had pointed directly to him. The crowd swarmed like African bees and had Will surrounded in seconds.

With any immediate danger to his person temporarily out of the way, Dallas wanted to see what had become of the two men who had been fighting. He knew both were injured and would require medical attention. 'Oh, bloody hell's teeth!' Will's driver sat astride Logan's injured skinner and, ignoring the pain of his own wounded arm, was squeezing his neck with grim enthusiasm. The other's eyes were bulging as he struggled feebly, banging his heels on the ground and squirming. The Zulu was not about to let go.

There was no time for finesse. Nor was Dallas in the mood for it. The adrenaline of a few moments earlier had been replaced by frustration and anger. Striding to them and swinging the barrel of his rifle, Dallas belted Will's man on the side of his head. He was not knocked out but the blow was sufficiently hard for him to lose interest in throttling the Sotho.

Gripping his skinner by an arm, Logan hauled the man to his feet. Dallas did the same with Will's driver. Propelling the dazed men in front of them, they shoved and pushed both to where the horses waited.

'Leave this to me,' Logan gritted.

'Gladly. I'll see if Will needs a hand.'

Having retrieved their money from the hapless Yorkshireman most of the crowd were making off, some still muttering under their breaths. Will, a little dishevelled though otherwise unscathed, flinched when he saw the look on Dallas's face. However, there was still enough bluster in him to complain. 'What did you go and do that for? I had upwards of ten quid in me hand.'

Ten quid! What price a man's life? The thought pushed Dallas's anger to bubbling point. He grabbed Will's shirt in both fists and shook him roughly. 'Give me one good reason not to fire you.' The words ground out. 'Just one will do.'

'I didn't mean no harm. Those boys were going to fight anyways. All I did –'

'You could have stopped them.' Dallas shoved and Will fell back against his horse.

'Not me,' Will babbled, shaking his head and pulling at his rucked shirt. 'You didn't see them. They was like madmen.' His look turned sly. 'Anyways, what's best? Get it done with now or have trouble on the trip? Those two haven't finished, not by a long shot. You don't know the natives like I do. They've started something and neither will rest until it's over. Better sooner than later if you ask me.'

Despite a near overwhelming desire to pick Will up and hurl him under a passing span of oxen, Dallas realised he spoke some truth. But there was still the matter of taking bets.

'Someone was going to run a book,' Will went on, reading his thoughts. 'Why not me?'

Immoral? Indecent? Not the done thing? Oh Jesus! Dallas was unsure. His idea of principles seemed meaningless in this part of the world, yet he found himself deeply affronted by Will's actions. Unable to adequately express his feelings in a way that would be understood by the little trader, Dallas sought rationale through authority. 'If they wish to kill each other I can't stop them. If you choose to run a book on the outcome, I can't stop that either. But by God, sir, you will not do it while in my pay. There is no place on this team for ill will. If your boys start trouble I expect you to stop it. Fail and you are no use to me. This is the only warning you'll get. Do I make myself understood?'

Will nodded. 'Are you going to tell him that?' He jerked a thumb towards Logan.

'I think you'll find, if you last that long, that my feelings on this matter will be clear to everyone before the hour is out. There is no need to trouble yourself with thoughts of favouritism. Now, do we have all that is needed for fetching the oxen?'

'I think so.' Will was taken aback by the sudden change of topic.

'Well, do we or don't we?'

'I'll check.' Will's expression was guilty.

'Can you control your driver?'

'Yes.' Will looked sullen.

'Good. See to his arm and make sure we have enough medicine to treat him until it heals. And when you have done that, please explain to your men the rules of this expedition. They are to be left in no doubt that my word is law and at the first sign of trouble, not only do they lose their jobs but you lose yours as well. Any questions?'

Will shook his head.

'Then kindly get to it.'

Dallas turned and let out a slow breath. Now for Mr Burton.

Logan was letting rip in Zulu and cuffing heads none too gently. Will walked past, snapping his fingers, and his driver and two others trotted after him. Dallas watched briefly, hoping the man had taken his threat seriously. He addressed Logan. 'Tell your men we leave today. If your skinner is badly hurt he'll have to stay behind. That decision is between you and him. If he comes with us make sure his wound is kept clean. It will be your responsibility to tend him.'

Surprised by the tone but making no comment, Logan spoke briefly to his Africans before turning back to Dallas. 'That was one hell of a shot. Was it a fluke?'

'No.'

'Good. Because I've told my boys that if there's any more fighting you'll shoot their cods off just as easily as that finger. Talk about being shit-scared of you. What with your face looking the way it does and now this, they're saying you are a man who never walks from trouble. You've certainly got their respect, old boy, you'll have a praise name before you know it.'

Dallas had no idea what Logan was talking about and in no mood to ask. 'Terrific!'

'They also think you're bewitched.'

Dallas got down to the point he wished to make. 'I've straightened things out with Will, so now it's your turn. If you don't like it, feel free to leave.' He treated the man to ninety seconds of ire.

To his surprise, Logan took it on the chin. 'Fair enough,' he said when Dallas fell silent. 'So long as you mean it.'

'Every word.'

Dallas had assumed that their oxen would be young and male. For a start, they were larger and stronger than females. Pregnant cows and newborn calves would not, he believed, be a good idea on such an arduous trip.

For once in accord, Logan and Will had different reasons for including cows.

'We can trade any calves for ivory,' Will said.

'Won't need to,' Logan countered.

'Then why take females?' Dallas asked. 'Surely it's better to have castrated bulls?'

'And when they die, as some will? Or are stolen? What then?'

Will added, 'We trade some things for native cattle but they are wild. No good for working as a team. Logan's right. It's best to have back-up.'

'Calves born will be too young,' Dallas protested.

'Yoke them behind their mothers and you'd be surprised how well they work,' Logan persisted. 'Isn't that right, Will?'

'Yes.' Will sounded doubtful. 'Their main use, though, is for trade.'

A squabble erupted but, since each man saw the sense of what the other was saying, soon petered out.

'Do others take cows?' Dallas asked.

'Some do, some don't.'

It wasn't much of an answer, but with no experience behind him, Dallas had to accept his two partners' advice.

Although they'd been unable to buy as many oxen as Will insisted would be needed, seventy-six looked a formidable number as the herd boys brought them together. The Africans had identified three that might prove troublesome but, by and large, all were obedient and easy to move. Dallas was impressed by the calm confidence and soft words the Zulus used in their handling of the animals. Logan saw his appreciation and explained the ritual significance of cattle.

'They're not just meat and milk, old chap. A man's wealth is measured by the number of cattle he owns. He pays debts with them, trades for wives, swaps some for favours. Sure, they have practical applications – clothing, body decorations, shields, that sort of thing – but there's an even greater value than any economic considerations. The Zulus believe that cattle are their link with ancestors. At all important tribal ceremonies when ancestral blessings are sought, a beast is always sacrificed. It's one of the ways they make contact with the spirits.'

As Logan spoke, Dallas watched the men working with the oxen with renewed interest. It wasn't just experience the Africans used. There was respect too. And the cattle responded to it.

'It's only the men,' Logan went on. 'There are all kinds of taboos preventing women from having anything to do with cattle. For example, they believe that should a woman go near the herd when it's her time of the month cows will suffer a loss of milk, become sick and even die. If you ever see a woman in the cattle kraal, chances are she'll be quite old and probably the most important female of that family.'

'Kraal?' Dallas queried.

Logan raised his eyebrows. 'Sorry. You make me realise how much I take for granted. Zulu families live together within a circular stockade. It's called a kraal. Inside that is another circle where cattle are kept for the night.'

'The cattle kraal?'

'Correct.'

Will rode up to them. 'What did I tell you? Aren't they beauties? Strong and healthy. The boys are already naming them.'

At a questioning look from Dallas, Logan explained. 'Nothing fanciful about it. Translated, you'd find the names describe a particular feature, like colour or horn shape. It's how the Zulus identify their cattle. If the boys are naming this lot it means they are prepared to look after them as their own.'

'Not like personal possessions, I hope.' Dallas had visions of his oxen mysteriously disappearing.

'Don't worry about that,' Logan assured him with a laugh. 'That's another taboo. They wouldn't dream of it.'

'What's to stop them?'

'The old spoor-law. Where the tracks of stolen cattle stop, so too does the life of whoever lives there. Cattle theft is punishable by death and Zulus take the crime seriously. If your cattle went missing, these boys would turn themselves inside out to find them, if for no other reason than to prove their own innocence.'

'But you said the oxen could be stolen.'

'Not by our boys, they're responsible for them. There's nothing to stop others, though. It's a way of life for these people. A crime it might be, but if they think they'll get away with it, they'll try.'

Dallas couldn't understand how relaxed Logan was over what could be a catastrophe.

The older man saw his confusion and laughed. 'Don't worry. Zulus don't usually steal from other Zulus. If we leave their territory, that's when we have to be careful. Other tribes are not bound by Zulu laws.'

Dallas had to accept the flimsy explanation but he didn't like it much. The pitfalls for the inexperienced that Will had spoken of were more serious than he had imagined.

Will rode on ahead to open the gate of a holding pen at the back of Cato's store. The oxen walked sedately through as if they'd been doing it all their lives.

With the cattle secure, spare horses in an

enclosure nearby and the wagons waiting outside Cato's, all that remained to do was buy supplies and stock up on goods they could trade. Here, Will came into his own, even Logan being content to let him take charge. There was only one slight altercation over how many bags of coffee they'd need – Will said one, Logan wanted three and Dallas decided to split the difference.

Leaving Will haggling over the price of beads, Logan and Dallas went outside to evaluate the ever-present throng of Africans in search of work. Dallas needed a driver and two others. 'It's important that you get a more senior man for the wagon because he'll be in charge,' Logan advised as they approached a group of maybe forty men.

'Will any of them speak English?' Dallas asked, beginning to feel frustrated by being at someone else's mercy in order to communicate.

'Not many.' Logan called out in Zulu and three men stepped forward.

'They claim to. Try them out.'

All three had crouched and were looking up at Dallas with unreadable expressions. He sensed that the next few seconds were critical, his authority judged by words and actions, a first impression which, once formed, nothing he could do would change. An empty effort to impress was not going to work. The lack of interest on their faces was in contrast to an evident tension in each motionless body. They reminded Dallas of a theatre audience – quick to show contempt if an actor let them down.

'I need an experienced wagon driver.' When in

doubt, state your case and be done with it. Dallas had learned a thing or two watching his father deal with tenant farmers on their estates in Scotland.

One of the men smiled. 'Yebo.'

Another thumped his chest with a clenched fist and announced, 'Jesus.'

The third clapped his hands together softly as if drawing attention to himself. 'I can drive.'

'We will be away for three to six months.'

Yebo repeated himself. 'Yebo.'

Jesus grinned, revealing teeth like old headstones.

The one who said he could drive nodded. 'I am ready.'

It was no contest really. Yebo might have some knowledge of English but it was scant. Jesus had none. Besides, the third was well presented while the other two were ragged and none too clean.

Dallas turned to him. 'What is your name?'

'Mister David, master.'

The other two were given one last chance. 'Your names, please.'

Blank stares met his request.

Dallas drew Logan to one side. 'I'd say it was obvious. What do you think?'

Logan looked resigned. 'If you insist.'

'What's wrong with him?'

'He sounds mission educated.'

'Surely that's better than the alternatives?'

'Not necessarily. They're often resented by the others. Look, I understand why you want him – you haven't much option, really – just as long as you know they can cause trouble.'

'I'll have to take that chance. There's no point employing someone if we don't understand each other. The other two don't seem to speak English at all, despite any claims to the contrary.'

'I agree, but you'll have to learn some Zulu pretty damned fast.'

'I will. In the meantime, I'll take Mister David. At least I know he can drive. Lord knows if the others can.'

'Ask them.'

'You speak the language. Would you do it for me?'

'You're employing them. They expect to be questioned by you. If you leave it to me, they'll think I'm in charge and you'll have the devil's own job getting them to obey you.' Logan glanced over at the three squatting Africans. 'Whichever one you choose, don't take the others. Let your man select the rest.'

'Why?'

'Two reasons. Discipline.'

Dallas waited but Logan had finished. 'That's one.'

'Two, actually. The natives know you pick a boss boy first. Those three put themselves forward for the job. The man you decide on would have his work cut out telling the others what to do since they consider themselves as equals. Secondly, your head boy will pick men he can control, not necessarily those with experience. That's the way it works. Some of the best boys are those who only know how to take orders. It's a hierarchy system and very efficient.' Logan waved to someone walking past then went on. 'Pick your head man wisely and you'll have a smooth-running expedition. Choose a wrong'un and you'll have nothing but grief for the entire trip.'

'Well, who would you take?'

'In your position I'd take my chances with Mister David. If he's no good you can always get rid of him.'

That was what Dallas had already decided for himself. He went back to the three waiting men. 'Mister David, your English is very good.'

'Thank you, master.'

'Where did you learn it?'

'At the mission, master.'

Dallas heard Logan mutter, 'Sweet Jesus, I thought so. That's all we need.' The African must have heard too but showed no sign of having done so.

'Have you worked as a driver before?'

'Yes, master. For six years I work with Master Leslie.'

Logan, who had moved closer, whistled and nodded. Clearly, the name meant something to him.

'Why do you no longer work for this master?' Dallas slipped subconsciously into a vernacular many Europeans used to communicate with Africans. He slowed down his speech, enunciating each word carefully, keeping everything simple. He even heard himself imitating the man's accent.

It was Logan who replied. 'He's gone missing.'

'Who is he?'

'Trader, hunter, explorer. Same as everyone else. One of the best. Hasn't been seen for a while.'

Dallas looked back at Mister David. 'Where is he now?'

'Tongoland, master.'

'Up near Portuguese territory,' Logan volunteered.

'Why did you not go with him?'

'I was sick, master. The fever.'

Dallas threw Logan a questioning look.

'If he's spent six years with David Leslie, he's okay,' Logan responded in an undertone. 'Provided the fellow's not lying, of course.'

Dallas replied as softly, 'Must know him reasonably well to take on the name Mister David.'

'He'll be calling himself Mister Dallas within a day if he thinks it will get him anywhere.'

'Master?' Mister David held a piece of paper in his hand. 'Master Leslie tell me give this to my new master.'

It was a reference that praised the African lavishly. Logan read it over Dallas's shoulder. 'Looks genuine enough,' he said. 'David Leslie obviously thought highly of him.'

That clinched it as far as Dallas was concerned. 'Okay. I'll take him on.'

'First establish what tribe he's from.'

'Why?'

'You saw the trouble this morning. That was tribalism at its best.'

Dallas turned back to a now-standing Mister David. The other two, sensing rejection, had drifted away. 'Are you a Zulu?'

'Yes, master.'

'Mr Logan is coming with us. His skinner is a Sotho.'

A wide grin spread over Mister David's face. 'No problem for me, master. My father's sister is a Sotho.'

Dallas registered Logan's derisive snort. Although curious to know why, now was not the time to ask. Instead, he informed Mister David that the job was his, outlined expectations and conditions, then added, 'I need two good boys to come with us.'

'I find them, master.'

'Good. Meet us back here in two hours.'

Logan interrupted. 'That he won't understand.'

The pleasant look on Mister David's face didn't alter. 'I understand, master.' He indicated the ground and, with his heel, drew a line in the dirt. 'The shadow of that tree will be here.' With that, Mister David ran off to the holding pen where a group of men were admiring Dallas's oxen.

'Time will tell with that one,' Logan said darkly as they walked towards Cato's.

Dallas made no comment. Time would tell with them all.

At the store, Will's bartering and buying spree was going very well. Dallas had Logan go to the blacksmith next door with instructions and a list of supplies. He concentrated on cooking and eating utensils, medical supplies and a more suitable rifle. He would have to take advice on black powder, lead and tin for making bullets.

The standard list prepared by Cato's was the result of the shop having kitted out literally hundreds of similar ventures and, as such, extremely comprehensive. It included everything the men would need for their own well-being – two cases of French brandy being considered a basic requirement. In addition, through trial and error, bartering goods were in proportion to their popularity, with tobacco and beads topping the list, followed by coils of copper wire, blankets, umbrellas and bolts of cloth. With few exceptions, Will followed it to the letter and, by three that afternoon, their provisions were ready for loading.

Spans of eighteen oxen were yoked and hitched to each wagon. Hindsight, in this instance, being both mother and father of prudence, the spare horses wore rope halters and were tethered to the sides. Additional oxen would be driven. Gregarious by nature, they kept bellowing to join their yoked companions. The chance of them wandering from the main party was small.

The wagons had to be loaded so that each span pulled approximately the same weight, about seven thousand pounds, with essentials such as food, water, cooking pots and bedrolls easily accessible. All three African drivers proved experienced and efficient, each team working independently yet with close cooperation to spread the loads fairly.

Dallas noticed that Will's driver and Logan's skinner, both bandaged yet each working steadily with no outward show of discomfort, took great care to remain as far away from each other as possible. No words, or even eye contact, passed between them. If resentment still simmered, neither allowed it to show. Despite this, Dallas had the uncomfortable feeling that he was watching a volcano in its initial stages of preparing to blow.

The Africans recruited by Mister David proved to be willing and cheerful. One, a handsomely proud yet fierce-looking fellow, with teeth so perfectly white and square they didn't seem real, was called July. The other, equally impressive in appearance, had his good looks marred by a walleye. He, if Mister David could be believed, answered to the name Tobacco. The three worked well together and even Logan commented that Dallas seemed to have a good team.

They were standing back watching the loading. 'Tobacco! What a name.'

Logan laughed. 'He will have chosen it himself. Most natives adopt an English word to use when working with us. I once had a boy called Nostril.'

'Why do they do it?'

'It's quite normal for them to have more than one. At birth, they are given an *igamu*. That's their great name, but usually they pick up a pet name as well. Believe it or not, some even receive what's called a fancy name, one that is supposed to keep alive the memory of whoever first fancied the word. There are names devised by peer groups – through the various stages of a boy growing up.'

'Such as?'

'At around five they become herd boys, tending the cattle during the day. They give each other names. When they're a bit older they learn stick-fighting. That brings another one.'

'So, they're like nicknames?'

'Sort of. They only get really serious about it when they join their fighting regiment. As a man gets older, provided he's brave of course, he can also earn a variety of praise names. One of Nostril's was *Ihloboshi-eli vimbe-esangiveni-kwapungula; umakazi-abantwana-ba-ya-kupuma-ngopi-na.*'

The words rolled easily off Logan's tongue. He grinned at the expression on Dallas's face. 'It means "Adder which obstructs the doorway in the village of Phungula; by what way then shall the children go out?"'

'What does all that mean?'

'I have absolutely no idea. It was a hell of a lot easier to call him Nostril. Besides, one is never quite sure of the significance in a name. Some can only be used by certain members of the family or by men of the same fighting regiment. You have to be a bit careful, so it's usually safer to use the one they give you.'

Will joined them. 'We should be under way soon. Won't get far tonight but I know a good place we can set up a camp. Plenty of grass for the horses and cattle. Water, too.' He looked at Dallas. 'That's important. Best to give the stock as much of a head start as possible; country gets rough soon enough. Shelter, too. Storm could come in later. If we protect the team –'

'What the hell are you going on about?' Logan demanded suddenly.

'Boy's got to learn,' Will defended himself.

Logan bit down on his cigar, shifted it sideways in his mouth and growled, 'He'll do that without your help. Probably faster.' He glanced at Dallas. 'We outspan, my boy. That's the word here. "Outspan". When we pack up and leave, it's "inspan". Got it?'

'I think so,' Dallas said, grinning. 'When we come in for the night, we *out*span. Go out for the day, we *in*span. Simple, really.'

'Told you.' Will sounded triumphant. 'You can't expect him to know these things.'

'Oh, shut up!' Logan stomped away, unconvinced. 'The boy's no fool.'

Logan and Will had already had a difference of opinion on the best route to take. Logan wanted to get into Zululand quickly, by the coast road. Will argued for inland, saying that way saw few, if any, traders which meant better potential. Neither, because their interests were so diverse, would budge. Dallas could see the sense of travelling a lesser-used route and his decision to take Will's advice had Logan grumbling at every chance he got.

'There are better resting places along the coast.'

'Good ones inland, too.'

'The going is easier.'

'The rivers might be up.'

'Better feed for the oxen.'

'Sour grass.'

'Your way will take longer.'

'What's the rush?'

'To find elephant, man. They're all up north.'

'Rubbish! I was talking to someone only the other day who said he'd seen herds numbering hundreds on both sides of the river near Umvoti.'

'Pah!' Logan dismissed the comment. 'These rumours always fly.'

Will went on undaunted. 'The elephants up north are skittish.'

Dallas could not offer an opinion but he was heartily sick of the constant bickering. 'We're going inland.'

'Where there are no tracks and probably no elephants either.' Logan was determined to make his point. 'Don't say I didn't warn you.'

Will wanted the last word. 'If we follow the river there's villages and elephants aplenty. You'll see.'

'Why take this risk?' Logan was wavering. 'Don't know of anyone who heads for the midlands either to trade or shoot. You've heard the stories. Our black brethren up there are none too friendly.'

'Is that what you're afraid of?'

'Afraid! Me? How dare you, sir.'

The argument flared again, ranging back and forth until Dallas, exasperated, asked Mister David if they were wasting their time going inland to reach Zululand.

'No, master. There are a lot of villages. Master Green is right, they do not see many traders. Some of the tribes fight each other but you they will welcome.'

'And elephant?'

'The meat is much valued, master. You will be shown where to find them.'

Dallas was itching to get on the road. Logan and Will continued arguing. After a final check that everything had been securely tied down, Dallas swung onto Tosca's back and, with his horse prancing in nervous excitement as she sensed they were about to move off, shouted, 'Let's go.'

Mister David smiled widely, flicked his whip and the yoked team, as one, leaned into their harnesses. Straining against the weight they pulled, powerful muscles bunched with effort. Once rolling, all eighteen oxen settled to a leisurely pace as the spoked wheels turned freely on heavily greased axles.

Dallas brought Tosca alongside. 'Tell July to help with the cattle.'

Mister David translated and one of the Zulus dropped back.

As he rode, Dallas was aware of stares from passers-by. Most men showed envy, others admiration, while a few shook their heads in apparent disapproval, of what he had no idea. Women smiled and waved. Children ran alongside. No-one, it seemed, remained indifferent to the sight of a young man setting off into the wilderness to face whatever danger, hardship or excitement that might come his way. In Scotland Dallas had enjoyed life to the full, but never once had he felt so completely alive as he did now.

After five minutes a quick check behind

confirmed that both Will and Logan had their wagons rolling. Spare cattle, controlled by several men including July, brought up the rear.

Will saw Dallas looking back, raised his hat and waved it cheerily in acknowledgment. Obviously, the anticipation of adventure had him in fine fettle. Dallas was glad to see the excitement did not diminish with repetition.

He was too intoxicated by a cocktail of feelings to stay in one place for long. From point, Dallas turned Tosca and rode back at a full gallop, easing only when he reached the last wagon. 'You'll wear yourself out at that rate,' Will warned, though his own eyes were alive with enthusiasm.

'Does it always feel this good?' Dallas wanted to whoop with joy.

'Aye, at first. Short-lived it is too.'

Dallas didn't need to hear anything negative right at that moment and was quickly off again to rejoin Mister David. He had only felt such excitement once before – on his first train journey from Edinburgh to the unknown city of London when he was fourteen. Then, parents were on hand reminding him not to fidget, to sit up straight or adjust his cravat. Now no-one could tell him what to do. This was one expedition where he could do what he damned-well pleased.

The euphoria waned as they climbed clear of town. It didn't disappear completely and a sense of well-being remained as Dallas used those first few miles to check equipment, man and beast for signs of weakness. He was well pleased with his inspection.

At the rear, three Africans easily managed the twenty-two unharnessed oxen. In front of each spanned team, another Zulu walked ready to lend a hand in difficult terrain. The nine spare horses, tethered on short ropes to the wagons, had no option but to follow where they were led. They seemed perfectly happy with the arrangement. The loads were well packed, rattled little and barely shifted when the ground became uneven. Pots and gridirons lashed to the rear frame of each wagon swung wildly but did not impede progress. Also slung under the wagons were chicken coops.

'We eat a few and trade the rest,' Will explained.

'What do they eat?' Dallas asked.

'Whatever they find. We let them out once we've outspanned for the day.'

He sounded so matter of fact that Dallas didn't comment on how, in his experience, chickens didn't take kindly to being rounded up. He'd just have to wait and see.

An innovation all found extremely convenient was the addition of square canvas bags that hung along each side of the wagons and were packed with day-to-day essentials. This had been Will's suggestion. Each sling was secured snugly against the timber, allowing hardly any movement.

The wagons themselves were solid and strong. Dallas had expressed concern over their somewhat basic harnesses but, as Will reassuringly explained, accidents would happen regardless. What they had was the result of much trial and error by explorers and traders who had gone before. Once away from civilisation, irrespective of any modern equipment they started with, the sun and rain would take their toll. Running repairs relied on materials available in the bush. The length of trek chain which held everything together was the only part that would be difficult to replace. Will had taken a long time to choose theirs, examining each in minute detail and rejecting several he thought had weak links. Everything else could be improvised until they reached a town.

Yokes, fitted at intervals along the chain, were as thick as a curtain pole and about five feet in length. Saplings could easily be substituted for them. *Skeis*, wooden pegs slipped through holes at either end of every yolk, were used to fasten a *reim* under the neck of each beast. Replacements could easily be fashioned. The *reim* itself was made of raw hide, soft to touch yet dried to the strength of rope. They carried an extra four in case some broke before any game was shot for the cooking pot. Once they'd done that, a night-time task would be to make more *reims* from the animal skins.

Oxen were yoked together in pairs, the trek chain running between them joining to the *düssel-boom*, a stout pole in front of the wagon and behind the last two beasts. There were no reins with which to steer. In hard-to-negotiate conditions, an African would walk with the yoked oxen guiding them from in front, with a small *reim* attached to the trek chain for that very purpose. At all other times, the driver's shouting, whistling and liberal use of his whip seemed to be the way it was done.

For a young man fresh from Britain, inexperienced in trekking, out of his depth in unfamiliar territory, surrounded by dangerous animals and strange inhabitants – both black and white – Dallas felt he was pretty well prepared.

Under a sky dark with sultry storm clouds, the air was close and clammy as they turned onto the Old Dutch Road. Dallas could smell rain. Gulls wheeled and screeched overhead, a sign that the weather had turned bad out to sea. It certainly looked impressive, as if a massive grey wave was boiling its way inland.

They'd been travelling for perhaps an hour and a half when Will rode up alongside Dallas. 'Storm's coming in fast. Best we outspan for the night and get the oxen settled. We should turn off here.'

'Where?'

'See those trees? There's good feed and water.'

Dallas glanced at the sky. It had turned a threatening purplish black and the wind was getting stronger by the minute. 'Good idea.'

Will rode ahead, beckoning the three drivers to follow. They quickly formed a semicircle, sheltering on the open side of an overgrown tangle of wild figs. Even so, the wind picked up and pounced. The horses twitched and fidgeted nervously and oxen bunched together against the windbreak of trees.

'It's going to dump on us at any minute,' Logan predicted. He shouted something in Zulu and the Africans ran to stretch tarpaulins over the wagons, pegging each into the ground to prevent them blowing away. Everyone huddled under the canvas, waiting for nature to vent its fury.

Within minutes the heavens opened. Dallas had never seen a storm like it. The rain came as a solid wall of water whipped in all directions by a wind determined to shred their flimsy cover. Thunder rolled and crashed with barely a break. Low clouds, tumbling and boiling, almost touched the ground as they rolled past, thrown into relief by lightning that danced incessantly across the sky in crazy, skittering patterns of raw power. Trees, weighed down by rain, were flung back and forth, branches whipped to breaking point. Daylight turned to dark in a matter of minutes.

Sodden horses and cattle turned their backs to the wind and stood, eyes closed, streaming wet, muscles flinching involuntarily. The storm pounded them for a good twenty minutes before tapering off to a steady rain.

'Well,' Logan announced cheerfully, his voice louder than necessary in the returning calm, 'that's that for tonight. It'll stop soon and the boys can get a fire going.'

It did. Abruptly. The weather in Africa, like everything else, didn't hold back but there was a predictability about it. No pretence. When it rained, it poured. When it stopped, that was it. No coy little afterthoughts or days of dismal drizzle.

Emerging from cover, Dallas was surprised to see expressions of pure terror on the faces of the Africans as they peered out from shelter. He beckoned Mister David who, with obvious reluctance, crawled from protection and, glancing nervously around, joined Dallas. 'Tell the boys to start a fire. There's dry wood in Master Green's wagon, they can get it going with that.'

'I will tell them, master.'

Mister David sounded so doubtful that Dallas was quick to reprimand him. 'If they will not follow your instructions, you are of little use to me.'

'Please, master.' Mister David cast a fearful look towards the sky. 'We are not protected. We must wait.'

It suddenly dawned on Dallas that he might be blundering into an area of superstition or taboo. 'Get back under cover, Mister David. I will call you in a short while.'

His driver needed no second bidding.

Dallas sought explanation from Logan and Will. 'Could one of you please tell me why the Africans are so scared?'

Will shrugged. 'Bloody natives. Any excuse not to work. All their talk of heaven doctors is crazy.'

'No it's not,' Logan contradicted. 'It may be different from what we understand but there's a lot of commonsense in what they believe.'

'Sure,' Will sneered. 'Sap, bird fat and bark smeared on a wooden peg to ward off lightning. That's quite logical, I suppose.' He winked at Dallas. 'Or how about the fat and feathers of a lightning bird? If you're quick, you'll find one where lightning strikes the ground.'

'Don't make fun of what you fail to understand,' Logan warned. 'Anyway, you've got it wrong. The lightning bird is used to initiate a heaven doctor. It's not used by him.'

'How pleased I am to have asked the question,' Dallas cut in with heavy sarcasm. 'I've thoroughly enjoyed listening to the two of you bicker. Thank you.'

Will snorted. 'Load of mumbo jumbo, if you ask me.'

It was Logan who supplied an answer of sorts. 'Best I keep it simple, old chap. For the moment, it's enough for you to understand that the Zulus have a variety of medical and magic specialists. I don't know them all, but there are three main doctors in every village. One is basically a herbalist whose skills are handed down from father to son. By and large these doctors, or *inyanga* as they're called, are just like our apothecaries. In fact, I'd go so far as to say most are more knowledgeable.'

Logan scowled at Will, who was grinning. 'Laugh if you like. In a lot of cases their medicines are a damned sight more effective than ours.'

'You're welcome to them,' Will told him. 'I'll take my chances with something more civilised.'

Logan ignored Will's comment and went on. 'The most prestigious *inyanga* are known as *sangoma*. They have extensive knowledge of herbs and roots but are essentially diviners who have been, or so the Zulus believe, possessed by spirits. Their function is primarily to read omens and predict the future. The third kind of *inyanga* is a heaven doctor or heaven herd. He is said to be in sympathy with heaven and can protect animals, individuals or entire villages from severe storms. There are a whole lot of superstitions about thunder and lightning that are deeply entrenched in all Zulus. That's why our boys are scared. They had not been protected by a heaven herd.'

'Thank you,' Dallas said sincerely. 'Your explanation has saved me from making an embarrassing mistake. When can we reasonably expect them to emerge from under the wagons?'

Will scrambled from cover. 'They'll come out now if they know what's good for them.'

'No!' Logan's voice turned sharp. 'It would be best if we showed by example that it's quite safe.'

All three stood together on the sodden and steaming ground. The afternoon air had turned soft and cool. Crickets and tree frogs were in full voice. Black clouds rolled westwards. Above and behind them a late afternoon sun fanned shards of light into a clearing sky. Cattle and horses had spread out to graze hungrily. There was a pungent aroma of wet earth in the tranquil stillness. If the Zulus could be coaxed into starting a cooking fire, Dallas thought everything would be perfect.

The unexpected appearance of a man on horseback dispelled any feeling of well-being. 'Will Green! Get this mangy lot off my land or I'll set the dogs on you.'

Will offered a sick smile. 'Nice to see you again, Mr Carruthers.'

The irate owner's ferocious expression did not waver as he glared at Will. 'Go on. Clear off, the lot of you.'

Dallas approached the horse and rider.

The farmer shifted his ire to Dallas. 'And who are you?' He didn't wait for a response. 'How dare you people presume to use my land without permission.'

Will had a look of injured innocence on his face and was about to object. Dallas just knew that whatever he was about to say would not sit well with this man. Will gasped with pain as the heel of a boot made sharp contact with his ankle. Ignoring him, Dallas smiled up at the farmer. 'Dallas Granger, at your service, sir. Please accept my apologies for any presumption. I was given to understand that we were welcome to outspan here for the night?'

The swift kick had not gone unnoticed but Mr Carruthers confined his satisfaction to a grim smile. 'Then you are very much mistaken, Mr Granger, for I do not need the likes of Will Green anywhere near my land. Last time I allowed that scoundrel to camp here he scarpered without so much as a thank you.'

'In that case, I fully sympathise with your displeasure.'

Dallas's quiet voice and manner were getting through to the farmer. 'Why should I trust him again?'

'Sir, Mr Green is employed by me now. While I cannot vouch for his past debts I will most certainly pay whatever you ask for us to remain here.'

Disarmed, Mr Carruthers ummed and erred before grudgingly allowing them to stay on condition that Dallas settle in advance. 'Be gone by first light,' he warned as a parting shot. 'I'm not running a charity.' A finger pointed at Will. 'You still owe me a pound from last time.'

'I meant to pay, honest. It's just that we was in a hurry and didn't know how to find you.'

'That is an outright lie, Green. Do not heap insult on top of dishonesty.' The farmer scowled at Will. 'I was here well before sun-up. Such an explanation is unacceptable. You had no intention of honouring our arrangement.'

Will went to argue but Dallas interrupted. 'Pay him,' he ordered.

'But –'

'Pay him, by God, or I'll take it out of your hide.'

Grumbling, Will produced a dirty, torn note and reluctantly handed it over.

The farmer snatched it and examined Will's offering closely before folding the note and placing it in a pocket.

'Mr Carruthers,' Dallas addressed the now much placated owner. 'I do hope that this unfortunate incident has not soured you against future dealings between us. This meadow is most pleasant, for both man and beast.'

'Aye. It's here for the benefit of travellers. Those that pay, that is. I'm not a greedy man, understand, but neither do I give away good feed, water and shelter. It's been a pleasure doing business with you, young man. You are welcome to use this place in future. Good day to you, sir.' Without another glance at Will, Mr Carruthers rode off.

Dallas closed his eyes in frustrated anger. Where was the end of Will's duplicity? He was sick to death of ferreting for the truth in everything the man said. Openly allowing annoyance to show, he spoke coldly. 'I'm reasonably certain that you have, by now, concocted some kind of feeble excuse. I do not wish to hear it. You, however, will listen to what I have to say. As a man of honour, I do not take kindly to being tarnished by someone else's knavery. In fact, Will, I won't tolerate it. Do you understand what I'm saying?'

'I –'

'Is that clear?' Dallas thundered.

'Yes.' Will took on the look of a child caught raiding the pantry.

'Good. Please keep this warning at the forefront of your forgetful mind.' Dallas turned away. 'If indeed you have one,' he muttered to himself.

Damn the man! As he walked over to where a fire now flickered, Dallas had to admit that Will's little aberrations were not that different from his own past escapades. No malice intended, simply a recurring habit of offending others or things blowing up in his face. The only difference, so far as he could see, was that Will's conscience and his had taken different forks in the road. No, that was unfair. In his heart of hearts Dallas could see the difference between dodging a fee for the use of private land and . . . The memory of Lord de Iongh's shocked face came into focus. Was he seriously searching for a favourable comparison for himself?

A man of honour. His very words to Will. His mother had once said of a guest, 'The ghastly man speaks so endlessly of his own honour that, I swear, it makes me want to check the silver after he's gone.'

Troubled by his thoughts, Dallas went to where Will was examining the surcingle on his saddle.

Will looked up, wary yet open.

'Can we make a deal?'

Will nodded.

'No more surprises.'

Such an idea was obviously alien to the Yorkshireman. 'Well now, I never meant to mislead you. A man forgets.'

There was no guile that Dallas could see. 'You forgot you owed him money?'

Will shrugged and looked defiant. 'Course not. With the storm and that, I didn't think he'd see us. Where was the harm?'

'Dishonesty, Will, especially if you're on the receiving end, does not make a man your friend. We needed the safe haven. Your previous actions made us unwelcome. Can't you see the harm in that?'

'Wouldn't have been none if we'd got away with it. You'd have saved a pound.' Will looked aggrieved. 'And so would I.'

Dallas huffed a breath. 'Don't test me,' he said lamely.

Logan looked amused when Dallas returned to the fire. 'You're wasting your time, old chap. The man's a rogue.'

'We're all that, one way or another,' Dallas reflected flatly. 'The fact that Will isn't clever enough to hide his duplicity probably makes him less deceitful than those who can.'

Logan whistled. 'That's profound.'

Dallas smiled. 'Must be the open air.'

Will joined them. 'I was just thinking . . .'

Two pairs of eyes skewered him.

'What? What have I said?'

'Old boy, you have just stated the height of impossibility.'

'Well!' Will was affronted. 'If you don't want to hear it . . .'

'I can hardly wait,' Logan intoned with heavy sarcasm.

'Tomorrow night,' Will went on with dogged determination. 'I know this man . . .' He saw doubt on Dallas's face. 'I don't owe him money. Honest.'

EIGHT

Will had spoken the truth. He had, however, omitted to mention a small matter of the man's sister. As they hastily beat a retreat the next evening, Dallas was imagining all the painful things he'd like to do to his partner. 'Jeez! How was I to know she thought I'd marry her?' were very nearly the last words Will ever uttered.

'That's it,' Logan fumed once they were out of rifle range. 'From now on we outspan anywhere but where Will suggests.'

The route they travelled was much used by hunters and adventurers, hardy individuals in search of wealth or new horizons. Most would trek north-west to the highveld country but it was at Colenso, just over a hundred miles from Durban, where the Thukela seriously began its journey to the Indian Ocean, that Will recommended they turn off and work the two hundred meandering miles back to the river mouth. North of the Thukela lay traditional royal-house-ruled Zulu-land. While Zulus also lived to the south, in English-governed Natal Province, they were

266

regarded as exiles. Will's plan, at least in theory, was to find suitable river crossings and trade on both sides. It was Logan who, rather belatedly Dallas thought, pointed out that Thukela actually meant 'the startling one' because of its unpredictable habit of rising with no warning. Those they met along the way didn't add to Dallas's confidence level. They offered advice and information in abundance but their opinions varied wildly. It soon became obvious that, with very few exceptions, not many could quote first-hand experiences. Most, however, recommended a change of plans. It seemed that everyone knew someone who had ventured into the Thukela river system, never to be seen again.

Having objected to their intended route from the outset, Logan took each new story seriously and tried, time and again, to have them turn back. Will remained optimistic and would not be swayed. Dallas suspected that most tales told owed their substance to over-vivid imaginations. Seeking practical information from Mister David was a waste of time. His knowledge, or lack of it, also stemmed from hearsay, exacerbated by tales told by other drivers as they sat around the campfire. What Dallas found increasingly and worryingly obvious was that while Will's suggestion had merit and made practical sense from the point of view of trading, the Yorkshireman didn't actually have a clue about the country, the people or anything else they might encounter along the way.

Will's track record, to date, hadn't exactly been

exemplary. The closer they came to Colenso, the more Logan fretted. Will remained adamant and Dallas had no idea if they were doing the right thing or not.

Five days into the trip he spoke of his dilemma. Predictably, this set off an argument that, like most others on the same topic, seemed to go around in an endless circle.

Sick of it, Dallas cut into the bickering. 'For God's sake, both of you, shut up.'

He had their attention.

'We decide. Once and for all. Now! After that, no more dissent. Agreed?'

'Agreed.'

Dallas glared at Logan. He *looked* as if he agreed. He turned his eyes to Will. Was it too much to hope for? Will certainly didn't sound committed when he said, 'Sure.'

'You'd better be.' Dallas spat out each word clearly. He'd had enough of these two and made no attempt to hide it.

Will's eyes dropped. 'I am.'

Logan produced three coins. 'What about we flip?'

'Flip! This isn't a bloody game.'

Logan grinned. It wasn't a very nice one. More of a snarl, really. 'What is it, then? You tell me. I've never seen a more hit-and-miss enterprise than this. One common-as-muck little crook and a benighted, wet-behind-the-ears doob. Why not toss a coin? It makes as much sense as anything else on this ridiculous venture. Come on. You're both gambling men. Let's decide our fate with a little help from Lady Luck. I'm game.'

Dallas and Will exchanged glances. In the Yorkshireman's eyes was temptation. Logan was talking his language. Will's hand went out to accept a coin.

What the hell? Dallas thought, a strangely daredevil feeling inside him. He put out his own hand.

'Right.' Logan stood poised to flip. 'On the count of three. Two or three heads and we carry on. Tails we go back to the coast.'

'Just a minute.' Will wanted to examine each silver florin.

'Satisfied?' Logan asked heavily.

'I am now.'

'One, two, three.' The coins spun high into the air and were left to land on the ground. 'Heads!' Will yelled. 'Two are heads.'

In defeat, Logan was gracious. 'Very well. You'll hear no more from me. We go on. I'll have my money back, Will, if you don't mind.'

Will retrieved the coins from his pocket, shrugged, and handed them over with a sheepish smile.

So they went on. Logan was as good as his word, uttering not one complaint or caution. After a couple of days, however, Dallas came to realise that the man's face could be more expressive than any stated comment.

Their decision finally taken, Dallas turned his attention to learning more about his new home. While Logan's assessment that he was ignorant and inexperienced had hit home, he was damned if the man could accuse him of being uneducated. A doob, indeed! He'd show them.

He took to sitting on the wagon for a large proportion of each day, using the opportunity to quiz Mister David on matters of Zulu political and social history. It didn't take long for him to realise that while people like Will and Logan could readily quote facts, their assimilation of them fell woefully short of the mark.

Sitting around the fire at night, Dallas would hear dramatic tales of past kings and their deeds from his two white companions. The next day, Mister David filled in the details. Will and Logan gave him the shape and colour while the Zulu added contrast and reason.

'Is it wrong to speak of your king?' Dallas asked his driver, seeking to clarify a comment of Will's from the previous evening that to even look at a Zulu king the wrong way was courting death.

Mister David settled himself. A born storyteller, he enjoyed educating this white master. 'No, but to say his name is considered disrespectful. We call him "our father". This is so because he is the only one among us who can act for our ancestors.'

'I thought a *sangoma* could do that.'

'They speak to the ancestors and receive messages from them. Our father is like one of them only he is here with us.'

Dallas saw an immediate similarity between this man's position and the Pope. A representative on earth.

'He lives in a big kraal which we call *isigodlo*. All

his wives, children, many soldiers and servants live with him. It is forbidden to enter unless you are summoned.'

'What happens if you go there uninvited?'

'It is taken as a sign that you mean harm. You would be killed.'

'That sounds a bit harsh.'

Mister David nodded. 'To you, maybe. I do not know why you should find it so. We learn these things as small boys. Only the foolish or unfortunate invite death, unless you are one of our father's personal attendants. Then it would be an honour to die with him.'

'You mean when a king dies his servants are killed?'

'Of course.'

Egyptians had once done something similar. Dallas wondered if the custom could have come south in ancient times. There was little point in asking Mister David. It was clear that Zulus accepted tribal authority without question. They never challenged tradition, simply went along with it. He asked another question. 'If I met your current ruler, King Mpande, the man you call father, how should I behave? It would be easy for me to do something wrong.'

Mister David laughed. 'Our father understands that white people are not the same as us. He would treat you differently.'

'How?'

The driver thought for a while, then gave a comparison. 'If you were invited to eat with our father you would sit with him, talk, and be treated as if you, yourself, were a king. I must lie at his feet and accept food without touching it with my hands. An *inceku* would feed me.'

'*Inceku*?'

'One of the servants who helps prepare our father's food.'

'What else can't you do?'

'I may not be seen to sneeze, cough or spit while our father is eating, even if I am not in the *isigodlo*. Should our father send word that he wishes to see me, I must approach so that my head is below his. When I leave, I must do so on my knees, facing our father. No Zulu may laugh in the *isigodlo*.'

'Would that apply to me?'

Mister David shrugged. 'I think you would be forgiven for not understanding our customs.'

Dallas nodded slowly.

'The king is not so strict all the time. In periods of hardship people turn to our father for cattle and grain. These are given freely, for although very wealthy, he holds everything for his people not for himself.'

'Even so, it seems as though the king can order your death for just about anything.'

'That is right. A strong king makes his people strong too. Only the weak allows disrespect to go unpunished.'

Sometimes Will's and Logan's straightforward explanations were preferable to Mister David's more convoluted answers. The Zulu had a tendency to rattle off unfamiliar names of people and places which were near impossible to remember. Succession to Mpande's throne was one subject where Dallas definitely preferred a simple answer.

He'd noticed that one topic seemed to dominate whenever white men gathered and their conversation turned to Zulu matters. With Mpande's health failing, his son, Cetshwayo, was generally accepted as the rightful heir to his throne. Speculation on the ramifications of this event, both for Zulus themselves and white settlers, ranged from optimistic to dire predictions of war.

Cetshwayo was a man in his mid-forties who had long believed his destiny lay in becoming fourth king of the Zulus. To achieve this, he knew that a powerful ally would not go astray. Both Boers and the British coveted the fertile country known as Zululand. The Boers viewed Zulus as potential slaves, a bonus when they could settle the area. Britain, with similar aspirations, also needed naval supremacy in the Indian Ocean. This could only be secured if the interior, beyond Zululand's coastal strip, remained orderly and manageable. Cetshwayo, though unsophisticated and illiterate, understood that hostility between the Boers and British could be used to his own advantage. He was playing one against the other.

Depending on their political leanings, Europeans had varying opinions about Cetshwayo. Some argued that the fourth king would honour his father's ceding of land east of Blood River to the Transvaal Boers. Others predicted he wouldn't, foreshadowing conflict with the Zulus, possibly even a spillover to all-out confrontation between the Boers and British. Many more said that all Cetshwayo wanted was to rule his own people. Logan believed that the dictum laid down by Shaka, the founding father and first king of the Zulus, was still fully enforced – that the ultimate duty of Zulu men was to protect their nation – and that this would ensure trouble of some kind.

'Look, they're warlike enough as it is,' he was fond of saying. 'How would you feel if diversions like marriage were outlawed until you reached forty or were granted special dispensation from the king? In my view, enforced celibacy makes matters worse. Any man under forty who receives permission to marry has earned that privilege through blooding his spear in battle. They'll fight at the drop of a hat just so they can take a wife or two. Trouble is coming, you mark my words.'

All this was very interesting and Dallas wanted to know more. Asking Mister David brought the inevitable realisation that nothing was that easy, particularly if it were to do with the Zulus. Listening to the more simplistic understanding achieved by most Europeans was at least a way to establish an initial comprehension of the situation. Even then, Dallas battled with things that the old hands accepted as perfectly normal. The guts of the tale, as far as he could tell, was mayhem, murder, betrayal and greed – not all that different from European history, simply more direct in its savagery. And at every twist and turn in the story were accounts of Dutch or British treachery.

'There's only one common denominator,' Logan pronounced. 'Land.'

For a change, Will agreed. 'Aye. Same as anywhere.'

Logan elaborated. 'Shaka formed the Zulu nation to protect its clans from other tribes intent on taking territories traditionally held by them. A noble cause with practical reasons. No land, no food. Petty skirmishes had been going on for centuries. All Shaka did was unite related clans against a common enemy so making them stronger and virtually impossible to conquer. He had no quarrel with white men. The British were way down in the Cape. Dutch settlers remained within the Cape Colony under British protection. Shaka didn't see either as any kind of threat. Britain was kept busy defending the Cape against raiding tribes in the south. Shaka had his work cut out keeping Zululand free of traditional enemies from the north. Neither encroached on the other so Shaka was perfectly happy to ignore any strange white foreigners. Then the fun started. In 1824, two Englishmen landed near Durban and met with Shaka. They tricked him. The Zulu king thought he was signing a document giving permission for a trading settlement but in fact he had ceded outright title to Port Natal and 3500 square miles of surrounding land. It was immediately proclaimed British territory. A few settlers drifted in and by 1835 they had renamed the place Durban. Britain's Governor of the Cape Colony wasn't all that interested in extending his responsibilities into Natal and the new territory was initially left to fend for itself.'

'Did Shaka retaliate?' Dallas was trying to remember what, if anything, he'd been taught at school about those earlier days.

'No. Even though he'd been tricked, Shaka wasn't worried by a handful of settlers in a part of the country that was not strategically important. He never lived to see the consequences of his generosity. Four years later Shaka was murdered by his half-brother, Dingane. The new king remained amiably disposed towards the British, more interested in lording over his own people than anything else. Ruthless discipline and the endless warring of Shaka's day had taken their toll and Zulus welcomed the chance to rest and recover. Durban grew and Dingane seemed perfectly happy to allow it.' Logan shrugged. 'Nothing lasts forever.'

'So what happened?'

'Those who live by blood and violence need the protocol of tension or their warlike tendencies will find other outlets. The breakdown of discipline is what happened. Mischief, disregard for a king they did not respect, disobedience in the ranks set off reprisal. Dingane realised, too late, that his people needed to be ruled with an iron fist. To compensate, he overreacted, murdering anyone who disagreed with him, including all but one of his own brothers.'

'And since he's still alive, that would have to be Mpande?' Dallas ventured.

'Correct. Mpande was considered no threat for the simple reason that they believed him to be mentally feeble.' Logan paused to gather his thoughts.

Will leapt into the silence. 'Bloody Boers ruined it. Damned Dutchmen weren't satisfied living under the British. If it hadn't been for them –'

'Oh, do be quiet,' Logan snapped. 'You have no idea what you're talking about.'

Will shrugged, smiled and fell obediently silent.

'In a way, he's right,' Logan conceded. 'The Boers wanted to govern themselves so they started trekking north. Most made for the Orange Free State and the Transvaal but a small group, led by a man called Piet Retief, came over the Drakensberg Mountains and approached Dingane for permission to settle. Retief had about fifteen men with him. Dingane didn't think so few would present a problem.'

'But it was British territory,' Dallas commented.

'Not really. North of the Thukela wasn't. And that's what the trekkers wanted. You see, the Boers had started thinking of Zululand as the Promised Land. They were eager to farm there. At around the same time Dingane was starting to find fault with the British. He wanted guns so his *impi* could finish off their enemies once and for all. Britain remained adamant that no native force was to be armed. When Retief and his small band of men asked for land, Dingane agreed. He thought they might provide him with rifles. It didn't worry him that it was the same land he'd previously granted to a handful of Englishmen.' Logan broke off, smiling at Dallas's confusion. 'I know. At times the Zulus seem childlike in their simplistic manner of doing things. At others, they appear to go out of their way to complicate matters. Don't even try to liken it to our ways.

'You have to understand that Zulus have a different way of thinking. All land is owned by the king. He grants its use to others but if they don't work it, or he's fallen out with them for some reason, he'll let somebody else take over. It was like that with Retief. Dingane wanted proof of his friendship and good intentions. All the Boers had to do for land was retrieve cattle stolen by enemy raiders from further north and driven out of Zulu territory.'

'What happened?' Dallas asked, fascinated.

'Retief agreed and set off. Unfortunately, hundreds of impatient trekkers decided not to wait and without Dingane's permission, set themselves up inside Zululand. Although greatly offended, the king decided to wait for Retief to return. And here, my young friend, comes a classic example of misunderstanding.'

Dallas waited in silence for Logan to continue.

'The Boer trekkers had insulted a Zulu king. Not a good idea, I'm afraid. In good faith, he had granted certain land in return for a favour. Instead of a few whites gratefully accepting what was generously given by Dingane, he now had hundreds, with more arriving each day, taking anything they fancied. Understandably, the man felt betrayed and was furious.'

'And Retief?' Dallas prompted impatiently.

'He had no idea how much he'd offended Dingane. He found the cattle and drove them back into Zululand. Then, instead of simply returning them with no fuss, he took seventy-one men with him to the king's kraal. Retief believed that a show of force would impress. It had quite the opposite effect. The Boers broke every rule in the book. They brought the cattle back, then put on a military display for the king's benefit. Regrettably for Retief, the Zulus use fire and smoke in certain of their ceremonies. With Piet and his men charging around on their horses and firing at will into the air, gunpowder smoke lingered in the king's kraal. The cordite smell made Dingane suspect some kind of witchcraft. The Boers galloped right round the kraal, symbolically surrounding it. This was taken as aggression. Retief should have known better.'

'How was he supposed to know?'

'Thomas Halstead was with him as an interpreter, a man experienced in native affairs. He'd witnessed the results of European ignorance before and must have warned against such a display.'

'Retief sounds like a fairly arrogant individual.'

'Probably was. That wouldn't have worried Dingane. The king understood arrogance, even admired it. No, the real undoing of Retief was the way he refused to arm the Zulus. Dingane's request was a serious one and should have been taken that way. Instead, Retief laughed.'

'And you're not supposed to laugh in the *isigodlo*.'

Logan raised eyebrows. 'Correct. Though in this case he might have been forgiven if he hadn't tugged at his beard. The implication was not lost on Dingane. Retief was telling him that only a foolish child would arm the Zulus. Three days later, after lavish entertaining of Retief and his men with singing, dancing and feasting, the Boers were seized and taken to *kwaMatiwane*, the hill of execution.' Logan dragged a finger across his throat. 'No-one was spared.'

'What happened to the trekkers who had already moved into Zululand?'

'Eleven days after Retief and his men were executed, the Zulus struck each settlement. Only a handful survived. All up, about six hundred of the first Boer trek party into Zululand were killed – men, women and nearly two hundred children. More than half were white. A sad state of affairs and one that affected not only the Boers. The British administration was shocked that whites were targeted in such a way. I believe, as do many others, that revenge has yet to be extracted for what some still see as a terrible betrayal.'

'Didn't anybody strike back at the time?'

'Oh yes. The Boers sent three hundred and fifty men into Zululand. They lost eleven, including the joint commander of the force. The British joined in too, sending officers and eight hundred or so Zulu exiles, only half of which were armed. On Dingane's orders, they were ambushed by Mpande. Most were killed. After that, Dingane launched an attack against Durban itself. For a while, the place was a ghost town. Many European settlers scuttled back to the Cape.'

'When was this?'

'Thirty years ago.'

'So Dingane made enemies of both the Dutch and us?'

Logan smiled. 'Stop thinking like a white man.'

Dallas rolled his eyes. 'Forgive me for finding it difficult not to. I was under the impression I was one.'

'Dingane kept raiding Boer settlements that continued to establish in Zululand. At the same time he actively sought a resumption of friendly relations with the British. Not that he preferred us over them, mind, it was just that the Boers seemed more intrusive at the time. We, of course, jumped at the chance. London wanted dominance of South Africa while all poor old Dingane needed was an ally in his quest to keep Zululand free of white intrusion. There was a lot of rhetoric from White-hall, mainly mouthing off about protecting the Zulus from slavery, although somebody did decide to send out the 72nd Highlanders. Under this guise, Britain's real aim was to prevent Zululand being overrun by the Boers. They had no intention of committing men to battle on behalf of Dingane. A message was sent to Andries Pretorius, the leader of a Boer *kommando* unit intent on paying Dingane back for the betrayal of Retief and the trekkers. I believe the communication said something along the lines of desist and withdraw. As you can imagine, the Boers were hardly likely to be quaking in their boots. They pressed on and camped on the Ncome River.'

Will volunteered, 'It's now called Blood River.'

'Only by whites.' Logan frowned at the interruption. 'The Zulus had spies out. They knew Pretorius and his men were there.'

'How many did he have?'

'About four hundred and fifty all up. Most were farm boys who grew up with a rifle. They also had cannons. Dingane sent about ten thousand *impi* against them. Some were armed with weapons they'd taken from Retief but the Zulus believed that bullets would curve in flight like their *assegais*. They tried to compensate for this and missed everything fired at. The Ncome was too deep for the Zulus to cross. A wide chasm stopped them coming in from the south. They had only one approach – between the river and the ditch. It was open country but the Boers took their stand at the narrowest point. The Zulus attacked four times and on each occasion were mown down. It's estimated that three thousand warriors died at the Battle of Blood River. The Boers lost no-one.'

'What did Britain do?' Dallas asked, not sure he wanted to know.

Logan smiled sardonically. 'The jolly old Crown,' he said derisively. 'Let me put it this way. When Dingane asked for their help he was thinking of troops and guns. What he got from the garrison commander in Port Natal was laughable. The British sent a message to Pretorius regretting the slaughter and warning of displeasure should further aggression occur. They let Dingane down badly. After the loss of so many at Blood River, Zulus started to question their king's authority. Support for Dingane began to wane. And guess who was waiting in the wings?'

'Mpande.'

'Right. A sitting duck for the machinations of politics. He already had quite a following. The Boers were still worried by Dingane's diplomatic relations with the British so they set up their own with Mpande. There were several clashes between Dingane and Mpande, but the rot had set in. Dingane's followers began to decamp by the thousands. Eventually the old guard fled north and Mpande became third king of the Zulus.'

'And now he is dying.'

'After thirty years of mainly peaceful rule, yes.'

'And now?'

'Not so fast, old chap. Remember there were both Boer and British interest in Natal. It's important to understand what happened to secure it all as a British province.'

'Good point. What was it?'

'Simply this. Zulus who had fled in order to escape Shaka's and Dingane's tyranny began to come back. We played politics and encouraged them. The Dutch didn't like it, but wouldn't run the risk of war with Britain. After some protest that they were being overrun by savages, the settlers packed up and left.'

'And now the likely successor to Mpande is Cetshwayo?' Dallas nodded in understanding of his newfound facts.

'There's no choice really. He killed the only other contender.'

'Charming.'

'He's a Zulu.'

Logan's acceptance of what sounded like murder showed Dallas how much he still had to learn. But it would have to wait. Yawning, he crawled into his bedroll. 'How long did it take you to pick up and understand all that?'

Logan's face was unreadable in the dying firelight. 'A few years. You'll hear all kinds of versions. They can't all be true. Listen and learn. Make up your own mind.'

'I will. Goodnight.'

Dallas was asleep within seconds. Shadowy Zulu kings leapt through his dreams, pursued by dour-faced Boers and Englishmen with fake smiles.

Every day Dallas would take a portion of what he'd been told by Logan or Will and discuss it with Mister David. This way he was able to look at a picture without becoming lost in its colour. Having been told by Logan how Mpande didn't actually like his son, Cetshwayo, Mister David explained why. It was a complicated tale of love, loyalty and sibling jealousy. Dallas was glad he understood the basics before tackling more intricate detail.

When the driver finally fell silent, Dallas asked how he felt about white men explaining his people's history. Could their knowledge ever be as profound as that of a Zulu?

Mister David took so long in replying that Dallas was beginning to wonder if he would. Then, unexpectedly, he made a comment that seemed unrelated. 'Do you see that tree?'

'I see it.' Dallas wondered what the man was talking about.

'If you ask what it is, I can say it is a tree.'

'That's because it is one.'

'Or I can tell you about how we eat the fruit, why *inyanga* use its bark and leaves for medicines, what birds and animals seek it for shelter or food. From me you will learn what part of the tree is useful for building our houses and whether we burn its wood for cooking. I can say how long it takes to grow and how big it will be when it is very old.'

'Yes,' Dallas said slowly, beginning to see sense in what Mister David was getting at.

'Do you wish to learn these things or is it enough to know it is a tree?'

Dallas laughed. 'I see your point, Mister David. Remember I am new to this country. To hear first of fruit and leaves I may never learn from which tree they come.'

His driver chewed that over before nodding thoughtfully. 'I too can tell you it is nothing but a tree.'

Dallas wanted Mister David to understand why he preferred most of his information diluted by white ignorance. He strove to explain. 'Have you heard of Queen Victoria?'

'The great white queen. Yes, I have heard of him.'

Dallas let that go. Africans, he'd come to learn, often mixed their genders. 'What do you know about her?'

Mister David shrugged. 'He is very powerful. Our king praises him.'

'Can you tell me the name of her husband? How many children they had before he died? Who will be the next king? Where she lives? Who are her main advisers?'

'Why should I know these things?'

'No reason. I could tell you, though, because she is my queen.'

The Zulu laughed. 'My head would be too sore if you did that.'

'Exactly so, Mister David. As would mine if I tried to understand everything about the Zulus. Or your tree, if you like.'

The driver repeated, 'I can say it is a tree.'

'Yes, but you would think I already knew what it was. Let me put it this way. What if I told you that Victoria was a fine queen until she lost her beloved husband, Albert? The Prince of Wales causes her much concern?'

'Master?'

'Oh, come. Don't you understand? I know these things, why don't you?'

'Ah!'

'A Zulu might say that a great white queen lives across the big water in a place called London. He might even tell you that her husband is dead and a son worries her greatly. You would understand this?'

'Yes.'

'Then, with this knowledge, you could come to me and ask who are the husband and son and why is she worried? I would answer that her husband was Albert, who died ten years ago. The son is Edward who spends too many idle hours in pleasure and does not take seriously that, one day, he will be king.' Dallas smiled. 'That would answer the question and your head would not be sore because you already knew a little part of the story.'

The African smiled back. 'I hear you. To understand the end we must first know of the beginning. Without this we will forever look through the eyes of a child.'

'Yes, but a mother teaches her young in a manner she knows they will understand. Too much talk and the child will become confused.'

'There is much truth in what you say. Very well. The white man can tell you it is a tree. That is the beginning. When you ask me about that tree I will know your ears are open.'

Mister David nodded slightly and returned his attention to the oxen. Dallas was only just beginning to realise how wide a cultural gap existed between whites and blacks. Could any European come close to bridging it? From what he'd seen, there were Africans willing to help close it. Unfortunately they seemed to be the only ones braving the chasm.

They'd been on the road for just over a week when they reached the Howick Falls. It was midafternoon and threatening skies brooded away to the south. The waters of the Mngeni River were muddy brown as they swirled past to plunge three hundred and fifty feet into the gorge below.

'Been some rain in the Berg,' Will commented, referring to the Drakensberg Mountains which appeared on their left like a great purple wall of basalt rock.

Logan shielded his eyes as he searched the opposite bank. 'No flag,' he grunted. 'We should make it.'

Dallas eyed the ford with some concern.

'They fly a red flag if it's too dangerous,' Logan explained.

'It doesn't look very safe to me,' Dallas replied.

Will pointed to the other side where a white man had approached. He was carrying a piece of red material. 'Looks like the river's rising.'

The man saw them and waved their wagons over. With sign language he indicated that more rain had fallen and they should hurry.

'Come on, let's go,' Will urged. 'Any messing about and we could be stuck here for days.'

The three drivers did not question his wisdom. One at a time, whips cracking, they put their nervous oxen at the ford. Several beasts stumbled but being yoked, the others carried on, momentum allowing the fallen to regain their footing. The spare horses danced and shied with no option but to go along. One wagon, the last to cross, kept slightly further from the edge and tilted crazily as two wheels slipped off a rock shelf that formed the crossing. Only a few feet away, the rushing water disappeared into the abyss below. Ignoring risk to life and limb, half-a-dozen Africans were quickly to hand and disaster was averted. Loose cattle baulked, bellowed and hesitated before being encouraged from behind with sticks. One of Will's Zulus slipped and rolled twice before scrabbling fingers took hold and he was able to drag himself to safety.

'Let's go,' Logan shouted. 'Don't think about it.' He heeled his horse forward, a look of grim determination on his face.

'This is madness,' Dallas muttered, following without hesitation. Tosca plunged gamely into the flow, hooves slipping as she strived to stay upright. Instead of wading, his horse preferred to rear up and, with a thrust from both hind legs, surge forward. In this manner, they reached the other side. Will was right behind.

Logan and a group of onlookers, children mainly, were waiting for them. 'River's coming down tonight. We'll be the last to cross.'

The track sloped gently away from the falls to an open area with good grass and water. Knowing the animals would benefit from a rest, Dallas decided not to press on further. The horses and oxen needed no second bidding when Logan selected a suitable area to outspan for the night. Even if the river did flood, they were well clear of any danger. Two Zulus, armed with *assegais* and knobkerries, were posted as guards. Several others were busy setting up camp, washing clothes and preparing food for the night.

Will had shot a buffalo that morning. They'd salted and rolled the skin before loading it onto a wagon. Four Africans were busy cutting most of the flesh into strips to make biltong, a process which required the meat be rubbed with salt before soaking overnight in a mixture of spice and vinegar. Then it was strung to dry in the sun. Each wagon would be festooned with drying strips of meat until an outer crust formed and then, depending on personal preference as to how moist or dry one preferred biltong, eaten as snacks.

Mister David had been charged with the making of extra *reims*. Strips of animal skin had to be stretched, twisted, unravelled and then greased. It was not a complicated process but very time consuming, because it took several days of repeating it over and over before the skin had the strength yet softness needed to restrain the oxen's movement without rubbing. Most of the *reims* would be sold for about two shillings each when they reached a town.

As the afternoon shadows lengthened, and listening to the conversations in Zulu as the Africans worked, a feeling of contentment settled on Dallas. Exile might have been a harsh word but in reality, despite a few minor problems along the way, life wasn't all that bad. All being well, he would make money from this trip. His companions were experienced even if they did squabble like children. He had a driver who spoke English and was willing to talk about the lifestyle and culture of his people. It was all so different. The weather would be hell once they reached the Thukela Valley, but this part of the country was high enough to avoid the worst of the heat. Days were hot, not humid, with nights cool and crisp as fine champagne. The country, soft sometimes yet dramatic in its beauty, rising to a horizon of distant, weather-sculptured peaks.

Dallas hadn't expected such diversity. Africa, if he'd thought about it at all before coming here, was steamy jungles, wild rivers and savage animals. The area around Howick was not unlike parts of Scotland, if one discounted the cacophony of sounds that filled the air, especially at night. In a very short time, he had learned that most had a reassuring explanation.

Strange and once frightening noises were less threatening when they could be identified and understood. Dallas had heard lion roar at night, often quite close and terrifyingly savage. Already he could detect differences in the sound. Some, he had discovered, were inquiring grunts to the rest of a pride. Other sounds told of territorial disputes, sexual frustration or contentment, even just plain making a noise because they felt like it. The proximity of predators didn't necessarily mean danger. Dallas learned to watch and take his cue from the cattle. They either ignored the presence of lion or became extremely nervous. He also learned how to judge their distance from camp.

'Have a guess, double it and double it again,' Logan told him. 'Sound travels out here.'

Dallas put the theory to Mister David. 'I do not

understand how you measure distance,' his driver admitted. 'The *ngonyama* we heard last night would take as long to reach as a morning from sleep to the road.'

That tallied. They could break camp within thirty minutes. Dallas, using Logan's method, had already worked out that the lion must have been about four miles away. He was becoming familiar with myriad strange sounds heard in the darkness. The *nyaaa ya ya ya ya* howl and yip of jackal. A fiery nightjar's call that sounded like *good-Lord-deliver-us*. The warning *waa-hoo* bark of baboon or the hoarse, high-pitched scream of hyena at dusk. He could tell the difference between a common river frog – *krik-krik-krowww* – and the shy bubbling kassina – *quoip* – that sounded like a large bubble bursting. Dallas learned to recognise the docile yet deadly puff adder and aggressive, venom-spitting cobras. Despite the nightmarish look of some, he soon relaxed at the unexpected appearance of spiders. Only one could kill a man and that was the female black button spider, seldom found outside of the Cape Colony. With knowledge grew acceptance. Each day became a classroom with Will, Logan and Mister David acting as his teachers.

The major worry was conflict between Will's driver and Logan's skinner. They kept their distance from each other and never exchanged a word, but with gestures and body language, the animosity was clear to all. Twice, Will had to speak sharply to his driver, who listened, nodded polite acceptance then went straight back to deliberate, yet silent, provocation. Of the two Africans, the Sotho skinner seemed best able to keep his feelings under control.

This did not reassure Logan. 'I know him well. He can't keep this up. He'll strike. When he does, no-one will see it coming.'

Dallas knew there was little he could do to prevent trouble. Logan and Will acted as though it was inevitable and, in the main, appeared unconcerned. He'd have to take his lead from them.

His musings were interrupted by a sharp outburst from Logan. 'What's that bloody fool up to?'

Dallas, so busy with his thoughts, had neither seen nor heard two approaching wagons. The lead team was being urged on by a white man. Next to him sat two women. The wagon behind was driven by an African. Neither showed any sign of slowing down.

'Wait,' Logan shouted, scrambling up from a position next to the fire and waving his arms. 'There's a red flag flying.'

The driver of the first wagon had no option but to stop. 'I can see that.' He was probably in his early fifties, well dressed and spoken. 'We must get across today.'

Logan shook his head. 'Our wagons came over more than an hour ago and it was difficult enough then. The river has risen nearly a foot since. You have women with you. Don't be a fool, man.'

The wagoneer's expression set stubbornly. 'I'd advise you to keep a civil tongue in your head, sir.'

Next to him, a woman of similar age kept both

eyes averted. A girl on the other side of her, around seventeen years old, with pale blonde ringlets and an impatient look in her wide blue eyes, leaned over and clasped the man's arm. 'Come, Papa. Do not delay.'

'Beggin' your pardon, miss.' Will stood suddenly, whipping his hat off as he spoke. Frizzy strands of dark red hair straggled around his face. 'Mr Logan here is right. It's far too dangerous.'

The girl tossed her head but the man jumped down from his driver's seat. 'Jack Walsh.' A hand extended in greeting.

'Logan Burton.'

Walsh nodded. 'I've heard of you.'

Logan introduced Dallas.

'Delighted.' Walsh's handshake was firm.

Then Will.

The newcomer inclined his head but did not offer his hand. The snub was not lost on Will who glared sourly back.

'If your boys could help we can still make it.'

'What's the rush?' Will challenged. 'It's not worth the risk.'

Another girl, similar in age to the first, poked her head from behind the second wagon. Deep russet ringlets framed her heart-shaped face. 'It doesn't look safe, Uncle Jack. Perhaps we should wait.'

'Don't be stupid, Sarah,' snapped the other girl. 'I *must* get to Pietermaritzburg.'

'There, there, calm yourself, Caroline,' the middle-aged woman soothed.

Caroline shook off her mother's hand.

Jack Walsh smiled. 'My daughter is getting married there, gentlemen, hence our determination to cross.'

'It looks dangerous,' wailed the girl called Sarah. 'Please, Caroline, can't we wait?'

The flagman had put in an appearance and overheard. 'There have been big rains in the Berg. The river could be up for days.'

'Please, Papa.' Caroline sounded tearful. 'The wedding is on Saturday. There's still so much to do.'

The girl's concern left Logan unmoved. 'If you don't mind my saying so, young lady, better to delay your wedding than be swept over the falls.' Logan smiled as he spoke.

His charm and words of advice were to no avail. Caroline ignored both. 'Send Thulani ahead. Then we can see how deep the water is.'

Jack Walsh smiled indulgently. 'Such is the impatience of youth. My daughter is determined.' He called to an African and spoke to him in Zulu.

The man eyed the river fearfully.

'Go, Thulani,' Caroline insisted. 'You will be quite safe.'

Dallas could see the Zulu was terrified and he spoke without thinking. 'Your servant seems to have more sense than you, Miss Caroline. To cross now would be foolish in the extreme.'

'Oh for heaven's sake,' Caroline snapped. 'Don't any of you understand?' She leaned over and snatched up the whip. Before anyone could stop her she flicked it expertly, urging the team towards the swollen river.

Jack Walsh jumped onto the rolling wagon. 'You and Thulani stay here,' he yelled back to Sarah. 'I'll call you over if it's safe.'

Will scratched his head. 'Bet ya a florin they come to grief.'

With no guiding hand to reassure the team, wagon and all were more than likely to do just that. Reaching the rock ledge directly above the falls, Walsh's oxen stopped dead in their tracks. Without waiting to think, Dallas ran towards the river and straight into the raging water.

'Come back, you bloody idiot,' Logan yelled.

But Dallas didn't hesitate, forcing his way forward until he reached the lead beast and grabbing the *reim*. Hanging on grimly as the team tossed their heads in terror, he pulled with all his might, encouraging them to cross. To his intense relief, first Mister David, then July and Tobacco appeared. Slapping, whistling and tugging, they got the team moving again. The surging water came up to the men's hips, its force so great that it was difficult to stay upright. Once rolling, the oxen were as keen to leave the river as were the men helping them. They surged towards the far bank and hauled the wagon clear. Flanks heaving, eighteen exhausted animals stood trembling on dry land.

Jack Walsh looked grim and angry but made no comment to his daughter. 'Thank you,' he said to Dallas. 'We were afloat for a moment there.'

With every passing minute, the river rose higher. 'I saw her starting to swing,' Dallas replied. 'The other wagon won't make it.'

Walsh was well aware of the fact and nodded unhappily. 'Then, Mr Granger, I have little option but to entrust you with the safe return of my niece to her parents in Colenso.'

With that, Dallas turned to recross the raging river. 'On my honour, sir, I will see that no harm comes to her.'

Walsh's parting words, 'Much obliged,' floated to him as he pushed back into the water.

The drag had increased alarmingly, even at the edges, but there was nowhere else to cross. Locking wrists, Dallas and the three Zulus stepped cautiously into deeper water. The roar was deafening. Spray billowed from the bottom of the falls like fine rain. Chocolate-brown water swirled around Dallas's waist. He felt his boots sliding on the smooth, water-polished rock. They weren't going to make it. Inch by painful inch, the distance became less. Each relied on the others. When one slipped, it was imperative that his companions had firm footholds. Glancing up, Dallas saw Will and Logan standing knee deep, about twenty feet away. Logan was swinging a rope which he hurled upriver, allowing it to snake towards them in the torrent. Dallas lunged, his fingers missing the lifeline as it was swept past.

Again his feet slipped. This time he went under. Next to him, Mister David also lost his footing. Faces contorted with effort, the other two men hauled them back to their feet. They were right in the middle of the ford, the deepest part. Dallas saw Logan swing the rope again. This time it flew high, uncoiling towards them. With his free hand Dallas grabbed and held on.

'Master!'

July, his features slack with fear, was losing the grip he had on Mister David. Dallas managed to feed the rope behind all four of them. Tobacco grabbed the end and passed it back on their upriver side. Fingers fumbling with cold and wet, Dallas was able to secure a slip knot. Bound together like sticks of firewood, and pulled ashore by willing hands, they were finally free of the flooding river.

And just in time. Turning to look back, Dallas saw an uprooted tree swirl past before disappearing over the falls.

Shivering slightly, with water still running in rivulets down his body, Dallas went to where Sarah and her driver, Thulani, waited, apprehension clear in both of them. 'You cannot possibly get over,' he told them, fingers brushing wet hair off his face.

They looked considerably relieved.

'Caroline is a madcap,' Sarah ventured. 'She won't listen to anyone.'

'Your uncle has charged me with returning you home. It is on our way and would be my pleasure. We will spend the night here and move off in the morning. If the river has gone down and your uncle is still on the other side, we can assist your crossing. Will that be acceptable?'

'Thank you. I should be sorry to miss my cousin's wedding but if I must then your protection would be most welcome.'

Dallas inclined his head. 'You will no doubt be

hungry. We have plenty of food and you are welcome to join us. Your driver may eat with our men.'

'You are most kind.' She held out a hand and Dallas helped her down from the wagon. In doing so, he couldn't avoid taking a deeper breath to enjoy the scent of flowers that seemed to surround her. On the ground, she faced him. 'Your name, sir?'

'Dallas Granger. Come and meet the others.'

'From where do you hail, Mr Granger?'

'Scotland.'

'Oh. I travelled there once.'

'Were you born here?'

'Yes. My parents came out twenty years ago. They're from Sussex.' She ducked her head and giggled. 'Forgive me. I am Sarah Wilcox.'

They reached the fire where Logan and Will were trying to get dry. Dallas made the introductions and explained that they would be escorting Miss Wilcox back to her parents in Colenso. Sarah curtsied to each, much to Will's obvious delight, and apologised for her impetuous cousin. 'I'm sure Caroline didn't realise that it would be so dangerous,' she concluded.

Logan was magnanimous. 'No harm done.'

Will was less so. 'The young lady needs a boot –'

'Will!' both Logan and Dallas chorused.

'So she may not sit down for a week,' Sarah Wilcox murmured demurely. 'Have no fear, Mr Green. My uncle will undoubtedly take care of that.'

Dallas bent his head to hide a smile.

Sarah Wilcox, in spite of her tender years, turned out to be a charming companion. In the company of three strange men, at least one of whom had manners bordering on troglodytic, she affected no airs and graces. When it was time for her to turn in she calmly said, 'I would appreciate it if none of you ventured past my wagon for the next ten minutes so that I may make preparation for sleep.'

'What a charming young lady,' Logan pronounced quietly after Sarah had left them.

'She's all right,' Will conceded. 'Just our luck to be landed with taking her home.'

'We're going to Colenso anyway,' Dallas reminded him. 'It's not out of our way. And I could hardly refuse to help.'

'Well, it's still a nuisance,' Will grumbled.

Logan winked at Dallas. 'He's upset because he'll have to mind his manners for the next few days.'

'I can mind my manners with anyone,' Will said angrily. 'Don't need no women on a trek.'

'It's not her fault,' Dallas put in mildly. 'Leave it alone, Will. She's with us whether you like it or not.'

'That'll be right. I saw you gawping at her. You and your fancy ways.' Will mimicked Dallas. 'Try a piece of this, Miss Wilcox, it's particularly tender. Are you sure you're comfortable, Miss Wilcox? Warm enough, Miss Wilcox? Miss Wilcox this, Miss Wilcox that. Why don't you say what's on your mind? How's about a –'

'Will!' Logan and Dallas hissed at him.

He edged a stray log into the fire with his boot before saying grumpily, 'I prefer my women honest, that's all.'

Dallas ignored the comment. Will sounded more jealous than put out. Although Sarah Wilcox had accorded him the same pleasantries as Logan and Dallas, their conversation had left Will behind. Perhaps it was that. Whatever, the Yorkshireman seemed thoroughly out of sorts.

It took five days to reach Colenso and deliver Sarah to her parents. She travelled in her own wagon with Thulani, joined the others for refreshments, and made no fuss whenever a delay was caused by swollen streams or running repairs. One morning she calmly dealt with the appearance of a snake from under her wagon by stepping out of its way and watching it leave. 'It's harmless,' she told Dallas. 'See the black spots down its spine? They call them garden snakes because they eat snails and slugs. No point in killing it.'

Even Will was thawing.

Dallas liked Sarah. She was pretty, in a doll-like way, plump and nicely rounded, nipped in at the waist with hips and breasts emphasised. Having an eye for the female form, Dallas felt that given a few years she would earn the description 'full-bodied'. He enjoyed their conversations, finding her down-to-earth mannerisms and way of speaking refreshing. He liked her wide smile, dancing dark eyes and the way her brows arched over them. She was, in fact, perfect farmer's wife material. She was not, however, Lorna. Dallas had no interest whatsoever in pursuing a romantic attachment. Jette had been different – a mature woman who wanted the same as him, no strings attached. Sarah would be looking for a husband. She'd have to cast her aspirations somewhere else.

Sarah, perhaps because she felt he'd saved her aunt, uncle and cousin from certain disaster, seemed to develop a crush on Dallas. She said nothing directly but it was there in her smile, the tilt of her head and a look in her eyes. Thinly disguised hints became quite frequent. 'Oh, I do hope you'll call on us whenever you are passing, Mr Granger. My parents would make you most welcome.' Or, 'You should look to buying land near Colenso, Mr Granger. The pasture is particularly fine there.'

Logan teased him unmercifully. 'Better keep an eye on the *Natal Mercury*, old chap, or we'll miss the banns being published.'

Will was more pragmatic. 'Keep your hands to yourself with that one, Dallas. One little touch and she'll have you down the aisle so fast you'll wonder how you got there.'

To all of this Dallas would smile and shake his head. His heart was in another place. Sarah was in no danger from him.

Sarah's father, a rather round figure of a man with brusque manners and a habit of glaring from beneath beetle brows, seemed less than grateful for the safe return of his daughter and regarded the trio of men with a good deal of suspicion. He quickly cut short Dallas's explanation. 'Get inside, missy. I'll speak to you later.'

Dallas stopped mid-sentence, more than a little surprised by his accusing tone.

'You have placed my daughter in a most untenable position, sir. When news of this circulates, her reputation will be in tatters.'

'I assure you, sir –'

'Your assurances are useless. Why didn't you take her across the river?'

'Her uncle –'

'Pah! The fool.' Mr Wilcox glowered. 'My wife's brother allows that uppity daughter of his to lead him around by the nose.'

Logan intervened. 'Would you prefer if Sarah had been swept over the falls? The river was rising fast. Mr Granger risked his life for your brother-in-law.'

The man's eyes bulged. 'Don't take that tone with me, sir. My daughter would be in Pietermaritzburg if you hadn't interfered. That's where she's supposed to be.'

Dallas had heard enough of his rudeness. He raised his hat. 'We'll bid you good day, sir.'

'Not so fast, young man. What do you intend to do about the situation?'

'I beg your pardon?'

'My daughter. No decent man will look at her now. You have ruined her good name.'

'Don't be ridiculous, sir. We have delivered Sarah safely home as requested. Any impropriety is within your own thoughts. Good day.' Dallas turned to Mister David. 'Get this team rolling,' he muttered.

The last they saw of Mr Wilcox he was standing outside his house waving a fist at them. 'You'll hear more of this, by God you will.'

Logan rode up alongside. 'What a lovely man.' He grinned. 'Just what you need for a father-in-law.'

'Why me? Why not you, or Will?'

'Do be sensible, dear boy. I'm too old and Will's too . . . Well, let's just say that of the three of us you presented the best credentials.'

'If anything's an impediment to the poor girl's suitability for marriage it's her father,' Dallas said darkly.

'You could do a lot worse.'

'Coming from you, that's almost blasphemy.'

Logan laughed. 'Put it behind you, lad. That's the last you'll see of the Wilcox family.'

NINE

Having escaped the odious Mr Wilcox they drove their wagons into the town of Colenso for a final topping up of supplies. Very little was known about the Thukela Valley but one fact was abundantly clear, even to Dallas. For the next few months, until they reached the river mouth, anything overlooked now would be something they'd have to go without.

Colenso wasn't much to look at. It had evolved in order to supply inland-bound travellers who, from this point, either headed north towards the Transvaal or west to the Orange Free State. A few businesses, a couple of dozen houses and an hotel made up the town. The stores were every bit as well stocked as Cato's in Durban and, if one had run out of an item, its owner seemed only too happy to suggest an alternative source of supply. Dallas sold their excess *reims* and received two and sixpence apiece.

The British Hotel, run by a courtly gentleman called Captain Dickinson, was the town's meeting place. Tales and advice were swapped, dusty throats soothed by fine ale and stomachs satisfied by plain but good fare. Captain Dickinson did a roaring trade, particularly during the wet summer months. West of the town, depending on rainfall in the Drakensberg, the bridgeless Thukela River could hold up travellers for many days until a crossing could safely be made.

Purchases finalised, wagons outspanned and watched over by the African staff, it was time for a little relaxation. They made their way to the hotel, where men of like mind always gathered. They were a diverse lot, from all parts of the world, who shared but one thing – a love of adventure. Logan and Will knew many of them and were soon caught up in conversation. By now, Dallas had learned enough about the Zulus and Natal to join in some of the discussions. Nevertheless, he still felt very much an outsider. Several times he had the distinct impression that most there regarded him with something akin to amusement. Standing close by was a young man of similar age to himself.

'It takes several years for them to accept you,' the fellow traveller told Dallas. 'They expect you to fail, you see. Until you've proved yourself there's no point in getting to know you.'

Dallas turned and held out his hand. 'Dallas Granger.'

His gesture was firmly reciprocated. 'Stephen Holgate.'

'And how do you prove yourself?'

'Stay alive.' Holgate shrugged and smiled. 'Simple, really.'

'If many of the stories I've heard are to be believed, that's not a foregone conclusion.'

'Pah!' Holgate dismissed the dangers with a wave of his hand. 'Don't listen to rumour. Half the things they say are to put off competition.'

'How long have you been trading?'

'About four years. I hear you're planning to follow the Thukela through to the Indian Ocean.'

Spontaneous mirth was the response of most within earshot.

'Are you insane?'

'Got a death wish, old chap?'

'Old Johnny Derby went down there last year. Hasn't been seen since.'

Stephen Holgate eyed Dallas with a degree of speculation. 'I've thought of doing that trip myself, once or twice in fact. Could never find someone willing to come with me. There's a bit of superstition among the natives about going there, has been since Shaka's days. Anything connected to he who created the Zulu nation is regarded as sacred.'

'Our boys have said nothing.'

'Times are changing. Zulus who work regularly with whites know if they wish to continue doing so they have to drop a lot of the mumbo jumbo. Doesn't mean they don't believe it. What puts most traders off the Thukela route is a real possibility that the Kaffirs will suddenly remember their superstitions once they're into the valley. You don't want that happening, believe me. If your boys slink off one night and leave you to it that's real trouble.'

'What is it that could worry our Africans, yet doesn't bother those who live there?'

Holgate hesitated, twisting his handlebar moustache thoughtfully before answering. 'Old rivalries. They may all be Zulu now, but in Shaka's day, they certainly weren't. Those who came south were regarded as cowards. The stories became embellished over the years and it's hard to know where truth ends and legend begins. You see, at the turn of this century there was a major drought. It caused conflict among tribes who had previously lived in harmony. Some fled to the Thukela Valley but they found a harsh life compared to further north. A few turned to banditry but most fought for territory. It's rumoured that there are great mounds of human remains all over the place.' Holgate stopped, frowning in concentration. 'Have you heard of Zulu praise poems?'

Dallas nodded. 'They seem to have many.'

'Indeed. Praises are sung through every stage of a boy's transition to manhood. Once grown up, he can only win praise by brave deeds. The more praise poems a warrior has, the more he is admired. As you can imagine, the king has hundreds, which, in a way, are a record of his deeds. The upheavals that saw tribes fleeing towards the Thukela are attributed to Shaka's crushing of his rivals. If I can remember it, his praise poem to celebrate what was, at the time, regarded as a victory, went something like this:

The newly planted crops they left still short,
The seed they left among the maize-stalks,

The old women were left in the abandoned sites,
The old men were left along the tracks,
The roots of the trees looked up at the sky.

Holgate smiled mirthlessly. 'Stirring stuff which only adds to a northern Zulu's belief that his southern cousin is a coward. But it's more complicated than that. You probably know how important ancestors are to the Zulu?'

Again Dallas nodded.

'The whole Thukela basin is believed to be crawling with lost ancestors. Enemy ancestors, not a friendly lot. Get the idea?'

'So how do we deal with it?'

'It won't be easy and really depends on how civilised your Kaffirs are. Stay firm, but at the same time, you must be seen as understanding. You're in good company. Will Green is one of the best traders around and Logan Burton has earned respect as an elephant hunter. The Kaffirs listen to them. I assume they know where you're heading?'

'Yes.'

'Then you'll probably be all right. Don't let them weaken your resolve, but if they appear genuinely frightened, listen to what they're saying then act accordingly.'

Dallas looked reflective. 'There's more to Africa than I ever imagined.'

Holgate grinned at him. 'If you can say that, you're halfway to belonging. Some people never stand confidently on this continent. They remain confused, unwilling to learn and accept the complexities.'

'Anything else I should know about the Thukela?'

Stephen Holgate didn't hesitate. 'Listen to what local natives tell you. They know the way. You can't just follow the river. It's too steep and rocky.'

Another man had overheard and joined their conversation. 'He's right. Those who live there know the place intimately. You must heed any advice but . . .' The stranger spread his hands and shrugged. 'Trouble is, the locals can't always be trusted. If they're friendly with the next village you'll get reliable information on how best to reach it. If not, God help you. They'll do anything to stop trade goods reaching a rival clan even if it means your dying in the process. It's risky, young man. Have you got a Zulu who you trust?'

Dallas nodded. 'Several.'

'Then let them advise as well. They'll know when you're being lied to.'

'Are we likely to encounter many hostile natives?'

'They're all hostile. I wouldn't want my life in any of their hands. But they do like to trade. You'll be fine as long as you have what they want.'

The talk went on in that vein for some time. Logan joined them and quickly adopted an 'I-told-you-so' look on his face. That is, until someone mentioned elephants.

'I'm telling you, man, the place is crawling with them.'

Logan brightened considerably at the news.

Dallas could have listened to these men all

night, but like most who are up with the sun and put in a demanding day's work of at least twelve hours and very often much more, by seven-thirty the majority had drifted off to find their bedrolls. A few hardy souls stayed on, Will among them, but by nine o'clock the volume of alcohol consumed meant that conversations had become repetitive and rambling. Dallas and Logan left Will to it.

In the morning, had Dallas been receptive to omens, he would have been reassured by the weather. It was perfect. A cloudless blue sky, hot sun teasing out the pleasant sweaty odour of oxen and horses, and a light breeze. All augured well for their journey. The scenery was a different matter. In the distance, running east to west, the Drakensberg Mountains reared skyward, a silhouette, rendered featureless in the dusty air, misty and mysterious. Almost lost against this ghostly bulk, closer hills seemed insignificant, their contours blurred by shimmering heat. Nearer town, stretching to infin-ity where the mountains didn't block its path, the Colenso plain bared its flat, stony countenance making Dallas wonder what on earth caused Sarah to claim that this was good farming country.

Logan rode up beside him. 'Bit boring,' he com-mented, staring out. 'Thank God we're not staying here. Whenever I pass through this place it reminds me of a crossroads to better things. Whichever way you go from here, the scenery only improves.'

They reached the Thukela around midday. Its waters flowed swift and brown but signs were that the river level was dropping. For once, Logan and

Will were in agreement. For now, they should stick to the Thukela's southern bank. The river's name, as Dallas already knew, meant 'the startling one' – a reference to sudden floods which could sweep, with no warning, through the valley. At such times, crossings were virtually impossible. Since they planned to trade mainly with the unexploited southern tribes, it made sense to start on their side of the river. Admittedly, Will's agreement with that might have been tempered by the fact that he was decidedly ill.

The man had barely spoken all morning. Unusually for him, he'd chosen to ride on the wagon rather than his horse. Once settled beside the driver, he pulled down a battered hat for shade, folded his arms and slumped everything – head, shoulders and spine. Dallas could have sworn that even his ears drooped. Snores and groans of protest whenever the steel-rimmed wheels hit uneven ground were the only indication that Will was actually alive.

'Here we go,' he croaked as they turned off the road. 'One of them fellows yesterday was telling me there's a big village about ten mile from here. Good place to start.' The effort cost Will dearly and he winced with pain. Having contributed that one burst of enthusiasm, he subsided, yet again, into the misery of his hangover.

Mister David confirmed the location. 'I have never visited this place but the village Master Green mentions is known to me. I have a brother living there.'

Dallas hitched Tosca to the side of the wagon and jumped up next to Mister David. 'You seem to call many people your brother. In my culture, only the children of my own parents are called brother or sister.'

'Hau!' Mister David seemed surprised. Then he smiled. 'To understand the tree, you must go to its seed.'

'The father?' Dallas guessed out loud.

'*Baba*,' Mister David confirmed. 'We call this father, the man who planted his seed inside our mother, *baba*. But he is not the only father we have. All his brothers and sisters are also our father. We respect these fathers as much as *baba*. Sometimes even more.'

'Why?'

'If such a person is older than our *baba*, he must be shown greater respect.'

'What if he is an older sister?' Dallas asked, understanding for the first time that Mister David did not necessarily mix up his pronouns.

Mister David wagged his head ambiguously. 'Not so much.'

'These fathers,' Dallas ventured, feeling his way. 'Must they be from the same mother?'

'No. Only from the father of *baba*. It is possible to have a father younger than yourself if he was born of a young wife to the grandfather.'

'Does this also apply to your mother?'

'Yes. A birth mother is called *umame*. Her sisters and brothers are also our mother.'

'Doesn't this get confusing?'

'We have different names that tell us who is who.'

'Tell me a few. The important ones. What do you call your father's older brother?'

'*Ubaba omkhulu.* If he is younger, he is called *ubaba omncane.* If he is a sister, *ubabekazi.* A sister of *umame* is *umamekazi.* Her brother is *malume.* All the children of our father's brothers and our mother's sisters are our own brothers and sisters. But the children of a sister of our father or the brother of our mother are called *umzala.*'

Dallas had to guess that this word had the same meaning as cousin. When he put the question to Mister David, the Zulu looked blank and shrugged.

'Do you know the word *isibongo*?' he asked by way of a response.

'No.'

'I will try to explain. It is a praise name that all those coming from the same ancestor use. So if I meet a man who gives his praise name and it is the same *isibongo* as mine, then he is a brother.'

'Even if you've never heard of him?'

'Of course. It would be a great insult for me not to treat him as such.'

'How is the brother in this village we go to your brother?'

'He has the same *isibongo.* Otherwise, I do not know.'

'How come you know about him?'

'My mother told me.'

'Which mother?'

314

Mister David laughed. '*Umamekazi*.'

'Your birth mother's sister?'

'Yes. You are learning.'

Dallas shook his head. 'Slowly, Mister David. It is not easy.'

The normally expressionless eyes of his driver glanced at him. There was a look of approval in them. 'You at least try to understand. That is very good.'

The village, which Mister David referred to as Chief Ngetho's, came into sight a little before four-thirty. By then, Dallas had been told what to expect and how to behave.

'You will see that what Master Green calls a village has many different kraals. We call them *umuzi*. Because some *umuzi* are close together, white people make the mistake of thinking they are all part of the same village. This is not so. When *umuzi* are close we are of the same tribe, this is true. But each has a chief.'

'How many people would there be in one *umuzi*?'

'Some are big. Others not so big. The chief, his wives and children. His younger brothers and their wives –'

'When you say brothers, do you mean all brothers or only those from his *umame* and *baba*?' Dallas interrupted.

'All brothers. There is no difference with us.'

'So a kraal or *umuzi* can be very large indeed.'

'Some sons also stay. Even non-related people

can place themselves under a chief's protection. If the *umuzi* is very big then its chief will be an important man.' At a questioning glance from Dallas, Mister David explained. 'He must be very rich to afford many wives and take care of so many people.'

'The *umuzi* we go to now, how many people will live there?'

Mister David shrugged. 'I am not knowing but it will be too very big. Chief Ngetho is an important man.'

Dallas had heard his driver use the words 'too very' on more than one occasion when he was trying to indicate that something was on a large scale. For some reason, most Africans resorted to these words, always in a surprised tone, rather than use a more appropriate word that gave an accurate indication of size, importance or numbers. So he knew that by saying the *umuzi* was 'too very' big was not a criticism, rather a description. A small point of understanding but every bit as significant in the learning process as tribal matters. 'Will they make us welcome?'

'Yes.'

'Because of your brother with the same *isibongo*?'

'That is so. When that is learned we will be invited to enter.'

Dallas was concerned with making a good impression. He had no wish, through ignorance, to insult anyone. 'Tell me the things to remember so that I show good manners.'

'You must expect the same. That is important.

You will be offered refreshment. It should come from the *inkosikazi* or you have been insulted.'

'Who is this *inkosikazi*?'

'The great wife of a chief.'

'Great wife?'

'A chief has many wives but only one can bear him a son who will become chief when he dies. She is the great wife, selected after much consultation with others because it is her duty to look after the ancestors.'

'How do I know which one is the great wife?'

'Her house will be the largest in the kraal. You will also see that it is at the back of the *umuzi*, exactly opposite the entrance.'

Dallas was coming to realise how much discipline and order existed in a society that, to an outsider, appeared to lack any kind of structure or formality.

'If you are invited into a dwelling you must sit here.' Mister David waved his right hand. 'This is the side for a man. Women and children will be on the other. Do not go to the back, opposite the entrance, for it is here that a place is kept for the spirits. It is called *umsamo* and no-one is allowed to sit there. Never linger in the doorway, go immediately inside.'

'Why is that?'

'When a house is built we bury medicine there to protect against evil and also lightning. It is bad manners to stand on that place.'

Dallas nodded. 'Go on.'

'A mat will be provided. Do not sit on the bare

floor. And you must sit like this.' Mister David demonstrated, drawing his knees up. 'When you eat always wait until the chief has started. It is bad manners to place your fingers over the rim of a pot containing food. If you are offered beer, hold the bowl with your right hand and its saucer with the other. Never stand to drink and always remove your hat. To show you like the beer, rub your stomach or make a loud wind noise.'

Dallas was still digesting this information when Mister David continued. 'Remember to walk behind the chief. If you pass other men be sure to show them your strong side.'

'My strong side?'

Mister David indicated his right arm. 'It is with this hand that you hold any weapons. Present it empty to another man and he knows you pass in friendship.'

Good grief! Dallas thought. Ignorance won't just insult these people, it could get one killed.

Mister David saw his look of confusion and smiled. 'Do not worry. People will know you are a stranger to our ways. If you are seen to be trying they will forgive any mistakes.'

It was as his driver said. Had it not been for Mister David's explanation that each circular stockade was an *umuzi* in its own right, self-contained, self-supporting and entirely different from the next, Dallas would have mistaken the distant kraals as belonging to one village. Chief Ngetho's *umuzi* was quite large, housing some forty or more huts.

By the time their wagons rumbled to a stop, a large number of curious onlookers had gathered at the entrance to watch their approach. Excited murmurings came from the assembled crowd. Children peeped shyly from behind their mothers, dogs barked hysterically, chickens and pigs scratched on unconcerned, rummaging for sustenance. The scene was primitive, but to Dallas, whose rudimentary knowledge of these people allowed him to look deeper, it was tranquil and not in the least threatening.

The children were naked, save for a string of beads many wore around their waist. They looked plump and well nourished, bright-eyed and happy. Dallas noticed several girls, no more than six or seven years old, with babies strapped to their backs. Mister David had explained that one of the tasks performed by young girls was to babysit for their mothers. The ease with which they appeared to carry out this duty said much for their sense of responsibility.

Teenagers covered their genitals – the boys with leather strips, girls using grass or bead aprons. The girls, bare-breasted, showed no embarrassment, or indeed boastfulness, over that which to them was a natural bodily feature. Some older women wore a complete covering of cowhide and cloth, while others displayed a colourful strip of material across their breasts. Mister David's explanation enabled Dallas to know that fully covered women were married, bare-breasted girls remained single and those with a short skirt and breast-wrap had been promised to a man. Dallas could see now why the beads they carried with them were an important trading item. As well as their skirts, all the women decorated themselves with necklaces and headbands.

Older men, though less colourful than the women, were nonetheless resplendent in animal skins and feathers. Modestly covered front and back by strips of leather or an apron of monkey tails, most displayed armbands and leggings of teased ox tail. Many wore a headband to which they had affixed the feathers of a male ostrich or cockerel.

Some of the men and a large number of women bore evidence of scarification on their cheeks and upper arms. Two or three rows of no more than six small round scars to each. Dallas knew that the initial cuts were self-inflicted with a knife, then covered with cow dung before a burning cinder was placed on top to penetrate the manure and scorch underlying flesh. There was no cultural significance to this form of decoration and not everyone indulged in it.

Watching the ever-growing group who silently scrutinised the new arrivals, Dallas wondered what he'd have made of them without the education he was receiving from his driver. He would have considered them uncivilised, most certainly. But even with no understanding of these people he could not have failed to see a dignity and pride in their bearing. They had a culture probably older than his and far less concerned with meaningless convention.

Theirs was a tough life in which ways had evolved to accommodate circumstances. Doffing a hat in greeting as a mark of respect back home seemed such an empty gesture compared to revealing your strong side as a demonstration of friendship.

Mister David jumped down from the wagon and made his way towards the entrance. Those crowding around it parted to let him to pass. Squatting to one side, just outside the kraal, he spoke in Zulu. Logan, who had reined in next to Dallas, quietly told him what was happening.

'He's told them his praise name and requested that we be granted an audience with the chief.'

'What happens now?'

'We wait.'

Out of the corner of one eye, Dallas saw Will come awake, stretch, yawn and open his mouth to speak. Immediately the driver clamped a hand on Will's arm and shook his head in silent warning. Will looked around, saw where they were, took in the silent crowd, then sat back and said nothing.

Logan, who had also been watching, nodded slightly in approval.

An older man, more decoratively attired than most, made his way through the entrance to where Mister David waited.

'Ah!' Logan breathed quietly. 'A member of the council is here.'

'Council?'

'An elder. Not as important as the chief but one who advises him.'

'How can you tell?'

'Younger Zulus wear less decoration. It gets in the way of their activities. Once a man gains full maturity, he is not expected to work as hard physically. His main duties are as a member of council. He can wear his clothing longer. See how the skins around his legs touch the ground.'

Dallas was still admiring the man's attire when Mister David beckoned. 'Show's about to start,' Logan muttered. 'Don't, whatever you do, sit on the left inside a hut.'

'Women's side.'

Logan glanced at him. 'Good. Keep learning.'

Mister David did not accompany them to see the chief. Dallas caught a glimpse of his driver walking hand-in-hand with another young man, presumably his 'brother'. They were clearly delighted to meet each other and their conversation rang loud and clear so that all around knew this was a meeting of kinsmen and, as such, the newcomer should be treated with every respect.

Chief Ngetho was waiting for them. After the build-up, Dallas found himself somewhat disappointed. He had expected strength, maybe even a streak of cruelty. The wrinkled old man with a pot-belly and bowed legs came as a bit of a surprise. His eyes, however, were shrewd and alert as he sized up the strangers. '*Sanibona*,' he said eventually.

'*Yebo, baba*,' Logan replied.

Will remained silent so Dallas also said nothing.

A lengthy conversation followed between Logan and the chief. Without understanding what was being said, Dallas could see that Logan initiated none of it. Chief Ngetho asked a question, Logan responded then fell silent waiting for the next. Dallas's newfound knowledge also explained why the chief spoke only to Logan and why Logan behaved as if he were the leader of their expedition. He was the oldest of the three white men. Will obviously understood that too, for although he could follow the conversation, he made no attempt to join in. Finally, Logan turned to Dallas. 'We are invited to drink beer. The chief suggests we sit outside in the shade where his council will join us. A social occasion in honour of our visit.'

With no obvious sign from anyone, a woman appeared bearing a large clay pot. She knelt in front of Chief Ngetho, holding out the vessel for his approval. When he nodded, she began to skim froth off the top and onto the ground. 'Offering to the spirits,' Will muttered in an undertone.

After stirring the beer the woman poured some into a small gourd from which she drank before refilling it for the chief. When he had sampled the brew, a larger container was filled to the brim and handed to the chief who took a long drink before passing it on. Dallas noticed that Logan, as the African had done, held the gourd in his right hand and the saucer in his left, just under his chin. Will, on the other hand, displaying a surprising lack of formality, grasped the gourd with both hands and ignored the saucer which Logan had placed on the ground in front of him. Dallas noticed the chief's disapproval. When it was his turn, he copied Logan.

The 'beer' was like nothing he'd ever tasted. It

was reddish in colour and cloudy in appearance with a raw, freshly brewed smell. Dallas sipped and was pleasantly surprised by the taste. 'Ummm!'

Everyone laughed and Logan leaned towards the chief, saying something to him. The man responded. Logan nodded and translated. 'Chief Ngetho says you are a man who, in white man's culture has enough years to wear the *isiCoco* and therefore you are old enough to drink *utshwala*. Your appreciation amuses him.'

Utshwala was obviously beer. The *isiCoco* would have to wait.

Dallas passed the beer on and, by the time the gourd reached him a second time, it was nearly empty. He looked at it dismayed. Would it be bad manners to finish it? Logan spoke briefly to Chief Ngetho before coming to the rescue. 'Drink what's in there then hand it to the *inkosikazi* with the opening pointing upwards.'

Dallas nodded, remembering that *inkosikazi* was the great wife. He drained the gourd and did as Logan instructed. It was refilled and handed back to him. He wondered how to indicate that he'd had enough but worried about insulting their host. The gourd had been refilled three times and Dallas was beginning to feel he would burst when the chief finally passed it empty to the *inkosikazi* with the opening pointing down. The beer drink was over.

Expressing appreciation came easily to everyone. The fermented corn did its stuff and all belched with gusto.

Dallas was surprised that he didn't feel more intoxicated. If he'd had as much ale back home, especially in such a short space of time, he'd be well and truly inebriated by now. All he felt was mildly relaxed. He listened and observed as Logan and Chief Ngetho began the process of trade. It took several hours and night had fallen by the time they'd finished.

'We are invited to eat with the chief tonight,' Logan told Dallas as they made their way to the wagons. 'Several sleeping huts are at our disposal. This has gone very well. Some of the younger men will come with us tomorrow to show us where to find elephants. To repay the chief for his kindness, they will keep the meat. It's an early start tomorrow.'

Dallas had no idea what exactly they had traded and what, if anything, would be given in return. Logan was the obvious one to ask, but once at the wagons, he busied himself with preparations for the following morning's hunting. Realising that Will would have followed the bartering process, Dallas decided to ask him. Before he did, however, he queried how the normally vociferous Yorkshire-man had managed to remain silent throughout the negotiations.

Will looked slightly put out by the question. 'I know when to hold my tongue,' he responded with a touch of asperity. 'You'll get nowhere with the natives if you don't follow their rules.'

'Then why did you guzzle the beer like that?'

'I was thirsty.'

'The chief didn't like it.'

'Bugger the chief.' Will looked defiant. 'It doesn't hurt to demonstrate that you know the rules but nor does it do any harm to show you're not necessarily going to follow them. You'll learn soon enough that if you give a Kaffir an inch, he'll want a bloody yard.'

Dallas was inclined to disagree, but since Will was supposed to be such a good trader, said nothing. 'So you were happy with Logan's bargaining?'

'It was all right,' came the grudging reply.

'Would you have interrupted if he seemed to be giving too much away?'

'Not then.' Will looked briefly angry. 'But he'd know about it by now, let me tell you.'

'Then what have we traded?'

'For every four green or yellow beads, we will be given a chicken.'

'A chicken! For four cheap glass beads! That's outrageous.'

Will chuckled, his sense of humour restored. 'Only the high-born can wear yellow and green. It's believed they grow on trees in a magic place. Others tell you they're from the sea. Those little beauties are worth far more to a Zulu than gold or ivory.'

'But I've seen many of the people here wearing yellow and green around their neck.'

'Not as decoration. Only in love letters, where each colour has a special significance.'

'Such as?'

'That you'll have to ask David. I don't know. By

the way, when you are counting out beads tomorrow, remember that they prefer the smallest.'

'Have we traded the other colours?'

'All of them. But by weight. Depending on colour, we'll get a bull or a cow for one or two pounds of beads.'

No wonder traders can become rich! Dallas could not believe that coloured glass could have such a value. He said as much to Will.

'In the old days,' his partner explained, 'Kaffirs wore woven and dyed grass, strings of snail shells, horns, even animal gall bladders stuffed with fat. Those who could afford it also used copper and brass. To get the colours they wanted meant mixing dyes. It was a lengthy process and most would fade in the sun or run when wet. That's why glass beads became so popular and they're prepared to pay handsomely for them.'

'Doesn't it bother you? These beads are ten a penny.'

'Value,' Will said portentously, 'is in the eye of the buyer.'

The meal that night was filling but not especially enjoyable. It consisted of a mealie meal porridge and several unfamiliar vegetables in a green liquid. Using hands, squeezing the dough-like substance into a ball then scooping up some of the rest and popping it into one's mouth, was the acceptable way to eat. The main course was followed by different varieties of wild berries. Immediately after they had eaten, the chief excused himself.

Once he had gone, Logan and Will looked knowingly at each other.

'What is it?' Dallas asked.

'No meat,' Will said.

'Perhaps they have none.'

'Oh, they have, and plenty of it. We are not important enough to justify killing a beast. No matter, the trading went well.'

'Bed,' Logan said. 'Most of the village is already asleep. This way.'

'How do you know where we're supposed to sleep?' Dallas hadn't seen anyone show Logan their accommodation.

'Visitors are always allocated huts to the right of a kraal's entrance, next to where the younger men sleep.'

He might have known. The Zulu sense of order again.

Zulu huts, the like of which Dallas had only seen from the outside, had a cosy yet rustic interior. Comfort proved to be an entirely different matter. A structural backbone was formed by bent saplings, lashed to three central poles supporting the roof. The sides and roof were of thatched grass with no windows and an arched doorway so small that they had to crawl through it on hands and knees. Inside, the floor was made from a mixture of soil from ter-mite mounds, mixed with clay then beaten flat and hard with stones. It had been covered with cow manure and polished to a smooth glass-like finish. Round sleeping mats were rolled and fastened to the wall with cowhide. Wooden headrests, a kind of bench design, stood on the ground under each of them. Otherwise, save for a cooking fire, the hut was empty.

Dallas went to move the three-stone hearth that was situated centrally in a space between the hut's supporting posts. With three grown men sleeping on the floor he felt the fireplace would be in the way.

'Don't touch that.' Will and Logan's sharply spoken words, for once in unison, stayed his intention.

'Why? We'll need all the space we can get.'

Logan shrugged. 'The Zulus are superstitious about one of those rocks. I can never remember which, so best to leave them all where they are.'

Will supplied the answer. 'It's this one.' He indicated the stone behind the pillar, closest to the entrance. 'It's called *umLindiziko*. They always leave it, no-one dares touch it.'

'Any reason?' Dallas asked.

'There are always reasons,' Logan replied. 'Some long forgotten, leaving nothing but superstition. I suspect this is one such example because I've yet to find someone who can explain it properly. Trust what we say, though. Move that stone and God help you.'

Following his companions' example, Dallas took a sleeping mat from the wall and rolled it out. He eyed the headrest. Two blocks of wood with a narrow, yet solid, suspension bridge between them. 'Can they really sleep on that?'

'Apparently.' Logan removed his shirt, rolled it up and put it under his head. 'I tried once. Woke up with a neck so damned stiff I suffered for days.'

Dallas also used his shirt. The floor was hard but not much different from the ground. Curled comfortably on his mat, he decided that the pleasant smell of thatch which offered protection from the elements was as good a sleeping chamber as any. How wrong he was! Since the hut was reserved for guests, its cooking fire was rarely used. The lack of smoke, essential to rid the thatched roof of its less welcome inhabitants, meant that they shared the place with all manner of bugs.

Several hours later, as he slapped away yet another unidentified creepy-crawly, Dallas asked anybody who would listen, 'Do you think it would be rude if we gave up on Zulu hospitality and slept out in our own bedrolls?'

'Very,' came back Logan's sleepy reply. 'Just try not to lie on your back and snore. Anything could end up in your mouth.'

In a hut close by, Mister David and the three others in there with him were having no such qualms. Sonorous sounds filled the night. 'They might at least make that racket in unison,' Dallas grumbled, having long since given up trying to sleep on the rock-hard floor. Both hips ached and his back cried out for what now seemed like a spongy bed in the open veld. Mosquitoes attacked incessantly and something had taken more than a passing interest in one finger which now itched, burned and, on inspection in the pitch dark, felt twice its normal size. Eventually he slept, if you could call it that – more an uneasy truce called between a tired body and suspicious mind. Dallas tossed, scratched and swiped his way through the rest of the night.

The next morning he was bleary eyed and out of sorts. It was of little comfort to discover that whatever munched on his finger had left no long-term ill effects. On leaving the hut, Dallas's eyes adjusted to the light and he became aware that the inhabitants of Chief Ngetho's kraal had been up and about for some time. The ground was swept clean of leaves, calabashes stood full to the brim with water collected from the river, and women were leaving for the fields with hoes. A group of men sat under a shady tree, talking. Logan and Will were already at the wagons supervising the unloading of trade goods.

'Sleep well?' Logan asked teasingly.

'No.' It was an answer as short as his temper.

Logan nudged Will. 'Do you think the young master got off the wrong side of the floor?'

'Very funny,' Dallas said sourly. 'Where's Mister David?'

'Here, master.' His driver's head appeared round the corner of a wagon.

'What is an *isiCoco*?' No messing around and keep it simple, his tone implied.

'It is the headring worn by married men,' Mister David told him.

'Thank you.'

Chief Ngetho arrived as they finished unloading. He inspected the wares, prodding, nodding and grunting as he went. Umbrellas and blankets were highly prized, but by far the most sought-after items were beads. The deal confirmed, two bulls, six cows, three goats and a dozen chickens joined the expedition, along with an assortment of skins and several elephant tusks.

By midmorning, and with a group of young men ready to go with them, the wagons were rolling. Dallas twisted in his saddle and looked back at the village, his first experience of traditional African life. The *umuzi*, yesterday afternoon a collection of conical huts surrounded by a fence of closely packed branches, was much more than that now. He had learned so much and yet, he knew the process had only just begun. Despite the lack of sleep his spirits had risen and he found himself mentally comparing the Zulus and their ways with all that had been familiar a few short months ago. The man he might have become had once been predictable. Now, nothing could be anticipated, barring one inescapable fact. If he made old bones, his creaky brain would hold memories that most men couldn't even dream of. Surely, in the stepladder of life, the experiences he was having now had him standing several rungs higher than others his own age? The thought brightened what so far had proved to be a somewhat dismal day.

The crowds of smiling, waving children who had chased after the wagons eventually turned back, skipping and giggling, the diversion of a trading party overtaken by chores awaiting each and every one of them. Young as they were, all understood that the fine line between full and empty bellies meant shared responsibility – a lesson taught by example – so ingrained that none ever considered challenging the logic of it.

Even as he had these thoughts, Dallas was aware that with continued exposure to European ways, time-honoured traditions would eventually become diluted. He couldn't decide whether that would be a good or a bad thing.

A small brown puppy, thin and undernourished, kept coming even when the children had turned back. Unsteady on its feet, sometimes moving more sideways than forward, the obviously sick animal seemed determined to follow. No-one called it back and the puppy stumbled after their wagons as if on an invisible leash. Dallas watched in sympathy. Each step was obviously an effort. 'Go home,' he shouted, waving an arm.

The animal stopped, blinked, then came on.

'Clear off.' Dallas tried again.

Will, carrying his rifle, rode up beside him. 'This should do it,' he muttered, raising the weapon.

'Don't be stupid,' Dallas snapped. 'You can't just shoot someone else's animal.'

Will looked surprised. 'Why not? The Zulus only use dogs as leopard bait.'

'I don't care. Don't shoot it.'

'Fine.' Will looked disappointed. 'You deal with it.' With that he rode off towards the leading wagon.

Great! The puppy abruptly sat down, its dark eyes locking onto Dallas, a plea in the animal's expression.

You don't want a dog. Don't look in its eyes. Sucker! It's only a dumb animal.

'Ralph!' The high-pitched yip was wavering and uncertain but the pup obviously enjoyed the sound enough to try a repeat performance.

'Ralph, ralph.'

'Friend of yours?' Logan had ridden up to see what was going on.

'Did you hear that? It said "ralph".'

'Ralph!' The animal obliged once more.

They watched while the puppy, with some difficulty, rose and came closer.

'Could have rabies,' Logan said. 'It's certainly not a happy chappy.'

'It looks starving.'

Mister David called to Dallas. 'It is a present to you from my brother.'

'Gosh, thanks,' Dallas muttered.

'Are you going to keep it?' Logan asked, watching the runt with some distaste. 'It'll be covered with fleas, probably have all kinds of skin disease. It's a Kaffir dog. Inbred to buggery and not a brain in its head.'

'Do I have a choice?' Dallas cursed himself for a soft touch. 'I can't refuse the gift,' he added, in a voice that didn't convince even himself.

The puppy finally made it to where Logan and Dallas sat on their horses. Tosca skittered nervously at its proximity. No more than eight weeks old, the animal stared up at Dallas, one ear cocked, the other floppy, head tilted to one side.

'Ralph,' Dallas spoke to the animal. 'Very well, Ralph. Let's see if we can make anything of you.' He dismounted and gently picked up the dog. It was little more than skin and bone. Fleas scurried in all directions. The puppy wriggled and tried to lick his face. As canines went, Ralph had to be the most unsavoury and pathetic specimen Dallas had ever seen. Naturally, that organ which pumped blood as its prime function and occasionally admitted feelings for others, missed a beat, did the latter and embraced one trembling and thoroughly disgusting bag of flea-covered bones, no questions asked. 'Mister David, do we have any of that corn porridge made up?'

'Yes, master.'

Dallas carefully handed the puppy to his driver. 'Give him some.'

'Ralph,' Logan said, laughing. 'You're not seriously going to call him that, are you?'

'Why not? It's his name. Ask him.'

Logan rode away, shaking his head.

Dallas joined Mister David on the wagon. 'You drive. I'll feed Ralph.'

The puppy inhaled porridge with such gusto that Dallas could only assume that the poor little thing had had to fight for every morsel of food ever to pass its lips. Sustenance was followed by some serious paw-licking and five minutes at least of vigorous flea-stirring before Ralph curled himself into a ball, winked one eye at Dallas, then fell asleep on the seat between his new owner and Mister David.

Something in the way the Zulu kept glancing down at Ralph alerted Dallas to the fact that his reaction to such a present was unusual. 'Why did your brother give me a gift?'

Mister David answered warily. 'To help with the hunting.'

Dallas stared at his driver, who shrugged and added, 'Perhaps not.' After more silent eye contact, the Zulu miserably owned up. 'He did not give you this dog.'

'Who did?'

'No-one.'

'No-one! You mean I've stolen someone's animal?'

'No.'

Realisation dawned. 'They are pleased I took it?'

'The village has many dogs.'

'So to return it would not be rude but thoughtless?'

Mister David nodded.

Dallas took a deep breath. 'Very well. I will keep it. But you have to understand that white men treat their dogs with love and respect.'

'I have seen this happen.'

'And I expect you to do the same.'

Unhappy but cornered, Mister David again nodded.

Changing the subject, Dallas used the opportunity to learn more about the significance of Zulu beadwork. Relieved, his driver was only too happy to oblige.

'Each colour has a meaning. Together they are used to tell a story.' He fingered a small square of beads around his neck. 'I will test you with this.'

'Is that a love letter?'

Mister David looked shy suddenly. 'Yes,' he said simply.

Dallas wasn't sure if he should push for more details or not. His driver laughed. 'Read this and you will know the secrets of my heart.'

Dallas smiled and waited.

'To understand you must know that a girl may not give a love letter until she is allowed to have a sweetheart. For today I will only tell you that it takes a long time for this to happen. A young man may not declare his feelings for a girl until after the *buthwa*. So your head does not become too very sore, we will start with the tree.'

'Good idea.'

Mister David touched his love letter. 'We call this *inCwadi*. Each colour has a name and a meaning. White is called *iThambo* which, in our language, means bones. It also stands for love and honesty. Black is *isiTimane*, a darkness or shadow which prevents us being together. The red bead, *umGazi*, is blood but can tell us that the eyes are red from weeping or looking in vain for the one you love. Yellow are called *iNcombo*, our word for young corn. It stands for riches. To a Zulu this means many cattle.'

'Is that why only the high-born usually wear it?'

'Yes. They are the holders of our wealth.'

'And green?'

Mister David looked uncertain. 'Our word is *oBuluhlaza,* meaning new grass. Alone, it is a symbol of good times for our cattle. I do not know why but when we put green in love letters it means we are feeling lonely or our hearts are full of jealousy.'

Amazing! Dallas thought. The green-eyed monster certainly gets around. How is it that this colour means the same thing in his culture and mine? It must come from one primary source – but what, where? To Mister David all he said was, 'You have a lot of blue in your love letter.'

'That is for *iJuba*, the dove. A sign of faithfulness and loyalty.'

'And the pink?'

'Ah! That one is very bad. It tells of poverty. Her father cannot meet the bride price.'

'What is the word?'

'We call them *ubuMpofu*, poor ones.'

'We've also brought brown and striped beads, though I see none in your love letter. What do they mean?'

'Brown is *umLilwana*, a low fire that does not burn brightly. It is our word for disappointment. The other is like the striped grasshopper and tells of doubt. We call it *iNtotoviyane*.'

Dallas scrutinised Mister David's love letter. 'How do I read it?'

'Start at the outside. The pattern leads to the centre.'

Feeling a bit like he was reading someone's private mail, Dallas did as he was told. 'White. She loves you. Blue, she is faithful. White, she loves you. Green, she is jealous.' He broke off. 'Why is she jealous?'

'It is hard to explain. Her feelings are as if she is jealous. She feels sick because we are not together.'

Dallas continued his reading. White featured prominently, as did black, blue and red. The girl's message was repeated over and over, ending with a solid block of white beads.

Mister David beamed approval. 'Tomorrow I will show you another love letter and you will tell me the story using Zulu words for each colour.'

Dallas reached behind for his diary. 'Then you'd better tell me again so I can learn them.' He wrote the words phonetically. When he showed them to his driver and asked if they were properly spelt, Mister David shrugged. 'I do not know.'

'But you went to school.'

'Yes, where I only learned to spell in English.' Mister David hesitated, then asked, 'Please do not be angry but, as you want to learn about the Zulu, I too wish to know more about the white man.'

'That is good. I will try to help. Did Master Leslie teach you anything?'

'He was a very busy man,' Mister David said in defence of his previous employer. 'Sometimes he spoke of a home but in his words I am thinking there was much sorrow.'

'Was there anything to stop him going back?' Dallas wondered if, like himself, David Leslie was also in exile.

The Zulu shook his head. 'No. One time Master Leslie go back and I not see him for two full seasons. Then he was happy to return here.'

'So what do you think made him sad?'

Mister David shrugged. 'I think his heart lied. It whispered of home but all he found was strangers living in houses with no shadows.'

Dallas tried some lateral thinking. Shadow and darkness were represented by black beads, in the language of love letters, a colour that told of sadness. Strangers in a house with no shadows might mean the absence, or even distortion, of distant memories. He decided to try his deduction. 'Master Leslie's heart remembered how it used to be yet his eyes told him how much it has changed?'

'That is part of it. And with time to think, he found that he too had changed.'

Strangers in houses with no shadows. How perfectly logical. Dallas nodded his understanding, then asked, 'What do you wish to know of my people?'

Mister David looked uncertain. 'We can speak of anything?'

'Anything you like.'

'And you will remember the tree?'

Dallas smiled. 'Of course.'

'Tell me then why it is that you wear so many clothes?'

Glancing at the Zulu in surprise, for he was dressed European style in shorts and a singlet, Dallas then took in his own attire. Boots, socks, long trousers, long-sleeved shirt, braces and a waistcoat. He thought of so many different ways he could answer the question. Convention, modesty, fashion, none of it made much sense out here. Practicality might work. 'In England it is very cold.'

'But here it is not so cold.'

The Zulu way of looking at life – the sheer commonsense of everything they did – was, Dallas knew, going to make a nonsense of any answer he could give. Still, he had to regard the question as seriously as his driver treated those asked by him. 'You are right. But it is our custom.'

Mister David threw him a quizzical look.

Dallas had a brainwave. 'When you eat you sit differently from a woman. Why?'

'Hau! A woman cannot sit with her knees drawn up. It is immodest.'

'Why don't you sit with your legs on one side like a woman?'

'Others would point and laugh. It is not our way.' He broke off. 'Ah! I understand.'

'That is the tree,' Dallas went on. 'It is called custom.'

Mister David nodded. 'We have a saying that means it is as dangerous to change nothing as it is to try and change everything. Some things were meant to be left alone while others cry out for us to make them better. I understand this tree you call custom. It is good to respect the things you are taught. But like Master Leslie saw for himself, his past has not stood still for him. The day will come for him to stop being sad and find happiness in a new life. As a grown man, this may not happen quickly. In the minds of his children the distance to England will seem greater. And, too, for the children's children. Africa will see to that.' Mister David smiled suddenly. 'Forgive me. I ask a question and fail to wait for your answer.'

'You seem to know it anyway.'

'I have one other thing that puzzles me greatly. Our women are more attractive to us when their . . .' He hesitated, then demonstrated with his hands the ample proportions of a well-rounded posterior. 'White women are not so lucky. They make themselves look bigger with too many clothes. Why do they do this? Is it to make themselves more attractive?' The Zulu gave a self-conscious laugh. 'For us, this does not work.'

Dallas was helpless to prevent the laughter that burst from him. Personally, he found a woman's bustle the most ridiculous fashion accessory he'd ever seen. Mister David, once sure he'd caused no offence, joined in. When he could, Dallas managed to address the question. 'Some of your women have scars on their faces. Why?'

'They think it makes them beautiful.'

'Does it?'

'Many like it. I do not.'

'Why?'

'It changes nothing. Inside, that woman is as she was born.'

'So, it's a fashion?'

'Fashion?' Mister David's brow furrowed.

'It is liked by others so they do it?'

'This I can see.'

'So is the bustle some white women wear behind them. Fortunately for us, fashion changes. Five years from now, no-one will like it.'

'Hau! Then they might dress for heat and comfort.'

Dallas shook his head. 'I doubt it. Do your women cover anything that men are not supposed to see?'

The Zulu looked surprised yet answered calmly. 'Only the tops of their legs at the back.'

'Then you are lucky. In my society a woman covers herself from neck to feet.'

'Hau! So white men excite easily.'

Dallas grinned and let that go.

'The tree. It is custom. One branch is what you call fashion. Another can be modesty.'

'Correct.'

'I see it more clearly now. Thank you.' Mister David went to say more but, at that moment, Ralph's stomach rebelled against the unexpected feast of porridge and he unceremoniously dumped it between the two men. Mopping up, Dallas wondered why tribal culture made so much sense while his own seemed to contain nothing more than silly rules and regulations. He felt dissatisfied with his answers. The Zulu had a deep understanding and acceptance of those things that governed day-to-day life. All Dallas could do, indeed, all he had ever done, was buck the system because, although unknown to him at the time, he disagreed with most of it.

They found evidence of elephant around midafternoon the following day. Their guides from Chief Ngetho's kraal had led them to a steep-sided gorge. Approaching the narrow entrance, no clue was given that there may be a way through. The hills beyond folded together, creating the impression of a solid barrier.

Logan dismounted and crouched to examine the first droppings they found. Picking up one of the soup plate-sized balls he broke it in half, sniffed and tested the firmness with his fingers. 'Five or six hours old,' he told Dallas.

'How can you tell?'

'Fresh dung is yellowish and has a stronger smell. Rather like cattle. Then it goes dark like this, although it retains some moisture. Anything older dries out, starts to bleach and gets broken down by beetles.' Logan spoke to one of the villagers and listened intently to his reply before translating for Dallas's benefit.

'Apparently there's a good-sized herd living here. This track leads into a valley and back to the river. For the past month or so, elephants have been in residence. Must be good feed for them. They don't usually stay so long in one spot.' Logan straightened, brushing the already drying dung from his hands. 'It's a big area and the Thukela runs along the base of those hills to the north. That's where we'll find them.' He swung back into the saddle. 'I suggest we go on a bit then leave the wagons and proceed on foot.'

The narrow neck that allowed access to the valley beyond was barely wide enough to pass through.

'Jesus!' Involuntary appreciation of the sudden change in vegetation burst from Dallas. Framed on all sides by rock-strewn hills of all shapes and sizes that were dotted with stunted trees, it was a valley of perhaps five miles wide that stretched far into the distance, twenty miles or more. Forest fringed the base of the hills – noticeably thicker where the river ran – enclosing a dead flat plain. Almost park-like, the trees in the valley were large and majestic. The grass was lush and long. Everything glowed gold and green in the afternoon sun. And, as far as the eye could see, herds of zebra, springbok, impala, wildebeest, buffalo and many more species grazed leisurely or simply lazed in the late afternoon sun. Haughty giraffe trimmed abundant acacia trees to perfect umbrellas better than any gardener could. None seemed in the slightest concerned by the presence of strangers.

Heat and humidity pressed down. No cooling wind found its way into this place, just the occasional hint of a breeze. Sweltering temperature, turned muggy by the presence of water, settled around the men with a lover's ardour. Their clothes, wet with perspiration, stuck like flypaper. Sweat stung their eyes and turned fingers slippery.

'The Garden of Eden,' Logan commented dryly, riding up beside Dallas. 'Wherever you think it might be, God throws in a flaw.'

Dallas grunted. He had no energy suddenly to do anything else.

They outspanned the wagons, allowing cattle and horses to graze. The smell of distant water drew their thirsty animals towards the river. Three Zulus went with them to ensure they didn't wander too far.

'Do you think the wagons are safe here?' Will worried. 'What if the elephants decide to turn this way?'

'If this is the only way into the valley then you may rest assured it's the only way out and they'll most certainly come in this direction.' Logan had little patience for Will's nervousness. 'That's why we're well off the track they use.' Rummaging in one of his wagon's side canvas pouches, Logan produced a crumpled pair of long, grey trousers and a dark shirt which he pulled on in place of the shorts and white top that he'd been wearing.

'Why are you doing that?' Will's question seemed superfluous to Dallas but Logan answered it anyway. 'An elephant's eyesight is bad, though they're far from blind. We'll be in thick bush and I'd like to remain as invisible as possible.'

'So you *are* scared,' Will crowed.

'Cautious,' Logan said shortly, turning to test a vagrant scrap of breeze that suddenly ruffled the grass. 'Couldn't be better. Straight in our faces.'

'I'd like to come with you.'

Logan was preparing two enormous eight-bore muzzle-loading single shot rifles. He paused and looked at Dallas. 'What did I tell you back in Durban?'

'To do as I was told.'

'Right. So now I'm telling you no.'

'That's not acceptable. I'll do as I'm told but I'm coming with you.'

'You don't have a gun.'

Dallas indicated his ornate Yellow Boy.

Logan laughed derisively. 'You won't knock down an elephant with that toy.'

'I also bought this in Durban.' Dallas produced a breech-loading Rawbone .577 double hammer gun.

Logan grunted. 'Better. But those folded metal cases can be difficult to extract. Ever fired it?'

'No, but it can't kick that much.'

'That's another reason why you're not coming.'

The two of them locked eyes. 'I can shoot,' Dallas said coldly. 'And I don't panic easily.'

'You'd know that, would you? Been charged by a few wounded ducks, have you? Stood your ground, did you? Bravo!'

'I have to start somewhere,' Dallas pointed out reasonably.

'Not in thick bush, you don't. Open country, maybe, but this will be hairy.'

'Then another gun could be useful.'

'We're not grouse shooting, you dumb bastard.' A kind of controlled tension had come over the older man. It was in his eyes and voice. 'You bloody well stay here.'

Logan's uncharacteristic anxiety was not about Dallas. From past experience he knew that in conditions like these there would be considerable danger. A build-up of nerves always brought Logan to the brink of an adrenaline rush. It had saved his skin on more than one occasion. However, how could he explain this to an inexperienced youngster whose courage was not in doubt but, should things go bad, remained an unknown quantity just as likely to shoot Logan as an elephant? Yet, the boy had a point. He had to start somewhere.

The logic of Dallas's next words seemed to sway Logan. 'You were once as raw as I am now. Who taught you?'

'No-one,' Logan answered shortly.

'Then I'm one up on you.'

He had to concede the point, but Logan wasn't about to give in easily. 'Think so? Out there you're on your own. Me? I'll be taking care of number one.' He jabbed his chest with a thumb and coughed once as the gesture tickled something inside. Frowning, he went on. 'So listen and listen good. Where would you shoot an elephant?'

'Heart. Brain. Lung. Any one should stop him.'

Logan grunted. 'True. And where exactly would you expect to find them?'

'Usual places. Head or just behind the shoulder.'

Logan smiled sourly. 'An elephant's heart lies more or less at the front of its chest cavity. The lungs are just above. From either side, a leg obscures most of them. From in front, their trunk is often in the way. The brain? Well now, you'd think in a head that size it would be easy to hit. It isn't. Proportionately, an elephant's brain is quite small and surrounded by a honeycomb of protective bone. It lies between the earholes. For a side shot, you bust him midway between the ear and eye. From the front aim below the eyes, roughly third wrinkle down the trunk, though that depends on how close you are. Unfortunately, the earholes can't be seen when the bloody thing is facing you. Miss, and you're in a heap of trouble. A good brain shot is the only one that will drop him immediately. Hit him in the heart, and even if he's dead on his feet, he'll run. Sometimes that means straight at you. And there's another problem. The rest of the herd aren't going to stand around waiting their turn. Once the first shot is fired, all hell breaks loose. You need a cool head to stay in one piece.'

Dallas ignored the dramatic outburst, confident that, when the time came, he could stay calm. 'So what would *you* aim for?'

'Like you said, heart, brain or lung, depending on the angle. The difference between you and me is that I know where to find them.'

'Then let me come with you. I won't even carry a rifle. Just watch what you do.'

Something between a grunt of disbelief and a snort of reluctant acceptance burst from Logan. 'You come with me, my boy, you carry a rifle and make damned sure you're prepared to use it. Got that?'

Dallas nodded happily.

'You walk when and where I walk. You stop when I stop. You shoot only if *I* tell you and then you fire immediately. You run like hell on my command and that you do before the words are out of my mouth. Understand?'

Another nod.

'Keep your gun loaded and both barrels cocked, your finger well away from the triggers. Got that?'

'Yes.'

'You fire without a good reason, and I *mean* one like I'm about to get stomped, and my gun bearer will have orders to shoot you. Got that?'

'Fine.'

'Fine.' Logan continued to load his rifles, patching and ramming a solid spherical ball down each barrel.

'Just one thing.'

The older man sighed.

'I want to shoot an elephant.'

Without looking up, Logan replied, 'How did I know you were going to say that?'

'Just one.'

'We'll see. If I tell you it's not safe, will you listen?'

'Yes.'

Logan bellowed to Mister David. 'Did you shoot elephants with David Leslie?'

'Yes, master.'

'Good. You can come with us. What about you, Will? I don't suppose you want to join us. Let's make this a party, why don't we?'

Will shook his head vigorously. 'You're welcome to them bastards. I'm staying right here. First shot I hear I'm up a tree.'

Logan, lighting a cigar, glanced at him and gave a sardonic smile. 'Got a decent rifle?'

'For elephants?' Will shook his head. 'Only a Hayton Cape gun.'

'What combination?'

'Twelve bore and Snider .577.'

'That'll do.' Logan jerked his head towards Dallas. 'He'll need back-up. Give it to David.'

'What about me?' Will whined.

'You'll be up a tree, remember? Borrow the Yellow Boy. That should take care of the leopard.'

Will's eyes widened.

Logan shook his head and chuckled.

One of the young men from Chief Ngetho's *umuzi*, who had gone into the trees to scout, came running back. '*Ndhlovu*,' he panted, pointing.

After listening for some time and questioning the African, Logan translated. 'They're about three miles away and moving towards us.' He squinted at the sun. 'They'll browse for a couple of hours yet then head for water. Normally I'd wait for them to drink but with our cattle here it could make them nervous.' He ground the cigar under his heel. 'Right. No more talking,' he said tersely and moved off.

The five young villagers, armed only with spears, went ahead. Logan and his gun bearer followed some twenty yards behind, the former stopping whenever a slight breeze reached them to check its direction with powdered ash from a pouch on his belt. Four Zulus from the trading party, carrying nothing more than *assegais*, were next. Dallas and Mister David brought up the rear. They crossed immediately to the treeline on their left and followed it east, towards the elephants, keeping to the plain for easier walking.

The heat never let up and sweat ran freely down Dallas's face, stinging his eyes. He didn't bother to brush it away. Moving at a fast pace, his own momentum created a cooling effect that brought relief of sorts.

Thirty minutes later, the Africans in front stopped. Logan did the same, indicating that Dallas should remain where he was. They listened. The sound of a breaking branch nearby told them that the men intent on taking life were converging with the animals who were concentrating only on sustaining it.

Slowly now, silently, they moved on. Dallas could only guess at Logan's intentions. They had to stay upwind but the elephants would instinctively try to flee in that direction since it was their only escape from the valley. So, inexperienced as he might be, once the first shot was fired Dallas knew they could reasonably expect a panicked stampede with any number of animals heading straight for them. He was grateful suddenly for the hours his father had spent teaching him that a gun was to be treated as an extension of his arm. He could shoot as well as the next man. But could he remain calm?

Entering the trees, Logan beckoned and waited for Dallas to join him. Chief Ngetho's warriors, together with their own boys, melted away, presumably to a safer location. They would not reappear until the shooting stopped.

'They're just ahead,' Logan whispered.

Peering through the gloom of dappled shade, Dallas could see nothing. But he heard them – a rumbling-stomach sound, breaking branches. And he could smell them – a pleasant manure odour, not unlike the stables at home, coupled with the sharper, almost astringent, tartness of urine. His eyes scanned the bush. How could such large animals so near to them remain invisible?

'There,' Logan hissed. 'Big male.'

An elephant's head came into view over a tree at least ten feet tall. It was browsing on the tender top leaves, wrapping its trunk around several branches, stripping them of foliage then placing it in its mouth. Almost immediately a searching trunk hovered over the tree again, selecting, stripping and delicately devouring the find. Dallas estimated that the animal was no more than twenty feet from where he, Logan and the two Zulus stood frozen. With what little breeze there was wafting towards them, and the sound of breaking branches loud in the silence, the elephant had no idea they were there.

Logan raised his rifle. 'Get ready,' he mouthed.

Dallas nodded and eased a finger towards the triggers. A quick glance towards Mister David reassured him that the Zulu had Will's Cape gun at the ready.

Logan seemed to be taking a long time. The elephant's head was still clearly visible. What had his partner said about a side-on brain shot? A line between the ear and eye. That was it. Logan was waiting for the animal to present a better shot.

The sudden crashing retort caused Dallas to jump. Of the elephant there was suddenly no sign, but everything around them instantly exploded with trumpeting screams and the crashing of undergrowth.

'Back to back!' Logan shouted, changing rifles,

no longer concerned with caution. 'If anything comes for us, shoot it.'

From nowhere it seemed, the bush was suddenly alive with lumbering grey shapes. For a moment Dallas's mind froze and he had the fleeting feeling that he shouldn't be here, that he just had to close his eyes to be somewhere else – anywhere would do. The sight of a massive dark shape heading straight for them, fury exuding from the animal and boring deep into Dallas's soul, cleared his head in an instant. Forgetting sweat-stung eyes, awe, fear, and even his inexperience, Dallas instinctively fell into an ice-cold, precise, do-what-you-have-to-but-do-it-now state of mind. His actions were unhurried yet efficient, unpanicked though borne of urgency, and he recalled, with crystal clarity, everything Logan had told him about an elephant's vital organs.

Dimly aware that Logan had fired again, Dallas aimed and placed a shot between but below an elephant's eyes. The grey head reared and its hindquarters collapsed. A second animal appeared, turning at the sight of its fallen companion. Dallas found the area behind its front leg. A heart shot. The elephant stumbled, picked up speed, then after a few shambling steps, all four massive legs collapsed and the giant pachyderm went down.

Mister David snatched the empty rifle and reloaded. Will's Cape gun felt wrong in Dallas's hands but, with incredible speed, his own weapon was thrust back to him together with a shouted, 'Behind!'

Dallas whirled, gun raised.

Three of them. Even as he fired he was aware that one had dropped at a shot from Logan. A second fell to Dallas's first barrel and the third veered off to be swallowed up by the bush. A juvenile careered by, panicked eyes searching for its mother. By now the herd had located the source of their terror and all that remained was the crashing of their flight from whatever dreadful horror had visited the once peaceful valley. There was one long trumpeting scream in the distance and the bush went quiet. No-one moved for a few seconds.

'Insurance,' barked Logan, running to the nearest fallen animal and placing a shot at close range into its brain.

Dallas reloaded his empty barrel and did the same. Two were already dead but the heart-shot elephant shuddered as the 750 grain solid bullet snuffed out what little was left of his life.

'Good shooting, master.' Mister David pounded Dallas's left arm and smiled widely. His life had been dependent on the skill of a young unproven white man, but faith in him never wavered for an instant. The enormity of such a responsibility hadn't once crossed Dallas's mind and he nodded vaguely in the aftershock of action, staring down at the once mighty elephant. In death, it resembled nothing more than a mound of grey, wrinkled flesh. In life, it had been magnificent.

'Good ivory,' Mister David commented.

'Is it?' The tusks looked small to him.

'If it is longer than the ear, it is worth taking,'

Mister David told him. 'These ones are also thick. They should weigh around ninety pounds each.'

Logan joined them, a mixed expression on his face – relief, satisfaction and something that looked curiously sad. 'Not bad. Three each. You kept your head, well done. I know how difficult that can be when it's your first time, especially as conditions were far from ideal. It was easy to get close but once they panicked, bloody dangerous.' Logan looked down at the dead elephant. 'Shame,' he said in soft sympathy.

The Africans had reappeared and moved among the fallen elephants, hacking out the tusks. Their conversation was loud and happy.

'Full stomachs for some of them for a while. Let's leave them to it,' Logan said.

'Some of them? I thought so much meat would be plenty for all.'

'It is, but they have certain taboos that prevent young people from eating elephant meat.'

'Do you know why?'

'Young couples are afraid that the wife will give birth to an elephant if either of them eat it. I think it's because the animal seems to have many human traits. In times of famine, however, when they deliberately avoid pregnancy, they'll eat it fast enough.'

'So it's a superstition rather than any natural revulsion?'

'Oh, quite. And like most, has its origin in pro-creational myths.'

They emerged from the trees, about half a mile

from the wagons. Logan placed two fingers in his mouth and gave a shrill whistle. The remainder of their staff must have been waiting for the signal for they came at a run. Watching their bobbing figures, Logan chuckled. 'They'll want their share of the fat.'

'Fat?'

The older man nodded. 'They cook with it and eat it on bread.'

Dallas pulled a face.

'It's not that bad actually. You should try it.'

'I'm still coming to terms with biltong.'

Logan laughed. 'You'll get used to it.' He clapped Dallas on the back. 'I don't know about you but I need a drink.'

It was only then that Dallas realised he was feeling slightly weak at the knees. The size, proximity and sheer power of the elephants had caught him unawares. It was one thing to shoot deer back home. Out here, as Logan had pointed out on several occasions, a hunter's life is often on the line. A jammed gun, a moment's hesitation and the tables can turn against you.

'Do you ever get used to it?' he asked as they made their way back towards the wagons.

'Not in my experience. Back there was typical elephant country. You have to get in there with them and anything can happen. Even out in the open, if they get wind of you, anticipate a charge. Cows with young are the most dangerous. Bulls may be satisfied with scaring you off but females go for the kill.'

'How can you tell a male from a female, like

you did back there, when we could only see his head?'

'From its shape. Bulls have a rounded forehead where cows form a quite distinct angle. By the way, try not to shoot any more pregnant females.'

'I didn't have much option. She was coming straight at me.'

Logan nodded. 'Fair enough. It happens now and then.'

Dallas pulled a face. When he'd gone to deliver the coup de grâce he'd seen that what he'd thought was a bull had been heavy with calf. Despite his lack of choice, the fact that he had to kill a pregnant cow filled him with disgust.

Logan sensed his disquiet and tried to lighten the moment. 'I've yet to see an elephant hunter ask politely if his quarry would mind giving birth so he can collect her tusks with a clear conscience. There's no room in this business for sentimentality.' He gave a brief laugh. 'God knows why I keep hunting them. They scare the hell out of me every time.'

But Dallas still had his mind on the pregnant elephant. 'I'm not being sentimental. Well, maybe a little. A pregnant animal is hardly sport, is it?'

Logan stopped walking. 'None of this is sport,' he said sharply. 'It's trade. Business. A livelihood. That's all. You want sport, go hunt with the trophy seekers.'

'Sorry.' Dallas wondered what had upset the older man.

'If you think I enjoyed that back there, think

again,' Logan went on. 'If I could extract their bloody teeth without killing them, I would.'

'But –'

'There are no buts. An elephant is the most destructive beast God ever put on this earth. They raid the native crops, decimate the bush, strip and kill trees making food difficult to find for other animals. There are hundreds, no thousands, too many of them. Killing a few makes no difference. The tusks and skins give us a livelihood and their flesh feeds the local tribes.' Logan took a reflective breath. 'But if you've ever watched them take care of their wounded, look after the young, if you've witnessed their greeting rituals or methods of communication, if you've ever stood still and really looked at a herd, you'll know that the elephant is a gentle, intelligent and truly magnificent beast, worthy of our respect. That's why I hate killing them.'

'Then why –'

Yet again, Logan interrupted.

'Why? Money, old chap. The scourge of our modern world. I kill them because I must. Because it's the only thing I know how to do. But I don't have to like it.'

Dallas realised that Logan was angry with himself. 'If it bothers you that much, why not find something else to do?'

Logan started walking again. 'I can't,' he said softly. 'Nothing else matches it for excitement. And therein, my young friend, lies the paradoxical nature of man.'

Dallas was still pondering Logan's profundity

when they approached the wagons. Will didn't wait for them to reach him.

'You fuckin' bastards,' he yelled, shaking a fist.

Dallas and Logan exchanged a glance. What was bothering Will?

'You imbeciles. You shit-eating dog pricks. You . . . you . . .' Will ran out of steam.

'What's your problem?' Logan went straight to his wagon and, rummaging, produced a bottle of rum.

'Gimme that.' Will snatched, tore out the cork and upended the bottle.

'Hey!' Logan grabbed it back. 'Mine, I believe.' He took a swig and handed the rum to Dallas. 'What's got into you?'

'Those fuckin' elephants!' Will shouted. 'You did that on purpose.'

'Did what, for Christ's sake? What the hell are you talking about?'

Will pointed a shaking finger towards the trees. 'They came out right there. Ran straight at us. You deliberately chased them this way.'

Logan's head dropped and he pinched the top of his nose. He seemed to be counting to ten. When he looked up, Dallas could see the anger on his face. 'Next time we go after elephant, Will, I suggest you really do climb a nice big tree.'

'Think I won't?' Will sneered. 'I could have been killed.'

Logan walked away from the wagons and looked at the ground some forty yards away. 'Here are their tracks,' he called. Returning, Logan stood close in front of Will. 'They were running for their bloody lives, you spineless, gutless wonder. I doubt they even knew you were here.' He jerked a thumb at Dallas. 'This man could have been killed.' Another stab, this time towards himself. 'I could have been killed. The natives with us could have been killed. You? Why would they bother with a puny little weed like you?'

'You can't talk to me like that. We're supposed to be partners.'

Logan turned away, disgusted. 'Go to hell. Just keep out of my sight.'

'And you shouldn't –'

The speed with which Logan turned back and clutched Will's shirt front full in his fist was astonishing. He shook the man like a terrier would a rat. 'One more word,' he gritted, 'just one. That's all it will take and I'll break your fucking neck.' He threw Will aside and strode to the back of his wagon.

Will turned beseeching eyes on Dallas, who shrugged and also moved away. After the danger they'd encountered in the trees, Will's thoughtless complaint had angered him as well.

One of the young men from Chief Ngetho's village went to fetch the extra assistance that would be required to carry so much meat. Six elephants would take time to cut up. 'We'll outspan here,' Dallas announced.

Logan reappeared. 'Good idea. We'll probably need tomorrow as well.'

'What if the elephants come back?'

'Shut up,' Logan and Dallas yelled in unison. Then Logan added, 'If they do we'll make sure you're staked out right in their path.'

Dallas tossed Will some soap. 'Clean yourself up. The elephants won't be back.'

Will headed for the river without another word but took his Cape gun with him.

That night, the atmosphere remained strained. Will was still sulking. Logan disappeared to confront his conscience, while Dallas decided he wouldn't be killing any more elephants. Logan was welcome to do so and this would be reflected in a financial adjustment to his share of the profits. Fear hadn't brought Dallas to this decision. It was borne of respect for the elephant itself.

Ralph gorged on elephant meat and fell blissfully asleep by the fire. Dallas envied the dog. Sometimes, it seemed to him, the inability to reason must be a blessing.

TEN

It had taken five months to trade along the Thukela. They had gone at the worst possible time of year. Heat, storms, flooding, and a mysterious kidney disease that killed eight of their oxen were all caused by the fact that it was high summer. The valley, surrounded by one hill system after another, captured and held humidity, and in that climate, germs seemed to thrive. Insect bites and scratches from thorns invariably became infected. Daily inspections of cattle and horses were required to ensure they had not injured themselves, both being just as vulnerable as people to infection. Wagons bogging, food going off, lame horses and petty bickering were regular occurrences. Twice they became badly lost because the Africans refused to continue, insisting on a detour because an omen of some kind had been seen, supposedly a sign from wandering, unclaimed spirits waiting for their families to come and take them home.

Mainly they enjoyed courteous greetings and good trading relations but on three occasions they'd been driven away by angry inhabitants of a kraal. Once for unfortunate timing, which coincided with the death of a chief; another because, on the morning of their arrival, a calf lay down to sleep three times while its mother was being milked – a sign of impending disaster; and the third appeared to be caused by nothing more than jealousy that a rival clan had been visited before them.

The hatred between Logan's Sotho skinner and Will's Zulu driver seemed to be contained, but it simmered just below the surface causing Mister David to comment, 'It would have been better if one had killed the other in Durban. All the boys are scared.'

'Why?'

'It is difficult to explain.'

'Try.'

Mister David gave an apologetic shrug. 'Zulus believe that when someone dies it weakens any who are close. While we are weak the spirits can easily lead us after the one who is dead. We must make ourselves strong to stop this from happening.'

'How do you do that?'

'With black *muthi*. There are many things we use. Roots, bark from special plants, fats, powders, the flesh from some animals. We eat this medicine and put it in our water for drinking. Even the cattle must be smoked with it to protect them. We cannot eat *amasi* for one week.'

Dallas knew that *amasi* was a great delicacy, a kind of curdled milk with a cottage-cheese consistency, which was part of a Zulu's staple diet. Many taboos surrounded the eating of *amasi*, which was regarded as the food of a household and never shared with anyone who was not a member of the immediate family. To abstain from this greatly favoured food for a week showed the seriousness with which Zulus regarded death and the importance of taking a strengthening medicine. 'Do you know how to make this black *muthi*?' Dallas asked quietly.

'Yes, master.'

'Can you find the things you will need?'

'Yes, master.'

'Then I suggest you have them ready just in case.'

'Thank you. I will do as you say. The others will be comforted to know they can be protected.'

'I hope it won't be necessary.'

'I fear it will, master. What lies in wait is too strong to stop.'

Logan's Sotho skinner seemed unaffected by the finger he'd lost in Durban when Dallas broke up the fight. The hand remained bandaged for a week and then Dallas noticed the man brewing his own concoction to treat the wound. The healing process was swift and the man's dexterity with a skinning knife unimpaired. Dallas expected resentment from him. He was surprised, therefore, when it was obvious that the Sotho actually accorded Dallas great respect.

'He's grateful,' Logan said.

'Grateful! I shot his finger off.'

'Might have been his hand, old boy.'

Dallas supposed that was one way of looking at it.

Will's driver, too, treated Dallas with high regard. He'd lost a chunk of flesh from his upper arm. He bore the scar as if it were a badge of honour.

Logan explained, 'He now has proof of invincibility against the white man's gun. When he returns to his *umuzi* he will be greatly admired.'

Dallas shook his head. There was so much to learn about these people.

The animosity between Will and Logan hadn't changed either. In five months of trading and hunting, their mistrust of each other had neither grown or faded. It was simply there, although a grudging respect did exist between them for individual skills. Part of the trouble stemmed from social differences but the main cause of dissension, as far as Dallas could see, was that each was a loner and, as such, resented the other's presence. Dallas they tolerated. He, after all, was the one with the money.

Working their way down the Thukela River valley, despite any ongoing animosity, the expedition could be considered successful. Logan's ability as a hunter, combined with Will's judgment of goods and the bartering skills of both, ensured that as the wagons' loads lightened of beads and blankets, they were replenished by skins, horns and ivory. Even the cattle, sheep, goats, pigs and chickens traded along the way were exchanged for tusks.

Whenever they found a particularly pleasant place to outspan where good grazing and water were plentiful, Dallas would rest the animals for up to a week. Logan used these stops to take his recalcitrant Sotho and disappear, 'in search of elephants.' More often than not they'd go on foot, with little more than rifles, bags of bullets and powder, bedrolls and some biltong. Sometimes they stayed away for three or four days, usually returning with information about villages and elephant. Occasionally they'd return carrying a tusk each and, on one occasion, boys from camp had to go and help bring back ivory.

There was always something to do during these rest periods – running repairs to wagons and harnesses; *reims*, sjamboks and trek whips to be made for selling; loads sorted and restacked. Back in Edinburgh, any clothing repairs or adjustments had been made by a seamstress. Dallas became quite adept with needle and thread, though his efforts tended more towards strengthening a garment as opposed to improving its appearance.

Will displayed an unexpected practical side to his nature and was more than willing to teach Dallas things learned from years of experience. These were tricks of the trade, like how to prevent bees and wasps building nests down the barrel of a rifle, and how to make a poultice from bread and mustard to ease the extraction of acacia thorns that so often became embedded deep within the men's flesh. Will had the uncanny knack of knowing if a horse or one of the oxen was ailing well before the animal showed any obvious symptoms. 'It's easy,' he told Dallas. 'Their eyes go dull.'

Try as he might, when Will announced that Tosca wasn't well, he could see no difference in her eyes. The next day his horse had a bad attack of colic. Will force-fed the poor animal a mixture of castor oil and mealie porridge to prevent her developing a blockage in the intestine which would undoubtedly have led to a painful death. It worked, although Dallas worried that Will had been so heavy-handed with the treatment that Tosca was in danger of defecating to an early demise.

After their first experience of hunting elephant together, Dallas and Logan had a pithy discussion on the subject.

'I hear what you say about their destructive habits and I understand that the land can't support so many. Even so, we've heard that numbers have dropped dramatically in recent years. That aside, I have no problem with buying and selling tusks or your continuing to hunt. It's simply that I won't be shooting any more elephants.'

'Would you kill a mosquito or a fly?'

'Of course.'

'You'd happily shoot duiker and reedbuck?'

'Yes.'

'Is it the size? Killing smaller animals is fine but not big ones?'

'That has nothing to do with my decision.'

'What is your reason then?'

'I don't know.'

'Fear?'

'I was certainly frightened but it's not that either.'

Logan closed his eyes briefly, then admitted, 'I

envy you. You're a hypocrite, but who isn't? Okay, I'll do the shooting. One question, though. If I ask for back-up in a difficult situation will you give it?'

'Without hesitation.'

Logan nodded. 'Good.'

A few days later Dallas was to witness one of the rarest yet most touching sights Africa could offer. It was an event, Logan told him, that only occurred once in every seven or eight years. He'd never seen it before and knew of few who had. In fact, the phenomenon was discounted by most as hearsay.

The meeting of elephants.

They'd made camp between two small hills that sat on either side of the river. The Thukela wound, snake-like, between them. This part of the valley system had been over-grazed by local cattle and was virtually devoid of wildlife. A lone jackal buzzard soared hopefully in search of sustenance but otherwise Dallas and his companions had the area to themselves. Logan, who had scouted ahead, returned with news that the next village was some four miles away and that they'd be made welcome. Nobody had seen elephants for about three months.

As was usual, the Africans were up at first light. Instead of rekindling the fires for breakfast, collecting water and rounding up their oxen, comforting camp noises accompanied by quiet conversation that generally woke Dallas, on this morning it was a complete absence of sound which had the same effect. Something was wrong. He propped himself up in the bedroll, rubbing sleep from his eyes and yawning. The Africans were bunched together and staring wide-eyed in every direction. Looking beyond, Dallas's jaw dropped and he scrambled to join them.

'Christ! Where did they come from?'

Elephant, perhaps a thousand, stretching as far as the eye could see, with more arriving over the hills, up the river, down the river, all along the valley, a moving carpet of shuffling grey shapes.

Logan and Will, woken by Dallas's outburst, were equally stunned by the sight.

Dallas turned to Logan for an explanation, but his partner just stared in awe and said in a quiet voice, 'Mother of God!'

'Are we safe?' Will worried.

'They know we're here, if that's what you mean. As long as we stay put they'll give us our space.'

'But you said –' Will persisted.

'I know. No elephants.'

'So how come –'

'This is different. There's very little feed here for them. What you're seeing has either been pre-arranged or it's the result of some remarkable instinct. No-one knows. Christ! Hardly anyone has witnessed this.'

'There must be a theory of some kind,' Dallas said. 'What do people believe?'

'Most think it's a myth but I've heard others say that family groups can travel as far as two hundred miles for this event. It's thought that each matri-arch comes to do business, swapping their young bulls for others, as if they've worked out a way to avoid inbreeding. We're about to find out, gentlemen. We certainly can't go anywhere. Most of the family groups will have young and they'll be protective. All we can do is sit and watch.' With that, Logan turned to the still spellbound Zulus. 'Get this fire going. Stay away from the river, we've got enough water. Leave the cattle and horses to themselves. They won't wander far and any lions will be long gone. Don't make any unnecessary noise, just go about your work in camp as if the elephants weren't there.'

Hesitant at first, the Africans moved to do as instructed.

Logan settled himself comfortably into a camp chair. 'Join me,' he invited Will and Dallas. 'What we are seeing today puts us among a fortunate few in Africa.'

Dallas asked Mister David if he'd ever seen a meeting of elephants.

'I have heard of this thing but never seen.'

'I'm not sure how it makes us fortunate,' Will grouched. 'Look at the bastards. They're bloody everywhere.'

Logan ignored the comment and very soon, when it became apparent that the animals were not in the least bit interested in them, even Will relaxed.

They spent most of that day watching the elephants. In many respects, it was a lesson. Sibling rivalry, maternal love, grown male aggression, the confident majesty of a herd bull, playful youngsters – it was all on display. Sounds like stomach rumblings seemed to be one way they communicated, though there was much touching and intertwining of trunks as family greeted family, old friends who had not seen each other for many years. Semi-grown herd bulls sparred with much trumpeting, ear-flapping and butting of heads but their actions seemed more playful than aggressive. Dallas saw several examples of animals assisting injured or ailing companions.

'That one's on the way out,' Logan commented, indicating a large female obviously struggling to stay on her feet. Family had gathered around in a concerned group, leaning against the cow in an effort to hold her upright.

'Age?' Dallas asked.

'Probably. She looks old. The trip must have been too much.'

As they watched, the cow stumbled, both front legs collapsed and she toppled sideways.

'That's it,' Logan predicted. 'They'll not get her up now.'

It wasn't for want of trying. Others rallied to give assistance but to no avail, and eventually wandered away. During the next few hours, the fallen cow's family tried everything to get her to stand. Quite suddenly, all attempts ceased. The group of elephants had accepted the inevitable, occasionally laying their trunks gently on the animal as if comforting her. It was the most touching scene Dallas had ever witnessed.

'Look.' Will pointed.

Vultures were already circling, more spiralling in by the second.

'How do they know?' Dallas asked.

'They fly to a pattern a good two miles up. Each bird seems to have its own territory. When one drops towards a dead or stricken animal the rest soon follow.'

'They're out of luck for now,' Logan put in. 'The family will defend her.'

'For how long?' Dallas asked.

Logan shrugged. 'Don't know. Rest of the day, most likely. Sometimes elephants bury their dead beneath broken branches.'

Despite the crush of animals, some instinct caused others to leave a private space around the grieving family. Vultures waited patiently in the trees, but any daring to land on the ground were soon chased away.

Watching the elephants, Dallas fell in love. He marvelled at how such large animals could be so gentle. There were youngsters testing their mother's patience to the limit yet reprimands were rare and, when they did occur, softened with loving gestures. Elephants in the river squirted themselves and each other with water. Those drinking drew water into their trunks then curled the tip into a waiting mouth and drank slowly with great satisfaction. The operation was repeated over and over until an elephant had quenched its thirst.

'They can drink over twenty gallons in one session,' Logan told them.

Once sated, many an animal rolled on the churned-up riverbank, covering itself in wet mud.

'Keeps them cool and free of insects,' Logan said. 'Quite clever, really.'

The business of the gathering was yet another demonstration of an elephant's ability to communicate. Matriarchs met head-to-head, their rumbling conversation going on for anything up to an hour. At the end of their wheeling and dealing, a young bull from each group was called to come forward. Some were rejected. If that happened the deal was off, both family groups wandering away to bargain with a different unit. When an exchange was successfully concluded there were touching scenes of farewell followed by a joyous welcome from the new family.

One young bull, obviously reluctant to leave, started dragging his feet, constantly turning to look back. The family he was about to join waited patiently, as if understanding. His mother stood watching, making no effort to call him back to her side. At last she turned away and was immediately comforted by other females in her own group. Taking a cue from this, the youngster joined his new family and was greeted with affection. They moved off together quickly to lessen his sense of abandonment. The scene brought a lump to Dallas's throat.

At the end of that day the valley was still teeming with animals. The squealing, trumpeting and rumbling went on for most of the night, but come morning, only one group remained. During the dark hours all the rest had quietly departed, returning to their usual habitats. The elephants left were those still standing around the dead cow. They paid no attention as the wagons rolled past.

Dallas rode alongside Logan. 'After yesterday how can you still kill them?'

'Drop it.' Logan's response was full of suppressed anger. The older man's conscience waged a war within himself. Respect and admiration were pitted against the heady excitement of hunting. The conflict was so deep-seated and complicated that Logan was at a loss to explain it properly. Dallas found his attitude impossible to understand.

They travelled a rambling route, following pathways made by many different animals. Mister David explained that elephants would always find the most direct and convenient way through the hills. They seemed to know where to cross rivers, which outcrops to skirt and which to climb. Their droppings and destructive browsing were then followed by others. Local tribes used these routes for themselves, turning downtrodden grassy trails into well-used sandy tracks. And now the wagons added their impressions. Dallas knew that a road to the interior had been started the same way and found himself wondering if their path would be the forerunner of some future thoroughfare. He liked the idea. Somehow, it made him seem a part of this continent.

Will crowed constantly about how easy the trip had become. 'Told you,' he said, at least three times a day.

It was an extraordinary time. The freedom compared with Dallas's life in Scotland was intoxicating.

Absorbing all kinds of new and fascinating knowledge, seeing a wild land that far exceeded anything he could have imagined, the sounds and smells, the dangers and unspoiled beauty, all kept Dallas so engrossed that he wondered less and less about home.

Lorna was still with him, though. He thought of her at unexpected times. The call of a laughing dove one day, a bubbling series of descending notes, reminded him of her gentle laugh; the sand colour of dried grass moving slightly in shimmering heatwaves, her hair; the graceful movements of a lone female steenbok, her walk.

With these painful comparisons came memories of her. The day she defiantly climbed into the uppermost branches of a tree and then couldn't get down without his help. One rainy afternoon when Charlotte and Lorna, Charles and Dallas decided to try some claret left in the dining room. The boys had been twelve, the girls nine. All four became ill and were sent to bed in disgrace. The way she had looked at the ball given by his parents after Lorna and Charlotte had been presented to Queen Victoria. The smell of her skin and hair when he held her.

He tried to push the memories aside but she crept back and remained, like an aching void, in his heart.

Other recollections were less harrowing. Dallas had regrets – Charlotte and Charles, his mother, the security of family – but as time went by he felt more disconnected from them. Young, and busy embracing a new life, most of his past slipped into the background. He mentioned this fact one night as they sat staring into the hypnotic depths of flickering flame around the fire.

'I feel as though part of my life happened to someone else.'

Logan looked up from his contemplation. 'You've changed. Both Will and I have noticed. That's good. It's what you have to do.'

'You'd been back home when we first met. How was it?'

'Couldn't wait to leave. I only go to see family. Each time becomes more difficult. We've nothing in common. They think I'm too brash and rough. I find them pretentious and boring.'

'How about you, Will?'

'Ain't never been back. Worked me way here under canvas and you'll not see me set foot on one of them damned riggers again. Spent four years on the bastards.'

'What about your family?'

Will pulled a face. 'What about them? My father was a drunk, more often than not out of work. My mother took to religion. I'm one of twelve children, maybe more now for all I know. They were probably pleased to see the back of me – one less mouth to feed.'

'How old were you when you left?' Logan asked.

'Eleven.'

'Jesus!' Dallas couldn't relate to that. At such an early age he'd been a child. From the sound of things, Will hadn't enjoyed that privilege. His life must have been bad for him to leave home so young.

Will's next revelation confirmed it. 'Worked the pits since I was seven.' He shuddered. 'No choice. Out here a man owns himself.'

It seemed a good way of putting it.

'How old were you?' Will asked Logan.

'Twenty-three.'

'Don't suppose you had to work your way over?'

'No.' Logan chuckled. 'My father paid to get rid of me.'

'Bit of a tearaway, were you?'

'Not really. My mother died when I was twenty and he remarried a much younger woman. I think he wanted to get rid of any possible competition. Not that I was interested. She was pretty enough, I suppose, but the most disagreeable, whining bitch I've ever met. Nothing pleased her. Father ran himself ragged trying. In the end, it killed him.'

'Is she still alive?' Dallas asked.

'Yes, more's the pity. She makes my brother's life hell.'

'Did she have children by your father?'

'No. After the wedding night I don't believe he was allowed into her boudoir again.'

'You ever been in love?' Will asked suddenly.

Dallas and Logan glanced at each other. 'Yes,' Dallas said finally. 'She married someone else.'

Eyes turned to Logan. 'Once,' he admitted. 'It was a long time ago.'

'What happened?' Dallas asked.

'Tuberculosis,' Logan said briefly.

Both men looked at Will, who shrugged. 'Dunno. Felt like it. She wasn't interested.' Then he added, 'Plenty of women selling it in Durban.'

The three of them fell silent. Their conversation had come too close for comfort to the one thing missing from their lives. Contrary to popular belief, while Zulu men took as many wives as they could afford, and sexual experimentation was encouraged in children from an early age, the freedom seen by many Europeans as promiscuous was exactly the opposite. Within their own culture the Zulus were a moral and disciplined people. Any white man seeking a night's pleasure in mistaken certainty that a woman would be his for the asking was, at best, told to leave. Some paid the ultimate price for their lack of respect.

Neither Logan nor Will had quizzed Dallas about his past life. He was grateful for that. It saved him having to lie. Yet he wondered if their reticence was due to a respect for his privacy or because they suspected that he had something to hide. Will had speculated on it when they first met but hadn't mentioned it again. In a land where men often had nothing better to do around the fire at night than gossip, Dallas knew his secret should stay with him. Still, he was sorry he couldn't speak freely with these two. There were times when both men felt closer than family.

Tobacco broke into their reflections with an announcement that dinner was ready. Their food this night was a first for Dallas and he was not sure, despite positive assurances from the others, that he'd manage to eat anything. An abandoned termite mound had been modified to form a kind of oven and a fire lit in one of the chambers. Next to it, an area had been scraped out until it was large enough to accommodate the foot of an elephant. It was then left to cook for nearly five hours. When served, the meat resembled a glutinous mess, rather like liquid brawn. Wild yams and a green leafy spinach-type vegetable accompanied the delicacy.

Dallas took a tentative taste. Not bad. He had another. Bloody marvellous! Pushing aside his unease about its origin – the elephant was dead, its ivory stored in a wagon – being able to eat a part of the animal made more sense of its death than merely taking life for profit. Dallas tucked in. After all, a man had to eat.

Despite a dwindling stock of provisions, the men ate well. It was a varied diet of fresh meat, wild vegetables and fruit. Tobacco proved to be an innovative cook. A camp favourite was the small intestine of buck, turned inside out and made into a sausage stuffed with some of the animal's liver and kidney, chopped fine and flavoured with onion. Another popular dish was whatever fruit or berry could be found, served with wild honey. On one occasion Dallas accompanied Tobacco on his quest to find a hive and was astonished to discover that the African was guided by a bird. It fluttered in front of them, near enough to touch, its body bouncing, tail flickering, before flying on ahead to sit in a tree and wait for them to catch up. This process was repeated until they found a hive, all the time the bird making a rattling call which sounded like someone shaking a tinderbox. With a honey source located, the bird then sat in a nearby tree waiting patiently for its share of the prize. Tobacco lit a smoky fire to drive out the bees then extracted most of the comb and solemnly placed a piece to reward the bird nearby.

In Zulu, which Dallas now knew enough of to understand, Tobacco explained that they never took honey without thanking their guide. And they never cleaned out the hive completely.

The land was abundant with sources of sustenance if you knew where to seek out tubers, berries, fruit and herbs. Water in the Thukela and streams that flowed into it was pure, if at times muddy, and yielded the bonus of fresh fish which, while happy to catch and cook, the Zulus refrained from eating.

As the weeks went by and March became April, the weather improved. It was still hot by day but rain was less frequent and the air held a crispness at night that encouraged deeper sleep. The biting insects that had plagued them during the hotter months were more bearable and infection became less of a problem.

Their cattle, originally seventy-six in number, had suffered the loss of eight from disease, two from having broken legs, one while calving and seven to lion. That left fifty-eight and they needed fifty-four to pull the wagons. Eighteen calves had been born but were still too small to fit in the harness, so they mixed some of their traded animals with the experienced team. It worked reasonably well for, despite their wild nature, many of the native cattle had become used to a harness when ploughing to plant crops.

A frightening encounter with lion could have been much worse if a trembling Ralph hadn't raised the alarm by scooting into Dallas's bedroll. It woke him immediately and he could hear that oxen and horses were also nervous.

Eyes adjusting to the dark, Dallas was horrified to see that a pride was efficiently surrounding their animals. Any making a bid for freedom were quickly brought down. Cattle bellowed nervously and horses whinnied at a screaming pitch. The increasing panic woke everyone else.

The Zulus were fast to act. Seizing still-burning branches from the fires, and banging metal spoons against cooking pots, they stepped bravely into the midst of their terrified animals. The lions retreated, waiting. Dallas, Will and Logan loaded their rifles and went into the fray, shooting at every figure they could see slinking hopefully on the periphery. The lions were driven back but they were not about to give up their kills. With the guns keeping their tormentors at bay, the livestock were rounded up and brought closer to the wagons. The predators lost no time in claiming the seven already dead, even though bullets had reduced their numbers by three.

'We'd best post guards at night while we're in

this part of the valley,' Logan suggested. 'A couple of extra fires would help and it may even be necessary to kraal the animals with thorn branches. That's the biggest pride I've ever seen. They're bold and hungry. As long as we're in their territory they'll stalk us.' He issued instructions and three Zulus set about building extra fires. 'Should be all right tonight,' Logan added. 'If they eat their way through that lot they'll need to sleep it off.'

With improving weather, the night sky became a glittering canopy of winking lights of stars that seemed close enough to touch. They had colour too, something Dallas had never seen in the northern hemisphere. Some shone red, others orange. White, yellow and brilliant blue were also evident. Logan pointed out the Southern Cross, Orion and the horse-shaped Leo. One evening they witnessed a spectacular meteor shower which disturbed the Africans to such an extent that they crawled under the wagons and could not be coaxed out again.

'Bad omen, I suppose,' Dallas guessed.

'You should see them during an eclipse,' Logan told him. 'They think the sun and moon are sick, and even sing special songs and sacrifice cattle to make them well again.'

The next day Dallas decided to find out more.

Mister David explained that, to a Zulu, stars were the children of the sun and sky. He went on to tell Dallas his conception of the universe.

'The sky is a blue rock which surrounds us. On our side of this rock are the sun, moon and stars. The sun is a great chief and each day travels the sky. At night he follows a path under the sea. He has a summer house and a winter house. Every year the sun goes there.' Mister David pointed north. 'Further each day until the winter house is reached. He does not stay long as it is too cold and always returns to his summer house. The moon is a soldier of the sun. Some believe it is a hole in the rock but I do not think this is true. It is not so strong as the sun. The days devour it until it is thin and sick. Then the sun brings it back to life. When a new moon is first seen we beat drums and do not work our fields for, if we do, nothing will grow.'

Towards the end of their fourth month, two shocking events happened within seconds of each other.

The hatred between Logan's Sotho and Will's Zulu driver erupted with no warning: no-one saw it coming and there wasn't a thing anyone could do to prevent it. The other incident involved Ralph.

The morning, clear and cool, gave no indication of impending disaster. They had passed a pleasant night beside a small stream where both cattle and horses could spread out over the sweet, lush grass. No-one was in a hurry to get moving. Tree-studded hills rose on all sides, the silence broken only by the cry of guineafowl or baboon barking. A light breeze, bringing with it dung and dust-like scents of the bush, was drying clothes that had been draped over various small shrubs.

Dallas had spent time over the past months fruitlessly trying to teach Ralph a few tricks. The pup had grown from a skinny, worm-ridden fleabag to a chubby, bright-eyed youngster, full of bounce and pep. But that was the only improvement.

'You'll never train him, old chap. These Kaffir dogs are inbred with stupidity. Most of them have the brains of a chicken.'

Dallas was beginning to agree. Ralph, though cute, affectionate and apparently loyal, proved consistently impossible to control. With an unerring instinct for trouble, a disdainful disregard for socially acceptable places to relieve himself and a tendency to seek playmates in the middle of the night when everyone was asleep, he sorely tried the patience of all.

Ralph had a memory so full of holes that Dallas swore lessons learned escaped within three seconds. He forgot, time and again, that he couldn't walk on water. No-one could remember how many times he had to be rescued from the river. Their nightly fire proved to be another hazard. Ralph liked to hog the heat. He never made a connection between flames and a smoking coat of hair. Horses' hooves were there for yapping at, the dog quite forgetting kicks of objection that sent him tumbling – a yelping bundle of fur. Wagon wheels had to be nipped, despite a crushed paw that kept him limping for weeks. Burrows made by warthog or aardvarks were tailor-made for exploring, Ralph never remembering the numerous times he'd become wedged, needing to be dug out.

The dog was a glutton of the first order. He'd been known to brave fire just to knock over the stew pot and lap up spilled food. Once he gnawed his way through a bag containing sago and devoured the entire two pounds. Nothing was sacred. Boots and socks had to be placed out of reach at night. Logan tried to teach the animal a lesson by placing red-hot chillies in the toe of a sock and leaving it easily accessible. Both were gone by the following morning. For two days Ralph had the most horrible wind and deposited unspeakable things onto the ground. The experience taught him nothing.

'Sit.' Dallas held a finger over the dog's nose. A strip of biltong waited in his other hand, a reward if, by some miracle, Ralph obeyed.

Instead the animal lunged, grabbing the tidbit and pelting off into the grass to devour it.

'A lead suppository might help,' Will observed balefully.

What happened next was so fast that Dallas wondered for a moment if he was dreaming. No-one had noticed the leopard. That in itself was not surprising. Normally a night hunter, this rarely seen cat was capable of creeping unnoticed to its prey before moving in for the kill. One minute Ralph was tearing at the dried meat, enjoyment evident in his wagging tail and perky ears, the next there was a blur of dappled movement, a single yelp, and the leopard turned towards the treeline, Ralph held firmly in its jaw.

Dallas raced for his gun.

'Forget it,' Logan shouted. 'It's already out of range. Anyway, the dog will be dead by now.'

'Was that what I think it was?'

'Leopard,' Logan told him. 'I wondered why the baboon were so noisy this morning.'

'Look at it this way,' Will said pragmatically when he saw the look of sadness on Dallas's face. 'If Ralph had stayed in the village he wouldn't have lasted another week.'

'We'd better get moving,' Dallas said curtly. The dog had been a complete pain in the neck but he'd somehow wriggled his way into Dallas's affections and would be missed.

With the drama of Ralph holding everyone's attention, Will's driver had picked up a whip and flicked it lazily in the direction of his old adversary. Whether he intended it to be a challenge or not would never be known. The Sotho had been whittling some spare *skeis*, wooden pegs that secured leather *reims* under the necks of inspanned oxen. He came off the ground in one fluid motion, his hand thrust forward, burying the knife to its hilt into the stunned Zulu's heart. The wound pumped blood as he fell to the ground. Leaning down, Logan's skinner retrieved his blade, casually wiped it clean on the driver's shirt, sat down and resumed his whittling. The first anyone else knew of it was when Mister David went to his wagon to tie down the canvas.

He came running back, eyes wide, shouting. 'Trouble. Big trouble.'

Dallas was still thinking about Ralph. 'What is it now?'

'You come.'

Blood drained slowly from the body, which twitched spasmodically. 'Jesus!'

Logan and Will joined them, alerted by Mister David's panic.

They stared down at the dead driver then, almost in slow motion, four heads turned to seek out the obvious perpetrator. The Sotho kept whittling.

Logan spoke sharply to him.

The man raised defiant eyes and shrugged. 'He came at me with a whip.'

Seeing that the dead Zulu still clasped the handle in his right hand, there was no option other than to believe the story.

'We'll have to bury him,' Dallas said softly.

'Leave it to the Africans. They have special rituals.'

'Are they sacred?'

'Some. Though out here, with none of his family present, probably not.'

Dallas checked with Mister David and was allowed to observe the entire process.

Tobacco, who knew the driver's family slightly, went to gather leaves from a strong-smelling shrub. These he boiled, using the water, once cooled, to wash the driver's face. Tobacco then shaved the man's head. While still pliant, the body was propped against one of the wagon wheels in a sitting position, knees drawn up under the chin, arms down each side. Using a blanket, the corpse was firmly bound into that position.

'What happens now?' Dallas asked Mister David.

'We must wait.'

'Why?'

Mister David looked reluctant to tell him but eventually obliged. 'It is a common belief that wizards can use the dead for evil. If we bury a person after the sun has set, they cannot find them.'

A grave was dug – about four feet deep and five long with a terrace cut into one end. 'That is where the body will sit,' Mister David told Dallas. 'It is important that he faces his home.'

Just after sunset, the dead man was carried to his resting place. It was Tobacco who stepped into the grave and placed the man and his sleeping mat on the ledge inside. Into the hole then went the driver's wooden headrest, a snuffbox, the hair shaved from him earlier in the day and his clothes. The man's sticks and *assegais* were broken and also added to the grave. A flat stone was placed on his head, another at his feet. Then river stones were piled in front of the body. Once it had been hidden from view, the grave was filled in with earth before being covered by bundles of grass. On top of this, more stones were placed, one from each of the Africans.

'It is a final farewell,' Mister David explained, handing Dallas a stone. 'You are welcome to say goodbye.'

'Is he now an ancestor?' Dallas asked, placing the stone carefully.

'No. His spirit will wander for many years before then. He must be brought home. It is a special ceremony which only family can perform.'

Talk that night was minimal. Dallas didn't feel like it anyway, especially since learning that words were considered to be unlucky on the day of a funeral. Even Will, who was bursting to have it out with Logan's skinner, held his tongue. The looks he directed at the African's fire sent a clear message that the man had some explaining to do. Seemingly unbothered, the skinner burned some elephant flesh and a few roots of some kind, reducing them to ashes. These he ate before walking off to bathe in the river.

Logan quietly explained, 'He has to purify himself. If the Sotho are anything like Zulus, he's only done half a job. A full ritual needs the flesh of lion, baboon, jackal, hyena and hawk as well. Still, he's done his best.'

'What will happen to him now?'

'He'll probably take off, meaning we'll have lost two good men. All Zulu blood belongs to their king. Since this chap's of a different tribe any attempt to make good by bringing cattle will fall on deaf ears. He would be put to death immediately.' A sardonic grin. 'They'd keep the cattle, of course.'

'What about our other boys? Will they take justice into their own hands?'

'If one of them was a brother, he would feel morally obliged to avenge the death. Fortunately for us, these men are not related. No. It's the king, or, at the very least, the dead man's chief who makes those decisions. My skinner is safe enough at the moment but we'll wake up one morning and find him gone.'

Mister David was busy making the strengthening *muthi* to protect himself and the other Zulus from being drawn after the deceased. None was offered to the three white men, though all the oxen were smoked with it to keep them safe and well.

Logan's skinner slipped from camp two days before they arrived at the home of John Dunn, a friend of Logan's. With the Sotho's departure came a lightening of tension and it was a buoyed and happy party who reached their journey's end at the mouth of the Thukela.

Dallas had learned a great deal over the past five months. His understanding of the Zulu language was still basic, though good enough to greet and pass the time of day with others. Appreciation and respect for the native people of Natal grew proportionately to his understanding of their ways. And with that came the conclusion that while he might admire their customs, he would never be one of them. The differences were too great. Very few white men ever bridged the two cultures; those who did usually turned their backs on an earlier life. John Dunn, their host, was one such man.

Logan had described Dunn as 'a crabby old bastard. Thinks he knows everything. Bad enemy, good friend. Hates most people. Not shy about mentioning it, either. You get on his nerves, he'll let you know.'

There was no sign of a disagreeable nature in

Dunn's effusive greeting, leaving Dallas with the impression that while John Dunn might be a loner, he was also lonely. He lived as one with the Zulus. His kraal, five miles from the Thukela River, was as traditional as any *umuzi*. Yet Dunn plied them with fine wine, food that bridged Zulu and European tastes and mattresses on the floor of grass huts.

Despite Logan's description, Dunn was not old. A man in his late thirties, he dressed as a Zulu, which emphasised his thin and gangling physique. But piercing dark eyes and a full beard gave him a presence, his authoritive manner compelling. Tough, colourful and a total non-conformist, John Dunn had, to his intense irritation, become a legend. Dallas was fascinated by him.

Born in England, Dunn was only two years old when his family emigrated to Africa. His father bought a farm and, for ten years, young John Dunn lived happily and well, mixing with Zulu and Xhosa labourers to the extent that his command of both languages and understanding of their traditions was formidable. At the age of twelve, everything changed. His father was trampled to death by an elephant. Four years later, his mother died. John was seventeen when he took to the bush, hunting elephants and hiring out his services as a guide in the Thukela Valley.

If any man knew the future Zulu king, Cetshwayo, it was Dunn. The events leading to their friendship were strange yet typical of the Zulu ways Dallas had come to understand. Before he ever met Cetshwayo, Dunn had been friendly with his archrival for the throne of Zululand, a half-brother called Mbuyazi. A confrontation between Cetshwayo and Mbuyazi was considered inevitable. John Dunn, who had been offered land in return for his services, agreed to command a motley collection of Natal native border police to assist Mbuyazi in an attempt to rid himself of his most persistent competitor.

Cetshwayo had been expecting such an act of rebellion and massed about twenty thousand men to support him. Mbuyazi had only seven thousand. Confrontation between the rivals began on an unseasonably cold and misty morning in December 1856. Dunn was quick to see that Mbuyazi was seriously outnumbered and urged the Zulu to withdraw. Mbuyazi, however, with pride and ambition burning inside him, refused. In any case, it was too late by then. Cetshwayo's warriors pushed Mbuyazi back towards the Thukela River which, after recent storms, was swollen and raging. Many of his supporters who were not killed in the fighting were drowned trying to cross the muddy brown water, their bodies washed out to sea. John Dunn escaped in a boat which he'd prudently arranged to have waiting for him.

Considered an enemy by the prince regent, it might be expected that Cetshwayo would place a price on Dunn's head. However, this was not the Zulu way. As was custom, the spoils of war included an enemy's cattle. In the rounding up of these, some one thousand head belonging to various European traders were mistakenly taken by Cetshwayo.

John Dunn volunteered to try and get them back. First he went to Mpande. The old king was so afraid of Cetshwayo that he would only speak with Dunn in the centre of a cattle kraal where they could not be overheard. On hearing first-hand detail of the battle, Mpande was overcome with emotion at the loss of a son, yet he remained grateful to Dunn for his assistance. 'Go to the Mangweni kraal. Tell Cetshwayo I demand the return of any white man's cattle.'

The prince was well aware of Dunn's involvement with Mbuyazi but didn't mention it. The cattle were handed back with no fuss and Dunn was paid a reward of £250 by the grateful traders. With this money, John himself began trading in Zululand. He met Cetshwayo several times over the ensuing few years and a friendship developed between the two. Cetshwayo needed a white man he could trust to advise him, one who could write and read letters to and from the British. He offered the job to Dunn, who accepted and moved to land granted him by Cetshwayo. There he built a house and married Catherine Pierce, the daughter of a white father and mixed-race mother. As time went by, he also accumulated forty-nine Zulu wives. Some regarded Dunn as a white tribesman. The residents of Durban treated him as a disreputable outcast. Zulus respected the man, some even acknowledging him as their chief.

Once talk around the fire turned to Zulu politics, Dallas was content to listen and learn. 'What you have to understand about Cetshwayo is that he doesn't really have an allegiance to anyone but his own people,' Dunn told them in response to a question from Will about the Zulu heir apparent. 'He's a traditionalist. He'll go against other tribes but has no real desire to fight the white man.' He pulled a burning stick from the fire and relit his cigar.

'We've not heard much of him lately,' Logan said. 'What's he up to?'

'Biding his time mainly,' Dunn replied, sipping a particularly fine red wine he'd acquired from somewhere. 'I assume you've heard that Mpande has accepted the fact that Cetshwayo is his heir.'

'Does he have a choice? The prince has murdered all opposition.'

'Not quite.' Dunn puffed life into his cigar before going on. 'A couple escaped. Mind you, Zululand will be better off under Cetshwayo. At least he has the interests of his people at heart.'

'What are you saying?' Logan asked.

'The Boers are grooming one young heir to the throne. The British another. Think what that could mean.'

'Land-grabbing. We know the Boers want Zululand for themselves.'

'It's a well-established practice already. They encroach, the Zulus drive them off. Doesn't stop them coming back, though.'

'Be that as it may,' Logan said carelessly, 'I thought both sides acknowledged Cetshwayo as the next king.'

Dunn smiled thinly. 'Don't be so gullible, old

friend. The two princelings may never get a chance to challenge Cetshwayo. The Boers and British both know that. Then again, they might. Nothing is predictable save for one thing. The issue of land. It doesn't go away and never will. Mpande cultivates the Dutch, Cetshwayo prefers our countrymen. Do you think either has Zulu interests at heart? Only fools would say so. There is a dark cloud looming which cannot be ignored. This land has little time left. And, let me tell you, nothing will be resolved around a table. It is on the battlefield that the future of Zululand will be decided.'

'Does this come from Cetshwayo? Are you saying that the Zulus are preparing to fight?'

'The Zulus?' Dunn seemed surprised. 'Not yet, but yes, of course they will defend what is rightfully theirs. What would you expect them to do? They can't possibly win, although I doubt there's a man among them who would admit it. No, my friends, I'm referring to something more serious than that. An all-out confrontation between Boer and British. You mark my words, this country will run with the blood of us all, Zulu, English and Dutch alike. Make the most of this place while you can. I give it another ten years at best.'

'That's a bit pessimistic,' Logan objected.

Dunn waved his arm to indicate their surroundings. 'Look around you. Ever seen such fat cattle, such lush crops? This is God's own country.'

In a lull of contemplation that followed this comment, Dallas leaned forward. 'What is Cetshwayo actually like?'

Dunn's eyes twinkled. 'You have no idea,' the man said, smiling, 'how often I'm asked that.' Realising that Dallas was about to retract his question he held up a hand. 'No. If you are to make your life here, you should know.' He paused a second, then continued. 'For a Zulu, he is considered handsome. Quite a shy person or, at least, reserved. A man who speaks softly and is also able to listen. When it is required of him, he will speak out and is not afraid to challenge the opinions of others. More important than anything, however, is his belief in maintaining those principles which formed the Zulu nation.' Dunn shrugged his shoulders. 'I respect the man. He can hold his own with most whites and is not fooled by political machinations. Cetshwayo is generally well liked. What more can you ask of a future king?'

'And Mpande?'

Dunn chuckled. 'To European eyes he is a joke. All they see is an enormously obese man, too fat to walk. He is wheeled around in a little wagon. The king is fond of talking with traders and hearing their gossip. His people show respect, sing his praises and he is much loved, but we all know that the real power is Cetshwayo. Mpande will be remembered mainly for his peaceful reign, though, in the early days, he was more than capable of showing himself as a fine warrior.'

'Cetshwayo has a son, doesn't he?' Logan asked.

'Correct. Dinuzulu. He's already been named as his father's successor.'

'Will he get the chance to rule, do you think?'

'Nothing is certain save that the Zulus will always have a king. How much power he will wield beyond his own people is debatable.'

Logan glanced up at his friend. 'Where does all this leave you?'

John Dunn laughed. 'Me? I've known the best of Zululand. Younger men like Dallas here will see it for a while yet but, mark my words, his sons won't. The next Zulu king could well be the last. Oh, there'll be others, but it's my guess that in Cetshwayo we'll see the beginning of the end.' Dunn frowned. 'And let me tell you something else. It won't be the Zulus' fault.'

'What will you do if that happens?' Logan asked. 'Can't see you settling in Durban.'

'Ach, man!' Dunn reacted impatiently. 'Don't be stupid. What would I do in a town? I will stay. I'm more Zulu than English now. With luck, I won't live to see it end.'

His words sobered everyone until Will changed the subject. 'We head south from here. Our wagons are full. It's been a profitable trip. The Zulus still need to trade.'

John Dunn was not inclined towards optimism. 'Make the most of it,' he advised. 'Once the English or Dutch get their hands on this place there'll be no room for traders. They'll tame this land with roads and towns and the Kaffirs will have no need of you.'

Dunn's words stayed with Dallas all the way to Durban. He'd enjoyed the trip and wondered if Will and Logan would be prepared to join him for another. If the man regarded as a white Zulu was right and his predictions proved true, they might as well make as much money as they could while the opportunity still existed. Two nights out of Durban, he put the question to them.

Logan flatly refused. 'Don't take this personally, old chap, but I operate a hell of a lot better on my own. We'll clear enough with this load for me to pay you back and have some left over. I'm heading north.'

Disappointed, Dallas turned to Will.

'Who'll shoot elephants if he doesn't come?' Will asked.

It was a good point. Logan's expertise with a gun had brought in considerably more ivory than trading for it.

'I assume that means no.' Dallas tried to hide his feelings. 'Then I'll go on my own if I must.'

Logan grunted amusement. 'I wouldn't lose any sleep over it if I were you. It should take Will about three days to find himself broke again. He'll be with you.'

'Not this time.' Will shook his head vehemently. 'I'm going to finance my own trip.'

'And go where?' Logan challenged.

'South into Pondoland.' Will grinned. 'I hear it's wide open to traders.'

'Well,' Dallas said expansively, 'when you two run out of money, you'll know where to find me. I'm heading back to the Thukela Valley.'

'Fancy yourself as another John Dunn, do you?' Logan teased.

'Could do a lot worse,' Dallas replied soberly. 'I like that country.'

'So do the Zulus,' Will reminded him. 'And they got there first.'

'A man's got to have a plan,' Logan put in. 'Just don't tell God about it.'

'Why not?' Will was, surprisingly, quite a religious man.

'It makes him laugh.'

They spent the best part of a morning at Cato's warehouse laying out tusks and haggling over prices. The wagons went for repairs and were promised to be ready for use within two weeks. Dallas would keep two, the other having been bought by Logan. Oxen and the other cattle and spare horses were sold. 'More trouble than they're worth. Best to get rid of them and buy more when you leave.'

For once, Logan agreed with Will.

Mister David said he was going home for a visit. 'In ten days,' he told Dallas, 'if you need a driver, I will be outside the store waiting for you.'

Dallas felt a keen sense of separation as he said goodbye to each man who had been with them.

It was late afternoon when he mounted Tosca and turned towards the Berea. Mrs Watson's boarding establishment may not have a room for him, but with a bit of luck there would be letters from home. Eager as he was to hear from family, Dallas hoped above all that Lorna had written. A forlorn hope, he knew. She must hate him now.

Keeping Tosca at a steady walk, Dallas reflected on all he had learned since first arriving in Durban. Initial impressions had been tinged with anxiety and doubt. Now the sights seemed quite familiar and he felt at home. He'd been away nearly six months and the knowledge he'd acquired along the way far exceeded that which most people would pick up in a lifetime. When first setting foot on this land he'd been ignorant, awed and intimidated; now he was learning to love it.

In good humour – Dallas had more than doubled the monies outlaid at the onset of their trading expedition – he reined in outside Mrs Watson's gate. He paid scant attention to a fine-looking carriage drawn up outside. Anxious to see if there was any mail, Dallas hurried to the front door.

Mabel, the African maid, opened it and he greeted her in Zulu. Giggling with delight, she asked him to wait.

Ann Watson's expression alerted Dallas that something was amiss. 'Well now,' she said stiffly, blocking the doorway. 'A fine pickle you left behind. I'm surprised you have the nerve to show yourself after such scandalous behaviour. Did you think the whole thing would just blow over?'

'I beg your pardon?' Dallas actually took a step backwards, so surprised was he at her verbal outburst.

'You are a cad, sir.' Mrs Watson nearly shouted the words. 'That poor wee girl left alone to cry herself sick. The shame of it. How dare you walk back in here as if nothing ever happened?'

'Mrs Watson, I –'

'You'll not set foot in this house, sir, until I hear it from your own lips that you intend to do the honourable thing.'

'Honourable . . . what . . .' Dallas took a deep breath. 'I haven't the faintest idea what you're talking about.'

A bellow from within the house was so loud and full of fury it made Dallas jump. The squat, burly figure of Mr Wilcox was the last thing he expected to see, especially hurtling down the hall towards him with nothing short of murder his clear intention. 'I'll kill you with my bare hands, you damned Bluebeard. Vile seducer. You are an abomination, sir.' Mr Wilcox stopped next to Mrs Watson, panting with rage. 'I demand to know your intentions.'

'About what?'

Mr Wilcox, who was already a very unhealthy shade of red, went puce. 'My daughter, you ruiner of women. Sarah. I demand that you marry her as quickly as possible.'

'Sarah?' Dallas was still trying to work out what was going on. 'What on earth are you talking about?'

Mrs Watson tossed her head. 'Well, really, Mr Granger, I expected more from you than this.'

Mr Wilcox turned to Mabel, who was hovering, wide-eyed, nearby. 'Tell my daughter that her worthless lover has returned. She is to come downstairs immediately.' He looked at Mrs Watson. 'If you don't mind, madam, I would appreciate a few private minutes with the two of them.'

'Of course, Mr Wilcox.'

With a final look of disgust thrown at Dallas, Mrs Watson disappeared into the kitchen.

'Inside,' snapped Mr Wilcox.

Dallas followed him into the drawing room. The visibly perspiring man flung himself into a chair then, just as quickly rose and began to pace. 'I suppose you're going to deny seducing my daughter?'

'Seducing . . .'

'Seducing, sir. She is with child.'

'I . . .'

'You took advantage of an innocent young girl in her hour of need. You, who had been charged with her safe return. You . . .' Mr Wilcox was spluttering so hard he could barely speak. 'You – profligate. Of all the iniquitous acts of depravity, sir, I have heard of none worse. What do you have to say for yourself?'

Dallas's jaw fell at the news that Sarah was carrying a child, supposed, by her father, to be his. 'This has nothing to do with me, sir. I did not lay a finger on your daughter.'

His denial only spurred Mr Wilcox to greater fury.

Dallas cut across the man's outrage. 'Ask her. Sarah will confirm my words.'

'Ask her yourself, you corrupter of all things decent.'

Turning, Dallas saw Sarah hovering in the doorway. 'Sarah!'

She ran to him. 'Oh, my darling. I knew you'd

come back.' Her arms encircled his waist and she buried her face into his chest.

'Sarah!' Dallas eased the girl away. 'What . . . ?'

She looked up at him with shining eyes. 'Now we can be wed, for you promised that you would.'

'There, sir. Wriggle out of that if you can. I demand that you marry my daughter as quickly as possible.'

'Like hell!' Dallas was suddenly furious. 'I am not responsible for the child she carries.'

'My daughter is no liar, sir. She's scarcely more than a child herself. You will marry her, or by God, sir —'

'I want nothing to do with this. I have witnesses to prove that Sarah was returned to your care unsullied by me or anyone else in my party. I will not be forced into marrying her.'

Mr Wilcox smiled nastily. 'Oh, I think you will. I have the *London Times* shipped to me. There's an interesting story in one of their issues about a Lord Dallas Acheson and a certain Lady de Iongh's charge against him. The police seek him urgently. There's a reward for information regarding his whereabouts. The lithograph likeness looks remarkably like you, Mr Dallas Granger. Interesting, don't you think, that Lord Acheson's family home is the Grange in Edinburgh?' Mr Wilcox's smile turned triumphant. 'You have two choices, young man. Marry my daughter or be returned to England in chains. What say you?'

Ignoring him, Dallas turned to Sarah. 'Will you kindly tell your father the truth.'

'But Dallas . . .' Tears filled her eyes and her lips trembled. A credible performance by any standards.

'I made no promises and you know full well that the father of your child is not me. Why do you lie?'

Sarah buried her face in both hands and sobbed.

'Tell the truth, you foolish girl,' Dallas snapped. 'For I want no part of this deception.'

Sarah only sobbed harder.

'Enough, sir. I will not tolerate you bullying my daughter. You, and nobody else, are responsible for her condition, despite your cowardly and ungentlemanly denials. Do you intend to do the honourable thing, sir, or will it be necessary to send for the constabulary?'

'Sarah!' Dallas beseeched. 'For the love of God, will you please tell your father the truth.'

'Enough, I say,' Mr Wilcox roared. 'You have two choices and two seconds to make one. Which is it to be?'

Dallas stared at the man, hating him. He was left with little option. Marriage to a girl he didn't love who was carrying another man's child, or return to Scotland and the hangman's rope. 'Very well. I will marry Sarah. But be warned, sir, my name will be the only thing of mine she carries.'

He heard Sarah gasp with relief and felt her hand on his arm. It was all Dallas could do not to shake it off.

Sarah's father bounced once on his toes and nodded. 'There is no need for you to stay here further, Sarah. Go and pack. Now that Mr Granger has declared his intentions you can join your mother and me in town, at the hotel.'

Sarah, head bowed, moved to obey, not looking at Dallas or her father.

Mr Wilcox crossed the room, hand outstretched, his smile warming, though still calculating. 'Excellent. Welcome to our family, Dallas. I may call you Dallas, may I not?' Suddenly jovial, he made no effort to hide his obvious relief.

Dallas ignored the proffered hand, turned his back and moved to the window, staring out, seeing nothing.

'Come, young man. My daughter is as fine a catch as any. You will have no cause to regret your decision.'

Dallas spoke coldly. 'You give me little choice. I find it reprehensible that a father would willingly give his daughter to a man charged with rape. It tells me two things, sir. One, that you do not believe I committed such a crime. And two, you know full well I am not the father of Sarah's child. You are using a supposed crime against me for your own purpose. Talk of honour is a joke.'

Behind him, Wilcox began to splutter again.

'Save such false indignation for those who would believe it. You have me cornered. Congratulations. An expeditious solution to the quandary in which your daughter has placed you. I don't imagine Sarah came up with this answer on her own, though her willingness to participate says little for her character. I have no love for your

406

daughter and never will. Do not expect me to live and work alongside either of you. I intend to carry on trading.'

'But Sarah cannot be left on her own,' Wilcox objected.

Dallas still did not turn. 'Take her to Colenso. Do whatever you please. Frankly, I don't care. Two weeks from now I leave for the midlands with no expectation of returning for six months.'

'You cannot treat my daughter thus,' Wilcox shouted. 'She deserves the respect of her husband.'

'Do not tempt me to tell you what Sarah deserves.' Dallas spun back to face his future father-in-law. 'Damn you to hell, Wilcox. You and your conniving daughter.' Dallas strode from the room.

He almost collided with Mrs Watson, who hurriedly straightened up from where she had been listening outside the door.

'I'm certain you heard all that, madam.'

She was flustered but managed to say, 'Congratulations, Mr Granger. If you'll wait a moment, I have some letters for you.'

There were three. Without even glancing at them, Dallas stuffed the envelopes in a pocket, and left. At the gate, he swung onto Tosca and pushed her hard back into town. He needed a drink. In fact, he intended to get blind, stinking, falling-down drunk.

Dallas Granger married Sarah Wilcox six days later in a quiet civil ceremony with no guests other than her parents and Mrs Watson. Logan offered to be best man but Dallas curtly told him the term was inappropriate considering the circumstances.

'Are you sure, old boy, that you didn't –'

'I'm reasonably certain I'd have remembered,' Dallas said bluntly.

'Then why not refuse?'

'I can't.'

Logan stared at him. 'You're being blackmailed?'

'Precisely.'

'I won't ask –'

'Don't.'

The subject was dropped. Logan took the first wagon to be ready for use and headed north a day before the wedding.

Despite the circumstances, Sarah wore a white gown for the ceremony, which only served to emphasise her thickening waist. In fact, though knowing little of such things, Dallas thought the birth more imminent than her stated four months would indicate. Their wedding present from her parents was a modest house three doors distant from Mrs Watson, who promised to look in on Sarah while Dallas was away. Sarah's father had bought the place as an investment, intending to put in a caretaker landlady and run the establishment as a boarding house. Dallas barely acknowledged his new father-in-law's generosity, feeling that the house was just one more link in his heavy chain of captivity.

On their wedding night, alone together for the first time, he and Sarah finally spoke of the situation in which they found themselves. It came as no surprise to Dallas to learn that his new bride was as disenchanted with the arrangement as he. Dominated by her father to the extent that she was totally in awe of him, Sarah admitted that she'd simply allowed him to take control of her situation.

'No more secrets between us, Sarah. How far gone are you?'

'Seven months,' she whispered.

'So you knew you were pregnant when I took you home to Colenso?'

'I suspected.'

'Why did you not marry the father?'

'I couldn't. Father forbade it. Anyway, it would have been impossible. He –'

Dallas held up a hand. 'I have no interest in his identity. I daresay your dear father thought him beneath you.'

Tears filled her eyes.

'Are you in love with him?'

She bowed her head, unwilling to meet his gaze. Dark ringlets bobbed as she nodded.

Dallas let out a deep breath and groaned. 'Oh, Sarah! How could you agree to this marriage? You've made a mess of both our lives. I don't love you and you don't love me. Wasn't it enough that you ruined your own life? Why did you have to destroy mine too?'

'Father –'

'To hell with your father. Don't speak to me of that damnable man. I cannot abide him. He's bullied and blackmailed to get his own way, with no thought of anyone's satisfaction but his own. He may be your father, Sarah, but when I am here the man is not welcome in this house. I never wish to see him again.'

Sarah rose, crossed the room and sank down at Dallas's feet. 'I'm sorry. Forgive me. I'll try to be a good wife.'

Black despair settled on Dallas and he buried his face in both hands. Lorna's letter, one of the three given to him by Mrs Watson and which he had carried since then, should have filled him with joy. Looking at Sarah, he pulled the envelope from his pocket and waved it in her face. 'This is the woman I love. But for you, we would soon be wed. You have ruined my life. Go to bed, Sarah.'

She bit her lip then burst out, 'What about me? You are not the only one wronged. I am unhappy too.'

Dallas rose. 'Then, my dear,' he said cuttingly, anger making him cruel, 'perhaps you should have kept your legs together.'

Sarah gasped as though physically struck.

Remorse hit Dallas immediately. 'I apologise. That was unforgivable.'

She struggled to rise and he bent to help. Facing him, Sarah's eyes were steady. 'I know you are angry. I understand. I'm sorry. But, Dallas, many marry without love and still find happiness.'

'True,' he conceded. 'Love is often absent from a union. Then, too, so is deceit.'

'You are determined to hate me even though I offer to meet you halfway?'

Suddenly he felt weary. 'Perhaps in time, Sarah,

but not yet. I cannot pretend that which is not there.'

She nodded slowly. 'Then can we at least try to remain civil?'

Dallas frowned. She was trying hard, perhaps too hard. He remembered how she had flirted with him on the journey between Howick Falls and Colenso. A woman pregnant to a man she claims to love does not flirt with another unless . . . He spoke slowly, feeling his way. 'You are not in love with the father of this child, are you? I conveniently came along and provided a perfect way out. You told your father I'd seduced you. It was all your idea. That's the truth, isn't it, Sarah? Whether he believes it I cannot say. I suspect not.'

The look on her face gave him the answer.

'You're no better than your father. Don't speak of civility between us, it cannot be. I do not trust you.'

'Dallas!' Her hands stretched out imploringly. 'I fell in love with you.'

'Love?' Derision was strong in his voice. 'You don't know what it means.' He turned his back. 'Go to bed, Sarah. It's been a difficult day. No more lies. Just go.'

The voice behind him was small. 'Will you come too?'

Dallas nearly snorted in disbelief. 'No. I'll sleep in the other room.'

Sarah persisted. 'If you wanted to, I wouldn't mind.'

'I don't want to. Go to bed.'

She turned and left without another word.

Alone, Dallas opened Lorna's letter and read it for perhaps the hundredth time:

My dear Dallas,

Yesterday, during a visit to Edinburgh, I paid my compliments to your mother. Naturally, Lady Pamela would not divulge news of you and I refrained from placing her in a difficult situation by asking. I could not help, however, noticing a half-written letter on her escritoire and, whilst she was absent from the room, saw it was addressed to you. Yours to her lay underneath and, I confess, it was irresistible for me not to take a peek.

So much more is clear, my dear. I believed you had betrayed me. In a way, you had, and I find myself undecided as to the extent I can forgive you. I do know, however, that my love for you matches that which you profess for me. And so, I sit here now at Canongate urgently penning these words to you.

Lorna's letter was dated almost four months ago. It went on:

Mama's accusations are nothing more than a tissue of lies. I know you are incapable of such foul actions. It is your duplicity which vexes and torments me. I try so hard to understand that men are different but, Dallas, how could you? It is this that keeps me unsure. Do you truly love me? If you do, can I allow what is past to come between us? Is my love strong enough to forgive and forget? Were it not for both our circumstances, would you have continued the *affaire de coeur* with Mama?

I have good reasons to ask. You may reply to my Dumfries address knowing anything you write will remain between us. My marriage has proved to be a farce and it is news of this that behoves me to write to you for I do believe that you should know the truth.

Lord Dumfries suffered a stroke. He now hovers between life and death with little hope of recovery. My dear, he was struck down before making any demand to consummate our marriage. Our child grows strong within me. Soon my condition will begin to show. While my husband will know it cannot possibly be his, he is incapable of speech or indeed movement. No-one will guess and our son (for I am convinced it's a boy) will inherit all.

I know it is impossible that you return to Scotland, but on the demise of Dumfries there is no reason why I should not travel to Africa where we can be together at last.

You will be pleased to learn that Father has agreed to allow Charles and Charlotte to marry. I do believe that in his heart of hearts, Papa does not think you capable of the charges he was forced to lay against you. I'm afraid, however, that pride will never allow him to drop them.

Please reply as soon as you can. Until there is contact between us we cannot begin to rebuild the

*trust which we once enjoyed. I would appreciate
total honesty, Dallas, whether it be good news
or bad.*

> *Until then, I remain,*
> *Faithfully yours.*
> *Lorna*

The letter should have filled Dallas with the purest
happiness. Instead, he was consumed with despair.
What could he say? That he loved her but had been
blackmailed into a marriage he didn't want? She'd
never believe him, not after his past deceit. He
could not lie – he owed her the total honesty she'd
asked for. Did he have the strength to say he was
happily married now and that Lorna and their
child were a thing of the past? No, he couldn't do
that either. Did he just ignore the letter? How?
That wasn't fair. And, oh God, how he ached to see
her again.

Dallas Granger spent his wedding night in deep
contemplation of a wine decanter which, for some
unaccountable reason, seemed to require regular
refilling. By the time he fell into bed he was, to his
intense satisfaction, as drunk as a lord.

Ten days later, Dallas set off again for the Thukela
Valley. Logan, he thought, would be well into
Zululand by now, having taken the quicker coast
road. Of Will there had been no sign, although
Dallas did hear he'd gone south as planned. Mister
David, good as his word, had been waiting at Cato's
store. Tobacco and July also opted to go with

Dallas. With two wagons, a second team was needed. Having learned his lesson the hard way, those employed were all Zulus.

Dallas was anxious to leave Durban, craving the order and simple commonsense of Zulu company. He longed for solitude in the Thukela Valley, the purity of a star-studded sky, the honesty of animals and the earthiness of other traders. Anything would be better than staying with Sarah and her anxious eyes, which he trusted no more than the words she spoke.

In those ten days before he left, Dallas spent more time than was necessary in town, most of it frequenting grog shops and taverns seeking the company of strangers who asked no questions because their lives were no better than his and didn't need the burden of another's woes. In one such establishment he encountered Jeremy Hardcastle. The former first officer was full of resentment; Dallas, of anger. Both had been drinking rum. The inevitable fight was shambling but vicious, Dallas winning the encounter by breaking Hardcastle's jaw.

Police arrived to arrest the sailor who had managed to elude them since being erroneously released after his previous attack on Dallas. Knowing he would be shipped back to France to face charges for breaking his contract, Hardcastle again slipped away and could not be found. Nobody looked very hard for him. The case was of little relevance in Africa and besides, British and French relations were strained to say the least.

Dallas received a warning for public brawling and Tosca, who was growing used to returning home with him sprawled across her neck, obliged yet again.

Dallas knew he was behaving badly. He could barely bring himself to speak with Sarah. She tried hard to please, keeping the house clean, preparing meals that, more often than not, he was too drunk to eat. With the physical work being done by the gardener, she established a small vegetable patch and tried hard to elicit Dallas's approval when she proudly showed him the neat rows, each identified by a stake bearing a description of what lay under the soil. He stared at it, shrugged his shoulders and returned inside. Each night she timidly intimated that if he wished to enter her bed she would make him welcome. He seldom bothered to reply and always slept alone.

He wrote a short letter to Lorna, agonising over every word.

My dearest love,
Once again, circumstances conspire against us. I cannot bring myself to explain. It is best that you forget me for I am, indeed, unworthy of your love and respect.
Know this, my darling, I have always loved you and always will. The miles that so cruelly lie between us make little difference. My heart breaks for that which we cannot have. It is my heartfelt wish, however, that you will, one day, find the happiness you so richly deserve.

Oh, that I could hold you and our child in my arms. It cannot be.
Yours forever,
Dallas.

On the morning of Dallas's departure he was hungover and silent.

'When will you be back?' Sarah asked.

'Don't know.'

'How long do you think?' she persisted.

'Four to six months.'

'Oh!'

'Why so surprised? Some traders are away longer.'

'Yes, but –'

'But nothing. This is what I do. Get used to it.'

Sarah bit her lip. 'Do you mind if my mother stays here? At least until the baby's born?'

'I mind everything about your parents. What you do while I'm not here is up to you. Just make sure she's gone before I get back.'

'Dallas, can you not at least leave in friendship?'

'I offered that. Look where it got me.'

Sarah flushed and her eyes slid away.

Dallas touched his hat. 'Farewell.' He turned Tosca and rode away. It was conscience that had him stop and look back. Sarah still stood, just outside their gate, watching his departure. Dallas returned to her side. 'I'm sorry, Sarah. I resent being forced to marry you, and cannot forgive your part in this. One day we might work things out but now it's too soon for me. Time apart may help. Then again, it may not. I wish you well with the birth. Your baby will have my name though never my heart.'

'And me? Is that all you offer?' Tears sprang into her eyes.

'I won't lie to you, Sarah. Don't expect more. It's the best I can do.'

She turned and half-ran, half-waddled, back to the house. Dallas thought she looked like a hippopotamus, ungainly out of the water, with a heavy stomach and awkward movements. The front door slammed so loudly that Tosca skittered in alarm.

'What was I supposed to say?' Dallas asked his horse, flicking lightly on the reins.

Tosca pricked her ears at the question.

'And how was I supposed to tell Lorna?' he added miserably. 'Damn it to hell. My wife makes me feel guilty when, in truth, it is she who should be penitent.' Dallas nudged Tosca's flanks with his heels and she responded by breaking into a canter. 'Ah, to hell with it!' he shouted, feeling the release of constraint as his horse gathered speed. 'Let's go back to the bush.'

The trip went well. Dallas was remembered and made welcome. His command of Zulu had improved, though he kept Mister David by his side for difficult negotiations. Although refusing to hunt elephant, many villages had a stockpile of ivory that had once belonged to those who had developed a penchant for mealies, the Zulus' most important source of food. Having less ivory was compensated for by the fact that he had no partners with whom to share a percentage of its value. They often lingered longer than necessary when finding a pleasant place to outspan. There was no hurry and it became a relaxed and contented journey. On two shillings a day, plus food, the Africans were well pleased with the pace.

They skirted the spot where Will's driver had been buried. The Zulus refused to go near it, superstitious dread of the unclaimed dead stronger than any order from this world. Dallas understood and they outspanned in the next valley. Alone, he rode back to make sure the grave remained undisturbed. The place was as they left it.

The elephant that had died during the great meeting had provided a feast for the scavengers of Africa, both large and small. A hollow-skinned carcass, white with droppings of vultures, was all that remained, save for well over a hundred pounds of ivory. The tusks required little effort to remove. Dallas strapped them on either side of Tosca's back, took the reins and walked the distance back to camp.

So far as he could tell, no-one had traded in the valley since his first trip. That was fine with him. Dallas felt connected to the place, almost regarding it as his own territory. He took to scouting the hills, solitude and space allowing the peace denied by recent events back in Durban.

Midway through the trip, Mister David and the others became strangely nervous. There were, they said, many bad omens to be found. Yet, at each kraal they visited, they were welcomed with courtesy.

'There is something bad,' Mister David told

Dallas as they left one *umuzi*. 'The people are afraid to tell what it is. They say the king is indisposed.'

'He is an old man. Sickness is to be expected.'

Mister David shook his head. 'I am thinking that the king is dead.'

'What makes you say that?'

'Cetshwayo has summoned all the princes. I cannot say more. We are forbidden to speak of it until a new king declares himself.'

Dallas planned to call on John Dunn. Surely he would know if Mpande was dead?

He was pleasantly surprised to find Logan there too, although all was not well with his one-time partner. Logan was recovering from an encounter with a protective lioness. She'd ripped his left arm open, from shoulder to elbow, severing muscle and tendons alike before the knife he wielded with his right hand found tender flesh and she decided to back off.

'Silly bastard still didn't kill her,' Dunn observed witheringly.

'She had cubs,' Logan protested.

'Yes. And a fair proportion of your arm dangling from her mouth.'

Dallas was keen to ask about Mpande, but before he could, Dunn and Logan were determined to give him all the gory details of the injury.

Out towards Nkwalini, far from medical help, Logan had allowed tribal treatment of his injuries. But the teeth and claws of a lion carry all kinds of germs, and a raging fever soon set in. Logan had insisted he be taken to John Dunn and the fifty-odd miles were covered at breakneck speed, a race against time.

Dunn took one look at his friend, decided there was nothing to lose, and sent for a local *inyanga*. On arrival, the medicine man immediately cut open the suppurating sores, draining enough black blood and pus to almost fill a small gourd. Logan had little use of his left arm. The Zulus had long been aware of the healing powers to be found in penicillium, a bluish-green fungus that grows on stale fruit. The *inyanga* stuffed Logan's wounds with a mixture of his own making that contained a large proportion of this mould.

Although the patient's recovery was slow, he was getting better. Logan had been at Dunn's kraal for nearly two weeks and was itching to get moving. 'Can't do much with this bloody arm, old boy, so my hunting days could well be over. Still, I can get by on trading.'

Finally, Dallas was able to ask about Mpande.

John Dunn looked thoughtful for a moment, as if trying to decide how much to say. 'How much have you heard?'

'Nothing. Just that Mpande is indisposed. Mister David says it means he is dead but refuses to elaborate.'

'Hmmm.' Dunn glanced over towards where Mister David sat with Tobacco, July and several others. 'That's a good Kaffir you've got there. I'm surprised he told you that much. No-one is supposed to speak of a king's death until his successor announces it. That can't happen until the corpse has dried out.'

'Dried out?'

'It's their custom. They bind the body of a king into a squatting position and wrap it in the skin of a young steer. Then a fire is lit and kept alight. They burn wood that gives off a pleasant smell which is supposed to disguise the stench. Doesn't work. You can smell it a mile off.'

'You've been to the *isigodlo*?'

'I heard that the inner council had shaved their heads. It is a sign of mourning. Then I, too, was told the king was indisposed. I went to see for myself. I don't know how those poor devils live with that awful smell.'

'So he is dead?'

'You didn't hear it from me.'

'I suppose they'll kill off his body-servant and several women to go with him when he's buried.' Logan clearly disapproved.

'Bound to.' Dunn shrugged it off. 'It's the way they've always done it.'

Once again, Dallas realised that while a lot of the Zulu ways made sense, there were some customs he simply could not accept. This was one of them. John Dunn, perhaps because he had been exposed to them from a very early age, didn't appear to have difficulty in adopting these strange aspects of Zulu culture. He was welcome to them.

Dallas and Logan returned to Durban together. They had both been away for nearly six months. At Cato's, the two men found a prosperous-looking Will and all three of them set out to celebrate.

Reluctantly, two days later, Dallas bid his friends farewell and returned to the cottage. To his annoyance, Sarah's parents were there.

His wife met him as he came through the front door. She didn't greet him and appeared nervous. 'Mother and Father –'

'I know. I saw the carriage.'

'Dallas!' boomed a voice from within. 'Pleased to see you, my boy. Heard you were back.' Mr Wilcox sounded unnecessarily hearty. With reluctance, Dallas went into the parlour where his father-in-law waited. 'Welcome home. Sarah, what about some tea for the lad, he must be parched.'

Mrs Wilcox glanced up at Dallas then looked quickly away.

'Madam,' Dallas said bluntly. There was no way he would, or even could, call the woman Mother.

She nodded, still not looking at him, glanced fearfully at her husband, then dropped her head.

Fine, Dallas thought. I don't want to speak with you either.

Sarah brought tea and cake. Dallas ignored both and poured himself a whisky, no doubt a present from his in-laws, then turned to face his silent audience.

'No-one has mentioned Sarah's child, though obviously there is one, since my wife is no longer pregnant.'

Mr Wilcox coughed nervously, his wife dabbed her eyes and Sarah sat down suddenly.

'The child is born. A boy,' Wilcox said finally.

'Oh.' Dallas looked at him politely.

'He was born four months ago. Prematurely,' Sarah said.

Dallas nodded and waited.

'I owe you an apology.' Mr Wilcox bowed his head and it took Dallas some moments to realise that the man was weeping. They all were.

'Was he stillborn? Is he ill? What is wrong with you all?'

Wilcox wiped his eyes, fumbled in a pocket, produced a handkerchief and blew his nose with a loud trumpeting sound. 'The baby is hale,' he said, wiping nose and mouth vigorously.

Sarah's eyes could not meet Dallas's. 'Please try to forgive me.'

Dallas put down his glass. 'Where is the boy?'

Eyes darted around the room, as if seeking a victim who would break the news. Wilcox himself provided the answer. 'The baby's father has him. It's for the best.'

Clarity dawned, so obvious it was a wonder Dallas hadn't thought of it before. And, if true, it provided the way out of this loveless marriage. 'How very unusual,' he said softly. 'A seducer would not want his bastard son. Nor, I suggest, would a man who already has a wife. That leaves but one other option, doesn't it? The father is African.' He glared at Sarah. 'Am I right?'

Her mouth opened but no sound came.

'Thulani,' Dallas guessed. 'The Zulu who drove your wagon. He's the father, isn't he?'

Sarah nodded reluctantly.

'So, my dear, you carried a bastard Zulu child

which you thought to pass off as mine. I swear, I don't know if you are innocent, devious or just plain stupid. You fall pregnant, produce a child which can't possibly belong to the man you blackmail into marriage, ruin his life, then ask forgiveness.' Dallas turned to Wilcox. 'And you, sir, were party to this deceit? You knew?'

All the puff and wind had gone from his father-in-law. 'I had no idea who . . . It was as much of a shock to me as it must be to you.'

Dallas downed the rest of his whisky and gave a short laugh. 'It comes as no shock to me, I assure you. Your entire family has connived and lied with no regard for the feelings of others. I detest you all.'

'Son –'

'I am not your son, sir, nor will I ever be.' Dallas turned to leave the room.

'Where are you going?' Sarah cried.

'To find a lawyer.'

'A lawyer!' Mr Wilcox looked dumbfounded. 'Why?'

Dallas stopped and threw him an astonished look of his own. 'I intend to divorce your daughter. Our marriage has never been consummated and this child is all the proof I need of her infidelity. Good day to you, sir.'

'Wait!'

Dallas looked him up and down, his contempt evident. 'There's nothing left to be said.'

'You will not divorce my daughter, Mr Granger. The scandal would be horrendous. I forbid it.'

'Try and stop me.'

'Very well, since you insist. I still hold information that can send you to the gallows. Force my hand and I'll go straight to the police.'

'After what she has done?' Dallas flung an arm in the direction of Sarah. 'Are you totally mad? Have you no shred of decency?'

'I understand your anger, son.'

'Stop calling me that. I want nothing to do with you or your daughter.'

'You will remain married to Sarah.' The older man's jaw set obstinately.

'The gallows would be preferable.'

'Don't test me. You have been wronged, I agree, but, mark my words, I will not allow a scandal.'

Dallas could see he meant it. 'You leave me little choice. Sarah can keep my name, though that will be all. I refuse to live under the same roof and will have nothing more to do with any of you.'

'Dallas!' Sarah had started crying. 'How could I tell you?'

'Obviously you have great difficulty separating the truth from your lies. Good day, madam.'

There was only one place he could think of going. Mrs Watson's. Her welcome surprised him. 'You received my message. Good. I've put your visitors in the big front room.'

Dallas had received so many shocks that day, one more didn't seem to matter. 'What visitors?'

'Why, the Marchioness of Dumfries and her son, here from Scotland. They arrived a month ago.'

ELEVEN

It took a while for his brain to make the connection. Lorna! Could it be? Dallas felt as though his feet had been glued to the doorstep. 'Here?' he managed.

Mrs Watson's lips were pressed together. 'Spirited young thing,' she managed tightly. 'Said she'd stay until you returned. Made no effort to call on your wife.'

'She knows –'

'Of course. I appraised her of your marital status as soon as she asked after you. I must say, Mr Granger, your behaviour is peculiar to say the least. It seems you have no interest in the marriage or news of your child, *and* now there is a young lady looking for you, acting for all the world as if she has every right. Tongues are wagging, let me tell you. She may be a marchioness, Mr Granger, but her ladyship has been far from discreet. I understand she's recently widowed but you'd never know from her manner of dress. Not one single sign of mourning. Were it not for her ladyship's station, she would not remain in my house.'

Mrs Watson's ostentatious use of Lorna's title

told Dallas that, despite disapproval, she was sufficiently awed to make allowances.

'Is she here at the moment?'

'Her ladyship has not been out since hearing of your return. Indeed, the whole of Durban has been wondering when you intended going home to your wife. The poor girl is bereft at the loss of your child.'

So! Sarah and her father's duplicity continues. It came as no surprise. They'd have had to concoct some explanation for the baby's disappearance.

'Such a pity,' Mrs Watson continued. 'Born two months early, no doubt due to worry over you, and then to lose the poor wee thing.'

Dallas wondered what this good woman would think if she knew the truth.

His thoughts were beginning to take on some kind of order. 'In the first place, Mrs Watson, my private life is nobody's business but my own. In the second, is it so inconceivable that I would have had friends before coming to this land? Your tendency to reach ill-informed conclusions and think badly of me is tedious to say the least.'

Mrs Watson looked shocked by the outburst. 'What was I supposed to think?'

'Whatever you like, Mrs Watson. Thought is the operative word. Especially as you of all people know the circumstances of my marriage. That is, unless you are also hard of hearing.'

'Well, really, Mr Granger!' Mrs Watson was flushed but determined to make her point. 'It takes a gentleman to make the best of things. Your callous disregard of a wife leaves me no option but to question whether such a description applies to you.'

Dallas rubbed two fingers across his eyes. On top of the argument he'd just had with his father-in-law, the cumulative effects of scotch whisky were not taking kindly to this confrontation. He made no further comment.

Mrs Watson looked disappointed. She turned and picked up a bundle of mail. 'These came for you.'

Dallas took the envelopes and placed them in a coat pocket. 'Thank you. I would like to see the marchioness, if you please.'

She hadn't finished with him. 'Under the circumstances, Mr Granger, I find that I am unable to store your possessions here any longer. I would also be obliged if you would refrain from using this address for further correspondence.'

Dallas stared her down. 'The marchioness, if you please.'

Mrs Watson nodded stiffly. 'Wait here. I'll call her.' With that she turned and shut the door in his face.

Dallas waited, mixed emotions strong in him. Lorna here! In one respect, it was a dream come true, but she had come too late. He was married. Their relationship could not continue, yet it was the only thing he craved. It had been the one constant in his life, despite all that conspired against it. Despair competed with the heady excitement of seeing her again. Oh God, if only he were free!

He heard footsteps clattering down the stairs.

The front door swung open and there she was, just as he remembered her. With no thought of who might see them, Lorna flung herself at him, wrapping her arms tightly around his neck. Dallas held her close, smelling the sweet scent he'd never forgotten, burying his face in her hair, feeling her warm, lithe body tight against his. 'Oh, my darling, my darling,' he murmured.

She moved back suddenly, her eyes scanning his. 'You still love me,' she said quietly. 'I can see it.'

'I never stopped.' She was so beautiful. Motherhood had matured the soft innocence of the young girl he'd left behind, but her face remained fresh, yet to develop the angular planes which would turn youthful purity into classic beauty. His arms ached to hold her again but he kept the distance she'd put between them, horribly aware that space was not what kept them apart.

'Dallas!' she cried out. And in that one word was her pain.

Mrs Watson's voice came from within the house, as did a sniff of disapproval. 'The little boy is crying, your ladyship.'

Lorna dragged her eyes from his. 'Thank you.' She drew herself up and, in that instant, Dallas saw Alison, her mother, a woman for whom society's rules had not been written. 'If you don't mind, Mrs Watson, Dallas and I would like to speak in private. My son is disturbed and I have no wish to trouble you further. We will go to my room.'

'My lady, it really would not be seemly,' Mrs Watson objected feebly.

Lorna smiled graciously. 'Seemly! Are you suggesting impropriety, Mrs Watson?'

In the face of such regal disregard for convention, disapproval crumbled into uncertainty. 'No, no, of course not, your ladyship. I'm sure it will be perfectly proper. After all, you are old friends. Er, would you care for some tea? I'll have Mabel bring it upstairs.'

'Thank you, but no,' Lorna said firmly. 'We do not wish to be disturbed. Have no fear, Mrs Watson, all will be above board.'

Dallas followed Lorna upstairs to the room that had once been his. He could feel the landlady's eyes boring into his back. *What was Lorna thinking?* Her disregard for what was proper would be all over Durban inside of six hours. For his own sake he didn't care, but Lorna's reputation would be in danger. And it didn't seem to bother her. She smiled and opened the door.

A lace-lined cot stood in one corner, the baby in it red-faced and wailing. His tears stopped immediately Lorna entered the room and his face lit up with smiles. 'Mama.' Chubby arms lifted towards her.

'Mama is here, my precious.' Lorna moved swiftly across the room, plucked her son from the cot and turned to Dallas, her eyes sparkling. 'He's quite precocious for nine months. I swear, he'll be walking soon.' She kissed the child's downy head, before saying, 'May I present your son, the Marquis of Dumfries, Cameron Keith Adair Dallas Kingholm. I call him Cam. Nanny will be back soon. She'll take

Cam for a walk. Then we can talk. There is much to be said between us. You have deceived me, Dallas, yet again. Frankly, I am furious with you.'

'Lorna –'

Her eyes glittered with anger. 'We will wait for Nanny.'

There was Alison again. The steely resolve. Do it my way. Fly in the face of convention. It was not arrogance, although, Lord knows, that's how it sounded. But Dallas had known Lorna all her life and he sensed her uncertainty. He felt apprehension stir. She was here but, despite her welcome downstairs, forgiveness was a long way off – perhaps even impossible. He didn't blame her for that but it scared him. She could be so stubborn that no amount of reasoning would sway her. Then again, he'd seen her forgive her brother when he insisted on putting her beloved pony at a jump Lorna said was too high. The horse gamely tried, stumbled and broke a leg, necessitating that it be destroyed. Lorna had been heartbroken but Charles was forgiven 'because she loved him'.

Unsure of himself, Dallas moved towards her, fascinated by the baby who smiled, revealing two perfectly formed teeth. Dallas felt his stomach flip over. Cam had blond curls and blue eyes, and was the image of his mother. Something in those baby-blue depths drew him closer and he felt a bonding of blood so powerful it took his breath away. It transcended emotion, a fiercely protective instinct, deep within his gut. Dallas knew he would commit murder to keep this child safe.

'My son,' he whispered, holding out his arms.

Lorna handed him the baby.

'My son,' Dallas whispered again, smelling the aching innocence of babies, a combination of sleep, powder and a wet napkin – the scent of trust and dependence. 'Hello, Cam.' He looked over the child's head to Lorna. 'He's beautiful.'

She smiled, briefly dropping her guard. 'And ours. How could he be anything else?'

As if sensing that the man who held him had nothing but good intentions, Cam snuggled into Dallas's shoulder, babbling baby talk, one hand grabbing a fistful of his father's hair.

Dallas laughed as his son tugged. 'He's strong.'

Lorna extricated the baby's fingers. 'Come, my darling. Dry clothes for you.'

Cam gurgled and blew bubbles.

'He's a fine wee laddie,' Dallas commented as Lorna drew off the soaked napkin. 'And has the makings of quite a man,' he added, grinning.

She frowned up at him. 'If memory serves, he takes after his father.'

A lock of hair had fallen over her eyes and she blew upwards, trying to move it. Dallas reached out and smoothed back the curl, desire flooding through him. 'Lorna –' His voice was deep, eyes dark with longing.

She tossed her head, shaking his hand away. 'Wait, I said.'

A knock on the door announced the nanny's arrival. To Dallas's surprise, she was Lorna's old nanny.

'Lord Acheson,' the woman said, face expressionless but disapproval evident in her stiff voice.

'Nanny Beth,' he replied, unconsciously using the name she'd allowed when he was a child. 'How lovely to see you again.'

Nanny Beth did not respond.

'Cam needs a hat,' Lorna said briskly. 'Then a walk, I think. The fresh air will be good for him. Don't go far and have him back here in fifteen minutes.'

'Yes, my lady.'

By the look on Lorna's face, Dallas guessed that she too was, in some way, out of favour with the straitlaced woman.

As soon as the door shut behind Nanny Beth and Cam, Lorna wasted no time. 'Married, Dallas? I take it this was what you could not bear to explain in your letter?' She gave a bitter smile. 'It was my belief you were referring to past indiscretions. Silly me. If you'd made it plainer I would never have embarrassed us both by turning up here.'

'Let me explain now.'

'Indeed you shall, Dallas, for I find it impossible to believe you should twice treat me so shabbily.' Lorna stood ramrod straight, eyes on his. 'I came here in good faith. Your apparent deceit weighs heavily on my heart. Explain, if you can. No lies. You owe me that much.'

'Not a day has passed –'

Lorna turned her back and stared out of the window. Eventually she spoke quietly. 'Do not treat me as a fool.'

'I'm not.'

She spun back. 'Then for God's sake, do not dare expect me to believe you could not forget me. You are married, Dallas. Another woman bears your name. I could have forgiven you my mother, but this . . .' She broke off, tears threatening.

Dallas went to her and drew her to the bed. 'Sit down and I will tell you. Please listen, Lorna, for nothing is as it seems. May I sit next to you?'

She nodded and the two of them sat side-by-side, Lorna making sure there was some distance between them.

Dallas began to speak. Lorna's eyes never left his. He did not embellish the tale, telling her only the facts. 'When your letter arrived, it was too late. Wilcox was threatening to reveal my whereabouts to the police. I was filled with despair when I wrote to you.' He stopped, jaw working with emotion. 'I love you, Lorna,' he said finally in a husky voice. 'I never ceased to love you. I didn't mean to deceive you.'

Lorna sighed deeply. 'And now you have a wife.'

'Yes,' he said. 'She has my name.'

'And the child?'

'His father took him.'

Lorna looked surprised. 'What kind of a mother is that?'

'Sarah is a very confused girl. It was for the best. For what it's worth, I came here today to try and get my old room back. I had no idea you were here. I simply cannot bear to live with Sarah.'

Dallas held his breath. Lorna was chewing her

bottom lip. A sure sign she was coming to a decision. 'Divorce?' she asked finally.

'Unlikely.'

She nodded, still chewing. 'You've left her?'

'Yes.'

'For good?'

'Yes.'

'Swear to me, Dallas, that you are telling the truth.'

He placed a hand over his heart. 'I swear.'

Lorna stopped worrying her lip. 'I left Scotland against my father's express wishes. Family and friends find my actions unfathomable and slightly shocking, though they would be far more horrified if they knew the real reason for my travels. In other words, Dallas, I have already, to some extent, tarnished my reputation.' She sighed. 'I don't completely trust you any more. You have caused me a great deal of pain. Yet I remember the Dallas I thought I knew. I love that man. Is he still there?'

Acting purely on instinct, for this was a Lorna who had matured greatly and he was less certain of her now, Dallas knew she wanted reassurance but that it had to come from the sincerity of his words, rather than loving gestures. 'Yes, he is,' he said quietly, his eyes not leaving hers. 'And he loves only you.'

Tears filled her eyes suddenly. 'He'd better,' she burst out. 'Because my heart cannot take any more.'

He reached for her, a hard lump of emotion in his throat. 'I love you, my darling. So very, very much. Forgive me, I beg you. I will never cause you pain again.' He held her while she sobbed, stroking her hair, his hands gentle and caring. 'I'm so sorry,' he whispered again and again.

She quietened eventually and pulled back. Even hiccupping and sniffing, her eyes swollen and red, she was beautiful. 'What will we do?' she asked.

'We have two choices, my darling.'

Lorna nodded. 'I cannot bring myself to consider one of them. Despite all that has happened, we belong together.'

A release of tension, in the form of a shuddering breath, came from Dallas. 'Be very sure.'

Lorna leaned into him. 'If you are by my side I can be strong.'

Dallas felt his heart soar. He drew her closer and kissed her, a long and yearning kiss of promise and love. 'With you by my side I need nothing else,' he told her when they drew apart.

Her smile was watery. 'It will take a while before –'

He placed a finger over her lips. 'I will spend the rest of my life proving my love, if needs be.'

'When I learned you were wed I nearly took the next boat home.'

'I'm glad you didn't. What stopped you?'

'The tone of Mrs Watson's voice. She said nothing of the circumstances but I sensed there was more . . . something left unsaid. That decided me to stay.'

Dallas traced her jaw and chin with a finger. 'Thank God,' he said quietly.

They heard Cam and Nanny Beth returning.

'She will be even more disapproving,' Lorna said, mischief flaring briefly.

The middle-aged Scotswoman was more than that. Clucking her tongue, she made an ostentatious display of smoothing the bed. 'Will ye be needing my services again today, my lady?'

Lorna went to her and placed an arm around the thick waist. 'Nanny Beth.' Her voice was gentle. 'You have known us since we were born. Can you find it in your heart to understand?'

'You will do what pleases you both, as usual, I'm sure. Any appeal for common decency will fall on deaf ears.' She pulled away from Lorna.

'Would you prefer to return home?' Lorna asked.

'If you please, my lady.'

'Very well. I can see that we cause you much distress. I would not prolong your displeasure. You may stay on at Mrs Watson's until I secure a berth for your return. I shall, of course, honour our contract. You will be paid for the full six months.'

'Thank you, my lady.' With no other word, and no look towards Dallas, or even Cam, Nanny Beth left the room.

'Ouch!' Lorna commented. She went to remove Cam from his carriage.

'Let me do that.' Dallas unstrapped the boy and swung him into the air. Cam laughed with delight.

Lorna giggled, for the first time sounding like her old self. 'There's something I wish to show you.'

'What is it?'

'You'll see. It's not far.'

She would say no more and Dallas was content for her to keep it a secret.

Mrs Watson stood by the front door, pretending to be polishing a brass knocker already kept sparkling bright by Mabel. 'Your carriage has arrived, my lady. Will you be back for dinner?'

'I think not. In fact, we'll be moving out tomorrow. Nanny Beth will stay here for a while.'

Ann Watson's face fell. Having such nobility staying in her home, irrespective of the most recent turn of events, which she could hardly wait to pass on, had been quite a coup for her. 'As you wish, your ladyship.'

A pony and trap waited outside, the driver standing ready to assist Lorna and Cam. 'Can you speak Zulu?' Lorna asked.

'Some.'

'Then kindly tell Thomas to hop in the back. You can drive.'

Thomas's face fell when Dallas related the instruction. 'The madam likes to drive,' he commented, jumping lightly into the back. Then, as Dallas hitched Tosca behind, he added, 'It is the man who should drive.'

'I will do it today,' Dallas told him.

Ego restored, Thomas settled back for the ride. Dallas helped Lorna and Cam onto the seat next to him and took the reins. Lorna tucked an arm through his. With Cam on her lap, they were a picture of carefree happiness.

'Where to?' Dallas asked, conscious of the effect

it would have three doors down if they were to drive past his house in this manner.

'That way.' Thankfully Lorna pointed in the opposite direction.

He turned the horses and they set off. It was not far. 'Slow down,' Lorna told him ten minutes later. 'See that driveway. Go in there.'

Dallas had noticed the house before and often wondered to whom it belonged. Set well off the road, behind a low stone wall, mature trees lined a curved driveway. The two-storeyed Regency-style house, so popular in England in the early part of the century, would have looked out of place but for the fact that its stucco rendering had been painted a sand colour and the iron balconies white, giving the building an almost tropical appearance. 'Who owns this place?'

'I do.'

'You!'

Lorna grinned, delighted at his surprise. 'I bought it a few days after my arrival.'

'Whew! It must be the most expensive house in the whole of Durban.'

'It is, my dear. What else would you expect from such a grand lady?'

They laughed and, for a moment, Dallas was transported back to the carefree days of his youth, to a time where responsibility was up to the adults and life a succession of pleasant interludes. It was so like Lorna that once the drama, whatever it happened to be, was over and she'd spoken her mind, she reverted to normal. She could never hold a grudge. He had let her down badly, and yet, difficult as it must have been, she was able to put the hurt aside so their problem could be faced with as little emotional interference as possible. Dallas's respect and love for Lorna had never been as great as it was at this moment.

'Why buy a house if you planned to return home?'

Lorna gave a wry smile. 'Just let's say I'm an eternal optimist.' Her eyes were warm with love as she looked over at him. 'Besides, I could not bear to be on the other side of the world from you.'

Dallas, aware of the Zulu behind them, confined his response to a small grin of pleasure.

The drive led them past several ornate water features, a number of well-planned and planted rockeries, flowerbeds and large open areas of lawn. 'I adore the plants here,' Lorna said. 'They're so colourful.' Zulu women worked in the garden. 'The men don't want to work,' Lorna commented. 'Strange, isn't it?'

'It's not that,' Dallas told her. 'Traditionally, cultivating is women's work. An old man may grow tobacco for himself but he never plants crops. In the fields it has changed a bit since Europeans introduced the plough. Today men have to till the soil because women are forbidden to work with cattle. A decorative garden like this is unheard of in Zulu society – it has no use at all.'

He called a greeting to two women who were weeding, receiving shy acknowledgment, delivered with heads averted and eyes lowered.

'Why don't they look at you?' Lorna asked. 'It's quite disconcerting.'

'Respect,' Dallas replied. 'Normally, a visitor would not greet a woman but, if he did, she would avoid eye contact. It's considered bold.' He reined in, jumped down and helped Lorna alight. 'Do you have a groom?'

As if on cue, a short, wiry man appeared, his flaming red hair a clash with the scarlet livery he wore. 'Will ye be needin' 'em agin, missus?'

'Not today.' Lorna turned to Dallas. 'May I present Mr Bruce Buchanan? I've employed him to train up a groom and driver, as well as a butler. Mr Buchanan returns home next month.' She glanced at the diminutive Scot. 'Mr Buchanan, this is –'

'Granger,' Dallas cut in.

'Pleased tae meet yer, sir.'

Dallas found his hand gripped in a surprisingly strong handshake.

The driver appeared from the back. 'There ye be, ye lazy Kaffir. Sittin' there loik royalty, I see.'

Thomas understood not a word. He simply grinned and led the horses and trap away.

Buchanan shook his head. 'No point in speaking Zulu to him. He dinnae ken a word.'

Dallas was hardly surprised. If the man's Zulu was anything like his English, Thomas must be one very confused driver.

'The bay'll be needin' a shoe, missus. I'll attend to it, the Kaffir hasn't a clue. Best ye seek the services of a farrier once I'm awa.'

'Keep trying, Mr Buchanan. The butler is coming along nicely.'

'Aye, well, I can but do ma best.'

He looked after the retreating Thomas. 'Nice mare,' he commented of Tosca. He touched his forehead. 'Aye well, best be aboot ma duties.' He bowed slightly and left them.

Lorna smiled at Dallas's expression.

'Where on earth did you find him?'

'He presented himself here the day I took possession. Dishonourable discharge from the 45th Regiment. Apparently he had a physical disagreement with one of the officers. Quite open about it. Told me I couldn't possibly find proper staff on my own. Probably right, too. Anyway, I've not regretted taking him on even though Nanny Beth was speechless with horror at the mere idea.'

Dallas shook his head. Lorna's willingness and ability to take control of her life was remarkable. Most women in her situation wouldn't have known where to start. Mr Buchanan might be of questionable character but, freshly arrived in this strange new land, Lorna's instinct was to hire someone from home who could help her settle in. It made sense.

If Dallas found Bruce Buchanan startling, it was nothing compared with the apparition that greeted them inside. The butler spoke no English, wore an ill-fitting heavy linen suit and a cotton shirt. He was barefoot and bore the Zulu insignia of maturity and marriage, the *isiCoco* – a circlet of fibre and animal tendons – which had been sewn into his hair and dressed with honeycomb wax before being greased and polished. Normally, as hair grows, it is cut and the *isiCoco* remains a regulation size. The circlet on Lorna's butler was raised, unkempt and, judging by the smell, in dire need of replacement.

Dallas greeted him respectfully. 'I see you.'

'Yes, I see you too.'

There was dignity and pride in the old man's face.

'This is Percy,' Lorna explained. 'Neither of us understands a word the other says but he's marvellous at giving orders to the girls.'

'Percy!' Dallas muttered. He turned to the Zulu. 'What is your *igamu*?'

Percy smiled, showing a row of broken and stained teeth. 'My great name is Ndaba.'

Translated, Ndaba literally meant 'matter' and usually referred to a quarrel or a meeting of significance.

He explained. 'I was born during the great *indaba* between our *baba*, Shaka, and the white men who came from the sea.'

Dallas knew there had been many meetings but guessed the one to which Percy referred had taken place when the first traders entered Natal and negotiated permission from the first Zulu king to travel and trade within his kingdom. It would tie in with his guess that Percy was about fifty.

'Are you the *induna* in this household?' Dallas asked, wishing to know if Percy regarded himself as being in charge and if he received due respect for his position.

'*Yebo.*'

'Are any of the women here your wife?'

'They are all my wives.'

Dallas was willing to bet that Lorna neither knew this fact nor was aware of the pitfalls. She should not be employing both a man and his wives since family members tended to collude with each other and would often rob their employer. 'The madam speaks no Zulu. She is not familiar with your ways.'

'He is a good madam,' Percy responded. 'He treats us fairly.'

Well, at least Lorna was given the respect usually reserved for men.

Cam chose that moment to grizzle and a young African girl appeared. 'He's hungry,' Lorna told her. The girl nodded, smiled, spoke softly to the baby in Zulu and bore him off to the kitchen. Percy melted away as well.

'What was all that about?' Lorna wanted to know. 'Percy looks a little odd but I'm happy with him. The girls jump when he speaks.'

'That's because they are his wives.'

'All of them?' Her eyes widened.

'Yes.'

'My, my. A busy man indeed.' She smiled. 'Speaking of which, would you care for a grand tour?' One eyebrow arched. 'Of the house, of course.'

His hungry eyes provided her answer. The tour would have to wait.

It was the first time they'd made love in a bed, not having to worry about being caught. The pleasure of slowly undressing each other, finding familiarity in each other's bodies, their enforced separation and despair that they'd never be together again, made it a special afternoon. Lorna's longing for Dallas equalled the yearning he had for her. Time and necessity had compelled him not to think of the silky softness of her skin, the yielding warmth of her lips. Now he luxuriated in the feel of both, in the musky scent of her most secret parts, in her low moans of pleasure as she found release. Nothing was withheld, no gesture or words too intimate. In Scotland, Lorna had seemed like a naughty girl breaking the rules. Defiance had motivated her then. In a way it still did, but longing and distance had enhanced her memories, and now that she was in his arms, Lorna would accept nothing less than perfect honesty.

Dallas needed that as well. Love, thwarted by convention and events, might so easily have slipped past them, a haunting memory only, thought of in moments of wistful sadness. Yet by some miracle, here was a second chance. Dallas would never be so awed by love's raw power as he was that afternoon.

Shadows stretched long on the lawn outside by the time either of them thought of their son.

'He'll be fine,' Lorna whispered, sending a shiver through him as her breath tickled his ear. 'Queenie is very good with him. She's the only one who speaks any English.' Lorna stretched and yawned. 'The servants will be gossiping but I don't care. I couldn't have waited any longer.'

'Mmmm!' He nuzzled a bare shoulder.

She propped herself on one elbow. 'There's so much to tell each other.'

'I know.' His fingers played with her hair.

'Will you stay the night?'

'Every night. You are my wife in everything but name. And, God willing, you shall have that one day.'

Lorna kissed him. 'Is that a proposal, Lord Acheson?'

'You mustn't call me that. I have no title here. It's for the best.' He tickled her nose with one of her own curls. 'And, yes, it's a proposal.'

'I accept. I shall call myself Mrs Granger and to hell with those who carp about morality.'

He smiled. 'You've changed.'

'So have you.' She kissed him again.

Dallas spoke against her mouth. 'I like the new you.'

'Do I shock you?'

'A little.'

'Perhaps I have more of my mother in me than you suspect.'

Dallas grabbed her shoulders and wrestled her underneath him. She was laughing up at him, eyes soft. He loved her so much. 'You have only Lorna in you. Do not compare yourself with others, for they would come off second best.'

'Dallas?' She was suddenly serious.

'Yes, my darling Lorna.'

'I meant what I said. I don't care a fig what people say about us. It's you I want. Everything else can be worked out.'

He kissed her deeply, ready with words of agreement, but she responded to him and thoughts of everything save the moment deserted them.

When they finally left the bedroom and went in search of Cam, they found him strapped, Zulu-style, to Queenie's back, held snug by a blanket. He was dozing as she prepared vegetables for dinner but came awake on hearing his mother's voice. 'Let's take him outside,' Dallas suggested.

In the cool and shaded garden, Dallas played with Cam while Lorna looked on. 'You are so good with him,' she commented.

'He is my son,' Dallas said simply.

Cam yawned suddenly.

'And he's wearing me out,' Dallas added, picking up the baby. 'Come, little man. Your beautiful Mama and very handsome Papa will put you to bed.'

After dinner, with servants gone for the day and their son tucked into his cot upstairs, they finally spoke of all the other things that had been on both their minds. Lorna wanted all the details of his escape. She shivered as he described the cold and wet journey south from Edinburgh in an open wagon with Victor.

'The weather was foul in Scotland. I kept imagining how awful it must have been for you.'

He told her of Cousin Adrian's assistance and of his narrow escape from detection aboard the *Newcastle Lady*.

'Oh, Dallas! If they'd caught you I'd have died.'

Dallas tightened an arm around her.

'Tell me of Sarah. I know how you met. What is she like?'

Dallas sighed. 'Sarah. Now there's one young lady I really should have avoided.' He glanced at Lorna. 'Sure you want to know?'

'Yes. I don't feel she's a threat to me now.'

'Never was,' he said lightly. 'I'll try to describe her but I'm not sure I know myself. I liked her well enough when we met. Having little choice in the matter of returning home and missing her cousin's wedding, Sarah could so easily have been difficult and demanding. As it was, she seemed to accept the situation and proved good company. None of us, not Logan, Will nor myself, gave the slightest indication of anything other than protectiveness. I swear, I didn't lay a finger on her.'

'I believe you. It's in your voice.'

As best he could, Dallas gave a physical description of Sarah and attempted to explain her personality. The latter wasn't easy – he'd seen so many sides to it, yet still didn't know if he was even close to understanding her. 'Can you imagine how I felt, returning to Durban and finding Wilcox blaming me for the fact that his daughter was with child? And Sarah went along with it. It wasn't until her son was born that the truth could no longer be concealed.'

'What do you mean?'

He hadn't mentioned it before but now he told her. 'The father was African.'

Lorna sat up excitedly. 'Dallas, my darling, surely that's grounds enough for divorce?'

'I thought so. But Wilcox is using the same blackmail tactics he employed in forcing me to marry her. The damned man wants to avoid a scandal, that's all he cares about. I can't even begin to know what Sarah wants. She's told so many lies I believe nothing she says. I had no choice but to marry her. And now there is no option but to stay married. Her father knows of the charges that stand against me. He has *The Times* sent out from England, saw a report of my supposed crime and has threatened to tell the police.'

'Will he make trouble for us?'

'Believe me, Lorna, I loathe the man so much I would do him an injury if he tries. Now that we're together, nothing and no-one will be allowed to come between us. When I arrived at Mrs Watson's I'd already told Sarah and her parents that all I could give was my name. Anyway, that's the only thing any of them wanted. They were hardly bothered by my refusal to be a proper husband.'

'But when Sarah's father hears of us, what will he do?'

'Nothing, if he knows what's good for him.'

'How can you be sure?'

'I know who is the father of Sarah's child. He would not be hard to find. Wilcox will do anything to keep that a secret.'

Lorna tilted her head back and looked at him.

Dallas shrugged helplessly.

'Softie,' she said quietly.

'Perhaps, my darling,' he apologised. 'Admittedly I have grounds and could prove it. The question is, could I then live with myself? Sarah is a pawn in her father's manipulations. I could never be that much of a cad, darling.'

'You'd have every right to be.'

'It's the sheep in me.'

'No.' Lorna shook her head. 'I know you too well. Despite our escapades when we were growing up, you never shied from responsibility. There was a time you even took the blame for me. Remember?'

They both laughed. Lorna had been ten, Dallas fourteen, and the incident in question was a mischievous idea to hurl eggs from inside a turret at the Grange, their target, gardeners pruning rose bushes. By some fluke, Lorna's first shot was a bullseye. They discovered the hard way that an egg, even thrown from a great height, does not necessarily break on impact. What suffered on this occasion was the gardener's head. Pandemonium broke out below as the man collapsed, blood streaming from a broken nose. No-one knew what had caused his injury. The egg, having done its worst, bounced once and rolled away into the flowerbed.

Convinced they'd killed the man, Dallas and Lorna went straight to Lord Dalrymple. Being used to his son's pranks, he jumped immediately to the conclusion that Dallas had thrown the offending projectile.

Lorna, four years younger than Dallas and in awe of Lord Dalrymple's formidable ire, became hysterical. Dallas took the leather-strap whipping without a murmur. Later, Lorna crept to his room with cream buns, a jug of lemonade and whispered thanks.

Remembering, Dallas kissed her cheek. 'Lord! How far back we go together.'

'We do, don't we?' She briefly looked angry. 'That's why no conniving, trumped-up, pretentious little commoner is going to come between us.' Her right hand was raised, palm towards him. 'Pact?'

He placed his palm against hers. 'Pact.'

It was something they'd done as children and it hadn't lost its meaning.

'Will you keep trading?'

'For the moment. Profit aside, I like the country and its people.'

He told her of the Thukela Valley. 'It's so beautiful, Lorna. One day I will own some of that land.' He smiled at himself. 'If you're not careful I'll turn into a boring farmer, just like my brother.'

'Never. You are far too wicked.'

Dallas talked about the Zulus and his growing respect for them. 'There's a man up north called John Dunn. He's turned his back on most Europeans and lives among the Africans as one of them. He's the happiest, most contented person I've ever met.'

They were snuggled together in an enormous overstuffed armchair, built for one yet accommodating the two of them with room to spare. Dallas kissed Lorna. 'Your turn. I've hogged the conversation long enough.'

'You had more to tell.'

'I still can't believe that you don't hate me.'

She smiled. 'The day you left giving no explanation I went back to the house. My father was shouting at Mama. I didn't know why but soon learned. I hated you then.'

'I'm sorry.'

'I know you and Mama . . . It had been going on for some time. I understand that. But if you loved me, why did it continue after that day by the river?'

'I was sick with misery over your betrothal. I knew you couldn't be mine even before then. I had no prospects. Your parents would have forbidden a marriage between us. But suddenly you were further out of reach. That day at the river . . . I should have been stronger. But you were so miserable and so sure of what you wanted. And I . . . Well, I loved you. Probably always have. It only hit me the night of the debutante ball. You were so grown-up suddenly, so beautiful and serene.'

'Serene! More like quaking with fear that you wouldn't ask me to dance.'

'What a couple we are.'

Lorna kissed him on the cheek. 'One of the things I've always admired about you, Dallas, is that you rarely allow convention to get in your way. I'm the same. If you recall, my family always saw me as a tomboy. At home I always felt as if I were acting a part. Out here, I feel more myself than ever before. There are so many real people who can't be bothered with convention and petty rules. That's one of the reasons I took on Mr Buchanan, he's a real character.'

Dallas nodded. 'Wait until you meet my ex-partners.'

'I want to meet everyone you know, to make my home here. If we cannot marry, we can at least live as man and wife. I'm sure many do the same.'

'Probably.' He grinned. 'You're going to look very fetching in a bead skirt.'

'A what?'

The grin widened. 'It will have to cover the backs of your thighs or I'll become quite excited. However, your breasts mean nothing to me.'

'Dallas, whatever are you talking about?' One eyebrow was up.

He laughed outright. 'Zulu tradition, my darling. I'm full of happiness and babbling nonsense.' He hugged her tightly. 'It's your turn to talk.'

Lorna told him of the days leading up to her wedding. 'I was sick with fear for you. I thought you'd be caught and hanged. I begged Mama to tell the truth but she wouldn't. Father simply refused to listen, though he did say, "If that boy is half as clever as I think, he's well away from harm." I spent days in my room, dreading news that you'd been arrested.'

She shuddered at the memory. 'I hardly remember the wedding. It was a hideous day. All I wanted to do was die. I seriously considered throwing myself from the roof. The only thing stopping me was our baby. As time passed, I began to believe that Father had been right and you'd somehow managed to get out of Britain. It gave me the strength to stay alive. I knew, in my heart of hearts, that if you had escaped then one day we'd be together.'

'Like this?'

'Exactly like this.' Lorna took a deep breath. 'Lord, my love, how different it is here with you. I loathed that old goat – his voice, his touch, everything.' She shivered again, picked up one of Dallas's hands and held it close to her chest before going on. 'After the wedding we travelled by carriage to Dumfries. It took three days. As we set off, the first thing he said was, "If you can bear to wait, my dear, I'd prefer that our firstborn be conceived at home." He acted as though I was desperate to be in his bed, yet I hadn't looked at or spoken a word to him since the ceremony. The man must have realised how foul I found him.' A deep frown crossed her forehead. 'Arrogant bastard!' she burst out passionately.

Dallas wasn't shocked. As children he and Lorna had swapped swearwords which they'd picked up from some of the family servants.

'The trip was ghastly. Each hour took me further from home, each mile more distant from wherever you might be. We always stayed in second-rate inns. He'd refused my request to bring a maid, so at night I would lock the door of my room and have no-one to talk to. All the while we drew closer to the time when he would insist on his conjugal rights. That's what he called it, Dallas. He went on and on about it.'

The memory was upsetting her but Dallas knew she needed to purge herself of it.

'We arrived at his estate around four in the afternoon. It looks most impressive from the outside. The main house has four floors and is much larger than Canongate or the Grange. There are two wings, south and north, connected by glass pavilions. God knows why he built them. As far as I know they were never used. The old fossil lived quite frugally with the bare minimum of furniture and hardly any creature comforts. His whole house was freezing, the food awful and servants rude. A tweeny showed me to my bedchamber. A tweeny, Dallas! When I demanded a proper lady's maid the marquis told me to train up the little slut. Train her! I could barely understand a word she uttered. The girl was useless. Clumsy, lazy – why, Percy has more breeding. I told her to light the fire and bring hot water. She refused. Apparently, the marquis disdained what he called pampering. By the time I went down to dinner I was ready for battle.'

He'd seen her in that state before. Formidable, from memory.

'The food arrived cold,' she went on. 'I tried to send it back but *he* overruled me. As soon as we were alone I told him that if I were to be mistress of his house then he should allow me some authority. He laughed. Said his home had been good enough for over sixty years and I wasn't to change a thing. My presence was tolerated only for the heirs I would bear. I looked down the long table at him and something inside me died. I was his prisoner, one towards whom the servants would have little respect and certainly no loyalty. I had hated him before but suddenly the spirit in me shrivelled. It was replaced by such despair and fear that, in an instant, I became little more than a shell. His callous indifference kindled such loathing, yet I felt helpless, alone.'

Dallas smoothed hair off her wet cheeks. 'Fucking bastard!' His quiet voice carried the venom of hatred searing his heart.

She gave a watery smile. 'Thank you.'

'You didn't lose your spirit, my darling, although I can see why you thought you had. What happened? When did he suffer his stroke?'

'Later. At dinner he drank rather a lot. I retired early, hoping he'd be too drunk.' She laughed derisively. 'Too much to hope for, as it turned out. At around midnight he staggered into my room, terribly drunk, weaving and shouting, a footman holding him up. Dallas . . .' She was weeping. 'I realised that the servant had been instructed to remain. He was to help . . .' Lorna broke off, leaning into Dallas for strength.

'Dear God!' Totally shocked, he felt a raw anger towards her father. A man who would condemn his daughter to such a fate! Lord de Iongh may have been much admired by his peers but Dallas began to see a reason for Alison's unfaithfulness. Her husband was as cold as any fish. He tightened his arms around the girl he loved.

'Lorna, you don't have to go on with this if it distresses you.'

She shook her head. 'You must know. There can be no secrets between us.' She wiped at her eyes, took a breath and went on. 'I threw the biggest tantrum of my life. Screamed, swore, and chucked everything I could get my hands on at the two of them. Finally, the footman was dismissed. By then, my dearly beloved husband was himself in a towering rage, shouting, calling me a bitch, tearing off his nightshirt. I realised then that I had the means of getting even. He couldn't stand being disobeyed or made a fool of. Beyond caring what might happen to me, I laughed at him, called him every horrible thing I could think of. His vanity sent him into an even greater rage. I made fun of his bald head and wrinkled skin, even his smell. When he was completely naked, I pointed at his . . . his . . . shrivelled-up . . . and asked what he hoped to achieve with it. That was it. He went mad, frothing at the mouth, pulling at himself trying to make it bigger, shouting what he wanted me to do. I suppose I was scared but I was also full of hatred. I laughed and laughed, just to goad him.'

Lorna was still clutching Dallas's hand and he could feel the strength of those terrible memories in her fingers. 'Go on,' he said softly. 'Get rid of it all.'

'I don't think he was aware of anything other than his fury. One moment my husband was standing there slobbering like a dog, bellowing at me; the next, with no warning, he clutched at his head and collapsed on the floor.'

'Thank God.'

'The sudden silence is what I remember most. After all that screaming, the marquis made no sound at all. He just lay there; his mouth opened and shut, yet no words came. I knew that something serious must have happened. After what seemed like ages, I took a couple of steps closer. His eyes begged me to send for help.' Her voice broke. 'I just stood there and told him to die. I said it over and over in a whisper. I could see he understood. He was frightened, shaking all over but helpless, unable to move even his hands. I went to the bureau, poured myself some wine, then sat where he could watch me drink. Time passed – it must have been over an hour. I hoped that the longer I delayed the more damage was likely. Dallas, there was not a shred of sympathy in me. Eventually, I pulled on a gown and opened the door. That beastly footman was still there, waiting down the hall. I told him the marquis appeared to be unwell and instructed him to fetch a doctor. He was suspicious but went anyway. When the family physician finally arrived, he more or less implied that Lord Dumfries should have known better than to take such a young wife. He assumed that physical exertion had brought on the attack. I didn't enlighten anyone. Even the footman had to accept the diagnosis.'

Dallas felt the tension leave her body. 'Your letter said he lived.'

'He lasted three months.'

'Did he know of our child?'

'I told him. It had the desired result. I suppose

you could say he lost his temper. It was difficult to know. His eyes bulged and he turned bright red. Suddenly he just . . . died.' She shrugged. 'After his funeral I took revenge on the staff and fired the lot. For three months I'd had to live with their flagrant insubordination. Now, as mistress of the estate, they had no choice other than to accept my authority. A few did try to find favour but I detested them all. With new staff selected by me installed, I decided to stay only until our child was born. Knowing I'd never live there, it gave me great pleasure to spend a small fortune on the house. My staff were pleasant and loyal. The months passed in a most agreeable way. For every penny I spent, I could imagine the marquis turning in his grave. May he rot in hell!'

'And everyone believes that Cam is his?'

'Those who must, yes. Cam inherits everything. No-one has questioned his legal rights. Everyone believes the marquis died as the result of begetting an heir.'

'What will you tell our son?'

'*We* will tell him the truth.'

Dallas smiled at the determination in her voice. 'Good.'

'I only hope Cam understands.'

'He will if we raise him our way.'

'Meaning?'

'To be true to himself and respect the right of others to do the same.'

'What if he decides we are bad people?'

'Bad is a state of mind perceived differently by

everyone. If he loves us, he won't think that. Anyway, in ten years our situation won't matter to anyone. With a bit of luck Sarah will find another and grant me a divorce. Then I can make an honest woman of you.'

Lorna's response was immediate. 'I'm honest enough to please myself. Being the same for you is all that matters to me now.'

Dallas wagged a finger at her. 'I do declare, my love, that your position gives you confidence to question the constraints of society.'

'And why not? Don't you think I have earned the chance to please myself? If my title makes people too intimidated to express disapproval, then so be it. Who cares for them anyway?' Turning from the harrowing tale of her wedding night, Lorna switched to other news. 'Mother has taken another lover.'

At the mention of Alison, Dallas felt guilty. 'How is it that you have so readily forgiven me?'

'I love you. Why waste years being resentful? What's the point?'

'Does your father know about the new one?'

'Probably. I think he's always known and turned a blind eye.'

'Until me. He could hardly ignore what was right under his nose.'

Lorna dug him in the ribs with an elbow. 'I may have forgiven you but that doesn't mean I wish to be reminded. Can we not speak of it again?'

'I wanted to end it after you and I . . . She wouldn't allow it.'

'My dear Dallas, the word is *no*.' There was steel in her voice which told him that forgiveness hung by a thread.

Dallas dropped his head. 'It taught me a lesson.'

Lorna gave him a tiny smile. 'I want to be the only one.'

'And so you shall be. From this night to the end of my life.' He placed a hand over his heart. 'I promise that for as long as I have you there will be no other.'

The smile grew and she snuggled closer. 'Good,' she murmured.

'Charlotte and Charles?' Dallas asked, wanting to know he'd done no lasting damage to his best friend's and sister's chances of happiness.

'Two peas in a pod, my dear. Father eventually gave in. He's always had a soft spot for Charlotte. The wedding was very discreet with only a few family and friends. It was the way they wanted it. They live quietly in Perthshire and rarely come to Edinburgh. Charlotte is expecting a baby; it may even be born by now. When they heard I was coming out here, both sent their love.'

'Thank God. After betraying you, the knowledge that I had ruined their lives as well was especially hard to take. When I read in your letter that they were, after all, allowed to marry, I was filled with joy for them. And your father? How did he react to your coming out here?'

'He knew why I wanted to find you.'

'You told him?'

'No. Mother did.'

'How did she know?'

'She took one look at Cam. Everyone says he looks like me but Mother saw straight through that. I saw no reason to lie. Now she can barely stand me to be in the same room as her.'

'I'm sorry.'

'I'm not. We were never close. Anyway, she couldn't care less where I went. At least Father tried to talk me out of it until I reminded him of the callous indifference he'd shown for my happiness, giving me to . . . that old man. Then he caved in.' Lorna gave a cynical laugh. 'What choice did he have? The Dumfries estates border with our own in that part of Scotland and his grandson is the sole heir. Land means more to Father than flesh and blood, always has.'

Dallas tightened his arms around her. 'It doesn't to me.'

'Should that ever change, you may rest assured that I will remind you,' she told him in the sweetest of voices.

'Tch! I can see our life together will never be dull.'

Lorna looked serious. 'What will you tell Sarah?'

'The truth. She probably doesn't deserve it but I'll not deceive her any more than is necessary. Anyway, I told her about you on our wedding night. We have never slept in the same room, let alone bed.'

'Another blissfully happy couple,' Lorna commented dryly. 'Thank God we're of like minds,

Dallas. Life is too short to be miserable. Others have interfered enough. From now on we make our own decisions. If they're wrong, we'll have only ourselves to blame.' She changed the subject. 'Lady Pamela sends her love. Lord Dalrymple, his blessing.'

'Do they know about Cam?'

'No. I thought it best to keep it a secret from them for now.'

Dallas agreed, though it hurt not to be able to claim the boy as his own to his parents. 'How are my brothers? Do you know?'

'Thomas . . .' She hesitated, then grinned. 'Oh, bother it! Why not tell the truth? He's a dear man but such a bore. You're an uncle again, did you know? They've had another son.'

Dallas smiled at her accurate assessment of his oldest brother. 'There's a letter in my pocket from Mother. The news is probably in there. Something quite beautiful, irresistible and compelling rather took my mind off any mail. Not to mention meeting my son for the first time.'

'Read it now.'

He shook his head. 'Later. Right now I'd rather listen to you.'

Lorna's eyes shone approval. 'Boyd is still in the army.'

'I hope he kept his commission.'

'Yes. Your father intervened. Said that the sins of a younger brother should have no bearing on another's impeccable career.'

Dallas looked guilty. 'The earl is a good man. I fear I've sorely tried him over the years.'

'A sweetie,' Lorna agreed. 'And quite impressive when his dander's up. Boyd's commanding officer nearly fell over himself to oblige.'

Dallas laughed. Though Lord Dalrymple was not his natural father he felt a rush of filial affection for him. The man was stern, not very demonstrative, but always there when needed.

'How's Glendon?'

Lorna glanced at him from under raised eyebrows. 'Something odd happening there.'

'Odd?'

'Glendon has been sent to India. We don't know why. All your parents are certain of is that the engagement has been called off, the ex-fiancée refuses to give a reason and her uncle, the bishop, seems unwilling to explain Glendon's sudden disappearance. There's been no word from Glendon.'

'Foul play? Surely not.'

'Cover-up, more likely.'

Their eyes met, as they both remembered the rather foppish young man who had gone so readily into a church environment, not for glory, but through a genuine wish to help others. Had he fallen foul of a less-than-perfect regime, or was Glendon himself guilty of some crime which necessitated his removal from public scrutiny?

'Don't worry about your brother. Lord Dalrymple is asking a lot of questions. If anyone can get to the bottom of the mystery, it's your father,' Lorna reassured Dallas. 'Glendon is probably in the south trying to convert the Tamils.'

'One shudders to imagine —'

'Into what!'

Lorna threw back her head and laughed. It was such a good sound, warm and earthy. Dallas knew her so well and yet there was so much more to learn. Charles had been his closest friend, Lorna Charlotte's. Different ages, different interests, different sexes, although their paths crossed regularly and they'd always got on well. Without this childhood fraternalism to strengthen their relationship, the obstacles they faced might well prove too great. As it was, each knew they could depend on the other – an essential ingredient in any friendship, although Dallas had some work to do in regaining Lorna's total trust – leaving deeper feelings free of the usual constraints that exist when strangers fall in love. Perhaps the absence of doubt would give them the courage they'd need.

'You were lucky to find a room with Mrs Watson. I know she's an old busybody but the place is clean.'

'I wanted to stay where I knew you'd come back to for mail. This house has been ready to move into for the past week. Now it needs to be lived in. I'll collect my things from Mrs Watson tomorrow.'

He kissed her hair. 'I'm planning another trip. Come with me.'

'Try and stop me. I'm itching to see this country.'

'It's not always easy. Are you sure?'

'Very. I'm not made of glass and neither is our son.'

He could see she meant it. 'Cam should grow up understanding the Zulus.'

She snuggled into him. 'He'll need brothers and sisters too.'

'Indeed he will.'

'And not too much younger either.'

'Perish the thought.'

She was reaching for him. 'Don't think me wanton or anything, my darling, but if we don't go upstairs right now, I could very well ravish you here and now.'

Dallas rose hastily. 'Oh, all right,' he pretended to grumble, then reached down and lifted her in his arms. 'I love you very much,' he whispered.

TWELVE

The next morning, anxious to hide nothing from Sarah lest she accuse him of deception, Dallas tethered the carriage outside Mrs Watson's boarding house and, while Lorna was busy packing and organising the loading of both their possessions, walked the three doors to the house he had been expected to call home. There was no sign of his in-laws' buggy. The maid admitted him and Dallas found Sarah in the front parlour. She greeted him warily.

'Where are your parents?'

'They left early this morning for the farm.'

'Good.' He chose a chair opposite her and sat down. 'I have something to tell you.' Now the moment had arrived, Dallas found he was quite calm. He owed his wife nothing, not even respect.

Sarah's eyes were accusing.

'Why do you look at me as if I have let you down?'

She lowered her lids. 'Because you have.'

'I?' Dallas couldn't believe his ears. 'You have a strange way of regarding responsibility, Sarah. How, in your estimation, have I disappointed you?'

'We are married,' she whispered. 'You took vows.'

'Yes,' he agreed. 'With one arm twisted up my back.'

'Many are forced into wedlock. They make the best of it.' She raised her eyes to his, and he saw determination on her face. 'You promised to love, honour and keep safe –'

'It was preferable to the gallows.' Dallas found he was growing angry.

'Can we not try?'

He waited a moment for his irritation to subside. Sarah was her father's daughter all right. No sign of contrition, only concern for herself. 'I have less inclination to try now than ever,' Dallas said finally. 'On our wedding night I showed you a letter and told you it was from the only woman in this world I could ever love.'

Sarah nodded.

'She's here.'

'What?' The single word carried fear.

'After leaving here yesterday I went to seek my old room at Mrs Watson's. Lorna was there. I had no idea.'

'A fine story,' Sarah snapped. 'Surely you don't expect me to believe it.'

'Believe what you like. I care little for your so-called sensitivities. The truth escapes you so often it may be hard to recognise.' Dallas kept his tone mild but Sarah behaving as a wronged wife was intensely annoying. 'You will hear the gossip soon enough. I'm telling you so that you are prepared, though, God knows, you don't deserve that courtesy. Lorna and I will be living together. In all but name, she is my wife. We already have a son. Though circumstances in Scotland did not allow us to be together, out here we have no intention of hiding our love. I wish you no embarrassment, Sarah, and I'm not trying to hurt you. We would never have lived together, you know that.'

'I had hoped –'

Dallas shook his head. 'You've told too many lies, Sarah.'

She hung her head. 'My father –'

Dallas sprang from his chair, frustration bursting to the surface. 'God damn it, Sarah. Despite your responsibility for this farce you have the audacity to threaten me with exposure. To hell with your bloody father. I have no wish to stoop so low, but you force my hand. Thulani would be easy to find. If needs must, I will make public the entire sordid story. Tell your damned father I said so.'

'No!' The word was wrung from her. 'I'm trying to warn you.'

He paced. 'Unless I miss my guess, your father is well satisfied. Your happiness means as much to him as mine did. He cares for his reputation, nothing else. If his son-in-law behaves badly, he will go out of his way to play the martyr. In a way, that would suit him better than acting the doting father-in-law. He likes me no more than I care for him. If he so much as squeaks one word against me I will make good my promise to reveal the truth.'

'I'll deny it.'

'Try. The baby's colour will speak for itself. Thulani's evidence will do the rest. There are only so many midwives in this town. Whatever your father may pay to buy silence, I can afford to double. Threaten my happiness any further than you already have and you will be forced to leave Africa, never to see your son again. Don't make this harder than it already is, Sarah. You've done enough harm.'

'It's not fair,' she cried out. 'Nobody loves me. Thulani hates me too.'

In a moment of clarity, Dallas saw the real Sarah. An only child, she'd been spoiled rotten. On the surface she appeared well adjusted and sweet, yet underneath lay a selfishness that would have been easy for her father to manipulate. Between them, they'd hatched a solution to Sarah's self-imposed predicament – he to protect reputation, she for something deeper and more devious. Dallas had no idea whether her relationship with the Zulu was founded on love or lust. Sarah had been willing enough to invite him into her bed for those few nights Dallas stayed in this house. She had gambled and lost. The reality of that left her with nothing, capable only of self-pity. He stood in silence, wondering how far she would go to try to keep him from leaving.

Sarah's dark eyes filled with tears and she dabbed at them with delicate little movements. Furtively she kept glancing at Dallas to see his reaction. When she finally spoke, it was all he could do not to laugh outright at a blatant last-ditch attempt to get her way which was so transparently untrue that even Sarah didn't look as though she believed it. 'I could have loved you. I liked you well enough.'

'Enough to lie, as we both know.'

'I had no choice.'

'Of course you did.'

'You don't know my father.'

'Oh, I think I do.'

Tears flowed unchecked. 'It wasn't my fault. Thulani forced himself on me.'

Dallas shook his head. 'Don't try to make more trouble, you silly girl. For God's sake, Sarah, stop deluding yourself. You played with fire and the inevitable happened. Face it.'

She licked at the salty liquid running past her mouth. 'I know what you think of me, Dallas, but I do love my child and it breaks my heart that Thulani took him away. I can't go home, the baby is there.'

'And well cared for.' Dallas didn't believe this story either. Sarah's play-acting was getting on his nerves. He felt anxious to leave, get back to Lorna and all that was honest. 'What will you do now? When the rumours start to circulate it will be very difficult for you here.'

'My cousin, Caroline, has invited me to live with her in Pietermaritzburg. I said I'd wait and see. Now I may as well accept.'

Dallas nodded and moved towards the door. Caroline was welcome to her. 'With your permission I will remove my belongings from here.'

'You can take them now. They're packed and ready.'

Mock martyrdom didn't suit her any more than false repentance, outrage or pathos.

'One day, for your own sake, Sarah, I hope you discover the person you really are. I give up. I confess, you completely confuse me. Goodbye. Stay well.'

She turned her face away.

Dallas found his things in two suitcases under the stairs. He supposed she'd packed everything. They were easy to carry the short distance to Mrs Watson's, where he put them into the carriage with their other possessions. Lorna stood in the doorway saying goodbye to the landlady. He joined them, took Cam from Lorna and placed him on his shoulders.

The baby crowed with pleasure.

'Are you ready to leave, my dear?'

Lorna had been watching his face, trying to gauge how the meeting with Sarah had gone. She smiled, reassured. 'Yes, darling.'

'Then we'll say goodbye, Mrs Watson. And thank you for everything.' He caught a whiff of something and removed Cam from his shoulders. 'I do believe our son has a present for you, my love.' When he looked back the solid wooden door was slamming shut. Its ultimate impact rattled several windows. 'Nice knowing you, Mrs Watson.' He grinned at Lorna. 'Let's go. We have the rest of our lives to live.'

Arm in arm they walked towards the carriage. 'The news will be all over Durban within twenty-four hours,' Lorna guessed.

'I hate to contradict you, my darling, but try six.'

'Who cares?' Lorna flung off the hat she'd been wearing and shook out her lustrous blonde hair. The pale skin Dallas remembered had taken on a light tan since coming to Africa. It brought out the blue in her eyes.

'Your eyes used to be grey,' Dallas commented.

'Must be a reflection of the sky,' she said gaily. 'I've never seen such a beautiful colour.' Lorna hesitated. 'How did it go?'

'I have no idea.'

She lifted an inquiring eyebrow.

Dallas shrugged. 'Honestly, I don't know. She went through every emotion known to women and didn't mean any of them. Will you promise me something?'

'If I can.'

'Be honest. If you're cross, be cross. If you're sad, cry. Happy, laugh. Sorry, apologise. Will you do that? And could you do something else? Put Cam on the other side. He stinks.'

Lorna moved the baby, then slid closer to Dallas, kissing his cheek. 'I promise to be honest but you'll have to get used to the smell. Babies are like that.'

Dallas rolled his eyes in mock horror.

'Da,' Cam said happily.

'Hear that?' Dallas grinned. 'He said dada.'

'Rubbish.'

'Da.'

'There. He said it again.'

'That's just babbling.'

Dallas gave his best lordly look. 'I do believe you're jealous.'

'Am not.'

'Dada.'

Lorna tickled then kissed their son. 'Disloyal little brat.'

Dallas wondered how a person as small as Cam could smell that bad. He was amazed that it didn't seem to bother Lorna. Looking over at her, at the flawless skin, the fashionable clothes, the erect way she sat, she might have been any one of a dozen girls he knew back in Edinburgh. But she was exceptional in every respect and Dallas knew he was a very lucky man.

'You're staring.'

'Have you eyes in the side of your head?'

'No.'

'Then how did you know?'

'The carriage is nearly off the road.'

Dallas would have been happy to relax and enjoy every moment of each day with Lorna and Cam but he had much to organise for the next trip. It was all very well for him to rough it but he couldn't expect a woman and baby to do the same. An extra wagon would be needed, properly kitted out for comfort and privacy, provisions less basic. The list of baby requirements was astonishing.

'He needs all that?'

'Yes.'

Her tone said she was not prepared to compromise. Dallas bought the lot.

Although their domestic arrangement had tongues wagging, neither Lorna nor Dallas knew enough people to worry about whether they were being snubbed. As Lorna put it, 'If you have a fist full of money to spend, it's amazing how quickly shop-keepers fall over themselves to sell their wares.' While reputations were one thing, Dallas was known as a man who paid his bills and due deference was shown to both him and Lorna. What was said behind their backs, they neither knew nor cared.

Cam thrived under his father's attention. 'He needed a man in his life,' Lorna said one night. 'I suspect there's more than a streak of stubbornness in him. As his mother, I usually give in. You make him put it to good use; I can see that when you play with him. If Cam doesn't get his way, instead of crying, he approaches whatever it is from a different direction. Guess who wins every time?'

Dallas looked skeptical. 'Are you sure? He's only a baby.'

'A miniature combination of you and me, my love.'

'Good grief! What have we done?'

Lorna giggled. 'Unless I'm mistaken, we've done it again. I'm two days late.'

Dallas folded her close. 'Mmmm!' He nuzzled her neck. 'Perhaps we should make sure.'

She nodded solemnly. 'I agree. One should always have a contingency plan.'

Two days before they were due to leave, on his way into town, Dallas, reacting to nothing more than a spur-of-the-moment whim, took a different route and rode past Jette's aunt's house. He nearly fell off Tosca on seeing the beautiful Danish thief outside in the garden. He reined in and sat still, watching her. She was picking flowers.

Jette must have sensed something because she straightened suddenly and turned to look. 'Dallas!' Her voice held pleasure, nothing more.

'Jette.'

She walked towards him, stopping just inside the gate. 'How well you look.'

He nodded curtly. 'You too, madam. That's a lovely brooch you are wearing.'

Jette looked down briefly. 'Isn't it?' Her gaze challenged his. 'An admirer gave it to me.'

'He must have admired you greatly.'

'Oh, he did.'

Dallas dismounted and walked closer. She watched him approach, a tiny, unreadable smile on her face.

Dallas found no rancour in him. Her gaze held steady with his and, instead of anger, he felt curiosity. 'Why did you do it?' he asked quietly.

There was no guilt on her face. 'I'm a thief, what else was I to do?'

'Our time together meant nothing?' Inwardly, Dallas winced at his masculine need for reassurance. It was pathetic, he knew that.

Jette's smile grew. 'The others on board offered slim pickings indeed. Mr Logan was obviously financially embarrassed. Soldiers and sailors have never been my style. And the wretched Mr Arnaud was a bore. You were young, good looking and secretive about your past. It intrigued me. I expected nothing more than a pleasant interlude and, I freely confess, found myself far from disappointed.'

Dallas was only human, a fact he'd had reason to acknowledge in the past. The smile that spread across his face came quite spontaneously.

Jette continued, her eyes sparkling with amusement at his reaction. 'Having discovered the two pouches, I nearly left them. You were so ill my initial instinct was to take pity. Fortunately or not, I pride myself on professionalism.'

'You have good reason,' Dallas rejoined.

She gave a tinkling laugh. 'Touché. If it makes you feel better, I have occasionally entertained a guilty conscience about mixing business with pleasure.' Jette shrugged. 'It soon passes.'

Her candour was appealing. 'Do you have any of it left?'

'All of it. Not due to any feelings of shame, I assure you. I'm a woman who loves beautiful things. But I'd have sold them in an instant if I'd been short of funds. Fortunately my finances improved dramatically in Morocco.' She pouted slightly. 'I suppose you want them back?'

'They are family heirlooms, the only contact I have with my father.'

'How touching! You're introducing an element I find tedious – there is no place for emotion in my business.'

'Very well. Like you, I need the money.'

Jette laughed again, totally relaxed. 'You are

indeed fortunate, Dallas. For once, Lady Luck has chosen to favour me and I am no longer in the predicament I was. Take back what is rightfully yours. A small request, however. May I keep this brooch?'

He smiled. He couldn't help it. She was so brazen. 'You're right about one thing. I admired you greatly. Yes, keep the brooch.'

Jette clapped her hands. 'Thank you, for I am exceedingly fond of it. Tether that fine horse and come inside.'

He could hardly believe his good fortune. 'I did consider asking your aunt if she knew where you might be.'

'You met her?'

'No. Logan gave me the address but I never took the matter further.'

'I'm pleased you didn't speak to her. She had no idea of my . . . ah, profession.'

'That's what stopped me. You say *had*?'

'She died.' No explanation, just the facts.

'I'm sorry.'

Jette shrugged that it didn't matter. 'I hardly knew her. She left me this house and a decent inheritance. My aunt was a widow and yours truly is her only living relative. Today I am quite comfortably off.'

Dallas didn't ask how. He could imagine it well enough. All he said was, 'Sultans are known for their generosity.'

Jette inclined her head, indicating that they were.

'How did you get away?'

'That was easy. I simply slipped out at night and disappeared into the darkness.'

'You were lucky not to be caught. I understand that harems are closely guarded.'

Jette frowned. 'Is that what you think of me? Dallas! I thought you held me in *some* esteem. Obviously not.'

'What else am I to think?'

'That's up to you. With lack of knowledge nothing is a foregone conclusion. Hasn't life taught you that?' She shook her head. 'No matter. As to my escape, I did have some help.'

'Another conquest?'

'There you go again. I would not entrust my safety to a mere admirer. Their thinking is invariably muddled by emotion. I needed a cool head, local knowledge and greed.' She grinned. 'Commodities easily bought in Morocco.' Abruptly, Jette changed the subject. 'Wait here. I'll be down in a moment.'

Dallas looked around the room while he waited. He had no idea how long Jette had lived here but noticed no attempt to erase what was obviously her aunt's taste in decoration. Perhaps she didn't intend to stay; someone like Jette would quickly grow bored. Her willingness to return his possessions had come as a complete surprise. If she were to be believed, the decision to take his jewels had been almost casual. Did the same apply to giving them back? Or was it the risk of reprisal? He didn't think so. Jette seemed to fear nothing.

She returned and found him studying the portrait of an exquisitely beautiful woman, dressed entirely in black, an expression of haughty arrogance on her face. 'My mother. Cold as ice, harder than steel, selfish as a cat and a bitch of the first order. She was younger than my aunt.'

Dallas turned and saw that she held the two pouches his mother had given him. 'You were obviously fond of her.'

Jette's eyes flicked to the portrait. 'Actually I was. At least she was honest. Never once in her life did my mother pretend to be nice.' She shrugged and handed him the bundles. 'If you hadn't found me I'd have made no attempt to return these. Everything's there but this.' She fingered the brooch. 'A pity I must lose the rest. There are some exquisite pieces there.'

Dallas took the pouches. He did not insult Jette by checking their contents. Somehow, he knew she told the truth.

'Can you stay a moment?'

'Not for long. I'm heading north in a couple of days and have matters to finalise.'

'A couple of minutes only. I'd like you to meet someone.'

She waited for his nod of agreement then swirled from the room, leaving only a hint of spicy perfume and an image of rustling silk. Jette returned a minute later with a sleepy baby. 'His name is Torben. He is your son.'

Dallas could see that. As Cam was a replica of his mother, Torben resembled Dallas with an uncanny likeness. He experienced a slight dizziness and shook his head, blowing out a long breath.

'Jette, I had no idea.' Dallas felt stupefied. This was the last thing on earth he had expected.

'Of course you didn't.' She laughed lightly. 'A woman of my experience usually takes precautions. You'd have expected that. My trouble was that for some years now I've had a strange yearning for a child. I expected to conceive while married but . . .' She spread her hands expressively. 'It didn't happen. When my husband died it made my desire for a baby greater than ever. I felt time was passing me by and soon it would be too late.'

Surprise quickly turned to anger. 'You intended this?'

'Yes.'

'With no consideration of my wishes?'

'Would you have agreed?'

'Probably not. Frankly, Jette, you are hardly the kind of woman who should bring up a child, especially my son.'

'Don't be so priggish. This has nothing to do with you.'

'Nothing . . .' Dallas was dumbfounded. 'You call theft nothing, for that's what it amounts to.'

Jette laughed. 'I hadn't thought of it that way.' Her eyes turned soft and she kissed the baby's downy head. 'Forgive me, Dallas, for I truly did not think beyond my own need. Would you have preferred not to know?'

He ran a hand through his hair. 'How can I answer that? Confound it, woman, how dare you stand there and calmly introduce me to my own son? Did you think it would have no meaning?' Dallas's eyes were drawn to the child. It fascinated him to see such a perfect mirror image of himself. He groaned. 'This has complicated my life beyond measure.'

Jette came closer, her expression one of concern. 'It doesn't need to. I shouldn't have told you, I'm sorry. Torben is such a joy and I wanted to thank you. Believe me, no-one need know.'

'You've only got to look at him.'

'Well, yes, I didn't anticipate that.'

'And what do you expect of me?'

'As I told you, nothing. I did very well in Morocco. I'm turning respectable, my dear. I intend opening a dress shop catering for the wealthy, those willing to pay through the nose for something imported. It should make a fortune.' She smiled. 'Especially when a little factory I'm also starting begins to produce copies.'

Despite everything, Dallas had to chuckle. 'You are incorrigible, Jette. No doubt you'll do very well. I swear, you have the scruples of a knave.'

'Thank you, I'll take that as a compliment.'

His laugh was spontaneous and surprisingly hearty. 'Dammit, Jette,' Dallas said when he could. 'Now what?'

'Well, to be honest, I do feel quite affectionate towards you. There is no man in my life.'

He cut her off. 'There is a woman in mine.'

Jette nodded acceptance. 'A pity. Is she special?'

'Very.'

'I can see that duplicity sits uneasily with you. I withdraw the offer. However, should you part company, perhaps it will be made again.'

'We have a child. He's a few months older than Torben.'

'Ah! The reason you left home, no doubt.'

'No.'

She waited, then added, 'It's none of my business, of course.' When he still said nothing, Jette shrugged. 'Honourable, too. A trait I pray has been passed on to my son.'

Now he had to know. 'Exactly what did you do in Morocco?'

'It bothers you? What I did or the fact that it was done while carrying your child?'

Dallas pulled a wry face. 'The latter.'

Her tinkling laugh sounded slightly forced. 'How very droll. Very well, since you insist, I was employed by the sultan to set up and run a small gambling house. It required some experience in that area, which I possess. He paid me handsomely, though I confess to helping myself to a share of the profits. It was not a situation that could continue undetected. I knew the consequences would be terminal, sultans do not take kindly to being robbed. Judging the moment was about to come, I left. Simple as that.'

He couldn't help but admire her. 'I'm sure it wasn't.'

'Perhaps not,' she admitted. 'It's in the past. Today Torben and I are safe.'

'And the dress shop? For how long will that keep you happy? You'll be bored in no time.'

She shook her head. 'It's different now. Torben has changed me somewhat. I have never worried about what people think of me but youth needs the security of acceptance. Being a bastard is an unfair burden for any child. That's why I tell people his father is dead. It could be true. You have no need to fear that the truth will out. The secret can remain between us. In fact, I beg you to keep it.'

No secrets between us. That's what Lorna had said to him. 'I will have to tell Lorna.'

'Your woman? Why? It can only upset her.'

'I'm sure it will. When I return home with these, I will have to tell her everything. If she ever meets you and Torben; well, the boy looks so much like me. Lorna will do the calculations. She's no fool.'

'Will she be discreet?'

'Yes.'

'Very well. Do what you must. For my part, Torben's father died before his birth. An accident at sea. He will grow up believing that.'

Dallas stared at the dark-haired little boy. The pull he'd felt immediately on seeing Cam was missing. But Dallas had known that Lorna was pregnant with his child. Torben came out of the blue. While fascinated by the baby and his incredible likeness to himself there was little emotional connection. He had no doubt that it would come, given the right circumstances. But Jette had made it plain. Torben was hers and hers alone. It was probably best for all concerned that way.

Jette took a step forward, stood on tiptoe and kissed him. 'Thank you for my wonderful child.'

Dallas moved back. 'My pleasure.' He knew it was the wrong response but, dammit, it had been a pleasure.

Jette appreciated the remark and laughed. 'I'll walk you to the gate.'

All day, Dallas worried about Lorna's reaction, vacillating between lying by omission and telling the truth. If he lied and Lorna found out, she would not forgive him. This fact alone gave him the strength to be honest. He waited until they were alone after dinner.

'Whatever is wrong, Dallas? You are like a bee in a bottle this evening.'

By way of an answer, he produced the two pouches and dropped them in her lap. Lorna stared at the contents. 'Where on earth did these come from?'

'It's a bit complicated.'

She looked at him a long while, then patted the sofa. 'Come and sit. From your expression and behaviour it would seem you have something to tell me.'

Dallas told her the whole story, from his mother's revelation when she gave him the jewellery, to his involvement with Jette on board ship, to unexpectedly seeing her that day and discovering he had fathered her child.

Lorna heard him out in silence, her fingers playing with the sparkling pieces still in her lap. When he finally faltered into uneasy silence, she asked quietly, 'Have you told me everything?'

'Yes, I swear.'

'This woman Jette, have you feelings for her?'

'Other than a sense of betrayal, no.' He did not think it prudent to confess that, despite her actions, he found it impossible to hate the Danish woman.

'You must have admired her. After all, you took her to your bed.'

'A man . . .' He saw Lorna's look of distaste and broke off. 'I'm sorry, my love, but it's different for men.'

'Why?' she asked coldly.

'We are capable of . . . of . . .'

'Fornication.' Lorna supplied the word curtly.

'Yes.' Dallas looked down at his hands, which he realised were gripping his knees. 'A man who is not committed to another –'

'Oh!' Her expression was not encouraging. 'But, Dallas, it was my understanding that you loved me. Is that not commitment?'

'You were wed. Somehow, I knew not how, I had to forget you.'

'In another woman's arms?'

'If that's what it took, yes,' he said a trifle defiantly. 'I did not believe I would ever see you again.'

Lorna's expression softened slightly, but her words were hard. 'Well, Dallas, the loss of your true father's property would seem to be something brought on by your own foolishness. As usual, you have triumphed over adversity. I wonder if it has been worth it.'

'What do you mean?'

'You have a son. How do you feel about that?'

'Furious. I felt she'd stolen more than what lies in your lap.'

Lorna pressed her lips together and he could see she was very angry. 'Stolen only what you freely gave. That is hardly theft.'

'She deceived me.'

'And I? Did I deceive you as well?'

'No,' he cried in anguish. 'With you it was different. I confess, my darling Lorna, I knew there was every chance you might conceive our child. I wanted it to happen. If I couldn't have you then at least we could share something precious.' Dallas buried his face in his hands. When he looked up, his eyes were moist. 'I have behaved badly, I know. I've been selfish, thinking only of my own desires. If truth be known, I'm still doing that. A gentleman would have accepted the position in which Sarah placed him and made the best of it. He would have sent you home, your reputation unsullied. Around you, Lorna, I cannot think of anything but a desperate desire to spend my life with you. I love you so much I cannot consider anything other than us being together. Of that I am guilty.' He had run out of words, despair strong in him.

Lorna took her time, chewing her lip. Finally she said, 'You are not a weak person, Dallas, yet you have behaved in a most surprising manner. Why?'

'I don't know,' he admitted miserably. 'I had lost you. Nothing else seemed to matter.'

'I can accept that you had a liaison with another. But a child, Dallas. She has something of yours that I believed was my exclusive right. It makes a difference.'

Oh God, don't let me lose her, not after all we've been through. 'Not to us. I implore you, don't let it affect us.'

'Can't you see it? There's a child, your child. Of course that changes things.'

'No.' He took her hands. 'How was I to know? Jette wants nothing from me. When I saw him there was none of the affection I felt immediately for Cam. I didn't even hold him.'

'He's still yours. Surely you experienced some emotion?'

Dallas shook his head. 'It's difficult to explain. Knowing you were pregnant with our child I loved you both. It felt natural, right. Jette was . . . a diversion.'

Lorna gave a very unladylike snort.

'It's true. If she hadn't stolen from me I'd not have given her another thought. I'm sorry, my darling, I didn't see it as being unfaithful, and I certainly didn't expect a child as the result. Maybe that's why I feel nothing.'

Hard eyes turned grey, or perhaps ice blue, bored into his. 'Could there be more?'

'What!' He hadn't expected that question.

'Babies. Could there be any more out there?'

'No. I swear.'

'There'd better not be.'

'There are no more secrets. Not one. I've been something of a lost soul but that has changed. Since you came back into my life I have purpose, a reason to live. I have no need of anything else, my darling, save you and our children. I will devote my life to us as a family. It is all I ever wanted.'

The lip-chewing stopped. 'I must love you a great deal, for it is in my heart to believe you. But be warned, Dallas, I will not tolerate further surprises of this nature. If we are to be together there can be no other, past or present. I hope you understand that. I mean every word. I've forgiven you so much already. There are limits.'

He took her in his arms and was relieved when she stayed there. 'There's no-one else. I've made a mess of my life and paid dearly for it. Now that we are together, I'll not betray you. I have no interest in other women. In fact, Jette offered and I turned her down.'

'Because of me?'

'Yes.'

'And if I hadn't been here?'

Dallas didn't flinch. 'I probably would have said yes.'

'So,' Lorna smiled though her eyes remained cold, 'I have competition.'

'None. I want no-one but you. That's the truth.'

She searched his eyes and he looked back, willing her to believe him. Finally, her expression softened. 'You could always get around me.' She looked down at the rings, bracelets, necklaces and other fine pieces. 'What about these?'

'They're yours. They'll pass on to our children.'

She picked up a diamond-crusted tiara and held its glittering beauty so that a spectrum of brilliant colour reflected the dancing candlelight. 'Do you think I'll ever wear this?'

'It would look wonderful with a bead skirt.' He waited anxiously. Was the flippancy too soon? *Oh God, Lorna, laugh, please laugh.*

She did and he breathed more easily. 'And this ring will go so well with broken fingernails.' Once again, with the crisis behind them, she was able to move on.

'Do you mind, my darling, that I cannot offer you the country estates and high life of Scotland?'

'Mind? Of course not. I mean that, Dallas. Everything out here seems so vibrant. I feel totally alive. I'm so excited about the trip I can hardly wait for it to start.'

He held her face between his hands. 'I promise you, there are no more surprises.'

Her eyes searched his for the truth. 'You are like a drug,' she said finally. 'One I cannot live without.'

'You will never need to.' He drew her close and kissed her.

A loud rapping on the door made both of them jump. 'Who on earth is that at this hour?' The mantle clock had just chimed ten-fifteen.

Dallas rose. 'Only one way to find out. Put those baubles out of sight, no telling who it might be.' He left the room, crossing the wide entrance hall to the front door.

'You're a hard man to find,' Logan said by way of greeting.

Will was next to him, grinning like a fool. 'Mrs Watson sends her regards.'

Dallas could just imagine it. The poor woman usually retired at eight. He stepped aside. 'Come in.'

'Who is it, darling?' Lorna stood silhouetted in light from the sitting room beyond.

Dallas made the introductions.

Logan barely managed to respond, his eyes meeting those of a gaping Will, who nodded before the older man turned to Dallas.

'If you don't mind my asking, dear chap. What happened to Sarah?'

'Long story.'

'Don't mind us,' Logan responded cheerfully. 'We've got all night.'

'That's what scares me,' Dallas shot back. 'Come on, you two. Thirst is written all over you.'

They moved into the sitting room, where Logan immediately spotted a whisky bottle that Dallas had not bothered to decant. 'Smith's Glenlivet, as I live and breathe,' Logan whispered reverently. '*The* Glenlivet.'

Dallas poured him half a glass. Logan sniffed appreciatively then sipped. 'Ah! Not another like it. The most complete of them all, dear boy. Nose and flavour superb. If the Highlands never contribute another thing to this world, they need not worry. And this,' he held up the glass, 'is how it should be served. In fine crystal glass from a generous hand. Cheers, old chap. Forgive me for not waiting.'

While Logan waffled on and on about the joys of Smith's Glenlivet, Dallas poured Will a glass of claret, for which he knew the Yorkshireman had a particular weakness, and whisky for himself and

Lorna. Topping up Logan's depleted drink, Dallas saw surprise on the older man's face that a woman, obviously a well-bred one, would drink straight spirits.

Lorna saw it as well. 'Do you disapprove, Mr Burton?'

'Not at all, dear lady,' Logan said hastily, though clearly he did.

Lorna smiled. 'Many pleasures are denied women in the name of propriety, Mr Burton. Would you not agree? If truth be told, gender-specific codes of behaviour were designed almost exclusively by men. One has to ask, of what are they so afraid?'

Dallas knew that Lorna's words were more about seeing what made Logan tick than throwing out a challenge. God help his old partner if he chose to patronise her. Thankfully, he didn't.

'Indeed, madam. In the matter of malt, more than likely they feared not enough would be left for themselves.'

Lorna laughed and turned to Will. 'Mr Green, Dallas tells me you have taught him a thing or two about trading. May I ask how you came to be a trader?'

'Trial and error, miss . . . er . . . missus,' Will growled, his words clipped by the embarrassment of being singled out. He was not at ease.

'Right,' Lorna said briskly, when it became obvious Will had given all he intended. 'You asked about Sarah, Mr Burton. If you gentlemen will excuse me, I shall retire.' She kissed Dallas on the cheek. 'Don't be long, darling.' Nodding to the others, Lorna drained her glass and left.

The silence hung heavy with curiosity. Dallas sighed. 'Let me freshen your drinks. Sit down and don't interrupt.' He told the two men some of his story.

Will was far from convinced. In fact, with the ladylike marchioness gone from the room, he became quite vocal. 'You left this one in Scotland, about to marry an old man, and carrying your child. So you married another, also with child, this time not yours. Then the first one reappears, your wife obligingly lets you live with her but refuses a divorce. Am I right?'

'Yes.'

'I don't get it. There's something you're not telling us.'

'Perfectly simple, old chap,' Logan said.

'Yeah? Then perhaps you'd be good enough to explain, seeing as how you know so much.'

Dallas had never heard such garbled guessing come so close to the truth.

'Why leave this beauty? They are so obviously deeply in love.' Logan turned to Dallas. 'I'm not asking, dear boy, just woolgathering.' He looked back at Will. 'Our young friend here is the type to adopt a stiff upper lip and get on with things. For some strange reason, he didn't do that. Instead, he left her and came out here. Now, it's a sad but true fact that the aristocracy rarely marry for love. The British Isles are positively drenched by bleeding hearts. His lady becomes betrothed to a man she

494

doesn't love. Dallas cannot marry her himself. What does this tell you? They're aristocrats.'

'You've only got to listen to them to know that.'

Logan frowned and went on. 'But why leave?' He held a finger up, ready to make his point. 'Our young and probably titled friend has another reason. What, I hear you ask? Ah, well, that could be any number of things but I suspect keeping one step ahead of the law had something to do with it.' He cocked an eye at Dallas. 'A duel? Illegal in Britain now. Shot somebody? No? Something else, then. Let's move on.'

Will was starting to look impatient.

'Bear with me.' Logan anticipated his interruption.

'You're guessing,' Will accused.

'Indeed. And our young, probably titled, escapee friend's silence tells me I might be on the right track.'

'Close enough,' Dallas muttered.

Logan looked smug. 'For some reason, he marries Sarah. Why? As you and I both know, Will, Dallas paid no more romantic attention to the girl than either of us. So, perhaps the ghastly Mr Wilcox discovered our young, probably titled, escapee friend's secret and forced him to marry his daughter. Blackmail. How can that be? We now find our hero's up and left his wife to set up house here. Suddenly, he is no longer concerned with whatever Sarah's father held over his head. Could that mean Dallas has something to hold over his?' Two very intelligent eyes bored into Dallas's. 'The threat of scandal. Yesssss! Where is the baby?'

'Enough,' Dallas cut in.

Logan nodded, making one last guess. 'Thulani.'

'The Kaffir driver!' Will was outraged. 'That's disgusting. They should shoot the –'

'No, dear fellow. Don't tell me you haven't indulged.'

'That's different.' Will turned to Dallas. 'Is it true?'

'Don't ask,' Logan advised. 'You'll force him to lie.'

Uncomfortable in the ensuing silence, Dallas changed the subject. 'What brings you two here?'

'We're broke,' Will said flatly.

'Come, come, let's not be crude.'

'What would you call it then?'

Logan ignored the question. 'You're leaving again soon. If you could see your way clear to offer the same conditions as before, we'd both be most grateful.'

'I don't need partners.'

Two beseeching expressions confronted Dallas. He couldn't help smiling. 'Very well. Same deal as before. We leave in two days. Do either of you have a wagon?' The looks on their faces gave him the answer. 'Then get organised, and quickly. Put them on my bill. If you're not ready to leave when I am, the deal's off.'

Lorna was still awake when Dallas went up to bed. 'Are they coming with us?'

'Do you mind?'

'No. I liked them. Do hurry, Dallas. I've been lying here thinking the most lascivious things.'

He grinned, slid into bed and kissed her deeply.

Logan and Will must have worked around the clock because both men were ready and waiting when Dallas arrived at Cato's to pick up trading goods and supplies.

'Is she coming with us?' Will asked in an undertone.

Dallas heard. 'She is. So is the baby. They are my family. Any other questions?'

Will backed off. 'No. Just asking.' When Dallas adopted that tone there was no point in discussing matters.

THIRTEEN

Lorna and Cam took well to the road. The wagon was comfortable and a makeshift barrier had been erected to prevent the baby from falling out. Mister David, Tobacco and July were once again only too happy to accompany them. In every respect save one, the three worked well as a team. They argued good-naturedly, even displaying petty jealousy, over time spent with Cam. Mister David usually won since he drove Dallas and Lorna's wagon. The youngster adored sitting on the Zulu's lap as they rolled along and often curled into Mister David's chest taking a quick nap.

When outspanned, Tobacco and July would vie for favour, and as their bickering became more heated, Lorna was forced to intervene, suggesting they take it in turns – one day each. This solution had not occurred to either man and they happily accepted the compromise.

Logan, Will and their Africans also claimed a share of Cam's attention. Each had his own way of entertaining the child. With constant company, not to mention that of his parents, the little boy remained happy and stimulated.

'He was always a contented baby,' Lorna told Dallas. 'Now he's positively enraptured. It must be good for him.'

'How different from our upbringing.'

She pulled a face at the memory. 'I'd have loved to grow up like this.'

Dallas laughed at her whimsy. 'You're wild enough as it is.'

And she'd laughed with him, knowing he wouldn't want her any other way.

If there was a sour note, it had to do with Logan. The man was, in one respect, being an obstinate fool. Zulu and European alike tried to dissuade him, but to no avail. Lorna came closest, using feminine wiles, until she went too far and Logan saw through it.

'Nice try,' he told her, 'but I happen to be impervious to expressions of devotion from a woman who is so obviously bound until death to another. I know you mean well, but my mind's made up.'

'Fine,' Lorna snapped, frustrated. 'Kill yourself. See if I care.'

'What will be, will be,' Logan responded blandly. 'Our fate is written the day we are born.' Then he grinned. 'And you *would* care.'

Lorna threw up her hands in disgust.

Logan's left arm had healed quite well. Although there was practically no feeling from elbow to shoulder, he could, with difficulty, lift and fire a rifle. This led to the announcement that perhaps his hunting days weren't over after all, a statement that worried everyone. They could see how slow he had become, something that could get him killed if he went after elephants. Which was exactly what Logan intended.

Otherwise, it was proving a dream trip. Will had a new wagon master, his other boys the same as before. Logan's murderous skinner had never reappeared, and his replacement was an excellent tracker and gun bearer. Squabbles, normal among the Africans, were minimal and easily diffused. All in all, Lorna could not have been introduced to a trader's life under more agreeable circumstances.

Will, who firmly believed that he alone could purchase the required quality and quantity of trade goods, had cast his experienced eyes over Dallas's stock and nodded approval. 'You've learned well. You're one of us.'

The compliment, casually made to sound like a mere observation, coming from someone who normally looked for negatives, filled Dallas with a level of self-respect and satisfaction he'd never anticipated. Respect shown him in the past had largely been due to who he was, not what he'd done. This was different.

Before setting off, rebellion from Lorna over the matter of clothes had Dallas almost speechless with amazement. He knew she was different from most women and this latest idea, outstanding in its audacity, made the utmost sense. Still, he didn't know whether to applaud or try to talk her out of it. In the end, because he could see how determined she was, Dallas went along with her.

'God help the women of Durban,' he said dryly. 'They'll be having the vapours in public when they see this.'

Secretly, he thought she looked wonderful.

It all stemmed from Lorna's refusal to ride side-saddle. 'It's too uncomfortable. You have to keep changing sides to avoid backache. That means dismounting, adjusting the stirrups and remounting. It wastes so much time.'

'Travel on the wagon.'

'No. I want to ride with you. I like the freedom of having my own horse.'

Dallas thought that was wonderful too.

Lorna found a local seamstress to improvise with store-bought calico dresses, turning skirts into trousers and tops into pinafores under which she could wear a light blouse. Not for her the fashionable bustle and leg-of-mutton sleeves, which were both hot and cumbersome. The horrified seamstress tried to talk her into at least allowing the leg covering to remain full and billowing, caught in at the ankle to give some impression of modesty. But no. Lorna insisted on straight legs, tight fitting, with pockets like those in a man's trousers. And that was what she proudly wore when they went to provision at Cato's. The sight of a woman in such a shockingly revealing outfit tested a disapproving Durban society that grudgingly had to accept that the aristocracy seemed to do, and get away with, anything they damn-well pleased.

Dallas, who had long since discarded his impractical attire for lighter store-bought clothes, couldn't fault Lorna's thinking and decided her courage deserved his encouragement. 'You'll start a new fashion, my darling. Fetching and practical.'

She'd grinned. 'As long as you don't think of me as a man.'

'With that beautiful hair and lovely face? I think not.'

'You're biased.'

'Guilty.'

'I've packed a couple of good outfits just in case. Are you sure you don't mind my dressing this way?'

Dallas leered. 'I know what's underneath.'

'Naughty!'

They bantered constantly. It was part of their fun and Dallas delighted in the way Lorna could give as good as she got. And quickly. Her mind was sharp and she wasn't afraid to speak it. When he thought back, their friendship had always been peppered with incidents where each tried to get the better of the other. Much to Dallas's amusement, Lorna would swear like a trooper when the occasion called for it. She didn't hold back either. Logan and Will were shocked that a woman could be so outspoken, but Lorna quickly won them over. Even so, they were careful with their own language in her company.

The Africans were enchanted by her hair. Long, shining blonde curls were a rarely-seen thing. Most European women wore theirs up, covered with a hat. Lorna liked her hair to flow freely, only using a hat when the sun became too hot. So, hatless, locks tied loosely by a ribbon at the base of her neck, dressed in cream with a blue shirt underneath and wearing soft handmade riding boots, Lorna became a talking point on trails from Durban to the Thukela. Further north, those they met along the way either didn't care what she wore or were too polite to mention it.

Mister David needed to overcome a deeply held belief that women were put on earth to bear children, cook meals, brew beer and tend crops before he would talk with Lorna of Zulu ways, as he had with Dallas. Her questions differed, tending to focus on the woman's role. He would speak from a man's viewpoint, surprisingly unlearned about how Zulu women actually felt, what their main concerns were or even what was discussed when they spent time alone together. Lorna had to be content with an overview but became determined to learn Zulu so that her curiosity could be satisfied.

She readily accepted some of Mister David's advice regarding Cam's mode of dress. He convinced her to discontinue the use of a napkin during the day. 'It is not normal for him to be wet or dirty. The boy must do his toilet as our children. On the ground.'

For practical reasons – Cam slept snuggled into his parents – Lorna still insisted on a napkin at night.

Their routine was only marginally different from the first time the three white men had worked together. The freedom of bathing in streams and wandering naked back to the wagons could not continue. Frank conversations about the female sex were strictly off-limits. Dallas outspanned their wagon well apart from the others, his excuse being that should Cam wake in the middle of the night they didn't want to disturb anybody. The truth was rather more basic. Lorna and Dallas's delight in each other was often clearly audible. Add to that a rocking wagon and no-one had any doubts about the goings-on inside. As for Cam, he obligingly slept through it all.

Will had many concerns about bringing a woman and child along, but as the days passed and both thrived on the experience, he was forced to admit that Dallas had an extraordinary family. Lorna was accepted as Dallas's wife. After all, Cam was his son and neither Will nor Logan had thought Sarah particularly suitable, particularly since learning something of the circumstances.

The journey to Pietermaritzburg went without incident. Their oxen and horses were from good salted stock, the wagons in fine condition. Although the weather remained hot and sultry, the trip was timed so that, once they reached the Thukela, the nights at least would be starting to cool down.

In Pietermaritzburg they topped up supplies and Dallas bought a second double rifle, just in case. News of his marriage to Sarah had reached the town, but intimidated by Lorna's title, no-one mentioned it to them, although it was obvious from sidelong looks and smirks that tongues were wagging. Lorna breezed through such disapproval with a nonchalant air that belied her vulnerability. Dallas knew he was responsible for most of her uncertainty, and went out of his way to support and reassure her when they were out and about together.

They were both pleased to leave Pietermaritzburg behind. Being the administrative centre for Natal, the town was largely populated by devotees of British-style red tape. Everyone lived strictly according to rules and codes that gave them comfort borne of familiarity, sorely needed by most in a strange land. To these people the rumours circulating about Dallas and Lorna were scandalous. To Dallas and Lorna, the town and the people in it were most tedious.

Back on the road, riding together, Lorna voiced what was on both their minds. 'I never thought that being different would be so hard.'

'Do you care what they think?'

'Yes and no.'

Dallas smiled. 'We all seek approval. Some of us conform, and receive it. But from whom? People we respect?'

Lorna smiled back. 'You're right. Logan's and Will's support is far more meaningful.' She glanced over at him. 'Thank you.'

'For what?'

'You know very well for what. You give me confidence.'

'You already have that in abundance. You were wonderful.'

'Without you there –'

'That will never happen.'

She leaned sideways and kissed his cheek. 'I feel so happy.'

He grinned his pleasure. 'Me too. It's like no-one can touch us.'

'Um . . . Dallas?'

Something was in her voice. He gave her a long look. 'Am I going to like this?'

'I don't know.'

He was still watching her. 'Well?' he demanded.

'Don't be so bossy.'

'You're hedging. Come on, out with it.'

'I'm definitely with child.' It came out in a rush, as if she were scared of his response.

Dallas was instantly concerned. 'Are you positive? How will you cope? The Thukela can be pretty rough. Perhaps we should return to Durban.'

'I knew you would say that. I'm not returning anywhere. I'll be fine. It's you I'm thinking of. How do you feel about it?'

His smile was soft. 'Nothing special. Just overjoyed.'

She laughed. 'Is that all?'

He laughed with her but was still worried. 'If anything should go wrong . . . Promise you'll take it easy.'

'Dallas.'

'Yes.'

'Do me a favour.'

'Anything.'

'Don't be such an old woman.'

He ducked his head, smiling. But he was serious as he spoke to her. 'I'll be right there, should you need me.'

'I know,' Lorna said softly. 'That is what makes me so happy.'

In Colenso, they again restocked. To Dallas's intense relief there was no sign of Mr Wilcox. However, he was quite certain that their passing through would be reported back to him. Reaching the Thukela River they left the road north and headed into Zululand. 'Here we go,' Dallas told Lorna. 'This is where it starts.'

She smiled, but it was strained and her face pale.

'Are you all right?' he asked anxiously. Lorna had been quiet all morning.

'It's the early month's sickness,' she explained. 'Bloody nuisance. I'll be fine. It will pass in a few weeks.'

'Why not lie down in the wagon?'

'And miss all this magnificent scenery! Not a chance. Don't fuss, Dallas, I'll be fine.'

And indeed, as the day progressed, Lorna improved. The next morning she was sick again. 'Perhaps we should stop somewhere until you're over this.' Dallas was becoming increasingly concerned. 'It worries me, seeing you so ill.'

Lorna straightened from a bout of retching and wiped her mouth. Perspiration shone on her forehead and her pallor was alarming. 'Don't treat me like a bloody invalid,' she snapped. 'I might start behaving like one.'

Dallas pressed his lips together to stop smiling. Humour, in Lorna's current frame of mind, was definitely not a good idea. But it always amused him when she swore. It was not the words themselves so much, as the refined accent in which she delivered them. She could make her language sound both respectable and shocking at the same time. 'Have it your way,' he said, not unkindly.

'Thank you. I intend to.' Lorna bent double and brought up more watery liquid, swearing under her breath – frustration the most likely cause. 'Help me,' she said suddenly.

He was beside her in an instant, an arm giving support.

'Sorry to be such a miserable wretch.'

'You can't help it.'

'It's so frustrating, Dallas. I loathe feeling off-colour, that's what makes me difficult.'

Dallas kissed her hair. 'Stubborn would be a better word.'

She leaned into him. 'I think I might lie down for a bit.'

'Good idea.'

'Will you stay with me?'

'Of course.'

She slept for several hours and, on waking, was back to the old Lorna.

Logan and Will stayed well away from Dallas's domestic difficulties. They had guessed that Lorna was pregnant and knew there was nothing they could do for her. Both men feared her vitriol when she was in a bad frame of mind and were more than happy to let Dallas deal with it. Mister David too, went out of his way to remain silent whenever Lorna was out of sorts. He did speak to Dallas about her welfare, and on being told that she had dreamed of crossing a swollen river – Dallas having put this down to her lack of enthusiasm at crossing the Howick Falls after she'd learned it was there that he'd met Sarah – Mister David had shaken his head. 'No. That dream is a sign that she carries a female child.'

'Do Zulu women also become sick?'

'It can happen.'

'Do you have any way to prevent it?'

'Not this. It is normal. Our women are protected from other things.'

'Such as?'

Mister David had become quite comfortable telling Dallas about evil spirits. 'They must be protected from wizards with a medicine that only an *inyanga* can make. If you like, I can ask for some at Chief Ngetho's kraal.'

'Thank you.' Although Dallas didn't know what Lorna would make of it, anything was worth a try. 'What else?'

'The madam is far from home.' Mister David reached inside the canvas cover of the wagon. 'I find this to keep her safe.' He held up some small weeds bearing tiny leaves and yellow flowers. 'It is called the *umKhondo* plant. She should wear it round her ankles.'

Dallas took the wilting weeds. Wearing them would probably appeal to Lorna, the novelty of doing so far outweighing any reason behind it.

'Madam must not stand when she eats.' Mister David looked distressed. 'That would be very bad.'

'Why?'

'Then the baby also stands and will arrive by its feet.'

This was beyond Dallas's understanding. He had no idea which part of a baby was supposed to emerge first. Calves presented front feet and their heads at the same time, although he suspected that human babies might be different. 'Oh,' was the best he could do.

Mister David was warming to his subject. 'And you must keep out of the river, for it will carry you away.'

'How am I expected to wash?'

'I will bring water.'

He seemed so serious that Dallas nodded agreement.

'I will make up some *isiHlambezo* closer to her time of birth.'

It was a word Dallas had not encountered before and he asked for an explanation.

'We soak special plants and keep them covered in a pot. A small spoonful each day will make it an easy birth. Be careful not to allow anyone other than yourself to look on this medicine for if they do, the child will resemble them, not you.'

For all Dallas's admiration of the Zulus and their traditions, some of what Mister David was telling him seemed to fit with what he would have called old wives' tales.

Lorna agreed. 'I'll wear the flowers and sit to eat

if it makes Mister David happy. But that's it. I will not swallow any witchdoctor's concoction. As for you being carried away in the river, one has to ask how that would be possible.'

The Thukela was showing distinct signs of drought, its flow reduced to a trickle of shallow water. The next morning, however, rain in the Drakensberg Mountains had turned the river into a swirling brown maelstrom. Lorna looked at it in amazement. 'Where are those weeds?' she managed. 'Tell Mister David to keep picking.'

By the time they reached Chief Ngetho's *umuzi*, Lorna had been well-schooled by Mister David as to matters of etiquette. Very often, Dallas joined in their discussions. Up until then, all the advice his driver had given was for a man. Women were different. They were a man's property and Lorna would not be viewed as anything else. She could not join a beer drink, sit in with the bartering process, go anywhere near the cattle or speak until spoken to. A woman had to be demure and modest at all times, not engaging in eye contact, nor even eating with the men.

It pleased Dallas greatly to see her accepting and adopting Zulu ways which were so different from everything the two of them had grown up with. He had worried that Lorna might object to the lowly status accorded to women. Although ahead of her time herself, and knowing she could never accept a Zulu woman's place in her own society, Lorna could see no reason to question age-old tradition. She was able to look beyond the superficial and see sense in the underlying reasons, although, like Dallas, she privately rejected some of the more superstitious customs.

A Zulu woman's life seemed hard by anybody's standards. Not only did she cook and clean but worked in the fields for hours on end, toiling in the hot sun to grow the mealies that made up her family's staple diet. She had to be amenable at all times, especially towards her husband, male members of his family, and any of the wives who were regarded as socially superior. She could not dream of so much as looking at another man. The very real threat of execution was there to ensure her good nature. She bore children with the minimum of fuss, suffering total isolation in a special hut for anything up to eight days until the child's navel string fell off, but was still expected to pull her weight hoeing and weeding, often back in the field the day after giving birth. The collection of water and washing of clothes in crocodile-infested rivers was cheerfully undertaken by her, despite the regularity with which African women lost their lives to these ferocious and much-loathed killers. Firewood was also her responsibility and she regularly carried heavy loads on her head, walking vast distances under a boiling sun and braving whatever wild animal she might encounter.

By comparison, the men seemed to have an easy time, spending long hours in pleasurable conversation in the shade, drinking beer one of the wives had made, eating their food and rotating sexual favours. However, each man old enough to belong to a regiment – and the ages ranged from about sixteen to seventy and beyond – was obliged to defend his king, his clan and his chief. Deaths during battle, particularly once the white man arrived with firearms, were many. The Zulu warrior went against bullets with nothing more than a shield and *assegai*. They died in their tens of thousands. Not accounting for as many deaths, but certainly as responsible for a considerable depletion of their numbers, were casualties from ongoing tribal skirmishes.

The result – more women than men.

A husband was a very desirable asset. He was obliged to feed, clothe and provide shelter for each wife. Cattle being taboo for women, and hunting a man's domain, if women wanted milk and meat they had to rely on a husband to provide them. He also gave her children, who would take care of her as she grew older. Unmarried women were rare and regarded as outcasts. The death of a husband did not necessarily mean an end to security – more often than not, one of his brothers would take on the responsibility of his wives. Therefore, a married woman was reasonably assured of continued protection throughout her life.

With so many wives to control and keep happy, a strict pecking order had developed. Severe penalties kept women obedient and children and chores kept them occupied. It was a system that had worked well for centuries. So Lorna kept quiet, observed, and learned from Mister David, and came to respect the rules of Zulu society. Arguments would break out, but were always resolved with humour and dignity. Esteem was given freely and received humbly. Discipline that seemed harsh did serve to remind people of their manners.

The treatment of her son was another matter entirely. Cam, as a young male child, was indulged every moment. For the two days they spent at the *umuzi*, Dallas grew used to the sight of his son strapped to the back of a young *in Tombazana*. Cam would be taken to the river to bathe and play, or to a hut to taste food specially prepared by the girl's mother.

Lorna's and Cam's hair colour continued to be a constant source of fascination to everyone. Etiquette did not allow any man to approach Lorna, but young Cam's head was constantly touched and his hair pulled in playful wonder – sometimes with too much enthusiasm, in which case his tears caused great consternation, and even led to reprisal if the offender was a child. Women, except for the great and right-hand wives, treated Lorna's locks to even more attention, several even begging for a snippet. These Lorna would happily have given were it not for Dallas's warning that she could very well end up with no hair at all.

Lorna spent most of her time at Chief Ngetho's *umuzi* learning how to make a love letter for Dallas. This provided hours of giggling entertainment for the *ntombi*, girls eligible for marriage but as yet unpromised. Lorna's insistence on using mainly white beads amused everyone. 'I love him very much,' she would protest in the most basic Zulu, bringing on yet another bout of merriment and many lewd comments over Dallas's ability to keep her satisfied.

It was of some concern to the older women that Cam had not been cleansed of *isiGwenba* at birth. Through Mister David's interpreting, they told Lorna that, unless the procedure were performed, he would grow up to be unusually lecherous or have a tendency towards eczema. The cure was to take the stem of a castor oil leaf, thrust it roughly into the baby's rectum and twirl it until copious quantities of blood became evident. Lorna was horrified at the prospect, especially when Mister David informed her that many babies bled to death after the treatment. Dallas intervened, explaining that Cam had been born in Britain where similar customs were carried out. He described, with embellishment, the purification ceremony – basically baptism – and how by dousing a baby with specially blessed water that child was protected from *isiGwenba*. The women remained unconvinced until Dallas improvised and gave details of a completely fictitious ritual that was similar enough to the Zulu way to satisfy them.

When the time came to leave Chief Ngetho's *umuzi,* Lorna had made friends with so many women and children that the morning's work was left undone as they crowded around to say goodbye. Riding alongside Dallas, she was in high spirits. 'Are all these people so friendly?'

'Not always. Mister David has a brother living there. They've sort of adopted the rest of us. Don't forget, Colenso is not that far away. White faces are nothing new. As we go further down the valley, that changes.'

'Will any of them be hostile?'

'It's possible. We've been chased away a couple of times. Most kraals like to trade but that's no guarantee that a welcome on one trip will mean the same next time round. The further we get from civilisation, the more superstitious people become. We could be refused entry for something quite simple, like an owl hooting on the roof of a hut the night before.'

'You've learned so much. Sometimes I feel I'll never catch up.'

'You'd better not. You're a woman. It would be unseemly.'

She laughed; then, without warning, her face drained of colour. Lorna leaned sideways, retching.

Her morning sickness had grown no worse or better. She would wake feeling fine but within half an hour become cranky and ill. That state lasted several hours then, quite suddenly, Lorna would be back to her normal self. Dallas became used to these mornings and learned the only way to deal with them was to disappear. Fussing only made her more irritable.

Keeping Cam out of the way helped. He loved riding with his father, tucked comfortably in front of him on the saddle. Dallas enjoyed it too. The child seemed to be growing before his very eyes, baby babble rapidly turning into Zulu or English words. Dallas felt such love whenever Cam's eyes lit up with recognition and he said 'Dada'. Having missed the first nine months of his son's life, Dallas was more than happy to make up for lost time.

Aside from the inconvenience of morning sickness, Lorna loved being out in the bush. Life under canvas was predominantly a masculine preserve for the very good reason of its discomfort. The fact that it was something most women had enough sense to avoid was a challenge Lorna took on with grim determination to succeed.

There were a few intrepid women out and about in wagons with their husbands. Not many hunted, although some developed a dexterity with firearms that matched that of their menfolk. Other hunters adopted the attitude of sailors – that having a woman along encouraged bad luck. Lorna typified the free spirit required for a woman to be enticed from the safety and comfort of home into the unknown and dangerous world of adventurous men. Whatever drove her, she pooh-poohed the idea of bringing misfortune.

'Utter rubbish,' she'd snapped when Will raised the subject.

'I'm only saying that some believe it.'

'Do you?' she challenged.

In Will's opinion Lorna could do no wrong. 'Of course not.' His voice belied his words.

Her eyes danced with mischief. 'Yes, you do, Will. Go on. Admit it.'

Will looked embarrassed and shrugged.

'If you expect trouble it will always find you.' Lorna turned to Logan. 'Isn't that so?'

'I daresay,' Logan agreed, chuckling at the other man's discomfort. 'Though Will is right in one respect. Having a woman along leaves more scope for misadventure. And before you climb on your high horse, let me point out that a man feels obliged to protect his woman. It means he cannot fully concentrate on protecting himself. Understandably, accidents happen. That's all I'm saying.'

'I take your point,' Lorna said in a subdued voice. 'I never thought of it in such a way.'

'But you're no trouble,' Will put in, eager to show loyalty.

The ease that existed between everyone was largely due to Lorna's ability to cut through formality. She was not exactly one of the boys, no-one's imagination being that good, but never once did she use femininity as an excuse. Lorna was quick to realise that when nausea hit, the best place for her was in the wagon. As her illness subsided, she got on with things and made no mention of it. Still, Lorna refused breakfast because she could not keep it down. No-one tried to coax her, knowing she would eat when she felt better. Dried strips of biltong, wild fruit and berries, comprised the midday meal, and the culinary skills of their cook made for dinners everyone could appreciate, despite the strangeness of some concoctions. Cam seemed to be a bottomless pit when it came to food. Dallas watched with pride as his son's small body grew sturdy and brown. At the end of each day, full to the brim with fresh air, endless stimulation, unlimited exercise and plenty to eat, Cam fell asleep in someone's arms as he listened intently to campfire conversations. His life was healthy, secure and free. He responded with a happy nature and endless curiosity.

Will and Logan still bickered but the bite had gone from their exchanges. Each, it seemed, had developed respect for the other's expertise. Either would die rather than admit it, though.

Despite regular practice with his rifle, Logan's arm continued to be a concern. 'It's not your aim,' Dallas said one night. 'That's never been better. It's speed. You're too slow.'

'Rubbish,' Logan snapped back. 'I'm as fast as I ever was.'

'No, you're not. And in a tight situation with elephants, you could be seriously hurt.'

'We need the tusks.'

'We're trading a few.'

'Not enough. I'm going back into that valley and you can't stop me.'

Dallas blew air and reluctantly gave voice to a decision he had made a few days earlier. 'No, that I can't. But I can come with you.'

The look of relief on Logan's face told everyone that he too had been worried.

They reached the valley of Dallas's only elephant hunt near sunset two days after leaving Chief Ngetho's *umuzi*. It was as beautiful as Dallas remembered. Hemmed in by hills with lush grass, a belt of trees following the river, game dotted over an open plain stretching away some twenty miles. A hunter's paradise.

To Will it was threatening, the narrow access gorge their only way in or out. Evidence of elephant activity was hard to miss.

It was as sultry as before. The humidity and heat pressed down, faces ran with sweat and clothes stuck to their bodies. Almost immediately, Cam came out in a rash and grew uncharacteristically fractious. Lorna mixed a calamine paste and rubbed it over his body. Mister David boiled a concoction of crushed leaves and chopped roots, let the brew cool and applied it liberally. Whether it was the calamine, Zulu *muthi* or a combination of the two no-one would ever know but Cam improved and the rash never came back.

Late that afternoon the elephants came. More than last time. There were about a hundred, making their stately way to a favourite drinking spot at the river, spread out for the best part of a mile. The sight stopped everyone. Outspanned and shaded by trees, the wagons, cattle and horses presented no threat. The elephants ignored them.

They were led by an old matriarch. Youngsters scurried to keep up. Dallas counted at least six mature bulls with good ivory, and young males jostled and scrapped between themselves.

'They're beautiful,' Lorna breathed.

'Unusual,' Logan muttered. 'There's plenty of food and water around. What has made so many families join forces?'

'Hunters?'

'I hope not,' Logan responded. 'They'll be damned aggressive if that's the case.'

'They're showing no sign of nervousness,' Dallas observed. 'It may be the good grazing.'

'Perhaps.' Logan sounded doubtful. 'There are some big boys among them. If we're lucky, we'll be in the money.'

'No heroics,' Dallas warned. 'Take them in the open.'

Logan threw him a hard look. 'We'll take them where we damned-well can. Tomorrow.'

The presence of so many elephants worried Dallas. Family units tended to number between ten and twenty. They were happy to greet other herds but usually parted company again. This was not a massed gathering as they'd seen last year. What outside pressure had made these animals stick together?

Will, who decided to go out of the oppressive humidity of the valley and shoot something for their supper, provided the answer. 'Hunters,' he said, on his return. 'Found a couple of carcasses. The tusks are gone. Wheel tracks head off into the hills. Couple of weeks ago, I'd say.'

'Hngh!' Logan grunted. 'No sign of them in the valley. That's something at least.'

In their wagon later that night, Lorna asked Dallas about the dangers. He didn't try to hide his concern. 'It depends where they are and if they've been shot at before. Some of the forest along the river is pretty dense. You have to get close. If they're in the water or out in a clearing it's easier.'

'Why not shoot as they come into the valley?'

'No cover. We'd never get near enough. Besides, after the first shot they'll panic and run for the gorge. It's best to give them space to get away.'

'Do we have to kill them?'

Dallas pulled her into his arms. 'Were it up to me, no. I feel the same as you. We're in the minority, I'm afraid. Most hunters have no feelings one way or another for elephants. They represent money, that's all. Logan's not like them but he's not like us either. I don't know what it is with him. It's as if he has to prove something. This time it's different.'

'How?'

'Well, normally he gets out there, shoots what he can, becomes moody as if nursing a guilty conscience, then goes back the next day to do it all again. He once said nothing beats it for excitement. Perhaps it is as simple as that, I don't know. This time I think he feels his reputation is at stake. He's a proud man. And stubborn. That arm isn't reliable and he knows it. That's why I can't let him go after them on his own. With elephants running everywhere, you need at least two effective rifles. Even with his gun bearer loading for him, Logan might be too slow.'

'Can't someone else do it?'

'Will is scared witless of elephants. And most Zulus are no good with guns.'

She stirred, tightening her arms around him. 'I can shoot.'

'I know. You're a damned good shot. But this is dangerous. You're not coming with us.'

It was pitch dark in the wagon. Dallas felt her hurt.

'I'm sorry, darling, you're too precious to place in danger. What would happen to Cam if we were both –'

'Don't.' Her hand clapped over his mouth. 'Don't even think about something like that.'

'I hate killing elephants,' Dallas went on, kissing her fingers. 'Once was enough. They're almost human in some respects. I swore I'd never shoot another. Now . . .' His voice tailed off.

'If anything happens to you, I'll kill Logan.'

The conviction in her voice made Dallas smile. 'You and Cam will be safe with the wagons. As soon as you hear the first shot, make sure you both lie low in here. The elephants will come this way making for the gorge. They won't charge a wagon but if you're on the ground, you could be in trouble. Promise me you'll do as I ask.'

'You'll be on the ground, though, won't you?'

'Behind a tree with a loaded gun in my hand.'

'I'm scared. There were an awful lot of them.'

'They may be gone by tomorrow.'

'God, I hope so.'

The elephants stayed. It was barely light when Mister David quietly woke Dallas. '*Ndhlovu* still here. Those we saw yesterday and more.'

Dallas's guts knotted as nerve ends tightened. There were too many. It was madness to think that two puny men with guns could take on such numbers.

He dressed and joined Logan at the fire. 'Still with me?' the older man asked.

'Do I have a choice?'

Faded eyes flicked to his then down to the rifle he was checking. 'You know you do.'

Dallas shook his head. 'And you know I don't.'

'Who needs a damned wet nurse?' Logan loaded both his single barrel eight-bores with spherical lead projectiles that had been hardened with tin. 'Stay here with your wife and son.'

'You're crazy. You know that, don't you?'

Logan's smile was tight but he made no comment.

Dallas could see that getting into the right frame of mind was proving harder than it had in the past. 'We don't have to do this.'

'You don't. I do.' Logan's shaggy head turned and his eyes bored into Dallas's. 'I need the money. I'm not getting any younger. Don't you understand? This is my last chance.'

'That's rubbish and you know it. You can make a decent living by trading.'

'It's not the same.'

Dallas left it. They'd had this conversation before, and despite his words to Lorna last night, he didn't understand Logan's reasoning any better this time. The man seemed determined to court danger, test himself against the odds. In some ways, Dallas was no different, questioning, even flaunting, many of the rules people were expected to live by. But this went further. He'd seen his partner take risks but now there was a kind of desperation in him. Perhaps Logan really did believe it was his last chance and for that reason chose to ignore the overwhelming evidence that it might be suicidal.

'Relax,' Logan advised Dallas. 'They're still too close to the wagons. We'll let them browse a while longer.'

It was over an hour before they set off after the elephants. Logan's mood swung from taunting to tense and back again. Dallas's feelings weren't much more stable. Committed to going with Logan, he couldn't come to terms with the fact that he'd never been more scared in his life.

'Let's go,' Logan said finally, handing a loaded eight-bore to his African gun bearer. Mister David was ready with one of Dallas's lighter double rifles. 'It will take a while to get into position,' he told Will and Lorna. 'When you hear shots, go straight to the wagons and stay there. You'll be quite safe.'

'Take care.' Lorna kissed Dallas hard on the mouth, anxiety in her eyes. 'You too.' She pecked at Logan's cheek.

Dallas noticed that Logan had the silliest grin on his face as they walked away.

The elephants were a good couple of miles away, spread out and browsing in the trees. Dallas could see none but heard them quite clearly. In some places, the dense bush was several hundred yards deep. There was not a breath of wind. Logan's gun bearer led them silently towards the river. Firing from that direction would force the elephants out onto the plain.

'We could do with somebody else shooting,' Logan commented. It was his only concession to the danger they faced.

Dallas focused his mind on the job at hand. This

was no time for sympathy or aversion to the havoc they were about to wreak on so many unsuspecting animals. That luxury could come later. Right now, his main objective was to keep everybody alive. He was helpless to prevent the build-up of tension as they crept stealthily forward. Dallas's hands remained steady but, in his guts, the flutters felt as if he were trembling. Mister David was one pace behind, holding his second gun. Logan's man remained out in front. Well back and strung out over a hundred yards or so, came the African skinners armed only with *assegais* and knives.

Reaching the river at a point where the elephants were probably half a mile away, Logan's gun bearer froze and nodded. A small herd of zebra had just left the water and were making their way back through the trees to graze on the open plain beyond. The zebra hadn't spotted them, but with excellent eyesight and a nervous disposition, if they did, and panicked, they could easily spook the elephants. Luckily, the herd disappeared giving no sign that they'd seen anything threatening.

A storm was building, dark clouds rolling in over the distant hills. It brought an unwanted breeze into the valley causing leaves to rustle overhead in restless relief. Logan took up the lead and started forward again. He moved in slow motion, the rifle held across his body, each foot carefully placed to avoid making a sound.

A breaking branch. Dead ahead. Freeze. Ignoring the streaming, salt-laden sweat and forgetting the persistent moisture seeking flies, they froze and listened. Another branch. To the left. *What's that? Shadow? No. Something moved.* A crawling sensation crossed Dallas's scalp. As his eyes adjusted to the dappled light, he began to look through, rather than at, the bush. Indistinct shapes came vividly into focus. Feeding elephants were all around them, some as close as twenty feet away. They had somehow walked right into the middle of them.

Dallas saw Logan slowly turn. His chin lifted. 'Back off.' The gesture was clear. Dallas looked behind. *No good. Elephants. Christ! How many can there be?* Freeze.

Sweat, suddenly icy cold, ran down Dallas's chest and back. His throat felt dry, gut constricted, each heartbeat thundered in his chest. *Get ready.* He eased a thumb towards the hammers of his uncocked rifle. *I'm dead. They're too close. Too many of them.*

Dallas could smell them, hear their stomach rumblings. A bull to his left stopped feeding. The animal remained perfectly still. *Flap your ears. Eat. Do something.*

'Wind's shifted,' Logan warned, his voice absurdly, suicidally, shockingly loud. 'Look out, they're on to us.'

For an instant nothing happened as man and beast tried to assimilate their proximity to each other. The ramifications were deadly for both. Then all hell broke loose.

Reacting instinctively, Dallas and Logan turned back-to-back, their eyes everywhere, rifles up and ready, gun bearers beside them. Both men were right-handed and, with no words spoken, each covered an area ahead and to their left.

Shutting his mind to everything save a basic instinct for self-preservation, Dallas sensed a large cow to his right lift her trunk. Her eyes latched onto the intruders. With little or no hesitation, she tucked up her trunk, a foot swung back once, her head shook violently and outstretched ears flapped wildly. Then, with a shrill trumpet, she came. Every sense heightened, Dallas ignored her. The elephant was on Logan's left. Even while focused on his own field of fire, a corner of Dallas's mind remained aware of his partner's actions.

Logan's heavy rifle thundered. Still she came. He grabbed for his other gun and took aim. Before he could fire, the cow collapsed. Smoothly, with no break in concentration, Logan raised the muzzle and fired again. Another cow dropped, just behind the first. Two shots, two down. Dallas registered Logan reaching for the other rifle with his bad arm, fumble, then drop it. Without conscious thought, he covered them both until his partner was ready to fire again. It seemed as if, instead of trying to flee, some of the elephants were actually seeking them out. Enraged screams filled his head. Deadly shapes bore down. Animal and man were driven by one single thought. Kill or be killed. Neither wanted to die. The nerves of moments ago had been replaced by a cool and certain knowledge that if he didn't get them, they'd get him. And all the while, for every single second of the mayhem that had erupted, Dallas felt like an observer. He missed nothing. He felt nothing.

One of the skinners had turned and tried to run. He was overtaken, picked up like a piece of tinder and flung higher than the trees. Dallas saw him land, with bone-breaking impact, back on the ground. Two more elephants fell to brain shots before he could look back. The young bull was kneeling on his victim, shrieks of agony louder than the trumpeting all around. Dallas hesitated. A fraction of time was all it took. If he killed the animal, it might fall on the Zulu. If he didn't, the man was dead anyway. It was more instinct than thought which drove him. He fired. A knee shot. The elephant tried to move forward, stumbled and fell. The skinner was free of the crushing weight but didn't move. Dallas's mind clicked over. *Out of action. The Zulu was unnaturally flat and covered in blood. Elephant twitching, trying to stand. Finish him later.*

Logan yelled something. Dallas glanced behind. The hunter was swearing loudly. His gun had failed to fire. Three elephants were converging on them. Logan's hand reached back for his other rifle. Dallas fired and brought one animal down. He turned to the next and fired again. Hand back. The second double slapped into his waiting left hand. Snatch. Cock. Aim. Fire. Where's Logan? Cock. Aim. Fire. Hand back. He and Mister David were like machines. *Where's fucking Logan?* Slap. Reloaded gun. Cock. Aim. Fire. Turn. Cock. Aim. Fire. Hand back. *Not so many now.* Fire. *Got you.* Dallas had no idea how long the carnage lasted or how many animals he'd killed. What did register was that his partner's guns had fallen silent.

Sudden, painfully loud silence. *They've gone. Where's Logan?* In slow motion, rifle ready, Dallas turned, his eyes scanning. Dust hung in the air heavy with the smell of burnt gunpowder. Fear hovered then pounced. Logan had been right behind him. Now there was nothing but dusty space. Dallas was shaking, swearing, crying. 'Logan?' he croaked.

Nothing. Deathly still. The kind of silence to dread. The depth of it spelt disaster.

'Fuck it, Logan. Where are you?'

Mister David's hand found his arm and squeezed gently. The African nodded, his eyes looking away to the left. Logan! Leaning against a tree. Sitting. *How did he get there?* Legs straight out, rifle in his lap, head slumped to one side. *Something wrong. Too quiet.*

Then Dallas noticed the blood. It welled from a gaping wound in Logan's chest. Realisation dragged at his guts. On legs of jelly, Dallas ran to his fallen partner. Logan was still breathing.

'Logan. Jesus, man, talk to me.'

One eye opened. A grimace crossed his face and a deep groan escaped. 'Bastard got me,' he whispered, his words hardly audible as he struggled to breathe. 'One too many.' Logan gagged as bright lung blood frothed from his mouth.

Dallas knelt beside him. The tusk had probably missed Logan's heart, though the damage it caused would be just as fatal.

'Stay with me.' Logan's voice was nothing more than a whisper as life ebbed from him. 'Good . . . good way to go.'

Sweat and tears poured down Dallas's face. There was nothing he could do, nothing anyone could do. He reached out a hand and gripped Logan's shoulder. It felt hard and solid. Dependable. Alive. Sobs threatened and Dallas swallowed them away. Logan raised pain-filled eyes. 'Cheers, old boy.' Moments later, a shudder ran through the old hunter and he was gone.

Not possible. Seconds before, Logan had been thinking, feeling, breathing. Now nothing. Even his staring eyes showed nothing. The impartial lack of emotion that is death. *Where do you go? Life can't stop just like that.*

Dallas jumped as he heard more firing. A part of his mind registered approval. Mister David was delivering a coup de grâce to those that needed it. No point in a 'dead' elephant coming back to life and killing them. *Not that it would bother you, old friend.* Logan's sightless eyes couldn't have cared less. Lucky or not? Dallas didn't know.

Ten minutes later, when Mister David returned, Dallas was still on his knees, still gripping his friend's shoulder, somehow trying to reassure the man that he was there. Tears, a combination of grief and spent fear, had come and gone. Dallas needed to think, take action, but the ability to do either escaped him.

'Sixteen,' Mister David announced.

'What?' Dallas glanced up, eyes unfocused.

'Sixteen elephants,' Mister David repeated patiently, understanding the paralysis that gripped his employer. To the Zulu, Dallas had become a hero. Already, words for a praise poem were forming in the African's mind. 'Two other men are dead. The rest are gone, run away.' Mister David's lip curled. 'Women!' he said contemptuously.

Dallas didn't blame them. At least they were alive.

Nineteen lives snuffed out. As the number sank in Dallas gave a low groan of despair. *All for what? Profit?* He rose and looked down at Logan, a man who had died doing what he loved. There was an almost fatalistic justice in that. What about the two Zulus? They lost their lives because of blind faith that the white men's guns would keep them safe. Dallas assumed that the other man who had died would be Logan's gun bearer. He stayed till the end. What did hunters say? A good Kaffir is one who doesn't run. It made sense around the campfire. Reality was something else. And the elephants? Oh yes, they had a choice. Two in fact. Kill or be killed. Escape or be killed. Either way, sixteen now lay dead.

He was breathing more normally. Thinking. Things to be done. Bury the dead. Cut out tusks. Distribute the meat. Get out of this dreadful place.

Distant shots sounded from where the wagons waited. Lorna! Cam! He'd left them there with two Africans and Will, the former unarmed, the latter no doubt scared half to death. Panicked elephants, too frightened to be cautious. Oh Jesus!

Dallas ran, uncaring of the thorns that tore his clothes and flesh, unaware of the stifling midday heat, indifferent to a protesting body that had already absorbed more than any man should. He ran as though pursued by some unspeakable evil. The firing stopped and still he ran, lungs bursting as they burned up oxygen in that sultry, humid hell. 'Lorna?' Her name wrung from him, high and wavering in fear and exertion. 'Lorna?' He ran the full three miles, in every step a fear so great it nearly choked him.

Fifty yards from the wagons, he came across the first body. 'Lorna?' It was a scream of sheer panic. Another body. Dallas ran on.

'Dallas?'

Oh God, sweet Jesus! The surge of relief rolled over him like a tidal wave. She was safe. There, running to him, blonde hair streaming. Neither stopped. Dallas caught her up, holding as tightly as he dared. His breath came in torturous gasps, lungs straining, chest heaving, legs trembling. He held on to her for dear life. She was crying and shaking but she was alive and in his arms.

Dallas had pushed himself to the limits yet he had to know about the bodies. 'What happened?' he croaked, staring over her head at three grey shapes lying close to the wagons.

'Cam,' Lorna whispered, clutching at him. 'He was so hot. Tobacco took him to the river. They were on their way back when we heard your first shots. Then the elephants came. Dear God, Dallas, I've never seen anything like it. Cam was right in their path. Tobacco ran with him but I knew they weren't going to make it. I grabbed your Winchester and let fly.'

'Is Cam all right?'

He felt her head nodding.

'You shot these elephants? With the Yellow Boy?'

'At them, yes. It was Will who stopped them.'

'My God!'

Lorna pulled away, bent double and retched. The enormity of what she had gone through hit Dallas with a force that left him filled with horror. Pregnant, sick and afraid, she had stood her ground to face dozens of panic-filled, stampeding elephants. She had put herself in danger in order to save their son from certain death. When she straightened he caught her close. 'Never again. Never. I know I said the same thing last time but I do mean it. Never, ever again.'

She sagged against him. 'I've never been so scared. Everything happened so quickly. There was no time to think.'

Dallas felt her hot tears, and as they clung to each other he became very angry, furious with Logan and his ridiculous pride, disgusted with himself for deserting everything that was precious to him. The elephants weren't to blame, people were. Those God had given the gift of reason. Reason! There was nothing remotely reasonable about today.

Over Lorna's head, he saw Will coming towards them. Still carrying his Cape gun, Will looked as angry as Dallas felt. 'How many times do I have to say it?' he roared. 'Elephants are dangerous. Now perhaps that idiot friend of yours will listen.' Seeing the look on Dallas's face, he stopped. 'What?'

Dallas tightened his arms around Lorna. 'Logan's dead.'

He felt her quick intake of breath and saw the colour drain from Will's face.

'We lost two of the boys as well.'

Will Green, that wily little Yorkshireman whose word could never be counted on, who would lie, cheat, even rob when he thought he could get away with it, suddenly had moisture in his eyes. He scrubbed it away angrily but the tears came back and trickled down his face. 'No,' he whispered. 'Not Logan. It's not possible.'

Dallas saw Will's struggle to accept what had happened. They had both believed that Logan was indestructible. The fact that this had proved not to be somehow was more shocking than his actual death. It felt like betrayal.

Yet in the void that had been raw terror, something quite unexpected revealed itself. Will made no secret of looking out for himself first, yet despite a very real fear of elephants, when time came to stand up and be counted, he had not let Lorna down. Danger, less to himself than to two others he'd come to care about, brought out bravery noone, least of all himself, would have expected. With it had come confidence. Will, uncharacteristically and with surprising authority, took charge. Blowing his nose vigorously, he nodded to Dallas. 'Take care of her.' Striding off, Will summoned the straggle of skinners who were just starting to reappear. 'Come with me. There's work to be done. You, bring shovels. You, go back to Chief Ngetho's. There's meat here for his people. You, get my Bible. 'Tis God's blessing that damned man needs, whether he wants it or not. You, get the fire going. We'll want coffee with our rum.'

Dallas could not believe the change in Will. He was grateful for it, though. He had to spend time with Lorna and Cam. A man for whom he held great affection had been snatched from him today. Now Dallas needed the company of two others. It wouldn't bring his friend back, but it had made him realise that nothing should be taken for granted. He and Lorna walked slowly, arms around each other, back to their wagon. Cam, blissfully unaware of the danger he'd been in, sat playing with wooden building blocks. Tobacco stood nearby.

'Sir.' The African's eyes were downcast. 'I am sorry, master.'

'Don't be. You were not to blame.'

Tobacco hung his head. 'I should not have taken him to the river.'

'I asked you to,' Lorna reminded him quietly. 'I thought we'd have time. It's not your fault, it's mine.'

Dallas could see the Zulu did not understand Lorna's English. He eased her from him and went to the man, placing hands on his shoulders. 'Cam loves the water and the weather is very hot. You did the right thing. I do not blame you. We would like you to keep taking him. We trust you.'

Lorna joined them. 'Please, Tobacco. It could have been your life too. Your actions made it possible for the guns to save our son.'

Dallas translated for her.

'Madam.' Tobacco looked up. He was struggling to express himself and failing. The moment was made difficult by centuries of tradition. A man who allows his life to be saved by a woman is an object of scorn. In recent years, exposure to Europeans had brought with it grudging acceptance of technical and medical expertise hitherto unknown in Zulu society. The whites had strange customs, though no-one doubted their cleverness. They also provided employment, a necessary evil if the much-coveted goods brought with them were to be purchased. In that valley, and on that day, respect competed with a still popularly held belief that women were inferior. 'You are my sister now,' was the best compliment Tobacco could manage without compromising masculine superiority.

Lorna, quick to understand, knew that a reciprocal gesture was required, one that would allow the Zulu to keep face. 'As Cam will be your brother,' she responded.

A wide smile of acceptance told her she'd got it right.

Later, Dallas tried to explain that the brother-sister thing was quite complicated and he wasn't certain that Tobacco was entitled to take on a new brother and sister without permission from his chief. Lorna would have none of it. 'He can call us what he likes. We are indebted to each other. That's enough for me.'

Logan was buried in the valley, Zulu-style, in a sitting position, facing home, his rifles and skinning knife interred with him. Will insisted on saying a requiescat of his own invention. It was short and sweet. 'Dear Lord, even if he ain't religious, he's a good man. Don't blame him for shooting elephants. Someone has to seeing as they eat too much. You made them big, an' I ain't blamin' you for that. Anyways, take care of him, Lord, may he rest in peace. An' if you wouldn't mind, Lord, find him a friend. He was lonely down here. Thank you.' Will looked defiantly around, waiting for someone to laugh. No-one did.

'Amen,' Dallas said.

'Yeah, sorry, Lord. Amen.'

Mister David organised burial of the crushed skinner and Logan's gun bearer. The latter had died in similar fashion to his employer after being impaled and carried on a tusk for several hundred yards. Empty spaces around the fires that night kept everyone subdued. The Africans had their own beliefs which kept them silent. Dallas, Lorna and Will each reflected on Logan's absence. Sleep seemed like a good idea for everyone.

Chief Ngetho's men arrived early the next morning and began the gruesome task of cutting up nineteen elephants. The meat had already begun to spoil in the heat. Vultures, jackal, hyena and ants had, during the night, begun to make inroads on some. But even with their voracious appetites, the volume of meat was too much. The men worked hard. It was hot and dirty toiling, made difficult by scavengers equally determined to keep their share. Dallas and Will supervised extraction and weighing of the tusks. They were all anxious to leave the valley with its oppressive temperature and tragic memories. Two days later, the ivory loaded onto Logan's wagon, they were rolling again.

As they left the valley, elephants were seen once more, creatures of habit, tempted back by an abundance of good food and water. At the sight of the wagons, the smell of men and cattle, fear spread through the herds in an instant. Turning as one, they fled towards the distant hills and disappeared. Watching them, Dallas's heart contracted with sympathy.

Lorna, whose nausea seemed a little improved that morning, sat next to Dallas as he had a spell driving their wagon. Young Cam lay talking to his toes behind them. 'Do you think Logan would approve of where he's buried?'

'The man loved that valley as much as anywhere else in Zululand. Just about his last words were that it was a good way to go. He meant out in the bush, not in a town. Logan was a loner. He'll be happy. I think he always expected to die like that.'

'We should have stopped him.'

'How? You saw his determination. He'd have gone alone if necessary.'

'It was terrifying. How could Logan have found it exciting?'

'Challenge,' Dallas suggested. 'Some people need that. You and I do in a different kind of way.'

'I suppose so.' She sounded doubtful. 'Did he have family?'

'Yes, in England. They didn't get along and I have no idea how to contact them.'

'We must try. If he had any papers they could be in his wagon.'

'I'll check. If there's anything that gives me an address, I'll write to them.'

Lorna was silent.

'What's troubling you?'

'Us. If we died out here, who would tell our families?'

'You're upset, darling. So am I. Logan was a friend, a good one. I'll miss him a great deal. But try to remember, he wouldn't have wanted to go any other way.' Dallas put an arm around her. 'Anyway, we're not going to die. We're going to buy land and become fat and boring.'

Lorna's eyes looked into his. 'Fat and boring sounds fine to me.' She leaned her head on his shoulder, ready at last to talk about the valley. 'I thought you were dead. When the elephants turned towards us, one had blood all over its tusks. I was scared to death for Cam. Something – I have no idea what – took over. I grabbed the rifle, even thought to take extra ammunition, and ran towards them. I think I was screaming. Then I just stood there and fired. I couldn't have cared less about myself. Will was suddenly next to me and the two of us seemed to be acting as one. When the first animal dropped I felt nothing but satisfaction. We brought down the other two and the rest swerved away. It wasn't until I got back to our wagon that the reaction hit me. This is a strange place, Dallas. So beautiful, yet there's danger everywhere.'

'What happened back there was our fault. Logan's and mine. You can't blame the elephants.'

'I know.' She burrowed into him, her arms gripping his waist. 'I love you. If anything took you from me I'd want to die too.'

Cam was sound asleep. Dallas called up Mister David. 'Take over.' Jumping down, he unhitched Tosca and Lorna's bay mare, then rode up alongside the wagon. 'Feel like a ride?'

'Yes, please.' Lorna needed no help. She leaned over and made the transition from wagon to horseback with the ease of a young boy. 'Where to?'

'Up there.' Dallas pointed ahead. 'There's some country over those hills I want you to see. We'll be gone a few hours. Will Cam be all right?'

Lorna glanced at Mister David, who nodded. 'When he wakes, I shall call Tobacco to sit with him.'

'Let's go.'

They kept the horses to a leisurely pace. Although Lorna scoffed at the idea, Dallas felt her condition was too delicate for her to ride faster than a walk. He was gently insistent and Lorna, surprisingly, gave in. They followed the river then crossed at a wide, sandy bend, stopping to let their horses drink. Veering away from the water, Dallas led them towards two small hills. Beyond, the land dropped dramatically, stretching away into a haze of purple and blue. 'Look.' His wave took in the entire scene spread out before them. 'See that river? It's the Ndaka. The name means muddy. Follow it as far as you can and you'll just make out another.'

'Over there.' Lorna pointed.

'Yes. That's the Thukela. It makes a wide sweep northwards and meets with the Ndaka.'

Lorna shaded her eyes to scan an endless thorn-veld plain of sandy soil and waving yellow grass. Heat shimmered and danced forming mirages, large sheets of water that no-one in their wildest imagination could believe were real. Small dust devils blew across the hot land. She took a long time before glancing at Dallas. 'You're joking.'

He grinned. 'Patience. All will be revealed. The Thukela then turns due east and is joined by several major rivers as it makes its way down to the sea.'

'How far away is that?'

Dallas shrugged. 'About a hundred miles, at a rough guess.'

'And?' Lorna prompted.

'The last fifty miles interest me. It's sufficiently far enough inland and high enough to avoid the humidity of the coast. The area is bordered by two rivers – the Nsuzu to the north and the Thukela. It's some of the most beautiful country I've ever seen.'

'Why bring me here then?'

'You had cobwebs in your head. I wanted to blow them away.'

Lorna laughed. 'You're right. And it's worked. I thought you were telling me that you wanted to live here.'

'For myself, I wouldn't mind. I love the sense of space up here, the roughness of it. But, my darling, as I also happen to love you, this is probably too isolated.'

She shot him a questioning look. 'Just how isolated are we?'

'See for yourself. Nothing moves out there.'

Lorna leaned the distance between the two horses and kissed him. 'Good,' she said softly.

By the time they reached John Dunn's kraal at Mangethe, Will was firmly of the opinion that Logan's spirit travelled with them, bringing good luck, fair weather and excellent trading. He'd even taken care of Lorna's morning sickness. And when Cam came within inches of stepping on a puff adder, instead of striking as it normally would have done, leading to almost certain death, the snake uncharacteristically up and left. 'Logan,' Will pronounced.

Under his breath, Dallas muttered, 'Thanks, old boy.'

The weather improved daily. Warm dry days with nights cooling most agreeably. All slept better as a result.

Their supply of trade goods ran out at the village before John Dunn's. As well as ivory, skins and a mass of trek-made leather goods, they had accumulated an impressive collection of cattle, goats and poultry. Dunn bought all their excess livestock.

They had been travelling for almost five months. Cam, who had grown nearly three inches, was a brown and sturdy toddler who preferred running to walking and could now out-talk the best of them. Lorna, tall and naturally slender, carried her pregnancy with barely a bulge. She'd foregone the enjoyment of riding two months earlier, either travelling on the wagon or, when the terrain was easy, walking with long, loose-limbed strides. Her face and arms were unfashionably brown, she exuded excellent health and happiness shone from her eyes.

John Dunn made them most welcome, insisting they stay at least three nights in a newly built European-style guesthouse. The news of Logan's death saddened their host greatly. An adventurer himself, one who had hunted and traded in Zululand, he was blunt but accurate. 'He died as he liked to live. A gun in his hand, miles from so-called civilisation, doing what he did best. He gambled, lost, and to be perfectly honest, it's the way he expected to go. What more could a man of the bush ask? I'll miss him, but in a way, I envy him.'

Conversation inevitably turned to politics. Will began it on their first night there, when he queried British recognition, or rather lack of it, for the self-proclaimed Zulu king.

Dunn rolled his eyes. 'Cetshwayo is still waiting for the British to acknowledge him. Shepstone is due up here any day to officially crown him in the name of Her Majesty. Cetshwayo has not been impressed by the delay. In truth, he couldn't afford to wait. A couple of months ago he declared the period of mourning for Mpande was over and moved the royal kraal up to Ulundi, which they're calling the heart of Zululand. As we speak, a new *isigodlo* is being built next to his father's old one.'

Dallas wanted to know why Cetshwayo couldn't wait for Shepstone.

'Two reasons. He's a traditionalist first and a politician second. It was important that his subjects saw him crowned the old way. Of more concern, though, was the discovery that several northern chiefs together with five of Mpande's younger sons who live in Natal under British protection were plotting against him. He had to act quickly. I went with him, which turned out to be just as well.'

'Why?' Dallas asked.

Dunn looked momentarily defiant. 'Rifles. Some of the Zulus were armed.'

'You supplied them?'

'Why not? It was legal. I had permits.'

'But how did you get the authorities to agree?'

'I told them the truth. Cetshwayo needed to establish authority over his own people. Mind you, I omitted to mention that I offered to train some of his *impi*.'

Dallas nodded. 'I imagine a few hunters and traders helped as well.'

Dunn's glare became suspicious. 'How did you know?'

Dallas laughed. 'Fact or fiction, news travels.'

'Do you want to hear what happened or not?'

'Sorry. Please continue.'

Dunn threw Lorna a resigned look and continued.

'On our way north we had to have a purification hunt. The Zulus believe that a time of mourning allows evil influences to descend on them. Before a new king is crowned they must protect him and themselves by washing their spears in blood. In the Mhlathuze Valley thousands spread out, forming a ring about five miles across. They closed in, killing everything. After that we continued on to Mtonjaneni to await the northern chiefs. It was here Cetshwayo received the first sign of ancestral blessing. His warriors cornered and killed a lion. This good omen encouraged him to proceed towards the Perfumery.'

At a questioning look from Dallas and Lorna, Dunn explained. 'The tradition goes back to Shaka's ancestors. The Perfumery is where kings and their immediate household were anointed with sweet-smelling herbs. During his reign, Mpande rebuilt the place and it has great tribal significance. Anyway, after a few days there we moved on to where the crowning ceremony would take place. It put us on open ground and Cetshwayo's followers were nervous, especially when a large contingent came into view led by one of the chiefs who aspired to the throne. They formed into battle order about a mile from where we waited. As if that wasn't enough, two more contenders arrived and we were virtually sandwiched between rival clans.'

'What happened?' Lorna asked, fascinated.

'Cetshwayo remained quite calm. He sent advisers to talk with each of the chiefs.'

'They must have had a pretty persuasive argument,' Dallas commented with a grin.

Dunn smiled. 'The sight of armed Zulus and about two hundred rifle-carrying white men put pepper in it,' he agreed. 'The rival parties came in peacefully, though it was still rather tense until Cetshwayo sacrificed some special cattle for his ancestors. After that, no-one could question his right to the throne.'

'How were the cattle special?' Lorna wanted to know.

'They'd been brought from *kwaNobamba* – the Place of Unity and Strength. It is where the sacred ring of the Zulus is kept. In a secret ceremony the cattle had been washed, imparting spirits from the Zulu nation's birthplace. By sacrificing them, Cetshwayo symbolically bound together his right to be king and his people's allegiance. That tied a knot far stronger than any ambitions his rivals might have had. Cetshwayo, in the eyes of the entire Zulu nation, is now king and will remain so until his death.'

Lorna's eyes were bright with interest. 'It must be tedious being asked to explain that which you know so well. Thank you.'

John Dunn, whose preference for Zulu women was obvious – he'd taken forty-nine as wives – had fallen under her spell. 'Not at all, dear lady. It pleases me greatly to see such genuine interest.'

'Will recognition from Britain come at a price?'

Dallas asked, quietly amused by the lack of Dunn's usual brusqueness.

'Most certainly. I hear rumours that they want some aspects of control taken from the chiefs. If Cetshwayo agrees, as he surely will, he'll meet resistance, possibly outright rebellion. Allow that and the respect of his people will be lost.'

'What would the chiefs have to give up?' Will wanted to know.

'Specifically, the British object to what they regard as indiscriminate killing. The push is for fair trials and the right of an individual to appeal to his king for leniency. They also insist that no life be taken without Cetshwayo's consent. There's even talk of a fine system for minor crimes.'

'Clever but dangerous,' Dallas remarked. 'So much for a chief's authority.' He gave a short laugh. 'After all, the power of life and death is a pretty sure way to keep law and order. If that responsibility is Cetshwayo's alone and he is allied with the British, the king becomes their puppet. Other tribes could rebel against what they perceive as interference with their tribal system. I wonder if that's wise?'

'I've tried to warn him. He won't listen. Cetshwayo wants supreme power and will not entertain the idea that it could go against him. If it does, watch the fur fly. What we've got is a three-edged sword – Shepstone, who claims to know what he is doing; the British, who have put their trust in him; and Cetshwayo, who has no intention of allowing outsiders to dictate the way he rules.

You wait. If this so-called coronation takes place and Cetshwayo agrees to the conditions, Britain will find a way to use it against him. And that can only spell disaster. They overestimate Shepstone's so-called expertise and conveniently forget the Zulus' pride in their nation. It will be war, my friend, and a bloody one.'

'Where would that leave you?'

'Interesting question. I see no choice. Circumstances change. One way or another, I'd have to leave Zululand. The British insist I do and the Zulus make it plain what will happen if I don't.' He smiled, and in his eyes there was a terrible sadness. 'I may be allowed back in time. My future here lies in the heart and soul of some, in the greed of others.' Dunn threw up his hands. 'So be it.'

'You and every white face this side of the Thukela would have to leave,' Will predicted ominously.

'Not at all,' Dunn contradicted. 'I would have to leave because of my close friendship with the king. I couldn't fight for him, much as I might like to, in a war against my own people. Those who have settled here, especially the farmers, would be left alone. The Zulus have little quarrel with them.'

Lorna leaned forward. 'I know you have no crystal ball but seeing you mention settlers, there is land between the Thukela and the Nsuzu that interests us greatly. It belongs to Zululand, does it not?'

'Correct. And your interest is well justified. It's good country.'

'How would we go about acquiring some?'

'You'd live there? Even after hearing what you have this evening?'

'Yes.'

Dunn's eyebrows went up. 'Well,' he said reflectively, pulling at an earlobe, 'the king would have to grant you the use of it. These days, I'm afraid, he usually seeks weapons in return. Even then, there's no guarantee that once you supply them he'll honour the deal. If he did, you'd never own it outright. I'd advise you to look elsewhere for land.'

Lorna's eyes met Dallas's, seeking support.

John Dunn laughed. 'A determined young lady. I like that. Very well, I'll speak to the king. You'll have to meet with him. Are you prepared to travel back here if I send word?'

'Of course,' Dallas answered.

'He may say no,' Dunn warned.

'We can but ask,' Lorna pointed out, remaining positive.

'Indeed,' John Dunn smiled. 'And I wish you success. All I can do is repeat your request. I have no influence in this regard.'

Word came from Dunn ten days after they returned to Durban. Cetshwayo was prepared to discuss a trade. A grant in return for rifles. The king claimed that he needed guns to keep the ever-encroaching Boers off Zulu territory. 'I can arrange rolling block Snider conversion Enfields,' Dunn had written. 'It remains only a matter for your own conscience.'

'What does he mean by that?' Lorna asked.

'If Britain and the Zulus go to war they would be used against our troops.'

'But the Zulus become better armed by the day. If they don't get guns from us, there must be many others ready and willing to provide them in return for favours or land. Why, even John Dunn admits to supplying Cetshwayo.'

'I know. My conscience remains clear. I find it difficult to imagine a confrontation. Cetshwayo actively promotes good relations with the British.'

'So, do we do it?'

Dallas smiled. Lorna's enthusiasm remained a constant delight to him. 'I'll go and speak to the king. See what he wants and what land he proposes to trade.'

'I'm coming with you.'

'My darling, that would not be wise.'

Warning signs crossed her face. 'Why not?'

'You are nearly seven months with child.'

'So what? Mister David can give me some *muthi* to help with the birth. I'll be fine.'

Dallas took her in his arms. 'And, my dearest, you are a woman. Have respect for these people. Your presence would be an affront to the king.'

Lorna closed her eyes, knowing he was right. 'Are you suggesting that I stay here, alone, and have our child while you go gallivanting around the country having a good time?'

'I'll be back well before the baby arrives.' He tightened his arms and kissed away the frown. 'Promise.'

'It's not fair.' Lorna stamped her foot, though there was little anger in the gesture, merely disappointment.

'A pity Mr Buchanan is no longer here. I'd feel happier if you had reliable company.'

The Zulu Bruce Buchanan tried to train had proved lazy and unreliable. In the end, it was agreed that Mister David be offered the position of groom. 'Later, if we are granted land, we'd like you to come with us. There will be much work and I'll need a man I can trust.'

'Where is this place?'

When Dallas told him of the area he hoped to farm, Mister David's face split into a broad grin and he fingered the love letter around his neck.

'Ah!' Dallas smiled back. 'I see the idea pleases you.'

'That is the tree,' Mister David replied gravely. 'It has many branches. Some you will learn of, most are none of your business.'

Dallas's smile grew wider. 'Fair enough, Mister David. But for now, I wish you to remain here and take good care of the madam.'

'It will be an honour, for he is a good madam.'

'I should be back in two or three weeks.'

'You will find me here, master.'

'Thank you. Tell Tobacco and July there will be work for them too, if they wish.'

Dallas travelled light back into Zululand, taking the quicker coastal route. The roads were dry and most rivers easy to cross. He reached John Dunn's kraal four days after setting off. His host was brusque. 'You have made good time. We leave in the morning. The king is expecting us.'

That night Dallas found he was full of excitement and hope. To live in such beautiful country with Lorna and their children promised everything he could ever have hoped for. He did not regret having to end his trading days. They'd been fun, sometimes dangerous and richly rewarding, but with a family he could not continue in that way of life. Dallas had learned a great deal about the Zulus and their country, enough to live and work comfortably beside them. A war between native and European might never happen. Even if it did, Dallas was not going to allow mere speculation to prevent him from carving out a future in his adopted land.

FOURTEEN

The meeting with Cetshwayo had gone well. The Zulu king granted him use of the land he asked for and, while Dallas could never own it, for as long as he respected and nurtured it, the land was, to all intents and purposes, his to use as he pleased. After the meeting, Dallas had spent several days with John Dunn who proved to be most helpful, providing advice on where to buy the best cattle, what Zulu workers he would need, how to deal with Chief Gawozi, who ruled that part of the country, and many other issues that would require Dallas's attention.

For five years now, Dallas, Lorna and their ever-expanding family had lived in peace with their Zulu neighbours. And now, the rumblings of war threatened this idyllic lifestyle. Dallas and Lorna had seen it coming but tried to convince themselves it was nothing more than sabre rattling. Until this morning when a letter arrived, making it impossible to misinterpret British intentions.

Squabbling voices cut through Dallas's concentration and he frowned, trying to ignore them. It was the fourth time he'd read the letter and still found its contents impossible to take in. Britain had declared war on the Zulu nation and he was expected to volunteer his considerable knowledge as interpreter, scout and guide.

Dallas had been anticipating a polite request, not a demand. As a resident of Zululand, he did not qualify for the obligatory call to arms that adult male colonists living in Natal received. The strongly worded recommendation that he 'remember his duty to Queen and country' came as something of a surprise. Dallas didn't need reminding that his Queen and country of birth probably still had a price on his head. Joining a volunteer unit would put him perilously close to official British red tape and he doubted that his real identity would remain a secret for long. If he had to serve – and Dallas didn't particularly want to – he'd be better off joining one of the small commando groups made up mainly of Boers who offered their services out of a basic dislike of all African races. Even this held little appeal. Dallas didn't hate the Zulus, but had profound respect for them and a genuine liking for the nation founded by Shaka.

The clamour outside had grown in volume to the point where he had to investigate.

'You did that on purpose.' Cam.

'Did not. You got in the way.' Torben.

'No, he didn't. I saw you.' Ellie.

'Mama! Cam is bleeding.' Kate.

Something was more amiss than usual. Dallas sighed and rose, leaving his official summons on the kitchen table. Lorna was nowhere to be seen – probably attending to the baby. He stepped out onto the deeply shaded stone stoop to be confronted by four sets of eyes – one defiant, one pain-filled and two indignant. 'What happened?'

He should have known better. Everyone spoke at once, until he held up a hand for silence.

'Cam, how did you cut yourself?'

'Torben hit me with the bat.'

Dallas turned his gaze to the accused.

'It wasn't my fault. Cam moved too close.'

'He did not.' Ellie was only five but a mature sense of fair play meant that her parents usually looked to her for the truth. 'Torben hit him on purpose.'

Three-year-old Kate removed a thumb from her mouth, nodded vigorously, causing golden curls to bounce around her face, and sidled closer to her older sister as if seeking protection.

'Inside,' Dallas said sternly, alarmed by the volume of blood running down Cam's face and dripping onto his bare chest. Two wolfhounds and a bull terrier – family pets of such soppy personalities that their breeds sounded like a joke – were busily cleaning up any drops fallen onto the stone floor.

The four children trooped past.

Dallas had two choices of assistant. Torben or Ellie. Kate, though willing, was too young. Torben would be reluctant. He looked at his older daughter, who gazed calmly back. 'Ellie, your mother is busy so you'll have to help.' Despite her extreme youth, Ellie could be relied on to make ready whatever was required. He turned to his eldest son. 'Up onto the table, young man.'

Cam, taller than most boys his age, vaulted backwards, landing on the smooth stinkwood surface with a resounding plop. Still the blood flowed down his face.

'Will it need stitches?' Ellie asked, filling a dish with water from the kettle. She placed it on a tray, alongside a bottle of iodine, some cottonwool, gauze, a bandage, tweezers and a safety pin and carried it carefully to where her father waited.

Dallas dipped a wad of cottonwool in the lukewarm water and gently wiped Cam's forehead. Despite copious bleeding, the wound was superficial – a wide but not deep gash. 'I think we'd better amputate his head,' Dallas informed everyone, winking at his patient.

At seven, the joke was appreciated by Cam, who grinned. 'Is it that bad?'

Kate asked, 'What's apootate mean?'

'Amputate, silly. And it means cut it off,' Torben said with malicious enjoyment.

Kate's soft heart melted and she began to cry. Ellie put an arm around her and glared at Torben.

'Papa is only joking,' Cam told Kate. 'Don't cry.'

Alerted by the continuing commotion, Lorna appeared supporting six-month-old Duncan on one hip. 'What happened?' she asked, taking in the scene and accurately guessing who had done what to whom. Handing Duncan to a hovering nanny, she moved swiftly to the table and confirmed that the injury looked worse than it really was. 'Iodine please, Ellie. And some . . . Oh, I see you've already got everything. Good girl.'

Looking as pleased as she felt at the compliment, Ellie moved closer to watch her mother dab at the slowing flow of blood. The older their first daughter became, the more it was obvious to Lorna and Dallas that Ellie had a fascination for blood and guts. When animals were slaughtered or game shot, a farm worker injured, even after an incident like today's, Ellie's nose was inevitably as close as she could get, her solemn eyes missing nothing. She displayed a clinical detachment that many a trainee doctor or budding Florence Nightingale would have given anything to develop. Irrespective of the severity of a wound – once she had minutely inspected the burns, welts and charred flesh of a young Zulu boy who had been killed by lightning, a sight that had brought Dallas close to nausea – Ellie's interest seemed more concerned with anatomy than a macabre fascination. 'You missed a bit,' she informed Lorna.

'So I did. Would you clean it, dear, while I prepare a dressing?'

Lifted onto the table, Ellie efficiently took over. Cam remained composed, showing no outward sign of discomfort.

Kate looked up at the table, tears of compassion in her large blue eyes. Unlike her older sister, she took any adversity to heart, suffering almost as much as the victim. A little hand crept up to hold one of Cam's, who looked down at her serious expression and smiled. 'It's not sore.'

'It will sting.'

'Only a little.' He could not prevent a wince as the iodine did its worst.

'There.' Lorna deftly bandaged his forehead and straightened from her task, dropping a light kiss on Cam's head, pronouncing him a brave little warrior who would probably live to tell the story of how he killed a lion with his bare hands.

Jumping from the table, and ignoring Torben, who stood against the Welsh dresser, arms folded and a bored look on his face, Cam suggested to the girls that they might like him to read them a story. The three traipsed off together towards the sitting room. With the drama over, the girls were so impressed with their brother's bravery they had bestowed on him the status of temporary hero.

Dallas hooked one foot around the leg of a chair and pulled it out. 'Sit.' Torben's saunter bordered on insolence but his father made no comment. Instead, with the dresser now vacated, he and Lorna joined forces in front of it waiting for Torben to do as he was told.

The boy sat, facing sideways.

'Don't push your luck, young man,' Dallas barked. 'And don't be rude.'

Reluctantly, Torben turned towards them.

Clamping down on exasperation, Dallas chose his tactics and began. 'There's no point in lying. You hit Cam quite deliberately. I'm not going to ask for an explanation – you probably don't even know why you did it.'

Torben looked surprised.

'However,' Dallas went on, moving to stand in front of him, 'I would like it understood that what you did might have killed your brother.' He reached down and tapped Torben's temple firmly enough so that the boy blinked in pain. 'If you'd hit him there, he could be dead. Do you have anything to say for yourself?'

The head shake was silent.

'How about an apology?'

'Sorry.'

Dallas shook his head. 'It's not me you hit.'

Defiance showed in the boy's set mouth.

Dallas moved back beside Lorna, their eyes locking in silent despair. Turning to face Torben, Dallas chose another tack. 'Cam isn't perfect. No-one is. Did he do something to annoy you?'

'Would you punish him if he did?' Torben challenged.

'That would depend on what it was.'

'You always take his side.'

'I'm giving you the chance to explain.'

'What good will that do? No-one understands.'

'I'm trying to,' Dallas said gently. 'Unless you meet me halfway, I'm afraid you're on your own.'

'I'm not apologising. He asked for it.'

'How? For goodness sake, son, speak to me.'

Tears sprang to Torben's eyes and he angrily scrubbed them away with his knuckles. 'The girls like him better than me. He knows that and waits until we're playing then comes and takes over. I'm not sorry I hit him.'

Dallas sighed. He'd get nowhere trying to force

an apology. 'I'll leave it up to your conscience.' He reached to the top of the dresser, taking down a leather strop. 'Your explanation is no excuse for something which might have killed him. If you weren't so mean to the girls they might like you better. Unless there's another reason for your behaviour, you'll have to be punished.'

Dallas waited but Torben just stared at him.

'Very well. Stand up and bend over.'

Lorna hastily left the room. She had no stomach for the very occasional call for corporal punishment, although in most cases when Dallas considered it necessary, she agreed.

Torben took the six lashes like a man, his furrowed brow and clenched fists the only signs of suffering. In truth, although his son didn't know it, Dallas never used much force. Just enough so that whichever boy, and it was usually Torben, was being punished knew about it. 'Now go to your room and stay there. You may join us for meals but other than that you are to remain there for two days.'

Without a word, Torben did as he was told. Dallas watched him go. As he passed the sitting room door Torben could not resist a dig. 'Sissy.'

If Cam responded, Dallas didn't hear what he said. Cam was no angel. No doubt he'd get even at some stage.

Dallas sank onto one of the kitchen chairs with a sigh. Try as he might, he could not get close to Torben. No-one could. The boy had a chip on his shoulder and not one member of the family could get rid of it. 'Must be the Danish in him,' Dallas had said on one occasion.

As a toddler he'd been prone to tantrums and dark moods, but was at least reachable.

Cam's cheerful, easygoing temperament only served to show how difficult Torben was. As the two boys grew older, their differences were becoming more apparent. Dallas and Lorna realised that, given his nature, Torben would find it easy to believe he was being picked on. This, in turn, only made him more defiant.

Just after his sixth birthday, Torben's moodiness and lack of communication became much worse. It was then he learned that Lorna wasn't his real mother.

'Do you think he remembers Jette?' Lorna asked, often in despair.

'How can he?' Dallas responded. 'He was still a baby.'

When Dallas had arrived home from his meeting with Cetshwayo, Mister David's anxious face warned him that something was amiss.

'What's wrong, my friend?'

'It is nothing, master.'

'Oh, come! Do not expect me to believe that. Have you had bad news?'

The Zulu deflected his question. 'Is the king well?'

'He is in excellent health. I have been granted land in Chief Gawozi's region.'

Satisfaction gleamed in Mister David's eyes. 'That is good.'

'He is your chief, I understand.'

'Yes.'

'And you wear a Mpungose maiden's love letter?' Mister David's fingers fondled the beaded message.

'So you will be pleased to hear that we will probably move north after the birth of our child.' Dallas smiled. 'Tell me then, since I bring good news, what is it that troubles you?'

Mister David's eyes would not meet his. 'It is not my business.' He turned, leading Tosca to the stables. 'But,' the words came over his shoulder, 'the madam is anxious to speak with you.'

Lorna had heard him arrive and was standing at the front door. In response to his wide grin and open arms, she tossed her head and retreated inside.

Mystified, Dallas followed.

She waited, hands on hips, at the foot of the stairs. When he went to kiss her, she fended him off.

'What's wrong, darling? Have I angered you in some way?'

'No. It is I who might cause you concern.'

Dallas took Lorna's arms, pulling her to him. 'You could never do that.' He breathed in the clean smell of her hair. 'Mmmm. It's good to be home.'

'Dallas!' She struggled to free herself. 'You'd better come with me.' Turning, she swept up the stairs.

Dallas followed, wondering what on earth was going on. She hadn't even asked about the grant.

From the landing, Lorna turned into Cam's room. 'We have company.'

Dallas could only gape. Sitting in the cot with their child was Torben. 'Where the hell did he come from?'

Queenie, the Zulu girl, who had taken on a nannying role since she was the only indoor servant who spoke English, sat by the cot, her eyes wide with apprehension. She knew that Torben was the master's son. What she couldn't anticipate was how he would take to the child's unexpected appearance. Lorna shook her head at Dallas's question and said, 'We'll talk downstairs.'

In the parlour, she poured him a large scotch and a slightly smaller one for herself. 'Don't I get a kiss?' he asked, taking the glass.

She ignored his words and sank into a chair. 'Talk first. We have a problem.'

'Torben?' He could have bitten his tongue. Clearly, Lorna was in no mood for frivolity and their problem was obvious.

She frowned and got straight to the point. 'Quite,' Lorna agreed crisply. 'To put it mildly, the boy has been dumped on us.'

Dallas ran a hand through his hair. The appearance of Jette's child was one thing. That he was more than a one-day visitor, quite another. 'It would appear that damned woman has no scruples whatsoever.'

'I'm inclined to agree, although I admit she seemed extremely distressed.'

Dallas took a seat opposite Lorna. 'You'd better tell me what happened,' he said quietly.

Lorna sipped her drink, sighed deeply and told

him. 'Five days ago Mister David came to tell me that a Mr Jeremy Hardcastle, accompanied by Mrs Jette Petersen and a small boy, waited at the gate. They requested entrance. Naturally, I invited them in.'

'Naturally? Even though you knew who she was?'

'I was curious to see this other son of yours. And to be truthful, I was more than slightly intrigued at the prospect of meeting the boy's mother.'

Dallas suppressed a grin. On more than one occasion Lorna had tried to get information about Jette. He'd always been vague, believing it the lesser of two evils. Any slip of the tongue had been pounced on and shaken, not satisfied until she knew everything. Wary now, Dallas kept the conversation centred on actual details rather than risk tripping over Lorna's Achilles heel. She'd comment on Jette soon enough. 'You say she was with Jeremy Hardcastle?'

'Yes. Ghastly man. I think she was frightened of him.'

Dallas let that go. Jette knew the one-time ship's officer well enough to avoid him if she wished.

'Mrs Petersen was in quite a state. Something about a sultan who had managed to locate her and threatened revenge unless she returned his money. What was that all about, do you know?'

'I told you Jette jumped ship in Casablanca. Apparently she'd accepted a commission from the Sultan of Morocco to set up a small gambling casino in Rabat. Typical of her, she robbed him and fled.'

'Why didn't you tell me that before?'

'Darling, you seem to feel threatened by Jette. You have no need, you know. I try to say as little as possible about her so you don't wonder if I carry any feelings for her.

'You must have had some. Torben is living proof of that.'

'I was lonely. She was attractive. That's all.'

Lorna rubbed fingers over her eyes and nodded. 'Sorry. I am jealous, I confess, especially after meeting her. She's really quite beautiful.' Her eyes bored into his.

'Can I come over and sit next to you?'

'No.'

'Very well. Let's clear this up once and for all. Yes, Jette is beautiful. Yes, I slept with her and thoroughly enjoyed myself. We've gone through all this before. Inside Jette, however, there is something quite unattractive. Oh, she can be charming, no doubt about it. But I wouldn't trust her. She takes, never gives. Compared with you, she hasn't a chance.' Dallas broke off and shook his head. 'I don't know any more words to try and convince you. I love you. You are my life. No-one else.'

Lorna tried to smile. 'I hear your words and am desperate to believe them. It may take a while, now that I've met her.'

'Is this connected to the fact that I had an affair with your mother at the same time as –'

'Yes, of course it is,' Lorna snapped. 'Women don't get over such a thing easily, try as they might.'

She had a point.

Lorna sighed. 'How did we get off the subject? I do trust you, Dallas, really. I know you love me.'

'Please let me sit next to you.'

'Not yet. Let's finish talking about Torben and his mother. Mrs Petersen was very scared. I don't think she cared much about herself but she was certainly concerned for Torben. I got the distinct impression that Mr Hardcastle was somehow involved.'

'That doesn't surprise me. The man's obsessed with Jette. He'd do anything to have his way. That includes placing lives in danger.'

'He didn't say much while they were here. Just kept glancing at his fob watch as if impatient to get going. She said that bringing Torben to you was his idea. She was obviously most distressed at the thought of leaving her baby here, but could see no other option. I was to tell you that a trust fund had been set up for Torben which would mature when he was twenty-five.' Lorna handed Dallas an envelope. 'The details are in here. The news definitely came as a surprise to Mr Hardcastle. He became quite angry, accusing Mrs Petersen of withholding information and demanding that he be responsible for the fund. That was the only time I saw her stand up to him. She was adamant that you administer the trust and completely ignored his rantings. While she was obviously intimidated by the man, nothing he could do or say would induce her to hand him control of Torben's inheritance. It showed me just how terrified she was that harm would befall her son. As they left she said she hoped you would forgive her and take the boy to your heart.'

Dallas swallowed a decidedly large gulp of scotch. 'You mean she casually called by to drop off her son and leave him with us . . . forever?' he asked, his throat burning, shaking his head. 'I don't believe it! Isn't she coming back for him at all?'

'No.'

Dallas jumped to his feet and paced in agitation. 'This is ridiculous. I fathered the boy, as you know, with no idea that Jette deliberately used me for that purpose. She expected no other involvement from me. Torben was hers and hers alone. Now he's passed on like a discarded possession. Dammit, Lorna, why didn't you say no?'

'I couldn't. The poor woman. It was no act, her heart was breaking. Torben looks so like you. If I'd refused, you might have resented that too.'

Dallas knelt in front of Lorna. 'Cam is my son. I love him.' He placed a hand on the swell of her belly. 'And this little one is ours too.' He stroked gently. 'But Torben? I don't know how I feel about him. And what about you? The child is my flesh and blood but he's nothing to you.'

She smiled slightly. 'That's not strictly true. He's a mirror image of you. My heart went out to him. It's not his fault. He's just a pawn in whatever his mother and that Hardcastle man are up to. I have heard that the two of them went north to the Gold Coast. There is no doubt in my mind that Mrs Petersen fully believed Torben's life to be in danger. She was very frightened. I also think Mr

Hardcastle holds something over her. It was plain she didn't like him very much.'

'Nobody likes the man. He's a scoundrel of the first order.' Dallas sighed with frustration. 'I wish I'd been here, Lorna. Perhaps I could have helped her. The woman's a thief with the scruples of a street harlot but at least she's honest about it. Despite all I said before, and I meant every word, I still liked her.'

'So did I. That's probably the main reason I agreed to take Torben. She was telling me the truth.'

'So suddenly we've got a second son.'

For the first time since he'd arrived home, Lorna looked, if not happy, more relaxed. 'It would seem so.'

'What's he like?'

'Fairly quiet. Not open and happy like Cam. His English is atrocious. He seems to have moods where he refuses to communicate. Hopefully he'll snap out of those before too long. Perhaps he's missing his mother. For all that, he's a dear little chap. Cam is delighted to have company.' Lorna leaned towards Dallas and kissed him. 'Welcome home. I missed you.'

'Didn't look like it when I got here,' he grouched.

'Sorry. I was feeling a trifle fragile over Jette. And I wasn't sure what your reaction would be about Torben.'

'I'm not happy about it,' Dallas admitted. 'It's the last thing I expected.' He kissed her back. 'That's two adjustments we'll have to make.'

'Two?'

'Torben and Zululand.' He was unprepared for her enthusiastic lunge. The two of them fell on the floor, Lorna splayed out on top of him. 'Careful, my darling.'

Her eyes were shining. 'When? When do we go? Tell me more.' The problem of Torben and Jette slipped away as happiness engulfed her.

Dallas grinned. 'Any time you like, though there's a house to be built and a lot to organise. I think we'd better stay in Durban until the baby arrives. And if you two don't get off me, that could happen at any moment.' He eased Lorna onto her back, leaned down and kissed her deeply. 'I love you,' he told her quietly. 'You have a very big heart.'

That was just over five years ago. There were times when Dallas wished he'd never laid eyes on Jette. What single woman, irrespective of the circum-stances, would deliberately fall pregnant only to relinquish responsibility to the father when life became a little tough? Jette didn't need the likes of Jeremy Hardcastle, regardless of what threats he might have made. She was a woman of the world who, by her own admission, had plenty of money. Surely she could have slipped away – after all, she'd done it before – taking Torben somewhere they'd both be safe.

Shaking his head at the complexities of human nature, Dallas picked up the official letter and gave further consideration to his current headache. What was he to do? The contents were hardly news. A brief history stating it was considered necessary to subdue the Zulus in order to unite them under a confederation administered by Britain. Dallas probably knew more than most about recent machinations and how they affected the Zulus. The fact that this communication contained any kind of information was, in itself, a form of justification for what Dallas knew to be a gross overreaction.

Events over the past five years had occurred as John Dunn predicted. Cetshwayo, having accepted the terms and conditions laid down by Shepstone at the time of his coronation, was now finding them working against him. Despite doing nothing to threaten British interests in Zululand and keeping his fifty thousand strong *impi* out of other African uprisings, Cetshwayo had run into trouble over the increasing number of executions he considered essential to maintain law and order among his regiments. The main difficulty originated from Cetshwayo's insistence that traditional laws regarding marriage for warriors be maintained. No man, unless he'd washed his spear in blood or reached the age of forty, could take a wife. The king's peaceful policies gave no opportunity for bloodshed and disputes over women became commonplace. Frustrated Zulus fought and killed each other over women they were not permitted to marry. Naturally, murder had to be punished. Executions increased. The administration were as appalled by the numbers as they were by the methods, which to them seemed barbaric in the extreme. Clubbing or spearing were barely tolerated. But when news reached them of stakes being driven into a culprit's anus until they reached his neck, disgust turned to outrage. These events came to the attention of Sir Henry Bulwer. The Lieutenant-Governor of Natal was forced to speak to Cetshwayo about them, reminding him of his promise to Shepstone at the time he was crowned king.

Cetshwayo's response had been entirely predictable, 'Why does the Governor of Natal speak to me about my laws? Do I go to Natal and dictate to him about his laws? While wishing to be friends with the English I do not agree to give my people over to be governed by laws sent to me by them.'

This response was accepted by Bulwer, who understood the Zulus well enough to respect their desire for independence. But to the newly appointed High Commissioner for Native Affairs in South Africa, Sir Bartle Frere, it was a declaration of war. Frere's response was to ask Britain for reinforcement troops, a request that was denied. Two days before the refusal reached him, and acting with certainty that he would soon receive at least two more battalions and cavalry to swell existing British regular troops and colonial volunteer units, Frere took the first steps towards what would ultimately end the Zulu empire. He acted without the support of his government and from a desire to expand British influence north of the Thukela River. His urgent need to gain control of fertile Zulu-held territory was compounded by the fact that the Boers were also contemplating action against the Zulus in order to grab their lands.

Frere announced that Blood River, hotly contested between Boer and Zulu since twelve thousand *impi* had been defeated some forty years earlier defending land that had been annexed without their permission, was to be returned to the Zulus. However, Frere had allowed himself some freedom. In return for recognition of sovereignty, he'd ignored advice, and instead of the Boers being compensated for loss of land by the Transvaal, those who left the area would receive recompense from the Zulus.

In addition, any Zulus who had been involved in border skirmishes with the Boers over the Blood River territory were to be handed over within twenty days with fines totalling six hundred head of cattle paid at that time. Within thirty days, summary executions without trial were to cease. The Zulu army was to be disbanded and their military system broken up. Young men were free to marry on reaching maturity. A British Resident would be located in Zululand to enforce these requirements and no-one was to be expelled from Zululand without his express permission. Any dispute involving a European would be heard in front of both the king and the Resident.

Cetshwayo accepted that those guilty of raids against Boer settlers should be handed over to the British. He even agreed to pay the stipulated fines, despite finding the demand for six hundred head of cattle totally unreasonable. As for the rest of it, the king contemptuously dismissed the British dictums as arrogant interference and a threat to the Zulu way of life.

Because of seasonally flooded rivers, Cetshwayo said it would take him longer than the stipulated twenty days to hand over the men and cattle. Frere took this as evasion and replied that the ultimatum stood. If the king had not complied within the required time, British troops would have no option but to advance into Zululand. Cetshwayo maintained a dignified silence and, on 11 January 1879, Lord Chelmsford's forces crossed the Thukela.

John Dunn had been advised by Cetshwayo to 'stand aside'. Settlers in Zululand, Dallas and Lorna among them, were, in the main, undecided about what to do. Zululand was home. The majority enjoyed good relations with their African neighbours. Word had come out that those who took no action against the Zulus need not fear for their safety. But most had deeply rooted connections with Britain. Unlike the generous offer of Cetshwayo that settlers who chose to stay would remain unharmed, Britain used emotional blackmail. It was up to the conscience of every man, the letter stated. They could stay in Zululand and be regarded as traitors, or volunteer their services to a severely understrength British force in its noble quest to gain outright administration of Zululand, thus protecting the very lives of those who lived there.

Stirring rhetoric unless one knew, as Dallas did only too well, that it was all a cover-up for simple land-grabbing greed. He did not approve of the invasion and so, for a time, did nothing. But now came this letter and its blatant patriotic appeal.

'What are you going to do?' Lorna had returned to the kitchen and found him, head in hands.

'About Torben or this?' He looked up and waved the letter.

'That.'

'Christ! I honestly don't know.'

She joined him at the table. 'It's not fair. Why can't they leave us out of it? The Zulus are willing to.'

'The Zulus don't want war. The British declared it and are determined to win at any costs.'

'Then you have no option, do you?'

'Not really. Refuse and I'll be considered a traitor. If I join up, we lose everything here. Cetshwayo granted us this land in good faith and we've kept our side of the bargain. This crazy fool, Frere, is hell-bent on war and every able-bodied man is expected to volunteer. I'm no traitor, Lorna, but for the life of me I can't see the sense of confrontation unless all else has failed. Frere knows he can only push Cetshwayo so far and he's deliberately exceeding the limits. He's forcing the Zulus into a war they can't win. It's criminal.'

'And it won't end there, will it?'

Dallas shook his head. 'With the Zulus defeated, Britain will have control over the whole region. The Boers won't stand for that.'

'Bloody man,' she burst out, referring to Frere.

'Damn him and his arrogant Queen and country mentality.'

Dallas often agreed with Lorna's plainly expressed sentiments. She frequently speculated on what state the world might be in if it were controlled by women. When others pointed out that Britain already was, she would tartly reply that Queen Victoria was nothing but a figurehead surrounded by male advisers.

But the decision was out of Dallas's hands. Reluctant as he was, he knew he had no option. 'We'll have to pack up and leave,' he told Lorna. 'You and the children can live in Durban until it's over.' He screwed up the letter in anger. 'Damn it! Whichever way you look at it, we're betraying someone.'

Lorna stood behind him and wrapped her arms around his shoulders, resting her chin on his head. 'Even John has become a scout,' she said, referring to their friend John Dunn.

'What else could he do?' Dallas asked. 'Cetshwayo's council of chiefs and princes blame him for the breakdown in communication between Britain and the Zulus. They threatened to kill him. He had nowhere to go but south. Once John was in Natal he had no option. The same will happen to us. I either remain here on the farm and hope for the best, or seek safety in Durban and become eligible for duty. Not much of a choice, is it?'

'Oh, Dallas.' She reached over and took his hands in hers. 'Just when everything is going so well.'

Dallas kissed her fingers, then rose from the kitchen table, his mind made up. 'Start packing,' he told Lorna. 'Like it or not, we really have no choice. Might as well make the best of it.' He jammed a hat on his head and left to speak with Mister David.

Riding Tosca, the green rolling hills, a wide, picture-blue sky and sparkling rivers seemed to mock him. He'd been warned it couldn't last. Young, he'd paid no heed, confident that if a time came for him to move on, he could do so without a backward glance. Dallas hadn't anticipated that the land would creep inside his heart and soul, that his love for the farm would become inextricably enmeshed with love, laughter, children and Lorna until it was impossible to think of one without the other. Leaving hurt. It wasn't the cattle. In anticipation of this moment, he'd sold most of them. Those left would, he knew, disappear into Zulu hands the moment his back was turned.

It wasn't the house either, although, God knows, enough blood, sweat and back-breaking labour had gone into its building. It was the memories. Spring mornings, the air crisp and clear, the call of an eagle, the contented lowing of cattle, the smell of wood fires on the day Kate drew her first breath. It was family picnics by the river, the velvet depth of night, smells after rain and a million small recollections blended together in a mosaic backdrop to the life he had chosen. That was it. He had made a choice and now faceless ambitious idiots

were interfering. Dallas accepted that to live without outside influence would be near impossible.
He did not, however, have to like it.

In a sour frame of mind, he located Mister
David and dismounted. The two men greeted each
other then stood side-by-side not speaking, looking out over the distant hills, their thoughts finding
a similar theme.

Finally, his *induna* broke the silence. 'The king
has sent more runners.'

Dallas nodded. 'I don't blame him. He needs
every man he can get. Have you been called?'

'Yes. We leave tomorrow.'

Dallas shaded his eyes and stared out at the
beauty that was his land. 'What becomes of this
place?' he asked softly. 'Whoever wins this damned
war, Zululand will never be the same.'

'I fear you are right. It is not our custom to own
land, only the king can do that. But if we are to
hold it, our ways must change. We will need your
paper proof that it is ours.'

Dallas gave Mister David a questioning glance.
'What if you lose?'

'It will not be so. Defeat has no place in our
hearts.'

'Nor in those of your enemy,' Dallas reminded
him.

Mister David shrugged. 'There is no point in
thinking this. No-one can run from the plans of
Unkulunkulu.'

Dallas raised his eyebrows and made no comment. *Unkulunkulu* was the old, old one who created

578

man, beast, flora, weather and all the geological features on earth. His achievements were acknowledged though he was not worshipped as an ancestor. In fact, although Zulus accepted that all men sprang from *Unkulunkulu*, they also believed he died so long ago that no-one could remember his praise poems. Being the first father of mankind, he was responsible for giving the Zulus the spirits of their ancestors. As such, *Unkulunkulu* had become a respected yet shadowy deity in Zulu custom.

'I see you chew long on my words,' the Zulu commented.

Dallas smiled. 'I was thinking earlier how I dislike the actions of others affecting my life. You make me see that it is not only the living who interfere. Sometimes we cannot see a reason. You are right. There is no point complaining about that which is beyond our control.'

'You will fight us?'

'I must.'

'So,' Mister David put out a hand and they shook, African-style, thumb, palm, thumb, clasp. 'Today we are friends. Tomorrow enemies. What is in our hearts will decide where we stand when the fighting finishes.'

'Stay safe, Mister David, for I would not like to lose your friendship to something that is not of our making.'

The Zulu looked surprised. 'If it must happen, it is better that way. In war, these things happen but to cause a friend to die in times of peace would be a burden of great sorrow.'

They walked together to the African kraals. No-one was attending to their duties, nor had Dallas expected it. A summons from the king required an immediate response. However, certain rituals were essential to guard a warrior from harm. Seeing that the men were absorbed, some with their cattle calling on ancestors, others leaping and mock fighting in preparation for battle or fashioning charms for protection, Dallas left them to it. At some stage during the night, they would all depart to join their regiments before assembling at the Great Place, the king's *isigodlo*, ready to do their great father's bidding.

Riding back to the house, Dallas found himself in a reflective mood.

Five years had passed. Better than none but not nearly enough. Would he be allowed back? Would he wish to return? Dallas didn't know but suspected not. If Britain won, as it surely must, Zululand would be fragmented. The conquerors would deliberately try to prevent unification, relying on old tribal jealousies to keep the country from rising as one. Without a king, the tribes would not bind together. The ensuing faction fighting would ensure that any white man's future there was uncertain. If, by some miracle, the Zulus prevailed, those settlers who had previously enjoyed both their friendship and Cetshwayo's protection could very well find themselves regarded as traitors by the Africans. Besides, if the British did lose this war they'd return and fight another day. Far better to walk away now.

Dallas took Tosca to the highest point on the farm. From there, spreading in all directions, was the land he'd come to regard as his. 'My mistake,' he told himself. 'It belongs to the king.'

His mind wandered back to the day Cetshwayo granted him the use of it. With John Dunn he had ridden to Ulundi, where the king was expecting them. After greeting Dunn warmly, intelligent eyes turned to Dallas, assessing the stranger even before introductions were made. Dallas noticed that although Cetshwayo was extremely relaxed in his treatment of John, the latter observed all formalities.

'Welcome,' the king said in a strong, deep voice. He looked at Dunn. 'Does your young friend speak our language?'

John indicated that Dallas should reply.

'I am still learning, *Baba*.'

Cetshwayo smiled. 'Then forgive me if I correct your mistakes for badly spoken Zulu is offensive to my ears.'

The king was casually dressed – that is to say, he was naked save for a slim strip of woven hide around his waist onto which had been sewn an animal skin flap at the back and a bush of genet tails at the front. His only adornments were the *isiCoco* and a brass bracelet. Although bordering on fat, his body appeared firm and well toned.

'I see you are surprised to find me looking like one of my less fortunate subjects,' he said, a twinkle in his large and shining eyes. He gave a laugh and his belly shook. 'I am at home,' he explained simply. 'For whom should I dress to impress?'

'No-one, *Baba*,' Dallas said hastily.

Again, the great belly laugh. 'Sit. We will drink beer.'

Dunn and Dallas sat on mats while Cetshwayo took a small wooden stool. Dallas remembered how impressed he'd been by the king's appearance. He had an open and good-natured face, made dignified by a short, neatly trimmed beard. His eyes roved restlessly as if afraid of missing something. He held himself erect and kept his head high, rather like royalty in England, so he always appeared to be looking down his nose. With skin darker than most Zulus, when he smiled, his teeth were startlingly white.

Beer was served, the pot passing between them several times before Cetshwayo raised the reason for their visit.

'I understand you seek land in the home of my people. Does Britain not have enough already?'

Dallas felt his heart sink. This was not a good start. 'It is true, *Baba*, the English hold much land. But it is here that my heart lies.'

'And mine, white man. This land belongs to me. Why should I deprive my own people by granting some of it to a stranger?'

'I would take care of it as if it were mine. I would employ many people who would be encouraged to establish their own kraals, cultivate fields and raise cattle for themselves. They would also receive payment for their work.'

Cetshwayo nodded slowly. 'You speak our words well, white man. By whom were you taught?'

'He is known to me as Mister David. He worked with David Leslie.'

'Ah. Then you have a good tutor. I know this man by reputation.' The king turned to Dunn. 'The land you spoke of is in the territory of Chief Gawozi kaSilwana. He must be consulted.'

'Unless I am mistaken, *Baba*, he has already given his consent,' Dunn replied.

Cetshwayo roared with mirth. 'You miss nothing, John Dunn, nothing at all. I had forgotten that three of your wives are of the Mpungose people,' he said finally, wiping his eyes and turning to Dallas. 'A good man, Gawozi. I rely on his judgment, though his body is worthless.'

Dunn explained. 'Chief Gawozi is a cripple. Paralysed. Despite this, he is highly respected. His mind is sharp and fair.'

'Yes, yes, yes,' Cetshwayo interrupted impatiently. 'It is true that Gawozi has no objections. However, I need to be convinced. Tell me, white man, what else do you bring in return for this land?'

'I will show you modern farming practices, yet learn of yours. I offer white man's *muthi* but respect the ways of Zulu medicine men. Women may be trained to work in a white man's house and garden, though encouraged to keep their own traditions at home. Children can learn from an English teacher alongside my own and I would hope that those who teach the Zulu ways would include my family so that the young know and understand both cultures. Your ceremonies and traditions will be upheld and respected. I propose to stock and run a trading store for the convenience of all who live and work on this land.'

Dallas fell silent. It had been a long speech to make completely in Zulu. He was aware of his shortcomings in the language and suspected he'd made many mistakes. Yet Cetshwayo regarded him with something akin to respect.

'Fine words, white man, if they are to be believed. Are they empty or real?'

'There is no intention to deceive. I have seen many Zulu ways and often they make more sense than my own.'

'The British want to take my land for themselves, as do the Boers. How do I know you are different?'

'I have no words to prove my sincerity, *Baba*.'

'Indeed, you do not. But the truth shines from your eyes. Tell me, white man, when this land is in flames, on which side of the river will you stand?'

There was no point in lying, Cetshwayo would see through any attempt to curry favour. 'On the side of my ancestors, *Baba*.'

A deep sigh rose from the bare, broad chest. 'Well said. The land is yours. Treat it respectfully.' The king looked at John Dunn. 'The terms are as we agreed. Two hundred rifles.'

'You will have them in ten days, *Baba*.'

Cetshwayo looked back at Dallas. 'One day, Mr Granger, the payment for your land may be turned against you.'

Dallas nodded agreement. 'In my culture, *Baba*,

there are those who cause change and others who think too much to do anything. I cannot control the future but I can live for the present. That is my way.'

'And the past?'

'That is for the conscience of those who lived then.'

'And when that time comes to you, white man? When your hair is grey and back bent, what will you regret?'

'Many things, I am sure, but I pray that this day will not be one of them.'

Cetshwayo proved to be quite a philosopher. He loved to gossip, insisting on all the latest news from Durban, tales of hunters and traders. With the business side of their meeting out of the way, the king kept both men talking for several hours before, with obvious reluctance, he had to dress more formally and attend to pressing tribal matters.

'Don't expect anything in writing,' John warned as they departed the *isigodlo*. 'The king's word is his bond until he decides otherwise.'

'Thank you for your help. I'd have been less successful on my own.'

'I disagree. The king was impressed by you.'

'Does he usually greet visitors dressed like that?'

Dunn laughed. 'Cetshwayo takes many by surprise, including his own people. How he presents himself seems to reflect the mood he's in, but in the company of friends, he tends to favour traditional dress. You have to agree, it's more comfortable.'

'I wouldn't know,' Dallas admitted. 'He wears it well. He's a fine-looking man.'

'Walks ten miles a day to keep fit.' Dunn changed the subject. 'Your woman, Lorna. She'll be pleased with the outcome.'

'Indeed. She's as anxious as I to move out of Durban.'

'Gossip is an ugly pastime. Unfortunately, rumours spread quickly. I hear tell you've already got a wife.'

'A young lady has my name,' Dallas responded tightly.

'And I know her father, slightly.'

'Then you will understand that I had no choice.'

'A man who dallies should expect to pay the price.'

'Ah! That is merely one side of the story.'

'Fair enough. You protect her good name. I'll say no more. As far as I'm concerned, Lorna is your wife. I just wanted you to know that.'

'Thank you.' Dallas laughed in good humour. 'And you?'

Dunn also laughed. 'Catherine is my great wife. The rest?' He shrugged and laughed again. 'They just happened. Actually, it was Cetshwayo who encouraged me to take more wives. Two are his sisters and you don't refuse an offer like that from the king.'

'I hope he never makes a similar offer to me. Lorna would not stand for such a thing.'

'He won't. Cetshwayo knows that it would offend.'

Dallas stopped reminiscing. He should be at the house helping Lorna. Yet sitting on the hilltop his thoughts returned to the past, to the day they realised that Torben was a fixture in their lives.

At first, Dallas and Lorna found themselves working hard to simply like the child. Jette had obviously indulged his every whim. Sharing with Cam was a concept Torben found totally alien. The boy demanded and took, never asking or showing gratitude. He would scream with frustration if Lorna's attention wandered from him.

Despite his best efforts, Torben did actually find a way into the hearts of his new parents. When happy, the youngster was delightful. By the time word reached Dallas and Lorna of Jette's and Jeremy Hardcastle's fate, Torben was as much a part of the family as the other children were.

The rumour was that Jette and Jeremy had been killed in a place called Kumasi, the Ashanti capital, inland in a British colony known as the Gold Coast. They were reputed to have been caught up in a tribal war between the Fanti people of the coast and the Ashanti. There was some doubt as to the accuracy of this story since the Fanti were not a warlike tribe. Clashes between them and the Ashanti were invariably close to the coast, where they did little more than defend themselves against their marauding northern neighbours.

As with many other incidents reported by visiting sailors, Dallas was uncertain whether this one was true. Attempts to find out met a brick wall. The Natal administration had little interest in what took place thousands of miles further north. All Dallas ever learned was that there had been an incident in which the name Jeremy Hardcastle featured and the man was believed to be dead. He could find out nothing more.

He was not surprised to learn that they had headed for the Gold Coast. Although Britain had been the dominant force there since the sixteenth century, the Danes were actively interested until 1850. The place would have suited both Hardcastle and Jette. If they were dead, a more likely cause would have to be that the sultan had finally caught up with Jette. Either that, or they'd been innocent victims when, in 1874, the British burned Kumasi to the ground. Given the reluctance of official sources in Natal to provide any details, Dallas was inclined to believe the latter.

When Cam and Torben were six, they were told the circumstances of their birth. 'I know they're still young,' Lorna said to Dallas, 'but it's best that we tell them before they work it out for themselves. With only two months' difference in their ages, I can't possibly pass myself off as Torben's mother.'

Dallas agreed and was more than willing to leave the job to Lorna. In the years they'd been together, individual strengths and weaknesses seemed to be equally divided between them and diplomacy tilted very definitely in her favour.

Cam took the news calmly. He'd always known Dallas to be his real father. The fact that his parents were not married was of little interest. They were together and both loved him. That was all that mattered. His mother's long-dead husband drew some curiosity. 'What's a marquis?'

'A member of the British peerage.'

'What's that?'

'In Scotland, it means he is a lord.'

'Like God?'

'Nothing like God. A marquis is usually very wealthy and owns lots of land.'

'How did he die?'

'He was quite an old man. His heart got tired and, one day, it just stopped.'

'What happened to all the land?'

'When you are older it could be yours.'

'Mine! Why?'

'People think the marquis was your father.'

Cam screwed up his nose. 'I'm glad he wasn't.'

'No more so than I,' Lorna said with heavy irony.

'So the land is mine?'

'Only if you wish to claim it.'

'How would I do that?'

'By acknowledging the Marquis of Dumfries as your real father.'

'But he wasn't.'

'That's right. People only think he was.'

'Then I don't want it.'

Lorna had smiled at that. 'You don't have to make up your mind right now. When you reach twenty-one, then you'll have to decide.'

'I've already decided.'

'Fine. It's really up to you.'

Cam looked reflective. 'Who is looking after this land?'

'My father.'

'Then let him keep doing it. I might change my mind.'

That was the end of it as far as Cam was concerned. As Lorna told Dallas later, his candid acceptance of the situation had been quite amusing.

Torben was a slightly different kettle of fish and Dallas lent Lorna support by sitting in on the conversation.

'You're not my real mother?'

'No, darling. We think she was killed in an accident.'

'Was I very young?'

'Yes.'

'Who is my father?'

'Dallas.'

Lorna could see the six-year-old mind trying to work it out. She tried to explain. 'I was married to someone else. Dallas met your mother and you were born. Your real mother loved you very much, as I do now.'

'Why didn't Father stay with my mother?'

'She didn't wish it.'

'Why?'

'It was her choice. Your father had no idea he had two sons until you were about seven months old.'

'Is that why he hates me?' Torben's eyes slid to Dallas to see his reaction and was rewarded with a bland expression.

'He doesn't hate you, darling. Your father loves you very much.'

'And Cam is Father's real son, too?'

'Yes, he is.'

'So why were you married to someone else?'

Lorna sighed inwardly. This was going badly. 'In Scotland, women don't always choose their husbands. Their parents do it for them. Sometimes that means that when a girl marries, she is in love with someone else. It was like that with your father and me.'

'What happened to the man you married?'

'He died.'

Torben chewed that one over for a while. Then, 'If you are not my real mother, I don't have to do what you tell me.'

'Yes you do,' Lorna said gently. 'Because learning is a part of growing up. If I don't correct your mistakes, how will you learn?' She could see one of the boy's moods becoming evident. They always began with a suffusion of scarlet spreading from his neck. 'Torben,' she went on quietly. 'You belong to this family every bit as much as everyone else. I may not be your real mother but I love you very much and want only the best for you. Do you understand that?'

'I don't like you.'

'You don't mean that.'

Lorna's ability to stay calm in the face of Torben's regular bouts of rudeness or disobedience never ceased to amaze Dallas. Usually, he stayed out of these confrontations, knowing that she was emotionally better equipped than he to deal with them. This occasion was too much.

'You apologise, young man. Immediately,' he snapped.

A clash of wills locked eyes across the room, the tension palpable. In the ensuing silence, Torben wavered first. 'Sorry.' But he hadn't finished. 'What am I supposed to call you?'

'What you've always called me. Mama.'

A small shake moved the mutinous head. 'No. You are not my mother.'

'Very well.' Lorna was brisk. 'If you prefer, call me Aunt Lorna.'

And Aunt Lorna she stayed. From that moment on, Torben took every opportunity to remind Lorna that she had no claim to him, nor control over him. It frustrated and angered Dallas to see the hurt such a young boy could inflict on the woman he loved. Lorna, if anything, became even quicker to defend Torben. It sometimes seemed as if she were trying too hard to be fair.

While Cam was delighted to live on the farm and mix with Zulu children, Torben went further into a shell. Cam thrived. Ranging all over the land dressed in nothing more than a pair of old shorts, he spent almost as much time in the Zulu kraals as he did at home. Torben, on the other hand, became engrossed in reading and rarely ventured outside. If he did, chances were he'd disrupt the others deliberately. This morning's incident had been a typical case in point.

The move to Zululand had gone smoothly.

After Eleanor was born – and she became Ellie within the first five minutes of her life and remained so – Lorna was filled with a restless impatience to start their new life in Zululand. Wagons and tents were their first home. Then they lived Zulu style, in beehive-shaped thatch huts, for another six months until their new house was habitable. Built mainly of stone, with wooden windows, floors and beams, a slate roof, and with a deep verandah running around three sides, it was a far cry from the stately homes Lorna and Dallas had grown up in. But, unlike their childhood surroundings, the house resonated with laughter and informality.

Mister David recruited men to work with the cattle. Both Tobacco and July were among the first to arrive. Life stretched ahead in pleasant anticipation of health, happiness and, God willing, peace and wealth. Katherine was born two years after Ellie. No-one called her anything but Kate. When Duncan came along Lorna insisted that he never be called Dunk.

As good as his word, life for Zulus on the farm Dallas and Lorna called *Ludukaneni* – the place where you get lost – remained traditional save for two exceptions. People were paid to work and children, if their parents chose, received education. Cattle belonging to the Africans were allowed to graze at will, fields still cultivated in the traditional manner. Hunting, provided it was for food and clothing and not profit, was permitted. The *umuzi* had resident *inyanga* and *sangoma* as well as various other *muthi* specialists. The head man, or chief, was too old to work and decided to make Mister David *induna* provided his authority be accepted once he returned to the *umuzi*.

A schoolroom was erected – upright poles, half walls of woven grass, a hard-packed dirt floor and a thatched roof. Desks and chairs arrived but few chose to use them, preferring to sit on the floor. The teacher, a middle-aged man who had come to Zululand as a missionary and found his efforts better valued imparting practical knowledge than matters ecclesiastical, arrived one day out of the blue. He had heard that *Ludukaneni* was looking for a teacher. He spoke fluent Zulu and German but his English was guttural and broken. Attempts to find a suitable teacher had, so far, failed. Since Dallas had promised Cetshwayo that the children would be taught English, he took the man on but insisted that lessons be conducted in that language. As a result, most of the school's pupils ended up with a heavily Germanic accent.

Cam and Torben joined the class when they turned five. Torben had a quick mind and enjoyed learning. Cam, on the other hand, was easily distracted and preferred to play with his Zulu friends. However, the stimulation of lessons did ease the constant battle of wills between the two boys.

Dallas and Lorna loved Zululand. Neither of them wished to leave. Their bond with *Ludukaneni* was eclipsed only by an ever-deepening love for each other and their growing family. Still unmarried, for despite many appeals, Sarah and her father steadfastly refused to consider her divorce from Dallas, the lack of formal recognition rarely bothered them. They had held a private ceremony shortly after moving to the farm, exchanging vows and rings. Each was as committed to the other as any married couple could be. Perhaps more so.

Nothing stays the same, however. Dark clouds of confrontation gathered south of the Thukela. Britain's war mentality was clear to all. Unrelenting, driven by hunger for land and power, urged on by ambitious officers eager to see their names adorn the pages of history, the halcyon days were rapidly coming to an end. Dallas and Lorna watched and waited. News reached them regularly. Within days of Sir Bartle Frere's ultimatum being read out, Dallas and Lorna also knew of its crushing terms and conditions. Realising that the Zulu king would never accept them, war seemed the most likely outcome.

Still they waited in hope. Cetshwayo did not wish to fight the British; it was this fact that kept them optimistic. And now the dreaded letter.

Nudging Tosca forward, Dallas rode back to the house with a heavy heart. What was inevitable in this land he loved would be nothing short of murder. Cetshwayo could mobilise thirty-three regiments, each with an average strength of fifteen hundred warriors. Despite this, the Zulus would be hopelessly outgunned. True, they had firearms. Apart from a very few who became crack shots, most never mastered the idea that it was better to take aim before firing rather than randomly discharging bullets until ammunition ran out or a case jammed in the breech.

In any event, the *impi* still had a preference for close-quarter combat, relying on their skill with shield and *assegai*. They were super fit, able to travel up to fifty miles in a day. Special ceremonies conducted by the king's doctors gave each man protection and made them invincible in battle, or so they believed.

Dallas thought otherwise. General Lord Chelmsford, the military commander of British forces in South Africa, might only have had access to seven battalions, just under eighteen thousand officers and men, but the Royal Artillery were armed with heavy cannons, rocket tubes and the newly introduced Gatling gun. Each infantryman carried a .450 calibre Martini Henry breech-loading single-shot rifle and bayonet. There was little doubt that Chelmsford's troops could destroy the Zulu capital and capture or kill Cetshwayo. It would be a bloodbath.

In the kitchen he found Lorna already well into the packing. She looked up and sighed. 'We can't take it all. It breaks my heart to leave so much of ourselves behind.'

He crossed the room and held her. 'We're not the only ones, my darling.'

She burrowed against him. 'I know.' Tears weren't far off. 'It's stupid to be so attached to possessions. It's just that everything I look at has a memory. Everything I touch is a piece of our past and, Dallas, it's so hard to decide.'

He felt hot tears against his chest. 'Come,' he eased her back, cupped her face in his hands and gently thumbed them away. 'We will choose together.'

Dallas, Lorna and the children left their farm on the morning of 21 January 1879. What they took with them was carried in three wagons. The three dogs trotted beside them and one haughty cat perched atop the piled-high belongings, or sprawled indolently on the seat next to whichever driver she had chosen to ride with that day. Dallas drove one wagon, Lorna another, Cam and Torben, young as they were, the third. No-one looked back. As they passed the kraals there was evidence that women and children remained. They did not stop to say goodbye. Nor did the inhabitants acknowledge their passing. Everyone, Zulu and white alike, was in shock. The war touched them all but in each and every heart remained one question. Why was it necessary?

Lord Chelmsford had invaded Zululand ten days earlier. Dallas and his family were stopped several times by British scouts who asked if they'd seen any signs of *impi* on the move. Although they had encountered similar Zulu scouting parties, Dallas could not bring himself to say so while still north of the Thukela. Treason? Perhaps. He didn't care. The Zulus had shown him and his family nothing but courtesy and kindness and he would not betray them on their own soil.

As they moved further south, rumours of a

British defeat at Isandlwana and subsequent victory at Rorke's Drift reached them. The tales varied wildly and claims ranged from a thousand to ten thousand deaths. Inclined to discount most of the stories as exaggerated gossip, the fact that they existed at all brought home the reality of war.

Their return to the house in Durban was sober and without joy. Percy, too old to respond to Cetshwayo's call to arms, had stayed on with his wives. Queenie, overjoyed to see the children, immediately took charge of them. Percy was full of news about Isandlwana but the rumour had travelled a long and pride-filled road before reaching his ears. Dallas listened respectfully. Inwardly he discounted much of it as hearsay.

He had good reason. The supposed Zulu victory at Isandlwana was on 22 January, the day after they left *Ludukaneni*. On that day two natural phenomena occurred that would have made the Zulus' willingness to fight unlikely. Firstly, it was the day of the dead moon, the day before a new moon appears. Traditionally, no important undertaking was ever commenced at such a time. As if that wasn't omen enough, during the afternoon there had been a partial eclipse of the sun. Zulus believed that this meant the sun was sick and they would normally have gone to great lengths, lamenting and making sacrifices, to shake it from lethargy.

But when Dallas presented himself at the garrison the day after arriving in Durban, he learned that there had indeed been two great battles fought on 22 January. Isandlwana, where fifteen hundred Zulus had died – most killed by rifle and artillery fire as they marched unflinchingly towards the British. Once within stabbing distance, the tables turned. Eight hundred regular troops, more than five hundred Natal Native Contingent soldiers, hundreds of wagon drivers and other noncombatants lay dead on the field as well.

Talk of the battle dominated conversation to such an extent that the bravery and ultimate victory of a handful of British soldiers who had defended the field hospital at Rorke's Drift and driven off some four thousand Zulus was, for a time, ignored. Eleven Victoria Crosses were ultimately awarded but, since valour in the field was expected, and anything other than total victory not anticipated, those in Durban spoke of little else but the Isandlwana trouncing.

At the garrison Dallas found that he, and many other colonial volunteers, were causing headaches. No-one knew quite where to send them. The main problem seemed to be a lack of communication from the field.

John Dunn, who had raised one hundred and fifty guides to ride with him, was currently attached to the Eshowe Relief Column. When Dallas requested secondment it was refused. 'We understand you are familiar with the Thukela Valley,' one officer commented. 'The Natal Guides need experienced men. We could send you to Colenso.'

It was the last place in the world Dallas wanted to go.

'Or you can scout along the coast up near Gingindlovu. We'll let you know.'

Everything was so vague, considering the urgency conveyed in the letter he'd received. Feeling disgruntled, Dallas returned to the Berea.

'When do you leave?' was Lorna's first question.

He shook his head. 'It's pandemonium at the garrison. No-one, least of all the commander, seems to know what's going on. For now, I wait.'

'Will you have to fight?' Cam asked.

'If I must.'

'What if you see one of our Zulus? What if it's Mister David?'

Dallas looked into the earnest young face of his eldest child. 'It's war, son. Mister David won't hesitate to kill me if he can.'

'But he's a friend.'

'He's a Kaffir,' Torben spoke harshly. 'If his blood is up, he'd kill you too.'

'As a warrior,' Dallas corrected Torben. 'It's his duty to defend the Zulu king and nation. Just as it's mine to defend Britain, much as I disagree with the whole damned issue. If Mister David and I survive this war we'll find each other and be friends again.'

'That's stupid,' Torben said. 'I wouldn't want to know anyone who tried to kill me.'

'That's because you don't understand the Zulus,' Cam burst out. 'You think you're better than them. You can't even speak their language.'

'Why would I? Half the time they just grunt.'

'They do not.'

Dallas could see a clash coming. 'That's enough, boys. We're at war and each man must do his duty. That's the end of it.'

Later that night, Lorna and Dallas were curled up together on the settee discussing the war. 'I can see Torben's point of view,' she said. 'When this is over could you really be friends with Mister David?'

'Of course,' he told her, remembering the Zulu's words as they had last stood side-by-side at *Ludukaneni.* "It is what is in our hearts." In Mister David's lay obligation to defend the only way of life he knew. In Dallas's, sympathy and understanding. War had been thrust between them but respect would remain long after the last gun fell silent and the last man died pointlessly in the name of glory.

'How do I fight these people? They're not my enemy, they're victims.' His words echoed the despair he felt.

'You said it earlier. Duty.'

'Duty.' Dallas repeated the word derisively. 'What authority has the God-given right to dictate where an individual's obligations must lie? Suddenly we're all supposed to remember our origins. Is that enough, I wonder? My heart and soul lie in Zululand, yet here I am supposedly volunteering to fight against the very people whose land is at stake. Land that is rightfully theirs. Frere can dress it up any way he wishes, it's still nothing short of robbery.'

'That's a bit harsh, darling. If Britain doesn't take it, the Boers will.'

'Yes,' Dallas agreed gloomily. 'And therein lies a story still to be written.'

Lorna kissed him. 'My, you're a sober-sides this evening.'

'Sorry. It's just that I've got the same feeling inside as when I fled from Scotland. I've left a part of myself behind. How many more times can that happen before my loyalties become so fragmented there's nothing left?'

Lorna smiled. 'Nothing?' she queried. 'How about the children and me?'

He pulled her closer. 'You're right. Thank God for that.'

A loud banging at the front door made Lorna jump nervously. Picking up his newly issued Martini Henry carbine, Dallas went into the hall and spoke through the front door. 'Who is it?'

'Me. Will.'

Dallas relaxed and let him in. He had seen Will Green only twice since their last trading trip. On both occasions, the wiry Yorkshireman had been returning from the Thukela Valley on his way to Durban and Dallas had purchased any superfluous livestock. 'Will! Come in, come in.'

He'd been caught in a downpour and dripped water. 'Better not.'

Lorna, recognising the accent, came to the door. 'Inside, Will Green, now if you please. You'll catch your death standing there.'

Grinning self-consciously, Will obeyed.

'Take off that coat. Give me your hat. Boots.' Lorna handled the bush-worn, non-too-clean garments with no show of distaste. 'I see you still have no stockings,' she commented on his bare feet.

'Something else to look after,' Will muttered.

Lorna bullied and bossed him into the parlour, but couldn't make him sit. 'I'm too wet.'

'Here.' She pulled up a wooden stool with interwoven cowhide strips serving as a seat. 'Sit on that.'

Shrugging helplessly, Will lowered himself and sighed with satisfaction.

Dallas handed him a goblet of red wine. 'Still in good repair?' he asked.

All three knew to what he referred. Will was the only one of them to revisit Logan's grave. 'Some elephant damage. Last trip the cairn had been spread around. Might have been baboon, though that's unlikely. Never seen them in that valley. Anyway, I fixed it.'

'Good.' Dallas fell silent for a moment, remembering the secret valley and that never to be forgotten day Logan Burton died. There were times, even now, when he still expected to look up and see the burly old hunter, cigar in mouth, ready with some sarcastic comment. 'What brings you here?' he asked finally.

'I called at the farm. I could see you'd left and assumed you'd be in Durban. Wondered what your plans are.'

Dallas shook his head. 'I've been to the garrison. Seems to me they've got more of us than they know what to do with.'

'You've got that half right. They need local knowledge badly, the more the better. Forming regiments from irregulars is their biggest problem. There aren't enough officers to go round and most of our lot expect a military rank.' Will shrugged. 'What use is that? Let's get out there, do the job and be done with it.'

'I quite agree,' Dallas said.

Will squinted up from his stool. 'Heard of Colonel Wood?'

'The 90th Light Infantry?'

Will nodded. 'Aye. That's him. Good man. He's calling for irregulars.'

'I heard they were all natives.'

Again, Will nodded. 'They were but he needs scouts. You know how unreliable the Zulus are. Wood is looking for white volunteers.'

'Where is he?'

'Covering the area between Hlobane Mountain and Kambula Hill. I'm joining him.'

'You!' Dallas was openly surprised. Will had never been the type to volunteer for anything.

There was a new confidence in Will's stare. 'Anything wrong with that?'

'No. It's just that I didn't expect . . . What made you choose Wood?'

'The rumours are that Chelmsford is preparing to attack Ulundi. Wood's responsibility is to keep the northern Zulus occupied.'

Dallas kept his gaze on Will.

The man's hands spread expressively as he shrugged. 'Wood was a navy man in the Crimea.

Then he joined the 17th Lancers and won himself a VC in India. After that he was with Wolseley in West Africa. That was six years ago.'

'So?'

'He's got Buller with him. China in the sixties and head of intelligence during the Ashanti War.'

'So you're covering your –' Dallas broke off and glanced at Lorna.

'Backside,' she supplied blithely.

Dallas smothered a grin. 'I hear he's deaf as a post.'

'Who? Buller or Wood?'

'Wood.'

Rumours always flew about prominent men and women and Dallas knew both officers by reputation. Evelyn Wood was known as a thorough professional despite recurring bouts of illness. The Zulus called him *Lukuni* after the wood from which they made their knobkerries. They respected his ability as a soldier and a leader of men. Redvers Buller was also an inspired leader, though less conventional. The man's temper had become legendary but a feel for the contribution that his somewhat free-spirited irregular scouts made to the war effort, and insightful use of such men, made him unique. Together, Woods and Buller were reputed to have a greater understanding of African warfare than any other combination of officers. Dallas could understand why Will wanted to join them. Far better to place your trust in such men than those lacking even a basic knowledge of the Zulus and their fighting capabilities.

'How do we join?'

'Tell the garrison commander and go. Either that or just leave anyway. We won't be missed. It's two less for them to worry about.' Will grinned. 'You did say *we*?'

'I might come with you.'

The grin widened, nearly splitting Will's face. 'Good,' he said simply, handing over his empty goblet for a refill. 'We can leave tomorrow.'

Lorna became brisk. 'I'll pack your things in the morning.'

'I won't need much.'

She nodded and he caught the sparkle of tears in her eyes as she turned to Will. 'You'll stay the night, of course.'

'Much obliged.'

'Provided you take a bath. Otherwise I'm afraid it's the stables.'

'That was good enough for Our Lord.'

Dallas raised his eyebrows. 'You're aiming a mite high there, my friend.'

Will's response was cut off by the appearance of a frustrated Percy. 'Master, there is a horse eating the vegetables.'

Dallas knew that the old Zulu was afraid of horses. 'Don't worry. We'll see to him ourselves. Could you please arrange some hot water for our guest.'

Looking vastly relieved, Percy bowed and left.

Will's raised eyebrows were a question.

'Don't ask,' Dallas advised. 'He's Lorna's, not mine.'

'There's nothing wrong with Percy,' Lorna said defensively. 'He's loyal and reliable.'

'Don't you have a stable hand?'

'We do,' Dallas said. 'He's probably drunk by now.'

'Damned Zulus,' Will said, without venom. 'I'll be glad when this thing is over.'

'Won't we all,' Dallas agreed. 'I have no stomach for betrayal.'

'Aye.' Will nodded. 'That's what this is, all right. Poor devils.'

It was typical of Will to criticise on one hand and sympathise on the other. In fact, most Europeans who lived and worked with Zulus did the same. That aside, let strangers make a disparaging remark and those who knew these proud people were quick to their defence.

'A toast.' Will held up his wine glass. 'To a speedy conclusion.'

'A speedy conclusion,' Dallas and Lorna repeated.

They all drank.

'And long live the king,' Will added.

'Amen to that,' Dallas agreed. Funny, he thought, sipping his scotch. Such a toast would only be understood by a handful of people. Yet it was one of the most sincere gestures he could remember making.

FIFTEEN

Rain. Would it ever stop?

'Why are we fighting for this damnable place?' someone asked peevishly.

A carpet of mud covered the ground, twelve inches thick in parts. Despite the wet conditions, temperatures remained high. Men and horses fell foul of the humidity. The soldiers had little immunity to diseases borne by the appalling weather. Nor did they relish food gone bad, rotting boots and mouldy uniforms. Tents dripped, bedding would not dry and the ever-present mud got into everything.

It was late March. British troops had been camped on Kambula Hill since news of the Isandlwana defeat reached them in late January. Inaction was exaggerating the men's already dwindling morale.

Dallas and Will joined the column five weeks earlier. It had rained for three of them.

The colonial volunteers were a mixed bag of some sixty men. Boer and British in the main – farmers, traders, hunters, guides – individuals used to living rough. They were a tough, independent group who preferred to trust their own initiative than follow orders. Lieutenant-Colonel Redvers Buller was the only exception they made. Second-in-command of the column, he was respected for his fearless courage, equestrian skills and leadership ability. They'd have followed him to hell if he'd asked, but only on their terms.

For his part, Buller shrewdly capitalised on the free-spirited nature of his irregulars. Most spoke Zulu, all possessed an invaluable understanding of African customs, none complained about the conditions and a few even had useful and influential contacts among the Zulu population. These he put to good use, turning several clans against Cetshwayo. To the last man, all were willing and able to act instinctively, never waiting to be told what to do.

They had been described by one journalist, quite unfairly, as '. . . broken gentlemen of runagate sailors, of fugitives from justice, of the scum of South African towns, of stolid Africanders . . . there were a few Americans . . . A greaser; a Chilean; several Australians; and a couple of Canadian voyagers from somewhere in the Arctic region.' Certainly, the writer's comments applied to some. But Redvers Buller was more than a match for those seeking thrills and a free meal. They soon found themselves on latrine duty, or something equally as mundane and distasteful, until they simply deserted and disappeared. As for the rest, Buller worked them well – scouting forays to assess the enemy's strength, raiding kraals, confiscating cattle and recruiting clans.

Colonel Evelyn Wood, overall commander of the column, busied his regulars with fortifying the camp at Kambula Hill. The lessons learned at Isandlwana had gone deep and he took no chances. The camp was well placed, high up with commanding views to the north and west.

A hexagonal-shaped laager had been constructed, wagons locked tightly together. Nearby was a secure cattle kraal. Both were protected by trenches and earth parapets, further fortified by a stone-built barricade a hundred yards out from the laager. Between the two lay a palisade roughly built from saplings. Four seven-pounders covered the north and two more faced north-east.

Events over the past two months had knocked the stuffing out of Chelmsford's planned offensive. A message reached Colonel Wood that he was on his own.

Buller had gathered his volunteers together to brief them. 'We've reliable information that an *impi* of some twenty thousand is gathering in Ulundi and preparing to march against us. For the moment, men, we're like a shag on a rock.' The man's strong voice matched his physique. 'There are no reinforcements coming. We are required to meet the whole damned Zulu army if needs must.'

Eyebrows raised. The regulars and volunteers on Kambula Hill totalled just over two thousand.

Buller hawked and spat before continuing. 'There's no question that these black bastards can move quickly. We know there's another four thousand, mainly *abaQulusi*, drilling on Hlobane.' He jerked a thumb backwards to indicate the hazy shape of a mountain some eleven miles east. 'I am reliably informed by some of you that they are disciplined, armed and familiar with the territory.'

Heads nodded agreement. From what had been observed and heard, the *abaQulusi* trained every day and remained doggedly loyal to Cetshwayo. The Zulu king had ordered that, should an opportunity present itself, they were to attack the British camp on Kambula Hill. No such chance had occurred and now, late in March, the *abaQulusi* were short of food, grazing for their cattle was decreasing despite incessant rain, and the warriors grew increasingly restless.

'The intention is for us to move against them now, before reinforcements arrive,' Buller went on. 'They are blocking any advance on Ulundi, we need to clear the way.'

'It'd be damned useful in retreat too,' a young Boer muttered, causing quiet amusement to those near him.

His father, the Boer commander Piet Uys, clipped his son's ear. 'Passop,' he warned. Be careful.

Will, standing nearby, overheard the exchange and grinned. 'He's right, though.'

'Ja,' Uys agreed. 'But the roineks won't admit it.'

Will ducked his head and chuckled. The expression 'red necks' was a direct reference to the way sensitive exposed skin on the backs of British soldiers' necks never seemed to go brown. Some suffered such sunburn that their skin resembled the scarlet tunics worn by infantrymen. This garment too, drew derision from the Boers. Coupled with gold braid and buttons, it made the troops extremely easy to spot. The Boers were openly scathing at the stupidity of such a uniform.

Stung by the description, the British responded by referring to Afrikaaners as either 'rock spiders' or 'hairy backs'. The insults didn't do much to cement relationships between British and Boer, and both were careful where and when they used the terms.

Buller was still talking. Up until this moment, he'd encouraged the volunteers' independence. Now it needed a lid. 'We'll attack during the hours of darkness. You men will be under my direct command.'

A ragged cheer started up, quickly stifled by Buller's ferocious scowl.

'Our task is to scale the eastern track and capture the Zulus' cattle. Lieutenant-Colonel Russell will take the western approach. Between us, we will cover all of Hlobane Mountain. This is a military operation, gentlemen. On this occasion you follow orders. Any man found guilty of disobedience will be court-martialled.'

Piet Uys had an expression of distaste on his face. 'I command my own men,' he shouted.

Buller didn't like that. 'And I command you,' he yelled back. 'Don't forget it.'

Someone at the back said, 'Fok yo,' and although Buller spoke not one word of Afrikaans, the meaning was crystal clear.

The military man flushed with anger.

Dallas wondered what the Boers would do next. Clearly, although they respected Buller, they disliked having to take more than casual orders from a British officer.

Uys stepped forward until he was no more than three feet from Buller. The two men squared up to each other. They were odd and unlikely-looking allies. Buller, hard-muscled and hatchet-faced, with impatience and ambition written all over him. Uys, slow-moving, slow-talking, almost benign by comparison. Until you looked into his eyes. He had volunteered along with four of his sons and forty burghers. Nothing special in that, the Boer commando system required that every adult male make himself available for duty whenever necessary. But Uys and his men were the only Transvaal Boers who gave their services with no request for payment. This fact alone made Piet Uys contemptuous of orders. He was there of his own free will, unpaid and motivated only by a fierce hatred of the Zulu. If the whim took him, there was nothing to stop Uys and his men leaving.

Buller knew this. 'Look here, I don't want a quarrel with you. We have to scale the eastern side of Hlobane and drive off the cattle. Those are my orders. If we run into trouble I don't want you and your men acting independently. There will be other troops coming in from the west.'

Uys hitched up his pants. 'Ja,' he said belligerently. 'But if my men see a Kaffir, he's a dead one.'

'You'll fire if, and when, I say. Not before.'

Uys turned and rejoined his men. 'I said nothing

about shooting.' He winked at the odd assortment of irregulars and whipped a skinning knife from his belt. 'A Kaffir dies just as easily with this.'

A murmur of appreciation greeted his remark. The burghers were the hardest of hard men, consolidated by a firm belief that Kaffirs were sub-human. After all, their Dominie had preached from the pulpit that a Kaffir's brain was much smaller than a white man's. On their farms, these men dispensed discipline to their Africans as they would to a dog – with a sjambok. The Boers took great pride in their toughness – it was a mark of manliness – and even young boys were encouraged to disdain the slightest hint of sensitivity.

Dallas sometimes wondered if, deep in their hearts, the Boers knew their attitude was wrong. Why else did they stick together with an almost fanatical dedication to each other and their religion? This stand by their commander – his flagrant and contemptuous dismissal of discipline followed by a display of solidarity – was typical. It said, 'We're with you but only on our terms.'

Buller had to leave it. A hard man himself, relying on the deeds and decisive action of others, as well as himself, to gain the esteem essential to lead men in battle, he had a high regard for Piet Uys. The man maintained the respect of his burghers and had proved himself time and again to be an excellent scout. Buller also knew that if pushed too far, Uys had it within his power to take his men and simply walk away. The lieutenant-colonel needed every man he could get.

'We leave at dawn tomorrow,' he said. Turning away, he barked, 'Granger, Green, come with me.'

Dallas and Will followed Buller to Colonel Wood's tent. The commanding officer glanced up at them then renewed his concentration on the maps spread out before him. Several minutes passed before he looked back. Stabbing a finger on the paper he said, with no preamble, 'Do either of you know this area?'

'No, sir,' Dallas responded.

'Been up there once or twice,' Will offered.

'Tell me about Devil's Pass.' His finger jabbed again.

Will was brief and informative. 'It's a way onto the plateau. Climbs about two hundred feet. Mainly scree with big boulders everywhere. No good for horses. Leads out onto open country higher up.'

'Hnghh!' grunted Wood, returning his attention to the map. Without glancing up he remarked, 'We know about the caves. Will the enemy use them?'

'They're Zulus. Of course they will.'

Colonel Wood worried his bottom lip with tobacco-stained teeth. Nobody said a word. The silence lasted a good half-minute. Suddenly the finger stabbed once more. 'You've been briefed?' He didn't wait for a reply. 'Buller will ascend here, Russell, here. I want to know where the *abaQulusi* defence is strongest. Can you two get that information for me?'

'Yes, sir.'

'Good.' Wood saluted absently. 'Dismiss.'

Outside, Buller didn't waste words. 'Leave under

cover of darkness. Get up there, find out what you can and get the hell out. Leave no calling card. Mustn't let the buggers know we're coming. Good luck, men.' With that he strode off towards his quarters.

Dallas speculated aloud on how Colonel Wood expected to get so many men to Hlobane without the Zulus seeing them coming. 'It's as if he's been ordered to create a deliberate diversion.'

'Perhaps he has,' Will said. 'Look out, here comes trouble.'

The Boer commander, Piet Uys, planted himself in front of them. 'Well?' he demanded, hands on hips.

'Well what?' Dallas replied, not liking the way Uys made out that he and his burghers were the only ones who mattered.

'Don't smart-talk me, man. Where are you going?'

'Hlobane,' Will said.

Uys regarded them for a moment. 'Then make damned sure you bring back the right information.'

'What's the matter?' Will challenged. 'Don't you think a couple of Englesmen can do it, eh?'

'No,' Uys said bluntly, turning away. 'I'd prefer to be protected by my own kind.'

'Charming!' Will muttered at his back.

'Forget it,' Dallas advised. 'He's annoyed that he wasn't asked.'

'The man only has himself to blame,' Will growled. 'We don't need dead Zulus all over the place at this stage.'

Back in his tent, Dallas treated himself to a wash and shave before lying down and trying to rest. The task they'd been given would probably take all night and he didn't want fatigue either to slow him down or cause him to make a mistake that could result in his and Will's deaths. He had no doubt that the *abaQulusi* would have rested and alert men on sentry duty. Acquiring the information Wood needed was not going to be easy.

Waiting for sleep, Dallas found himself wondering about Mister David and all the other Zulus he'd met and come to regard as friends. So many Africans were dead. Thousands more were too badly injured to fight again. Yet Cetshwayo still seemed able to summon new recruits. By now, the king had to be scraping the bottom of the barrel. Some of the regiments had been raised by Shaka. Their numbers, like the *uSixepi* or *umBelebele* Corps, were negligible, with an average age of seventy-nine. But Dallas had seen small groups of Zulus dressed for war made up of warriors barely into puberty. Was Cetshwayo so desperate that he was prepared to use old men and semi-trained boys?

He wondered how the Zulus themselves felt the war was going. There had been stunning defeats and victories on both sides. Dallas could not help but feel that the Zulus grew weary. Many clans had defected. A few even fought alongside the British.

The Zulus had their strategists, some exceedingly inspired. But they were not as flexible or experienced as the British whose officers had seen action in India, China and other parts of Africa. Despite underestimating the strength and will of his enemy, Lord Chelmsford's strategy – a three-pronged attack on the capital and subsequent capture of Cetshwayo – looked good on paper.

The centre column, to which Lord Chelmsford had attached himself, was nearly five thousand strong and commanded by Colonel Richard Glyn of the 24th Regiment. It was to cross into Zulu-land at Rorke's Drift and head straight for Ulundi. Glyn, a man of short stature and temperament, had distinguished himself during previous skirmishes in South Africa as an excellent, steady and sensible commander.

Simultaneously, a right-hand column, com-manded by Colonel Pearson of the 3rd Buffs, a veteran of the Crimean War, who had a similar number of men, was to cross the Thukela near its mouth and establish a fort on the Zulu side before moving forward to the mission station at Eshowe. There they were to await orders from the supreme commander to march on to Ulundi and assist in the final showdown.

The left-hand column, Colonel Wood's men, was also headed for the Zulu capital but from fur-ther north. Wood had a total of 2278 men. His brief was to keep the northern tribes occupied until he too answered the call to march south and join forces with Chelmsford and Pearson.

Pearson ran into trouble with the weather. It took five days to ferry his wagons and men across a swollen and fast-flowing Thukela. Once the construction of Fort Tenedos on its north bank was well under way, two divisions set off for Eshowe. No word had been received from Chelmsford, and Pearson, knowing nothing of events at Isandlwana and Rorke's Drift, assumed that the centre column was well advanced as planned. Pearson and his men encountered a few scattered groups of Zulus but their main problem was negotiating three more rivers and numerous drifts, all flooded. Then, almost at the hill on which Eshowe mission was sited, the column met fierce resistance from a force of six thousand *impi*. Attacking in their traditional horn-shaped formation, the Zulus held both the high ground and an element of surprise. Without the Gatling guns, it might have been a bloody defeat. As it was, only ten men were killed and sixteen wounded. The Zulus lost three hundred and fifty warriors before withdrawing under withering fire. On reaching Eshowe the following day, the British soldiers found it deserted.

Orders being orders, the British remained at the mission station. During the next few weeks it became increasingly obvious that the Zulus had effectively imprisoned them. The ever-present *impi* made no attempt to conceal their presence in the surrounding hills. The right-hand column was helpless, pinned down and useless.

Eight days earlier as planned, the centre column crossed into Zululand at Rorke's Drift. Leaving a reserve force there, the rest headed east towards Ulundi. Reaching Isandlwana, Chelmsford decided the town made an ideal advance base and set up camp. From there, before pushing on to the capital, he could send out patrols to reconnoitre the way ahead. Viewing it as a temporary stop only, and despite advice to the contrary, he refused to form a laager or build any kind of defence at all. Instead, he ordered that the reserve force left behind at Rorke's Drift move up to Isandlwana while the main body of troops, split into two groups, would try to locate a large Zulu force reputed to be in the area. The *impi* avoided detection and closed to within five miles of the camp. There, hiding in a valley, they were discovered by a mounted patrol. Having lost the element of surprise, the Zulus had no option but to attack. Despite superior fire power, the soldiers left at Isandlwana were no match for twenty thousand war-crazed warriors. Chelmsford, who returned late that afternoon with one of the scouting parties, was stunned. 'I can't understand it,' he said. 'I left a thousand men there.'

While the battle raged, four regiments of Zulus broke away and headed towards Rorke's Drift. Only one hundred and thirty-nine men remained to defend that camp. Barricades were built using anything they could lay their hands on, from bags of grain to biscuit boxes. Outnumbered by more than forty-to-one, the soldiers drove back wave after wave of Zulu warriors for twelve endless hours. Suddenly, at four in the morning, the *impi* silently withdrew, leaving exhausted and, in the main, wounded, defenders. They reappeared briefly at dawn, on the slopes of a nearby hill, a silent mass of black warriors who turned as one and disappeared back into Zululand. In later years, this gesture would be recorded as a tribute to the British soldiers' bravery. In truth, the Zulus had seen Lord Chelmsford's force returning and prudently left.

Dallas slept. He was still sound asleep when Will arrived. 'Ready?'

'Just a minute.' Yawning, he crawled from his bunk.

As he made ready, Dallas wished himself anywhere but in the here and now. He didn't want to spy on the Zulus. Nor did he wish to be overrun and killed by them. One cancelled out the other. The instinct of self-preservation strong, it didn't stop him resenting the position in which he'd been placed.

'Come on,' he said roughly, surprising Will. 'Let's get this done with.'

'Something bothering you?'

'Nothing that doesn't worry you too?' Dallas countered.

Will looked down at his sodden, mud-caked boots. 'A lot of things about this war worry me,' he said finally. 'But there's one thing that doesn't.'

'What's that?'

'My conscience,' Will replied. 'And you know damned well that Logan would have said the same.'

Dallas dropped his head, smiling. 'The pair of you couldn't muster half a conscience between you.' He looked back at Will. 'Thanks, friend.'

Will grinned too, then looked serious. 'I'm not like you, thinking everything through. On this occasion that helps. You can't take this war on your own shoulders. We're not responsible for it, so why burden yourself with guilt? Do it or die. That's all we need know.'

Dallas swung into the saddle. 'For once,' he said, when Will was mounted, 'you could just be right.'

As they rode he thought about Will's words. Just who was responsible? Who had such power over life and death? There were many, but three names stood out – Sir Bartle Frere, Lord Chelmsford and Cetshwayo. If there was a reckoning at the pearly gates, or wherever, Dallas hoped that Frere at least would have his work cut out trying to justify this war.

The rain continued to fall ceaselessly. It was a blessing in disguise. Obscuring their vision, it also prevented them from being seen. Not that they expected Zulu scouts to be off the mountain at night.

Although they were used to roughing it, the conditions tried both men. Water soaked every inch of them as surely as if they'd jumped fully clothed into a river. The horses continually shook their heads, trying to rid straining eyes of rain. Every noise they made seemed uncommonly loud. Underfoot, the ground squelched and sucked at every step.

Dallas shivered, despite the warm night.

'Have you heard from home?' Will asked softly.

'Two letters in Monday's mailbag. One from

Cam,' Dallas replied as quietly. Although seeming to be lost in the rain, their voices might carry.

'How are they?'

'Fine. Torben continues to disrupt everything. The others are well.'

'And my godson?' Will was godfather to Duncan and took his responsibilities seriously.

'Heathenistic.' Dallas grinned. 'He tore about thirty pages out of that Bible you gave him.'

'I'll get the lad another,' Will said firmly.

'I'd wait until he can read,' Dallas advised. 'He seems hell-bent on destruction at the moment.'

'He's only finding out how things work,' Will defended the youngster. 'Nothing wrong with that.'

'True,' Dallas agreed. 'It's also got a lot to do with the sound of paper tearing. He's stripped his bedroom of wallpaper as high as he can reach.'

Will chuckled indulgently. 'He's a fine wee laddie. Reminds me of Cam at that age.'

'Cam didn't try to destroy the house.'

'As I recall he didn't have one to destroy.'

They fell silent. Dallas smiled in the darkness thinking back to the day he met Will. Never in his wildest dreams would he have anticipated they'd become friends. He doubted Will would have believed it either.

The Yorkshireman hadn't changed. Will was still the same conniving chancer he'd always been. Just a bit more mature. Still too fond of a drink and addicted to gambling. Always broke and full of scheming ways to acquire money. However, he was devoted to Dallas and his family and, in his own way, had proved to be a loyal and reasonably honest friend.

'What are you going to do when this mess is over?' Dallas asked.

'Take my pay and open a trading store in Swaziland. You?'

Dallas shook his head. 'I don't know. Farm, I suppose.'

'*Ludukaneni*?'

'Depends. Who knows how Zululand will be carved up? If the land is decreed tribal it may not be allowed. The old days of seeking the king's permission are over.'

'Where then?'

Dallas sighed. 'I don't know, Will. Best wait and see.' He glanced at the dark profile next to him. 'Why Swaziland?'

'Just like the sound of it.'

Dallas smiled. As far as he was concerned, that gave as good a reason as any. 'Be careful who you swindle, my friend. The Swazis don't take kindly to mischief.'

'Swindle!' Will pretended outrage. 'I'll have you know –'

'That you are a pillar of society,' Dallas finished the denial for him with a chuckle. 'Of course you are, Will. I was merely making an observation.'

Will grunted and the two fell silent again.

They reached the western slope of Hlobane a little after nine-thirty. The rain had almost stopped. 'We'll leave our coats with the horses,' Dallas whispered. 'In fact, Will, I suggest we go native.'

'Good idea.'

It made sense. Their clothes and boots were waterlogged, more likely to be a hindrance than anything else. Barefooted and wearing only under-breeches, they would be more mobile and less likely to make a noise.

Swiftly, the two of them shed superfluous cloth-ing, stuffing it into their saddlebags. The horses they tethered in the bush. Camouflage was easy: mud, rubbed liberally over themselves.

'Rifles?' Will asked.

Leave no calling card Buller had said. Weapons were security, also an encumbrance. 'Knives,' Dallas decided. The *abaQulusi* had rifles but, with luck, would not be expecting visitors. With exceptional luck they'd be huddled around fires in shelters to escape the rain.

The western path, a steep rocky salient impos-sible for horses to negotiate, was almost as difficult for humans. Dallas and Will knew the Zulus would have sentries posted but there was no way to conceal themselves during the ascent. The lookouts would probably be positioned on the plateau, some eight hundred and fifty feet above. Depending on where, how alert they were, and how silently Dallas and Will could climb, lay the difference between success and failure. That aside, Lieutenant-Colonel Russell and his men could never hope to advance quietly. Even at night, the *abaQulusi* would hear them and casualties were likely to be heavy.

The two men had reached a projecting rock

ridge, well aware that one wrong step would see them over the side. Their way forward became steeper until they were forced to proceed on hands and knees. The wet rock was slippery. Small stones dislodged by their passing skittered and rattled back down the slope.

It was pitch dark. The rain had stopped completely, yet no moon or stars showed in the sky. Fortunately the Zulus' love of conversation and a habit of speaking loudly, alerted Dallas and Will that the plateau was just above. Lying full-length on the unyielding ground they listened, trying to pinpoint a direction.

'Dead ahead,' Will mouthed in Dallas's ear.

Nodding agreement, Dallas felt around for a suitable stone. 'Ready,' he whispered, hurling it as far as he could away from where they had to go over the top.

The voices above became excited and the sentries moved off to investigate.

'Go.' Dallas rose and scrambled over the lip, Will right beside him. They could see and hear the men now, six of them illuminated in the light of a flaming branch.

'*Mbili*,' one suggested, referring to the rock-dwelling rabbit-like creature, or dassie, which somehow managed to thrive in the harsh terrain.

Another disagreed. 'No. It is the rain. See here.' With his foot he pushed a large rock which obligingly came free and went crashing over the edge.

Dallas and Will melted into darkness, noting the makeshift shelters, each with a small fire burning at the entrance. To their surprise there were only three, apparently with two sentries in each.

Devil's Pass lay ahead. A seventy-yard, steep climb, strewn with boulders that formed a rough series of steps. The last leg to the top was narrow, dark and dangerous. Not surprisingly, there were no lookouts posted on this inhospitable ascent. What did amaze them was the absence of any security at the top.

'They're certainly not expecting an attack from the west,' Dallas observed.

'Why would they? Who in their right mind would try to bring soldiers up this way? Russell and his men will never get their horses up the ridge, let alone this far. Without mounts, they'll be cut to bits.'

'They're a diversion,' Dallas reminded him. 'Buller has the tough job.'

They set off across the plateau. Will estimated it to be about four miles long by one wide. It was here that the *abaQulusi* had their kraals. In the dark, Dallas and Will used their sense of smell to avoid them. Lingering wood smoke and the inevitable odour of cattle enclosed for the night made the task relatively easy. Once, however, they almost stumbled over a Kaffir dog with puppies. The female gave a startled yelp, leapt to her feet and loped away.

'So much for a mothering instinct,' Dallas muttered.

Avoiding the *umuzis* was not difficult, though there was nothing they could do about their own odours. Dogs and cattle would pick up the faintest alien smell and react. Dallas cursed his stupidity for the wash he had had earlier. Soap, toothpaste and shaving cream all left a lingering scent which, in the now cooler and still air, would be easily detected. Sure enough, a dog barked suddenly. They both froze. A sleepy voice called out to silence the animal, which promptly obeyed. Then another voice, older and more authoritative, added, 'Go see what disturbs that dog.'

Will grabbed Dallas and the two sank down. Someone was approaching, grumbling quietly. He passed quite close, stopping only to relieve himself. He wasn't away long, and returned still complaining about being woken, disappearing back into the *umuzi*. After waiting a good five minutes they cautiously rose and left as quickly as silence would allow.

Despite stopping to rub themselves down with cow dung, their presence was later detected by another dog. Unfortunately, this one decided to investigate. Barking half-heartedly, a sound to which no-one in the *umuzi* paid the slightest attention, it whimpered once as Will cut its throat.

'They seem pretty relaxed,' Dallas whispered. 'Still, we'd better lose that body. The rain should wash away the blood.'

'The land drops away about half a mile from here,' Will said. 'That should be far enough. It's a straight drop down. We can get rid of the dog there.' They walked in silence for ten minutes, moving further from the kraals. 'This is grazing land,' Will told Dallas. 'There'll be no-one around at this hour. He suddenly stopped. 'Careful. We're right on the edge.' He threw the dog over the side.

The noise seemed unnaturally loud as its dead weight made contact with the ground below and started rocks sliding on the steep slope. It seemed an age before silence returned. They waited several minutes before moving on.

Both men realised it was not as dark as before. Clouds had started to clear, the moon, in its first quarter, about to appear from behind them. If the clouds rolled away completely, out here with nothing to diffuse its brightness, it would provide too much light.

Crossing the plateau, they were able to establish an approximate number of people living there. Buller had said around four thousand warriors. Will and Dallas agreed with his estimate. The kraals were close to each other and they saw few with less than thirty beehive-shaped huts. In addition, they had to skirt a kind of military barracks that would easily house at least a thousand. The *abaQulusi*, it would seem, had called their clansmen together and constituted a formidable force.

They reached the plateau's eastern access. It was likely to be well guarded, since it was from this side that the *abaQulusi* would expect any attack. Surprisingly, the rim remained clear. Will found the well-worn path that ran down through sheer cliffs on either side. He knew that at the bottom lay a jumble of huge rocks, fallen there over the centuries, forming cave-like crevices and gaps. This had to be the Zulus' first line of defence. Hopefully, any sentries posted would be watching the way up, not down.

As they descended rain began to fall again. It quickly became obvious that the downpour might wash off their covering of mud. Praying that any sentries had taken cover, Dallas and Will inched their way down. They could hear muffled coughs, men clearing their throats and others speaking in undertones. From the caves, low firelight danced and flickered. The *abaQulusi* were not exactly disciplined in defence, but on this side of their mountain they were taking fewer chances. Dallas estimated there to be at least a hundred men hidden in the cave system. He counted around fifty tiny fires, so small they couldn't be seen from below.

Down on their bellies, Will and Dallas made excruciatingly slow progress past the caves. All it would take would be for one man to step outside his shelter, his eyes adjust to the dark, and they'd likely be discovered. The rain and the flickering fires helped to conceal them. Dallas looked both sides of the track, re-counting the telltale flames. Getting the numbers right on this track was crucial for Buller.

Will tapped his arm. Time to press on. Below them lay more steep slopes. The rain stopped as abruptly as it had started. The moon still threatened an appearance. As they moved forward, Will's foot slipped and stones clattered off into the darkness.

'Who is there?' demanded a rough voice.

'A man's got to piss,' Will responded in perfect Zulu.

Others laughed as he did exactly that. They reached the bottom with no more mishap.

'We'll have to get a move on,' Dallas warned. 'It's a good six miles round Hlobane and back to the horses.'

The two men set off in a loping run.

'They're on this side all right. What would you say, Will? A hundred at least in the caves?' They'd proceeded in silence for the last twenty minutes and were well away from the eastern path.

'I've seen that place in daylight. I'd double your estimate, but those rocks could hide ten times that number. If the Zulus see us coming you can bet they'll hide as many men as possible there. We could be cut to ribbons.'

'Shooting downhill is less accurate,' Dallas replied, not willing to speculate on the prospect of hand-to-hand combat. 'The horses would take the brunt of it.'

'Shit!' Will stubbed his toe, stumbled, and then regained his stride. 'My bloody feet are killing me.'

'Mine too.'

A loud warning hiss directly ahead stopped them in their tracks. 'What was that?' Dallas asked.

'I've only heard that sound once before,' Will told him. 'Under my bed. It's a fucking puff adder.'

Both men dived sideways off the track and gave it a wide berth for several minutes.

'They say it's a two-step death,' Will said

unnecessarily, once they had returned to the softer sand of the track. 'Two steps and you're dead.'

'At least it warned us,' Dallas commented. 'Nice of it.'

The horses were as they had left them. Dallas and Will wasted no time in returning to camp.

The British troops left Kambula Hill at dawn. Colonel Wood, relying on the intelligence gathered by Dallas and Will, decided there was no point in trying for an element of surprise. The *abaQulusi* were obviously anticipating an attack and he could not hope to move so many men without being detected. Making no attempt to conceal themselves, Russell, Wood and their men bivouacked three miles from the western ascent. Buller took up position five miles south-east of the other access route. Those watching on both sides of the mountain had more than enough time to warn the *impi*. By nightfall, warrior numbers on the western edge of the plateau had swollen to several hundred. In the rock caves, more than two thousand hid and waited.

Unbeknown even to his two most senior-ranking officers, Wood had sent a message to Lord Chelmsford that he was preparing to attack Hlobane and create the diversion his military commander asked of him. In it, he confessed, 'I am not very sanguine of success.'

Out on the plain looking through field glasses at the western escarpment which Russell and his men had to scale, Wood was even more doubtful. He kept such thoughts to himself.

Buller remained pragmatic about the outcome. He and his men had to reach the plateau. The Zulus, by now, knew they were coming. There would be casualties. But reach the summit he intended to do.

Dallas and Will were with Buller. They took the enforced wait as a chance to catch up on some much-needed sleep, as they'd had no chance to rest once they'd reached Kambula Hill. After a quick breakfast, they were heading back towards Hlobane.

At ten that evening Buller ordered that the fires be built up. Anyone observing them from Hlobane would hopefully believe that the enemy was still five miles away. As luck would have it, the ever-fickle weather played an ace of spades. A severe thunderstorm struck, delaying the troopers for hours. Undaunted, Buller advanced to the foot of Hlobane. It wasn't until three-thirty in the morning that they were ready to lead their horses up the trail. The storm still raged on around them, lightning giving away their positions. From the caves above, the Zulus opened fire.

Cursing the weather, Zulus, the mountain and horses in that order, the troopers doggedly pressed on. The *abaQulusi* had positioned themselves on either side of the path. The higher Buller and his men went, the more accurate Zulu crossfire became. Dallas felt a bullet pluck at his trousers and a stinging sensation followed. Around him, horses whinnied in fright and protest. Thunder crashed and rolled away, men shouted, guns roared, lightning flashed. It was the horses that suffered most. A larger target, and a Zulu tendency to fire in the general direction of whatever they wanted to hit, meant many were killed or wounded that night. Tosca was used to the sound but seemed to know that, this time, she was a likely victim. Dallas held her reins tightly and the horse, reluctantly, followed him up the rock-strewn path.

The storm raged for three hours. By the time troops reached the caves, the *abaQulusi* had abandoned that position and they were able to make the summit drawing only sporadic sniping fire. It seemed to Dallas that the Zulus were waiting for something. He felt a stirring of unease.

'What are they up to?' Piet Uys roared, equally as suspicious. 'Why are they just sitting out there?'

Those who still could had remounted. Buller galloped past, shouting orders. By now it was fully light. One troop of the Frontier Light Horse remained to keep the *abaQulusi* at bay and protect the rear. Native infantry were rounding up cattle ready to herd them towards the west.

'You won't get many down that way,' Dallas yelled at the British officer's retreating form. If Buller heard, he gave no sign.

'Bloody fool,' Will commented loudly.

That he certainly heard. Buller started to check his horse, decided against it and carried on.

'You'll be on the mat for that,' Dallas warned.

'Ah!' Will was disgusted. 'What's the point? The man refuses to listen.'

The Zulus' lack of response was disturbing Dallas. Why would they sit back and allow their cattle to be taken? 'There's something wrong,' he said to Piet Uys.

'Ja, man. I feel it too.'

Three hours after reaching the plateau, Buller had his first look at the hazardous descent down Devil's Pass and ordered they turn back for the eastern trail. At that moment, from his vantage point, he looked out and saw five columns of *impi* coming across the plain from the south-east. His jaw dropped. Moving steadily, and in absolute silence, they were advancing like a plague of locusts. 'Too late,' he bellowed. 'We'll have to take Devil's Pass.'

'This is what those black bastards were waiting for.' Uys was red-faced with anger. 'They knew the *impi* were coming.'

The *abaQulusi* had indeed been holding back to await reinforcements. At the appearance of twenty thousand men coming to their aid, they started using their rifles in earnest against the soldiers. On hearing increased gunfire, the advancing *impi* flowed effortlessly into their chest and horns battle formation and picked up the already punishing pace. They wanted to be waiting when the British made it to the plain.

Buller reacted immediately, realising that not only the men with him were at risk. Those left at the severely depleted garrison on Kambula Hill could very well find themselves facing another Isandlwana defeat. 'We have no choice,' he bellowed. 'It's Devil's Pass or nothing.'

Captured cattle and native infantry began the dangerous descent. Panic set in and spread. Urgency became a disorderly scramble for survival. Many animals and even a few men slipped and fell to their deaths. On the plateau there was no time to think of anything, other than the need to defend their position until everyone could start the descent. Dallas operated on pure instinct. In many ways, for him it was not unlike being in the middle of the elephants when Logan was killed.

'Here they come,' someone yelled as the *abaQulusi* made a determined rush. 'Thicker than grass and blacker than hell.'

'Fall back, men,' Buller urged. 'They're trying to delay us until the *impi* can cut us off. We must get down before they do.' The men seemed to be everywhere.

Piet Uys looked wildly around. He could see only three of his sons.

'Get going,' ordered Buller.

'My son!' the Afrikaner cried, ignoring him.

'Over you go,' Buller shouted at him.

'Son!' Contemptuously Uys turned his back and ran to where he had spotted his eldest boy. Dropping beside him, he cradled the injured lad in his arms.

Dallas spared a last look at the Boer commander before urging Tosca over the rim. He never saw Piet Uys again.

So many horses had been shot or fallen on Devil's Pass that, on reaching the bottom, the men had to double up. Will's horse had gone down to a stray bullet and he swung up behind Dallas on Tosca. Despite the arduous climb and frenzied descent, the animal seemed to know the worst was over. Miraculously, she had escaped injury, losing nothing more than two shoes in the mad scramble for safety. Will was also unscathed, though Dallas's thigh had begun to throb severely. He hadn't had time to examine the wound but it would need medical attention if infection were to be avoided.

As the last British troops straggled back to Kambula, the extent of their defeat became devastatingly clear. Fifteen officers and seventy-nine regular soldiers had been killed. The volunteers had lost Piet Uys and one of his sons. More than one hundred of the native infantry were dead. Those Africans who survived resented the dangerous retreat down Devil's Pass and the lack of covering fire they'd been given. What was left of the 2nd Battalion, a Zulu regiment, deserted. The Border Horse – mainly English settlers from the Transvaal – had somehow become separated from Buller. They met up with the descending troop of Frontier Light Horse who, having carried out Buller's orders to keep the *abaQulusi* at bay while the cattle were being herded down the mountain, were making their own way to the bottom. Together, because neither knew of the advancing *impi*, they rode south to assist any stragglers. This took them straight into the Zulus' right horn. Both detachments were driven back towards the mountain and massacred. Boer burghers, without a leader, returned to their homes. Mounted troops had been seriously weakened by the terrible loss of horses.

Kambula would be next. Dallas and Will, on Buller's instructions, attached themselves to Commandant Pieter Raaf's Transvaal Rangers. At dawn the next day, they rode out to try to locate the *impi*. The Zulus were camped on the eastern side of Hlobane. Dallas could see them making preparations for battle.

'They're getting ready, all right,' Will agreed.

A small fire had been lit, and whatever it was they burned in it, a great volume of smoke billowed out. Two at a time, the men passed through it and as they did, were sprinkled with *muthi*. A special war doctor then gave each man something to drink.

'They don't swallow it,' Will told Dallas. 'Watch. They'll walk away and spit it towards Kambula. The warriors believe it will make them safe against bullets.'

'I've seen enough,' Raaf said. 'They're about to take up formation. Let's go.'

Riding swiftly back to report, Dallas and Will agreed with Pieter Raaf that they had no more than five hours before the *impi* were ready to attack. They estimated the Zulus' strength to be more than twenty thousand and delivered this intelligence to Colonel Wood.

'Right,' the commanding officer said briskly. 'Enough time for dinner, gentlemen.'

The men who would be defending Kambula Hill sat down to eat. They could see the *impi* advancing, still six or seven miles away. Confidence had been restored despite the previous day's humiliating losses at Hlobane. The British were well prepared for this attack – fortification was good and every man knew his duties. They were armed with Martini-Henry breech-loading rifles, had more than enough ammunition and the support of heavy artillery.

After lunch, final preparations were swiftly made. Tents struck, ammunition boxes were opened and distributed, and troops took up their battle positions. The *impi* approached slowly, conserving energy, in five long columns still three miles away. The massed force halted and drew together for a final council of war. The decision – to wipe out the garrison on Kambula Hill before proceeding to the town of Utrecht – had to be made by those commanding the *impi*. Their king had instructed his army to attack Utrecht. But, on seeing the soldiers' tents being struck, the Zulus believed the British were preparing for flight. It was too tempting.

After debating tactics for nearly an hour, the *impi* advanced. The horns began to spread, like shadows in the grass. Dallas saw several men glance at the sky as if seeking a cloud that might account for it.

From one side to the other, with horns fully extended, warriors stretched for ten miles, moving in and around Kambula Hill so as to surround it completely. Out of range of the big guns they halted and divested themselves of all ceremonial covering, leaving only loincloths and necklaces specially made to provide the protection of tribal magic.

'Correct me if I'm wrong,' Dallas said dryly, trying to quell the nerves rising in his stomach. 'It seems to me that we might be somewhat outnumbered.'

Will grunted.

They were. Colonel Wood's force now totalled only two thousand, and of those, eighty-eight men were sick in the makeshift hospital.

'Here comes the right side,' Will observed, as he watched it advance. He sounded remarkably calm.

'Predictability will be their undoing one day,' Dallas replied, glad to hear his voice held none of the quivering he felt inside.

The Zulus since Shaka's day had attacked in a pincer-like formation. One horn usually made a mock charge which allowed those in the other to conceal themselves in long grass and sneak closer to the enemy. The chest, which had the greatest number of warriors, would then advance. Behind that lay a second large force. They would wait, their backs to the confrontation so that they could not observe it. This stopped them becoming over-excited, precipitating a premature charge. The chilling war chant, *uSuthu*, rang out. Thousand upon thousand baritone voices, raised in unison, had unnerved many a seasoned soldier. The entire battle would be overseen by a commanding officer who stayed well out of the fray, usually on a raised point of land, and was able to direct the action by sending runners with instructions.

Still out of artillery range, the right horn stopped again. Shouted taunts carried to the waiting British. 'We are the boys from Isandlwana.'

'What are they waiting for?' someone asked nervously.

Buller, well aware that with the right horn taking everyone's attention the left was probably in the process of creeping to within a hundred yards of them, went to Colonel Wood and suggested they provoke the right horn into a premature attack. Wood agreed.

'Come on, men. Let's show these bastards a thing or two.'

He took the Edendale troop of Natal Native Horse and those colonial forces still left to him, Dallas and Will among them. They rode boldly forward to within rifle range. Dismounting, the hundred or so men fired off a volley of shots against the two thousand *impi* of the right horn. Their audacity was too great and the Zulus swept towards them. Buller and his men mounted, fell back, dismounted and fired once more. In this way, they enticed the blood-lusting warriors well into range of the big guns before turning for the laager and galloping to safety. The Edendale Native Horse, who had been at Isandlwana and had no stomach for another resounding defeat, chose that moment to desert. They headed west.

The big guns opened up but their small bursting shells were more of an irritant than anything else. Still the swarming *impi* came on. As soon as they were within rifle range, the accuracy of

British marksmen took a devastating toll and finally forced them back. No-one, Zulu or European, realised at the time that disrupting the right horn's intention to join with the left, behind British lines, and effectively surround them, would become a turning point of the Zulu war. Warriors of the right horn were so demoralised they forgot orders and found cover in the rocky ground, resorting to rifle fire. Most only had single-shot muzzle-loaders. With their withdrawal, the chest and left horn immediately attacked.

'Christ!' someone yelled as seven-pounders blew huge holes in the Zulu ranks. 'Look at that. They just close up and keep coming.'

Dallas could hardly believe what he was seeing. The Zulus had little cover and no defence against artillery fire. Not once did they falter. Some even carried large stones on their heads which they threw to the ground and sheltered behind whenever firing in their direction became too intense. Wave after wave swept towards the garrison. Inevitably some made it into the laager, having miraculously survived the hail of shells and bullets.

One warrior, eyes red with fighting madness, a war chant emanating from deep within his chest, broke through and rushed at Dallas. It was *assegai* and shield against empty rifle and bayonet. Standing toe-to-toe, both men grappled for the upper hand. Dallas barely had time to register the shining black skin and rank odour of sweat before he was fighting for his life. Will was wrestling another Zulu next to him.

The Zulu was strong. Time and again he used his shield, deflecting the bayonet and trying to hook it so that he could pull the white man off balance and deliver an upward thrust with his *assegai*. Dallas knew he was weakening. Then, without warning, the African staggered backwards and slumped to the ground. Buller grimaced as he withdrew his bayonet from the man's back, then turned and dispatched Will's opponent in a similar fashion.

There was no time for thanks. Dallas rushed forward, knelt, reloaded and began firing again. The fighting continued for hours. At one stage the Zulus' left horn almost succeeded in overrunning the laager. They were driven off with bayonets.

Dallas, Will and the rest of the colonials were now firing under word of command. Buller, calm as can be, stood in the open, ramrod straight, snapping orders, never taking his eyes off the enemy. It was a courageous display of precision and discipline – attributes the *impi* had abandoned in the heat of battle – that turned the conflict in Britain's favour. With rifles nearly too hot to handle, the British coolly held their nerve and systematically repelled each new attack. By five in the afternoon, confidence had deserted the Zulus. They were preparing their retreat.

'Well done, men.' Buller's understatement went largely unheeded by the exhausted troops. Their commanding officer seemed indefatigable as he moved from man to man, slapping backs and sharing jokes. Suddenly, a long and loud cheer rang

643

out. The Zulus were falling back, turning to face a long walk to Hlobane. The garrison opened fire at will and what started as disciplined retreat became a desperate scramble to get beyond the range of rifle and artillery bombardment. But the Zulus' ordeal was far from over.

Bugles sounded 'to horse' and three columns led by Buller took off in hot pursuit after the fleeing *impi*. The cry rang out: 'No quarter, boys. Remember yesterday.'

Defeated and dispirited, not believing that all the strengthening and purification rites had let them down, the Zulus put up little or no resistance. For seven miles, Buller's men either shot them down or, in a display unworthy of the courage the *impi* had shown, speared them with their own discarded *assegais*. Dallas had no heart for it. Hundreds died during that retreat and he could not bring himself to account for even one of them. They deserved better.

Later, the morbid tally would reveal more than a thousand Zulus and eighteen British soldiers had died. Victory on Kambula Hill was the beginning of the end.

Well after dark, the garrison was still busy clearing the laager of dead or dying Zulus. Dallas, wandering aimlessly, found himself at the place where he'd gone hand-to-hand with a warrior. The man was still there. In the flickering light of burning torches he realised there was something familiar about the face frozen in death. One eye stared straight up, the other sideways. A sick feeling hit him in the guts as he crouched down next to the body. Tobacco had fought well. Dallas doubted the Zulu had recognised his foe.

'Shit!' The word wrung from him carried all the despair he felt about such a useless waste of life and a war that could so easily have been avoided.

Buller found him still crouched beside the body. 'Know him, do you, son?'

'Yes.' Dallas found his throat was tight. 'He saved my son's life.'

Buller squeezed Dallas on the shoulder. 'Hell of a business. We shouldn't be fighting these poor devils.'

Dallas dragged his eyes from his former employee, the man who had picked up Cam and run for the wagons in the face of charging ele-phants, and looked up. 'What happens now, sir?'

'We finish it,' Buller said firmly. 'Reinforce-ments have arrived from Britain. Lord Chelmsford has more recruits than he needs. Volunteers who wish to leave will be free to return home. Today we've demoralised half of Cetshwayo's army. Not many will take arms against us again.' Buller indi-cated Dallas's thigh. 'Get yourself to the hospital, Granger. I see you're wounded.' With that, he turned and walked away.

As Dallas rose, Will materialised from the dark-ness. 'Tobacco,' was all he said.

Will could only nod. He looked exhausted, and had a jagged gash across his forehead and a stab wound in one arm. His clothes were covered in grime and dried blood.

Dallas didn't doubt that he looked much the same. His thigh throbbed where the bullet had creased it at Hlobane. He presumed the wound had turned septic. There was a deep cut across his left palm and one boot had filled with blood after an *assegai* cut through the leather to flesh.

Suddenly everything ached. Dallas had a desperate need to lie down and close his eyes. 'Come on,' he said to Will. 'Let's get patched up.'

Will's arm needed stitches but his forehead was only bandaged. Dallas's thigh had turned red and ugly. The poison bubbled, fizzed and hurt like hell when an orderly poured peroxide into the wound. His hand and lacerated foot were cleaned up without difficulty.

The following morning, Will and Dallas were formally released from duty. Along with that of other volunteers, their departure further depleted British numbers on the battlegrounds of Zululand. Reinforcements were expected any day and the British wanted fully trained men for the final assault against Cetshwayo. The beautiful land of the past had gone. Bodies from the carnage of the day before still littered the ground. The garrison had cleared and buried only those close by. The rest were left for the scavengers and carrion eaters of Africa. It was a relief to turn away from such a distressing sight.

They took a chance and went to *Ludukaneni*. The kraals stood empty. What few cattle Dallas left behind were gone. Everything in the trading store had been stolen before the store itself was burnt to the ground. The schoolhouse also had gone up in flames. Surprisingly, the homestead was still standing, though many of its contents were no longer there.

The water pump still worked. They hand-pumped enough for baths and to wash their clothes. Feeling cleaner and more refreshed, Dallas found that the cellar had not been touched. Perhaps those who ransacked the house had decided not to bother with the dark cellar. Whatever the reason, dry field rations tasted so much better washed down by several bottles of decent red wine.

Whoever had taken most of the furniture had no use for beds. Dallas and Will slept on mattresses for the first time in nearly two months.

Just before drifting off to sleep, Dallas found himself wondering what Cetshwayo would do next. Would his army stand for more fighting? The tactics established by Shaka had made the Zulus unbeatable. Suddenly they faced the fact that these were no match for rifles and heavy artillery. The invincible *impi* and their famous *umkhumbi*, or horn formation, was a thing of the past. Some might fight again but would they ever muster the courage and tenacity that had so recently deserted them? They had been the stuff of legends in southern Africa. Now there was a superior force against which they had no response.

What about the king? Cetshwayo had done all he could to avoid a fight. But two things had worked against him. The British wanted his land, and his warriors, spurred on by a desperate need to wash their spears in blood in order to take wives, could not be contained. Today the once indestructible *impi* were returning to their kraals saying they had had enough. How could Cetshwayo still hope for victory? The best he could seek was a truce.

Would it be granted? Dallas didn't think so. Lord Chelmsford was determined to atone for the defeats at Isandlwana and Hlobane. He seemed consumed by a desire to capture the Zulu king. Perhaps the man believed that doing this would clear the stigma that attached to him over such an enormous loss of British lives.

Dallas and Will rode into Durban three days later. The two men said farewell outside Cato's store. Dallas turned a weary Tosca towards the Berea and home. He'd only been away a couple of months but it felt much longer. His body ached and his healing wounds itched. He longed to lie in a hot bath fragrant with one of Lorna's soothing herbal balms to soak away tension. He wanted the lingering smell of blood and sweat gone from his clothes, skin and hair. More than anything else, Dallas needed the softness of Lorna's perfumed body next to his, her sweet breath tickling his ear, her long, tapered fingers stroking tired muscles.

Tosca seemed to know they were headed home. She picked up her pace, ears pricked forward. Dallas imagined that she was thinking of a clean stable, soft straw, fresh water and the luxury of a good grooming. His mount had never let him down. He'd worked her hard and she deserved a little spoiling. Perhaps it was time for retirement, shady pastures and treats of apples and sugar.

He heard his children well before seeing them. They were playing on the front lawn – a game of cricket, by the sound of it. An unfamiliar male voice warned, 'Come on, Torben, that's not fair. Ellie can't handle that kind of speed. If you're going to play, then kindly remember she's only five.'

Frowning, because he recognised the voice but couldn't for the life of him think who it might be, Dallas turned into his front gate.

'Papa!' Cam spotted him first and came running. Ellie dropped the bat and was close behind. Torben took a couple of steps and stopped while little Kate hung shyly back, holding onto a man's hand.

Dallas dismounted just as Cam and Ellie launched themselves into his arms.

'You smell bad,' Cam said bluntly.

'He's been in a war, silly.' Ellie defended her father, although she kept one hand over her nose.

'Welcome home, Father.' Torben was formal.

'Yes, old boy, welcome home.'

Dallas finally recognised his brother. 'Where on earth did you come from?' He put Ellie and Cam down.

Boyd stepped up to Dallas and clapped him on a shoulder. 'Wanted to join in the fun. Requested a transfer to the 1st King's Dragoons. Seems like I've missed most of it.'

Dallas said nothing but picked up Kate. 'How's my little girl? I've missed you.'

Thumb in mouth, she snuggled into his chest.

He looked at his brother and boyhood memories skittered briefly through his tired brain. They had once been close. Had Boyd always squinted with his left eye? Was the gap between his two front teeth wider? Had his smile held a mocking quality all the time? Even his brother's accent sounded different, somehow out of place. It had been a total of eight, nearly nine, years since they'd seen each other. It was a shock to discover a breakdown in their connection – something Dallas had taken for granted. Where was the brotherly affection?

'When did you arrive?' he asked, more to give himself time to collect his thoughts than out of interest.

'Couple of weeks ago. Place is a bit basic, old boy. Don't know how you stand it.' Boyd flicked a small piece of lint from his scarlet tunic. 'So many damned savages,' he said, apropos of nothing, as if in those few words he could sum up the entire Zulu conflict.

'What about them?' Dallas found himself irritated.

Boyd shrugged carelessly. 'Time they were taught a lesson.'

He was spouting army rhetoric, repeating words like a performing parrot. Dallas supposed his brother was no different from other new arrivals. Why waste energy arguing with him? Boyd's bland acceptance of the status quo would most likely change once he'd seen the 'damned savages' in action. First his brother would have to shake off the arrogant belief that anything that wasn't British was simply not good enough. Realising he was staring, Dallas cleared his throat. 'Ulundi has to be taken but the Zulus are effectively defeated. I daresay you'll see action, if that is what you wish.'

'Well, yes, old boy, of course it is. We're heading north in a few days.'

'Good for you.'

The heavy irony was lost on Boyd. 'Where were you?'

'Kambula and Hlobane.'

His brother was envious. 'Lucky devil.'

'Lucky!' Impatient to see Lorna and preferring to greet his children than make conversation with a brother who saw action as an adventure, Dallas allowed his feelings to show. 'There's nothing lucky about mowing down a magnificent force of fighting men armed only with shields and spears. The Zulus didn't stand a chance.'

'They did well enough at Isandlwana.'

'Only because the British were stupid enough to think they were superior. They're not. Only their weapons are.'

Boyd looked surprised. 'Careful, old chap. That's treason you're talking.'

Dallas glanced towards the house. 'Where's Lorna?'

'Upstairs, at a guess. The little fellow isn't too well.'

'Duncan! What's wrong with him?'

'He's been sick for five days,' Cam told him. 'Mama has sent for the doctor several times.'

Dallas was suddenly, unreasonably angry. All he

wanted was to be at home with his family. He didn't want his youngest son to be ill, his wife distracted, or his brother waffling on about the excitement of war. 'Where's the groom?'

'You don't seem to have one, old chap.'

'I'll take Tosca,' Cam offered. 'Mister David is still away.'

Dallas nodded. It came as no surprise that Cetshwayo was reaching deep inside Natal for Zulu recruits.

'Here one day, gone the next,' Boyd put in, not understanding. 'Unreliable lot.'

Dallas's anger was reaching the explosive stage. With difficulty, he managed to control it. Boyd was, after all, his brother. 'Unreliable?' he queried. 'On the contrary.' His voice was harsher than intended. 'When the king calls he can rely on a full and immediate response.'

'The king?' Boyd's handsome face showed incomprehension.

'Cetshwayo,' Dallas said shortly.

'Oh, him.' Boyd dismissed the Zulus' ruler with the wave of a hand.

With sudden clarity, Dallas realised what was making him angry. Had he stayed in Scotland, he would most probably be exactly like Boyd. His brother had brought with him a shadow of the past that had no place in his life now. Dallas had moved beyond the mindless say-and-do formality of European society, thanks in no small part to the Zulu way of life. He turned to go. 'If you don't mind, I'd like to see Lorna.'

'And she's changed too,' Boyd went on, insensitive to Dallas's need to be with her. 'Just like her mother, if you ask me.'

Glancing at his brother, Dallas could see he had absolutely no understanding of, or willingness to accept, any kind of life outside a learned code of socially acceptable behaviour. His loss. Gently, Dallas put Kate down and she grabbed Boyd's proffered hand. Dallas turned and walked towards the house.

Percy greeted him in Zulu. With tears on his cheeks, he spoke. 'It is said that our *impi* are defeated.'

Dallas closed his eyes. He was weary. He wanted Lorna. 'They are still strong,' he responded gently. 'But in their hearts many are losing hope.'

'Why do you want war? What have we done?'

Percy's question was probably on every Zulu's lips. 'Why does the Zulu fight?' Dallas asked by way of answer. 'Is it not to gain cattle or land? Is it not to keep the enemy from getting too close? The British are no different.'

Percy bowed his head. When he looked up, his eyes were clear of moisture. 'It is so. Forgive me, master, for I am deeply troubled by our losses.'

Dallas knew he was speaking of land, rather than life. 'You have not lost anything, old man. It is still there but the time has come to share it.'

'Share!' Contempt shone briefly from Percy's eyes. 'The Zulu does not know this word. He conquers or is defeated. That is our way.'

'I know.' Dallas was full of understanding. This

man had probably fought more tribal wars than most and, in his breast, beat a heart filled with such pride that death would be preferable to defeat.

'Are we a lost people?' Percy queried.

Dallas owed him the truth. 'What did your great King Shaka say? " . . . You will not rule when I am gone, for the land will see locusts and white men come." I fear his words are true. The old days may be gone but your nation is established. Nobody can take that from you.'

'And what of now?'

'Now you taste the bitterness that Shaka fed to his enemies.'

'Then there is still a place for his people?'

'Yes, and always will be.'

'You understand,' Percy said slowly. 'Where others would cry in outrage. You are truly Zulu.'

Dallas smiled slightly. 'No. I cannot be one of you. But hear me well. Nothing stands still, old man. It is foolish to expect it to.'

'It would be unwise to believe we are a nation of the past. Many have underestimated us before and paid a heavy price,' Percy warned and changed the subject. 'Your youngest son is ill. The fever from mosquito is hot within him.'

'So I understand. I am anxious to see him.'

'I sent my daughters to the veld to sleep naked.'

'Thank you, old man. I appreciate what you have done.'

Percy turned and shuffled away. 'I will order hot water for your bath.'

Going up the stairs, Dallas was deeply touched

that, in spite of the war, Percy still cared enough to have his family try to assist Duncan. It was an old tradition, seldom seen these days. During an epidemic of any description, the young girls would leave their homes after dark to meet and sleep out in the open. They wore no clothes but, at daybreak, collected marsh grasses and made long skirts and capes to cover their shoulders and heads. Wearing these they returned home, singing and jumping over the very young children to protect them from becoming sick. The custom, called *umTshopi*, had probably been dropped as contact with Europeans made outbreaks of illness more prevalent, revealing the practice's inadequacies.

He could hear Lorna speaking softly to Duncan. She sat on the bed in his room, her back to the door. 'That's my little man. One more spoonful. Hold your nose and swallow.'

The medicine was quinine. The taste, as Dallas knew from experience, was terrible. Duncan, not surprisingly, had reached the same conclusion. Dallas moved further into the room. 'Hello, my darling,' he said softly.

Lorna looked round, startled. 'Dallas,' she breathed. 'Oh, thank God!'

Dallas gazed down at his youngest son. Gaunt and ill, he still had enough strength to wave off the spoon.

'How is he?'

'I've been desperately worried but he's over the worst. We're getting liquids into him and this morning he took a little porridge. Oh, Dallas, it is so good to see you. Can you stay? Will you be called away again?'

'I don't think so. The garrison is full to the brim with fresh-faced death-or-glory idiots. Let them mop up.'

Duncan's eyes were closing. Lorna rose from beside him. 'He'll sleep now. Poor little man.'

'Percy is arranging hot water. Come and scrub my back.' Dallas took Lorna's hand and they went to their room. The look on her face told him that if he tried to hold her, she'd object. He didn't blame her. Stripping, he could smell his own body odour.

With a towel around his waist, he watched the tub fill with steaming hot water. It looked so inviting. Percy came in with the last of it.

'Will the master be requiring these clothes?' he asked, indicating the discarded garments while testing the bathwater with one finger.

'Not those,' Dallas replied. 'Burn them.'

Percy picked up the clothing and held it as far away from himself as possible.

'You can shut the door, too.' Lowering himself into the tub, he could not prevent a sigh of delicious relief. 'Ahhhhh!'

Lorna returned and poured oil into the bath. The steam soon carried the refreshing scent of camphor, thyme and sassafras. She removed his bandages, fussing over the injuries. 'Was it bad?' she asked gently.

'The worst thing was knowing the Zulus didn't stand a chance. They knew it too. Their bravery was incredible.' He would not be drawn into details of battles and spared her the news of Tobacco's death.

She heard him out in silence. Then, her eyes anxious, she asked about Will.

'He's fine. I left him at Cato's. Says he's heading into Swaziland to start a trading store.'

Lorna looked relieved to learn that their friend was still alive. She busied herself washing Dallas's hair, cleaned the wounds, then called Percy. 'Tip this out and bring fresh water, please.'

Back in the bath, unashamedly enjoying such luxury, Dallas shaved while Lorna leaned on the side, watching him hungrily.

'I missed you,' she told him huskily.

He planted a wet, soapy kiss on her lips. 'And I you.'

She leaned forward and the kiss lengthened.

Dallas rose, dripping from the tub and scooped her up in his arms.

It felt so good to have her close to him. The past weeks slipped away. Desire competed with the need to savour their closeness. Desire won. Later, lying together, a jumble of arms and legs, they remembered Boyd.

'I met my brother downstairs. Is he staying here?'

'As good as. He seems to think he's in charge.'

'I'm sure you put him right.'

'I tried. Boyd doesn't seem to listen.' She frowned a little. 'Do you think he's changed?'

Dallas smiled. 'We're the ones who've changed.'

'If he calls me "my dear, gentle lady" one more time, I swear, darling, I'll shred him with my nails.'

He laughed and hugged her. A wave of happiness washed over him. This was his world. Here he felt completely at ease. Outsiders might interfere but for as long as Lorna and the children were beside him, they could do no harm.

Lorna snuggled into him. 'Mmm.'

'What's that supposed to mean?' he teased.

She arched an eyebrow at him. 'If it needs explanation, sir, forget I mentioned it.'

He pretended to leer. 'Give me fifteen minutes.'

'Fifteen! You're getting old, Dallas.' Her smile was wicked.

Before going downstairs they looked in on Duncan. He was sleeping peacefully. Lorna placed two fingers lightly against the baby's forehead. 'No fever.'

'He's very pale,' Dallas worried.

Queenie sat in one corner of the room, quietly crocheting. 'He will get better,' she told them without looking up. Beside her was a clay pot. Neither Dallas nor Lorna mentioned it but both felt comforted by its presence. Whatever brew the Zulus had mixed for their son, they knew it could only assist in the healing process.

'When he wakes, give him some barley water,' Lorna told her.

'I have prepared porridge.'

'Good. See if he'll have some. But he will need a lot of water as well.'

Arm in arm, they left the room and went downstairs. Boyd was standing in the parlour reading.

Every line of his erect body showed disapproval. 'Where are the children?' Lorna asked.

'In the kitchen,' he replied, not looking up from the book. 'The cook has made bread. Those little ruffians don't even let it cool down.'

Lorna laughed and Dallas grinned.

Boyd closed the book carefully and placed it on a table. 'I don't see anything funny about it,' he said, sounding put out. 'They need more discipline. They're little savages. Cameron will not use the bathroom. He . . . urinates wherever he likes. It's disgusting. Eleanor has begun to copy him. They're half naked most of the time. Running around barefoot can't be good for them either. What Mama and Papa would make of them is beyond comprehension.'

Dallas felt irritation rising inside him but it was Lorna who pounced on Boyd's criticism. 'Don't be such a stuffy old bore,' she said. 'They're the healthiest children in the world.'

'Really!' Boyd thought he'd found a weakness. 'I assume you include Duncan in that.'

'Duncan is recovering,' Lorna responded crisply. 'Malaria is a fact of life out here.' She hesitated, then added wickedly, 'In fact, Boyd, you're bound to suffer a bout or two in Zululand.'

He ignored that. 'If you kept the children covered and amused by indoor games, malaria wouldn't be a problem.'

'Indeed,' Lorna agreed. 'Wouldn't that be cruel in this beautiful climate?'

'I don't think you're listening,' Boyd said

scathingly. 'Others I've met are not so short-sighted with their children. How yours will ever take their place in society is beyond me. They don't know how to behave.'

Lorna pretended to yawn, tapping two fingers against her mouth in an elaborate 'ho hum' gesture.

Dallas had heard enough. That his brother disapproved was one thing, that he felt he had every right to openly criticise was quite another. 'You are welcome to visit our home,' Dallas told him, 'but on the condition you respect our private lives. Frankly, Boyd, I don't give a damn what you think of us.' He broke off as Percy appeared at the door.

'There is a madam asking to speak with you, sir. And a man who says he is her father.'

'Who is it?'

Percy looked uncomfortable. 'The madam is saying she is your wife.'

'Shit!' Lorna's expletive wasn't quiet and Boyd looked at her in horror. She stared right back. 'Shit!' she said again. 'Or would you prefer something more pithy?'

Boyd had been rendered speechless.

'Show them in,' Dallas told Percy. 'Let's see what brings them here.'

They heard Mr Wilcox before he entered the room. 'I will do the talking.'

'Yes, Father.'

Wilcox strode into the parlour like an aggressive bull mastiff, bandy legs, jaw thrust out, eyes bulging and teeth bared in what passed for a smile. He nodded curtly to Lorna. 'Madam.'

Lorna responded in kind. 'Sir.'

He stared pointedly at Boyd. Dallas introduced the father and daughter to his brother. He noticed how Sarah kept her eyes demurely down. She'd make a good Zulu, Dallas thought nastily.

Formalities over, Dallas waited for Wilcox to state his business. The man seemed reluctant. 'Granger, glad to catch you at home.'

'I've returned this very day,' Dallas responded somewhat bluntly. 'Would you care for refreshment?'

'No, no. We'll only stay a moment.'

Silence descended on the room – the mantle clock sounded loud and monotonous. Finally, Dallas asked, 'How may I help you, sir?'

Wilcox would not be drawn. 'Come, Granger, we've had our differences in the past. Can we not bury old hostilities, eh?'

This was too much. 'We have no regard for each other, sir. Kindly state the reason for your visit.'

The jovial facade cracked. Hatred flared briefly in the older man's eyes. When he spoke, his voice was hard. 'Is there anywhere we may speak in private?'

'My study.' Dallas led the way.

Alone, and with the door shut behind them, it was clear to Dallas that whatever had brought Wilcox was making him exceedingly uncomfortable. He seemed uncharacteristically unsure of himself and plainly didn't like it. 'Believe me, Granger, it gives me no pleasure to see you again.'

'The feeling is mutual.'

'Don't be insolent, you young puppy.'

'This is my home,' Dallas reminded him. 'For God's sake, man, tell me what brings you here and be gone.'

The blunt rudeness caused Wilcox to suck air between his teeth. He clenched both fists in an effort to remain calm. 'Do you wish to hear what I have to say?' he shouted suddenly. 'I did not come here to be insulted.'

Yes, but you make it so easy. Dallas did not allow his thoughts to show. He waited for Wilcox to calm down.

With a sigh, the man stated his reason for the visit. 'I came here tonight to offer you release from a contract you obviously have no intention of honouring.'

'In return for what?'

Wilcox glared at him. 'Upon my honour, sir, your disrespect knows no bounds.'

'Do not speak to me of honour,' Dallas said cuttingly. 'You have none. Nor, for that matter, do I respect you. What do you want?'

'You have ruined my daughter's life. Some compensation should be forthcoming. You are not a rich man, I know that. But the marchioness is very wealthy. What is freedom to marry her worth to you both?'

The rush of anger nearly overwhelmed Dallas. 'So,' he said in a hard voice, 'divorce has a price. I should have known. What a nasty piece of work you are, Wilcox.'

Anger darkened the older man's face. 'And as

for your honour, sir, you and that scarlet woman are the laughing stock of Durban.'

'Lady Lorna is no scarlet woman, you black-mailing bastard.' Dallas delivered the words with quiet venom. 'You and you alone forced us into this situation.'

Under the bluster, Wilcox was a coward. He backed away from outright confrontation. 'I have no desire to discuss this further,' he said, pale in the face of Dallas's anger. 'I have no reason to like you. You broke my daughter's heart.'

'Did I?' Dallas spoke coolly, despite an over-whelming desire to pick up the poker and bring it down on Wilcox's sweaty head.

'Indeed you did, sir.'

Dallas was suddenly tired of the charade. 'Get out. Take your conniving daughter and leave us be.'

'And the money?'

'What price would you pay for my continued silence about the real father of Sarah's child?'

'You wouldn't dare.'

'Push me too far, Wilcox, and I'll dare.'

'Then I would be obliged to contact the police about you.'

'Stalemate,' Dallas said softly.

'No, sir, you have more to lose than I.'

'Do I?' Dallas locked eyes with his father-in-law's.

The older man's eyes slid away. 'You will hear from me again, Granger. I will not permit you to treat Sarah in such a scurrilous manner. You *will* pay or, by God, the hangman's rope will be your last sight on this earth.'

Dallas turned his back and stared through the window into the dark beyond. 'Go to hell,' he said quietly. 'The sight of you sickens me.'

Wilcox was set to argue then nodded abruptly at the forbidding back. 'I bid you goodnight, sir.' He turned and left the room.

Fuming, Dallas remained in the study until he heard Sarah and her father leave. Would Wilcox carry through his threat? All the fine words about his daughter's reputation meant nothing to the man. Greed was what motivated him. Interesting, though, that when Dallas threatened him back, Wilcox lost confidence, resorting to bluff rather than demands. In a decidedly sour frame of mind, Dallas returned to the parlour.

Boyd's shocked reaction to the discovery that Dallas was married, not to Lorna as he'd supposed, but to another, was ill-timed and unwelcome. Dallas had no patience for it.

'Oh, do shut up,' he snapped. 'I'm not the slightest bit interested in your ridiculous posturing.'

Boyd blithely carried on. 'That poor, wee girl. Shame on both of you. It would seem that Africa has turned you against all that is decent.'

'If you don't mind,' Dallas ground out, 'there are some things Lorna and I need to discuss.' When Boyd made no move to leave, he added, 'In private.'

'Don't worry about me.' Boyd sat down and crossed his legs. 'As an older brother it is my beholden duty –'

'To realise when your presence is not welcome.' Dallas rubbed a hand over his eyes and relented.

'For God's sake, Boyd, you don't know the half of it. That little vixen lied and forced me to marry her. Her father blackmailed me to remain her husband. There is no love lost between any of us. I would marry Lorna in the wink of an eye were I free to do so. Your advice may be well meant but it is ill-advised.'

'Even so,' Boyd said stiffly, not hiding his hurt, 'you place the Marchioness of Dumfries in a most untenable position. I urge you both to remain apart until there is no impediment to your becoming husband and wife.'

Dallas's and Lorna's eyes met. In hers he saw a big, bad temper brewing. She was about to blow and Dallas didn't blame her.

Dallas intervened, although he didn't feel much calmer than Lorna.

'Since you seem impervious to suggestions that we'd like some privacy you leave me no alternative. Please go. I have been away for almost two months and wish to spend time with my family. As you seem incapable of anything other than criticism, that does not include you.'

Boyd turned to Lorna. It was a big mistake. 'Dear, gentle lady, can you not see the sense in what I'm saying?'

She faced him, fists clenched by her sides. 'I'll tell you what I see,' she cut back. 'Someone I once thought I knew and liked. My mistake. You are the most arrogant and boring bloody man I have ever had the misfortune of meeting. How dare you suggest that Dallas and I live apart? We have children, or have you forgotten them? Keep your opinions to yourself, Boyd. I, for one, don't wish to hear them.'

Mouth open, Boyd could only stammer, 'But, my lady.'

Dallas intervened before Lorna really blew her top. He pointed a finger at her. 'This is Lorna de Iongh, you idiot. Remember? You've only known her since she was born. Do stop all this nonsense. It has no place in our home.'

'Well, really.' Boyd stood and patted down his tunic. 'I can see there's no point in appealing to your morals, or anything else decent, for that matter. I'll bid you both goodnight.'

Rolling his eyes in relief, Dallas walked his older brother to the door. But Boyd had one more thing on his mind and, true to form, was determined to mention it. 'Will you be joining the final push on Ulundi?'

'No.'

'Why not?'

'I've done my bit.'

'But surely,' Boyd protested, 'you have a duty?'

Dallas ignored that. 'Chelmsford has more than enough men. Ulundi will be easy. In their own minds, the Zulus are already defeated. Nothing can save them now.'

'You sound as though you actually like them.' Boyd was ready for his soapbox again. 'They're the enemy, dear boy.'

'Not to me. They've shown me nothing but kindness, friendship and generosity. The Zulus are my friends. I have no wish to fight them.'

'Friends!' Boyd was astonished. 'They're savages, the whole lot. You've only got to look at them.'

'Oh, you'll be doing plenty of that, believe me. I hope your eyes are wide enough. When you see the *impi* stretched ten miles or more across the plain and hear twenty thousand voices shouting *uSuthu*, you may well think of them as savage. Look again. See the discipline as they flow into battle formation. Then, as your hair stands on end and a chill runs up your spine, you might just realise there's intelligence and experience in what you're seeing, so you'd better do something pretty damned quick or you'll be surrounded. See then if you still think they're savages. They are brave and determined adversaries, standing against us with little more than shield and *assegai*, knowing they're no match for soldiers' guns. God help you if they get close enough to use them. As you're fighting for your life you might actually realise that the Zulu is superior to you. It could well be the last thought you'll ever have, but if you survive and are forced down from that ivory tower, it might make you see sense. Then again, since you are so certain that right is on your side and the Zulus little more than animals, it might not.'

Boyd listened to the tirade with a slightly mocking expression on his face. He was hearing the words though their meaning was too far removed from everything he'd been told by others for him to grasp it. When Dallas paused, Boyd merely asked, 'What's got into you, old boy?'

'You,' Dallas said bluntly. 'You and your damned

arrogance, your stupid airs and graces, your biased opinions. Damn it, man, you've only just set foot in this place. What gives you the right to judge anybody? The Zulus or me. Get out there and take the blinkers off.'

That got through but the sardonic look remained. 'You've changed.'

'Yes,' Dallas agreed. 'I've found reality, and I'm happy to say, Lorna has too.'

'People are talking about you.'

'So what? Let them.'

Boyd picked up his cape, hat and cane from the hallstand. 'Why couldn't you stay with your wife? She struck me as being rather a nice little thing. Sort of filly I'd look for.'

'Help yourself,' Dallas said crudely, opening the front door. 'Oh, one more thing,' he added. 'If you do take up with Sarah, a point to bear in mind. She also likes Zulus.' With that, he bid his brother goodnight.

Lorna had heard his raised voice and come to investigate. When he turned towards her with a large and satisfied smile on his face, she had to ask why.

'Because,' he said, wrapping her in a bear hug, 'I'm a mean old thing.'

'You are not,' she protested loyally. 'Just a little excitable, perhaps.' She pulled back and looked at him. 'What did Sarah and her father want?'

Dallas filled her in. 'It would seem that the scandal of a divorce is of little concern compared with the whiff of money.'

'I have plenty –'

'No.'

She tilted her head and stared at him. 'You have a mulish look on your face.'

'So do you.'

'You're not going to pay him, admit it.'

'Not if I can help it.'

'Can we talk about it at least?'

He kissed her nose. 'Of course.'

'Dammit, Dallas,' Lorna burst out, stamping her foot. 'Stop being so bloody reasonable. If I can help, then why –'

A sudden shriek sounded from the kitchen, followed by a crash and the sound of Kate crying. 'Welcome home, my darling.' Lorna extricated herself from his arms. 'We can discuss this later. I'm going up to check on Duncan. You can deal with this.'

'You're too kind.' Dallas leaned forward and kissed her nose again.

She grinned at him. 'Will Sarah really divorce you if you pay?'

'So Wilcox says, and he appears to have control over her life.' Whatever was happening in the kitchen grew in volume until Dallas could no longer ignore it.

'Will we get married?'

'I'm supposed to ask.'

'So ask.'

'Will you marry me?'

'Damned right.' She turned and ran lightly up the stairs leaving him smiling like a fool.

'Master.' Percy appeared. He had undergone some kind of transformation. The Zulu was stark white from head to toe.

On closer inspection, Dallas discovered the reason. Flour. 'What happened?'

Percy told him in one word. 'Torben.'

Sighing, Dallas headed for the kitchen. Life was back to normal. In spite of Boyd's unwanted intrusion and that blackmailing son of a whore, Wilcox, Dallas couldn't have been happier.

SIXTEEN

Over the next few months Lorna and Dallas were in a kind of limbo. They were stuck in Durban until the war was over. It seemed to them that Lord Chelmsford was in no particular hurry to end the conflict.

This was not strictly true, however. Chelmsford himself commanded the relief of Colonel Pearson's right-hand column, which had been virtually imprisoned in the Eshowe mission for three months. It was why he ordered Colonel Evelyn Wood to create a diversion at Hlobane. Five days after Kambula Hill, Chelmsford was successful, his Gatling guns, rockets and rifles defeating some twelve thousand *impi*. In truth, the heart had already been torn from Cetshwayo's army. The battle lasted only twenty minutes and left a thousand of them dead and dying.

In Durban, John Dunn, who had personally scouted the Zulus' position and strength, told Dallas of the confrontation.

'Cetshwayo still forbids his *impi* to attack at night. They moved in at dawn under cover of a thick mist. As soon as it cleared, every man he had came at us.' Dunn gave a sardonic chuckle. 'Some of our boys had never seen action, let alone a bloody Zulu warrior. It was quite a sight, but the old spirit was lacking. They didn't get close enough to use *assegais*.'

'Poor bastards,' Dallas said quietly.

'Yeah.' Dunn sighed deeply, then gave vent to his frustration. 'I want this thing to stop. It's nothing short of murder. Why prolong the inevitable? Britain is being bloody criminal. I'm telling you, man, it may sound sentimental but this so-called war is a farce. Cetshwayo has tried to call it off. His *impi* are starting to refuse to stand against our weapons. Why doesn't Chelmsford take Ulundi and be done with it?'

'You could get out of it. Why stay?'

Dunn rubbed a hand over his face. 'There are reasons. I can't talk about them.'

Dallas could see that his friend was a man in deep emotional pain. Dallas himself had found it hard enough fighting a people he had come to respect. It would be so much more difficult for John.

It was another three months before Lord Chelmsford was ready to attack the capital. The delay was supposedly so that reinforcements had time to acclimatise. More importantly, though, horses accompanying the newly arrived troops were in poor condition after being confined on board ship for so long. They needed time to rebuild their strength.

Life, in the interim, drifted slowly for Dallas and

Lorna. Rumours reaching them indicated that, once Ulundi had fallen, Zululand would be segmented into smaller kingdoms or chieftainships, completely fragmenting the fragile bonds ruled over by Cetshwayo.

Boyd, who had anticipated action would occur much more quickly, remained in Durban and continued his moral crusade over his brother's living arrangements. (Mercifully, he was increasingly required at the garrison.) Time didn't help to change his attitude about the Zulus, either. Without understanding anything beyond a master and servant relationship, Boyd had formed judgment and condemned them as primitive, lazy and untrustworthy. Dallas and Lorna continued to find his company tedious in the extreme, only tolerating it because of family obligations.

The news of the sudden and unexpected death of Lorna's mother from tuberculosis did at least serve to cancel the warrant that still existed for Dallas's arrest. Lady Pamela wrote that Lord de Iongh had lost more than his wife. The man appeared to have given up interest in everything. After withdrawing an accusation he had always known to be false, he had retired completely from public life. Dallas was free to return to Scotland.

Lorna was not badly affected by the news, as she hadn't been close to either of her parents. Of more significance was the fact that Dallas's name had been cleared. 'Now at least we can go back for a holiday,' was all she said.

Dallas had become so used to the fact that

disgrace hung over his head he found it impossible to believe he was no longer a wanted man until a letter arrived from Lord Diamond, the British diplomat who had travelled to Africa aboard the *Marie Clare* with Dallas. In it was confirmation of everything Lady Pamela had written. Dallas was a free man.

Although the news was welcome, it was the freedom to marry Lorna that Dallas craved. He sent a brief note to the diplomat thanking him for taking the trouble to let him know. Lord Diamond responded with an offer of a position within the Cape Town administration. Dallas declined.

John Dunn, whenever he was in town, stayed at the Berea house. The young trader, Stephen Holgate, who Dallas had met in Colenso and talked of trading in the Thukela Valley, was another regular visitor.

The Zulu war had attracted world attention, drawing more adventurers to Africa than ever. Among them was Cecily Jerome, an American socialite. Lorna finally had a kindred spirit with whom she could discuss all the womanly things Dallas found trivial. Cecily was a breath of fresh air. Her first cousin, Jennie, had married Lord Randolph Churchill and produced one son – Winston. Lorna realised she'd met someone as plain-spoken as herself when Cecily blandly stated, 'The damned man is a political, social and intellectual bore. He hates women. Poor Jennie has a terrible life. And as for their son, God knows how he'll turn out – the boy spends all his time alone, playing with toy soldiers.'

Cecily had come to Africa with zoological and anthropological aspirations, having had the great misfortune of being born with a scientific mind. In her words, 'I can read and write, thanks to a governess. My needlework is exquisite. Endless tedious hours each week with the dreary and impoverished Miss O'Neill from Dublin saw to that. God I hated that woman. I play the pianoforte with daintiness and verve. Now there's a contradiction in terms.'

Lorna found her honest and amusing. 'Who told you that?'

'My tutor.' Cecily smiled wickedly. 'A gentle, dreamy young man of some rather aberrational sexual theories and very little talent. He taught music as if he was afraid of it.' Cecily made a moue. 'I begged to be taught Latin and Greek, pleaded with Father to find someone who could tutor me in physiology. All to no avail. Nice young ladies must never sully their minds with such masculine specialities. Heaven forbid that the male of our species feels intellectually inferior. It simply isn't done, my dear.'

Despite the lightness of her words, Lorna sensed an anger in Cecily. 'You must have had some tutoring?'

'Books,' Cecily said. 'I taught myself. That is why I'm never taken seriously.' She gave Lorna a wry grin. 'Bloody men and their egos.'

One such bloody man and his ego fell foul of Cecily's keen intelligence within seconds of meeting her. Boyd expressed patronising concern that she intended travelling to the rugged west coast with nothing but Africans for company. 'My dear lady,' he protested. 'Forget such foolishness.'

'Foolishness?' Cecily repeated, a steely glint in her eye.

Lorna and Dallas sat back and unashamedly enjoyed what amounted to a thorough shredding of Boyd's masculine prejudices. Cecily did such a good job that Boyd developed a sudden headache and begged off lunch, leaving the others relieved and unrepentant.

Dallas also liked Cecily. Not only had her company been good for Lorna, whenever she was around, the conversation was lively and stimulating. One day someone asked why she habitually wore a revolver tucked into her wide belt.

'I should have thought it obvious,' she replied coolly. 'One hopes not to need it but one is aware that if one does, one needs it bloody fast.'

It was a sad day indeed when Cecily, dressed on Lorna's recommendation in trousers, set off on her travels. They heard, via the gossip grapevine, that on crossing the falls at Howick, she encountered Stephen Holgate heading for Durban with ivory. Cecily and Stephen had heard of each other from Lorna and Dallas but, so far, had not met. So taken was the trader with the American woman that he entrusted the load of ivory to his gun bearer and joined her. Scandalised ladies of quality and vaguely envious gentlemen of excellent breeding eagerly repeated snippets of rumour that filtered back to Durban. Cecily and Stephen behaved, 'for all the world as though they were wed'.

Lorna and Dallas were delighted.

Boyd left Durban for Zululand in the middle of May 1879, his being the only squadron of the 1st King's Dragoon Guards to join Lord Chelmsford. The rest of his regiment, under the command of Major-General Hugh Clifford, was responsible for administration and keeping the communication lines open between Durban and the Zululand border.

'Bit of luck, old chap,' Boyd enthused. 'I'd have been awfully miffed to come all this way only to miss out.'

Dallas had long since given up trying to talk sense to his brother. He shook Boyd's hand, wished him well and was damned glad to see the back of him.

It was suddenly obvious that the planned attack on Ulundi was imminent. After what had seemed like delaying tactics, events moved swiftly. John Dunn and his scouts crossed into Zululand at the Lower Thukela Drift. Under the command of Major-General H.H. Crealock, a coastal column would advance to St Paul's mission station, twenty-five miles from the royal kraal at Ulundi.

Colonel Evelyn Wood and his men, having advanced from Kambula Hill, were already in position and waiting to join forces with Chelmsford.

The overall commander and his Ulundi column crossed Rorke's Drift and detoured some forty-five miles in order to avoid Isandlwana where, four months after the battle, British corpses still lay scattered on the ground.

The British closed on the capital like a giant predator with arms outstretched. Cetshwayo, desperate to avoid a final confrontation, sent gifts and messages to Lord Chelmsford. In return, he received demands that were impossible to meet. It seemed that nothing could prevent the final crushing blow. Two days after Chelmsford entered Zululand, an event took place that sealed the fate of the Zulu nation more effectively than anything which had taken place already.

From Durban, Dallas and Lorna followed this build-up with horror but also an increasing impatience for the war to end. Little news reached them about Cetshwayo. The king had gone quiet, presumably attending to affairs put on hold over the past months. Then, in May, they heard that runners had been dispatched, summoning warriors to Ulundi. They also learned that Cetshwayo had found it necessary to repeat the command before his army agreed to muster.

Even as the king called his *impi,* he never let up trying to negotiate a peaceful solution. As messenger after messenger returned to Ulundi with refusals or impossible demands, Cetshwayo was in despair. He sent a plea to Chelmsford. 'What have I done? I want peace – I ask for peace.'

The response was more demanding than ever.

'They knew he'd never agree. They want him crushed,' Dallas said angrily. 'The British will settle for nothing less.'

As they witnessed the inevitable death of a

nation, other matters also came to the fore. Dallas had one last, thoroughly agreeable, confrontation with his father-in-law. Invited for a drink, Sarah's father arrived looking suspicious. It was the first time ever that his son-in-law had requested a meeting.

In the study, Dallas turned to face the man he disliked above all others. 'All charges against me in Britain have been dropped,' he began.

Wilcox's expression changed to one of apprehension.

'Therefore,' Dallas went on, 'you no longer represent any kind of threat to my freedom.'

'Come, come,' Wilcox tried to bluster. 'A gentleman's word and all that.'

'A divorce will go through which you will instigate immediately. If you try to disrupt the proceedings I shall make a public statement in my defence. It won't make pretty reading. Sarah's reputation, which you claim to be so concerned with, will be in tatters. I can even produce the child. And you, sir, can expect to be charged with blackmail. The choice is yours.'

'Dallas . . . son . . . you don't mean it.'

'Every word.'

Wilcox knew he was beaten. He left the Berea house and Dallas never saw him again.

Defeat, however, did not prevent the man, through lawyers, from trying to milk all he could from his son-in-law. There were times when Dallas felt that things were actually going backwards.

'Don't get so angry,' Lorna told Dallas.

'I want to marry you, damn it,' Dallas fumed. 'Is that so hard to understand?'

Lorna giggled, and after some moments of trying to remain serious, Dallas also saw the funny side.

'Sorry.' He grinned slightly, ashamed of taking his frustration out on her.

'So you should be,' she said. 'A woman in my condition deserves more respect.'

'Another one? Good God, woman, you're like a rabbit.' He held her close. 'My rabbit. I love you.'

'After this, no more,' she mumbled around his lips. 'I'm losing my figure.'

'You are not.' His hands slid down over her buttocks. 'You still have the body of a young girl.'

It was true. Dallas never tired of watching Lorna. He delighted in her enthusiasm for life, disregard for society's rules and obvious love for him. She was as beautiful now as the debutante who had first captured his heart. Dallas continued to love her with his entire soul.

The children were another source of pleasure. Torben continued to be disruptive but had found some satisfaction in his passion for learning. He thrived in Durban, stimulated by the energy of a growing city. Lorna and Dallas sometimes worried about his solitary nature – the boy seemed to have no friends – yet, in the main, he was content.

Cam was also of concern to his parents, with his obvious reluctance to take on anything remotely resembling education. The lad loved animals and the bush. He had many friends but preferred the company of Zulu children. Cam couldn't wait for the war to be over so they could move back to Zululand.

Ellie's fascination with matters medical continued. Cecily Jerome had totally fallen in love with her and, if anything else were needed to cement the friendship between Lorna and Cecily, it was Lorna's determination that, should Ellie wish it, her interests would be actively encouraged.

Kate had become a tiny replica of Lorna. Physically, that is. Otherwise, she was gentle and compliant. 'Where did that come from?' Lorna asked Dallas more than once. 'She's not the least bit like us.'

'No, she's her own person,' Dallas always replied. 'Nothing wrong with that.'

Duncan recovered from malaria and went back to stripping wallpaper. Paper, as far as he was concerned, was for tearing. All their books had to be kept under lock and key. Likewise, important personal documents. Give Duncan a *Natal Mercury* and he was in baby heaven.

'Do you think he'll grow out of it?' Lorna worried.

'I sincerely hope so,' Dallas said. 'He's getting taller. The paintings will be next.'

In his increasing impatience for a return to Zululand Dallas sought an interview with the newly appointed High Commissioner, General Sir Garnet Wolseley, who had been sent out to hasten the end of the war.

It was generally acknowledged that, at long last, Britain wanted the Zulu conflict to be over and done with. Isandlwana and Hlobane were embarrassing defeats. The prolonged siege of Eshowe had been humiliating. If Chelmsford couldn't deliver victory, Wolseley, according to him, would. As he was such a busy man, Dallas was surprised that the High Commissioner agreed to see him.

'I've read your submission,' Wolseley said, shaking Dallas's hand. 'How can I be of assistance?'

'A simple yes or no would do it,' Dallas replied. He had asked about the possibility of returning to his farm when the war was over.

Wolseley nodded. 'No.'

Taken aback by the blunt response, all Dallas could manage was, 'Thank you.'

Wolseley fiddled with a waxed end of his moustache. With the other hand, he tapped a finger on Dallas's written request. 'When this is over, Zululand will need men like you. That's why I agreed to this meeting.' He rose and went to a map on the wall, smiling slightly at the expression on Dallas's face. 'No doubt you've heard the rumours. As you can see by these red ink lines, Zululand is to be divided into thirteen chieftainships.'

'You can't be serious!' Dallas was appalled to have this confirmed. 'There will be anarchy. Within months, the clans will be fighting each other.'

Wolseley shrugged. 'Zululand will eventually be annexed to Britain. Some breakdown of law and order would serve our purpose admirably.' His finger traced the southern extremities of the territory from east to west. 'This is where you should look for a farm.'

Dallas stared at the map. John Dunn's land, all of it. Was this why John had continued to offer his services as a scout? 'You would make Dunn a chief?'

'A king, if he so wishes.'

'Just to create a convenient buffer between the Zulus and Natal?'

Wolseley inclined his head.

'What would happen to Cetshwayo's heir?'

'Dinuzulu? That's up to Her Majesty.' Wolseley tapped a coastal stretch. 'I hear you're a cattle man. Take some good advice. Sugar. The climate here is perfect for it. Any request for land to grow sugar-cane will be favourably viewed by Dunn.'

'He's a cattle man too.'

'So I believe.' Wolseley permitted himself a small smile. 'It was nice to meet you, Granger.' His out-stretched hand signalled an end to the meeting.

Lorna was shocked when she heard. 'So John has sold out.'

'What else could he do? They threw him a very tempting carrot. A chieftainship ensures his contin-ued lifestyle, the only one he wants.'

'It won't be easy. He'll have to jump whenever the administration says. Become their puppet. I would never have expected that of him.'

'Don't judge John too harshly, darling. I think even Cetshwayo would understand. Besides, know-ing John, he'll find ways to get around red tape.'

News broke the next day of the event that has-tened a final confrontation and an official end to the Zulu war. Lord Chelmsford, much to his dismay, had been given responsibility for the safe keeping of the French Prince Imperial, Louis Napoleon, son of the late Napoleon III and Empress Eugenie. Louis came from a fiercely proud military background. At twenty-three years of age, he had spent the last nine of those exiled in Britain with his mother. Four years earlier, he had passed out seventh in a class of thirty-four from the Royal Military Academy at Woolwich. Desperate for active duty, the Prince Imperial had to be content with theoretical manoeuvres at Aldershot. Disraeli was not prepared to accept responsibility for any mishap that might befall a young man regarded as Napoleon IV by many of his countrymen.

When reinforcements left Britain for South Africa, Louis wanted to go too. Disraeli refused to allow it. Faced with pressure from the queen, and much against his better judgment, the British Prime Minister was forced to change his mind. He insisted, however, that the prince go under his own volition and as a spectator only.

Louis presented himself to Chelmsford bearing a letter from the Duke of Cambridge asking that he be allowed to observe as much field activity as was possible. He also bore a testimonial from the Governor of Woolwich, which praised his military qualities. Both letters of recommendation contained warnings that the prince was inclined to be impetuous. Faced with his obvious backing by Queen Victoria and the Prime Minister, Lord Chelmsford had no option but to graciously, though reluctantly, accept him as an aide-de-camp.

Realising how serious the ramifications would be should anything happen to this claimant of the French throne, a country that was not exactly fond of Britain, Chelmsford placed Louis in the care of his most trusted officer. Lieutenant-Colonel Redvers Buller took the prince on one patrol. He refused to take him out again. When pressed for a reason, Buller bluntly stated that the prince's hot-headed disobedience under fire could cause a serious incident for which he saw no reason to take responsibility.

The job then fell to a Lieutenant Carey. While out on a routine patrol, they came under sporadic rifle fire from Zulus hiding in a rocky outcrop. The prince again ignored a command to stay back. Instead, he drew his great-uncle's sword and charged into the fray. His dice with death worried Chelmsford but the experience only whetted Louis's enthusiasm for action.

On 1 June, the Prince Imperial of France got more than he bargained for.

The charismatic force of Louis's personality, and his total disregard for orders, proved a disastrous combination. The prince, with an escort of six including Lieutenant Carey, were heading for an area between the Ityotosi and Lombokola rivers so that Louis could sketch. On reaching the place, Louis pointed out a deserted kraal and said, 'We can collect water from the river. There should be wood here. Coffee would be most welcome.'

Carey refused. 'See how the corn grows thick

on three sides? A hundred Kaffirs could hide in there. It's too dangerous.'

'Rubbish, my friend. The place is deserted. Come, we would all appreciate some refreshment.'

Carey was not Buller. He agreed.

Thirty armed Zulus were hidden in the mealies. They waited. Soldiers dismounted, knee-haltered their horses and the animals began to graze. They watched as the men lit a fire to boil water. When the Zulus judged the time to be right, firing and yelling, they burst from cover. The prince and two of his escort were killed.

Lieutenant Carey made it to safety. Out of rifle range, he reined in and looked back, wondering what to do next. After some minutes, and with more than twenty Zulus circling trying to cut off retreat, he decided that the Prince Imperial must be dead, and left.

Dallas and Lorna heard the full story from their butler, Percy. The ever-reliable Zulu grapevine ensured any attempt at a cover-up by the British would fail. The fact was that Lieutenant Carey might have saved Louis's life.

As the Zulus attacked, one man's horse bolted leaving him stranded. He was killed by an *assegai*. A second soldier was shot as he rode away. Louis tried to escape, running alongside his horse, attempting to vault onto the saddle. The advancing natives saw the prince's foot slip as his mount reared in fright. He grabbed at a holster attached to the front of his saddle and tried to swing up. The holster ripped away and Louis fell to the ground, badly injuring his right hand. His horse galloped off. The prince rose to his feet as seven Zulus approached, *assegais* raised.

Percy, who coincidentally bore the same name as Louis's horse, related the story with drama and respect for the man's bravery. 'He stood and tried to find his own *assegai*,' the Zulu told Dallas, referring to the prince's sword. It had fallen to the ground. With only a revolver he ran to higher ground but with his injured hand he could not use the gun. 'A warrior threw an *assegai* which went in here.' Percy indicated his thigh. 'The prince pulled it out and ran straight at them. He was a very brave man to attack seven Zulus. Another spear struck him here.' Percy tapped his chest. 'That's when he was surrounded and killed. The prince's *assegai* has been given to King Cetshwayo.'

Dallas knew that the Prince Imperial would have had his stomach ritually slit open. He wondered what French royalists would make of the fact that the great Napoleon's sword was now in the hands of a besieged Zulu king somewhere in the wilds of Africa.

On hearing the news Buller was furious with Lieutenant Carey. 'You deserve to be shot, and I hope you will be. I could shoot you myself.' The unfortunate Carey was court-martialled eleven days later for his failure to defend the prince.

Any chance Cetshwayo had of achieving a peaceful end to the war was effectively ruined. Lord Chelmsford had to accept ultimate responsibility for the prince's death. Coming so soon after earlier disasters, he needed a swift success. Nothing else would do.

As for the dead Louis, he was sent home amid solemn ceremonies. The news reached Europe by telegraph long before the prince's body. Shock and horror erupted in both England and France, the former due to embarrassment; the latter, patriotic resurgence of latent royal support. Far more publicity was accorded this one death than the reputed thirteen hundred at Isandlwana.

There were some pragmatic observations, however. One man publicly commented that, 'The Zulus had inadvertently solved one of the most difficult problems of French history.'

John Dunn arrived unexpectedly in Durban around the middle of July, ten days after Ulundi had fallen. He told Lorna and Dallas of the Zulus' defeat. To combat the effectiveness of Cetshwayo's bull's horn strategy, Chelmsford had formed his men into a rectangle. Five companies comprised the front and side faces while two closed up the rear. Within this square, as it was called, were staff headquarters, mule carts carrying reserve ammunition, several hospital wagons, volunteers and a troop of the King's Dragoon Guards. The force numbered five thousand three hundred and seventeen. They marched in this formation to within a mile and a half of the royal kraal. There they halted.

Nothing happened. The clash that Chelmsford had wanted for so long, might, it seemed, once again elude him. Nervous new recruits, who had listened to seasoned regulars tell tales of Zulu might and ferocity, found the empty landscape unnerving. More than one asked, 'Where are they?' Silence buzzed in their ears, the only sound their own heartbeats.

Mounted scouts rode out, seeking an enemy that seemed to have melted away.

'They were there, all right,' John said. 'We couldn't see them but the place throbbed with life. It was eerie, an almost tangible expectancy hung in the air. Twenty thousand men had hidden in the grass and we couldn't find one.' He shook his head. 'When they chose to reveal themselves it was done one regiment at a time. I've never seen anything like it. We were completely surrounded. They just stood there in complete silence, holding their shields in front of them. God!' He shook his head again, eyes moist at the memory.

Dallas was deeply moved by the image. The courage of those men, many of whom had already seen how easily shells and bullets brushed aside cowhide shields and smashed defenceless bodies.

John was openly weeping. 'The greatest warrior race in the world. They knew what to expect, yet they ranked against us and did not falter. As one, the foot stamping and rattle of *assegais* against shields started. The sound was so loud it got inside our heads. Then the war cry went up and they came at us.

'Jesus Christ, Dallas, the dumb bastards were falling as if they'd been tipped from a cart. The nine-pounders ripped through them, Gatlings cut them to shreds and still they bloody near reached us.' He brushed impatiently at his wet cheeks. 'Half an hour. Thirty minutes. That's all it took to turn them, break them. The 17th Lancers and King's Dragoon Guards went after them as if they were pig-sticking.'

Dallas had seen the same after Kambula Hill, a sight that had disgusted him. He wondered if Boyd was there. Probably.

'They burned the royal kraal. I believe Wolseley will headquarter there until the king is captured. Chelmsford has requested that he be returned to England. It's over.'

John spent the night. After dinner, weary, and more than slightly drunk and angry, he admitted his true feelings. The three sat sprawled in front of a logfire. Outside, unseasonal drizzle fell. It was not, strictly speaking, cold outside – although it looked it. The fire was a comforting diversion. Coming from upstairs, the children's voices were, for once, in accord.

'What now, John?' Dallas asked. 'Any word of the king?'

Dunn shook his head. 'He moves from kraal to kraal. His supporters lay false trails.'

'It can't continue.'

'Cetshwayo knows that. By evading capture, he is trying to give his people their pride back. The king has always put his nation and the House of Shaka before anything else.' Dunn rose unsteadily and swayed to the sideboard, banging his glass down and reaching for a decanter. Turning, he leaned back for support and went on. 'The Zulus have dominated southern Africa for centuries.' Dunn wagged a finger at his friends. 'So what's it to be? Do we defeat them only to sit back while they rise again, more powerful than before? Or have we lost something that can never be replaced?' He didn't wait for a reply. 'Let me tell you what I think. The British aren't stupid. They plan to fragment the Zulu people under different chiefs. They have chosen well, selecting those who already fight among themselves. When it doesn't work, Wolseley, or whoever, will claim the Zulus cannot run their own affairs, annex the territory and take control. These people need their king and unity if they are to remain strong. That will be impossible.'

John was only confirming what Dallas already knew. 'I believe that you are to be one such chief.'

'How the hell do you know?'

'I spoke to Wolseley. He made no secret of it. Even suggested that I approach you for land.'

John moved back to his chair and sunk into it. 'Idiotic man.' He took a large swallow of scotch. 'And I agreed,' he slurred. 'Me! The one who tried to warn Cetshwayo not to trust the British.' Bleary eyes turned towards Dallas. 'They give a mealie with one hand then take a whole bloody field with the other. Yes, I will be responsible for a kingdom.' He sneered at the word. 'That was the prize. I fell for it, as they knew I would. Then the conditions came.' He fell silent, staring moodily into the fire.

'I saw a map in Wolseley's office. Your land is the buffer zone.'

'Got it in one, my friend.' He held up his glass. 'Would you mind?'

Dallas rose and topped it up. If anyone deserved to get totally drunk, it was John.

'Thanks.' He took another gulp. His eyes became slits as he tried to stay awake. 'Chief John Dunn,' he mocked, saluting himself. 'Any idea how many clans live in that chunk of land? Five. Where the hell do they go when it's taken from them by the British?' His head dropped. 'I've sold them out,' he mumbled.

Dallas lunged as the crystal glass slipped from the man's fingers.

Lorna brought a footstool. They removed his boots, covered him with a blanket and left him snoring.

Cetshwayo eluded capture for nearly two months. He was finally found in the Ngome forest, north of the Black Mfolozi River, and taken to Ulundi. There, Wolseley informed the Zulu king that he had been deposed. He was sent to Cape Town, where he remained a prisoner for three years.

Wolseley wasted no time. He told the two hundred or so clan chiefs that Zululand would be sectioned into thirteen kingdoms, the rulers of which would be chosen by him. New rules and regulations were announced. British rules which only the British understood. Bewildered Zulus could only attempt to comply with them.

Boyd returned to Durban with no more understanding of Africa and her people, black or white, than he had when he arrived. He spoke excitedly of a glorious victory, never once acknowledging Zulu courage or the fact that they were completely out-gunned. Instead, he tended to denigrate Cetshwayo's *impi* as being brainless buffoons who had got what they deserved.

He turned up one day with a young man who looked vaguely familiar. It was Nesbit Pool, who had been a co-traveller on the *Marie Clare* and who had joined the 17th Lancers in Cape Town.

'Says he knows you, old boy,' Boyd said.

Dallas stared at the young man, at his red-rimmed eyes, shaking hands and a nervous habit of shrugging first one shoulder then the other. He'd arrived in Africa a fresh-faced, keen ensign. He was now a lance corporal with shot nerves. 'Pleased to see you again,' said Dallas.

'Y-y-yes,' Pool stammered.

'Bit shell-shocked,' Boyd explained comfortably, as if it were the most natural thing in the world. 'Spot of home leave will put him right.'

Dallas doubted it. The barely controlled hysteria in Pool's eyes bordered on madness.

'He was at Isandlwana,' Boyd added in an undertone.

'Don't tell me they sent him to Ulundi in this state?'

'Of course, old boy. Where else? A man has his duty.'

He belongs in a straitjacket. Dallas didn't voice his

thought. Pool's condition was simply another example of suffering. There'd been plenty of that.

Just before Boyd returned to Scotland, Dallas told him that Lord de Iongh had dropped the charges against him. Boyd was flabbergasted when both his brother and Lorna said they intended to stay in Africa and that Scotland was the last place in the world they wanted to be.

'But, dear lady, your inheritance.'

'Bugger it,' Lorna said carelessly. 'My father lives on the estate now. It means nothing to me.'

Boyd left Africa convinced that his brother and the woman who lived as his wife were both completely mad.

Dallas and Lorna acquired land, nearly two thousand acres, on the Mhlathuze River, near the tiny coastal settlement of Richard's Bay. It was as Wolseley had said. Mention sugar, and land would be found. John Dunn was delighted to have them there. They were two people he could count on, who understood the Zulus and would help them adjust. When it became obvious that Dallas had little interest in planting cane – only one-fifth of his property carried the crop, the rest ran cattle – Dunn conveniently ignored the terms of his friend's title. Both he and Dallas knew that Zulu men would refuse work in canefields as being beneath them, though they would happily tend to cattle.

The farm was called Morningside, after a district of Edinburgh. Lorna and Dallas took up residence two months after Frazer was born.

A few weeks before the move, Cecily Jerome returned from her west coast wanderings to write up all she had seen and learned. With her was Stephen Holgate, still smitten despite being fifteen years the woman's junior. Lorna and Dallas were invited to lunch.

'No cracks about age,' Lorna warned as their carriage turned into Cecily's drive.

'Who, me?'

Cecily and Stephen waited on the front steps, arm-in-arm.

'Hello, old girl, nice to have you back.' Dallas only just managed to contain a grunt of pain as Lorna's elbow found his ribs.

'Right.' Cecily came down the steps and stood, hands on hips. 'Very funny, Dallas. Let's get this straight. Stephen is twenty-eight. I'm forty-three. We don't have a problem with it. What's yours?'

'Just teasing.' Dallas threw Lorna an injured look. 'Honest,' he added when she refused to glance at him.

'Oh, for God's sake, you two.' Cecily turned and strode back to a grinning Stephen. 'Are you coming in for lunch or not?'

It turned into an hilarious and relaxed afternoon. Cecily and Stephen, far from trying to justify their relationship, acted as though it was nothing out of the ordinary. The two were obviously in love and didn't care who knew it. Late in the afternoon Lorna and Dallas returned home in mellow mood.

Approaching their house, Dallas noticed a carriage standing outside. It drove off in great haste as they approached. Dallas frowned. Instinct told him something was amiss and he urged the horses to go faster. Driven by an African, the lone occupant was little more than a shadowy figure, his hat pulled down, coat collar turned up. As their carriage drew closer, Dallas felt a shiver of apprehension. There was something familiar about the man. He slowed the horses and turned into their drive.

'Did you see the man in that brougham? I could have sworn . . .' Dallas shook his head. 'It can't be. He's supposed to be dead.'

'No, and I've no idea who you are talking about.'

'Jeremy Hardcastle.'

'What!' Lorna had turned quite pale. 'It can't be. Anyway, why would he be hanging around here?'

'I don't know, but if it was him, there's bound to be a bad reason for his appearance.'

Inside, all appeared well. Queenie was attending to Frazer. Duncan, Kate and Ellie were playing pick-up-sticks in the parlour. Cam had gone to a friend's house and Torben sat in his room reading. There had been no callers and no-one had seen anything suspicious.

Dallas pushed his concerns aside. The rumours that Jette and Hardcastle were dead had been convincing. The hasty departure of a carriage changed nothing; it was probably nothing more than a coincidence.

Two days later, Percy announced that a Mr Jeremy Hardcastle was calling on them.

While they waited for him to be shown in,

Lorna and Dallas instinctively drew together. The visit could only mean one thing – Torben.

As he entered the room Lorna could not hold back a gasp of surprise. Hardcastle walked slowly, with a pronounced limp. He leaned heavily on a cane, without which the man would possibly have fallen. The left side of his face was badly scarred, the skin livid and puckered. A continuous scar ran through one eye down to his neck. The eye itself appeared sightless, a strange milky colour. It was pulled out of shape, the lid stretched and stuck in a half-closed position. His mouth was also twisted. There were no lips from one corner until nearly the centre of it. Teeth and gums showed through in a permanent grimace. Whatever had caused such injuries should have killed the man.

Hardcastle was only a few years older than Dallas but his hair had turned white. It grew thick on the right side but at the top and left, only small tufts poked through the shiny evidence of severe burns.

Despite a history of distrust and dislike between them, Dallas felt some sympathy for the man. He had obviously suffered terribly. 'We heard you were dead.'

'As you can see, I'm very much alive.' The voice was a rasp, the words, forced through lips that didn't work properly, ill-formed and indistinct.

'Please sit down.'

'Thank you.' Hardcastle juggled the stick with limbs unwilling to do his bidding. Dallas had to force himself not to assist. The man might resent it. He wondered how Hardcastle managed to get in and out of a carriage. Settled at last, his relief was evident. Standing obviously hurt.

'Jette sends her regards.' It was almost a whisper.

'What the hell happened to you?'

Hardcastle swallowed with difficulty. 'Fire,' he said briefly. Then, 'Could I trouble you for a little wine? It helps ease my throat.'

Dallas poured and handed him the glass. He noticed that the man's left hand was also scarred, the fingers, or what was left of them, misshapen.

'What is it that you seek here?'

The ruined mouth stretched into what Dallas could only presume was a smile. 'Charming as usual, Granger.'

'We are not friends,' Dallas said bluntly. 'You have clearly suffered a great deal. For that, I am sorry. It does not, however, change anything between us. I repeat, what brings you here?'

Hardcastle drank some wine before replying. Some ran down his chin, which he dabbed at with a white handkerchief. He drank and dabbed again, although this time he had managed to swallow it all. Dallas realised that the man had little or no feeling left on his face and no idea whether he dribbled or not. Finally, Hardcastle answered the question. 'Jette wishes that her son be returned.'

In a rustle of silk, Lorna took up a determined stance in front of their unexpected guest. 'Just like that?' Her voice held anger. 'You drop him off here and then, eight years later, think you can walk in and take him from us. Think again, Mr Hardcastle, for it is not my inclination to oblige.'

Jeremy Hardcastle's right eye blinked. Something like panic passed across it. 'Jette is his mother.'

'And Dallas his father. We have fed, clothed, educated and loved Torben all this time. He is a part of our family. Have either of you considered his feelings? He believes his mother to be dead. Jette lost any claim to Torben when she abandoned him.' Bright flushes of pink glowed on Lorna's cheeks. 'I'll see you both in hell before handing him over.'

Hardcastle was unimpressed by her outburst. 'Beware, madam, for such words could turn and haunt you.'

'Is that a threat, Mr Hardcastle?' Lorna tossed her head.

Dallas intervened. 'Keep a civil tongue, Hardcastle. You are in no position to throw your weight around. I'll not tolerate you threatening my wife.'

'Wife!' the hoarse voice croaked. 'Hardly that.'

Lorna moved away, her expression one of resolve. 'It would seem,' she said to Dallas, as if no-one else was in the room, 'that Mr Hardcastle has learned few manners in his travels. He comes here demanding Torben, yet appears quite willing to insult those who have raised him. One would think – no, expect – that some humility might be appropriate. After all, abandoning the boy was his idea.'

'I had good reason,' Hardcastle rasped, allowing his anger to show. 'As you can see from my face, the sultan would do anything to punish Jette.'

'If that is so, it makes more sense for us to keep him here,' Lorna snapped.

Again, the mouth stretched in its parody of a smile. 'The sultan is dead. With him died his desire for revenge.' A fit of violent coughing overtook Hardcastle, quelled finally by his draining the glass of wine.

'Where is Jette?' Dallas demanded, almost snatching the glass to refill it. Handing the wine back, he added, 'Why did she not come for Torben herself?'

'She is . . .' Hardcastle's eyes slid away. 'Indisposed. Nothing serious. A slight cold.'

Suspicion now thoroughly aroused, Dallas sought to get rid of the man. 'I will not discuss this further. Jette would never allow a mere sniffle to prevent her from seeing her son. You're lying, Hardcastle. I don't know what you're up to, but I don't trust you. If Jette is party to your schemes and wishes to see Torben, then she is to come here herself. I will judge her sincerity.'

The scarred face turned puce. 'You'll give me the boy now or, by God, I'll take him myself.'

'That's it.' Dallas grasped Hardcastle's upper arms and pulled him from the chair. He saw pain pass over the ruined face but was too angry to care. 'Get out before I throw you out.'

'For God's sake, just let me take the boy,' Hardcastle pleaded, staggering slightly, then finding his balance.

'No!' Lorna shouted furiously. 'Torben is not a possession to be passed back and forth. He has made his life with us and I will not allow you to interfere.'

'Madam, you sorely try my patience. Were you mine I'd be teaching you a lesson with this.' He brandished his cane.

Dallas didn't wait. No-one threatened the woman he loved. One hand on Hardcastle's back, the other holding his good arm, he propelled the man through the front door and slammed it behind him. He was smiling slightly when he returned.

'What's so funny?' Lorna asked peevishly, still fuming.

'I don't believe he's moved that fast since he was hurt.'

She snorted, covered her mouth, then giggled through her fingers. 'You're terrible,' she managed.

'Dallas the dastardly,' he agreed amiably. 'No-one speaks to you like that. No-one.'

She wrapped her arms around him and snuggled against his chest. After only a few seconds, she pulled abruptly back. 'Torben! He's still at school but due home any moment. If Hardcastle sees him he might . . . Oh, Dallas!'

He was out of the room almost before she finished, riding to the school so hard his horse was a lather of sweat. Torben, about to leave, looked astonished to see his father. Dallas felt relief sweep over him that the boy was safe. Dismounting, he waited for Torben to reach him. 'Mind if I walk with you? There's something we have to talk about.'

Torben's expression was hard to read as Dallas told him that his mother might still be alive.

'According to Mr Hardcastle, she wants you back.' Dallas chose his words with care. 'I don't trust the man. However, it's only fair that you be apprised of the situation.'

'Would you give me back?' The voice held neither excitement nor apprehension.

'Only if it were your wish,' Dallas said cautiously. 'We would not stand in your way if you decided to live with your mother. But, my boy, I'd need to be satisfied it would be in your best interests.'

'So you would give me away?' This time there was confusion in the tone.

Dallas slapped a hand against his horse's still foaming flank. 'When we realised that Mr Hardcastle might see you coming home and try to take you with him, I rode like hell. Damn it, Torben, I don't want to lose you, son. It would break my heart if you went back to your mother.'

'What about Aunt Lorna?'

'Hers too. Believe me, she loves you as much as I do.'

There was a long silence. Then, in a small voice, Torben said, 'I want to stay with you.'

Dallas felt his heart soar. He stopped and smiled down at the anxious eyes. 'And so you shall.'

Relief glowed back. 'Will I see her?'

'Bound to, I have no doubt of that. Just remember, son, your mother did what she believed would be for the best. If you do meet her again, I would like to think that you will accept that and remain respectful.'

'I will, Father.'

'Good. Now, for the next few days it is my wish that you stay at home.'

Torben nodded his understanding.

'I wouldn't put anything past that man Hardcastle,' Dallas added. 'Come on, let's get back.'

At their gate, Torben stopped, kicked at a pebble, and looked up at his father. 'Aunt Lorna feels like my mother.'

'Son,' Dallas said, smiling. 'Are you too big for a hug?'

The following day Jeremy Hardcastle returned. Jette was with him, though she was not the woman Dallas remembered. It had been nearly seven years since he had seen her but she had aged twenty. Heavy make-up did not conceal the bruises on her face. Her eyes, once sparkling with mischief and amusement, had become dull. 'Hello, Dallas.' A front tooth was missing.

'Jette.' He kissed the offered cheek and, as he did, felt her body trembling.

'Are you satisfied?' Hardcastle looked smug. 'Here is the boy's mother.'

Dallas scrutinised the once beautiful face. Whatever catastrophe had caused Hardcastle's injuries had not afflicted Jette. Yet somehow she seemed more wounded than him. The once proud tilt of her head was gone. The erect body had a frailty of which loss of weight was not the cause. Once lustrous black hair, now streaked with grey, hung in lifeless proof that she was no longer concerned with her appearance. Dressed plainly, the quality of her clothes was good but her little touches of flair were not there.

'You wish to see Torben?'

'We intend to take him with us. Don't we, my dear?'

Dallas kept his eyes on Jette. 'I was speaking to the boy's mother.'

A gesture, so small Dallas wondered if he'd imagined it. A tiny shake of the head and a warning of some kind in her eyes. It was gone as quickly as it came. 'I want my son.'

There was no passion in the voice, no hint of longing. Instead, Dallas heard only despair. 'You may of course see him, for I would not deny you access. However, Jette, Torben has made it quite plain. He wishes to remain with us.'

A gleam of satisfaction shone briefly as she held his gaze. Then it was gone.

Jeremy Hardcastle who, until now, had remained leaning on his cane, had gone quite pale. 'Help me sit,' he demanded.

Jette obeyed immediately.

Once settled, he looked up at Dallas. 'You have poisoned the boy's mind against us.' The coughing spasm that followed was painful to watch. Lorna brought a glass of water, which Hardcastle drank greedily. 'Water, madam,' he said cuttingly when finished. 'Yesterday it was wine.'

'Yesterday,' she replied with spirit, 'I was unaware of exactly how vile you are, Mr Hardcastle. One only has to look at Jette to see what cruelty you are capable of. I would not place a mangy dog under your care, let alone a child.'

Jette remained standing next to the chair, hands

hanging listlessly by her side. At Lorna's reference to her appearance, she showed no reaction.

Hardcastle's good eye glared. 'The boy is rightfully hers. Return him to us and we shall leave you in peace. We will not go from here without Torben.' The cane, which now lay across his lap, whipped out suddenly, banging hard against Jette's leg. 'Tell him, you stupid woman.'

Showing no outward sign of pain, Jette kept her eyes lowered as she said in a voice devoid of expression, 'We want Torben.'

Dallas's and Lorna's eyes met. Whatever was being played out in front of them had nothing to do with any feelings of compassion on Hardcastle's part, and taking Torben certainly did not seem to be what Jette wanted.

'Damnation, woman!' Hardcastle tried to shout but failed. Furiously, he raised the stick. 'Tell him again.'

A sob rose in her throat as she cringed back from further abuse.

Dallas took two steps and snatched the heavy ebony cane, bringing it down hard across Hardcastle's shins. 'You bastard!' he shouted in fury.

Tears of pain welled from the man's right eye as he reached down and rubbed his legs. 'She is my woman.' The words came with no remorse. 'I'll treat her as I wish.'

'Not in my house.' Dallas turned and addressed Jette. 'You are welcome but he goes.'

'Wait,' Lorna said suddenly. She went to Jette and placed an arm around her. 'Better than that, stay with us. I extend an open invitation. What do you say, Jette?'

Slowly the Danish woman shook her head. 'Too late,' she whispered. 'Far, far too late.'

At that moment, the door opened and Torben stood looking at them.

'There he is,' Hardcastle crowed triumphantly. 'Get your things, boy. This is your mother. You're coming with us.'

Torben turned confused eyes to Dallas.

'Stay where you are, son. You will remain here as I promised.'

Jette kept her head turned away from Torben, unwilling to look at him.

'There's your son, dear.' Hardcastle seemed to be enjoying the moment. 'What a fine boy. Aren't you even going to greet him?' He stared at Torben, who stood transfixed in the doorway. 'Do forgive her. She's overcome with emotion.'

'Mother?' Torben's voice wavered. 'Is it really you?'

'Please,' Jette extended imploring hands towards Jeremy Hardcastle. 'Don't do it. I beg you, don't make me do this.' She fell to her knees in front of the chair. 'Please,' she cried brokenly.

'Get up,' he hissed, one hand roughly twisting and pulling her hair.

Dallas had seen enough. He plucked Jette away from Hardcastle. 'Get her out of here,' he said to Lorna. 'I'll see to this cretin. Take Torben and Jette somewhere they can be alone.'

Lorna tried to steer Jette from the room but she twisted away. 'No. You don't understand.'

Dallas had his attention focused on Jeremy Hardcastle. 'Out,' he ordered the Englishman. 'Leave my house immediately.' He moved towards him.

'Look out,' Jette screamed. 'He has a gun.'

Dallas saw the murderous intent on Hardcastle's face. He was aware that the man had produced a pistol and was pointing it at him. 'Run, Lorna,' he shouted desperately, lunging. It was too late. Just as the gun went off, Jette, screaming hysterically, dived between them. She crumpled to the floor.

'No!' This time Hardcastle managed to scream, a sound that was half-animal as it tore through the damaged tissue of his larynx. In disbelief he moaned, 'Jette, no. I didn't mean . . . Jette, get up.'

Dallas took advantage of his shock, easing the weapon from limp fingers.

Glancing swiftly over his shoulder Dallas saw that Lorna and Torben hadn't moved from the doorway. He dropped to one knee beside Jette. 'She's alive.'

Hardcastle was trying to rise from the chair. Without his cane he made little progress. Dallas pointed the pistol. 'Stay where you are.'

'Jette. I must help her.'

Dallas cocked the small revolver. 'One more move and I'll shoot you.'

The man slumped back, weeping.

Alerted by the gun going off, Cam burst into the room. 'What happened?' Big round eyes took in the scene, not comprehending. Behind him, Percy, Queenie and two other servants hovered nervously.

Outside, the three dogs set up a frenzied barking as they sensed all was not well in the house.

'Saddle up,' Dallas said tersely, knowing he could count on Cam to act sensibly. 'See if Doctor Grey is at home. Tell him to come immediately, someone's been shot. Then ride into town and fetch the police.'

Cam didn't hesitate.

Jette gave a pitiful cry. Easing her over, Dallas saw that the bullet had hit just above her right breast. 'The doctor is coming, Jette.'

'Torben?'

Lorna, her arm around him, drew the trembling boy to his mother's side. He clung to his step-mother, frightened and confused. 'It's all right, darling,' Lorna soothed. 'I'm right here.'

Jette finally allowed herself to look at her son. Tears damped the pain in her eyes. 'A day has not passed when I haven't thought of you,' she whispered. 'Don't be frightened. I never stopped loving you.' A shudder ran through her. 'I knew your father would protect you.'

Torben still stood next to Lorna, his face a mixture of disbelief, horror and a kind of denial. Dallas and Lorna had always told him how beautiful his mother was, yet what seemed to him to be an old woman at his feet was anything but. For years he'd held a shimmering image in his heart. This woman, and the scarred man who shot her, were so far removed from his fantasies that Torben wanted nothing to do with either of them. He buried himself closer to Lorna. 'She's not my mother.'

Jette heard. Hurt and understanding crossed her face. Pleading eyes sought Dallas. 'There were good reasons for leaving Torben here. What I didn't know was that Jeremy himself told the sultan where to find me. I was a fool, Dallas. Jeremy seemed to have changed and I believed we could be happy. Instead, he betrayed me. By the time I came to my senses it was too late.' She coughed and blood trickled down her chin.

Dallas gently wiped it away with a clean handkerchief. 'Hush. Don't tax yourself. The doctor will be here soon.'

Jette grimaced and shook her head slightly. 'I must tell you. The sultan sent a messenger saying I had two days to return the money. I couldn't, it was tied up in the shop and factory. My panic played straight into Jeremy's hands, as he knew it would. He suggested we disappear, leaving Torben with you for safekeeping. At first I refused. Then the factory burned down. I thought it a warning from the sultan, never suspecting for a minute that it was Jeremy's doing. Finally, I agreed it was too dangerous to remain in Durban. I was terrified Torben would be hurt. I thought my heart would break when I left him here.'

'Did the sultan do that to him?' Dallas asked, indicating Hardcastle.

'No. I know he told you differently but Jeremy was caught in a building when the British set fire to Kumasi.'

'You could have left him.'

'How? I had no money and Jeremy threatened

to reveal Torben's whereabouts. Moroccans are not particular how they take revenge. If the sultan couldn't find me, he'd get revenge through my son.'

'Then why come back for him?'

'The sultan died. We were safe, but it meant Jeremy's hold over me was also gone.' Jette gasped as pain flared in her chest. Slowly she went on. 'Jeremy's violence . . . well, it took its toll. I knew what he was up to, suggesting we get Torben back. It was power over me, the only thing he has to have. Dallas, I was desperate to see Torben and came up with a plan of my own.'

She was becoming upset in her urgency to explain.

'Enough, Jette. Save your strength.'

She managed a shaky smile. 'We both know where this will end. Let me tell the rest.'

Jeremy Hardcastle tried again to stand. Dallas didn't notice until he heard Lorna say, 'I'll break your legs with this cane if you move again.'

Dallas looked round and saw fury on the man's face.

'Don't listen to Jette. She's lying.'

Dallas passed Lorna the pistol. 'It's loaded. Don't hesitate to use it.'

Lorna's hand was steady. 'Not for a second,' she said calmly.

Dallas looked back to Jette. Beads of perspiration stood out on her forehead. The effort was costing her dearly, but he understood her need to tell the story. It was for Torben's sake. 'I planned to take our son and run. I had money here – it would have been possible. When we reached Durban I found that Jeremy had been one step ahead. False marriage and death certificates. He'd sent them to a lawyer years ago. Everything I own is in his name. There was nothing I could do.'

'You could have come to me.'

'Hadn't I done enough to you, Dallas?' She shivered. 'So cold. Is it getting dark?'

Dallas pulled a blanket off the back of the sofa and covered her.

'Thank you,' she whispered, her voice fading. 'You're a decent man. Take care of Torben. I've made such a mess of my life. He is the one good thing to come from it.'

'Please,' Hardcastle begged, 'let me be with her.'

'I think not. Jette has made it plain enough. She despises you.'

'Jette!' It was a cry of pure anguish. 'I love you.'

She turned her head away and closed her eyes.

Percy appeared at the door with Doctor Grey. When Dallas looked back at Jette, he could see it was too late.

Pronouncing Jette dead, the doctor asked about her bruises.

'The man who shot her,' Dallas said coldly. 'He has much to answer for.'

'No!' Hardcastle was beside himself, trembling, crying and shaking his head. 'I loved her. She was mine. I never meant to kill her. I didn't want to hurt her. I only did things when she . . . when I thought . . . I had to make her stay. Don't you see?'

A mad obsessiveness gleamed in his good eye. 'She needed me,' he sobbed. 'She had to be taught that.'

The doctor looked disgusted. He rose from Jette's side. 'I gather the police have been summoned. An autopsy will show how much this woman has suffered. I will send the cart.' With that, he turned towards Jeremy Hardcastle. 'As for you, sir, I hope you rot in hell.'

The police arrived soon after and took Hardcastle away in handcuffs. Two months later a court tried and convicted him of Jette's murder. In front of a jeering and mainly drunken crowd of spectators who had nothing better to do, Jeremy Hardcastle was hanged. Dallas and Lorna stayed well away.

Torben took some time to recover. Strangely, the fact that his mother was not the beauty he'd expected bothered him most. Almost immediately he stopped calling Lorna anything other than Mother. It was as if he needed her image to replace the reality of what Jette had become.

Despite patience, love and understanding from Lorna and Dallas, it was Cam who finally bridged the gulf between Torben and his siblings.

The two boys were having a rough and tumble in the garden. It started as fun but a blow to Cam's ear stung like hell and he responded in kind. The fight turned serious.

Lorna moved to stop it.

'Leave them,' Dallas said, some instinct telling him this was a defining moment in the boys' relationship.

They were identical in size and strength. Ten minutes later they were still slugging it out, both boys bloodied and bruised. It couldn't go on. Exhausted, they gave up, collapsing on the lawn and lying side-by-side, trying to get their breath.

Lorna couldn't stand back any longer. Skirts flying, she ran towards them. 'My God,' she cried. 'Look what you've done to each other. You're brothers. This is disgraceful.'

'We're not,' Torben managed.

'Oh, yeah!' Chest heaving from the physical exertion, Cam turned his head and looked at Torben. 'Sure feels like it from where I'm lying.'

Torben snorted.

Cam grinned, though it hurt his split lip.

Suddenly the two of them were laughing in earnest. They laughed until their bellies ached and heads hurt.

Lorna threw up her hands and walked away. 'When you've quite finished, come and get cleaned up in the kitchen.'

She and Dallas stood at the window, watching. They saw both boys on their hands and knees, then slowly rise. Cam hung an arm around Torben's neck and Torben held Cam's waist as they helped each other to the house.

What they didn't hear were Torben's words. 'You mean that?'

And Cam's reply. 'Hell, yes. Why else would I sometimes feel like killing you?'

It set them off laughing again.

The following day Dallas asked Cam what

they'd said to each other. Lorna failed to appreciate her son's reply but Dallas understood.

With impeccable timing, and a little help from the grapevine, Mister David presented himself at Morningside the day after Lorna, Dallas and the children arrived.

'I see you,' the Zulu greeted Dallas.

'I see you,' Dallas responded, delighted to see him again.

'I am thinking you will need an *induna*.' Mister David had a huge grin on his face.

'Indeed.'

Mister David's hand indicated a pregnant woman who waited patiently some distance away. 'My wife,' he said simply.

Dallas nodded. There was no point suggesting she join them.

'I need good men for the cattle.'

'I will find them.'

Mister David moved in.

Three days later, July arrived. He was hampered by a wounded leg. A bullet had shattered his right tibia. Tribal healing had been able to do little but fight off infection. He walked with the aid of a stick. Dallas put him in charge of farm equipment, a position that required July sit at a workbench for most of the day.

Will's trading store in Swaziland was a disaster. He simply could not settle in one place. Regular trading trips kept him away for months at a time. In his absence, the Swazi woman who Will had taken as a wife did her best. Unfortunately, tribal responsibilities were far stronger than any understanding of commerce. Will would return to find most of his stock given away or loaned out.

'The damned woman falls for every hard-luck story,' he complained on a visit to Lorna and Dallas.

'Does she have a choice?' Dallas asked.

'Not really,' Will admitted. 'She's obliged to obey all the male members of her family. I just didn't realise there were so many of them.'

'Get rid of the store. You're hardly ever there anyway.'

'Never!' Will looked horrified. 'She'd give away my things if I did that.'

'Then go and talk to John. See how he deals with it.'

Will said he might.

He kept the store and took a second Swazi wife. Whether it was Dunn's advice or his own canny idea, Dallas didn't know, but whenever Will went away, the store carried hardly any stock. It was a solution that pleased everyone. His wives could hardly give away something that wasn't there.

On 15 August 1881, one day after his divorce became official, Dallas married the only woman he had ever loved. Their honeymoon, children and all, was a trip home to Scotland.

It was strange to be back. The countryside, even the houses, seemed unfamiliar. They arrived late in October, the month the rains started in Zululand, a sticky, humid time of year. In Scotland, winter was creeping in. Chilly shadows stretched long over puddles bearing a thin covering of dull grey ice, the colour of cold. Autumn was long gone, the trees bare.

Dallas's parents met the train in Edinburgh. There were tears of joy as Lady Pamela greeted her favourite son, Lorna, whom she had always adored, and their six children. The earl was more restrained but he clasped Dallas's hand in a grasp hard enough to make him wince and his eyes softened as he was introduced to the children.

The Grange looked older and shabbier than it had in Dallas's memories. It was not, as Mister David might put it, a house with no shadows; rather, it was a place where Dallas no longer had a sense of himself. Ten years had passed. Dallas had moved too far from his old life to ever fully return to it. He found himself looking at everything through the eyes of a stranger.

He greeted the staff. When Dallas stood face-to-face with Victor, the memories of his escape flooded back. Ignoring the outstretched hand, the surprised head groom was pulled into a bear hug. 'I never did thank you,' Dallas said huskily.

'My lord, it was my duty.' Victor jerked back, a look of discomfort on his face. The aristocracy had no call to behave towards their servants with such familiarity.

The large house and white-skinned servants subdued the children. They were ill at ease. 'May we go outside and play?' Cam asked.

'Of course,' Dallas told them. 'But stay off the flowerbeds.'

Looking through the window a little later, Lady Pamela exclaimed, 'They have removed their shoes. They'll catch their death. Oh, do ask them to be careful, Dallas. I can see one of the girls in the top of a tree. Good gracious, what on earth are they up to now?'

Lorna joined her mother-in-law at the window, smiling at her horror. 'Catching fish,' she explained. 'Don't worry, they'll not harm them. I'm afraid you'll find our children a little wild.'

'No, no,' Lady Pamela said hastily. 'Merely different.'

Difference. It was everywhere. Stiff formality instead of natural and genuine laughter. Rigid rules in place of freedom. Servants who would rather die than show anything but deference, instead of Zulu staff who treated the children as their own.

In honour of their visit, Charles and Charlotte came down from Perthshire. They stayed at Canongate but spent the following day at the Grange. It was a disaster from start to finish. Dallas was keen to see his old friend but rather taken aback by his cool greeting. It was clear that Charles had not forgiven Dallas his liaison with Alison. Dallas didn't blame him but wondered why Charles had even bothered to make the effort to see him. He could easily have allowed Charlotte to visit on her own.

Their four impeccably behaved children seemed like wind-up dolls. They sat, hands folded in their laps, moving only when their parents suggested they might. Angus, the eldest, who was a year younger than Cam and Torben, at Charles's suggestion reluctantly went outside to join his cousins. He returned a few minutes later in tears. Cam and Torben had been stick-fighting, a traditional Zulu way in which personal differences are resolved. Children as young as five would practise with thin sticks. Angus had come off second-best, having been coerced into giving the game a try. A blow on the head, which Cam swore was only to show his cousin where to aim, was not appreciated, either by Angus or his parents.

Charlotte, ill at ease with a brother who appeared to have changed out of all recognition, kept the conversation on the topic of their childhood. It was the only point of contact they had left between them.

No-one, it seemed, had the slightest interest in hearing about Africa. When Lorna tried to tell everyone about Percy there were shudders all round.

'How perfectly awful that you can't find someone decent,' Charlotte responded.

'Recruit someone from here,' Charles advised.

'He sounds . . . different,' Lady Pamela murmured.

Thomas and his family came down from Tayside. Dallas had never been close to his eldest brother but now, if it hadn't been for Lady Pamela's desperate attempts, conversation would have ground to a halt within the first five minutes. Citing a full workload, Thomas left again the next day.

Boyd would be arriving at the weekend. Lord de Iongh would pay a brief visit at some stage.

By day six of their stay, Dallas and Lorna couldn't see how they'd get through the rest of their visit. To make matters worse, the weather had closed in and the children were bored. Torben, at least, found some diversion in the library. Ellie might have too but for the fact that the earl discovered the child with her nose buried deeply in a medical encyclopedia, minutely examining the male genitalia. Lord Dalrymple was scandalised. No amount of explanation about Ellie's scientific interests could persuade him to allow his granddaughter back into the library. Unfortunately for Torben, the ban extended to him. Ellie and Torben spent nearly a week at war.

Lorna and Dallas knew they couldn't blame their families. They were the ones who had changed.

When Lord de Iongh arrived, Dallas made himself scarce. The man had made it plain – he wished to see his daughter and grandchildren. Torben, he knew, was not Lorna's. Dallas, who found Torben's presence as natural as that of any of his other children, made no effort to justify it, which only served to spark further disapproval. The two of them went to Edinburgh for the day and Dallas spent several hours traipsing around behind a rapt Torben, visiting the castle, the National Gallery and various other places of interest. They returned to the Grange late in the afternoon bearing a number of books for Torben and smuggling in several medical reference books for Ellie.

Boyd's weekend visit was, by comparison with all the others, a breath of fresh air. He, at least, had been to Africa. Although his opinion of the place and people hadn't changed, there was some common ground.

Two days before they were due to leave for London, where they intended to spend a few days before boarding a ship home, Lady Pamela asked Dallas to have a private talk. They met in a small drawing room. A fire crackled cheerfully in the grate; outside, snow fell.

'You will be pleased to return home, I think.'

'I cannot lie, Mama. You are right. Zululand is home.'

His mother smiled. 'Do not think unkindly of us, I beg you. We do not have the benefit of your experience.'

'Would you consider a visit to us?'

'I would. The earl refuses. I fear he has been listening to Boyd.'

'A pity he doesn't also listen to me. Boyd wasn't there long enough to form a true impression. Nor would he open his eyes.'

'Not his fault, my dear.'

'Probably not.' Dallas poured them each some wine. 'Come on your own. You would be very welcome.'

'I cannot.'

'Why?'

'It is for this reason I asked for our talk. I have discovered that your father lives in Natal.'

'Natal! Where? What part?'

Lady Pamela sipped her wine. 'He farms near a place called Colenso.'

'How do you know this?' Dallas's heart beat wildly. Colenso, of all places.

'He wrote to me.'

'After all these years?'

His mother put her glass down. 'He is not well. He wanted to say goodbye.'

Dallas watched the composed face. Breeding prevented any show of emotion. 'How did you feel when you read the letter?'

She shrugged slightly. 'Confused, I suppose. It was so unexpected. With you gone all these years, I was no longer reminded of him. And his words . . . he didn't sound like the Jonathan I remembered.'

'One way or another, Africa changes people. Tell me his name, or does he use Jonathan Fellowes still? Do you think he would make me welcome if I called on him?'

'I told you, he is not well. Complications from a wound he suffered fighting the Zulus. From his letter I would say he is no longer on this earth.'

'A pity.' Dallas felt only slight regret. After all, he'd never met his real father. 'But, if this is so, how is it that you cannot visit?'

His mother looked down at her lap. 'What if he is still alive?' she whispered. 'It would be most awkward.'

'Awkward! Listen to yourself, Mother. Besides, I live in Zululand. Colenso is a long way from there.'

'No,' she said quietly. 'It would not be wise.

Besides, I would hate to travel without the earl and he will not come.'

Dallas left it but he felt hurt. Instead, he said, 'Tell me his name.'

'He went by the name of Walsh,' his mother said. 'Jack Walsh.'

The news hit Dallas in the solar plexus. Jack Walsh! The man whose life he had saved at Howick Falls. And Caroline was his daughter. Dallas's half-sister. Sarah's cousin. Which made Sarah's damnable father an uncle by marriage. 'I've met him,' he managed to say. He told his mother the circumstances.

'Oh, my dear,' she said, wiping her eyes once he'd fallen silent. 'It was meant to be.'

Later, when he told Lorna about the conversation, Dallas realised what his mother had meant. He had saved the life of the man who had given Dallas his. If nothing else had come from this trip to Scotland, there now existed a quid pro quo he'd never expected.

On board the ship that each day bore them closer to home, Lorna had some news of her own. 'Remember all those boring evenings you and I retired early simply to escape?'

'I'll never forget them,' Dallas replied with a grin, remembering. 'As good as it was to see everyone again, I've never been so pleased to leave anywhere. Why do you ask?'

'Out of boredom comes life,' Lorna said.

'Are you saying what I think you're saying?'

'I'm pregnant.'

'Oh God. Not another few months of your evil temper.' He grunted as she jabbed him in the ribs.

Margaret, known as Meggie, was born seven months later.

Their farm flourished as Zululand settled into a new order of things. Dallas did what he could to help the Zulus adapt. He employed as many as possible, men and women. Each received specialised training in one field or another. He built a school, paid the salaries of two teachers, and encouraged every African child on his farm to attend. Each step took them further from a culture that had existed for centuries. Dallas realised that, in order to survive, the Zulus had to change.

He said as much to Mister David.

'It is only a tree,' the Zulu replied.

Dallas's smile was tinged with sadness. Change might well be a tree but each year, as it grew, the leaves and fruit of Zulu tradition would wither and die.

Shortly after returning from Scotland, Mister David and Dallas spoke of the one thing they'd avoided mentioning. The war.

Mister David remembered. 'The red soldiers were few but how they fought.'

'You admire them?'

'Of course. We had more warriors and still we could not win.'

'Where did you fight?'

'Everywhere. Hlobane, Kambula . . .'

'You were at Kambula?'

'Yes. I was with the men of the chest.'

'Tobacco was there too.'

Mister David nodded. 'He was killed.'

'I know.' Dallas paused. 'I was there too.'

'Hau! You were a red soldier?'

'No. A scout.'

'Ah! Did you not think it wonderful? Every warrior shouted the war cry as he killed his enemy.'

'Yes, we were enemies. And yet you still choose to work for me.'

Mister David's response was simple. 'The war is finished. We are no longer enemies.'

'I admire your attitude. So many Zulus were killed. Your king has been captured and imprisoned. What becomes of everything the Zulus stood for?'

'We were strong. We can be so again.'

'No, my friend, you cannot. The British rule now. They will not accept any attempt to become the nation we once knew.'

Mister David thumped his chest. 'Here, we remain warriors. That cannot be taken away. Our women honour us and many new praise poems are sung. The Zulu heart beats with pride and that will always be so. There is not one man remaining who would not respond to our king's call. You may have beaten us on the battlefield and taken our laws, but in our heads and hearts we are still Zulus. No-one can change that.'

Listening, Dallas realised that Mister David truly held no malice. Nor was he issuing any kind of threat or warning. He was merely stating a belief he held with such sincerity that anything else was unthinkable. He was Zulu and proud of it. Out there, in a vast, largely untamed land that still carried the clan name, fragmented now by a colonial power who did not understand its people, every single man, woman and child held the same unshakeable belief. An enemy had dealt a blow to the Zulus as they themselves had to others in the past. It was something to be understood and accepted.

Within two years of the battle at Ulundi, it became apparent that Wolseley's rearrangement of Zululand was not working. Its people needed a common and respected authority to bind them together. The chiefs, on their own, were not enough. They sought their king.

It was at last acknowledged by London that Cetshwayo had tried to avoid war. The British were under pressure in the Transvaal, where friction with the Boers was getting out of hand. They had no time to intervene in skirmishes taking place within the boundaries of Zululand. Cetshwayo, suddenly seen as the obvious answer, made the journey to London and presented a case to both Queen Victoria and the Colonial Office for regaining his position.

His visit was a success. He became hugely popular with the British public and the government allowed him to resume sovereignty over his people.

It was not enough. Zulus of the past had been ruled and kept obedient by fear. On his return,

Cetshwayo found that with the power to order executions removed, he was no more effective than the chiefs had been.

On 8 February 1884, Cetshwayo suffered a convulsion and died. His family refused to allow a post-mortem, citing tribal tradition as the reason. The doctor called to issue a death certificate of suspected poisoning. Nothing was ever proved.

Cetshwayo spoke his last words to his half-brother, Dabulamanzi, who had led the Zulu *impi* at Isandlwana:

> *Dabulamanzi, there is my child; look after him for me. Bring him up well, for I have no other sons. Dinuzulu is my only son. There is your task, Dabulamanzi, to look after my child.*

Two years later, Dabulamanzi was shot and killed by Boers. Dinuzulu, then fifteen years old, became king of the Zulus.

His reign was short-lived. In 1889, after rebelling against British interference and increasing Boer settlements, he was exiled to the remote Atlantic Ocean island of St Helena, one thousand miles off the African mainland. The fact that Napoleon, whose great-grandson, Louis, had been killed in the Zulu war, had endured exile on that same island was of no interest to Dinuzulu, the two uncles who went with him, or their entourage of attendants and wives.

Ten years later, the fifth Zulu king was pardoned and returned to the land of his birth. By then, Britain's hold on Zululand was irreversible. The great nation created by Shaka was lost.

Or was it?

The pride remained. Quietly, but with determination, the Zulus kept their sense of identity.

'Do not underestimate us,' Percy had once said.

Dallas didn't. Not for one minute.

MORE BESTSELLING FICTION
AVAILABLE FROM PAN MACMILLAN

Beverley Harper
Storms Over Africa

Richard Dunn has made Africa his home. But his
Africa is in crisis.

Ancient rivalries have ignited modern political ambitions. Desperate poachers stalk the dwindling
populations of the game parks. For those of the old
Africa, the old ways, nothing is certain.

But for Richard – a man used to getting his own
way – the stakes are even higher. Into his world has
come the compelling and beautiful Steve Hayes. A
woman he swears he will never give up. A woman
struggling to guard her own dreadful secret.

Richard has no choice. He must face the
consequences of the past and fight for the future.
To lose now is to lose everything . . .

Beverley Harper
Edge of the Rain

The blood scent was fresh. Hunger ached in her belly . . . the lioness slid forward as close as she dared. The little boy seconds away from death was two, maybe three years old. He was lost in the vast, heat-soaked sand that was the Kalahari desert.

Toddler Alex Theron is miraculously rescued by a passing clan of Kalahari Bushmen. Over the ensuing years the desert draws him back, for it hides a beautiful secret . . . diamonds.

But nothing comes easily from within this turbulent continent and before Alex can even hope to realise his dreams he will lose his mind to love and fight a bitter enemy who will stop at nothing to destroy him . . .

From the author of *Storms Over Africa* comes a novel of courage and an unforgettable journey into the beating heart of Africa.

Beverley Harper
Echo of an Angry God

Likoma Island in Lake Malawi is renowned throughout Africa for its exotic and treacherous beauty – and its secret history of human sacrifice, hidden treasure and unspeakable horror. A history that cannot be hidden forever.

Lana Devereaux travels to Malawi seeking the truth behind her father's disappearance near Likoma Island fifteen years ago. But Lana soon finds herself caught in a web of deceit, passion and black magic that stretches back over two hundred years and has ramifications that reach well beyond the shores of Lake Malawi.

Beverley Harper is fast becoming one of Australia's most popular storytellers. *Echo of an Angry God* is her most thrilling adventure yet and follows the enormous success of her previous novels, *Storms Over Africa* and *Edge of the Rain*.

'a fast paced yet affecting thriller with . . . compelling authenticity'
WHO WEEKLY

'a terrific adventure'
GOLD COAST BULLETIN

Beverley Harper
People of Heaven

The poacher didn't shoot her. Bullets cost money
and a shot might alert the rangers . . . On the third
night, after enduring more agony than any man or
beast should ever have to face, the rhinoceros took
one last shuddering breath, heaved her flanks
painfully, and sought refuge in the silky blackness
of death.

In 1945 two returning soldiers meet on a train
bound for Zululand. They have nothing in common;
Joe King is a British–South African landowner,
Wilson Mpande a Zulu tribesman. Yet destiny will
link them for generations.

Michael King and Dyson Mpande, the sons of
enemies, share a precious friendship that defies
race and colour. But as the realities of apartheid
transform an angry South Africa, the fate of the
Zulu nation is as precarious as that of the
endangered black rhinoceros, hunted for its horn.
Each must fight for what he loves most.

And a great evil between their families will test their
friendship beyond imaginable limits.

Passionate, suspenseful, evocative, Beverley
Harper's fourth novel is a worthy successor to her
previous bestsellers, *Echo of an Angry God*, *Edge
of the Rain* and *Storms Over Africa*.

'Harper is Australia's answer to Wilbur Smith'
AUSTRALIAN GOOD TASTE

Beverley Harper
The Forgotten Sea

*Not a pretty sight. Certainly not one the authorities
on Mauritius, that gem of a tourist destination in a
trio of idyllic islands once known as the Mascarenes,
would like to become public knowledge. Their
carefully nurtured image was of sparkling blue sea,
emerald green palm fringes haphazardly angled
along pure white beaches . . . This was ugly, messy.*

When Australian journalist Holly Jones flies to
Mauritius to cover playboy adventurer Connor
Maguire's search for buried ancestral treasure, it
promises to be a relaxing two weeks in an exotic
island paradise. What she hasn't planned on is an
infuriating, reluctant subject with a hidden agenda.
Or one who stirs the fires in a heart grown cold.
But can she trust him . . .

After the body of a young woman is washed up on
a beach, Holly finds herself caught in a deadly
murder investigation and the island's darkest
secrets.

A compelling, passionate tale from Beverley
Harper, author of the bestselling *People of Heaven*,
Echo of an Angry God, *Edge of the Rain* and
Storms Over Africa.

'We have our own Wilbur Smith in the making here
in Australia'
SUN-HERALD

Beverley Harper
Jackal's Dance

Agony exploded in her knee. She staggered, tried to keep going, then nearly fell as a shocking pain rushed up her leg. Confusion and fear swamped her senses, escape suddenly essential. The tuskless cow turned and hobbled away, each step agonising torture. Her front right knee joint had been shattered by the single copper-jacketed bullet.

Man, her hated enemy, had just handed out a death sentence.

As the rangers and staff of a luxury lodge in Etosha National Park, Namibia welcome the last guests of the season, thoughts are predominantly on the three-month break ahead. Except for Sean, who is fighting his growing attraction for the manager's wife, Thea.

Camping in the park nearby, Professor Eben Kruger has his work cut out keeping the attention of the university students in his charge on the behavioural habits of the cunning jackal.

None of them could ever be prepared for the horrendous events about to take place. Each will be pushed to breaking point as the quest for survival becomes the only thing that matters.

Shocking, gripping, breathtaking, this is Beverley Harper at her best.